WILKIE COLLINS was born in London in 1824, the eldest son of the landscape painter William Collins. In 1846, having spent five years in the tea business, he was entered to read for the bar at Lincoln's Inn, where he gained the legal knowledge that was to give him much material for his writing. From the early 1850s, he was a friend of Charles Dickens, acting with him, contributing to *Household Words*, travelling with him on the Continent. Dickens produced and acted in two melodramas written by Collins, *The Lighthouse* (1855) and *The Frozen Deep* (1857). Of his novels, Collins is best remembered for *The Woman in White* (1860), *No Name* (1862), *Armadale* (1866) and *The Moonstone* (1868), which T. S. Eliot called 'the first, the longest, and the best of modern English detective novels'. Wilkie Collins, who braved Victorian morals by living with one mistress and maintaining another in a separate establishment, died in 1889.

JOHN SUTHERLAND, who has edited Anthony Trollope's *The Eustace Diamonds*, *Phineas Finn* and *Rachel Ray*, and William Thackeray's *The History of Henry Esmond*, all for Penguin Classics, is currently Northcliffe Professor of English Literature at University College London. His other publications include *Fiction and the Fiction Industry*, *Best Sellers: Popular Fiction of the 1970s*, *The Longman Companion to English Literature*, *Mrs Humphry Ward* and *Is Heathcliff a Murderer?*, a collection of essays.

ARMADALE

WILKIE COLLINS

EDITED WITH AN INTRODUCTION AND NOTES
BY JOHN SUTHERLAND

PENGUIN BOOKS

PENGUIN BOOKS

Published by the Penguin Group
Penguin Books Ltd, 27 Wrights Lane, London w8 5tz, England
Penguin Putnam Inc., 375 Hudson Street, New York, New York 10014, USA
Penguin Books Australia Ltd, Ringwood, Victoria, Australia
Penguin Books Canada Ltd, 10 Alcorn Avenue, Toronto, Ontario, Canada m4v 3b2
Penguin Books (NZ) Ltd, Private Bag 102902, NSMC, Auckland, New Zealand

Penguin Books Ltd, Registered Offices: Harmondsworth, Middlesex, England

First published 1864–6
Published in Penguin Classics 1995
5 7 9 10 8 6

Introduction and Notes copyright © John Sutherland, 1995
All rights reserved

The moral right of the editor has been asserted

Typeset by Datix International Ltd, Bungay, Suffolk
Filmset in Monophoto Baskerville
Printed in England by Clays Ltd, St Ives plc

CONTENTS

INTRODUCTION

'Like most of Collins' novels, *Armadale* has the immense – and
nowadays more and more rare – merit of never being dull' – T. S.
Eliot

'Nothing Boring about the Sensation Novel' – D. A. Miller

'Action! action! action!' – *Quarterly Review*, April 1863

Few novelists have made a reputation as suddenly and as spectacularly
as did Wilkie Collins with *The Woman in White* in 1859–60. With its
high-impact reportage style and new-fangled detective plot the novel
took the Victorian reading public by the throat. Thackeray sat up all
night reading it. Edward Fitzgerald (of *Omar Khayyám* fame) devoured
it three times, and named a herring-lugger he owned *Marian Halcombe*
'after the brave girl in the story.'[1] The Prince Consort sent a copy to
Baron Stockmar. Readers took bets among themselves as to what could
be Sir Percival Glyde's dreadful secret (illegitimacy, as it turned out).
Manufacturers took the opportunity to bring out *The Woman in White*
perfume, cloaks and bonnets. Music-shops displayed *The Woman in
White* waltzes and quadrilles and (most improbably) a 'Fosco Galop'.[2]
According to Nuel Davis, '*The Woman in White* was probably the most
popular novel written in England during the nineteenth century.'[3]

Popular in itself, *The Woman in White* popularized a new form of novel
– variously called the newspaper novel, 'matter-of-fact romance', the
bigamy novel and, most enduringly, the sensation novel. The term was
double-edged: it denoted 'sensation' as in *cause célèbre* but also in the
narrower psychological application of 'violent stimulation of the senses'.
Sensation fiction was felt as much as read – 'electrifying the nerves of
the reader' as one (indignant) commentator of the period put it. Its
practitioners exploited the same shock-horror stories as the penny press
of the day. Sensationalists specialized in a jagged style of narration that
impacted on the reader's sensibility like bullets. In the manuscript of
Armadale, Collins paid minute attention to details of interruptive typo-
graphy: the italics, white and black lines (i.e. line spaces and rules) and

dynamic paragraphing which break up the narrative flow are all of Collins's own devising. At times the narrative whispers, at others it shouts; volume, tempo and intensity are all controlled by narrative device and typographic effect. As a genre, sensation fiction works against the idea of the organic 'book' – preferring to fragment its narrative into segments (sometimes, as in *Armadale*, perversely called 'books'). The manuscript of *Armadale* also shows Collins revising his text to sharpen 'curtain lines' – instalment endings designed to keep the reader in suspense for a month. D. A. Miller (who has done much to bring sensation fiction back into critical fashion) claims plausibly that 'the genre offers us one of the first instances of modern literature to address itself primarily to the sympathetic nervous system, where it grounds its characteristic adrenalin effects: accelerated heart rate and respiration, increased blood pressure, the pallor resulting from vasoconstriction, and so on.'[4]

It is a feature of the sensation novel that it wholeheartedly embraced the century's new-fangled communications, its transport systems and its technological inventions (displayed to a wondering world at the Great Exhibition of 1851 – an event on the edge of *Armadale*'s narrative). The telegraph figures centrally in sensation fiction, and the terseness of the still-expensive medium (it costs five shillings to use the 'electrical fluids', a character notes in *Armadale*) conditions the writers' prose. So does the 'agony column' advertisement in the daily newspaper (another form of communication that cost by the word) – a precursor of today's computer bulletin board. In several sections of *Armadale*, characters exchange letters by the incredibly quick penny post, which from 1839 allowed same-day reply at near-fax speed. They routinely exploit the new transport and communications systems in ingenious ways. Take, for instance, the following passage from Lydia Gwilt's journal (7 o'clock, 8 August 1851):

> I have just come back from a long round in a cab. First, to the cloak-room of the Great Western, to get the luggage which I sent there from All Saints' Terrace. Next, to the cloak-room of the South Eastern, to leave my luggage (labelled in Midwinter's name), to wait for me till the starting of the tidal train on Monday. Next, to the General Post Office, to post a letter to Midwinter at the rectory, which he will receive to-morrow morning. Lastly, back again to this house – from which I shall move no more till Monday comes. (p. 508)

Lydia Gwilt uses the machinery of the modern metropolis with the expertise of a Victorian James Bond (she also anticipates the secret agent's 'dead drop' routine). On another occasion, as she goes off to be fitted for her wedding dress (part of a diabolic personation scheme) Lydia senses that something is wrong. Someone is tailing her:

> I drove straight to the milliner's shop – which I had observed, when I was there yesterday, had a back entrance into a mews, for the apprentices to go in and out by. I went in at once, leaving the cab waiting for me at the door. 'A man is following me,' I said; 'and I want to get rid of him. Here is my cab-fare; wait ten minutes before you give it to the driver, and let me out at once by the back way!' In a moment I was out in the mews – in another, I was in the next street – in a third, I hailed a passing omnibus, and was a free woman again. (p. 502)

If Collins had taken out a patent on this 'throwing the tail' gimmick, his heirs would be millionaires. It has become a cliché with thriller writers. Also interesting is the emancipatory 'I . . . was a free woman again'. Lydia is liberated from the traditional constraints on nineteenth-century women by the technologies of modern civilization which allow her to melt invisibly into the London crowd. (It is significant that in the country – where no escape into anonymity is possible – she feels caged and can find release only in suicidally excessive draughts of laudanum.)

Lydia loves new mid-century technology for its own complicated sake. When, at the grisly climax of the story, she plots to kill Allan Armadale, she spurns arsenic (the poison of choice for lesser women) as too primitive. With her ominous purple flask of carbonic acid (a chemical whose toxic applications were first explored in 1858) she generates a subtle poison gas which she elaborately wafts into her victim's room via a 'fumigation system' (i.e. air-conditioning vents). It is high-tech homicide, 1860-style, and far more complex than strictly required for the purposes of extermination. But Lydia wants a modish murder to crown her career – poisoning with style.

It is one of the characterizing features of the 'sensationalists' that they came as close as libel permitted to headline stories of the day. No moderately wide-awake reader of *Armadale* during its serial run, for instance, would have failed to make the connection between Lydia Gwilt's foster-mother, Maria Oldershaw ('Mother Jezebel'), and 'Madame Rachel' – i.e. Rachel Leverson. This lady, proprietor of a New Bond Street beauty salon (which opened in 1863, as Collins was laying the groundwork for *Armadale*), was accused of fraud in December 1865 and was, while Collins wrote, one of the most notorious and criminally glamorous figures in the country.[5] Shortly after the novel's publication she was to be sent to prison. Collins anticipates the jury's verdict and comes as near as he (or his publisher George Smith) dares to contempt of court. Behind her beautician's front Mother Jezebel is a blackmailer, a procuress and an abortionist. So was Madame Rachel Leverson. Collins broadly hinted as much to his readers, before they had juridical confirmation in the newspapers of 1867. Another headline item which hovers over the narrative of *Armadale* is the 'sensational' Yelverton bigamy case (Lydia Gwilt is – among her other criminalities – a skilled bigamist; see Book the Fourth, Chapter X, note 11). There is also multiple allusion in *Armadale* to the spectacular domestic poisoning trials of the 1850s which had all the country agog (Lydia poisons one husband and tries to poison the two other men in her life; there are hints that she may have had other victims over the years). The other chic crime of the day, 'personation', also figures centrally in the novel (Collins, I suspect, had caught wind of the Tichborne affair as it was brewing up; see Book the Third, Chapter XI, note 2). *Armadale*, in short, is a novel which reverberates to the headlines of the popular press in the 1850s and early 1860s.[6]

Sensationalists were sometimes called 'the school of Dickens' (in the 1850s and 1860s many of them worked on *Household Words* or *All the Year Round*, the 2d. weekly newspapers both edited by Dickens).[7] Collins was the Inimitable's favourite protégé. Although Dickens did not entirely approve of the over-engineered quality of Wilkie's plots (and took the maestro's privilege of telling him so) he had fostered his young friend's career. *The Woman in White* had been first serialized to huge effect in Dickens's new weekly paper, *All the Year Round*. But Dickens, for all his literary grandeur, did not have the financial resources of the mid-Victorian publishing giants. In the wake of *The Woman in White*'s success, Collins was approached in July 1861 by George Smith, founder of the *Cornhill Magazine* (edited by Dickens's great rival, Thackeray). Smith – legendary for the lavishness of his bids to writers – offered Collins £5,000 for a new serial (subject unspecified) to run in his monthly magazine. Collins accepted, with the proviso that he clear an outstanding commitment to Dickens (*No Name*, as it was to be).

Collins fairly crowed about the size of Smith's offer in a letter to his mother: 'Five thousand pounds for nine months or at most a year's work – nobody but Dickens has made as much.'[8] It was not quite true. At around the same time, Smith offered no less than £10,000 to George Eliot for *Romola* (serialized in the *Cornhill Magazine*, 1862–3). But George Eliot was no journalist happy to toss a novel off in a few months. Her tale of fifteenth-century Florence would be a Herculean labour of historical research – one which, as she later recorded, she would embark on as a young woman and emerge from as an old woman.

Armadale did, in the event, need much more than nine months to come to birth. For one thing, Collins resolved to make it something supremely good; his masterpiece. He wanted, in a word, to out-Dickens Dickens. This involved lengthy fore-planning. He undertook a wealth of primary research in exotic locations for what was to be – by comparison with *The Woman in White* – an extraordinarily far-flung narrative (the action starts in the Black Forest, jumps parenthetically to the Caribbean, returns to the English West Country, makes a gloomy excursion to the Isle of Man, plays out the main romantic plot among the flat waters of the Norfolk Broads, and climaxes bloodily in Naples and London's newest suburb, Hampstead). Collins also authenticated the medical, nautical and legal subplots in which the narrative abounds. While not as fetishistic about such research as his fellow sensationalist Charles Reade, Collins was very careful about eyewitness confirmation and getting technical details right.

Research was not, however, the main retardant to *Armadale*'s completion. Collins suffered a collapse of health before and during composition. His doctors (particularly his and Dickens's close friend, Frank Beard) had prescribed in early 1863 a total sabbatical from writing which put back the eventual publication of *Armadale* almost two years. George Smith, always the best-natured of employers, was patient. No one knows exactly what ailed Collins, and if he himself knew he was deliberately vague on the subject. He was not an old man (he turned forty during the composition of *Armadale*). His sexual athleticism might have been envied by men half his age. The term used to describe his chronic complaint – rheumatic gout – disguises more than it reveals. Like other gout sufferers Wilkie had excruciating pain in his joints (specifically he had a bad ankle and foot, which he alludes to in the characterization of Mr Neal in the first chapter). But when feeling well, he could go sailing with his journalist friend Edward Pigott. It was a sport which he loved, and which he projects on to the yacht-mad Allan Armadale the younger. Wilkie's most disabling symptoms seem to have been nervous. Light and sound were intolerably painful to him during his bad times. He was also prone to crippling bouts of depression. Writing exacerbated his symptoms (something he projects on to Ozias in the Naples episode of *Armadale*). He had what seems to be a major nervous collapse just before the publication of the novel's first number. During the subsequent composition of *Armadale*, he persuaded his physician Beard to refer him to a nerve and brain specialist. As is well known, Wilkie was intermittently (and while writing *Armadale*) addicted to opium – in the form of laudanum. In the short term, the narcotic soothed him; but in the long term he suffered the extra burdens of toxic overdose and withdrawal.

Wilkie's father had died prematurely (aged fifty-eight) of an unspecified disease. His brother Charley (who had married Dickens's daughter Kate) was slowly dying of cancer in the 1860s (he had also proved impotent after marriage – something that concerned his super-potent father-in-law). *Armadale* is a novel obsessed with fate, congenital doom and inherited blight. The sins of the novel's fathers (Ozias's mark of Cain and his 'negro blood', for instance) are relentlessly visited on their sons. It is significant, as Catherine Peters points out, that in the first episode the patriarchal Allan Armadale is clearly dying of tertiary syphilis. Put all this together and the hypothesis that Collins feared that he had inherited some venereal affliction (euphemistically called 'rheumatic gout') suggests itself irresistibly.

Whatever the reasons, *Armadale* is a novel obsessed with illness. It begins at a German *Kurort*, with the mayor of the place welcoming 'the first sick people of the season' (p. 10). There are many sick people to come in *Armadale*. The action ends in a sanatorium where Dr Downward (alias Le Doux) specializes in making well women unwell by his sinister regime of 'rest'. The plot opens with two invalids – one of them making his dying confession which the other less terminally sick man records. The bedridden and twisted Mrs Milroy is one of the finest side-studies in the book. Nor are principal characters immune. Ozias Midwinter is given Collins's nervous symptoms. Lydia Gwilt is given Collins's drug addiction (at one point in the action she blesses the sainted man who invented laudanum). The Reverend Brock dies of the English cholera (that was indeed rampant in England in 1851). The eerie Jacobean figure of Mrs Oldershaw ('Mother Jezebel') enamels over the marks of sickness in the general population with her cosmetics. (In the case in which Madame Rachel was indicted in December 1865 she had undertaken to remove the ravages of smallpox from the face of an American woman, in return for all that woman's jewellery.) There is disease everywhere in the world of *Armadale*.

Collins has his primary fame in literary history as the 'inventor' of detective fiction, particularly on the strength of his next work, *The Moonstone* (1868) – the first fully formed *roman-policier* in English. Fiction's love-affair with detection can be traced back to Oedipus and his fatally rigorous investigations into who murdered Laius. But as a genre with its well-defined rules and conventions, the detective novel pioneered by Wilkie Collins was formed by three main influences: the memoirs of the French detective E. F. Vidocq (and the imitations produced by bandwagon-following Scotland Yard detectives); the 1857 Matrimonial Causes Act which legitimized divorce on the production of the necessary 'evidence' (for which an army of private detectives was recruited); and the growing sophistication of criminals which in turn demanded a cleverer police force. Criminals, as Collins declared through the grandiose conception of Count Fosco in *The Woman in White*, were becoming very clever indeed – so clever that the old Dogberries and flatfoots of the traditional British law had no hope of catching them. What was needed was a new brand of criminal investigator – as resourceful and intelligent as the new artists in crime.

There are three kinds of detective encountered in Collins's fiction. First (and most prominent in the novels from *The Woman in White* to *Armadale*) are the amateur sleuths – intrepid individuals like Walter Hartright, Marian Halcombe, or the Reverend Decimus Brock who dedicate themselves to uncovering crime (Brock, even at death's door, is prepared to risk his professional reputation by trailing beautiful women round the streets of London). A second category – which only makes its appearance with Sergeant Cuff in *The Moonstone* – is the CID officer, the professional detective (oddly, not a single police officer, of any kind, appears at any point in *Armadale*). The last category is the private investigator (or 'confidential agent'). These 'spies' nauseated Collins, particularly at the time of writing *Armadale* – where the 'private eye' is represented by the obnoxious James Bashwood, with his army of hired snoopers. In the seventeenth number there is a denunciation of the private detective, whose rhetoric casts the genus into an even deeper pit of moral distaste than husband-poisoners like Miss Gwilt:

> No ordinary observation, applying the ordinary rules of analysis, would have detected the character of Bashwood the younger in his face. His youthful look, aided by his light hair, and his plump beardless cheeks; his easy manner, and his ever ready smile; his eyes which met unshrinkingly the eyes of every one whom he addressed, all combined to make the impression of him a favourable impression in the general mind. No eye for reading character, but such an eye as belongs to one person, perhaps, in ten thousand, could have penetrated the smoothly-deceptive surface of this man, and have seen him for what he really was – the vile creature whom the viler need of Society has fashioned for its own use.

There he sat – the Confidential Spy of modern times, whose business is steadily enlarging, whose Private Inquiry Offices are steadily on the increase. There he sat – the necessary Detective attendant on the progress of our national civilization; a man who was in this instance at least, the legitimate and intelligible product of the vocation that employed him; a man professionally ready on the merest suspicion (if the merest suspicion paid him) to get under our beds, and to look through gimlet-holes in our doors. (pp. 516–17)

So much for Sherlock Holmes, Sam Spade, Philip Marlowe and Magnum PI. Why is Collins so angry? Because he despised the divorce work which had brought these professional Peeping Toms into being after 1857. Collins's distaste was not impersonal: his own sexual life was highly irregular (he had two live-in mistresses in the 1860s, one of whom had a husband in the background). He was a fornicator, an adulterer and (probably) a consorter with ladies of the night. He was certainly sympathetic with Dickens who, in his fifties, had abandoned his wife and taken up with a young actress in her twenties, Ellen Ternan. Both novelists were probably targets of gimlet-boring peepers like James Bashwood – or feared they might be with all the hideous publicity that would ensue. In the event, Collins covered his tracks remarkably efficiently (as did Dickens) and – despite a huge expenditure of biographical effort – little is known of his secret life. But there certainly was an area of his life that he was determined to keep out of the public gaze.

Armadale depicts a world saturated in espionage. During the central section of the narrative Allan has set a man to spy on Lydia, who on her part is eavesdropping on Allan's love conversations with Miss Milroy in Thorpe-Ambrose Park. Meanwhile, bedridden Mrs Milroy has bribed her nurse to steam open her governess's letters. Lydia, on another front, has persuaded the love-besotted Felix Bashwood to spy on his employer, Allan, and report back to her. Bashwood has his son, James, investigate Miss Gwilt and report back to him (he feebly hopes to blackmail her into marriage). Bashwood has stationed men and women all round the capital. Pedgift is elsewhere investigating the mysterious Maria Older-shaw and her London aliases. Even Brock (the most easily deluded of these spies) is following suspicious women round the streets of London. It is, as Catherine Peters puts it, 'a nightmare world, in which even thoughts cease to be private, a picture of English society as a claustrophobic prison'.[9]

It is sometimes claimed that Collins is at his best with minor characters. *Armadale* certainly has a full cast of memorable *ficelles* and vignettes: the eccentric clockmaker Major Milroy (a variation on Dickens's maniac hobbyist Monsieur Manette); the 'no fool like an old fool', Felix Bashwood, parading like some seedy peacock in his finery to catch the eye of the deadly woman he loves (it is hard not to think that aspects of the Dickens–Ternan affair did not cross Collins's mind in this subplot); the garrulous gardener Abel Sage, who briefly and hilariously lightens the gloomy world of Thorpe-Ambrose, as does the ineffably wet Reverend Pentecost, who proves himself capable of getting seasick on a Norfolk Broad. The Pedgifts, father and son, are among Collins's finest lawyer creations – men so thoroughly conditioned by their profession that one suspects they have ink not blood in their veins.

For all this wealth of incidental characterization (it is a very populous novel), *Armadale* is dominated by its three Napoleons of crime: Dr Downward – the ladies' doctor who specializes in sinister anti-hysteria treatments; the painter of women, Maria Oldershaw (Collins has a misogynistic hatred of cosmetic art, associating it with moral corruption); and the Luciferian Lydia Gwilt. Each is a powerful creation, but as he tinkered with the plot in later life for stage adaptations, Wilkie distilled his creation down to a single portrait – 'Miss Gwilt'. The apotheosis of Lydia was logical. She is an extraordinarily complex creation. As allusions suggest, Lady Macbeth was in Collins's mind. Lydia's closer literary pedigree is easily traced. The good and bad governess had been stock types in the English novel for a quarter of a century. The dualism was set up by *Vanity Fair*'s Becky Sharp (gold-digger seductress, adulteress, adventuress, whore, poisoner) and – on the other side – plucky little Jane Eyre and her virtuous Brontean colleagues, Agnes Grey and Lucy Snowe.

The governess type changed melodramatically in the 1860s with three highly successful novels that twisted the characterization in startlingly new ways, blending good and bad inextricably. In Mrs Henry Wood's *East Lynne* (1861) the guilty wife, Isabel Vane (vain by nature as well as name), pays the price of her adulteries by losing her beauty in a catastrophic train crash. She returns – a shattered but chastened woman – to become the unrecognized governess ('Madame Vine') to the children she earlier abandoned. (One dies without knowing who she is, provoking the immortal 'dead! dead! and never called me mother!') In Mary Braddon's *Lady Audley's Secret* (1862) the governess Lucy Graham – a stunning Pre-Raphaelite beauty – catches the eye of rich old Sir Michael Audley of Audley Court. He marries and ennobles her.

But there is a secret in Lucy's past. A husband returns; she murderously pushes him down a well. Tracked down by a resourceful private detective (whom she attempts to kill by arson) Lady Audley is finally unmasked as the uxoricidal bigamist she is. She goes mad, and dies. In Joseph Le Fanu's intricately plotted *Uncle Silas* (1864), the horrific French governess Madame de la Rougierre specializes in killing her sleeping victims (a spiked hammer figures in the bloody climax). Wilkie Collins had himself complicated the stereotype with his sexually ambiguous Marian Halcombe – the resolute and 'manly' young governess who takes and vanquishes Count Fosco (winning his corrupt Italianate heart in the process).

This was fiction. Real life (as reflected in the newspapers) was dominated by another sexually ambiguous image – that of the domestic poisoner: the woman (bound by oath to love, honour, cherish and obey) who slips packets of arsenic into her unsuspecting husband's food and drink. 'There is probably no form of guilt', the *Annual Register* wrote in 1862, 'that strikes the mind of society with a deeper sense of disgust than that of secret poisoning'.[10] Poisoning by women, it principally meant. There was an epidemic of such crimes in the middle of the nineteenth century, as Mary Hartman records in *Victorian Murderesses*.[11] And there was the ineradicable suspicion (bolstered by the acquittal of clearly guilty women like Madeleine Smith in 1857) that innumerable other cases were never detected by the authorities.

There had been a whole series of highly publicized spousal poisonings in the 1850s. Sarah Chesham in 1851 (the year in which *Armadale* is set) was tried for no fewer than three murders before the law caught up with her. On being sentenced to hang she betrayed no emotion to watching eyes and 'walked with a firm step from the dock' to execution – a fate she met with equal impassivity. Constance Wilson, another career poisoner who was executed in 1862, was similarly inscrutable. She heard her sentence with 'an air of callous indifference' and was hanged at Newgate on 20 October 1862, before a crowd of 20,000 onlookers. What, most of them must have wondered, motivated this fiend in woman's shape? Many of those 20,000 spectators must have brought the same question to *Armadale* a few months later. Collins set out to give them an answer in his depiction of Lydia Gwilt, a mass poisoner seen from the inside.[12]

As Collins portrays her (and as she portrays herself in her journal) Miss Gwilt is an enigmatic figure. Her career has to be assembled from indirect (and occasionally deceptive) comments in the narrative, corroborated against James Bashwood's detective testimony (but even he, indefatigable though he is, cannot penetrate all her mysteries). It seems that Lydia Gwilt (strange name) came from nowhere. The first record we have is of her being the foster-child of Mrs Oldershaw (Mother Jezebel), in the early days when she and her apothecary husband sold potions from a horse and cart. The Oldershaws claim – wholly unconvincingly – to be Lydia's uncle and aunt. Until the age of eight Lydia was supported by payments, which then mysteriously stopped. She may be the daughter of a count, or a streetwalker, or both. She has a magnificent head of red hair (as Richard Altick reminds us, this colour of hair was profoundly disturbing to Victorians, see Book the Third, Chapter X, note 3). At twelve, Lydia catches the eye of rich young Jane Blanchard, who captiously decides she wants the flame-haired child as her maid. In the easygoing and morally lax Thorpe-Ambrose household Lydia is 'petted and made a plaything'. In an ingenious but unconvincing turn of plot, the pre-pubescent Lydia ('barely twelve years old') is persuaded by the most amoral of the novel's Allan Armadales (alias Ingleby) to forge a letter. The pretext is that he does not have Lydia's 'wicked dexterity' with the pen – but the real reason must be that forgery in 1832 is a capital offence, and Armadale-Ingleby is no fool. Reading between the lines, we assume that he sexually seduced the young maid. How else explain the curses heaped on her by the paternal Allan Armadale, as he lies dying. She is a more than leprous thing: 'I saw the girl afterwards – and my blood curdled at the sight of her. If she is alive now, woe to the people who trust her! No creature more innately deceitful and more innately pitiless ever walked this earth' (p. 34–5). (This, remind ourselves, is a twelve-year-old girl who did nothing more than imitate one adult's handwriting at the instigation of another adult.)

After the bloody consequence of her forgery, Lydia is bundled off to France. She is pensioned on condition that she never return to England. 'Unpleasantness' follows wherever she goes. A respectably married music teacher attempts suicide and goes mad. The still under-age Lydia has, apparently, seduced and ruined him. To protect the male sex, the young she-devil is confined to a religious establishment. Extreme in all things, she decides to take the veil. Better for the male sex had Lydia Gwilt been mewed up, as in earlier days. The nineteenth-century convent cannot reform or hold her, and Lydia Gwilt – now a dangerous woman – is loosed on the world to do her mischief. Already she has had an eventful enough life to fill several novels (some of them unpublishable in nineteenth-century England).

Lydia has only her red hair, her beauty, her musical talent and her unscrupulosity with which to make her way. Ever resourceful, she becomes a pianist in a 'low concert room in Brussels' where she is taken up by a Baroness who needs a beautiful young woman as bait for her card-sharping business. Five years pass. In Naples, Lydia entraps one of the Baroness's dupes, a rich young Englishman, into marriage. She returns to his home on the Yorkshire moors as a respectable lady, Mrs Waldron. But, corrupt to the core, she takes a Cuban lover – the magnificently disreputable Captain Manuel. Her cuckolded husband beats her with a horse whip; in return she poisons him. At this stage still inexpert in the murderer's skills she is apprehended, convicted, and – after furious (and sentimentally wrong-headed) protest from the papers – pardoned by the Home Secretary (for Collins's allusions to current events here, see Book the Fourth, Chapter XV, note 6). Spared the rope, Lydia is none the less obliged to serve two years in prison for theft. On her release, she makes an irregular 'Scotch marriage' with Manuel. But since he is already married, as she later discovers, the union is void. She blackmails her old employer, Mrs Armadale *née* Blanchard, and is in turn robbed and abandoned by the faithless Manuel. At this low point in her life she attempts a very public suicide, and in so doing sets off the series of deaths (but not her own) that lead to blue-eyed Allan Armadale inheriting Thorpe-Ambrose. The stage is set for the events of May to December 1851 which make up the body of the narrative.

However carefully we read *Armadale*, there remain tantalizing gaps in Lydia's history. Who *were* her parents? Did Collins keep this in reserve, and never get round to filling in the missing information? When – veiled, and with her distinctive red Paisley shawl flying – she threw herself from the first-class deck of the Thames steamer did she know that Arthur Blanchard, heir to Thorpe-Ambrose, was on board the vessel? Was it an attempt to lure him into a marriage trap, as she had other men? Or was she genuinely bent on self-destruction? At many points in the novel Lydia is baffling to the reader. She is also baffling to herself. Why, she wonders (as the reader might well wonder), does she keep a journal – something that may send her to the gallows:

> Why do I keep a diary at all? Why did the clever thief the other day (in the English newspapers) keep the very thing to convict him, in the shape of a record of every thing he stole? Why are we not perfectly reasonable in all that we do? Why am I not always on my guard and never inconsistent with myself, like a wicked character in a novel? Why? why? why? (p. 559)

Lydia is similarly perplexed by her uncontrollable love for her victim,

Midwinter. At other points in the narrative, she actually fears herself and wishes that – to spare the human race – she might be locked up. Why, she wonders, does she so hate Allan? Or does she hate him? Is it love gone wrong that makes her so vindictive? Do women love the men they poison? The 'Why? why? why?' is never satisfactorily answered.

Lydia's inability to fathom her own motives, her irrationalism and her fatal inability to control her temper (the typical weakness of redheads) leads her to commit a string of blunders – leaving her employment at Thorpe-Ambrose in a tantrum of rage against Neelie, for instance. Banished from the household, she has no hope of entrapping Allan in marriage. Steeping herself in laudanum is another inexplicable stupidity in one so calculating. Her strange refusal to shed her name for the purpose of disguise, which leads her into the absurdity of pretending to be 'the other Miss Gwilt', is bizarre. One of the most interesting and experimental sections of the novel is that in which Collins offers us a double perspective on the same crucial days in late July 1851: in the form of Lydia's confidential (but actually very guarded) letters to Mother Jezebel, and in the form of her more candid journal entries for the same days. But even with this binocular insight, Lydia remains invincibly mysterious.

The reviewers of *Armadale* hated Lydia Gwilt, and she was probably one of the reasons for the novel selling badly when it came out in volume form in May 1866. Mrs Oliphant (an inveterate foe to sensation fiction) had complained that in Collins's previous novel, *No Name*, the criminal heroine had been allowed to live. Collins would not make that mistake in *Armadale* (and his epigraph on the title page made it clear that Miss Gwilt was not to profit from her wrongdoing). None the less, his critics were unmollified. The *Spectator* foamed with rage at a novel which 'gives us for its heroine a woman fouler than the refuse of the streets'. Collins had overstepped the limits of decency and 'revolted every human sentiment'. This reviewer and others were particularly indignant that Lydia remained beautiful to the end – despite her evil ways. She would have been acceptable if, like Isabel Vane in *East Lynne*, she had been providentially disfigured (perhaps a rotted nose, or loss of teeth, or premature whitening of her red hair would have sufficed). In the *Athenaeum*, Collins's erstwhile friend Henry Chorley was, if anything, even more apoplectic in his denunciation of Lydia: 'one of the most hardened female villains whose devices and desires have ever blackened literature'. Wilkie, one suspects, was unrepentant (although he would doubtless have liked good sales). And most modern readers will have a more generous and thoughtful reaction to the fascinating Miss Gwilt than the affronted moral guardians of 1866.

If Lydia is the most interesting creation in the novel, Ozias Midwinter runs her close. He seems to have been initially conceived as a deliberate contradiction to elements in Thackeray's novel *Philip*, which ran in the *Cornhill Magazine* a couple of years before (1861–2). *Philip* sets up a tendentious opposition between the manly, Anglo-Saxon, blue-eyed, hearty hero of the title and his odious rival, the mulatto, Captain Grenville Woolcomb. Woolcomb (who is West Indian by origin) is sexually lascivious, rich, degenerate and corrupt. He steals the hero's intended wife and (black devil that he is) abuses her unspeakably. In the last chapters he stands for Parliament, under the slogan 'Am I not a man and a brudder?' The opposition between Philip and Woolcomb is virulently racist and politically weighted in the context of the civil war raging in America in the early 1860s. Thackeray's position on black Americans (whom he had seen in his 1852 and 1858 trips) was unequivocal and obnoxious: 'Sambo is not my man and brother', he frankly declared. His allusion, of course, is to the abolitionists' slogan, 'Am I not a man and a brother?' In his political sympathies Thackeray was strongly and virulently pro-South and anti-abolitionist. His prejudices were prominently expressed in the *Cornhill Magazine*, which he edited until March 1862 and to which he was the star contributor until his death at Christmas 1863.[13]

Ozias Midwinter has a Creole mother (whose first question, on learning that her husband loved someone before herself, is 'Was she a fair woman – or dark, like me?' (p. 31)). By setting the prelude in 1832 (the year before the emancipation of West Indian blacks), Collins ostentatiously stressed the point that Ozias is a child of slavery. On a number of occasions, the reader is reminded of Ozias's 'negro' appearance – particularly when he is aroused and the blood rushes to his face. His 'tawny' complexion is also the mark of Cain – Ozias is the son of a murderer and if he has racially tainted blood on one side of his parentage he has criminally tainted blood on the other. There is a telling episode, shortly after Ozias's first appearance in the novel, in which the Reverend Brock looks at him and is consumed with pathological disgust:

> His shaven head, tied up roughly in an old yellow silk handker-chief; his tawny, haggard cheeks; his bright brown eyes, preter-naturally large and wild; his tangled black beard; his long supple, sinewy fingers, wasted by suffering, till they looked like claws . . .

If this man was honest, his eyes showed a singular perversity in looking away and denying it. Possibly they were affected in some degree by a nervous restlessness in his organization, which appeared to pervade every fibre in his lean, lithe body. The rector's healthy Anglo-Saxon flesh crept responsively at every casual movement of the usher's supple brown fingers, and every passing distortion of the usher's haggard yellow face. (p. 64)

Brock's first inclination is to cast out this unclean, degenerate, mixed-breed thing. But eventually he comes to love, admire and trust Ozias. When the clergyman dies, it is to the mulatto's care that he leaves Allan. On his part, the fair-haired, blue-eyed Allan comes to see Ozias as his brother. There is a telling moment when the Creole and the Anglo-Saxon clasp hands on board the ominous ship (*La Grace de Dieu*) where the primal murder of one father by another took place, eighteen years before. 'The cruel time is coming,' Ozias warns Allan, 'when we shall rue the day we ever met. Shake hands, brother, on the edge of the precipice – shake hands while we are brothers still' (p. 126).

It is inconceivable that a novelist as aware as Collins would not know how this fraternal embrace of black and white as equals would be read in Civil War America – more particularly in the North (where *Armadale* was serialized in *Harper's New Monthly Magazine*).[14] In fact, the novel went down very well in the States – better than in Britain, where it was something of a sales flop. In dramatic versions of *Armadale*, Collins removed the negroid characteristics of Ozias, evidently feeling that the racial plot was not to English tastes.

There are interesting things happening on the edges of *Armadale*. Not least, Collins's own vexed private life was in turmoil as he assembled the novel's intricate plot. As one of his latest biographers (William M. Clarke) assumes, it was in 1864 that Collins complicated his irregular sexual affairs to an extraordinary degree. For the better part of a decade he had been living with Caroline Graves (the original woman in white). In 1864 she was just under thirty-five years old, and a widow. Caroline was a woman of the world who may, as a common-law wife, have lived for some periods 'bigamously' with Collins (her marital status has never been entirely clear). They moved house in 1864 and, after his bohemian fashion, Wilkie played the part of paterfamilias (Caroline had a young daughter, Harriet, by her first husband). Caroline was a sophisticated, cultivated woman who could evidently discourse to Wilkie on his work and hold her own socially with his literary friends.

Wilkie Collins was not, however, a man to be satisfied with one woman. In 1864 (as Clarke reckons) he met the simple Norfolk girl Martha Rudd (the meeting may be recalled in the Hurle Mere passage of *Armadale*, Book the Third, Chapters VIII–IX). Martha was just nineteen and very unworldly. Eventually (probably in 1867, a year after completing *Armadale*), Wilkie persuaded her to come to London. In a second household where he reigned as another paterfamilias, she bore him three children. He never made her an honest woman. As Clarke records, Collins contrived to live over the years with both women (apart from a brief and mysterious period during which Caroline was married to a third party). He was buried with Caroline – but Martha evidently had the greater claim to be his common-law wife.

For all the ingenious investigations and speculations of recent biography, we know tantalizingly little about Collins's private life. As Clarke observes: 'How he kept in touch with Martha [after 1864] and why he eventually persuaded her to move to London – and when – is shrouded in mystery. But that she was in the background during Caroline's continued efforts to persuade Wilkie to marry her is hardly in doubt. One can only marvel at his stamina in keeping his two women reasonably content'.[15] Some of the strains on his stamina can be deduced from *Armadale*. Much of Lydia's journal, in the central section of the narrative, is obsessed by her fury, as a 35-year-old woman of the world, against the little Norfolk chit, sixteen-year-old Neelie Milroy. Allan Armadale – the great male sexual prize in the novel – is attracted to both women, and at different times proposes marriage to both. Neelie, however, wins him. We have no records whatsoever of Collins's domestic life, what recriminations were exchanged in the sexual triangle set up after 1864. But it is hard not to think that Lydia's woman-of-the-world sarcasm at Neelie's schoolgirlish sexual immaturity and provincial gaucheness do not echo what was said (or what Collins feared would be said) by an enraged Caroline in their parlour at Melcombe Place. 'Am I handsome enough, to-day?' Lydia asks her journal. 'Well, yes', she answers, 'handsome enough to be a match for a little dowdy, awkward, freckled creature, who ought to be perched on a form at school, and strapped to a back-board to straighten her crooked shoulders' (p. 428).

For all the author's high hopes, *Armadale* never achieved very great things. Perhaps Collins tried too hard. But the novel was also damaged by the delay in publishing it. During the interval (1863–4) a massive anti-sensation-novel campaign was whipped up. Leading the charge was the *Quarterly Review*, with a broadside denunciation (taking in no less than twenty-four novels) in April 1863, alleging that the country was being debauched by the avalanche of trashy sensation novels loosed on it.[16] In exactly the same period, Dickens's *All the Year Round* lost readers in droves with Charles Reade's *Hard Cash* (3,000 as the author recorded) – a novel inevitably partnered in the public mind with *Armadale*. Dickens was impelled to publish a statement with Reade's last number, dissociating his journal from *Hard Cash*.[17] Circulation figures recorded by Smith show that, after a lift in November 1864, *Armadale* lost during its serial run about the same number of subscribers to the *Cornhill Magazine* as *Hard Cash* had lost Dickens.

George Smith, who was not a courageous publisher (even if he had published *Jane Eyre* fifteen years before), capitulated by serializing alongside *Armadale* two 'domestic' novels – Trollope's *The Claverings* and Mrs Gaskell's idyll *Wives and Daughters*. In Latin, as Reade pointed out, domestic meant 'tame', and these were excessively innocuous works that studiously avoided what Reade (in *Hard Cash*) called 'the dark places of England'. Collins himself was affected by the furore, and despite brave talk in his preface about 'Clap trap morality' took care to emphasize the 'Christian morality' of the book. In the body of the narrative, Collins ceded the moral centre to the excruciatingly preachy Decimus Brock. The novel ends with an invocation of the saintly Brock by Ozias as he addresses Allan in the happy-ever-after of his marriage to Neelie: 'God is all-merciful, God is all-Wise. In those words, your dear old friend once wrote to me. In that faith, I can look back without murmuring at the years that are past, and can look on without doubting to the years that are to come' (p.677). This priggishness (out of character in both Ozias and Wilkie) was a sop to the moral critics yapping at Collins's heels. They were not mollified: *Armadale* was mauled by the critics. Smith did not use Collins again (nor did he ever earn as much for any one novel again). In his next major piece of writing Collins avoided moral provocation and perfected the machinery of the detective novel, with his brilliant (and morally inoffensive) whodunnit, *The Moonstone*.

The main flaw in *Armadale* for many readers is its obtrusive 'theme'. George Eliot had made 'determinism' a fashionable topic for novelists in *Adam Bede* (1859), where in Chapter Sixteen Arthur Donnithorne and the Reverend Irwine debate whether a man has freedom of choice in his moral decisions, or whether he is nothing more than an automaton. This concern was, in part, a function of the growing sophistication of fiction as an explanatory tool for human behaviour. Novelists like Eliot and Collins could explain so much of motive and the influence of circumstance that their characters no longer seemed free agents – at least to the reader privileged with the narrator's god-like insight.

There are, however, deeper and less clear-cut aspects to the fatality theme in *Armadale*. The novel communicates a primitive sense of doom which one is tempted to connect with the sabbatarianism and religious austerity of Wilkie's father – a dominant influence on his sons' lives. William Collins exuded an atmosphere of imminent damnation for sinners. He was, for instance, 'convinced that both the outbreak of cholera and the Reform Bill riots of 1831 were God's judgement'.[18] Kenneth Robinson plausibly suggests that Wilkie's character (and life-long bohemianism) was largely formed in opposition to his father's religiosity. One suspects he may have been haunted by William Collins's posthumous condemnation. Wilkie embarked on an elaborate depiction of Ozias's Calvinist stepfather in the character of Alexander Neal which he subsequently deleted (see Book the First, Chapter II, note 5). It might have made the novel's moral design clearer had he kept it in.

When we encounter Ozias Midwinter for the first time he carries with him in his knapsack two volumes: the plays of Sophocles and Goethe's *Faust*. They are emblems of the free will–determinism conundrum that obsesses him. At one pole is Oedipus Rex, the man who cannot escape his fate, run as he will. At the other pole is Faust, who damns himself by clear-headed choice. Both tragic heroes are doomed, but the machineries by which they meet their doom are opposite. The 'Dream' (which Collins altered significantly in the manuscript) overlays the narrative as prophecy, its fulfilment as inevitable as the Delphic oracle's. But Ozias is not entirely convinced. His uncertainty as to whether his destiny is to be that of Oedipus or Faust, automaton or free agent, feeds into what is the most striking scene in the novel, when Major Milroy's elaborate clock goes wrong. As the hour chimes and the little figures crash into each other (the Major is meanwhile buried in the entrails of his machine) Ozias is seized with uncontrollable hysteria at the 'catastrophe of the puppets':

> His paroxysms of laughter followed each other with such convul-sive violence, that Miss Milroy started back from him in alarm, and even the patient major turned on him with a look which said plainly, Leave the room! Allan, wisely impulsive for once in his life, seized Midwinter by the arm, and dragged him out by main force into the garden, and thence into the park beyond.
>
> 'Good heavens! What has come to you!' he exclaimed, shrinking back from the tortured face before him, as he stopped and looked close at it for the first time.
>
> For the moment, Midwinter was incapable of answering. The

hysterical paroxysm was passing from one extreme to the other. He leaned against a tree, sobbing and gasping for breath, and stretched out his hand in mute entreaty to Allan to give him time. (p. 225)

It is a surreal episode, more so given Ozias's heroic self-control later in the novel. The reason that he reacts as he does at the débâcle of the Major's horological automaton can, however, be guessed at. It is a spontaneous and uncontrollable surge of relief that clockwork can actually go wrong. It is a hopeful catastrophe. Life's outcome is not necessarily ordained.

As T. S. Eliot (an unlikely admirer of the novel) said, *Armadale* has the great virtue of melodrama – that of 'delaying longer than one could conceive it possible to delay, a conclusion which is inevitable and wholly foreordained'.[19] In general this is true (we know that Allan must live happily with Neelie and that Lydia must come to an appropriately bad end). But *Armadale* none the less retains its ability to surprise us with regard to Ozias. To the very last page, Collins keeps us in suspense as to whether the narrative will climax with the deterministic vision of the dream (the fatal woman killing Ozias) or whether, like the Major's clock, the machine will break down, allowing Ozias to live. The manuscript suggests that Collins himself – for all his talk of foreplanning – was not entirely certain in his mind as to what Ozias Midwinter's end should be. It is one of the many features that make *Armadale* one of the most gripping of Victorian page-turners.

Notes

1. Kenneth Robinson, *Wilkie Collins* (London, 1951), p. 149. Following references are shortened to 'Robinson'.

2. Catherine Peters, *The King of Inventors: Wilkie Collins* (London, 1991), p. 227. Following references are shortened to 'Peters'.

3. Nuel Davis, *The Life of Wilkie Collins* (Illinois, 1956), p. 216. Following references are shortened to 'Davis'.

4. D. A. Miller, *The Novel and the Police* (Berkeley: California, 1988), p. 146. Miller's influential essay on Collins draws on a close reading of the texts and Foucauldian theory.

5. See Richard Altick, *The Presence of the Present* (Columbus: Ohio, 1991), pp. 540–45, for a description of Madame Rachel's notoriety in the 1860s. Following references are shortened to 'Altick'. For Collins and the newspapers see

Christopher Kent, 'Probability, Reality, and Sensation', *Dickens Studies Annual*, 20, 1991.

6. It will be noted, however, that Collins set *Armadale* in 1851. His motives for this slight antedating were probably to protect himself against accusations of libel.

7. The patriarchal role of Dickens in the school is argued in W. C. Phillips, *Dickens, Reade, and Collins: Sensation Novelists* (London, 1919).

8. Peters, p. 236.

9. Ibid., p. 275.

10. *Annual Register*, 1862, p. 453.

11. Mary S. Hartman, *Victorian Murderesses* (New York, 1977). Following references are shortened to 'Hartman'.

12. As Altick points out (pp. 525–6), Collins was evidently very influenced by the case of the poisoner Madeleine Smith. See also Hartman, Chapter Two.

13. For Thackeray's prejudices on race see Deborah Thomas, *Thackeray and Slavery* (Athens: Ohio, 1993).

14. Susan Balée touches on this subject in 'English Critics, American Crisis, and the Sensation Novel', *Nineteenth Century Contexts*, Spring 1993.

15. William M. Clarke, *The Secret Life of Wilkie Collins* (London, 1988), p. 112.

16. The article in the *Quarterly* was by the Reverend H. C. Mansel, April 1863, 481–514. For other attacks of the period, see Norman Page, *Wilkie Collins: The Critical Heritage* (London, 1974). Collins responds to these attacks in *Armadale* (see Book the Last, Chapter III, note 1).

17. See John Sutherland, 'Dickens, Reade, and *Hard Cash*,' *The Dickensian*, Spring 1985.

18. Robinson, p. 16.

19. See T. S. Eliot's long essay on Collins (1927), reprinted in *Selected Essays 1917–1932* (London, 1933).

FURTHER READING

For many years the standard critical lives of Collins were Kenneth Robinson's *Wilkie Collins* (London, 1951, reprinted 1974) and Nuel P. Davis's *The Life of Wilkie Collins* (Urbana: Illinois, 1956). These have been supplanted by two meticulously researched recent biographies: William M. Clarke, *The Secret Life of Wilkie Collins* (London, 1988) and Catherine Peters, *The King of Inventors: Wilkie Collins* (London, 1991). Clarke (a descendant of Collins by marriage) has dug up more than anyone thought possible about Wilkie's 'secret lives' (particularly his irregular sexual arrangements). Working independently, Peters has brought to light much new material on Collins's early home life and family background. Her book is particularly relevant to *Armadale* in its illuminating discussion of Collins's obsession with doubles, *doppelgängers*, stolen and recovered identity.

The traditional (and still informative) critical study of sensation fiction is Walter C. Phillips, *Dickens, Reade, and Collins: Sensation Novelists* (New York, 1919). Good summaries of the accumulated scholarship on Collins will be found in W. H. Marshall, *Wilkie Collins* (Boston, 1970) and Ira B. Nadel and William E. Fredeman, eds., *Victorian Novelists after 1885*, *Dictionary of Literary Biography* 18 (Detroit, 1983). A good selection of contemporary and later-nineteenth-century commentary is given in Norman Page, *Wilkie Collins: The Critical Heritage* (London 1974).

Coming closer to the present, the 1980s and 1990s have seen an explosion of interest in this school of fiction. Most useful to the editor of Collins are works which fill in the socio-historical-literary background. R. D. Altick's three books – *The Presence of the Present* (Columbus: Ohio, 1991); *Deadly Encounters* (Philadelphia, 1986); and *Victorian Studies in Scarlet* (New York, 1970) – supply an invaluable context to *Armadale*. So too does Mary S. Hartman's *Victorian Murderesses* (New York, 1976). The complex medical background to *Armadale* is illuminatingly dealt with by Jenny Bourne Taylor, *In the Secret Theatre of Home* (London, 1988). Nicholas Rance, *Wilkie Collins and Other Sensation Novelists* (London, 1991), is instructive on the political subtexts to the novel as is Philip O'Neill's *Wilkie Collins: Women, Property, Propriety* (London, 1988). As its title suggests, Winfred Hughes's *The Maniac in the Cellar: Sensation*

Novels of the 1860s (Princeton, 1980) directs its attention at the literary context; so does Sue Lonoff's informative *Wilkie Collins and his Victorian Readers* (New York, 1982).

Interviewers at the MLA conventions in the early 1990s noted a large number of Ph.D. theses in progress or just completed on Wilkie Collins. The inspiration for this fashionability is largely attributable to D. A. Miller's influential, Foucauldian *The Novel and the Police* (Berkeley: California, 1988) and Peter Brooks's *Reading for the Plot* (New York, 1985), both of which reappraise Collins in the light of 'theory'. A good example of the new wave of Collins criticism is Jonathan Loesberg, 'The Ideology of Narrative Form in Sensation Fiction', *Representations*, 13, Winter 1986. Feminist critics have also begun to examine the genre thoughtfully. See, for example, Elaine Showalter, 'Desperate Remedies: Sensation Novels of the 1860s', *Victorian Newsletter*, 49, September 1976. This line has been followed up by Tamar Heller, *Dead Secrets: Wilkie Collins and the Female Gothic* (New Haven: Connecticut, 1992).

On another front, it is noticeable that many of Collins's novels have been returned to print in the 1980s. There are two other editions of *Armadale* currently available: Catherine Peters's 'World's Classics' edition (Oxford, 1989) which has extremely valuable annotation and reproduces the 1869, one-volume text; and the 'Dover' edition (New York, 1977) which reproduces the *Cornhill* text – it has no annotation but offers the full range of George Thomas's illustrations.

The standard bibliographies of Collins's works are: M. C. Parrish and Elizabeth V. Miller, *Wilkie Collins and Charles Reade: First Editions described with Notes* (New York, 1940, reprinted 1968) and Kirk H. Beetz, *Wilkie Collins: An Annotated Bibliography* (Methuen: New Jersey, 1978).

A NOTE ON THE TEXT

The publisher George Smith offered Collins the large sum of £5,000 for the rights to a new novel (*Armadale* as it was to be) in July 1861. The letter in which he communicated the news to his mother records Wilkie's glee: 'Nobody but Dickens has made as much . . . if I live and keep my brains in good working order, I shall have got to the top of the tree, after all, before forty'.[1] As was common with writers at the top of the tree, no subject was specified at this stage. Wilkie Collins's name was sufficient. Smith's bid was evidently for the serial and first volume rights (the contract has not, apparently, survived). The proposed work was to be serialized in twenty monthly numbers of Smith's *Cornhill Magazine*, which had been launched in January 1860 with great fanfare. Smith was legendarily open-handed in his payments, and had recruited Thackeray as editor (he retired in March 1862) and all the great novelists of the day as contributors (less Dickens, who had started his own magazine, *All the Year Round*, in 1859). Collins's payment was more than the £3,500 Trollope received for *The Small House at Allington*, the novel which immediately preceded *Armadale*, but considerably less than the £10,000 George Eliot was offered for *Romola* (which none the less proved to be a failure as a serial for *Cornhill*, (January 1862–August 1863).

In July 1861 the expectation was that Collins would provide his new story for Smith to begin serialization in January 1863 or soon after. He had first to provide a new full-length work for Dickens (*No Name*). This, in fact, took somewhat longer than expected, running in *All the Year Round* from March 1862 to January 1863. *Armadale* was put back – initially a few weeks (Collins was quite capable of composing his story just ahead of the printer, although he liked to have time in hand at the beginning of the serial run). But Collins's health deteriorated badly in early 1863 and he was advised by his physicians to give up writing altogether until he recovered. On 19 March 1863 he recorded that the *Cornhill* novel was 'put off again . . . [Smith, Elder] have behaved most kindly and considerately about it'.[2] On 18 June 1863 he wrote with more precise dates: 'I have had a most kind and friendly letter from Mr Smith . . . allowing me until the 1st. of December next [1863] to send in the 1st. number of the new story for Cornhill.'³ He was in Strasbourg at the time and mysteriously declared 'I have *Got an Idea*!' (Major Milroy's clock may have been a small part of the idea.) He seems to have clarified this idea in Wildbad, where he went to take the curative waters in summer 1863. In July–August he visited the Isle of Man and in November he recorded: 'I am getting ideas as thick as blackberries'. By December he was convinced he had invented (but not yet started to write) 'an extraordinary story – something entirely different from anything I have done yet'. By January 1864 he was 'constructing my story' and again insisting that it was something 'entirely new'.⁴

Collins's delay must have been vexatious for Smith. Dickens began serializing Charles Reade's *Hard Cash* in *All the Year Round* in March 1863. Reade's novel would conclude in December 1863. Reade – who was another leading sensationalist – would thus overshadow Collins. It was a further vexation that Reade's novel (which features abominations perpetrated on patients in private lunatic asylums) went down very badly with the reading public, and lost Dickens 3,000 subscribers (as Reade calculated). Its failure cast a blight over Collins's forthcoming work (which also climaxes in a private lunatic asylum). While he was waiting for *Armadale*, Smith filled the gap in *Cornhill Magazine*'s pages with a hastily devised serial by his new editor, Frederick Greenwood, *Margaret Denzil's History* (November 1863–October 1864).

During the early part of 1864 Collins travelled on the Continent to recuperate his health. He thought out the plot for his new story in Rome, in February 1864. By March, when he returned to England, 'most of the important preliminary work was done'. After eighteen months' 'literary abstinence' he now felt well enough to write. On 20 April 1864 he told his mother: 'After much pondering over the construction of the story I positively sat down with a clean sheet before me, and began to write it on Monday last. So far my progress is slow and hesitating enough – not for want of knowing what I have to do, but for want of practice.' He instructed Smith that the new (and still unnamed) novel could be announced to start its serial run 'almost two years after the date first proposed'.⁵ The first sections were delivered to the printers (who approved of the story) in June 1864. Smith was very pleased. Dickens was sent an early set of proofs of the first number, and gave his approval.⁶ On 24 September 1864, however, just one week before publication of the opening number, Collins wrote in near panic to his friend Edward Pigott to report that 'The gout has affected my brain. My mind is perfectly clear – but the nervous misery I suffer is indescribable. Beard [his doctor] cannot yet decide when I can work again, or what is to be done about the Cornhill. With Smith away, and the first number made up on the first of the month, the disaster is complete'.[7] Evidently Collins somehow rode out this disaster. Keeping a month or so ahead of deadlines, and despite recurrent poor health, he finished writing on 12 April 1866, some six weeks before the last instalment was published. 'Miss Gwilt's death quite upset me', he recorded.[8]

The serial divisions of the novel in *Cornhill* are as follows: 1 (November 1864) Book the First, Chapter One; 2 (December 1864) Book the Second, Chapter One; 3 (January 1865) Book the Second, Chapter Two; 4 (February 1865) Book the Second, Chapter Four; 5 (March 1865) Book the Third, Chapter One; 6 (April 1865) Book the Third, Chapter Three; 7 (May 1865) Book the Third, Chapter Five; 8 (June 1865) Book the Third, Chapter Eight; 9 (July 1865) Book the Third, Chapter Ten; 10 (August 1865) Book the Third, Chapter Thirteen; 11 (September 1865) Book the Fourth, Chapter Three; 12 (October 1865) Book the Fourth, Chapter Five (up to this point in the run, *Armadale* was the first item in the magazine; after this point it was relegated to an inferior position); 13 (November 1865) Book the Fourth, Chapter Eight; 14 (December 1865) Book the Fourth, Chapter Ten; 15 (January 1866) Book the Fourth, Chapter Eleven; 16 (February 1866) Book the Fourth, Chapter Fourteen; 17 (March 1866) Book the Fourth, Chapter Fifteen; 18 (April 1866) Book the Fifth, Chapter One; 19 (May 1866) Book the Fifth, Chapter Three continued; 20 (June 1866) Book the Last, Chapter Three.

Collins had originally wanted *Armadale* to be illustrated by his close friend John Millais. But the artist was too busy (or perhaps too expensive), and Smith recruited the inferior George Thomas, who supplied one full-page and one vignette woodcut (to accompany the first paragraph) for each of the twenty numbers. It seems that Thomas had early proofs to work from, although some mismatches occurred between text and illustration (see Book the Second, Chapter I, note 7).

The *Cornhill* had been on a circulation slide ever since its launch (when it sold just under 110,000 copies). As *Armadale* started its run, monthly sales stood at around 41,000. Collins added a couple of thousand new subscribers, but by the end of *Armadale*'s serialization the magazine's sales had sunk to a new low of 36,000–38,000.[9]

Armadale was serialized a month later in America in *Harper's New Monthly Magazine*, from December 1864 to July 1866. It is likely that the American publisher was sent early proof sheets and Thomas's woodblocks, to forestall piracy. (Since not all *Harper's* instalments are illustrated, the timetable may occasionally have proved too tight.) The novel proved popular in America, and apparently revived the magazine's circulation, which had been badly hit by the Civil War. According to Nuel Davis, *Harper's* paid Collins between £500 and £750 for the serial and volume rights.

Smith, Elder released a 'Library Edition' of *Armadale* in two volumes in the second half of May 1866 (the break came between the ninth and tenth numbers). Essentially, it comprised the text and Thomas's twenty illustrations as they had appeared in *Cornhill Magazine*, with the addition of a title page designed by Collins. It contained a moralistic epigraph: '"Even my wickedness has one merit – it has not prospered. I have never been a happy woman." Miss Gwilt.' The two-volume edition also had a dedication to John Forster, an apologetic foreword by Collins and the 'Appendix' on the mysteriously prophetic events on the ship *Armadale*. There was some superficial reordering of materials: 'Book the First' became 'Prologue', with the following 'books' appropriately renumbered. Otherwise, the text was substantially as serialized, with a few errors and rough edges tidied up. The two-volume *Armadale* cost 26 shillings. Early reviews of the novel were extraordinarily and almost universally savage, and the edition did not, apparently, sell well (although evidently the librarian Mudie was obliged to order more than he initially intended).[10] The bibliophile Michael Sadleir notes that very few copies of the two-volume edition survive.[11] The surviving records of Smith, Elder record a print run of 1,286, of which 1,118 sold. Mudie took 500 at 15s. 6d. a copy. The relationship between Collins and George Smith did not prosper (Smith did not commission the novelist again, and may have regretted his expensive purchase of *Armadale*). A one-volume edition of the novel, priced six shillings, was brought out by Smith in November 1866, and by October 1869 this was being sold at the reduced cost of five shillings. It was, presumably, overprinted. In September 1871, Smith, Elder brought out a budget-priced two-shilling edition of *Armadale*. In the long run, George Smith (who evidently owned the copyright outright) probably got his money back. In America, *Harper's* brought out a one-volume edition in late 1866 at $1.60, with thirty-six illustrations by Thomas. Tauchnitz brought out a three-volume edition for the English-speaking European market in the same period.

This edition follows the first published version of *Armadale*, as published in the *Cornhill Magazine*, with the addition of the dedication, Collins's foreword, and the 'Appendix'.

Notes

1. Peters, p. 236.

2. Robinson, p. 179.

3. Sue Lonoff, *Wilkie Collins and his Victorian Readers* (New York, 1982), p. 33. Subsequent references are shortened to 'Lonoff'.

4. Lonoff, pp. 33–4.

5. Robinson, p. 187.

6. Lonoff, p. 34.

7. Peters, p. 268.

8. Robinson, p. 190.

9. See John Sutherland, '*Cornhill*'s Sales and Payments', *Victorian Periodicals Review*, 19, 3 (Fall 1986), p. 107.

10. Lonoff, p. 37.

11. Michael Sadleir in *XIX Century Fiction* (Cambridge, 1951), I, 376–7.

A NOTE ON THE MANUSCRIPT

The holograph manuscript of *Armadale*, comprising 577 leaves, is held at Henry E. Huntington Library, San Marino, California.[1] I am indebted to the library for permission to examine and quote from the manuscript. Like his mentor Dickens, Collins composed hyperactively and his pages are black with overscorings, marginal additions and interlineations. Typically he wrote in short spells with much cutting and pasting. Many of Collins's changes cannot be recovered from his obliterations. Those that can fall into four main categories. Most were simple improvements of the words on the page – sometimes changed as he went along, sometimes edited as he looked back over what he had written. Although Collins had the main lines of the plot clear in his mind from the first, he allowed himself considerable freedom with subplots, minor characters and incidental scenes: some of these changes of conception are recoverable and I annotate them in the explanatory notes. Like other sensation novelists, Collins was most attentive to suspense and effect, and the ends of instalments often show him sharpening up his 'curtain' lines on the 'Make 'em laugh, make 'em cry, make 'em wait' principle. Throughout his manuscript (which is also the copy text and contains the marks of Smith, Elder's printers) Collins is meticulous in instructions to the compositor on such things as white lines, black lines, new paragraphs, italics, small caps., etc.

Armadale was the first narrative Collins had written in monthly instalments, and he encountered a few problems with length, particularly towards the end of his composition. In the seventeenth and eighteenth numbers he miscalculated and was obliged to revise to fit the *Cornhill Magazine*'s length requirement. In a number of places he seems to have had to cut small amounts of material away in proof. The proofs themselves do not seem to have survived, but it is clear that Collins revised them carefully, improving local details with great skill and economy. Years of work for newspapers had trained him as a fluent and highly professional writer. The *Armadale* manuscript is an informative and still relatively unexplored document, and it is to be hoped that some enterprising doctoral student will undertake a thorough study of it.

Writing to a correspondent in October 1865, Collins declared: 'In the story I am now writing (*Armadale*), the last number is to be published several months hence [June 1866] – and the whole close of the story is still unwritten. But I know at this moment who is to live and who is to die – and I see the main events which are to lead to the end as plainly as I see the pen now in my hand ... the characters themselves were all marshalled in their places, before a line of *Armadale* was written. And I knew the end two years ago in Rome [February 1864], when I was recovering from a long illness, and was putting the story together'.[2] In his 'Appendix' to the novel, Collins refers more directly to a 'notebook' – presumably used in Rome – in which he forecast the plot (including the sanatorium murder) before embarking on the actual writing of the novel. This notebook seems not to have survived and it is possible that Collins slightly exaggerates the degree of preconception it contained. (There is, for instance, some reason for suspecting that the 'carbonic gas' episode was suggested at a later date by the prophetic suffocations on board the ship *Armadale* in November 1865.)

The Huntington Library also holds the manuscript version of Collins's first (1866) stage adaptation of *Armadale*,[3] and the unpublished – but printed and authorially corrected – second (1875–7) stage version, *Miss Gwilt*. Catherine Peters notes that the Parrish Collection at Princeton holds part of the French stage play which Collins devised with his collaborator François Régnier.

Notes

1. Call mark HM 33786.
2. William M. Clarke, *The Secret Life of Wilkie Collins* (London, 1988), p. 104.
3. Call mark HM 33790.

Facsimile of the title page of the first edition.

ARMADALE.

BY

WILKIE COLLINS.

WITH TWENTY ILLUSTRATIONS BY GEORGE H. THOMAS

IN TWO VOLUMES.

LONDON:

SMITH, ELDER AND CO., 65, CORNHILL.

1866.

FOREWORD[1]

Readers in general – on whose friendly reception experience has given me some reason to rely – will, I venture to hope, appreciate whatever merit there may be in this story, without any prefatory pleading for it on my part. They will, I think, see that it has not been hastily meditated, or idly wrought out. They will judge it accordingly – and I ask no more.

Readers in particular will, I have some reason to suppose, be here and there disturbed – perhaps even offended – by finding that 'Armadale' oversteps, in more than one direction,[2] the narrow limits within which they are disposed to restrict the development of modern fiction – if they can. Nothing that I could say to these persons, here, would help me with them, as Time will help me if my work lasts. I am not afraid of my design being permanently misunderstood, provided the execution has done it any sort of justice. Estimated by the Clap-trap morality of the present day, this may be a very daring book. Judged by the Christian morality which is of all time, it is only a book that is daring enough to speak the truth.

London, April, 1866.

BOOK THE FIRST[1]

THE TRAVELLERS

It was the opening of the season of eighteen hundred and thirty-two, at the Baths of WILDBAD.[2]

The evening shadows were beginning to gather over the quiet little German town; and the diligence was expected every minute. Before the door of the principal inn, waiting the arrival of the first visitors of the year, were assembled the three notable personages of Wildbad, accompanied by their wives – the mayor, representing the inhabitants; the doctor, representing the waters; the landlord, representing his own establishment. Beyond this select circle, grouped snugly about the trim little square in front of the inn, appeared the townspeople in general, mixed here and there with the countrypeople in their quaint German costume placidly expectant of the diligence – the men in short black jackets, tight black breeches, and three-cornered beaver hats; the women with their long light hair hanging in one thickly-plaited tail behind them, and the waists of their short woollen gowns inserted modestly in the region of their shoulder blades. Round the outer edge of the assemblage thus formed, flying detachments of plump white-headed children careered in perpetual motion; while, mysteriously apart from the rest of the inhabitants, the musicians of the Baths stood collected in one lost corner, waiting the appearance of the first visitors to play the first tune of the season in the form of a serenade. The light of a May evening was still bright on the tops of the great wooded hills watching high over the town on the right hand and the left; and the cool breeze that comes before sunset came keenly fragrant here with the balsamic odour of the firs of the Black Forest.

'Mr Landlord,' said the mayor's wife (giving the landlord his title), 'have you any foreign guests coming on this first day of the season?'

'Madam Mayoress,' replied the landlord (returning the compliment), 'I have two. They have written – the one by the hand of his servant, the other by his own hand apparently – to order their rooms; and they are from England both, as I think by their names. If you ask me to pronounce those names, my tongue hesitates; if you ask me to spell them, here they are letter by letter, first and second in their order as they come. First, a high-born stranger (by title Mister), who introduces

9

himself in eight letters – A, r, m, a, d, a, l, e – and comes ill in his own carriage. Second, a high-born stranger (by title Mister also), who introduces himself in four letters – N, e, a, l – and comes ill in the diligence. His excellency of the eight letters writes to me (by his servant) in French; his excellency of the four letters writes to me in German. The rooms of both are ready. I know no more.'

'Perhaps,' suggested the mayor's wife, 'Mr Doctor has heard from one or both of these illustrious strangers?'

'From one only, Madam Mayoress; but not, strictly speaking, from the person himself. I have received a medical report of his excellency of the eight letters, and his case seems a bad one. God help him!'

'The diligence!' cried a child from the outskirts of the crowd.

The musicians seized their instruments, and silence fell on the whole community. From far away in the windings of the forest gorge, the ring of horses' bells came faintly clear through the evening stillness. Which carriage was approaching – the private carriage with Mr Armadale, or the public carriage with Mr Neal?

'Play, my friends!' cried the mayor to the musicians. 'Public or private, here are the first sick people of the season. Let them find us cheerful.'

The band played a lively dance tune, and the children in the square footed it merrily to the music. At the same moment, their elders near the inn door drew aside, and disclosed the first shadow of gloom that fell over the gaiety and beauty of the scene. Through the opening made on either hand, a little procession of stout country-girls advanced, each drawing after her an empty chair on wheels; each in waiting (and knitting while she waited) for the paralysed wretches who came helpless by hundreds then – who come helpless by thousands now – to the waters of Wildbad for relief.

While the band played, while the children danced, while the buzz of many talkers deepened, while the strong young nurses of the coming cripples knitted impenetrably, a woman's insatiable curiosity about other women asserted itself in the mayor's wife. She drew the landlady aside, and whispered a question to her on the spot.

'A word more, ma'am,' said the mayor's wife, 'about the two strangers from England. Are their letters explicit? Have they got any ladies with them?'

'The one by the diligence – no,' replied the landlady. 'But the one by the private carriage – yes. He comes with a child; he comes with a nurse; and,' concluded the landlady, skilfully keeping the main point of interest till the last, 'he comes with a Wife.'

The mayoress brightened; the doctoress (assisting at the conference) brightened; the landlady nodded significantly. In the minds of all three the same thought started into life at the same moment – 'We shall see the Fashions!'

In a minute more, there was a sudden movement in the crowd; and a chorus of voices proclaimed that the travellers were at hand.

By this time the coming vehicle was in sight, and all further doubt was at an end. It was the diligence that now approached by the long street leading into the square – the diligence (in a dazzling new coat of yellow paint) that delivered the first visitors of the season at the inn-door. Of the ten travellers released from the middle compartment and the back compartment of the carriage – all from various parts of Germany – three were lifted out helpless, and were placed in the chairs on wheels to be drawn to their lodgings in the town. The front compartment contained two passengers only – Mr Neal and his travelling servant. With an arm on either side to assist him, the stranger (whose malady appeared to be locally confined to a lameness in one of his feet) succeeded in descending the steps of the carriage easily enough. While he steadied himself on the pavement by the help of his stick – looking not over-patiently towards the musicians who were serenading him with the waltz in *Der Freischutz*[3] – his personal appearance rather damped the enthusiasm of the friendly little circle assembled to welcome him. He was a lean, tall, serious, middle-aged man, with a cold grey eye and a long upper lip; with over-hanging eyebrows and high cheekbones; a man who looked what he was – every inch a Scotchman.

'Where is the proprietor of this hotel?' he asked, speaking in the German language, with a fluent readiness of expression, and an icy coldness of manner. 'Fetch the doctor,' he continued, when the landlord had presented himself, 'I want to see him immediately.'

'I am here already, sir,' said the doctor, advancing from the circle of friends, 'and my services are entirely at your disposal.'

'Thank you,' said Mr Neal, looking at the doctor, as the rest of us look at a dog when we have whistled, and the dog has come. 'I shall be glad to consult you to-morrow morning, at ten o'clock, about my own case. I only want to trouble you now with a message which I have undertaken to deliver. We overtook a travelling carriage on the road here, with a gentleman in it – an Englishman, I believe – who appeared to be seriously ill. A lady who was with him begged me to see you immediately on my arrival, and to secure your professional assistance in removing the patient from the carriage. Their courier has met with an accident, and has been left behind on the road – and they are obliged to travel very slowly. If you are here in an hour, you will be here in time to receive them. That is the message. Who is this gentleman who appears to be anxious to speak to me? The mayor? If you wish to see my passport, sir, my servant will show it to you. No? You wish to welcome me to the place, and to offer your services? I am infinitely flattered. If you have any authority to shorten the performances of your town band, you would be doing me a kindness to exert it. My nerves are irritable, and I dislike music. Where is the landlord? No; I want to see my rooms. I don't want your arm; I can get upstairs with the help of my stick. Mr Mayor and Mr Doctor, we need not detain one another any longer. I wish you good-night.'

Both mayor and doctor looked after the Scotchman as he limped upstairs, and shook their heads together in mute disapproval of him. The ladies, as usual, went a step farther, and expressed their opinions openly in the plainest words. The case under consideration (so far as *they* were concerned) was the scandalous case of a man who had passed them over entirely without notice. Mrs Mayor could only attribute such an outrage to the native ferocity of a Savage. Mrs Doctor took a stronger view still, and considered it as proceeding from the inbred brutality of a Hog.

The hour of waiting for the travelling carriage wore on, and the creeping night stole up the hill-sides softly. One by one the stars appeared, and the first lights twinkled in the windows of the inn. As the darkness came, the last idlers deserted the square; as the darkness came, the mighty silence of the Forest above flowed in on the valley, and strangely and suddenly hushed the lonely little town.

The hour of waiting wore out, and the figure of the doctor, walking backwards and forwards anxiously, was still the only living figure left in the square. Five minutes, ten minutes, twenty minutes, were counted out by the doctor's watch, before the first sound came through the night silence to warn him of the approaching carriage. Slowly it emerged into the square, at the walking pace of the horses, and drew up, as a hearse might have drawn up, at the door of the inn.

'Is the doctor here?' asked a woman's voice, speaking out of the darkness of the carriage in the French language.

'I am here, madam,' replied the doctor, taking a light from the landlord's hand, and opening the carriage door.

The first face that the light fell on, was the face of the lady who had just spoken – a young darkly-beautiful woman, with the tears standing thick and bright in her eager black eyes. The second face revealed, was the face of a shrivelled old negress, sitting opposite the lady on the back seat. The third was the face of a little sleeping child, in the negress's lap. With a quick gesture of impatience, the lady signed to the nurse to leave the carriage first with the child. 'Pray take them out of the way,' she said to the landlady; 'pray take them to their room.' She got out herself when her request had been complied with. Then the light fell clear for the first time on the farther side of the carriage, and the fourth traveller was disclosed to view.

He lay helpless on a mattress supported by a stretcher; his hair long and disordered under a black skull-cap; his eyes wide open, rolling to and fro ceaselessly anxious; the rest of his face as void of all expression of the character within him, and the thought within him, as if he had been dead. There was no looking at him now, and guessing what he might once have been. The leaden blank of his face met every question as to his age, his rank, his temper, and his looks which that face might once have answered, in impenetrable silence. Nothing spoke for him now but the shock that had struck him with the death-in-life of Paralysis. The doctor's eye questioned his lower limbs, and Death-in-life[4] answered, *I am here*. The doctor's eye, rising attentively by way of his hands and arms, questioned upward and upward to the muscles round his mouth, and Death-in-Life answered, *I am coming*.

In the face of a calamity so unsparing and so dreadful, there was nothing to be said. The silent sympathy of help was all that could be offered to the woman who stood weeping at the carriage door.

As they bore him on his bed across the hall of the hotel, his wandering eyes encountered the face of his wife. They rested on her for a moment; and, in that moment, he spoke.

'The child?' he said in English, with a slow, thick, labouring articulation.

'The child is safe upstairs,' she answered, faintly.

'My desk?'

'It is in my hands. Look! I won't trust it to anybody; I am taking care of it for you myself.'

He closed his eyes for the first time after that answer, and said no more. Tenderly and skilfully he was carried up the stairs, with his wife on one side of him, and the doctor (ominously silent) on the other. The landlord and the servants following, saw the door of his room open and close on him; heard the lady burst out crying hysterically as soon as she was alone with the doctor and the sick man; saw the doctor come out, half an hour later, with his ruddy face a shade paler than usual; pressed him eagerly for information, and received but one answer to all their inquiries, – 'Wait till I have seen him to-morrow. Ask me nothing tonight.' They all knew the doctor's ways, and they augured ill when he left them hurriedly with that reply.

So the two first English visitors of the year came to the Baths of Wildbad, in the season of eighteen hundred and thirty-two.

CHAPTER II

THE SOLID SIDE OF THE SCOTCH CHARACTER

At ten o'clock the next morning, Mr Neal – waiting for the medical visit which he had himself appointed for that hour – looked at his watch, and discovered to his amazement, that he was waiting in vain. It was close on eleven when the door opened at last, and the doctor entered the room.

'I appointed ten o'clock for your visit,' said Mr Neal. 'In my country, a medical man is a punctual man.'

'In my country,' returned the doctor, without the least ill-humour, 'a medical man is exactly like other men – he is at the mercy of accidents. Pray grant me your pardon, sir, for being so long after my time; I have been detained by a very distressing case – the case of Mr Armadale, whose travelling carriage you passed on the road yesterday.'

Mr Neal looked at his medical attendant with a sour surprise. There was a latent anxiety in the doctor's eye, a latent pre-occupation in the doctor's manner, which he was at a loss to account for. For a moment, the two faces confronted each other silently, in marked national contrast – the Scotchman's, long and lean, hard and regular; the German's, plump and florid, soft and shapeless. One face looked as if it had never been young; the other, as if it would never grow old.

'Might I venture to remind you,' said Mr Neal, 'that the case now under consideration, is MY case, and not Mr Armadale's?'

'Certainly,' replied the doctor, still vacillating between[1] the case he had come to see, and the case he had just left. 'You appear to be suffering from lameness – let me look at your foot.'

Mr Neal's malady, however serious it might be in his own estimation, was of no extraordinary importance in a medical point of view. He was suffering from a rheumatic affection of the ankle-joint.[2] The necessary questions were asked and answered, and the necessary baths were prescribed. In ten minutes the consultation was at an end, and the patient was waiting, in significant silence, for the medical adviser to take his leave.

'I cannot conceal from myself,' said the doctor, rising, and hesitating a little, 'that I am intruding on you. But I am compelled to beg your indulgence, if I return to the subject of Mr Armadale.'

'May I ask what compels you?'

'The duty which I owe as a Christian,' answered the doctor, 'to a dying man.'

Mr Neal started. Those who touched his sense of religious duty touched the quickest sense in his nature. 'You have established your claim on my attention,' he said, gravely. 'My time is yours.'

'I will not abuse your kindness,' replied the doctor, resuming his chair. 'I will be as short as I can. Mr Armadale's case is briefly this: He has passed the greater part of his life in the West Indies – a wild life and a vicious life, by his own confession. Shortly after his marriage – now some three years since – the first symptoms of an approaching paralytic affection began to show themselves, and his medical advisers ordered him away to try the climate of Europe. Since leaving the West Indies, he has lived principally in Italy, with no benefit to his health. From Italy, before the last seizure attacked him, he removed to Switzerland; and from Switzerland he has been sent to this place. So much I know from his doctor's report; the rest I can tell you from my own personal experience.[3] Mr Armadale has been sent to Wildbad too late: he is virtually a dead man. The paralysis is fast spreading upwards, and disease of the lower part of the spine has already taken place.[4] He can still move his hands a little, but he can hold nothing in his fingers. He can still articulate, but he may wake speechless to-morrow or next day. If I give him a week more to live, I give him what I honestly believe to be the utmost length of his span. At his own request, I told him – as carefully and as tenderly as I could – what I have just told you. The result was very distressing; the violence of the patient's agitation was a violence which I despair of describing to you.[5] I took the liberty of asking him whether his affairs were unsettled. Nothing of the sort. His will is in the hands of his executor in London; and he leaves his wife and child well provided for. My next question succeeded better: it hit the mark: "Have you something on your mind to do before you die, which is not done yet?" He gave a great gasp of relief, which said, as no words could have said it, Yes. "Can I help you?" "Yes. I have something to write that I *must* write – can you make me hold a pen?" He might as well have asked me if I could perform a miracle. I could only say, No. "If I dictate the words," he went on, "can you write what I tell you to write?" Once more, I could only say, No. I understand a little English, but I can neither speak it, nor write it. Mr Armadale understands French, when it is spoken (as I speak it to him) slowly, but he cannot express himself in that language; and of German he is totally ignorant. In this difficulty, I said, what any one else in my situation would have said: "Why ask *me*? there is Mrs Armadale at your service, in the next room." Before I could get up from my chair to fetch her, he stopped me – not by words, but by a look of horror, which fixed me by main force of astonishment, in my place. "Surely," I said, "your wife is the fittest person to write for you as you desire?" "The last person under heaven!" he answered. "What!" I said, "you ask me, a foreigner and a stranger, to write words at your dictation which you keep a secret from your wife!" Conceive my astonishment, when he answered me, without a moment's hesitation – "Yes!" I sat lost; I sat silent. "If *you* can't write English," he said, "find somebody who can." I tried to remonstrate. He burst into a dreadful moaning cry – a dumb entreaty, like the entreaty of a dog. "Hush! hush!" I said, "I will find somebody." "To-day!" he broke out, "before my speech fails me, like my hand." "To-day, in an hour's time." He shut his eyes; he quieted himself instantly. "While I am waiting for you," he said; "let me see my little boy." He had shown no tenderness when he spoke of his wife, but I saw the tears on his cheeks when he asked for his child. My profession, sir, has not made me so hard a man as you might think; and my doctor's heart was as heavy, when I went out to fetch the child, as if I had not been a doctor at all. I am afraid you think this rather weak on my part?'

The doctor looked appealingly at Mr Neal. He might as well have looked at a rock in the Black Forest. Mr Neal entirely declined to be drawn by any doctor in Christendom out of the regions of plain fact.

'Go on,' he said. 'I presume you have not told me all that you have to tell me, yet?'

'Surely you understand my object in coming here, now?' returned the other.

'Your object is plain enough – at last. You invite me to connect myself blindfold with a matter which is in the last degree suspicious, so far. I decline giving you any answer until I know more than I know now. Did you think it necessary to inform this man's wife of what had passed between you, and to ask her for an explanation?'

'Of course I thought it necessary!' said the doctor, indignant at the reflection on his humanity which the question seemed to imply. 'If ever I saw a woman fond of her husband, and sorry for her husband, it is this unhappy Mrs Armadale. As soon as we were left alone together, I sat down by her side, and I took her hand in mine. Why not? I am an ugly old man, and I may allow myself such liberties as these!'

'Excuse me,' said the impenetrable Scotchman. 'I beg to suggest that you are losing the thread of the narrative.'

'Nothing more likely,' returned the doctor, recovering his good humour. 'It is in the habit of my nation to be perpetually losing the thread – and it is evidently in the habit of yours, sir, to be perpetually finding it. What an example here of the order of the universe, and the everlasting fitness of things!'

'Will you oblige me, once for all, by confining yourself to the facts,' persisted Mr Neal, frowning impatiently. 'May I inquire, for my own information, whether Mrs Armadale could tell you what it is her husband wishes me to write, and why it is that he refuses to let her write for him?'

'There is my thread found – and thank you for finding it!' said the doctor. 'You shall hear what Mrs Armadale had to tell me, in Mrs Armadale's own words. "The cause that now shuts me out of his confidence," she said, "is, I firmly believe, the same cause that has always shut me out of his heart. I am the wife he has wedded; but I am not the woman he loves. I knew when he married me, that another man had won from him the woman he loved. I thought I could make him forget her. I hoped when I married him; I hoped again when I bore him a son. Need I tell you the end of my hopes – you have seen it for yourself." (Wait, sir, I entreat you! I have not lost the thread again; I am following it inch by inch.) "Is this all you know?" I asked. "All I knew," she said, "till a short time since. It was when we were in Switzerland, and when his illness was nearly at its worst, that news came to him by accident of that other woman who has been the shadow and the poison of my life – news that she (like me) had borne her husband a son. On the instant of his making that discovery – a trifling discovery, if ever there was one yet – a mortal fear seized on him: not for me, not for himself; a fear for his own child. The same day (without a word to me) he sent for the doctor. I was mean, wicked, what you please – I listened at the door. I heard him say: *I have something to tell my son, when my son grows old enough to understand me. Shall I live to tell it?* The doctor would say nothing certain. The same night (still without a word to me,) he locked himself into his room. What would any woman, treated as I was, have done in my place? She would have done as I did – she would have listened again. I heard him say to himself: *I shall not live to tell it: I must write it before I die.* I heard his pen scrape, scrape, scrape over the paper – I heard him groaning and sobbing as he wrote

– I implored him for God's sake to let me in. The cruel pen went scrape, scrape, scrape; the cruel pen was all the answer he gave me. I waited at the door – hours – I don't know how long. On a sudden, the pen stopped; and I heard no more. I whispered through the keyhole softly; I said I was cold and weary with waiting; I said, Oh, my love, let me in! Not even the cruel pen answered me now: silence answered me. With all the strength of my miserable hands, I beat at the door. The servants came up and broke it in. We were too late; the harm was done. Over that fatal letter, the stroke had struck him – over that fatal letter, we found him, paralysed as you see him now. Those words which he wants you to write, are the words he would have written himself if the stroke had spared him till the morning. From that time to this, there has been a blank place left in the letter; and it is that blank place which he has just asked you to fill up." – In those words, Mrs Armadale spoke to me; in those words, you have the sum and substance of all the information I can give. Say, if you please, sir, have I kept the thread at last? have I shown you the necessity which brings me here from your countryman's death-bed?'

'Thus far,' said Mr Neal, 'you merely show me that you are exciting yourself. This is too serious a matter to be treated as you are treating it now. You have involved Me in the business – and I insist on seeing my way plainly. Don't raise your hands; your hands are not a part of the question. If I am to be concerned in the completion of this mysterious letter, it is only an act of justifiable prudence on my part to inquire what the letter is about? Mrs Armadale appears to have favoured you with an infinite number of domestic particulars – in return, I presume, for your polite attention in taking her by the hand. May I ask what she could tell you about her husband's letter, so far as her husband has written it?'

'Mrs Armadale could tell me nothing,' replied the doctor, with a sudden formality in his manner, which showed that his forbearance was at last failing him. 'Before she was composed enough to think of the letter, her husband had asked for it, and had caused it to be locked up in his desk. She knows that he has since, time after time, tried to finish it, and that, time after time, the pen has dropped from his fingers. She knows, when all other hope of his restoration was at an end, that his medical advisers encouraged him to hope in the famous waters of this place. And last, she knows how that hope has ended – for she knows what I told her husband this morning.'

The frown which had been gathering latterly on Mr Neal's face, deepened and darkened. He looked at the doctor as if the doctor had personally offended him.

'The more I think of the position you are asking me to take,' he said, 'the less I like it. Can you undertake to say positively that Mr Armadale is in his right mind?'

'Yes; as positively as words can say it.'

'Does his wife sanction your coming here to request my interference?'

'His wife sends me to you – the only Englishman in Wildbad – to write for your dying countryman what he cannot write for himself; and what no one in this place but you can write for him.'

That answer drove Mr Neal back to the last inch of ground left him to stand on. Even on that inch, the Scotchman resisted still.

'Wait a little!' he said. 'You put it strongly – let us be quite sure you put it correctly as well. Let us be quite sure there is nobody to take this responsibility but myself. There is a mayor in Wildbad, to begin with; a man who possesses an official character to justify his interference.'

'A man of a thousand,' said the doctor. 'With one fault – he knows no language but his own.'

'There is an English legation at Stuttgart,' persisted Mr Neal.

'And there are miles on miles of the Forest between this and Stuttgart,' rejoined the doctor. 'If we sent this moment, we could get no help from the legation before to-morrow; and it is as likely as not, in the state of this dying man's articulation, that to-morrow may find him speechless. I don't know whether his last wishes are wishes harmless to his child and to others, or wishes hurtful to his child and to others – but I *do* know that they must be fulfilled at once or never, and that you are the only man who can help him.'

That open declaration brought the discussion to a close. It fixed Mr Neal fast between the two alternatives of saying, Yes, and committing an act of imprudence – or of saying, No, and committing an act of inhumanity. There was a silence of some minutes. The Scotchman steadily reflected; and the German steadily watched him.

The responsibility of saying the next words rested on Mr Neal, and, in course of time, Mr Neal took it. He rose from his chair, with a sullen sense of injury lowering on his heavy eyebrows, and working sourly in the lines at the corners of his mouth.

'My position is forced on me,' he said. 'I have no choice but to accept it.'

The doctor's impulsive nature rose in revolt against the merciless brevity and gracelessness of that reply. 'I wish to God,' he broke out fervently, 'I knew English enough to take your place at Mr Armadale's bedside!'

'Bating your taking the name of the Almighty in vain,' answered the Scotchman, 'I entirely agree with you. I wish you did.'

Without another word on either side, they left the room together – the doctor leading the way.

CHAPTER III

THE WRECK OF THE TIMBER-SHIP

No one answered the doctor's knock, when he and his companion reached the antechamber door of Mr Armadale's apartments. They entered unannounced; and when they looked into the sitting-room, the sitting-room was empty.

'I must see Mrs Armadale,' said Mr Neal. 'I decline acting in the matter unless Mrs Armadale authorizes my interference with her own lips.'

'Mrs Armadale is probably with her husband,' replied the doctor. He approached a door at the inner end of the sitting-room while he spoke – hesitated – and, turning round again, looked at his sour companion anxiously. 'I am afraid I spoke a little harshly, sir, when we were leaving your room,' he said. 'I beg your pardon for it, with all my heart. Before this poor afflicted lady comes in, will you – will you excuse my asking your utmost gentleness and consideration for her?'

'No, sir,' retorted the other harshly, 'I won't excuse you. What right have I given you to think me wanting in gentleness and consideration towards anybody?'

The doctor saw it was useless. 'I beg your pardon again,' he said resignedly, and left the unapproachable stranger to himself.

Mr Neal walked to the window, and stood there, with his eyes mechanically fixed on the prospect, composing his mind for the coming interview.

It was midday; the sun shone bright and warm; and all the little world of Wildbad was alive and merry in the genial spring time. Now and again, heavy waggons, with blackfaced carters in charge, rolled by the window, bearing their precious lading of charcoal from the Forest. Now and again, hurled over the headlong current of the stream that runs through the town, great lengths of timber loosely strung together in interminable series – with the booted raftsmen, pole in hand, poised watchful at either end – shot swift and serpent-like past the houses on their course to the distant Rhine. High and steep above the gabled wooden buildings on the river bank, the great hill-sides, crested black with firs, shone to the shining heavens in a glory of lustrous green. In and out, where the forest footpaths wound from the grass through the trees, from the trees over the grass, the bright spring dresses of women and children, on the search for wild-flowers, travelled to and fro in the lofty distance like spots of moving light. Below, on the walk by the stream side, the booths of the little bazaar that had opened punctually with the opening season, showed all their glittering trinkets, and fluttered in the balmy air their splendour of many-coloured flags. Longingly, here, the children looked at the show; patiently the sun-burnt lasses plied their knitting as they paced the walk; courteously the passing townspeople, by fours and fives, and the passing visitors, by ones and twos, greeted each other, hat in hand; and slowly, slowly, the crippled and the helpless in their chairs on wheels, came out in the cheerful noontide with the rest, and took their share of the blessed light that cheers, of the blessed sun that shines for all.

On this scene the Scotchman looked, with eyes that never noted its beauty, with a mind far away from every lesson that it taught. One by one, he meditated the words he should say when the wife came in. One by one, he pondered over the conditions he might impose, before he took the pen in hand at the husband's bedside.

'Mrs Armadale is here,' said the doctor's voice, interposing suddenly between his reflections and himself.

He turned on the instant, and saw before him, with the pure midday light shining full on her, a woman of the mixed blood of the European and the African race, with the northern delicacy in the shape of her face, and the southern richness in its colour – a woman in the prime of her beauty, who moved with an inbred grace, who looked with an inbred fascination, whose large languid black eyes rested on him gratefully, whose little dusky hand offered itself to him, in mute expression of her thanks, with the welcome that is given to the coming of a friend. For the first time in his life, the Scotchman was taken by surprise. Every self-preservative word that he had been meditating but an instant since, dropped out of his memory. His thrice-impenetrable armour of habitual suspicion, habitual self-discipline, and habitual reserve, which had never fallen from him in a woman's presence before, fell from him in this woman's presence, and brought him to his knees, a conquered man. He took the hand she offered him, and bowed over it his first honest homage to the sex, in silence.

She hesitated on her side. The quick feminine perception which, in happier circumstances, would have pounced on the secret of his embarrassment in an instant, failed her now. She attributed his strange reception of her to pride, to reluctance – to any cause but the unexpected revelation of her own beauty. 'I have no words to thank you,' she said faintly, trying to propitiate him. 'I should only distress you if I tried to speak.' Her lip began to tremble, she drew back a little, and turned away her head in silence.

The doctor, who had been standing apart, quietly observant in a corner, advanced before Mr Neal could interfere, and led Mrs Armadale to a chair. 'Don't be afraid of him,' whispered the good man, patting her gently on the shoulder. 'He was hard as iron in my hands, but I think, by the look of him, he will be soft as wax in yours. Say the words I told you to say, and let us take him to your husband's room, before those sharp wits of his have time to recover themselves.'

She roused her sinking resolution, and advanced half-way to the window to meet Mr Neal. 'My kind friend, the doctor, has told me, sir, that your only hesitation in coming here is a hesitation on my account,' she said, her head drooping a little, and her rich colour fading away while she spoke. 'I am deeply grateful, but I entreat you not to think of *me*. What my husband wishes—' Her voice faltered; she waited resolutely, and recovered herself. 'What my husband wishes in his last moments, I wish too.'

This time Mr Neal was composed enough to answer her. In low, earnest tones, he entreated her to say no more. 'I was only anxious to show you every consideration,' he said. 'I am only anxious now to spare you every distress.' As he spoke, something like a glow of colour rose slowly on his sallow face. Her eyes were looking at him, softly attentive – and he thought guiltily of his meditations at the window before she came in.

The doctor saw his opportunity. He opened the door that led into Mr Armadale's room, and stood by it, waiting silently. Mrs Armadale entered first. In a minute more the door was closed again; and Mr Neal stood committed to the responsibility that had been forced on him – committed beyond recall.

The room was decorated in the gaudy continental fashion; and the warm sunlight was shining in joyously. Cupids and flowers were painted on the ceiling; bright ribbons looped up the white window-curtains; a smart gilt clock ticked on a velvet-covered mantelpiece; mirrors gleamed on the walls, and flowers in all the colours of the rainbow speckled the carpet. In the midst of the finery, and the glitter, and the light, lay the paralysed man, with his wandering eyes, and his lifeless lower face – his head propped high with many pillows; his helpless hands laid out over the bed-clothes like the hands of a corpse. By the bed-head stood, grim, and old, and silent, the shrivelled black nurse; and on the counterpane, between his father's outspread hands, lay the child, in his little white frock, absorbed in the enjoyment of a new toy. When the door opened, and Mrs Armadale led the way in, the boy was tossing his plaything – a soldier on horseback – backwards and forwards over the helpless hands on either side of him; and the father's wandering eyes were following the toy to and fro, with a stealthy and ceaseless vigilance – a vigilance as of a wild animal, terrible to see.

The moment Mr Neal appeared in the doorway, those restless eyes stopped, looked up, and fastened on the stranger with a fierce eagerness of inquiry. Slowly the motionless lips struggled into movement. With thick, hesitating articulation, they put the question which the eyes asked mutely, into words.

'Are you the man?'

Mr Neal advanced to the bedside; Mrs Armadale drawing back from it as he approached, and waiting with the doctor at the farther end of the room. The child looked up, toy in hand, as the stranger came near – opened his bright brown eyes wide in momentary astonishment – and then went on with his game.

'I have been made acquainted with your sad situation, sir,' said Mr Neal. 'And I have come here to place my services at your disposal; services which no one but myself – as your medical attendant informs me – is in a position to render you in this strange place. My name is Neal. I am a Writer to the Signet in Edinburgh;[1] and I may presume to say for myself that any confidence you wish to place in me will be confidence not improperly bestowed.'

The eyes of the beautiful wife were not confusing him now. He spoke to the helpless husband quietly and seriously, without his customary harshness, and with a grave compassion in his manner which presented him at his best. The sight of the death-bed had steadied him.

'You wish me to write something for you?' he resumed, after waiting for a reply, and waiting in vain.

'Yes!' said the dying man, with the all-mastering impatience which his tongue was powerless to express, glittering angrily in his eyes. 'My hand is gone; and my speech is going. Write!'

Before there was time to speak again, Mr Neal heard the rustling of a woman's dress, and the quick creaking of castors on the carpet behind him. Mrs Armadale was moving the writing-table across the room to the foot of the bed. If he was to set up those safeguards of his own devising that were to bear him harmless through all results to come, now was the time, or never. He kept his back turned on Mrs Armadale; and put his precautionary question at once in the plainest terms.

'May I ask, sir, before I take the pen in hand, what it is you wish me to write?'

The angry eyes of the paralysed man glittered brighter and brighter. His lips opened and closed again. He made no reply.

Mr Neal tried another precautionary question, in a new direction.

'When I have written what you wish me to write,' he asked, 'what is to be done with it?'

This time the answer came:

'Seal it up in my presence, and post it to my Ex—'

His labouring articulation suddenly stopped, and he looked piteously in the questioner's face for the next word.

'Do you mean your Executor?'

'Yes.'

'It is a letter, I suppose, that I am to post?' There was no answer. 'May I ask if it is a letter altering your will?'

'Nothing of the sort.'

Mr Neal considered a little. The mystery was thickening. The one way out of it so far, was the way traced faintly through that strange story of the unfinished letter which the doctor had repeated to him in Mrs Armadale's words. The nearer he approached his unknown responsibility, the more ominous it seemed of something serious to come. Should he risk another question before he pledged himself irrevocably? As the doubt crossed his mind, he felt Mrs Armadale's silk dress touch him, on the side farthest from her husband. Her delicate dark hand was laid gently on his arm; her full deep African eyes looked at him in submissive entreaty. 'My husband is very anxious,' she whispered. 'Will you quiet his anxiety, sir, by taking your place at the writing-table?'

It was from *her* lips that the request came – from the lips of the person who had the best right to hesitate, the wife who was excluded from the secret! Most men in Mr Neal's position would have given up all their safeguards on the spot. The Scotchman gave them all up, but one.

'I will write what you wish me to write,' he said, addressing Mr Armadale. 'I will seal it in your presence; and I will post it to your Executor myself. But, in engaging to do this, I must beg you to remember, that I am acting entirely in the dark; and I must ask you to excuse me, if I reserve my own entire freedom of action, when your wishes in relation to the writing and the posting of the letter have been fulfilled.'

'Do you give me your promise?'

'If you want my promise, sir, I will give it – subject to the condition I have just named.'

'Take your condition, and keep your promise. My desk,' he added, looking at his wife for the first time.

She crossed the room eagerly to fetch the desk from a chair in a corner. Returning with it, she made a passing sign to the negress, who still stood, grim and silent, in the place that she had occupied from the first. The woman advanced, obedient to the sign, to take the child from the bed. At the instant when she touched him, the father's eyes – fixed previously on the desk – turned on her with the stealthy quickness of a cat. 'No!' he said. 'No!' echoed the fresh voice of the boy, still charmed with his plaything, and still liking his place on the bed. The negress left the room, and the child, in high triumph, trotted his toy-soldier up and down on the bedclothes that lay rumpled over his father's breast. His mother's lovely face contracted with a pang of jealousy as she looked at him.

'Shall I open your desk?' she asked, pushing back the child's plaything sharply while she spoke. An answering look from her husband guided her hand to the place under his pillow where the key was hidden. She opened the desk, and disclosed inside some small sheets of manuscript pinned together. 'These?' she inquired, producing them.

'Yes,' he said. 'You can go now.'

The Scotchman sitting at the writing-table, the doctor stirring a stimulant mixture in a corner, looked at each other with an anxiety in both their faces which they could neither of them control. The words that banished the wife from the room were spoken. The moment had come.

'You can go now,' said Mr Armadale, for the second time.

She looked at the child, established comfortably on the bed; and an ashy paleness spread slowly over her face. She looked at the fatal letter which was a sealed secret to her; and a torture of jealous suspicion – suspicion of that other woman who had been the shadow and the poison of her life – wrung her to the heart. After moving a few steps from the bedside, she stopped, and came back again. Armed with the double courage of her love and her despair, she pressed her lips on her dying husband's cheek, and pleaded with him for the last time. Her burning tears dropped on his face as she whispered to him. 'Oh! Allan, think how I have loved you! think how hard I have tried to make you happy!

think how soon I shall lose you! Oh, my own love! don't, don't send me away!'

The words pleaded for her; the kiss pleaded for her; the recollection of the love that had been given to him, and never returned, touched the heart of the fast sinking man as nothing had touched it since the day of his marriage. A heavy sigh broke from him. He looked at her, and hesitated.

'Let me stay,' she whispered, pressing her face closer to his.

'It will only distress you,' he whispered back.

'Nothing distresses me, but being sent away from *you*!'

He waited. She saw that he was thinking, and waited too.

'If I let you stay a little—?'

'Yes! yes!'

'Will you go when I tell you?'

'I will.'

'On your oath?'

The fetters that bound his tongue seemed to be loosened for a moment in the great outburst of anxiety which forced that question to his lips. He spoke those startling words as he had spoken no words yet.

'On my oath!' she repeated, and, dropping on her knees at the bedside, passionately kissed his hand. The two strangers in the room turned their heads away by common consent. In the silence that followed, the one sound stirring was the small sound of the child's toy, as he moved it hither and thither on the bed.

The doctor was the first who broke the spell of stillness which had fallen on all the persons present. He approached the patient, and examined him anxiously. Mrs Armadale rose from her knees; and, first waiting for her husband's permission, carried the sheets of manuscript which she had taken out of the desk, to the table at which Mr Neal was waiting. Flushed and eager, more beautiful than ever in the vehement agitation which still possessed her, she stooped over him as she put the letter into his hands, and, seizing on the means to her end with a woman's headlong self-abandonment to her own impulses, whispered to him: 'Read it out from the beginning. I must and will hear it!' Her eyes flashed their burning light into his; her breath beat on his cheek. Before he could answer, before he could think, she was back with her husband. In an instant she had spoken, and in that instant her beauty had bent the Scotchman to her will. Frowning in reluctant acknowledgment of his own inability to resist her, he turned over the leaves of the letter; looked at the blank place where the pen had dropped from the writer's hand, and had left a blot on the paper; turned back again to the beginning, and said the words, in the wife's interest, which the wife herself had put into his lips.

'Perhaps, sir, you may wish to make some corrections,' he began, with all his attention apparently fixed on the letter, and with every outward appearance of letting his sour temper again get the better of him. 'Shall I read over to you what you have already written?'

Mrs Armadale sitting at the bed-head on one side, and the doctor with his fingers on the patient's pulse, sitting on the other, waited with widely different anxieties for the answer to Mr Neal's question. Mr Armadale's eyes turned searchingly from his child to his wife.

'You *will* hear it?' he said. Her breath came and went quickly; her hand stole up and took his; she bowed her head in silence. Her husband paused, taking secret counsel with his thoughts, and keeping his eyes fixed on his wife. At last he decided, and gave the answer. 'Read it,' he said. 'And stop when I tell you.'

It was close on one o'clock, and the bell was ringing which summoned the visitors to their early dinner at the inn. The quick beat of footsteps, and the gathering hum of voices outside, penetrated gaily into the room, as Mr Neal spread the manuscript before him on the table, and read the opening sentences in these words:

I address this letter to my son, when my son is of an age to understand it. Having lost all hope of living to see my boy grow up to manhood, I have no choice but to write here what I would fain have said to him at a future time, with my own lips.

I have three objects in writing. First, to reveal the circumstances which attended the marriage of an English lady of my acquaintance, in the island of Madeira.[2] Secondly, to throw the true light on the death of her husband a short time afterwards, on board the French timber-ship, *La Grace de Dieu*. Thirdly, to warn my son of a danger that lies in wait for him – a danger that will rise from his father's grave, when the earth has closed over his father's ashes.

The story of the English lady's marriage begins with my inheriting the great Armadale property, and my taking the fatal Armadale name.

I am the only surviving son of the late Mathew Wrentmore, of Barbadoes. I was born on our family estate in that island; and I lost my father when I was still a child. My mother was blindly fond of me: she denied me nothing; she let me live as I pleased. My boyhood and youth were passed in idleness and self-indulgence, among people – slaves and half-castes mostly – to whom my will was law. I doubt if there is a gentleman of my birth and station in all England, as ignorant as I am at this moment. I doubt if there was ever a young man in this world whose passions were left so entirely without control of any kind, as mine were in those early days.

My mother had a woman's romantic objection to my father's homely Christian name. I was christened Allan, after the name of a wealthy cousin of my father's – the late Allan Armadale – who possessed estates in our neighbourhood, the largest and the most productive in the island, and who consented to be my godfather by proxy. Mr Armadale had never seen his West Indian property. He lived in England; and, after sending me the customary god-father's present, he held no further communication with my parents for years afterwards. I was just twenty-one before we heard again from Mr Armadale. On that occasion, my mother received a letter from him, asking if I was still alive, and offering no less (if I was) than to make me the heir to his West Indian property.

This piece of good fortune fell to me entirely through the misconduct of Mr Armadale's son, and only child. The young man had disgraced himself beyond all redemption; had left his home an outlaw; and had been thereupon renounced by his father at once and for ever. Having no other near male relative to succeed him, Mr Armadale thought of his cousin's son, and his own godson; and he offered the West Indian estate to me, and my heirs after me, on one condition – that I, and my heirs, should take his name. The proposal was gratefully accepted, and the proper legal measures were adopted for changing my name in the colony, and in the mother-country. By the next mail, information reached Mr Armadale that his condition had been complied with. The return mail brought news from the lawyers. The will had been altered in my favour, and in a week afterwards, the death of my benefactor had made me the largest proprietor and the richest man in Barbadoes.

This was the first event in the chain. The second event followed it six weeks aferwards.

At that time there happened to be a vacancy in the clerk's office on the estate, and there came to fill it, a young man about my own age, who had recently arrived in the island. He announced himself by the name of Fergus Ingleby. My impulses governed me in everything; I knew no law but the law of my own caprice, and I took a fancy to the stranger the moment I set eyes on him. He had the manners of a gentleman, and he possessed the most attractive social qualities which, in my small experience, I had ever met with. When I heard that the written references to character which he had brought with him, were pronounced to be unsatisfactory, I interfered, and insisted that he should have the place. My will was law, and he had it.

My mother disliked and distrusted Ingleby from the first. When she found the intimacy between us rapidly ripening; when she found me admitting this inferior to the closest companionship and confidence – (I had lived with my inferiors all my life, and I liked it) – she made effort after effort to part us, and failed in one and all. Driven to her last resources she resolved to try the one chance left – the chance of persuading me to take a voyage which I had often thought of, a voyage to England.

Before she spoke to me on the subject, she resolved to interest me in the idea of seeing England, as I had never been interested yet. She wrote to an old friend and an old admirer of hers, the late Stephen Blanchard, of Thorpe-Ambrose, in Norfolk – a gentleman of landed estate, and a widower with a grown-up family. After-discoveries informed me that she must have alluded to their former attachment (which was checked, I believe, by the parents on either side); and that, in asking Mr Blanchard's welcome for her son when he came to England, she made inquiries about his daughter, which hinted at the chance of a marriage uniting the two families, if the young lady and I met and liked one another. We were equally matched in every respect, and my mother's recollection of her girlish attachment to Mr Blanchard, made the prospect of my marrying her old admirer's daughter the brightest and happiest prospect that her eyes could see. Of all this I knew nothing, until Mr Blanchard's answer arrived at Barbadoes. Then my mother showed me the letter, and put the temptation which was to separate me from Fergus Ingleby, openly in my way.

Mr Blanchard's letter was dated from the island of Madeira. He was out of health, and he had been ordered there by the doctors to try the climate. His daughter was with him. After heartily reciprocating all my mother's hopes and wishes, he proposed (if I intended leaving Barbadoes shortly) that I should take Madeira on my way to England, and pay him a visit at his temporary residence in the island. If this could not be, he mentioned the time at which he expected to be back in England, when I might be sure of finding a welcome at his own house of Thorpe-Ambrose. In conclusion, he apologized for not writing at greater length; explaining that his sight was affected, and that he had disobeyed the doctor's orders by yielding to the temptation of writing to his old friend with his own hand.

Kindly as it was expressed, the letter itself might have had little influence on me. But there was something else besides the letter; there was enclosed in it a miniature portrait of Miss Blanchard. At the back of the portrait, her father had written half-jestingly, half-tenderly, 'I can't ask my daughter to spare my eyes as usual, without telling her of your inquiries, and putting a young lady's diffidence to the blush. So I send her in effigy (without her knowledge) to answer for herself. It is a good likeness of a good girl. If she likes your son – and if I like him, which I am sure I shall – we may yet live, my good friend, to see our children what we might once have been ourselves – man and wife.' My mother gave me the miniature with the letter. The portrait at once struck me – I can't say why, I can't say how – as nothing of the kind had ever struck me before.

Harder intellects than mine might have attributed the extraordinary impression produced on me to the disordered condition of my mind at that time; to the weariness of my own base pleasures which had been gaining on me for months past; to the undefined longing which that weariness implied for newer interests and fresher hopes than any that had possessed me yet. I attempted no such sober self-examination as this: I believed in destiny then; I believe in destiny now. It was enough for me to know – as I did know – that the first sense I had ever felt of something better in my nature than my animal-self, was roused by that girl's face looking at me from her picture, as no woman's face had ever looked at me yet. In those tender eyes – in the chance of making that gentle creature my wife – I saw my destiny written. The portrait which had come into my hands so strangely and so unexpectedly, was the silent messenger of happiness close at hand, sent to warn, to encourage, to rouse me before it was too late. I put the miniature under my pillow at night; I looked at it again the next morning. My conviction of the day before remained as strong as ever; my superstition (if you please to call it so) pointed out to me irresistibly the way on which I should go. There was a ship in port which was to sail for England in a fortnight, touching at Madeira. In that ship I took my passage.

Thus far, the reader had advanced with no interruption to disturb him. But at the last words, the tones of another voice, low and broken, mingled with his own.

'Was she a fair woman?' asked the voice, 'or dark, like me?'

Mr Neal paused, and looked up. The doctor was still at the bed-head, with his fingers mechanically on the patient's pulse. The child, missing his midday sleep, was beginning to play languidly with his new toy. The father's eyes were watching him with a rapt and ceaseless attention. But one great change was visible in the listeners since the narrative had begun. Mrs Armadale had dropped her hold of her husband's hand, and sat with her face steadily turned away from him. The hot African blood burnt red in her dusky cheeks as she obstinately repeated the question, 'Was she a fair woman – or dark, like me?'

'Fair,' said her husband, without looking at her.

Her hands, lying clasped together in her lap, wrung each other hard – she said no more. Mr Neal's overhanging eyebrows lowered ominously, as he returned to the narrative. He had incurred his own severe displeasure – he had caught himself in the act of secretly pitying her.

I have said – the letter proceeded – that Ingleby was admitted to my closest confidence. I was sorry to leave him; and I was distressed by his evident surprise and mortification when he heard that I was going away. In my own justification, I showed him the letter and the likeness, and told him the truth. His interest in the portrait seemed to be hardly inferior to my own. He asked me about Miss Blanchard's family, and Miss Blanchard's fortune with the sympathy of a true friend; and he strengthened my regard for him, and my belief in him, by putting himself out of the question, and by generously encouraging me to persist in my new purpose. When we parted, I was in high health and spirits. Before we met again the next day, I was suddenly struck by an illness which threatened both my reason and my life.

I have no proof against Ingleby. There was more than one woman on the island whom I had wronged beyond all forgiveness,[3] and whose vengeance might well have reached me at that time. I can accuse nobody. I can only say that my life was saved by my old black nurse; and that the woman afterwards acknowledged having used the known negro-antidote to a known negro-poison in those parts. When my first days of convalescence came, the ship in which my passage had been taken, had long since sailed. When I asked for Ingleby, he was gone. Proofs of his unpardonable misconduct in his situation were placed before me, which not even my partiality for him could resist. He had been turned out of the office in the first days of my illness, and nothing more was known of him, but that he had left the island.

All through my sufferings, the portrait had been under my pillow. All through my convalescence, it was my one consolation when I remembered the past, and my one encouragement when I thought of the future. No words can describe the hold that first fancy had now taken of me – with time and solitude and suffering to help it. My mother, with all her interest in the match, was startled by the unexpected success of her own project. She had written to tell Mr Blanchard of my illness, but had received no reply. She now offered to write again, if I would promise not to leave her before my recovery was complete. My impatience acknowledged no restraint. Another ship in port gave me another chance of leaving for Madeira. Another examination of Mr Blanchard's letter of invitation assured me that I should find him still in the island, if I seized my opportunity on the spot. In defiance of my mother's entreaties, I insisted on taking my passage in the second ship – and this time, when the ship sailed, I was on board.

The change did me good; the sea air made a man of me again. After an unusually rapid voyage, I found myself at the end of my pilgrimage. On a fine still evening which I can never forget, I stood alone on the shore, with her likeness in my bosom, and saw the white walls of the house where I knew that she lived.

I strolled round the outer limits of the grounds, to compose myself before I went in. Venturing through a gate and a shrubbery, I looked into the garden, and saw a lady there, loitering alone on the lawn. She turned her face towards me – and I beheld the original of my portrait, the fulfilment of my dream! It is useless, and worse than useless, to write of it now. Let me only say that every promise which the likeness had made to my fancy, the living woman kept to my eyes, in the moment when they first looked on her. Let me say this – and no more.

I was too violently agitated to trust myself in her presence. I drew back, undiscovered; and making my way to the front door of the house, asked for her father first. Mr Blanchard had retired to his room, and could see nobody. Upon that I took courage, and asked for Miss Blanchard. The servant smiled. 'My young lady is not Miss Blanchard any longer, sir,' he said. 'She is married.' Those words would have struck some men, in my position, to the earth. They fired my hot blood, and I seized the servant by the throat, in a frenzy of rage. 'It's a lie,' I broke out, speaking to him as if he had been one of the slaves on my own estate. 'It's the truth,' said the man, struggling with me; 'her husband is in the house at this moment.' 'Who is he, you scoundrel?' The servant answered by repeating my own name, to my own face: '*Allan Armadale*'.

You can now guess the truth. Fergus Ingleby was the outlawed son, whose name and whose inheritance I had taken. And Fergus Ingleby was even with me for depriving him of his birthright.

Some account of the manner in which the deception had been carried out, is necessary to explain – I don't say to justify – the share I took in the events that followed my arrival at Madeira.

By Ingleby's own confession, he had come to Barbadoes – knowing of his father's death and of my succession to the estates – with the settled purpose of plundering and injuring me. My rash confidence put such an opportunity into his hands, as he could never have hoped for. He had waited to possess himself of the letter which my mother wrote to Mr Blanchard at the outset of my illness – had then caused his own dismissal from his situation – and had sailed for Madeira in the very ship that was to have sailed with me. Arrived at the island, he had waited again, till the vessel was away once more on her voyage, and had then presented himself at Mr Blanchard's – not in the assumed name by which I shall continue to speak of him here – but in the name which was as certainly his as mine, 'Allan Armadale'. The fraud at the outset presented few difficulties. He had only an ailing old man (who had not seen my mother for half a lifetime), and an innocent unsuspicious girl (who had never seen her at all) to deal with; and he had learnt enough in my service to answer the few questions that were put to him, as readily as I might have answered them myself. His looks and manners, his winning ways with women, his quickness and cunning, did the rest. While I was still on my sick-bed, he had won Miss Blanchard's affections. While I was dreaming over the likeness in the first days of my convalescence, he had secured Mr Blanchard's consent to the celebration of the marriage before he and his daughter left the island.

Thus far, Mr Blanchard's infirmity of sight had helped the deception. He had been content to send messages to my mother, and to receive the messages which were duly invented in return. But when the suitor was accepted, and the wedding-day was appointed, he felt it due to his old friend to write to her, asking her formal consent, and inviting her to the marriage. He could only complete part of the letter himself; the rest was finished, under his dictation, by Miss Blanchard. There was no chance of being beforehand with the post-office this time; and Ingleby, sure of his place in the heart of his victim, waylaid her as she came out of her father's room with the letter, and privately told her the truth. She was still under age, and the position was a serious one. If the letter was posted, no resource would be left but to wait and be parted for ever, or to elope under circumstances which made detection almost a certainty. The destination of any ship which took them away would be known beforehand; and the fast-sailing yacht in which Mr Blanchard had come to Madeira was waiting in the harbour to take him back to England. The only other alternative was to continue the deception by suppressing the letter, and to confess the truth when they were securely married. What arts of persuasion Ingleby used – what base advantage he might previously have taken of her love and her trust in him to degrade Miss Blanchard to his own level – I cannot say. He did degrade her. The letter never went to its destination; and, with the daughter's privity and consent, the father's confidence was abused to the very last.

The one precaution now left to take, was to fabricate the answer from my mother which Mr Blanchard expected, and which would arrive in due course of post before the day appointed for the marriage. Ingleby had my mother's stolen letter with him; but he was without the imitative dexterity which would have enabled him to make use of it for a forgery of her handwriting. Miss Blanchard, who had consented passively to the deception, refused to take any active share in the fraud practised on her father. In this difficulty, Ingleby found an instrument ready to his hand in an orphan girl of barely twelve years old,[4] a marvel of precocious ability, whom Miss Blanchard had taken a romantic fancy to befriend, and whom she had brought away with her from England to be trained as her maid. That girl's wicked dexterity removed the one serious obstacle left to the success of the fraud. I saw the imitation of my mother's writing which she had produced under Ingleby's instructions, and (if the shameful truth must be told) with her young mistress's knowledge – and I believe I should have been deceived by it myself. I saw the girl afterwards – and my blood curdled at the sight of her. If she is alive now, woe to the people who trust her! No creature more innately deceitful and more innately pitiless ever walked this earth.

The forged letter paved the way securely for the marriage; and when I reached the house, they were (as the servant had truly told me) man and wife. My arrival on the scene simply precipitated the confession which they had both agreed to make. Ingleby's own lips shamelessly acknowledged the truth. He had nothing to lose by speaking out – he was married, and his wife's fortune was beyond her father's control. I pass over all that followed – my interview with the daughter, and my interview with the father – to come to results. For two days the efforts of the wife, and the efforts of the clergyman who had celebrated the marriage, were successful in keeping Ingleby and myself apart. On the third day I set my trap more successfully, and I and the man who had mortally injured me, met together alone, face to face.

Remember how my confidence had been abused; remember how the one good purpose of my life had been thwarted; remember the violent passions rooted deep in my nature, and never yet controlled – and then imagine for yourself what passed between us. All I need tell here is the end. He was a taller and a stronger man than I, and he took his brute's advantage with a brute's ferocity. He struck me.

Think of the injuries I had received at that man's hands, and then think of his setting his mark on my face by a blow!

I went to an English officer who had been my fellow-passenger on the voyage from Barbadoes. I told him the truth, and he agreed with me that a meeting was inevitable. Duelling had its received formalities and its established laws in those days;[5] and he began to speak of them. I stopped him. 'I will take a pistol in my right hand,' I said, 'and he shall take a pistol in his: I will take one end of a handkerchief in my left hand, and he shall take the other end in his; and across that handkerchief the duel shall be fought.' The officer got up, and looked at me as if I had personally insulted him. 'You are asking me to be present at a murder and a suicide,' he said; 'I decline to serve you.' He left the room. As soon as he was gone I wrote down the words I had said to the officer, and sent them by a messenger to Ingleby. While I was waiting for an answer, I sat down before the glass, and looked at his mark on my face. 'Many a man has had blood on his hands and blood on his conscience,' I thought, 'for less than this.'

The messenger came back with Ingleby's answer. It appointed a meeting for three o'clock the next day, at a lonely place in the interior of the island. I had resolved what to do if he refused; his letter released me from the horror of my own resolution. I felt grateful to him – yes, absolutely grateful to him – for writing it.

The next day I went to the place. He was not there. I waited two hours, and he never came. At last the truth dawned on me. 'Once a coward, always a coward,' I thought. I went back to Mr Blanchard's house. Before I got there, a sudden misgiving seized me, and I turned aside to the harbour. I was right; the harbour was the place to go to. A ship sailing for Lisbon that afternoon, had offered him the opportunity of taking a passage for himself and his wife, and escaping me. His answer to my challenge had served its purpose of sending me out of the way, into the interior of the island. Once more I had trusted in Fergus Ingleby, and once more those sharp wits of his had been too much for me.

I asked my informant if Mr Blanchard was aware as yet of his daughter's departure. He had discovered it, but not until the ship had sailed. This time I took a lesson in cunning from Ingleby. Instead of showing myself at Mr Blanchard's house, I went first and looked at Mr Blanchard's yacht.

The vessel told me what the vessel's master might have concealed – the truth. I found her in the confusion of a sudden preparation for sea. All the crew were on board, with the exception of some few who had been allowed their leave on shore, and who were away in the interior of the island, nobody knew where. When I discovered that the sailing-master was trying to supply their places with the best men he could pick up at a moment's notice, my resolution was instantly taken. I knew the duties on board a yacht well enough, having had a vessel of my own, and having sailed her myself. Hurrying into the town, I changed my dress for a sailor's coat and hat, and, returning to the harbour, I offered myself as one of the volunteer crew. I don't know what the sailing-master saw in my face. My answers to his questions satisfied him, and yet he looked at me and hesitated. But hands were scarce, and it ended in my being taken on board. An hour later Mr Blanchard joined us, and was assisted into the cabin, suffering pitiably in mind and body both. An hour after that, we were at sea, with a starless night overhead, and a fresh breeze behind us.

As I had surmised, we were in pursuit of the vessel in which Ingleby and his wife had left the island that afternoon. The ship was French, and was employed in the timber-trade: her name was *La Grace de Dieu*. Nothing more was known of her than that she was bound for Lisbon; that she had been driven out of her course; and that she had touched at Madeira, short of men and short of provisions. The last want had been supplied, but not the first. Sailors distrusted the seaworthiness of the ship, and disliked the look of the vagabond crew. When those two serious facts had been communicated to Mr Blanchard, the hard words he had spoken to his child in the first shock of discovering that she had helped to deceive him, smote him to the heart. He instantly determined to give his daughter a refuge on board his own vessel, and to quiet her by keeping her villain of a husband out of the way of all harm at my hands. The yacht sailed three feet and more to the ship's one. There was no doubt of our overtaking *La Grace de Dieu*; the only fear was that we might pass her in the darkness.

After we had been some little time out, the wind suddenly dropped, and there fell on us an airless, sultry calm. When the order came to get the topmasts on deck, and to shift the large sails, we all knew what to expect. In little better than an hour more, the storm was upon us, the thunder was pealing over our heads, and the yacht was running for it. She was a powerful schooner-rigged vessel of three hundred tons, as strong as wood and iron could make her; she was handled by a sailing-master who thoroughly understood his work, and she behaved nobly. As the new morning came, the fury of the wind, blowing still from the south-west quarter, subsided a little, and the sea was less heavy. Just before daybreak we heard faintly, through the howling of the gale, the report of a gun. The men, collected anxiously on deck, looked at each other and said, 'There she is!'

With the daybreak we saw the vessel, and the timber-ship it was. She lay wallowing in the trough of the sea, her foremast and her mainmast both gone – a waterlogged wreck. The yacht carried three boats; one amidships, and two slung to davits on the quarters; and the sailing-master seeing signs of the storm renewing its fury before long, determined on lowering the quarter-boats while the lull lasted. Few as the people were on board the wreck, they were too many for one boat, and the risk of trying two boats at once was thought less, in the critical state of the weather, than the risk of making two separate trips from the yacht to the ship. There might be time to make one trip in safety, but no man could look at the heavens and say there would be time enough for two.

The boats were manned by volunteers from the crew, I being in the second of the two. When the first boat was got alongside of the timber-ship – a service of difficulty and danger which no words can describe – all the men on board made a rush to leave the wreck together. If the boat had not been pulled off again before the whole of them had crowded in, the lives of all must have been sacrificed. As our boat approached the vessel in its turn, we arranged that four of us should get on board – two (I being one of them) to see to the safety of Mr Blanchard's daughter, and two to beat back the cowardly remnant of the crew, if they tried to crowd in first. The other three – the coxswain and two oarsmen – were left in the boat to keep her from being crushed by the ship. What the others saw when they first boarded *La Grace de Dieu*, I don't know: what *I* saw was the woman whom I had lost, the woman vilely stolen from me, lying in a swoon on the deck. We lowered her, insensible, into the boat. The remnant of the crew – five in number – were compelled by main force to follow her in an orderly manner, one by one, and minute by minute, as the chance offered for safely taking them in. I was the last who left; and, at the next roll of the ship towards us, the empty length of the deck, without a living creature on it from stem to stern, told the boat's crew that their work was done. With the louder and louder howling of the fast-rising tempest to warn them, they rowed for their lives back to the yacht.

A succession of heavy squalls had brought round the course of the new storm that was coming, from the south to the north; and the sailing-master, watching his opportunity, had wore the yacht, to be ready for it. Before the last of our men had got on board again, it burst on us with the fury of a hurricane. Our boat was swamped, but not a life was lost. Once more, we ran before it, due south, at the mercy of the wind. I was on deck with the rest, watching the one rag of sail we could venture to set, and waiting to supply its place with another, if it blew out of the bolt-ropes, when the mate came close to me, and shouted in my ear through the thunder of the storm, 'She has come to her senses in the cabin, and has asked for her husband. Where is he?' Not a man on board knew. The yacht was searched from one end to another, without finding him. The men were mustered in defiance of the weather – he was not among them. The crews of the two boats were questioned. All the first crew could say, was that they had pulled away from the wreck when the rush into their boat took place, and that they knew nothing of who they let in or who they kept out. All the second crew could say was, that they had brought back to the yacht every living soul left by the first boat on the deck of the timber-ship. There was no blaming anybody; but at the same time, there was no resisting the fact, that the man was missing.

All through that day the storm, raging unabatedly, never gave us even the shadow of a chance of returning and searching the wreck. The one hope for the yacht was to scud. Towards evening the gale, after having carried us to the southward of Madeira, began at last to break – the wind shifted again – and allowed us to bear up for the island. Early the next morning we got back into port. Mr Blanchard and his daughter were taken ashore; the sailing-master accompanying them, and warning us that he should have something to say on his return, which would nearly concern the whole crew.

We were mustered on deck, and addressed by the sailing-master as soon as he came on board again. He had Mr Blanchard's orders to go back at once to the timber-ship and to search for the missing man. We were bound to do this for his sake, and for the sake of his wife, whose reason was despaired of by the doctors if something was not done to quiet her. We might be almost sure of finding the vessel still afloat, for her lading of timber would keep her above water as long as her hull held together. If the man was on board – living or dead – he must be found and brought back. And if the weather continued to moderate, there was no reason why the men, with proper assistance, should not bring the ship back too, and (their master being quite willing) earn their share of the salvage with the officers of the yacht.

Upon this the crew gave three cheers, and set to work forthwith to get the schooner to sea again. I was the only one of them who drew back from the enterprise. I told them the storm had upset me – I was ill, and wanted rest. They all looked me in the face as I passed through them on my way out of the yacht, but not a man of them spoke to me.

I waited through that day at a tavern on the port for the first news from the wreck. It was brought towards nightfall by one of the pilot-boats which had taken part in the enterprise for saving the abandoned ship. *La Grace de Dieu* had been discovered still floating, and the body of Ingleby had been found on board, drowned in the cabin. At dawn the next morning, the dead man was brought back by the yacht; and on the same day the funeral took place in the Protestant cemetery.

'Stop!' said the voice from the bed, before the reader could turn to a new leaf and begin the next paragraph.

There was a change in the room, and there were changes in the audience, since Mr Neal had last looked up from the narrative. A ray of sunshine was crossing the death-bed; and the child, overcome by drowsiness, lay peacefully asleep in the golden light. The father's countenance had altered visibly. Forced into action by the tortured mind, the muscles of the lower face, which had never moved yet, were moving distortedly now. Warned by the damps gathering heavily on his forehead, the doctor had risen to revive the sinking man. On the other side of the bed the wife's chair stood empty. At the moment when her husband had interrupted the reading, she had drawn back behind the bed-head, out of his sight. Supporting herself against the wall, she stood there in hiding, her eyes fastened in hungering suspense on the manuscript in Mr Neal's hand.

In a minute more the silence was broken again by Mr Armadale.

'Where is she?' he asked, looking angrily at his wife's empty chair. The doctor pointed to the place. She had no choice but to come forward. She came slowly and stood before him.

'You promised to go when I told you,' he said. 'Go now.'

Mr Neal tried hard to control his hand as it kept his place between the leaves of the manuscript, but it trembled in spite of him. A suspicion which had been slowly forcing itself on his mind, while he was reading, became a certainty when he heard those words. From one revelation to another the letter had gone on, until it had now reached the brink of a last disclosure to come. At that brink the dying man had pre-determined to silence the reader's voice, before he had permitted his wife to hear the narrative read. *There* was the secret which the son was to know in after years, and which the mother was never to approach. From that resolution, his wife's tenderest pleadings had never moved him an inch – and now, from his own lips, his wife knew it.

She made him no answer. She stood there and looked at him; looked her last entreaty – perhaps her last farewell. His eyes gave her back no answering glance: they wandered from her mercilessly to the sleeping boy. She turned speechless from the bed. Without a look at the child – without a word to the two strangers breathlessly watching her – she kept the promise she had given, and in dead silence left the room.

There was something in the manner of her departure which shook the self-possession of both the men who witnessed it. When the door closed on her, they recoiled instinctively from advancing farther in the dark. The doctor's reluctance was the first to express itself. He attempted to obtain the patient's permission to withdraw until the letter was completed. The patient refused.

Mr Neal spoke next at greater length and to more serious purpose.

'The doctor is accustomed in his profession,' he began, 'and I am accustomed in mine, to have the secrets of others placed in our keeping. But it is my duty, before we go farther, to ask if you really understand the extraordinary position which we now occupy towards one another. You have just excluded Mrs Armadale, before our own eyes, from a place in your confidence. And you are now offering that same place to two men who are total strangers to you.'

'Yes,' said Mr Armadale – '*because* you are strangers.'

Few as the words were, the inference to be drawn from them was not of a nature to set distrust at rest. Mr Neal put it plainly into words.

'You are in urgent need of my help and of the doctor's help,' he said. 'Am I to understand (so long as you secure our assistance) that the impression which the closing passages of this letter may produce on us is a matter of indifference to you?'

'Yes. I don't spare you. I don't spare myself. I *do* spare my wife.'

'You force me to a conclusion, sir, which is a very serious one,' said Mr Neal. 'If I am to finish this letter under your dictation, I must claim permission – having read aloud the greater part of it already – to read aloud what remains, in the hearing of this gentleman, as a witness.'

'Read it.'

Gravely doubting, the doctor resumed his chair. Gravely doubting, Mr Neal turned the leaf, and read the next words:

There is more to tell before I can leave the dead man to his rest. I have described the finding of his body. But I have not described the circumstances under which he met his death.

He was known to have been on deck when the yacht's boats were seen approaching the wreck; and he was afterwards missed in the confusion caused by the panic of the crew. At that time the water was five feet deep in the cabin, and was rising fast. There was little doubt of his having gone down into that water of his own accord. The discovery of his wife's jewel-box, close under him, on the floor, explained his presence in the cabin. He was known to have seen help approaching, and it was quite likely that he had thereupon gone below to make an effort at saving the box.

It was less probable – though it might still have been inferred – that his death was the result of some accident in diving, which had for the moment deprived him of his senses. But a discovery made by the yacht's crew, pointed straight to a conclusion, which struck the men, one and all, with the same horror. When the course of their search brought them to the cabin, they found the scuttle bolted, and the door locked on the outside. Had some one closed the cabin, not knowing he was there? Setting the panic-stricken condition of the crew out of the question, there was no motive for closing the cabin before leaving the wreck. But one other conclusion remained. Had some murderous hand purposely locked the man in, and left him to drown as the water rose over him?

Yes. A murderous hand had locked him in, and left him to drown. That hand was mine.

The Scotchman started up from the table; the doctor shrank from the bedside. The two looked at the dying wretch, mastered by the same loathing, chilled by the same dread. He lay there, with the child's head on his breast; abandoned by the sympathies of man, accursed by the justice of God – he lay there, in the isolation of Cain, and looked back at them.

At the moment when the two men rose to their feet, the door leading into the next room was shaken heavily on the outer side, and a sound like the sound of a fall, striking dull on their ears, silenced them both. Standing nearest to the door, the doctor opened it, passed through, and closed it instantly. Mr Neal turned his back on the bed, and waited the event in silence. The sound, which had failed to awaken the child, had failed also to attract the father's notice. His own words had taken him far from all that was passing at his death-bed. His helpless body was back on the wreck, and the ghost of his lifeless hand was turning the lock of the cabin door.

A bell rang in the next room – eager voices talked; hurried footsteps moved in it – an interval passed, and the doctor returned. 'Was she listening?' whispered Mr Neal, in German. 'The women are restoring her,' the doctor whispered back. 'She has heard it all. In God's name, what are we to do next?' Before it was possible to reply, Mr Armadale spoke. The doctor's return had roused him to a sense of present things.

'Go on,' he said, as if nothing had happened.

'I refuse to meddle further with your infamous secret,' returned Mr

Neal. 'You are a murderer on your own confession. If that letter is to be finished, don't ask *me* to hold the pen for you.'

'You gave me your promise,' was the reply, spoken with the same immovable self-possession. 'You must write for me, or break your word.'

For the moment, Mr Neal was silenced. There the man lay – sheltered from the execration of his fellow-creatures, under the shadow of Death – beyond the reach of all human condemnation, beyond the dread of all mortal laws; sensitive to nothing but his one last resolution to finish the letter addressed to his son.

Mr Neal drew the doctor aside. 'A word with you,' he said, in German. 'Do you persist in asserting that he may be speechless before we can send to Stuttgart?'

'Look at his lips,' said the doctor, 'and judge for yourself.'

His lips answered for him: the reading of the narrative had left its mark on them already. A distortion at the corners of his mouth, which had been barely noticeable when Mr Neal entered the room, was plainly visible now. His slow articulation laboured more and more painfully with every word he uttered. The position was emphatically a terrible one. After a moment more of hesitation, Mr Neal made a last attempt to withdraw from it.

'Now my eyes are open,' he said, sternly, 'do you dare hold me to an engagement which you forced on me blindfold?'

'No,' answered Mr Armadale. 'I leave you to break your word.'

The look which accompanied that reply, stung the Scotchman's pride to the quick. When he spoke next, he spoke seated in his former place at the table.

'No man ever yet said of me that I broke my word,' he retorted, angrily; 'and not even *you* shall say it of me now. Mind this! If you hold me to my promise, I hold you to my condition. I have reserved my freedom of action, and I warn you I will use it at my own sole discretion, as soon as I am released from the sight of you.'

'Remember he is dying,' pleaded the doctor, gently.

'Take your place, sir,' said Mr Neal, pointing to the empty chair. 'What remains to be read, I will only read in your hearing. What remains to be written, I will only write in your presence. *You* brought me here. I have a right to insist – and I do insist – on your remaining as a witness to the last.'

The doctor accepted his position without remonstrance. Mr Neal returned to the manuscript, and read what remained of it uninterruptedly to the end:

*

Without a word in my own defence, I have acknowledged my guilt. Without a word in my own defence, I will reveal how the crime was committed.

No thought of him was in my mind, when I saw his wife insensible on the deck of the timber-ship. I did my part in lowering her safely into the boat. Then, and not till then, I felt the thought of him coming back. In the confusion that prevailed while the men of the yacht were forcing the men of the ship to wait their time, I had an opportunity of searching for him unobserved. I stepped back from the bulwark, not knowing whether he was away in the first boat, or whether he was still on board – I stepped back, and saw him mount the cabin stairs empty-handed, with the water dripping from him. After looking eagerly towards the boat (without noticing me), he saw there was time to spare before the crew were taken off. 'Once more!' he said to himself – and disappeared again, to make a last effort at recovering the jewel-box. The devil at my elbow whispered, 'Don't shoot him like a man: drown him like a dog!' He was under water when I bolted the scuttle. But his head rose to the surface before I could close the cabin door. I looked at him, and he looked at me – and I locked the door in his face. The next minute, I was back among the last men left on deck. The minute after, it was too late to repent. The storm was threatening us with destruction, and the boat's crew were pulling for their lives from the ship.

My son! I have pursued you from my grave with a confession which my love might have spared you. Read on, and you will know why.

I will say nothing of my sufferings; I will plead for no mercy to my memory. There is a strange sinking at my heart, a strange trembling in my hand, while I write these lines, which warns me to hasten to the end. I left the island without daring to look for the last time at the woman whom I had lost so miserably, whom I had injured so vilely. When I left, the whole weight of the suspicion roused by the manner of Ingleby's death, rested on the crew of the French vessel. No motive for the supposed murder could be brought home to any of them – but they were known to be, for the most part, outlawed ruffians capable of any crime, and they were suspected and examined accordingly. It was not till afterwards that I heard by accident of the suspicion shifting round at last to me. The widow alone recognized the vague description given of the strange man who had made one of the yacht's crew, and who had disappeared the day afterwards. The widow alone knew, from that time forth, why her husband had been murdered, and who had done the deed. When she made that discovery, a false report of my death had been previously circulated in the island. Perhaps I was indebted to the report for my immunity from all legal proceedings – perhaps (no eye but Ingleby's having seen me lock the cabin door) there was not evidence enough to justify an inquiry – perhaps the widow shrank from the disclosures which must have followed a public charge against me, based on her own bare suspicion of the truth. However it might be, the crime which I had committed unseen, has remained a crime unpunished from that time to this.

I left Madeira for the West Indies, in disguise. The first news that met me when the ship touched at Barbadoes, was the news of my mother's death. I had no heart to return to the old scenes. The prospect of living at home in solitude, with the torment of my own guilty remembrances gnawing at me day and night, was more than I had the courage to confront. Without landing, or discovering myself to any one on shore, I went on as far as the ship would take me – to the island of Trinidad.

At that place I first saw your mother. It was my duty to tell her the truth – and I treacherously kept my secret. It was my duty to spare her the hopeless sacrifice of her freedom and her happiness to such an existence as mine – and I did her the injury of marrying her. If she is alive when you read this, grant her the mercy of still concealing the truth. The one atonement I can make to her, is to keep her unsuspicious to the last of the man she has married. Pity her, as I have pitied her. Let this letter be a sacred confidence between father and son.

The time when you were born, was the time when my health began to give way. Some months afterwards, in the first days of my recovery, you were brought to me; and I was told that you had been christened during my illness. Your mother had done as other loving mothers do – she had christened her first-born by his father's name. You, too, were Allan Armadale. Even in that early time – even while I was happily ignorant of what I have discovered since – my mind misgave me when I looked at you, and thought of that fatal name.

As soon as I could be moved, my presence was required at my estates in Barbadoes. It crossed my mind – wild as the idea may appear to you − to renounce the condition which compelled my son as well as myself to take the Armadale name, or lose the succession to the Armadale property. But, even in those days, the rumour of a contemplated emancipation of the slaves[6] − the emancipation which is now close at hand − was spreading widely in the colony. No man could tell how the value of West Indian property might be affected if that threatened change ever took place. No man could tell − if I gave you back my own paternal name, and left you without other provision in the future than my own paternal estate − how you might one day miss the broad Armadale acres, or to what future penury I might be blindly condemning your mother and yourself. Mark how the fatalities gathered one on the other! Mark how your Christian name came to you, how your surname held to you, in spite of me!

My health had improved in my old home − but it was for a time only. I sank again, and the doctors ordered me to Europe. Avoiding England (why, you may guess), I took my passage, with you and your mother, for France. From France we passed into Italy. We lived here; we lived there. It was useless. Death had got me − and Death followed me, go where I might. I bore it, for I had an alleviation to turn to which I had not deserved. You may shrink in horror from the very memory of me, now. In those days, you comforted me. The only warmth I still felt at my heart was the warmth you brought to it. My last glimpses of happiness in this world, were the glimpses given me by my infant son.

We removed from Italy, and went next to Lausanne − the place from which I am now writing to you. The post of this morning has brought me news, later and fuller than any I had received thus far, of the widow of the murdered man. The letter lies before me while I write. It comes from a friend of my early days, who has seen her, and spoken to her − who has been the first to inform her that the report of my death in Madeira was false. He writes, at a loss to account for the violent agitation which she showed on hearing that I was still alive, that I was married, and that I had an infant son. He asks me if I can explain it. He speaks in terms of sympathy for her − a young and beautiful woman, buried in the retirement of a fishing village on the Devonshire coast;[7] her father dead; her family estranged from her, in merciless disapproval of her marriage. He writes words which might have cut me to the heart, but for a closing passage in his letter, which seized my whole attention the instant I came to it; and which has forced from me the narrative that these pages contain.

I now know, what never even entered my mind as a suspicion till the letter reached me. I now know that the widow of the man whose death lies at my door, has borne a posthumous child. That child is a boy – a year older than my own son. Secure in her belief in my death, his mother has done, what my son's mother did: she has christened her child by his father's name. Again, in the second generation, there are two Allan Armadales as there were in the first. After working its deadly mischief with the fathers, the fatal resemblance of names has descended to work its deadly mischief with the sons.

Guiltless minds may see nothing thus far but the result of a series of events which could lead no other way. I – with that man's life to answer for – I, going down into my grave, with my crime unpunished and unatoned, see what no guiltless minds can discern. I see danger in the future, begotten of the danger in the past – treachery that is the offspring of *his* treachery, and crime that is the child of *my* crime. Is the dread that now shakes me to the soul, a phantom raised by the superstition of a dying man? I look into the Book which all Christendom venerates; and the Book tells me that the sin of the father shall be visited on the child. I look out into the world; and I see the living witnesses round me to that terrible truth. I see the vices which have contaminated the father, descending, and contaminating the child; I see the shame which has disgraced the father's name, descending, and disgracing the child's. I look in on myself – and I see My Crime, ripening again for the future in the self-same circumstance which first sowed the seeds of it in the past; and descending, in inherited contamination of Evil, from me to my son.

At those lines the writing ended. There, the stroke had struck him, and the pen had dropped from his hand.

He knew the place; he remembered the words. At the instant when the reader's voice stopped, he looked eagerly at the doctor. 'I have got what comes next in my mind,' he said, with slower and slower articulation. 'Help me to speak it.'

The doctor administered a stimulant, and signed to Mr Neal to give him time. After a little delay, the flame of the sinking spirit leapt up in his eyes once more. Resolutely struggling with his failing speech, he summoned the Scotchman to take the pen; and pronounced the closing sentences of the narrative, as his memory gave them back to him, one by one, in these words:

Despise my dying conviction, if you will – but grant me, I solemnly implore you, one last request. My son! the only hope I have left for you, hangs on a Great Doubt – the doubt whether we are, or are not, the masters of our own destinies. It may be, that mortal freewill can conquer mortal fate; and that going, as we all do, inevitably to death, we go inevitably to nothing that is before death. If this be so, indeed, respect – though you respect nothing else – the warning which I give you from my grave. Never, to your dying day, let any living soul approach you who is associated, directly or indirectly, with the crime which your father has committed. Avoid the widow of the man I killed – if the widow still lives. Avoid the maid whose wicked hand smoothed the way to the marriage – if the maid is still in her service. And more than all, avoid the man who bears the same name as your own. Offend your best benefactor, if that benefactor's influence has connected you one with the other. Desert the woman who loves you, if that woman is a link between you and him. Hide yourself from him under an assumed name. Put the mountains and the seas between you; be ungrateful, be unforgiving; be all that is most repellent to your own gentler nature, rather than live under the same roof, and breathe the same air with that man. Never let the two Allan Armadales meet in this world: never, never, never!

There lies the way by which you may escape – if any way there be. Take it, if you prize your own innocence and your own happiness, through all your life to come!

I have done. If I could have trusted any weaker influence than the influence of this confession to incline you to my will, I would have spared you the disclosure which these pages contain. You are lying on my breast, sleeping the innocent sleep of a child, while a stranger's hand writes these words for you as they fall from my lips. Think what the strength of my conviction must be, when I can find the courage, on my death-bed, to darken all your young life at its outset with the shadow of your father's crime. Think – and be warned. Think – and forgive me if you can.

There, it ended. Those were the father's last words to the son.

Inexorably faithful to his forced duty, Mr Neal laid aside the pen, and read over aloud the lines he had just written. 'Is there more to add?' he asked, with his pitilessly steady voice. There was no more to add.

Mr Neal folded the manuscript, enclosed it in a sheet of paper, and sealed it with Mr Armadale's own seal. 'The address?' he said, with his merciless business formality. 'To Allan Armadale, junior,' he wrote, as the words were dictated from the bed. 'Care of Godfrey Hammick, Esq., Offices of Messrs Hammick and Ridge, Lincoln's Inn Fields, London.' Having written the address, he waited, and considered for a moment. 'Is your executor to open this?' he asked.

'No! he is to give it to my son, when my son is of an age to understand it.'

'In that case,' pursued Mr Neal, with all his wits in remorseless working order, 'I will add a dated note to the address, repeating your own words as you have just spoken them, and explaining the circumstances under which my handwriting appears on the document.' He wrote the note in the briefest and plainest terms – read it over aloud as he had read over what went before – signed his name and address at the end, and made the doctor sign next, as witness of the proceedings, and as medical evidence of the condition in which Mr Armadale then lay. This done, he placed the letter in a second enclosure, sealed it as before, and directed it to Mr Hammick, with the superscription of 'private,' added to the address.

'Do you insist on my posting this?' he asked, rising with the letter in his hand.

'Give him time to think,' said the doctor. 'For the child's sake give him time to think! A minute may change him.'

'I will give him five minutes,' answered Mr Neal, placing his watch on the table, implacably just to the very last.

They waited, both looking attentively at Mr Armadale. The signs of change which had appeared in him already, were multiplying fast. The movement which continued mental agitation had communicated to the muscles of his face, was beginning, under the same dangerous influence, to spread downwards. His once helpless hands lay still no longer; they struggled pitiably on the bed-clothes. At sight of that warning token the doctor turned with a gesture of alarm, and beckoned Mr Neal to come nearer. 'Put the question at once,' he said; 'if you let the five minutes pass, you may be too late.'

Mr Neal approached the bed. He, too, noticed the movement of the hands. 'Is that a bad sign?' he asked.

The doctor bent his head gravely. 'Put your question at once,' he repeated, 'or you may be too late.'

49

Mr Neal held the letter before the eyes of the dying man. 'Do you know what this is?'

'My letter.'

'Do you insist on my posting it?'

He mastered his failing speech for the last time, and gave the answer. 'Yes!'

Mr Neal moved to the door, with the letter in his hand. The German followed him a few steps, opened his lips to plead for a longer delay, met the Scotchman's inexorable eye, and drew back again in silence. The door closed and parted them, without a word having passed on either side.

The doctor went back to the bed, and whispered to the sinking man, 'Let me call him back; there is time to stop him yet!' It was useless. No answer came: nothing showed that he heeded, or even heard. His eyes wandered from the child, rested for a moment on his own struggling hand, and looked up entreatingly in the compassionate face that bent over him. The doctor lifted the hand – paused – followed the father's longing eyes back to the child – and, interpreting his last wish, moved the hand gently towards the boy's head. The hand touched it, and trembled violently. In another instant the trembling seized on the arm, and spread over the whole upper part of the body. The face turned from pale to red; from red to purple; from purple to pale again. Then the toiling hands lay still, and the shifting colour changed no more.[8]

The window of the next room was open, when the doctor entered it from the death-chamber, with the child in his arms. He looked out as he passed by, and saw Mr Neal in the street below, slowly returning to the inn.

'Where is the letter?' he asked.

Three words sufficed for the Scotchman's answer.

'In the post.'

THE END OF THE FIRST BOOK

BOOK THE SECOND

CHAPTER I

THE MYSTERY OF OZIAS MIDWINTER

On a warm May night, in the year eighteen hundred and fifty-one,[1] the Reverend Decimus Brock – at that time a visitor to the Isle of Man – retired to his bedroom, at Castletown, with a serious personal responsibility in close pursuit of him, and with no distinct idea of the means by which he might relieve himself from the pressure of his present circumstances.

The clergyman had reached that mature period of human life at which a sensible man learns to decline (as often as his temper will let him) all useless conflict with the tyranny of his own troubles. Abandoning any further effort to reach a decision in the emergency that now beset him, Mr Brock sat down placidly in his shirt-sleeves on the side of his bed, and applied his mind to consider next, whether the emergency itself was as serious as he had hitherto been inclined to think it. Following this new way out of his perplexities, Mr Brock found himself unexpectedly travelling to the end in view, by the least inspiriting of all human journeys – a journey through the past years of his own life.

One by one, the events of those years – all connected with the same little group of characters, and all more or less answerable for the anxiety which was now intruding itself between the clergyman and his night's rest – rose, in progressive series, on Mr Brock's memory. The first of the series took him back through a period of fourteen years, to his own rectory on the Somersetshire shores of the Bristol Channel, and closeted him at a private interview with a lady, who had paid him a visit in the character of a total stranger to the parson and the place.

The lady's complexion was fair, the lady's figure was well-preserved; she was still a young woman, and she looked even younger than her age. There was a shade of melancholy in her expression, and an undertone of suffering in her voice – enough, in each case, to indicate that she had known trouble, but not enough to obtrude that trouble on the notice of others. She brought with her a fine, fair-haired boy of eight years old, whom she presented as her son, and who was sent out of the way, at the beginning of the interview, to amuse himself in the rectory garden. Her card had preceded her entrance into the study, and had announced her under the name of 'Mrs Armadale'. Mr Brock began to feel interested in her before she had opened her lips; and when the son had been dismissed, he waited, with some anxiety, to hear what the mother had to say to him.[2]

Mrs Armadale began by informing the rector that she was a widow. Her husband had perished by shipwreck, a short time after their union, on the voyage from Madeira to Lisbon. She had been brought to England, after her affliction, under her father's protection; and her child – a posthumous son – had been born on the family estate in Norfolk. Her father's death, shortly afterwards, had deprived her of her only surviving parent, and had exposed her to neglect and misconstruction on the part of her remaining relatives (two brothers), which had estranged her from them, she feared, for the rest of her days. For some time past, she had lived in the neighbouring county of Devonshire, devoting herself to the education of her boy – who had now reached an age at which he required other than his mother's teaching. Leaving out of the question her own unwillingness to part with him, in her solitary position, she was especially anxious that he should not be thrown among strangers by being sent to school. Her darling project was to bring him up privately at home, and to keep him, as he advanced in years, from all contact with the temptations and the dangers of the world. With these objects in view, her longer sojourn in her own locality (where the services of the resident clergyman, in the capacity of tutor, were not obtainable) must come to an end. She had made inquiries, had heard of a house that would suit her in Mr Brock's neighbourhood, and had also been told that Mr Brock himself had formerly been in the habit of taking pupils. Possessed of this information, she had ventured to present herself, with references that vouched for her respectability, but without a formal introduction; and she had now to ask whether (in the event of her residing in the neighbourhood) any terms that could be offered would induce Mr Brock to open his doors once more to a pupil, and to allow that pupil to be her son.

If Mrs Armadale had been a woman of no personal attractions, or if Mr Brock had been provided with an entrenchment to fight behind, in the shape of a wife, it is probable that the widow's journey might have been taken in vain. As things really were, the rector examined the references which were offered to him, and asked time for consideration. When the time had expired, he did what Mrs Armadale wished him to do – he offered his back to the burden, and let the mother load him with the responsibility of the son.[3]

This was the first event of the series; the date of it being the year eighteen hundred and thirty-seven. Mr Brock's memory, travelling forward towards the present from that point, picked up the second event in its turn, and stopped next at the year eighteen hundred and forty-five.

The fishing village on the Somersetshire coast was still the scene; and the characters were once again – Mrs Armadale and her son. Through the eight years that had passed, Mr Brock's responsibility had rested on him lightly enough. The boy had given his mother and his tutor but little trouble. He was certainly slow over his books – but more from a constitutional inability to fix his attention on his tasks than from want of capacity to understand them. His temperament, it could not be denied, was heedless to the last degree: he acted recklessly on his first impulses, and rushed blindfold at all his conclusions. On the other hand, it was to be said in his favour, that his disposition was open as the day; a more generous, affectionate, sweet-tempered lad it would have been hard to find anywhere. A certain quaint originality of character, and a natural healthiness in all his tastes, carried him free of most of the dangers to which his mother's system of education inevitably exposed him. He had a thoroughly English love of the sea and of all that belongs to it; and, as he grew in years, there was no luring him away from the waterside, and no keeping him out of the boat-builder's yard. In course of time his mother caught him actually working there, to her infinite annoyance and surprise, as a volunteer. He acknowledged that his whole future ambition was to have a yard of his own, and that his one present object was to learn to build a boat for himself. Wisely foreseeing that such a pursuit as this for his leisure hours was exactly what was wanted to reconcile the lad to a position of isolation from companions of his own rank and age, Mr Brock prevailed on Mrs Armadale, with no small difficulty, to let her son have his way. At the period of that second event in the clergyman's life with his pupil which is now to be related, young Armadale had practised long enough in the builder's yard to have reached the summit of his wishes, by laying with his own hands the keel of his own boat.

Late on a certain summer day, not long after Allan had completed his sixteenth year, Mr Brock left his pupil hard at work in the yard, and went to spend the evening with Mrs Armadale, taking *The Times* newspaper with him in his hand.

The years that had passed since they had first met, had long since regulated the lives of the clergyman and his neighbour. The first advances which Mr Brock's growing admiration for the widow had led him to make, in the early days of their intercourse, had been met, on her side, by an appeal to his forbearance which had closed his lips for the future. She had satisfied him, at once and for ever, that the one place in her heart which he could hope to occupy was the place of a friend. He loved her well enough to take what she would give him: friends they became, and friends they remained from that time forth. No jealous dread of another man's succeeding where he had failed, embittered the clergyman's placid relations with the woman whom he loved. Of the few resident gentlemen in the neighbourhood, none were ever admitted by Mrs Armadale to more than the merest acquaintance with her. Contentedly self-buried in her country retreat, she was proof against every social attraction that would have tempted other women in her position, and at her age. Mr Brock and his newspaper, appearing with monotonous regularity at her tea-table three times a week, told her all she knew, or cared to know, of the great outer world which circled round the narrow and changeless limits of her daily life.

On the evening in question, Mr Brock took the arm-chair in which he always sat, accepted the one cup of tea which he always drank, and opened the newspaper which he always read aloud to Mrs Armadale, who invariably listened to him reclining on the same sofa, with the same sort of needlework everlastingly in her hand.

'Bless my soul!' cried the rector, with his voice in a new octave, and his eyes fixed in astonishment on the first page of the newspaper.

No such introduction to the evening readings as this had ever happened before in all Mrs Armadale's experience as a listener. She looked up from the sofa, in a flutter of curiosity, and besought her reverend friend to favour her with an explanation.

'I can hardly believe my own eyes,' said Mr Brock. 'Here is an advertisement, Mrs Armadale, addressed to your son.'

Without further preface, he read the advertisement, as follows:

If this should meet the eye of ALLAN ARMADALE, he is desired to communicate, either personally or by letter, with Messrs Hammick and Ridge (Lincoln's Inn Fields, London), on business of importance which seriously concerns him. Any one capable of informing Messrs H. and R. where the person herein advertised can be found, would confer a favour by doing the same. To prevent mistakes, it is further notified that the missing Allan Armadale is a youth aged fifteen years, and that this advertisement is inserted at the instance of his family and friends.

'Another family, and other friends,' said Mrs Armadale. 'The person whose name appears in that advertisement is not my son.'

The tone in which she spoke surprised Mr Brock. The change in her face, when he looked up, shocked him. Her delicate complexion had faded away to a dull white; her eyes were averted from her visitor with a strange mixture of confusion and alarm; she looked an older woman than she was, by ten good years at least.

'The name is so very uncommon,' said Mr Brock, imagining he had offended her, and trying to excuse himself. 'It really seemed impossible there could be two persons——'

'There *are* two,' interposed Mrs Armadale. 'Allan, as you know, is sixteen years old. If you look back at the advertisement, you will find the missing person described as being only fifteen. Although he bears the same surname and the same Christian name, he is, I thank God, in no way whatever related to my son. As long as I live it will be the object of my hopes and prayers, that Allan may never see him, may never even hear of him. My kind friend, I see I surprise you; will you bear with me if I leave these strange circumstances unexplained? There is past misfortune and misery in my early life too painful for me to speak of, even to *you*. Will you help me to bear the remembrance of it, by never referring to this again? Will you do even more – will you promise not to speak of it to Allan, and not to let that newspaper fall in his way?'

Mr Brock gave the pledge required of him, and considerately left her to herself.

The rector had been too long and too truly attached to Mrs Armadale to be capable of regarding her with any unworthy distrust. But it would be idle to deny that he felt disappointed by her want of confidence in him, and that he looked inquisitively at the advertisement more than once, on his way back to his own house. It was clear enough, now, that Mrs Armadale's motive for burying her son as well as herself in the seclusion of a remote country village, was not so much to keep him under her own eye, as to keep him from discovery by his namesake. Why did she dread the idea of their ever meeting? Was it a dread for herself, or a dread for her son? Mr Brock's loyal belief in his friend rejected any solution of the difficulty which pointed at some past misconduct of Mrs Armadale's, and which associated it with those painful remembrances to which she had alluded, or with the estrangement from her brothers which had now kept her parted for years from her relatives and her home. That night, he destroyed the advertisement with his own hand; that night he resolved that the subject should never be suffered to enter his mind again. There was another Allan Armadale about the world, a stranger to his pupil's blood, and a vagabond advertised in the public newspapers. So much, accident had revealed to him. More, for Mrs Armadale's sake, he had no wish to discover – and more, he would never seek to know.

This was the second in the series of events which dated from the rector's connection with Mrs Armadale and her son. Mr Brock's memory, travelling on nearer and nearer to present circumstances, reached the third stage of its journey through the bygone time, and stopped at the year eighteen hundred and fifty, next.

The five years that had passed had made little, if any, change in Allan's character. He had simply developed (to use his tutor's own expression) from a boy of sixteen to a boy of twenty-one. He was just as easy and open in his disposition as ever; just as quaintly and inveterately good-humoured; just as heedless in following his own impulses, lead him where they might. His bias towards the sea had strengthened with his advance to the years of manhood. From building a boat, he had now got on – with two journeymen at work under him – to building a decked vessel of five-and-thirty tons. Mr Brock had conscientiously tried to divert him to higher aspirations; had taken him to Oxford, to see what college life was like; had taken him to London, to expand his mind by the spectacle of the great metropolis. The change had diverted Allan, but had not altered him in the least. He was as impenetrably superior to all worldly ambition as Diogenes himself. 'Which is best,' asked this unconscious philosopher, 'to find out the way to be happy for yourself, or to let other people try if they can find it out for you?' From that moment, Mr Brock permitted his pupil's character to grow at its own rate of development, and Allan went on uninterruptedly with the work of his yacht.

Time, which had wrought so little change in the son, had not passed harmless over the mother. Mrs Armadale's health was breaking fast. As her strength failed, her temper altered for the worse: she grew more and more fretful, more and more subject to morbid fears and fancies, more and more reluctant to leave her own room. Since the appearance of the advertisement, five years since, nothing had happened to force her memory back to the painful associations connected with her early life. No word more on the forbidden topic had passed between the rector and herself; no suspicion had ever been raised in Allan's mind of the existence of his namesake; and yet, without the shadow of a reason for any special anxiety, Mrs Armadale had become, of late years, obstinately and fretfully uneasy on the subject of her son. At one time, she would congratulate herself on the fancy for yacht-building and sailing which kept him happy and occupied under her own eye. At another, she spoke with horror of his trusting himself habitually to the treacherous ocean on which her husband had met his death. Now in one way, and now in another, she tried her son's forbearance as she had never tried it in her healthier and happier days. More than once, Mr Brock dreaded a serious disagreement between them; but Allan's natural sweetness of temper, fortified by his love for his mother, carried him triumphantly through all trials. Not a hard word, or a harsh look ever escaped him in her presence; he was unchangeably loving and forbearing with her to the very last.

Such were the positions of the son, the mother, and the friend, when the next notable event happened in the lives of the three. On a dreary afternoon, early in the month of November, Mr Brock was disturbed over the composition of his sermon by a visit from the landlord of the village inn.

After making his introductory apologies, the landlord stated the urgent business on which he had come to the rectory, clearly enough. A few hours since, a young man had been brought to the inn by some farm labourers in the neighbourhood, who had found him wandering about one of their master's fields, in a disordered state of mind, which looked to their eyes like downright madness. The landlord had given the poor creature shelter, while he sent for medical help; and the doctor, on seeing him, had pronounced that he was suffering from fever on the brain, and that his removal to the nearest town at which a hospital or a workhouse infirmary could be found to receive him, would in all probability be fatal to his chances of recovery. After hearing this expression of opinion, and after observing for himself that the stranger's only luggage consisted of a small carpet-bag which had been found in the field near him, the landlord had set off on the spot to consult the rector, and to ask, in this serious emergency, what course he was to take next.

Mr Brock was the magistrate, as well as the clergyman, of the district, and the course to be taken, in the first instance, was to his mind clear enough. He put on his hat, and accompanied the landlord back to the inn.

At the inn-door they were joined by Allan, who had heard the news through another channel, and who was waiting Mr Brock's arrival, to follow in the magistrate's train, and to see what the stranger was like. The village surgeon joined them at the same moment, and the four went into the inn together.

They found the landlord's son on one side, and the ostler on the other, holding the man down in his chair. Young, slim, and undersized, he was strong enough at that moment to make it a matter of difficulty for the two to master him. His tawny complexion, his large bright brown eyes, his black mustachios and beard, gave him something of a foreign look. His dress was a little worn, but his linen was clean. His dusky hands were wiry and nervous, and were lividly discoloured in more places than one, by the scars of old wounds. The toes of one of his feet, off which he had kicked the shoe, grasped at the chair-rail through his stocking, with the sensitive muscular action which is only seen in those who have been accustomed to go barefoot. In the frenzy that now possessed him, it was impossible to notice, to any useful purpose, more than this. After a whispered consultation with Mr Brock, the surgeon personally superintended the patient's removal to a quiet bedroom at the back of the house. Shortly afterwards, his clothes and his carpet-bag were sent downstairs, and were searched, on the chance of finding a clue by which to communicate with his friends, in the magistrate's presence.

The carpet-bag contained nothing but a change of clothing, and two books – the Plays of Sophocles, in the original Greek, and the *Faust* of Goethe, in the original German. Both volumes were much worn by reading; and on the fly-leaf of each were inscribed the initials O. M.[4] So much the bag revealed, and no more.

The clothes which the man wore when he was discovered in the field were tried next. A purse (containing a sovereign and a few shillings), a pipe, a tobacco-pouch, a handkerchief, and a little drinking-cup of horn, were produced in succession. The next object, and the last, was found crumpled up carelessly in the breast-pocket of the coat. It was a written testimonial to character, dated and signed, but without any address. So far as this document could tell it, the stranger's story was a sad one indeed. He had apparently been employed for a short time as usher at a school, and had been turned adrift in the world, at the outset of his illness, from the fear that the fever might be infectious, and that the prosperity of the establishment might suffer accordingly. Not the slightest imputation of any misbehaviour in his employment rested on him. On the contrary, the schoolmaster had great pleasure in testifying to his capacity and his character, and in expressing a fervent hope that he might (under Providence) succeed in recovering his health in somebody else's house.

The written testimonial which afforded this glimpse at the man's story served one purpose more – it connected him with the initials on the books, and identified him to the magistrate and the landlord under the strangely uncouth name of Ozias Midwinter.

Mr Brock laid aside the testimonial, suspecting that the schoolmaster had purposely abstained from writing his address on it, with the view of escaping all responsibility in the event of his usher's death. In any case it was manifestly useless, under existing circumstances, to think of tracing the poor wretch's friends – if friends he had. To the inn he had been brought, and, as a matter of common humanity, at the inn he must remain for the present. The difficulty about expenses, if it came to the worst, might possibly be met by charitable contributions from the neighbours, or by a collection after a sermon at church. Assuring the landlord that he would consider this part of the question, and would let him know the result, Mr Brock quitted the inn, without noticing for the moment that he had left Allan there behind him.

Before he had got fifty yards from the house his pupil overtook him. Allan had been most uncharacteristically silent and serious all through the search at the inn – but he had now recovered his usual high spirits. A stranger would have set him down as wanting in common feeling.

'This is a sad business,' said the rector. 'I really don't know what to do for the best about that unfortunate man.'

'You may make your mind quite easy, sir,' said young Armadale, in his off hand way. 'I settled it all with the landlord a minute ago.'

'You!' exclaimed Mr Brock, in the utmost astonishment.

'I have merely given a few simple directions,' pursued Allan. 'Our friend the usher is to have everything he requires, and is to be treated like a prince; and when the doctor and the landlord want their money they are to come to me.'

'My dear Allan,' Mr Brock gently remonstrated. 'When will you learn to think before you act on those generous impulses of yours? You are spending more money already on your yacht-building than you can afford—'

'Only think! we laid the first planks of the deck, the day before yesterday,' said Allan, flying off to the new subject in his usual bird-witted way. 'There's just enough of it done to walk on, if you don't feel giddy. I'll help you up the ladder, Mr Brock, if you'll only come and try.'

'Listen to me,' persisted the rector; 'I'm not talking about the yacht now. That is to say, I am only referring to the yacht as an illustration—'

'And a very pretty illustration too,' remarked the incorrigible Allan. 'Find me a smarter little vessel of her size in all England, and I'll give up yacht-building to-morrow. Whereabouts were we in our conversation, sir? I'm rather afraid we have lost ourselves somehow.'

'I am rather afraid one of us is in the habit of losing himself every time he opens his lips,' retorted Mr Brock. 'Come, come, Allan, this is serious. You have been rendering yourself liable for expenses which you may not be able to pay. Mind, I am far from blaming you for your kind feeling towards this poor friendless man—'

'Don't be low-spirited about him, sir. He'll get over it – he'll be all right again in a week or so. A capital fellow, I have not the least doubt!' continued Allan, whose habit it was to believe in everybody, and to despair of nothing. 'Suppose you ask him to dinner when he gets well, Mr Brock? I should like to find out (when we are all three snug and friendly together over our wine, you know) how he came by that extraordinary name of his. Ozias Midwinter! Upon my life, his father ought to be ashamed of himself.'

'Will you answer me one question before I go in?' said the rector, stopping in despair at his own gate. 'This man's bill for lodging and medical attendance may mount to twenty or thirty pounds before he gets well again, if he ever does get well. How are you to pay it?'

'What's that the Chancellor of the Exchequer says, when he finds himself in a mess with his accounts, and doesn't see his way out again?' asked Allan. 'He always tells his honourable friend he's quite willing to leave a something or other—'

'A margin?' suggested Mr Brock.

'That's it,' said Allan. 'I'm like the Chancellor of the Exchequer. I'm quite willing to leave a margin. The yacht (bless her heart!) doesn't eat up everything.[5] If I'm short by a pound or two, don't be afraid, sir. There's no pride about me; I'll go round with the hat, and get the balance in the neighbourhood. Deuce take the pounds, shillings, and pence! I wish they could all three get rid of themselves like the Bedouin brothers at the show. Don't you remember the Bedouin brothers, Mr Brock? "Ali will take a lighted torch, and jump down the throat of his brother Muli – Muli will take a lighted torch, and jump down the throat of his brother Hassan – and Hassan, taking a third lighted torch, will conclude the performances by jumping down his own throat, and leaving the spectators in total darkness." Wonderfully good, that – what I call real wit, with a fine strong flavour about it. Wait a minute! Where are we? We have lost ourselves again. Oh, I remember – money. What I can't beat into my thick head,' concluded Allan, quite unconscious that he was preaching socialist doctrines to a clergyman,[6] 'is the meaning of the fuss that's made about giving money away. Why can't the people who have got money to spare give it to the people who haven't got money to spare, and make things pleasant and comfortable all the world over in that way? You're always telling me to cultivate ideas, Mr Brock. There's an idea, and, upon my life, I don't think it's a bad one.'

Mr Brock gave his pupil a good-humoured poke with the end of his stick. 'Go back to your yacht,' he said. 'All the little discretion you have got in that flighty head of yours, is left on board in your tool-chest. How that lad will end,' pursued the rector, when he was left by himself, 'is more than any human being can say. I almost wish I had never taken the responsibility of him on my shoulders.'

Three weeks passed before the stranger with the uncouth name was pronounced to be at last on the way to recovery. During this period, Allan had made regular inquiries at the inn; and, as soon as the sick man was allowed to see visitors, Allan was the first who appeared at his bedside. So far, Mr Brock's pupil had shown no more than a natural interest in one of the few romantic circumstances which had varied the monotony of the village life: he had committed no imprudence, and he had exposed himself to no blame. But as the days passed, young Armadale's visits to the inn began to lengthen considerably; and the surgeon (a cautious elderly man) gave the rector a private hint to bestir himself. Mr Brock acted on the hint immediately, and discovered that Allan had followed his usual impulses in his usual headlong way. He had taken a violent fancy to the castaway usher; and had invited Ozias Midwinter to reside permanently in the neighbourhood, in the new and interesting character of his bosom friend.

Before Mr Brock could make up his mind how to act in this emergency, he received a note from Allan's mother, begging him to use his privilege as an old friend, and to pay her a visit in her room. He found Mrs Armadale suffering under violent nervous agitation, caused entirely by a recent interview with her son. Allan had been sitting with her all the morning, and had talked of nothing but his new friend. The man with the horrible name (as poor Mrs Armadale described him) had questioned Allan, in a singularly inquisitive manner, on the subject of himself and his family, but had kept his own personal history entirely in the dark. At some former period of his life he had been accustomed to the sea and to sailing. Allan had, unfortunately, found this out, and a bond of union between them was formed on the spot. With a merciless distrust of the stranger – simply *because* he was a stranger – which appeared rather unreasonable to Mr Brock, Mrs Armadale besought the rector to go to the inn without a moment's loss of time, and never to rest until he had made the man give a proper account of himself. 'Find out everything about his father and mother!' she said, in her vehement female way. 'Make sure before you leave him that he is not a vagabond roaming the country under an assumed name.'

'My dear lady,' remonstrated the rector, obediently taking his hat, 'whatever else we may doubt, I really think we may feel sure about the man's name! It is so remarkably ugly, that it must be genuine. No sane human being would *assume* such a name as Ozias Midwinter.'

'You may be quite right, and I may be quite wrong; but pray go and see him,' persisted Mrs Armadale. 'Go, and don't spare him, Mr Brock. How do we know that this illness of his may not have been put on for a purpose?'

It was useless to reason with her. The whole College of Physicians might have certified to the man's illness, and, in her present frame of mind, Mrs Armadale would have disbelieved the College, one and all, from the president downwards. Mr Brock took the wise way out of the difficulty – he said no more, and he set off for the inn immediately.

Ozias Midwinter, recovering from brain-fever, was a startling object to contemplate, on a first view of him. His shaven head, tied up roughly in an old yellow silk handkerchief; his tawny, haggard cheeks; his bright brown eyes, preternaturally large and wild; his tangled black beard;[7] his long supple, sinewy fingers, wasted by suffering, till they looked like claws – all tended to discompose the rector at the outset of the interview. When the first feeling of surprise had worn off, the impression that followed it was not an agreeable one. Mr Brock could not conceal from himself that the stranger's manner was against him. The general opinion has settled that if a man is honest, he is bound to assert it by looking straight at his fellow-creatures when he speaks to them. If this man was honest, his eyes showed a singular perversity in looking away and denying it. Possibly they were affected in some degree by a nervous restlessness in his organization, which appeared to pervade every fibre in his lean, lithe body. The rector's healthy Anglo-Saxon flesh crept responsively at every casual movement of the usher's supple brown fingers, and every passing distortion of the usher's haggard yellow face. 'God forgive me!' thought Mr Brock, with his mind running on Allan, and Allan's mother, 'I wish I could see my way to turning Ozias Midwinter adrift in the world again!'

The conversation which ensued between the two was a very guarded one. Mr Brock felt his way gently, and found himself, try where he might, always kept politely, more or less, in the dark. From first to last, the man's real character shrank back with a savage shyness from the rector's touch. He started by an assertion which it was impossible to look at him and believe – he declared that he was only twenty years of age. All he could be persuaded to say on the subject of the school was, that the bare recollection of it was horrible to him. He had only filled the usher's situation for ten days when the first appearance of his illness caused his dismissal. How he had reached the field in which he had been found, was more than he could say. He remembered travelling a long distance by railway, with a purpose (if he had a purpose) which it was now impossible to recall, and then wandering coastwards, on foot, all through the day, or all through the night – he was not sure which. The sea kept running in his mind, when his mind began to give way. He had been employed on the sea, as a lad. He had left it, and had filled a situation at a bookseller's in a country town.[8] He had left the bookseller's, and had tried the school. Now the school had turned him out, he must try something else. It mattered little what he tried – failure (for which nobody was ever to blame but himself) was sure to be the end of it, sooner or later. Friends to assist him, he had none to apply to; and as for relations, he wished to be excused from speaking of them. For all he knew they might be dead, and for all *they* knew *he* might be dead. That was a melancholy acknowledgment to make at his time of life, there was no denying it. It might tell against him in the opinions of others – and it did tell against him, no doubt, in the opinion of the gentleman who was talking to him at that moment.

These strange answers were given in a tone and manner far removed from bitterness on the one side, or from indifference on the other. Ozias Midwinter at twenty, spoke of his life as Ozias Midwinter at seventy might have spoken, with a long weariness of years on him which he had learnt to bear patiently.

Two circumstances pleaded strongly against the distrust with which, in sheer perplexity of mind, Mr Brock blindly regarded him. He had written to a savings bank in a distant part of England, had drawn his money, and had paid the doctor and the landlord. A man of vulgar mind, after acting in this manner, would have treated his obligations lightly, when he had settled his bills. Ozias Midwinter spoke of his obligations – and especially of his obligation to Allan – with a fervour of thankfulness which it was not surprising only, but absolutely painful to witness. He showed a horrible sincerity of astonishment at having been treated with common Christian kindness in a Christian land. He spoke of Allan's having become answerable for all the expenses of sheltering, nursing, and curing him, with a savage rapture of gratitude and surprise, which burst out of him like a flash of lightning. 'So help me God!' cried the castaway usher, 'I never met with the like of him; I never heard of the like of him before!' In the next instant, the one

65

glimpse of light which the man had let in on his own passionate nature was quenched again in darkness. His wandering eyes, returning to their old trick, looked uneasily away from Mr Brock; and his voice dropped back once more into its unnatural steadiness and quietness of tone. 'I beg your pardon, sir,' he said. 'I have been used to be hunted, and cheated, and starved. Everything else comes strange to me.' Half attracted by the man, half repelled by him, Mr Brock, on rising to take leave, impulsively offered his hand, and then, with a sudden misgiving, confusedly drew it back again. 'You meant that kindly, sir,' said Ozias Midwinter, with his own hands crossed resolutely behind him. 'I don't complain of your thinking better of it. A man who can't give a proper account of himself, is not a man for a gentleman in your position to take by the hand.'

Mr Brock left the inn thoroughly puzzled. Before returning to Mrs Armadale, he sent for her son. The chances were that the guard had been off the stranger's tongue when he spoke to Allan; and with Allan's frankness, there was no fear of his concealing anything that had passed between them from the rector's knowledge.

Here, again, Mr Brock's diplomacy achieved no useful results. Once started on the subject of Ozias Midwinter, Allan rattled on about his new friend, in his usual easy light-hearted way. But he had really nothing of importance to tell – for nothing of importance had been revealed to him. They had talked about boat-building and sailing by the hour together; and Allan had got some valuable hints. They had discussed (with diagrams to assist them, and with more valuable hints for Allan) the serious impending question of the launch of the yacht.[9] On other occasions they had diverged to other subjects – to more of them than Allan could remember, on the spur of the moment. Had Midwinter said nothing about his relations in the flow of all this friendly talk? Nothing, except that they had not behaved well to him – hang his relations! Was he at all sensitive on the subject of his own odd name? Not the least in the world; he had set the example, like a sensible fellow, of laughing at it himself: deuce take his name, it did very well when you were used to it. What had Allan seen in him to take such a fancy to? Allan had seen in him – what he didn't see in people in general. He wasn't like all the other fellows in the neighbourhood. All the other fellows were cut out on the same pattern. Every man of them was equally healthy, muscular, loud, hard-headed, clean-skinned, and rough; every man of them drank the same draughts of beer, smoked the same short pipes all day long, rode the best horse, shot over the best dog, and put the best bottle of wine in England on his table at night;

every man of them sponged himself every morning in the same sort of tub of cold water, and bragged about it in frosty weather in the same sort of way; every man of them thought getting into debt a capital joke, and betting on horse-races one of the most meritorious actions that a human being can perform. They were no doubt excellent fellows in their way; but the worst of them was, they were all exactly alike. It was a perfect godsend to meet with a man like Midwinter – a man who was not cut out on the regular local pattern, and whose way in the world had the one great merit (in those parts) of being a way of his own.

Leaving all remonstrances for a fitter opportunity, the rector went back to Mrs Armadale. He could not disguise from himself that Allan's mother was the person really answerable for Allan's present indiscretion. If the lad had seen a little less of the small gentry in the neighbourhood, and a little more of the great outside world at home and abroad, the pleasure of cultivating Ozias Midwinter's society might have had fewer attractions for him.

Conscious of the unsatisfactory result of his visit to the inn, Mr Brock felt some anxiety about the reception of his report, when he found himself once more in Mrs Armadale's presence. His forebodings were soon realized. Try as he might to make the best of it, Mrs Armadale seized on the one suspicious fact of the usher's silence about himself, as justifying the strongest measures that could be taken to separate him from her son. If the rector refused to interfere, she declared her intention of writing to Ozias Midwinter with her own hand. Remonstrance irritated her to such a pitch, that she astounded Mr Brock by reverting to the forbidden subject of five years since, and referring him to the conversation which had passed between them when the advertisement had been discovered in the newspaper. She passionately declared that the vagabond Armadale of that advertisement, and the vagabond Midwinter at the village inn, might, for all she knew to the contrary, be one and the same. The rector vainly reiterated his conviction that the name was the very last in the world that any man (and a young man especially) would be likely to assume. Nothing quieted Mrs Armadale but absolute submission to her will. Dreading the consequences if he still resisted her in her feeble state of health, and foreboding a serious disagreement between the mother and son, if the mother interfered, Mr Brock undertook to see Midwinter again, and to tell him plainly that he must give a proper account of himself, or that his intimacy with Allan must cease. The two concessions which he exacted from Mrs Armadale in return, were, that she should wait patiently until the doctor reported the man fit to travel, and that she should be careful in the interval not to mention the matter in any way to her son.

In a week's time, Midwinter was able to drive out (with Allan for his coachman), in the pony-chaise belonging to the inn; and in ten days, the doctor privately reported him as fit to travel. Towards the close of that tenth day, Mr Brock met Allan and his new friend enjoying the last gleams of wintry sunshine in one of the inland lanes. He waited until the two had separated, and then followed the usher on his way back to the inn.

The rector's resolution to speak pitilessly to the purpose was in some danger of failing him, as he drew nearer and nearer to the friendless man, and saw how feebly he still walked, how loosely his worn coat hung about him, and how heavily he leant on his cheap clumsy stick. Humanely reluctant to say the decisive words too precipitately, Mr Brock tried him first with a little compliment on the range of his reading, as shown by the volume of Sophocles and the volume of Goethe which had been found in his bag; and asked how long he had been acquainted with German and Greek. The quick ear of Midwinter detected something wrong in the tone of Mr Brock's voice. He turned in the darkening twilight and looked suddenly and suspiciously in the rector's face.

'You have something to say to me,' he answered; 'and it is not what you are saying now.'

There was no help for it, but to accept the challenge. Very delicately, with many preparatory words, to which the other listened in unbroken silence, Mr Brock came little by little nearer to the point. Long before he had really reached it – long before a man of no more than ordinary sensibility would have felt what was coming – Ozias Midwinter stood still in the lane, and told the rector that he need say no more.

'I understand you, sir,' said the usher. 'Mr Armadale has an ascertained position in the world; Mr Armadale has nothing to conceal, and nothing to be ashamed of. I agree with you that I am not a fit companion for him. The best return I can make for his kindness, is to presume on it no longer. You may depend on my leaving this place tomorrow morning.'

He spoke no word more; he would hear no word more. With a self-control which, at his years and with his temperament, was nothing less than marvellous, he civilly took off his hat, bowed, and returned to the inn by himself.

Mr Brock slept badly that night. The issue of the interview in the lane had made the problem of Ozias Midwinter a harder problem to solve than ever.

Early the next morning a letter was brought to the rector from the inn, and the messenger announced that the strange gentleman had taken his departure. The letter enclosed an open note addressed to Allan, and requested Allan's tutor (after first reading it himself), to forward it or not at his own sole discretion. The note was a startlingly short one: it began and ended in a dozen words: 'Don't blame Mr Brock; Mr Brock is right. Thank you, and good-by. – O. M.'

The rector forwarded the note to its proper destination, as a matter of course; and sent a few lines to Mrs Armadale at the same time, to quiet her anxiety by the news of the usher's departure. This done, he waited the visit from his pupil, which would probably follow the delivery of the note, in no very tranquil frame of mind. There might or might not be some deep motive at the bottom of Midwinter's conduct; but, thus far, it was impossible to deny that he had behaved in such a manner as to rebuke the rector's distrust, and to justify Allan's good opinion of him.

The morning wore on, and young Armadale never appeared. After looking for him vainly in the yard where the yacht was building, Mr Brock went to Mrs Armadale's house, and there heard news from the servant which turned his steps in the direction of the inn. The landlord at once acknowledged the truth – young Mr Armadale had come there with an open letter in his hand, and had insisted on being informed of the road which his friend had taken. For the first time in the landlord's experience of him, the young gentleman was out of temper; and the girl who waited on the customers had stupidly mentioned a circumstance which had added fuel to the fire. She had acknowledged having heard Mr Midwinter lock himself into his room overnight, and burst into a violent fit of crying. That trifling particular had set Mr Armadale's face all of a flame; he had shouted and sworn; he had rushed into the stables; had forced the ostler to saddle him a horse, and had set off at full gallop on the road that Ozias Midwinter had taken before him.

After cautioning the landlord to keep Allan's conduct a secret, if any of Mrs Armadale's servants came that morning to the inn, Mr Brock went home again, and waited anxiously to see what the day would bring forth.

To his infinite relief, his pupil appeared at the rectory late in the afternoon. Allan looked, and spoke, with a dogged determination which was quite new in his old friend's experience of him. Without waiting to be questioned, he told his story in his usual straightforward way. He had overtaken Midwinter on the road; and – after trying vainly, first to

induce him to return, then to find out where he was going to – had
threatened to keep company with him for the rest of the day, and had
so extorted the confession that he was going to try his luck in London.
Having gained this point, Allan had asked next for his friend's address
in London – had been entreated by the other not to press his request –
had pressed it, nevertheless, with all his might, and had got the
address at last, by making an appeal to Midwinter's gratitude, for
which (feeling heartily ashamed of himself) he had afterwards asked
Midwinter's pardon. 'I like the poor fellow, and I won't give him up,'
concluded Allan, bringing his clenched fist down with a thump on the
rectory table. 'Don't be afraid of my vexing my mother; I'll leave you to
speak to her, Mr Brock, at your own time and in your own way; and
I'll just say this much more by way of bringing the thing to an end.
Here is the address safe in my pocket-book, and here am I, standing
firm, for once, on a resolution of my own. I'll give you and my mother
time to re-consider this; and, when the time is up, if my friend Midwinter
doesn't come to *me*, I'll go to my friend Midwinter!'

So the matter rested for the present; and such was the result of
turning the castaway usher adrift in the world again.

A month passed, and brought in the new year – '51. Overleaping that
short lapse of time, Mr Brock paused, with a heavy heart, at the next
event; to his mind the one mournful, the one memorable event of the
series – Mrs Armadale's death.

The first warning of the affliction that was near at hand, had
followed close on the usher's departure in December, and had arisen out
of a circumstance which dwelt painfully on the rector's memory from
that time forth.

But three days after Midwinter had left for London, Mr Brock was
accosted in the village by a neatly dressed woman, wearing a gown and
bonnet of black silk and a red Paisley shawl,[10] who was a total stranger
to him, and who inquired the way to Mrs Armadale's house. She put
the question without raising the thick black veil that hung over her
face. Mr Brock, in giving her the necessary directions, observed that she
was a remarkably elegant and graceful woman, and looked after her as
she bowed and left him, wondering who Mrs Armadale's visitor could
possibly be.

A quarter of an hour later, the lady, still veiled as before, passed Mr
Brock again close to the inn. She entered the house, and spoke to the
landlady. Seeing the landlord shortly afterwards hurrying round to the
stables, Mr Brock asked him if the lady was going away. Yes; she had

come from the railway in the omnibus, but she was going back again more creditably in a carriage of her own hiring, supplied by the inn.

The rector proceeded on his walk, rather surprised to find his thoughts running inquisitively on a woman who was a stranger to him. When he got home again, he found the village surgeon waiting his return, with an urgent message from Allan's mother. About an hour since, the surgeon had been sent for in great haste to see Mrs Armadale. He had found her suffering from an alarming nervous attack, brought on (as the servants suspected) by an unexpected, and, possibly, an unwelcome visitor, who had called that morning. The surgeon had done all that was needful, and had no apprehension of any dangerous results. Finding his patient eagerly desirous, on recovering herself, to see Mr Brock immediately, he had thought it important to humour her, and had readily undertaken to call at the rectory with a message to that effect.

Looking at Mrs Armadale with a far deeper interest in her than the surgeon's interest, Mr Brock saw enough in her face, when it turned towards him on his entering the room, to justify instant and serious alarm. She allowed him no opportunity of soothing her; she heeded none of his inquiries. Answers to certain questions of her own were what she wanted, and what she was determined to have: Had Mr Brock seen the woman who had presumed to visit her that morning? Yes. Had Allan seen her? No: Allan had been at work since breakfast, and was at work still, in his yard by the waterside. This latter reply appeared to quiet Mrs Armadale for the moment: she put her next question – the most extraordinary question of the three – more composedly. Did the rector think Allan would object to leaving his vessel for the present, and to accompanying his mother on a journey to look out for a new house in some other part of England? In the greatest amazement, Mr Brock asked what reason there could possibly be for leaving her present residence? Mrs Armadale's reason, when she gave it, only added to his surprise. The woman's first visit might be followed by a second; and rather than see her again, rather than run the risk of Allan's seeing her and speaking to her, Mrs Armadale would leave England if necessary, and end her days in a foreign land. Taking counsel of his experience as a magistrate, Mr Brock inquired if the woman had come to ask for money. Yes: respectably as she was dressed, she had described herself as being 'in distress'; had asked for money, and had got it[11] – but the money was of no importance; the one thing needful was to get away before the woman came again. More and more surprised, Mr Brock ventured on another question. Was it long since Mrs Armadale and her visitor had last met? Yes; as long as all Allan's lifetime – as long as one-and-twenty years.

At that reply, the rector shifted his ground, and took counsel next of his experience as a friend.

'Is this person,' he asked, 'connected in any way with the painful remembrances of your early life?'

'Yes, with the painful remembrance of the time when I was married,' said Mrs Armadale. 'She was associated, as a mere child, with a circumstance which I must think of with shame and sorrow to my dying day.'

Mr Brock noticed the altered tone in which his old friend spoke, and the unwillingness with which she gave her answer.

'Can you tell me more about her, without referring to yourself?' he went on. 'I am sure I can protect you, if you will only help me a little. Her name, for instance – you can tell me her name?'

Mrs Armadale shook her head. 'The name I knew her by,' she said, 'would be of no use to you. She has been married since then – she told me so herself.'

'And without telling you her married name?'

'She refused to tell it.'

'Do you know anything of her friends?'

'Only of her friends, when she was a child. They called themselves her uncle and aunt. They were low people, and they deserted her at the school on my father's estate. We never heard any more of them.'

'Did she remain under your father's care?'[12]

'She remained under my care – that is to say, she travelled with us. We were leaving England, just at that time, for Madeira. I had my father's leave to take her with me, and to train the wretch to be my maid—'

At those words Mrs Armadale stopped confusedly. Mr Brock tried gently to lead her on. It was useless; she started up in violent agitation, and walked excitedly backwards and forwards in the room.

'Don't ask me any more!' she cried out, in loud, angry tones. 'I parted with her when she was a girl of twelve years old. I never saw her again, I never heard of her again, from that time to this. I don't know how she has discovered me, after all the years that have passed – I only know that she *has* discovered me. She will find her way to Allan next, she will poison my son's mind against me. Help me to get away from her! help me to take Allan away before she comes back!'

The rector asked no more questions; it would have been cruel to press her farther. The first necessity was to compose her by promising compliance with all that she desired. The second was to induce her to see another medical man. Mr Brock contrived to reach his end harmlessly in this latter case, by reminding her that she wanted strength to travel, and that her own medical attendant might restore her all the more speedily to herself, if he were assisted by the best professional advice. Having overcome her habitual reluctance to seeing strangers by this means, the rector at once went to Allan; and, delicately concealing what Mrs Armadale had said at the interview, broke the news to him that his mother was seriously ill. Allan would hear of no messengers being sent for assistance: he drove off on the spot to the railway, and telegraphed himself to Bristol for medical help.

On the next morning the help came, and Mr Brock's worst fears were confirmed. The village surgeon had fatally misunderstood the case from the first, and the time was past now at which his errors of treatment might have been set right. The shock of the previous morning had completed the mischief. Mrs Armadale's days were numbered.

The son who dearly loved her, the old friend to whom her life was precious, hoped vainly to the last. In a month from the physician's visit all hope was over; and Allan shed the first bitter tears of his life at his mother's grave.

She had died more peacefully than Mr Brock had dared to hope; leaving all her little fortune to her son, and committing him solemnly to the care of her one friend on earth. The rector had entreated her to let him write and try to reconcile her brothers with her before it was too late. She had only answered sadly, that it was too late already. But one reference escaped her in her last illness to those early sorrows which had weighed heavily on all her after-life, and which had passed thrice already, like shadows of evil, between the rector and herself. Even on her death-bed she had shrunk from letting the light fall clearly on the story of the past. She had looked at Allan kneeling by the bedside, and had whispered to Mr Brock: '*Never let his Namesake come near him! Never let that Woman find him out!*' No word more fell from her that touched on the misfortunes which had tried her in the past, or on the dangers which she dreaded in the future. The secret which she had kept from her son and from her friend, was a secret which she carried with her to the grave.

When the last offices of affection and respect had been performed, Mr Brock felt it his duty, as executor to the deceased lady, to write to her brothers, and to give them information of her death. Believing that he had to deal with two men who would probably misinterpret his motives, if he left Allan's position unexplained, he was careful to remind them that Mrs Armadale's son was well provided for; and that the object of his letter was simply to communicate the news of their sister's decease. The two letters were despatched towards the middle of January, and by return of post the answers were received. The first which the rector opened, was written, not by the elder brother, but by the elder brother's only son. The young man had succeeded to the estates in Norfolk on his father's death, some little time since. He wrote in a frank and friendly spirit, assuring Mr Brock that, however strongly his father might have been prejudiced against Mrs Armadale, the hostile feeling had never extended to her son. For himself, he had only to add that he would be sincerely happy to welcome his cousin to Thorpe-Ambrose, whenever his cousin came that way.

The second letter was a far less agreeable reply to receive than the first. The younger brother was still alive, and still resolute neither to forget nor forgive. He informed Mr Brock that his deceased sister's choice of a husband, and her conduct to her father at the time of her marriage, had made any relations of affection or esteem impossible, on his side, from that time forth. Holding the opinions he did, it would be equally painful to his nephew and himself if any personal intercourse took place between them. He had adverted, as generally as possible, to the nature of the differences which had kept him apart from his late sister, in order to satisfy Mr Brock's mind that a personal acquaintance with young Mr Armadale was, as a matter of delicacy, quite out of the question, and having done this, he would beg leave to close the correspondence.

Mr Brock wisely destroyed the second letter on the spot, and, after showing Allan his cousin's invitation, suggested that he should go to Thorpe-Ambrose as soon as he felt fit to present himself to strangers. Allan listened to the advice patiently enough; but he declined to profit by it. 'I will shake hands with my cousin willingly if I ever meet him,' he said, 'but I will visit no family, and be a guest in no house, in which my mother has been badly treated.' Mr Brock remonstrated gently, and tried to put matters in their proper light. Even at that time – even while he was still ignorant of events which were then impending – Allan's strangely isolated position in the world was a subject of serious anxiety to his old friend and tutor. The proposed visit to Thorpe-Ambrose opened the very prospect of his making friends and connections suited to him in rank and age which Mr Brock most desired to see – but Allan was not to be persuaded; he was obstinate and unreasonable; and the rector had no alternative but to drop the subject.

One on another, the weeks passed monotonously; and Allan showed but little of the elasticity of his age and character, in bearing the affliction that had made him motherless. He finished and launched his yacht; but his own journeymen remarked that the work seemed to have lost its interest for him. It was not natural to the young man to brood over his solitude and his grief, as he was brooding now. As the spring advanced, Mr Brock began to feel uneasy about the future, if Allan was not roused at once by change of scene. After much pondering, the rector decided on trying a trip to Paris, and on extending the journey south-wards if his companion showed an interest in continental travelling.[13] Allan's reception of the proposal made atonement for his obstinacy in refusing to cultivate his cousin's acquaintance – he was willing to go with Mr Brock wherever Mr Brock pleased. The rector took him at his word, and, in the middle of March, the two strangely assorted compan-ions left for London on their way to Paris.

Arrived in London, Mr Brock found himself unexpectedly face to face with a new anxiety. The unwelcome subject of Ozias Midwinter, which had been buried in peace since the beginning of December, rose to the surface again, and confronted the rector at the very outset of his travels, more unmanageably than ever.

Mr Brock's position, in dealing with this difficult matter, had been hard enough to maintain when he had first meddled with it. He now found himself with no vantage-ground left to stand on. Events had so ordered it, that the difference of opinion between Allan and his mother on the subject of the usher, was entirely disassociated with the agitation which had hastened Mrs Armadale's death. Allan's resolution to say no irritating words, and Mr Brock's reluctance to touch on a disagreeable topic, had kept them both silent about Midwinter in Mrs Armadale's presence, during the three days which had intervened between that person's departure and the appearance of the strange woman in the village. In the period of suspense and suffering that had followed, no recurrence to the subject of the usher had been possible, and none had taken place. Free from all mental disquietude on this score, Allan had stoutly preserved his perverse interest in his new friend. He had written to tell Midwinter of his affliction[14] – and he now proposed (unless the rector formally objected to it) paying a visit to his friend, before he started for Paris the next morning. What was Mr Brock to do? There was no denying that Midwinter's conduct had pleaded unanswerably against poor Mrs Armadale's unfounded distrust of him. If the rector, with no convincing reason to allege against it, and with no right to interfere but the right which Allan's courtesy gave him, declined to sanction the proposed visit – then farewell to all the old sociability and confidence between tutor and pupil on the contemplated tour. Environed by difficulties, which might have been possibly worsted by a less just and a less kind-hearted man, Mr Brock said a cautious word or two at parting; and (with more confidence in Midwinter's discretion and self-denial than he quite liked to acknowledge, even to himself), left Allan free to take his own way.

After willing away an hour, during the interval of his pupil's absence, by a walk in the streets, the rector returned to his hotel; and, finding the newspaper disengaged in the coffee-room, sat down absently to look over it. His eye, resting idly on the title-page, was startled into instant attention by the very first advertisement that it chanced to light on at the head of the column. There was Allan's mysterious namesake again, figuring in capital letters – and associated, this time (in the character of a dead man) with the offer of a pecuniary reward! Thus it ran:

SUPPOSED TO BE DEAD – To parish clerks, sextons, and others. Twenty Pounds Reward will be paid to any person who can produce evidence of the death of ALLAN ARMADALE, only son of the late Allan Armadale, of Barbadoes, and born in that island in the year 1830. Further particulars, on application to Messrs Hammick and Ridge, Lincoln's Inn Fields, London.

Even Mr Brock's essentially unimaginative mind began to stagger superstitiously in the dark, as he laid the newspaper down again. Little by little, a vague suspicion took possession of him, that the whole series of events which had followed the first appearance of Allan's namesake in the newspaper six years since, were held together by some mysterious connection, and were tending steadily to some unimaginable end. Without knowing why, he began to feel uneasy at Allan's absence. Without knowing why, he became impatient to get his pupil away from England before anything else happened between night and morning.

In an hour more the rector was relieved of all immediate anxiety, by Allan's return to the hotel. The young man was vexed and out of spirits. He had discovered Midwinter's lodgings, but he had failed to find Midwinter himself. The only account his landlady could give of him was, that he had gone out at his customary time to get his dinner at the nearest eating-house, and that he had not returned, in accordance with his usual regular habits, at his usual regular hour. Allan had therefore gone to inquire at the eating-house, and had found, on describing him, that Midwinter was well known there. It was his custom, on other days, to take a frugal dinner, and to sit half an hour afterwards reading the newspaper. On this occasion, after dining, he had taken up the paper as usual, had suddenly thrown it aside again, and had gone, nobody knew where, in a violent hurry. No further information being attainable, Allan had left a note at the lodgings, giving his address at the hotel, and begging Midwinter to come and say good-by before his departure for Paris.

The evening passed, and Allan's invisible friend never appeared. The morning came, bringing no obstacles with it, and Mr Brock and his pupil left London. So far, fortune had declared herself at last on the rector's side. Ozias Midwinter, after intrusively rising to the surface, had conveniently dropped out of sight again. What was to happen next?

Advancing once more, by three weeks only, from past to present, Mr Brock's memory took up the next event on the seventh of April. To all appearance, the chain was now broken at last. The new event had no recognizable connection (either to his mind or to Allan's) with any of the persons who had appeared, or any of the circumstances that had happened, in the bygone time.

The travellers had, as yet, got no farther than Paris. Allan's spirits had risen with the change; and he had been made all the readier to enjoy the novelty of the scene around him, by receiving a letter from Midwinter, containing news which Mr Brock himself acknowledged promised fairly for the future. The ex-usher had been away on business when Allan had called at his lodgings, having been led by an accidental circumstance to open communications with his relatives on that day. The result had taken him entirely by surprise – it had unexpectedly secured to him a little income of his own for the rest of his life. His future plans, now that this piece of good fortune had fallen to his share, were still unsettled. But if Allan wished to hear what he ultimately decided on, his agent in London (whose direction he enclosed) would receive communications for him, and would furnish Mr Armadale at all future times with his address.

On receipt of this letter, Allan had seized the pen in his usual headlong way, and had insisted on Midwinter's immediately joining Mr Brock and himself on their travels. The last days of March passed, and no answer to the proposal was received. The first days of April came, and on the seventh of the month there was a letter for Allan at last on the breakfast-table. He snatched it up, looked at the address, and threw the letter down again impatiently. The handwriting was not Mid-winter's. Allan finished his breakfast before he cared to read what his correspondent had to say to him.

The meal over, young Armadale lazily opened the letter. He began it with an expression of supreme indifference. He finished it with a sudden leap out of his chair, and a loud shout of astonishment. Wondering, as he well might, at this extraordinary outbreak, Mr Brock took up the letter, which Allan had tossed across the table to him. Before he had come to the end of it, his hands dropped helplessly on his knees, and the blank bewilderment of his pupil's expression was accurately reflected on his own face.

If ever two men had good cause for being thrown completely off their balance, Allan and the rector were those two. The letter which had struck them both with the same shock of astonishment did, beyond all question, contain an announcement which, on a first discovery of it, was simply incredible. The news was from Norfolk, and was to this effect. In little more than one week's time, death had mown down no less than three lives in the family at Thorpe-Ambrose – and Allan Armadale was at that moment heir to an estate of eight thousand a year!

A second perusal of the letter enabled the rector and his companion to master the details which had escaped them on a first reading. The writer was the family lawyer at Thorpe-Ambrose. After announcing to Allan the deaths of his cousin Arthur, at the age of twenty-five; of his uncle Henry, at the age of forty-eight; and of his cousin John, at the age of twenty-one, the lawyer proceeded to give a brief abstract of the terms of the elder Mr Blanchard's will. The claims of male issue were, as is not unusual in such cases, preferred to the claims of female issue. Failing Arthur, and his issue male, the estate was left to Henry and his issue male. Failing them, it went to the issue male of Henry's sister; and, in default of such issue, to the next heir male. As events had happened, the two young men, Arthur and John, had died unmarried, and Henry Blanchard had died, leaving no surviving child but a daughter. Under these circumstances, Allan was the next heir male pointed at by the will, and was now legally successor to the Thorpe-Ambrose estate. Having made this extraordinary announcement, the lawyer requested to be favoured with Mr Armadale's instructions, and added, in conclusion, that he would be happy to furnish any further particulars that were desired.

It was useless to waste time in wondering at an event which neither Allan nor his mother had ever thought of as even remotely possible. The only thing to be done was to go back to England at once. The next day found the travellers installed once more in their London hotel, and the day after, the affair was placed in the proper professional hands. The inevitable corresponding and consulting ensued; and one by one the all-important particulars flowed in, until the measure of information was pronounced to be full.

This was the strange story of the three deaths:

At the time when Mr Brock had written to Mrs Armadale's relatives to announce the news of her decease (that is to say, in the middle of the month of January), the family at Thorpe-Ambrose numbered five persons – Arthur Blanchard (in possession of the estate), living in the great house with his mother; and Henry Blanchard, the uncle, living in the neighbourhood, a widower with two children, a son and a daughter. To cement the family connection still more closely, Arthur Blanchard was engaged to be married to his cousin. The wedding was to be celebrated with great local rejoicings, in the coming summer, when the young lady had completed her twentieth year.

The month of February had brought changes with it in the family position. Observing signs of delicacy in the health of his son, Mr Henry Blanchard left Norfolk, taking the young man with him, under medical advice, to try the climate of Italy. Early in the ensuing month of March, Arthur Blanchard also left Thorpe-Ambrose, for a few days only, on business which required his presence in London. The business took him into the City. Annoyed by the endless impediments in the streets, he returned westward by one of the river steamers; and, so returning, met his death.

As the steamer left the wharf, he noticed a woman near him who had shown a singular hesitation in embarking, and who had been the last of the passengers to take her place in the vessel. She was neatly dressed in black silk, with a red Paisley shawl over her shoulders, and she kept her face hidden behind a thick veil. Arthur Blanchard was struck by the rare grace and elegance of her figure, and he felt a young man's passing curiosity to see her face. She neither lifted her veil, nor turned her head his way. After taking a few steps hesitatingly backwards and forwards on the deck, she walked away on a sudden to the stern of the vessel. In a minute more, there was a cry of alarm from the man at the helm, and the engines were stopped immediately. The woman had thrown herself overboard.

The passengers all rushed to the side of the vessel to look. Arthur Blanchard alone, without an instant's hesitation, jumped into the river. He was an excellent swimmer, and he reached the woman as she rose again to the surface, after sinking for the first time. Help was at hand; and they were both brought safely ashore. The woman was taken to the nearest police-station, and was soon restored to her senses; her preserver giving his name and address, as usual in such cases, to the inspector on duty, who wisely recommended him to get into a warm bath, and to send to his lodgings for dry clothes. Arthur Blanchard, who had never known an hour's illness since he was a child, laughed at the caution, and went back in a cab. The next day, he was too ill to attend the examination before the magistrate. A fortnight afterwards, he was a dead man.

The news of the calamity reached Henry Blanchard and his son at Milan; and within an hour of the time when they received it, they were on their way back to England. The snow on the Alps had loosened earlier than usual that year, and the passes were notoriously dangerous. The father and son, travelling in their own carriage, were met on the mountain by the mail returning, after sending the letters on by hand. Warnings which would have produced their effect, under any ordinary circumstances, were now vainly addressed to the two Englishmen. Their impatience to be at home again, after the catastrophe which had befallen their family, brooked no delay. Bribes, lavishly offered to the postilions, tempted them to go on. The carriage pursued its way, and was lost to view in the mist. When it was seen again, it was disinterred from the bottom of a precipice – the men, the horses, and the vehicle all crushed together under the wreck and ruin of an avalanche.

So the three lives were mown down by death. So, in a clear sequence of events, a woman's suicide-leap into a river had opened to Allan Armadale the succession to the Thorpe-Ambrose estates.

Who was the woman? The man who saved her life never knew. The magistrate who remanded her, the chaplain who exhorted her, the reporter who exhibited her in print – never knew. It was recorded of her with surprise, that, though most respectably dressed, she had nevertheless described herself as being 'in distress'. She had expressed the deepest contrition, but had persisted in giving a name which was on the face of it a false one; in telling a commonplace story, which was manifestly an invention; and in refusing to the last to furnish any clue to her friends. A lady connected with a charitable institution ('interested by her extreme elegance and beauty') had volunteered to take charge of her, and to bring her into a better frame of mind. The first day's experience of the penitent had been far from cheering, and the second day's experience had been conclusive. She had left the institution by stealth; and – though the visiting clergyman, taking a special interest in the case, had caused special efforts to be made – all search after her, from that time forth, had proved fruitless.

While this useless investigation (undertaken at Allan's express desire) was in progress, the lawyers had settled the preliminary formalities connected with the succession to the property. All that remained was for the new master of Thorpe-Ambrose to decide when he would personally establish himself on the estate of which he was now the legal possessor.

Left necessarily to his own guidance in this matter, Allan settled it for himself in his usual hot-headed generous way. He positively declined to take possession, until Mrs Blanchard and her niece (who had been permitted, thus far, as a matter of courtesy, to remain in their old home) had recovered from the calamity that had befallen them, and were fit to decide for themselves what their future proceedings should be. A private correspondence followed this resolution, comprehending, on Allan's side, unlimited offers of everything he had to give (in a house which he had not yet seen); and, on the ladies' side, a discreetly reluctant readiness to profit by the young gentleman's generosity in the matter of time. To the astonishment of his legal advisers, Allan entered their office one morning, accompanied by Mr Brock; and announced, with perfect composure, that the ladies had been good enough to take his own arrangements off his hands, and that, in deference to their convenience, he meant to defer establishing himself at Thorpe-Ambrose till that day two months. The lawyers stared at Allan – and Allan, returning the compliment, stared at the lawyers.

'What on earth are you wondering at, gentlemen?' he inquired, with a boyish bewilderment in his good-humoured blue eyes. 'Why shouldn't I give the ladies their two months, if the ladies want them? Let the poor things take their own time, and welcome. My rights? and my position? Oh, pooh! pooh! I'm in no hurry to be squire of the parish – it's not in my way. What do I mean to do for the two months? What I should have done anyhow, whether the ladies had stayed or not; I mean to go cruising at sea. That's what *I* like! I've got a new yacht at home in Somersetshire – a yacht of my own building. And I'll tell you what, sir,' continued Allan, seizing the head partner by the arm, in the fervour of his friendly intentions, 'you look sadly in want of a holiday in the fresh air, and you shall come along with me, on the trial-trip of my new vessel. And your partners, too, if they like. And the head-clerk, who is the best fellow I ever met with in my life. Plenty of room – we'll all shake down together on the floor, and we'll give Mr Brock a rug on the cabin-table. Thorpe-Ambrose be hanged! Do you mean to say if you had built a vessel yourself (as I have), you would go to any estate in the three kingdoms, while your own little beauty was sitting like a duck on the water at home, and waiting for you to try her? You legal gentlemen are great hands at argument. What do you think of *that* argument? I think it's unanswerable – and I'm off to Somersetshire to-morrow.'

With those words, the new possessor of eight thousand a year dashed into the head-clerk's office, and invited that functionary to a cruise on the high seas, with a smack on the shoulder which was heard distinctly by his masters in the next room. The Firm looked in interrogative wonder at Mr Brock. A client who could see a position among the landed gentry of England waiting for him, without being in a hurry to occupy it at the earliest possible opportunity, was a client of whom they possessed no previous experience.

'He must have been very oddly brought up,' said the lawyers to the rector.

'Very oddly,' said the rector to the lawyers.[15]

A last leap over one month more, brought Mr Brock to the present time – to the bedroom at Castletown, in which he was sitting thinking, and to the anxiety which was obstinately intruding itself between him and his night's rest. That anxiety was no unfamiliar enemy to the rector's peace of mind. It had first found him out in Somersetshire six months since, and it had now followed him to the Isle of Man under the inveterately obtrusive form of Ozias Midwinter.

The change in Allan's future prospects had worked no corresponding alteration in his perverse fancy for the castaway at the village inn. In the midst of the consultations with the lawyers he had found time to visit Midwinter; and on the journey back with the rector, there was Allan's friend in the carriage, returning with them to Somersetshire by Allan's own invitation. The ex-usher's hair had grown again on his shaven skull, and his dress showed the renovating influence of an accession of pecuniary means; but in all other respects the man was unchanged. He met Mr Brock's distrust, with the old uncomplaining resignation to it; he maintained the same suspicious silence on the subject of his relatives and his early life; he spoke of Allan's kindness to him with the same undisciplined fervour of gratitude and surprise. 'I have done what I could, sir,' he said to Mr Brock, while Allan was asleep in the railway carriage. 'I have kept out of Mr Armadale's way, and I have not even answered his last letter to me. More than that, is more than I can do. I don't ask you to consider my own feeling towards the only human creature who has never suspected and never ill-treated me. I can resist my own feeling, but I can't resist the young gentleman himself. There's not another like him in the world. If we are to be parted again, it must· be his doing or yours – not mine. The dog's master has whistled,' said this strange man, with a momentary outburst of the hidden passion in him, and a sudden springing of angry tears in his wild brown eyes: 'and it's hard, sir, to blame the dog, when the dog comes.'

Once more, Mr Brock's humanity got the better of Mr Brock's caution. He determined to wait, and see what the coming days of social intercourse might bring forth.

The days passed; the yacht was rigged, and fitted for sea; a cruise was arranged to the Welsh coast – and Midwinter the Secret was the same Midwinter still. Confinement on board a little vessel of five-and-thirty tons, offered no great attraction to a man of Mr Brock's time of life. But he sailed on the trial-trip of the yacht nevertheless, rather than trust Allan alone with his new friend.

Would the close companionship of the three on their cruise, tempt the man into talking of his own affairs? No; he was ready enough on other subjects, especially if Allan led the way to them. But not a word escaped him about himself. Mr Brock tried him with questions about his recent inheritance, and was answered as he had been answered once already at the Somersetshire inn. It was a curious coincidence, Midwinter admitted, that Mr Armadale's prospects and his own prospects, should both have unexpectedly changed for the better about the same time. But there the resemblance ended. It was no large fortune that had fallen into his lap, though it was enough for his wants. It had not reconciled him with his relations, for the money had not come to him as a matter of kindness but as a matter of right. As for the circumstance which had led to his communicating with his family, it was not worth mentioning – seeing that the temporary renewal of intercourse which had followed, had produced no friendly results. Nothing had come of it but the money – and, with the money, an anxiety which troubled him sometimes, when he woke in the small hours of the morning.

At those last words he became suddenly silent, as if, for once, his well-guarded tongue had betrayed him. Mr Brock seized the opportunity, and bluntly asked him what the nature of the anxiety might be. Did it relate to money? No – it related to a Letter which had been waiting for him for many years. Had he received the letter? Not yet; it had been left under charge of one of the partners in the firm which had managed the business of his inheritance for him; the partner had been absent from England; and the letter, locked up among his own private papers, could not be got at till he returned. He was expected back towards the latter part of that present May, and if Midwinter could be sure where the cruise would take them to at the close of the month, he thought he would write and have the letter forwarded. Had he any family reasons to be anxious about it? None that he knew of; he was curious to see what had been waiting for him for many years, and that was all. So he answered the rector's questions, with his tawny face turned away over the low bulwark of the yacht, and his fishing-line dragging in his supple brown hands.

Favoured by wind and weather, the little vessel had done wonders on her trial-trip. Before the period fixed for the duration of the cruise had half expired, the yacht was as high up on the Welsh coast as Holyhead; and Allan, eager for adventure in unknown regions, had declared boldly for an extension of the voyage northwards to the Isle of Man. Having ascertained from reliable authority, that the weather really promised well for a cruise in that quarter, and that, in the event of any unforeseen necessity for return, the railway was accessible by the steamer from Douglas to Liverpool, Mr Brock agreed to his pupil's proposal. By that night's post he wrote to Allan's lawyers and to his own rectory, indicating Douglas in the Isle of Man as the next address to which letters might be forwarded. At the post-office, he met Midwinter, who had just dropped a letter into the box. Remembering what he had said on board the yacht, Mr Brock concluded that they had both taken the same precaution, and had ordered their correspondence to be forwarded to the same place.

Late the next day, they set sail for the Isle of Man. For a few hours all went well; but sunset brought with it the signs of a coming change. With the darkness, the wind rose to a gale; and the question whether Allan and his journeymen had, or had not, built a stout sea-boat was seriously tested for the first time. All that night, after trying vainly to bear up for Holyhead, the little vessel kept the sea, and stood her trial bravely. The next morning, the Isle of Man[16] was in view, and the yacht was safe at Castletown. A survey by daylight of hull and rigging showed that all the damage done might be set right again in a week's time. The cruising party had accordingly remained at Castletown; Allan being occupied in superintending the repairs, Mr Brock in exploring the neighbourhood, and Midwinter in making daily pilgrimages on foot, to Douglas and back, to inquire for letters.[17]

The first of the cruising party who received a letter was Allan. 'More worries from those everlasting lawyers,' was all he said, when he had read the letter, and had crumpled it up in his pocket. The rector's turn came next, before the week's sojourn at Castletown had expired. On the fifth day, he found a letter from Somersetshire waiting for him at the hotel. It had been brought there by Midwinter, and it contained news which entirely overthrew all Mr Brock's holiday plans. The clergyman who had undertaken to do duty for him in his absence had been unexpectedly summoned home again; and Mr Brock had no choice (the day of the week being Friday) but to cross the next morning from Douglas to Liverpool, and get back by railway on Saturday night, in time for Sunday's service.

Having read his letter, and resigned himself to his altered circumstances as patiently as he might, the rector passed next to a question that pressed for serious consideration in its turn. Burdened with his heavy responsibility towards Allan, and conscious of his own undiminished distrust of Allan's new friend, how was he to act in the emergency that now beset him, towards the two young men who had been his companions on the cruise?

Mr Brock had first asked himself that awkward question on the Friday afternoon; and he was still trying, vainly, to answer it, alone in his own room, at one o'clock on the Saturday morning. It was then only the end of May, and the residence of the ladies at Thorpe-Ambrose (unless they chose to shorten it of their own accord) would not expire till the middle of June. Even if the repairs of the yacht had been completed (which was not the case), there was no possible pretence for hurrying Allan back to Somersetshire. But one other alternative remained – to leave him where he was. In other words, to leave him, at the turning point of his life, under the sole influence of a man whom he had first met with as a castaway at a village inn, and who was still, to all practical purposes, a total stranger to him.

In despair of obtaining any better means of enlightenment to guide his decision, Mr Brock reverted to the impression which Midwinter had produced on his own mind in the familiarity of the cruise.

Young as he was, the ex-usher had evidently lived a wild and varied life. He had seen and observed more than most men of twice his age; his talk showed a strange mixture of sense and absurdity – of vehement earnestness at one time, and fantastic humour at another. He could speak of books like a man who had really enjoyed them; he could take his turn at the helm like a sailor who knew his duty; he could sing, and tell stories, and cook, and climb the rigging, and lay the cloth for dinner, with an odd satirical delight in the exhibition of his own dexterity. The display of these, and other qualities like them, as his spirits rose with the cruise, had revealed the secret of his attraction for Allan plainly enough. But had all disclosures rested there? Had the man let no chance light on his character in the rector's presence? Very little; and that little did not set him forth in a morally alluring aspect. His way in the world had lain evidently in doubtful places; familiarity with the small villainies of vagabonds peeped out of him now and then; words occasionally slipped off his tongue with an unpleasantly strong flavour about them; and, more significant still, he habitually slept the light suspicious sleep of a man who has been accustomed to close his eyes in doubt of the company under the same roof with him. Down to the very latest moment of the rector's experience of him – down to that present Friday night – his conduct had been persistently secret and unaccountable to the very last. After bringing Mr Brock's letter to the hotel, he had mysteriously disappeared from the house without leaving any message for his companions, and without letting anybody see whether he had, or had not, received a letter himself. At nightfall, he had come back stealthily in the darkness – had been caught on the stairs by Allan, eager to tell him of the change in the rector's plans – had listened to the news without a word of remark – and had ended by sulkily locking himself into his own room. What was there in his favour to set against such revelations of his character as these – against his wandering eyes, his obstinate reserve with the rector, his ominous silence on the subject of family and friends? Little or nothing: the sum of all his merits began and ended with his gratitude to Allan.

Mr Brock left his seat on the side of the bed, trimmed his candle, and, still lost in his own thoughts, looked out absently at the night. The change of place brought no new ideas with it. His retrospect over his own past life had amply satisfied him that his present sense of responsibility rested on no merely fanciful grounds; and having brought him to that point, had left him there, standing at the window, and seeing nothing but the total darkness in his own mind faithfully reflected by the total darkness of the night.

'If I only had a friend to apply to!' thought the rector. 'If I could only find some one to help me in this miserable place!'

At the moment when the aspiration crossed his mind, it was suddenly answered by a low knock at the door; and a voice said softly in the passage outside, 'Let me come in.'

After an instant's pause to steady his nerves, Mr Brock opened the door, and found himself, at one o'clock in the morning, standing face to face on the threshold of his own bedroom with Ozias Midwinter.

'Are you ill?' asked the rector, as soon as his astonishment would allow him to speak.

'I have come here to make a clean breast of it!' was the strange answer. 'Will you let me in?'

With those words he walked into the room – his eyes on the ground, his lips ashy pale, and his hand holding something hidden behind him.

'I saw the light under your door,' he went on, without looking up, and without moving his hand; 'and I know the trouble on your mind which is keeping you from your rest. You are going away to-morrow morning, and you don't like leaving Mr Armadale alone with a stranger like me.'

Startled as he was, Mr Brock saw the serious necessity of being plain with a man, who had come at that time, and had said those words to him.

'You have guessed right,' he answered. 'I stand in the place of a father to Allan Armadale, and I am naturally unwilling to leave him, at his age, with a man whom I don't know.'

Ozias Midwinter took a step forward to the table. His wandering eyes rested on the rector's New Testament, which was one of the objects lying on it.

'You have read that Book, in the years of a long life, to many congregations,' he said. 'Has it taught you mercy to your miserable fellow-creatures?'

Without waiting to be answered, he looked Mr Brock in the face for the first time, and brought his hidden hand slowly into view.

'Read that,' he said; 'and, for Christ's sake, pity me when you know who I am.'

He laid a letter of many pages on the table. It was the letter that Mr Neal had posted at Wildbad nineteen years since.

CHAPTER II[1]

THE MAN REVEALED

The first cool breathings of the coming dawn fluttered through the open window as Mr Brock read the closing lines of the Confession. He put it from him in silence, without looking up. The first shock of discovery had struck his mind, and had passed away again. At his age, and with his habits of thought, his grasp was not strong enough to hold the whole revelation that had fallen on him. All his heart, when he closed the manuscript, was with the memory of the woman who had been the beloved friend of his later and happier life; all his thoughts were busy with the miserable secret of her treason to her own father which the letter had disclosed.

He was startled out of the narrow limits of his own little grief by the vibration of the table at which he sat, under a hand that was laid on it heavily. The instinct of reluctance was strong in him; but he conquered it, and looked up. There, silently confronting him in the mixed light of the yellow candle-flame and the faint grey dawn, stood the castaway of the village inn – the inheritor of the fatal Armadale name.

Mr Brock shuddered as the terror of the present time, and the darker terror yet of the future that might be coming, rushed back on him at the sight of the man's face. The man saw it, and spoke first.

'Is my father's crime looking at you out of *my* eyes?' he asked. 'Has the ghost of the drowned man followed me into the room?'

The suffering and the passion that he was forcing back, shook the hand that he still kept on the table, and stifled the voice in which he spoke until it sank to a whisper.

'I have no wish to treat you otherwise than justly and kindly,' answered Mr Brock. 'Do me justice on my side, and believe that I am incapable of cruelly holding you responsible for your father's crime.'

The reply seemed to compose him. He bowed his head in silence, and took up the confession from the table.

'Have you read this through?' he asked quietly.

'Every word of it, from first to last.'

'Have I dealt openly with you so far? Has Ozias Midwinter—'

'Do you still call yourself by that name,' interrupted Mr Brock, 'now your true name is known to me?'

'Since I have read my father's confession,' was the answer, 'I like my ugly alias better than ever. Allow me to repeat the question which I was about to put to you a minute since – Has Ozias Midwinter done his best, thus far, to enlighten Mr Brock?'

The rector evaded a direct reply. 'Few men in your position,' he said, 'would have had the courage to show me that letter.'

'Don't be too sure, sir, of the vagabond you picked up at the inn till you know a little more of him than you know now. You have got the secret of my birth, but you are not in possession yet of the story of my life. You ought to know it, and you shall know it, before you leave me alone with Mr Armadale. Will you wait, and rest a little while? or shall I tell it you now?'

'Now,' said Mr Brock, still as far away as ever from knowing the real character of the man before him.

Everything Ozias Midwinter said, everything Ozias Midwinter did, was against him. He had spoken with a sardonic indifference, almost with an insolence of tone, which would have repelled the sympathies of any man who heard him. And now, instead of placing himself at the table, and addressing his story directly to the rector, he withdrew silently and ungraciously to the window-seat. There he sat – his face averted; his hands mechanically turning the leaves of his father's letter till he came to the last. With his eyes fixed on the closing lines of the manuscript, and with a strange mixture of recklessness and sadness in his voice, he began his promised narrative in these words:

'The first thing you know of me,' he said, 'is what my father's confession has told you already. He mentions here that I was a child, asleep on his breast, when he spoke his last words in this world, and when a stranger's hand wrote them down for him at his death-bed. That stranger's name, as you may have noticed, is signed on the cover – "Alexander Neal, Writer to the Signet, Edinburgh." The first recollection I have is of Alexander Neal beating me with a horsewhip (I daresay I deserved it), in the character of my stepfather.'

'Have you no recollection of your mother at the same time?' asked Mr Brock.

'Yes; I remember her having shabby old clothes made up to fit me, and having fine new frocks bought for her two children by her second husband. I remember the servants laughing at me in my old things, and the horsewhip finding its way to my shoulders again, for losing my temper and tearing my shabby clothes. My next recollection gets on to a year or two later. I remember myself locked up in a lumber-room, with a bit of bread and a mug of water, wondering what it was that made my mother and my stepfather seem to hate the very sight of me. I never settled that question till yesterday, and then I solved the mystery, when my father's letter was put into my hands. My mother knew what had really happened on board the French timber-ship, and my stepfather knew what had really happened, and they were both well aware that the shameful secret which they would fain have kept from every living creature, was a secret which would be one day revealed to *me*. There was no help for it – the confession was in the executor's hands, and there was I, an ill-conditioned brat, with my mother's negro blood in my face, and my murdering father's passions in my heart, inheritor of their secret in spite of them! I don't wonder at the horsewhip now, or the shabby old clothes, or the bread and water in the lumber-room. Natural penalties all of them, sir, which the child was beginning to pay already for the father's sin.'

Mr Brock looked at the swarthy, secret face, still obstinately turned away from him. 'Is this the stark insensibility of a vagabond?' he asked himself, 'or the despair in disguise of a miserable man?'

'School is my next recollection,' the other went on. 'A cheap place in a lost corner of Scotland. I was left there, with a bad character to help me at starting. I spare you the story of the master's cane in the school-room, and the boys' kicks in the playground. I daresay there was ingrained ingratitude in my nature; at any rate, I ran away. The first person who met me asked my name. I was too young and too foolish to know the importance of concealing it, and, as a matter of course, I was taken back to school the same evening. The result taught me a lesson which I have not forgotten since. In a day or two more, like the vagabond I was, I ran away for the second time. The school watch-dog had had his instructions, I suppose: he stopped me before I got outside the gate. Here is his mark, among the rest, on the back of my hand. His master's marks I can't show you – they are all on my back. Can you believe in my perversity? There was a devil in me that no dog could worry out; I ran away again as soon as I left my bed; and this time I got off. At nightfall I found myself (with a pocketful of the school oatmeal) lost on a moor. I lay down on the fine soft heather, under the lee of a great grey rock. Do you think I felt lonely? Not I! I was away from the master's cane, away from my schoolfellows' kicks, away from my mother, away from my stepfather; and I lay down that night under my good friend the rock, the happiest boy in all Scotland!'

Through the wretched childhood which that one significant circum- stance disclosed, Mr Brock began to see dimly how little was really strange, how little really unaccountable, in the character of the man who was now speaking to him.

'I slept soundly,' Midwinter continued, 'under my friend the rock. When I woke in the morning, I found a sturdy old man with a fiddle, sitting on one side of me, and two dancing dogs in scarlet jackets on the other. Experience had made me too sharp to tell the truth, when the man put his first questions. He didn't press them – he gave me a good breakfast out of his knapsack, and he let me romp with the dogs. "I'll tell you what," he said, when he had got my confidence in this manner, "you want three things, my man; you want a new father, a new family, and a new name. I'll be your father; I'll let you have the dogs for your brothers; and if you'll promise to be very careful of it, I'll give you my own name into the bargain. Ozias Midwinter, junior, you have had a good breakfast – if you want a good dinner, come along with me!" He got up; the dogs trotted after him, and I trotted after the dogs. Who was my new father? you will ask. A half-bred gipsy, sir; a drunkard, a ruffian, and a thief – and the best friend I ever had! Isn't a man your friend who gives you your food, your shelter, and your education? Ozias Midwinter taught me to dance the Highland fling; to throw somersaults; to walk on stilts; and to sing songs to his fiddle. Sometimes we roamed the country, and performed at fairs. Sometimes we tried the large towns, and enlivened bad company over its cups. I was a nice lively little boy of eleven years old – and bad company, the women especially, took a fancy to me and my nimble feet. I was vagabond enough to like the life. The dogs and I lived together, ate and drank, and slept together. I can't think of those poor little four-footed brothers of mine, even now, without a choking in the throat. Many is the beating we three took together; many is the hard day's dancing we did together; many is the night we have slept together, and whimpered together, on the cold hill-side. I'm not trying to distress you, sir; I'm only telling you the truth. The life with all its hardships was a life that fitted me, and the half-bred gipsy who gave me his name, ruffian as he was, was a ruffian I liked.'

'A man who beat you!' exclaimed Mr Brock, in astonishment.

'Didn't I tell you just now, sir, that I lived with the dogs? and did you ever hear of a dog who liked his master the worse for beating him? Hundreds of thousands of miserable men, women, and children would have liked that man (as I liked him) if he had always given them what he always gave me – plenty to eat. It was stolen food mostly, and my new gipsy father was generous with it. He seldom laid the stick on us when he was sober; but it diverted him to hear us yelp when he was drunk. He died drunk, and enjoyed his favourite amusement with his last breath. One day (when I had been two years in his service), after giving us a good dinner out on the moor, he sat down with his back against a stone, and called us up to divert himself with his stick. He made the dogs yelp first, and then he called to me. I didn't go very willingly – he had been drinking harder than usual, and the more he drank the better he liked his after-dinner amusement. He was in high good-humour that day, and he hit me so hard that he toppled over, in his drunken state, with the force of his own blow. He fell with his face in a puddle, and lay there without moving. I and the dogs stood at a distance, and looked at him: we thought he was feigning, to get us near and have another stroke at us. He feigned so long that we ventured up to him at last. It took me some time to pull him over – he was a heavy man. When I did get him on his back, he was dead. We made all the outcry we could; but the dogs were little, and I was little, and the place was lonely; and no help came to us. I took his fiddle, and his stick; I said to my two brothers, "Come along, we must get our own living now;" and we went away heavy hearted, and left him on the moor. Unnatural as it may seem to you, I was sorry for him. I kept his ugly name through all my after-wanderings, and I have enough of the old leaven left in me to like the sound of it still. Midwinter or Armadale, never mind my name now – we will talk of that afterwards; you must know the worst of me first.'

'Why not the best of you?' said Mr Brock, gently.

'Thank you, sir, – but I am here to tell the truth. We will get on, if you please, to the next chapter in my story. The dogs and I did badly, after our master's death – our luck was against us. I lost one of my little brothers – the best performer of the two; he was stolen, and I never recovered him. My fiddle and my stilts were taken from me next, by main force, by a tramp who was stronger than I. These misfortunes drew Tommy and me – I beg your pardon, sir, I mean the dog – closer together than ever. I think we had some kind of dim foreboding on both sides, that we had not done with our misfortunes yet; anyhow, it was not very long before we were parted for ever. We were neither of us thieves (our master had been satisfied with teaching us to dance); but we both committed an invasion of the rights of property, for all that. Young creatures, even when they are half-starved, cannot resist taking a run sometimes, on a fine morning. Tommy and I could not resist taking a run into a gentleman's plantation; the gentleman preserved his game; and the gentleman's keeper knew his business. I heard a gun go off – you can guess the rest. God preserve me from ever feeling such misery again, as I felt when I lay down by Tommy, and took him, dead and bloody, in my arms! The keeper attempted to part us – I bit him, like the wild animal I was. He tried the stick on me next – he might as well have tried it on one of the trees. The noise reached the ears of two young ladies, riding near the place – daughters of the gentleman on whose property I was a trespasser. They were too well brought up to lift their voices against the sacred right of preserving game, but they were kind-hearted girls, and they pitied me, and took me home with them. I remember the gentlemen of the house (keen sportsmen all of them) roaring with laughter as I went by the windows, crying, with my little dead dog in my arms. Don't suppose I complain of their laughter; it did me good service – it roused the indignation of the two ladies. One of them took me into her own garden, and showed me a place where I might bury my dog under the flowers, and be sure that no other hands should ever disturb him again. The other went to her father, and persuaded him to give the forlorn little vagabond a chance in the house, under one of the upper servants. Yes! you have been cruising in company with a man who was once a footboy. I saw you look at me, when I amused Mr Armadale by laying the cloth on board the yacht. Now you know why I laid it so neatly, and forgot nothing. It has been my good fortune to see something of Society; I have helped to fill its stomach and black its boots. My experience of the servants' hall was not a long one. Before I had worn out my first suit of livery, there was a scandal in the house. It was the old story; there is no need to tell it over again for the thousandth time. Loose money left on a table, and not found there again; all the servants with characters to appeal to except the footboy, who had been rashly taken on trial. Well! well! I was lucky in that house to the last; I was not prosecuted for taking what I had not only never touched, but never even seen – I was only turned out. One morning, I went in my old clothes to the grave where I had buried Tommy. I gave the place a kiss; I said good-by to my little dead dog; and there I was, out in the world again, at the ripe age of thirteen years!'

'In that friendless state, and at that tender age,' said Mr Brock, 'did no thought cross your mind of going home again?'

'I went home again, sir, that very night – I slept on the hill-side. What other home had I? In a day or two's time, I drifted back to the large towns and the bad company, – the great open country was so lonely to me, now I had lost the dogs! Two sailors picked me up next; I was a handy lad, and I got a cabin-boy's berth on board a coasting-vessel. A cabin-boy's berth means dirt to live in, offal to eat, a man's work on a boy's shoulders, and the rope's-end at regular intervals. The vessel touched at a port in the Hebrides. I was as ungrateful as usual to my best benefactors – I ran away again. Some women found me, half-dead of starvation, in the northern wilds of the Isle of Skye. It was near the coast, and I took a turn with the fishermen next. There was less of the rope's-end among my new masters; but plenty of exposure to wind and weather, and hard work enough to have killed a boy who was not a seasoned tramp like me. I fought through it till the winter came, and then the fishermen turned me adrift again. I don't blame them – food was scarce, and mouths were many. With famine staring the whole community in the face, why should they keep a boy who didn't belong to them? A great city was my only chance in the winter time; so I went to Glasgow, and all but stepped into the lion's mouth as soon as I got there. I was minding an empty cart on the Broomielaw,[2] when I heard my stepfather's voice on the pavement-side of the horse by which I was standing. He had met some person whom he knew, and, to my terror and surprise, they were talking about me. Hidden behind the horse, I heard enough of their conversation to know that I had narrowly escaped discovery before I went on board the coasting-vessel. I had met, at that time, with another vagabond boy, of my own age; we had quarrelled and parted. The day after, my stepfather's inquiries were made in that very district; and it became a question with him (a good personal description being unattainable in either case) which of the two boys he should follow. One of them, he was informed, was known as "Brown", and the other as "Midwinter". Brown was just the common name which a cunning runaway boy would be most likely to assume; Midwinter, just the remarkable name which he would be most likely to avoid. The pursuit had accordingly followed Brown, and had allowed me to escape. I leave you to imagine whether I was not doubly and trebly determined to keep my gipsy master's name after that. But my resolution did not stop here. I made up my mind to leave the country altogether. After a day or two's lurking about the outward-bound vessels in port, I found out which sailed first, and hid myself on board. Hunger tried hard to force me out before the pilot had left; but hunger was not new to me, and I kept my place. The pilot was out of the vessel when I made my appearance on deck, and there was nothing for it but to keep me or throw me overboard. The captain said (I have no doubt quite truly) that he would have preferred throwing me overboard; but the majesty of the law does sometimes stand the friend even of a vagabond like me. In that way I came back to a sea life. In that way, I learnt enough to make me handy and useful (as I saw you noticed) on board Mr Armadale's yacht. I sailed more than one voyage, in more than one vessel, to more than one part of the world; and I might have followed the sea for life, if I could only have kept my temper under every provocation that could be laid on it. I had learnt a great deal – but, not having learnt that, I made the last part of my last voyage home to the port of Bristol in irons; and I saw the inside of a prison for the first time in my life, on a charge of mutinous conduct to one of my officers. You have heard me with extraordinary patience, sir, and I am glad to tell you, in return, that we are not far now from the end of my story. You found some books, if I remember right, when you searched my luggage at the Somersetshire inn?'

Mr Brock answered in the affirmative.

'Those books mark the next change in my life – and the last, before I took the usher's place at the school. My term of imprisonment was not a long one. Perhaps my youth pleaded for me; perhaps the Bristol magistrates took into consideration the time I had passed in irons on board ship. Anyhow, I was just turned seventeen, when I found myself out on the world again. I had no friends to receive me; I had no place to go to. A sailor's life, after what had happened, was a life I recoiled from in disgust. I stood in the crowd on the bridge at Bristol,[3] wondering what I should do with my freedom now I had got it back. Whether I had altered in the prison, or whether I was feeling the change in character that comes with coming manhood, I don't know; but the old reckless enjoyment of the old vagabond life seemed quite worn out of my nature. An awful sense of loneliness kept me wandering about Bristol, in horror of the quiet country, till after nightfall. I looked at the lights kindling in the parlour windows, with a miserable envy of the happy people inside. A word of advice would have been worth something to me at that time. Well! I got it: a policeman advised me to move on. He was quite right – what else could I do? I looked up at the sky, and there was my old friend of many a night's watch at sea, the north star. "All points of the compass are alike to me," I thought to myself; "I'll go *your* way." Not even the star would keep me company that night. It got behind a cloud, and left me alone in the rain and darkness. I groped my way to a cart-shed, fell asleep, and dreamed of old times, when I served my gipsy master and lived with the dogs. God! what I would have given when I woke to have felt Tommy's little cold muzzle in my hand! Why am I dwelling on these things? why don't I get on to the end? You shouldn't encourage me, sir, by listening so patiently. After a week more of wandering, without hope to help me, or prospects to look to, I found myself in the streets of Shrewsbury, staring in at the windows of a bookseller's shop. An old man came to the shop-door, looked about him, and saw me. "Do you want a job?" he asked. "And are you not above doing it cheap?" The prospect of having something to do, and some human creature to speak a word to, tempted me, and I did a day's dirty work in the bookseller's warehouse, for a shilling. More work followed at the same rate. In a week, I was promoted to sweep out the shop, and put up the shutters. In no very long time after, I was trusted to carry the books out; and when quarter-day came, and the shopman left, I took his place. Wonderful luck! you will say; here I had found my way to a friend at last. I had found my way to one of the most merciless misers in England; and I had risen in the little world of Shrewsbury by the purely commercial process of underselling all my competitors. The job in the warehouse had been declined at the price by every idle man in the town – and I did it. The regular porter received his weekly pittance under weekly protest. – I took two shillings less, and made no complaint. The shopman gave warning on the ground that he was underfed as well as underpaid. I received half his salary, and lived contentedly on his reversionary scraps. Never were two men so well suited to each other as that bookseller and I! *His* one object in life was to find somebody who would work for him at starvation wages. *My* one object in life was to find somebody who would give me an asylum over my head. Without a single sympathy in common – without a vestige of feeling of any sort, hostile or friendly, growing up between us on either side – without wishing each other good-night, when we parted on the house stairs, or good-morning when we met at the shop counter – we lived alone in that house, strangers from first to last, for two whole years. A dismal existence for a lad of my age, was it not? You are a clergyman and a scholar – surely you can guess what made the life endurable to me?'

Mr Brock remembered the well-worn volumes which had been found in the usher's bag. 'The books made it endurable to you,' he said.

The eyes of the castaway kindled with a new light.

'Yes!' he said, 'the books – the generous friends who met me without suspicion – the merciful masters who never used me ill! The only years of my life that I can look back on with something like pride, are the years I passed in the miser's house. The only unalloyed pleasure I have ever tasted, is the pleasure that I found for myself on the miser's shelves. Early and late, through the long winter nights and the quiet summer days, I drank at the fountain of knowledge, and never wearied of the draught. There were few customers to serve – for the books were mostly of the solid and scholarly kind. No responsibilities rested on me – for the accounts were kept by my master, and only the small sums of money were suffered to pass through my hands. He soon found out enough of me to know that my honesty was to be trusted, and that my patience might be counted on, treat me as he might. The one insight into *his* character which I obtained, on my side, widened the distance between us to its last limits. He was a confirmed opium-eater in secret – a prodigal in laudanum, though a miser in all besides. He never confessed his frailty, and I never told him I had found it out. He had his pleasure apart from *me*; and I had my pleasure apart from *him*. Week after week, month after month, there we sat without a friendly word ever passing between us – I, alone with my book at the counter: he, alone with his ledger in the parlour, dimly visible to me through the dirty window-pane of the glass door, sometimes poring over his figures, sometimes lost and motionless for hours in the ecstasy of his opium trance. Time passed, and made no impression on us; the seasons of two years came and went, and found us still unchanged. One morning, at the opening of the third year, my master did not appear as usual to give me my allowance for breakfast. I went upstairs, and found him helpless in his bed. He refused to trust me with the keys of the cupboard, or to let me send for a doctor. I bought a morsel of bread, and went back to my books – with no more feeling for *him* (I honestly confess it), than he would have had for *me* under the same circumstances. An hour or two later, I was roused from my reading by an occasional customer of ours, a retired medical man. He went upstairs. I was glad to get rid of him, and return to my books. He came down again, and disturbed me once more. "I don't much like you, my lad," he said; "but I think it my duty to say that you will soon have to shift for yourself. You are no great favourite in the town, and you may have some difficulty in finding a new place. Provide yourself with a written character from your master before it is too late." He spoke to me coldly. I thanked him coldly on my side, and got my character the same day. Do you think my master let me have it for nothing? Not he! He bargained with me on his death-bed. I was his creditor for a month's salary, and he wouldn't write a line of my testimonial until I had first promised to forgive him the debt. Three days afterwards, he died, enjoying to the last the happiness of having over-reached his shopman. "Aha!" he whispered, when the doctor formally summoned me to take leave of him, "I got you cheap!" – Was Ozias Midwinter's stick as cruel as that? I think not. Well! there I was, out on the world again, but surely with better prospects, this time. I had taught myself to read Latin, Greek, and German; and I had got my written character to speak for me. All useless! The doctor was quite right; I was not liked in the town. The lower order of the people despised me for selling my services to the miser, at the miser's price. As for the better classes, I did with them (God knows how!) what I have always done with everybody, except Mr Armadale – I produced a disagreeable impression at first sight; I couldn't mend it afterwards; and there was an end of me in respectable quarters. It is quite likely I might have spent all my savings, my puny little golden offspring of two years' miserable growth, but for a school advertisement which I saw in a local paper. The heartlessly mean terms that were offered, encouraged me to apply; and I got the place. How I prospered in it, and what became of me next, there is no need to tell you. The thread of my story is all wound off; my vagabond life stands stripped of its mystery; and you know the worst of me at last.'

A moment of silence followed those closing words. Midwinter rose from the window-seat, and came back to the table with the letter from Wildbad in his hand.

'My father's confession has told you who I am; and my own confession has told you what my life has been,' he said, addressing Mr Brock, without taking the chair to which the rector pointed. 'I promised to make a clean breast of it when I first asked leave to enter this room. Have I kept my word?'

'It is impossible to doubt it,' replied Mr Brock. 'You have established your claim on my confidence and my sympathy. I should be insensible indeed if I could know what I now know of your childhood and your youth, and not feel something of Allan's kindness for Allan's friend.'

'Thank you, sir,' said Midwinter, simply and gravely.

He sat down opposite Mr Brock at the table for the first time.

'In a few hours you will have left this place,' he proceeded. 'If I can help you to leave it with your mind at ease, I will. There is more to be said between us than we have said up to this time. My future relations with Mr Armadale are still left undecided; and the serious question raised by my father's letter is a question which we have neither of us faced yet.'

He paused and looked with a momentary impatience at the candle still burning on the table, in the morning light. The struggle to speak with composure, and to keep his own feelings stoically out of view, was evidently growing harder and harder to him.

'It may possibly help your decision,' he went on, 'if I tell you how I determined to act towards Mr Armadale – in the matter of the similarity of our names – when I first read this letter, and when I had composed myself sufficiently to be able to think at all.' He stopped, and cast a second impatient look at the lighted candle. 'Will you excuse the odd fancy of an odd man?' he asked, with a faint smile. 'I want to put out the candle – I want to speak of the new subject, in the new light.'

He extinguished the candle as he spoke, and let the first tenderness of the daylight flow uninterruptedly into the room.

'I must once more ask your patience,' he resumed, 'if I return for a moment to myself and my circumstances. I have already told you that my stepfather made an attempt to discover me some years after I had turned my back on the Scotch school. He took that step out of no anxiety of his own, but simply as the agent of my father's trustees. In the exercise of their discretion, they had sold the estates in Barbadoes (at the time of the emancipation of the slaves, and the ruin of West Indian property) for what the estates would fetch. Having invested the proceeds they were bound to set aside a sum for my yearly education.

This responsibility obliged them to make the attempt to trace me – a fruitless attempt, as you already know. A little later (as I have been since informed) I was publicly addressed by an advertisement in the newspapers – which I never saw. Later still, when I was twenty-one, a second advertisement appeared (which I did see) offering a reward for evidence of my death. If I was alive, I had a right to my half share of the proceeds of the estates, on coming of age; if dead, the money reverted to my mother. I went to the lawyers, and heard from them what I have just told you. After some difficulty in proving my identity – and, after an interview with my stepfather, and a message from my mother, which has hopelessly widened the old breach between us – my claim was allowed; and my money is now invested for me in the funds, under the name that is really my own.'

Mr Brock drew eagerly nearer to the table. He saw the end now, to which the speaker was tending.

'Twice a year,' Midwinter pursued, 'I must sign my own name to get my own income. At all other times, and under all other circumstances, I may hide my identity under any name I please. As Ozias Midwinter, Mr Armadale first knew me – as Ozias Midwinter he shall know me to the end of my days. Whatever may be the result of this interview – whether I win your confidence, or whether I lose it – of one thing you may feel sure. Your pupil shall never know the horrible secret which I have trusted to your keeping. This is no extraordinary resolution – for, as you know already, it costs me no sacrifice of feeling to keep my assumed name. There is nothing in my conduct to praise – it comes naturally out of the gratitude of a thankful man. Review the circumstances for yourself, sir; and set my own horror of revealing them to Mr Armadale out of the question. If the story of the names is ever told, there can be no limiting it to the disclosure of my father's crime; it must go back to the story of Mrs Armadale's marriage. I have heard her son talk to her; I know how he loves her memory. As God is my witness, he shall never love it less dearly through *me*!'

Simply as the words were spoken, they touched the deepest sympathies in the rector's nature: they took his thoughts back to Mrs Armadale's death-bed. There sat the man against whom she had ignorantly warned him, in her son's interests – and that man, of his own free-will, had laid on himself the obligation of respecting her secret for her son's sake! The memory of his own past efforts to destroy the very friendship out of which this resolution had sprung, rose, and reproached Mr Brock. He held out his hand to Midwinter for the first time. 'In her name, and in her son's name,' he said warmly, 'I thank you.'

Without replying, Midwinter spread the confession open before him on the table.

'I think I have said all that it was my duty to say,' he began, 'before we could approach the consideration of this letter. Whatever may have appeared strange in my conduct towards you and towards Mr Armadale, may be now trusted to explain itself. You can easily imagine the natural curiosity and surprise that I must have felt (ignorant as I then was of the truth) when the sound of Mr Armadale's name first startled me as the echo of my own. You will readily understand that I only hesitated to tell him I was his namesake, because I hesitated to damage my position – in your estimation, if not in his – by confessing that I had come among you under an assumed name. And, after all that you have just heard of my vagabond life and my low associates, you will hardly wonder at the obstinate silence I maintained about myself, at a time when I did not feel the sense of responsibility which my father's confession has laid on me. We can return to these small personal explanations, if you wish it, at another time; they cannot be suffered to keep us from the greater interests which we must settle before you leave this place. We may come now—' his voice faltered; and he suddenly turned his face towards the window, so as to hide it from the rector's view. 'We may come now,' he repeated, his hand trembling visibly as it held the page, 'to the murder on board the timber-ship, and to the warning that has followed me from my father's grave.'

Softly – as if he feared they might reach Allan, sleeping in the neighbouring room – he read the last terrible words which the Scotchman's pen had written at Wildbad, as they fell from his father's lips.

Avoid the widow of the man I killed – if the widow still lives. Avoid the maid whose wicked hand smoothed the way to the marriage – if the maid is still in her service. And, more than all, avoid the man who bears the same name as your own. Offend your best benefactor, if that benefactor's influence has connected you one with the other. Desert the woman who loves you, if that woman is a link between you and him. Hide yourself from him, under an assumed name. Put the mountains and the seas between you; be ungrateful; be unforgiving; be all that is most repellent to your own gentler nature, rather than live under the same roof, and breathe the same air with that man. Never let the two Allan Armadales meet in this world; never, never, never!

After reading those sentences, he pushed the manuscript from him, without looking up. The fatal reserve which he had been in a fair way of conquering but a few minutes since, possessed itself of him once more. Again his eyes wandered; again his voice sank in tone. A stranger who had heard his story, and who saw him now, would have said, 'His look is lurking, his manner is bad; he is every inch of him, his father's son.'

'I have a question to ask you,' said Mr Brock, breaking the silence between them, on his side. 'Why have you just read that passage in your father's letter?'

'To force me into telling you the truth,' was the answer. 'You must know how much there is of my father in me, before you trust me to be Mr Armadale's friend. I got my letter yesterday, in the morning. Some inner warning troubled me, and I went down on the sea-shore by myself, before I broke the seal. Do you believe the dead can come back to the world they once lived in? I believe my father came back in that bright morning light, through the glare of that broad sunshine and the roar of that joyful sea, and watched me while I read. When I got to the words that you have just heard, and when I knew that the very end which he had died dreading, was the end that had really come, I felt the horror that had crept over him in his last moments, creeping over me. I struggled against myself, as *he* would have had me struggle. I tried to be all that was most repellent to my own gentler nature; I tried to think pitilessly of putting the mountains and the seas between me and the man who bore my name. Hours passed before I could prevail on myself to go back and run the risk of meeting Allan Armadale in this house. When I did get back, and when he met me at night on the stairs, I thought I was looking him in the face as *my* father looked *his* father in the face when the cabin door closed between them. Draw your own conclusions, sir. Say, if you like, that the inheritance of my father's heathen belief in Fate is one of the inheritances he has left to me. I won't dispute it; I won't deny that all through yesterday *his* superstition was *my* superstition. The night came before I could find my way to calmer and brighter thoughts. But I did find my way. You may set it down in my favour that I lifted myself at last above the influence of this horrible letter. Do you know what helped me?'

'Did you reason with yourself?'

'I can't reason about what I feel.'

'Did you quiet your mind by prayer?'

'I was not fit to pray.'

'And yet something guided you to the better feeling and the truer view?'

'Something did.'

'What was it?'

'My love for Allan Armadale.'

He cast a doubting, almost a timid, look at Mr Brock as he gave that answer; and, suddenly leaving the table, went back to the window-seat.

'Have I no right to speak of him in that way?' he asked, keeping his face hidden from the rector. 'Have I not known him long enough; have I not done enough for him yet? Remember what my experience of other men had been, when I first saw his hand held out to me; when I first heard his voice speaking to me in my sick room. What had I known of strangers' hands all through my childhood? I had only known them as hands raised to threaten and to strike me. *His* hand put my pillow straight, and patted me on the shoulder, and gave me my food and drink. What had I known of other men's voices, when I was growing up to be a man myself? I had only known them as voices that jeered, voices that cursed, voices that whispered in corners with a vile distrust. *His* voice said to me, "Cheer up, Midwinter! we'll soon bring you round again. You'll be strong enough in a week to go out for a drive with me in our Somersetshire lanes." Think of the gipsy's stick; think of the devils laughing at me when I went by their windows with my little dead dog in my arms; think of the master who cheated me of my month's salary on his death-bed – and ask your own heart if the miserable wretch whom Allan Armadale has treated as his equal and his friend, has said too much in saying that he loves him? I do love him! It *will* come out of me – I can't keep it back. I love the very ground he treads on! I would give my life – yes, the life that is precious to me now, because his kindness has made it a happy one – I tell you I would give my life—'

The next words died away on his lips; the hysterical passion rose, and conquered him. He stretched out one of his hands with a wild gesture of entreaty to Mr Brock; his head sank on the window-sill, and he burst into tears.

Even then, the hard discipline of the man's life asserted itself. He expected no sympathy; he counted on no merciful human respect for human weakness. The cruel necessity of self-suppression was present to his mind, while the tears were pouring over his cheeks. 'Give me a minute,' he said, faintly. 'I'll fight it down in a minute; I won't distress you in this way again.'

True to his resolution, in a minute he had fought it down. In a minute more he was able to speak calmly.

'We will get back, sir, to those better thoughts which brought me last night from my room to yours,'[4] he resumed. 'I can only repeat that I should never have torn myself from the hold which this letter fastened on me, if I had not loved Allan Armadale with all that I have in me of a brother's love. I said to myself, "If the thought of leaving him breaks my heart, the thought of leaving him is wrong!" That was some hours since – and I am in the same mind still. I can't believe – I won't believe – that a friendship which has grown out of nothing but kindness on one side, and nothing but gratitude on the other, is destined to lead to an evil end. I don't undervalue the strange circumstances which have made us namesakes – the strange circumstances which have brought us together, and attached us to each other – the strange circumstances which have since happened to us separately. They may, and they do, all link themselves together in my thoughts; but they shall not daunt me. I *won't* believe that these events have happened in the order of Fate, for an end that is evil – I *will* believe that they have happened in the order of God, for an end that is good. Judge, you who are a clergyman, between the dead father, whose word is in these pages, and the living son, whose word is now on his lips! Which am I – now that the two Allan Armadales have met again in the second generation – an instrument in the hands of Fate, or an instrument in the hands of Providence? What is it appointed me to do – now that I am breathing the same air, and living under the same roof with the son of the man whom my father killed – to perpetuate my father's crime by mortally injuring him? or to atone for my father's crime by giving him the devotion of my whole life? The last of those two faiths is my faith – and shall be my faith, happen what may. In the strength of that better conviction, I can face you resolutely with the one plain question, which marks the one plain end of all that I have come here to say. Your pupil stands at the starting-point of his new career, in a position singularly friendless; his one great need is a companion of his own age on whom he can rely. The time has come, sir, to decide whether I am to be that companion or not. After all you have heard of Ozias Midwinter, tell me plainly, will you trust him to be Allan Armadale's friend?'

Mr Brock met that fearlessly frank question by a fearless frankness on his side.

'I believe you love Allan,' he said; 'and I believe you have spoken the truth. A man who has produced that impression on me, is a man whom I am bound to trust. I trust you.'

Midwinter started to his feet – his dark face flushing deep; his eyes fixed brightly and steadily, at last, on the rector's face. 'A light!' he exclaimed, tearing the pages of his father's letter, one by one, from the fastening that held them. 'Let us destroy the last link that holds us to the horrible past! Let us see this confession a heap of ashes before we part!'

'Wait!' said Mr Brock. 'Before you burn it, there is a reason for looking at it once more.'

The parted leaves of the manuscript dropped from Midwinter's hands. Mr Brock took them up, and sorted them carefully until he found the last page.

'I view your father's superstition as you view it,' said the rector. 'But there is a warning given you here, which you will do well (for Allan's sake, and for your own sake,) not to neglect. The last link with the past will not be destroyed when you have burnt these pages. One of the actors in this story of treachery and murder is not dead yet. Read those words.'

He pushed the page across the table, with his finger on one sentence. Midwinter's agitation misled him. He mistook the indication, and read, 'Avoid the widow of the man I killed – if the widow still lives.'

'Not that sentence,' said the rector. 'The next.'

Midwinter read it: 'Avoid the maid whose wicked hand smoothed the way to the marriage – if the maid is still in her service.'

'The maid and the mistress parted,' said Mr Brock, 'at the time of the mistress's marriage. The maid and the mistress met again at Mrs Armadale's residence in Somersetshire, last year. I myself met the woman in the village, and I myself know that her visit hastened Mrs Armadale's death. Wait a little, and compose yourself; I see I have startled you.'

He waited as he was bid, his colour fading away to a grey paleness, and the light in his clear brown eyes dying out slowly. What the rector had said had produced no transient impression on him; there was more than doubt, there was alarm in his face, as he sat lost in his own thoughts. Was the struggle of the past night renewing itself already? Did he feel the horror of his hereditary superstition creeping over him again?

'Can you put me on my guard against her?' he asked, after a long interval of silence. 'Can you tell me her name?'

'I can only tell you what Mrs Armadale told me,' answered Mr Brock. 'The woman acknowledged having been married in the long interval since she and her mistress had last met. But not a word more escaped her about her past life. She came to Mrs Armadale to ask for money, under a plea of distress. She got the money, and she left the house, positively refusing, when the question was put to her, to mention her married name.'

'You saw her yourself in the village. What was she like?'

'She kept her veil down. I can't tell you.'

'You can tell me what you *did* see?'

'Certainly. I saw, as she approached me, that she moved very gracefully, that she had a beautiful figure, and that she was a little over the middle height. I noticed, when she asked me the way to Mrs Armadale's house, that her manner was the manner of a lady, and that the tone of her voice was remarkably soft and winning. Lastly, I remembered afterwards, that she wore a thick black veil, a black bonnet, a black silk dress, and a red Paisley shawl. I feel all the importance of your possessing some better means of identifying her than I can give you. But, unhappily—'

He stopped. Midwinter was leaning eagerly across the table, and Midwinter's hand was laid suddenly on his arm.

'Is it possible that you know the woman?' asked Mr Brock, surprised at the sudden change in his manner.

'No.'

'What have I said, then, that has startled you so?'

'Do you remember the woman who threw herself from the river steamer?' asked the other – 'the woman who caused that succession of deaths, which opened Allan Armadale's way to the Thorpe-Ambrose estate?'

'I remember the description of her in the police report,' answered the rector.

'*That* woman,' pursued Midwinter, 'moved gracefully, and had a beautiful figure. *That* woman wore a black veil, a black bonnet, a black silk gown, and a red Paisley shawl—' He stopped, released his hold of Mr Brock's arm, and abruptly resumed his chair. 'Can it be the same?' he said to himself, in a whisper. '*Is* there a fatality that follows men in the dark? And is it following *us* in that woman's footsteps?'

If the conjecture was right, the one event in the past which had appeared to be entirely disconnected with the events that had preceded it, was, on the contrary, the one missing link which made the chain complete. Mr Brock's comfortable common sense instinctively denied that startling conclusion.[5] He looked at Midwinter with a compassionate smile.

'My young friend,' he said kindly, 'have you cleared your mind of all superstition as completely as you think? Is what you have just said worthy of the better resolution at which you arrived last night?'

Midwinter's head drooped on his breast; the colour rushed back over his face: he sighed bitterly.

'You are beginning to doubt my sincerity,' he said. 'I can't blame you.'

'I believe in your sincerity as firmly as ever,' answered Mr Brock. 'I only doubt whether you have fortified the weak places in your nature as strongly as you yourself suppose. Many a man has lost the battle against himself far oftener than you have lost it yet, and has nevertheless won his victory in the end. I don't blame you, I don't distrust you. I only notice what has happened, to put you on your guard against yourself. Come! come! Let your own better sense help you; and you will agree with me, that there is really no evidence to justify the suspicion that the woman whom I met in Somersetshire, and the woman who attempted suicide in London, are one and the same. Need an old man, like me, remind a young man, like you, that there are thousands of women in England, with beautiful figures – thousands of women who are quietly dressed in black silk gowns and red Paisley shawls?'

Midwinter caught eagerly at the suggestion; too eagerly, as it might have occurred to a harder critic on humanity than Mr Brock.

'You are quite right, sir,' he said, 'and I am quite wrong. Tens of thousands of women answer the description, as you say. I have been wasting time on my own idle fancies, when I ought to have been carefully gathering up facts. If this woman ever attempts to find her way to Allan, I must be prepared to stop her.' He began searching restlessly among the manuscript leaves scattered about the table, paused over one of the pages, and examined it attentively. 'This helps me to something positive,' he went on; 'this helps me to a knowledge of her age. She was twelve at the time of Mrs Armadale's marriage; add a year, and bring her to thirteen; add Allan's age (twenty-two), and we make her a woman of five-and-thirty at the present time. I know her age; and I know that she has her own reasons for being silent about her married life. This is something gained at the outset, and it may lead, in time, to something more.' He looked up brightly again at Mr Brock. 'Am I in the right way now, sir? Am I doing my best to profit by the caution which you have kindly given me?'

'You are vindicating your own better sense,' answered the rector, encouraging him to trample down his own imagination, with an Englishman's ready distrust of the noblest of the human faculties. 'You are paving the way for your own happier life.'

'Am I?' said the other, thoughtfully.

He searched among the papers once more, and stopped at another of the scattered pages.

'The Ship!' he exclaimed suddenly, his colour changing again, and his manner altering on the instant.

'What ship?' asked the rector.

'The ship in which the deed was done,' Midwinter answered, with the first signs of impatience that he had shown yet. 'The ship in which my father's murderous hand turned the lock of the cabin door.'

'What of it?' said Mr Brock.

He appeared not to hear the question; his eyes remained fixed intently on the page that he was reading.

'A French vessel, employed in the timber-trade,' he said, still speaking to himself; 'a French vessel, named *La Grace de Dieu*. If my father's belief had been the right belief – if the Fatality had been following me, step by step, from my father's grave – in one or other of my voyages, I should have fallen in with that ship.' He looked up again at Mr Brock. 'I am quite sure about it now,' he said. 'Those women are two – and not one.'

Mr Brock shook his head.

'I am glad you have come to that conclusion,' he said. 'But I wish you had reached it in some other way.'

Midwinter started passionately to his feet, and seizing on the pages of the manuscript with both hands, flung them into the empty fireplace.

'For God's sake, let me burn it!' he exclaimed. 'As long as there is a page left, I shall read it. And, as long as I read it, my father gets the better of me, in spite of myself!'

Mr Brock pointed to the match-box. In another moment, the confession was in flames. When the fire had consumed the last morsel of paper, Midwinter drew a deep breath of relief.

'I may say, like Macbeth: "Why, so, being gone, I am a man again!"' he broke out with a feverish gaiety. 'You look fatigued, sir; and no wonder,' he added in a lower tone. 'I have kept you too long from your rest – I will keep you no longer. Depend on my remembering what you have told me; depend on my standing between Allan and any enemy, man or woman, who comes near him. Thank you, Mr Brock; a thousand, thousand times, thank you! I came into this room the most wretched of living men; I can leave it now as happy as the birds that are singing outside!'

As he turned to the door, the rays of the rising sun streamed through the window, and touched the heap of ashes lying black in the black fireplace. The sensitive imagination of Midwinter kindled instantly at the sight.

'Look!' he said, joyously. 'The promise of the Future shining over the ashes of the Past!'

An inexplicable pity for the man, at the moment of his life when he needed pity least, stole over the rector's heart, when the door had closed, and he was left by himself again.

'Poor fellow!' he said, with an uneasy surprise at his own compassionate impulse. 'Poor fellow!'

CHAPTER III

DAY AND NIGHT

The morning hours had passed; the noon had come and gone; and Mr Brock had started on the first stage of his journey home.

After parting from the rector in Douglas Harbour, the two young men had returned to Castletown, and had there separated at the hotel door, – Allan walking down to the waterside to look after his yacht, and Midwinter entering the house, to get the rest that he needed after a sleepless night.

He darkened his room; he closed his eyes – but no sleep came to him. On this first day of the rector's absence, his sensitive nature extravagantly exaggerated the responsibility which he now held in trust for Mr Brock. A nervous dread of leaving Allan by himself, even for a few hours only, kept him waking and doubting until it became a relief, rather than a hardship, to rise from the bed again, and following in Allan's footsteps, to take the way to the waterside which led to the yacht.

The repairs of the little vessel were nearly completed. It was a breezy, cheerful day; the land was bright, the water was blue, the quick waves leapt crisply in the sunshine, the men were singing at their work. Descending to the cabin, Midwinter discovered his friend busily occupied in attempting to set the place to rights. Habitually the least systematic of mortals, Allan now and then awoke to an overwhelming sense of the advantages of order – and on such occasions a perfect frenzy of tidiness possessed him. He was down on his knees, hotly and wildly at work, when Midwinter looked in on him; and was fast reducing the neat little world of the cabin to its original elements of chaos, with a misdirected energy wonderful to see.

'Here's a mess!' said Allan, rising composedly on the horizon of his own accumulated litter. 'Do you know, my dear fellow, I begin to wish I had let well alone.'

Midwinter smiled, and came to his friend's assistance with the natural neat-handedness of a sailor.

The first object that he encountered was Allan's dressing-case, turned upside down, with half the contents scattered on the floor, and with a duster and a hearth-broom lying among them. Replacing the various objects which formed the furniture of the dressing-case one by one, Midwinter lighted unexpectedly on a miniature portrait, of the old-fashioned oval form, primly framed in a setting of small diamonds.

'You don't seem to set much value on this,' he said. 'What is it?'

Allan bent over him, and looked at the miniature.

'It belonged to my mother,' he answered; 'and I set the greatest value on it. It is a portrait of my father.'

Midwinter put the miniature abruptly into Allan's hands, and with-drew to the opposite side of the cabin.

'You know best where the things ought to be put in your own dressing-case,' he said, keeping his back turned on Allan. 'I'll make the place tidy on this side of the cabin, and you shall make the place tidy on the other.'

He began setting in order the litter scattered about him, on the cabin table and on the floor. But it seemed as if fate had decided that his friend's personal possessions should fall into his hands that morning, employ them where he might. One among the first objects which he took up was Allan's tobacco-jar, with the stopper missing, and with a letter (which appeared by the bulk of it to contain enclosures) crumpled into the mouth of the jar in the stopper's place.

'Did you know that you had put this here?' he asked. 'Is the letter of any importance?'

Allan recognized it instantly. It was the first of the little series of letters which had followed the cruising party to the Isle of Man – the letter which young Armadale had briefly referred to as bringing him 'more worries from those everlasting lawyers,' and had then dismissed from further notice as recklessly as usual.

'This is what comes of being particularly careful,' said Allan; 'here is an instance of my extreme thoughtfulness. You may not think it, but I put the letter there on purpose. Every time I went to the jar, you know, I was sure to see the letter; and every time I saw the letter, I was sure to say to myself, "This must be answered." There's nothing to laugh at; it was a perfectly sensible arrangement – if I could only have remembered where I put the jar. Suppose I tie a knot in my pocket-handkerchief this time? You have a wonderful memory, my dear fellow. Perhaps you'll remind me in the course of the day, in case I forget the knot next.'

Midwinter saw his first chance, since Mr Brock's departure, of usefully filling Mr Brock's place.

'Here is your writing-case,' he said; 'why not answer the letter at once? If you put it away again, you may forget it again.'

'Very true,' returned Allan. 'But the worst of it is, I can't quite make up my mind what answer to write. I want a word of advice. Come and sit down here, and I'll tell you all about it.'

With his loud boyish laugh – echoed by Midwinter, who caught the infection of his gaiety – he swept a heap of miscellaneous encumbrances off the cabin sofa, and made room for his friend and himself to take their places. In the high flow of youthful spirits, the two sat down to their trifling consultation over a letter lost in a tobacco-jar. It was a memorable moment to both of them, lightly as they thought of it at the time. Before they had risen again from their places, they had taken the first irrevocable step together on the dark and tortuous road of their future lives.

Reduced to plain facts, the question on which Allan now required his friend's advice, may be stated as follows:

While the various arrangements connected with the succession to Thorpe-Ambrose were in progress of settlement, and while the new possessor of the estate was still in London, a question had necessarily arisen relating to the person who should be appointed to manage the property. The steward employed by the Blanchard family had written, without loss of time, to offer his services. Although a perfectly competent and trustworthy man, he failed to find favour in the eyes of the new proprietor. Acting, as usual, on his first impulses, and resolved, at all hazards, to install Midwinter as a permanent inmate at Thorpe-Ambrose, Allan had determined that the steward's place was the place exactly fitted for his friend – for the simple reason, that it would necessarily oblige his friend to live with him on the estate. He had accordingly written to decline the proposal made to him, without consulting Mr Brock, whose disapproval he had good reason to fear; and without telling Midwinter, who would probably (if a chance were allowed him of choosing) have declined taking a situation which his previous training had by no means fitted him to fill. Further correspondence had followed this decision, and had raised two new difficulties which looked a little embarrassing on the face of them, but which Allan, with the assistance of his lawyers, easily contrived to solve. The first difficulty, of examining the outgoing steward's books, was settled by sending a professional accountant to Thorpe-Ambrose; and the second difficulty, of putting the steward's empty cottage to some profitable use (Allan's plans for his friend comprehending Midwinter's residence under his own roof), was met by placing the cottage on the list of an active house-agent in the neighbouring county town. In this state the arrangements had been left when Allan quitted London. He had heard and thought nothing more of the matter, until a letter from the lawyers had followed him to the Isle of Man, enclosing two proposals to occupy the cottage – both received on the same day – and requesting to hear, at his earliest convenience, which of the two he was prepared to accept.

Finding himself, after having conveniently forgotten the subject for some days past, placed face to face once more with the necessity for decision, Allan now put the two proposals into his friend's hands, and, after a rambling explanation of the circumstances of the case, requested to be favoured with a word of advice. Instead of examining the proposals, Midwinter unceremoniously put them aside, and asked the two very natural and very awkward questions of who the new steward was to be, and why he was to live in Allan's house?

'I'll tell you who, and I'll tell you why, when we get to Thorpe-Ambrose,' said Allan. 'In the meantime, we'll call the steward X. Y. Z., and we'll say he lives with me, because I'm devilish sharp, and I mean to keep him under my own eye. You needn't look surprised. I know the man thoroughly well; he requires a good deal of management. If I offered him the steward's place beforehand, his modesty would get in his way, and he would say – "No." If I pitch him into it neck and crop, without a word of warning and with nobody at hand to relieve him of the situation, he'll have nothing for it but to consult my interests, and say – "Yes." X. Y. Z. is not at all a bad fellow, I can tell you. You'll see him when we go to Thorpe-Ambrose; and I rather think you and he will get on uncommonly well together.'

The humorous twinkle in Allan's eye, the sly significance in Allan's voice, would have betrayed his secret to a prosperous man. Midwinter was as far from suspecting it as the carpenters who were at work above them on the deck of the yacht.

'Is there no steward now on the estate?' he asked, his face showing plainly that he was far from feeling satisfied with Allan's answer. 'Is the business neglected all this time?'

'Nothing of the sort!' returned Allan. 'The business is going with "a wet sheet and a flowing sail, and a wind that follows free".[1] I'm not joking – I'm only metaphorical. A regular accountant has poked his nose into the books, and a steady-going lawyer's clerk attends at the office once a week. That doesn't look like neglect, does it? Leave the new steward alone for the present, and just tell me which of those two tenants you would take, if you were in my place.'

Midwinter opened the proposals, and read them attentively.

The first proposal was from no less a person than the solicitor at Thorpe-Ambrose, who had first informed Allan at Paris of the large fortune that had fallen into his hands. This gentleman wrote personally, to say that he had long admired the cottage, which was charmingly situated within the limits of the Thorpe-Ambrose grounds. He was a bachelor, of studious habits, desirous of retiring to a country seclusion after the wear and tear of his business hours; and he ventured to say that Mr Armadale, in accepting him as a tenant, might count on securing an unobtrusive neighbour, and on putting the cottage into responsible and careful hands.

The second proposal came through the house-agent, and proceeded from a total stranger. The tenant who offered for the cottage, in this case, was a retired officer in the army – one Major Milroy. His family merely consisted of an invalid wife and an only child – a young lady. His references were unexceptionable; and he, too, was especially anxious to secure the cottage, as the perfect quiet of the situation was exactly what was required by Mrs Milroy in her feeble state of health.

'Well! which profession shall I favour?' asked Allan. 'The army or the law?'

'There seems to me to be no doubt about it,' said Midwinter. 'The lawyer has been already in correspondence with you; and the lawyer's claim is, therefore, the claim to be preferred.'

'I knew you would say that. In all the thousands of times I have asked other people for advice, I never yet got the advice I wanted. Here's this business of letting the cottage as an instance. I'm all on the other side myself. I want to have the major.'

'Why?'

Young Armadale laid his forefinger on that part of the agent's letter which enumerated Major Milroy's family, and which contained the three words – 'a young lady'.

'A bachelor of studious habits walking about my grounds,' said Allan, 'is not an interesting object; a young lady is. I have not the least doubt Miss Milroy is a charming girl. Ozias Midwinter of the serious countenance! think of her pretty muslin dress flitting about among your trees and committing trespasses on your property; think of her adorable feet trotting into your fruit-garden, and her delicious fresh lips kissing your ripe peaches; think of her dimpled hands among your early violets, and her little cream-coloured nose buried in your blush-roses! What does the studious bachelor offer me, in exchange for the loss of all this? He offers me a rheumatic brown object in gaiters and a wig. No! no! Justice is good, my dear friend; but, believe me, Miss Milroy is better.'

'Can you be serious about any mortal thing, Allan?'

'I'll try to be, if you like. I know I ought to take the lawyer; but what can I do if the major's daughter keeps running in my head?'

Midwinter returned resolutely to the just and the sensible view of the matter, and pressed it on his friend's attention with all the persuasion of which he was master. After listening with exemplary patience until he had done, Allan swept a supplementary accumulation of litter off the cabin table, and produced from his waistcoat-pocket a half-crown coin.

'I've got an entirely new idea,' he said. 'Let's leave it to chance.'

The absurdity of the proposal – as coming from a landlord – was irresistible. Midwinter's gravity deserted him.

'I'll spin,' continued Allan, 'and you shall call. We must give precedence to the army, of course; so we'll say Heads, the major; Tails, the lawyer. One spin to decide. Now, then, look out!'

He spun the half-crown on the cabin table.

'Tails!' cried Midwinter, humouring what he believed to be one of Allan's boyish jokes.

The coin fell on the table with the Head uppermost.

'You don't mean to say you are really in earnest!' said Midwinter, as the other opened his writing-case and dipped his pen in the ink.

'Oh, but I am, though!' replied Allan. 'Chance is on my side, and Miss Milroy's; and you're outvoted, two to one. It's no use arguing. The major has fallen uppermost, and the major shall have the cottage. I won't leave it to the lawyers – they'll only be worrying me with more letters; I'll write myself.'

He wrote his answers to the two proposals, literally in two minutes. One to the house-agent: 'Dear sir, I accept Major Milroy's offer; let him come in when he pleases. Yours truly, Allan Armadale.' And one to the lawyer: 'Dear sir, I regret that circumstances prevent me from accepting your proposal. Yours truly, &c., &c.' 'People make a fuss about letter-writing,' Allan remarked, when he had done. '*I* find it easy enough.'

He wrote the addresses on his two notes, and stamped them for the post, whistling gaily. While he had been writing, he had not noticed how his friend was occupied. When he had done, it struck him that a sudden silence had fallen on the cabin; and, looking up, he observed

that Midwinter's whole attention was strangely concentrated on the
half-crown, as it lay head uppermost on the table. Allan suspended his
whistling in astonishment.

'What on earth are you doing?' he asked.

'I was only wondering,' replied Midwinter.

'What about?' persisted Allan.

'I was wondering,' said the other, handing him back the half-crown,
'whether there is such a thing as chance.'

Half-an-hour later, the two notes were posted; and Allan, whose close
superintendence of the repairs of the yacht had hitherto allowed him
but little leisure-time on shore, had proposed to wile away the idle
hours by taking a walk in Castletown. Even Midwinter's nervous
anxiety to deserve Mr Brock's confidence in him, could detect nothing
objectionable in this harmless proposal, and the young men set forth
together to see what they could make of the metropolis of the Isle of
Man.

It is doubtful if there is a place on the habitable globe which,
regarded as a sight-seeing investment offering itself to the spare attention
of strangers, yields so small a per-centage of interest in return, as
Castletown. Beginning with the waterside, there was an inner harbour
to see, with a drawbridge to let vessels through; an outer harbour,
ending in a dwarf lighthouse; a view of a flat coast to the right, and a
view of a flat coast to the left. In the central solitudes of the city, there
was a squat grey building called 'the castle'; also a memorial pillar
dedicated to one Governor Smelt,[2] with a flat top for a statue, and no
statue standing on it; also a barrack, holding the half company of
soldiers allotted to the island, and exhibiting one spirit-broken sentry at
its lonely door. The prevalent colour of the town was faint grey. The
few shops open were parted at frequent intervals by other shops closed
and deserted in despair. The weary lounging of boatmen on shore was
trebly weary here; the youth of the district smoked together in speechless
depression under the lee of a dead wall; the ragged children said
mechanically, 'Give us a penny', and before the charitable hand could
search the merciful pocket, lapsed away again in misanthropic doubt of
the human nature they addressed. The silence of the grave overflowed
the churchyard, and filled this miserable town. But one edifice, prosperous to look at, rose consolatory in the desolation of these dreadful
streets. Frequented by the students of the neighbouring 'College of King
William',[3] this building was naturally dedicated to the uses of a pastrycook's shop. Here, at least (viewed through the friendly medium of the

window), there was something going on for a stranger to see; for here, on high stools, the pupils of the college sat, with swinging legs and slowly-moving jaws, and, hushed in the horrid stillness of Castletown, gorged their pastry gravely, in an atmosphere of awful silence.

'Hang me if I can look any longer at the boys and the tarts!' said Allan, dragging his friend away from the pastrycook's shop. 'Let's try if we can't find something else to amuse us in the next street.'

The first amusing object which the next street presented was a carver-and-gilder's shop, expiring feebly in the last stage of commercial decay. The counter inside displayed nothing to view but the recumbent head of a boy, peacefully asleep in the unbroken solitude of the place. In the window were exhibited to the passing stranger three forlorn little fly-spotted frames; a small posting-bill, dusty with long-continued neglect, announcing that the premises were to let; and one coloured print, the last of a series illustrating the horrors of drunkenness, on the fiercest temperance principles. The composition – representing an empty bottle of gin, an immensely spacious garret, a perpendicular Scripture-reader, and a horizontal expiring family – appealed to public favour, under the entirely unobjectionable title of The Hand of Death. Allan's resolution to extract amusement from Castletown by main force had resisted a great deal, but it failed him at this stage of the investigations. He suggested trying an excursion to some other place. Midwinter readily agreeing, they went back to the hotel to make inquiries. Thanks to the mixed influence of Allan's ready gift of familiarity, and total want of method in putting his questions, a perfect deluge of information flowed in on the two strangers, relating to every subject but the subject which had actually brought them to the hotel. They made various interesting discoveries in connection with the laws and constitution of the Isle of Man, and the manners and customs of the natives. To Allan's delight, the Manxmen spoke of England as of a well-known adjacent island, situated at a certain distance from the central empire of the Isle of Man. It was further revealed to the two Englishmen that this happy little nation rejoiced in laws of its own, publicly proclaimed once a year by the governor and the two head-judges, grouped together on the top of an ancient mound, in fancy costumes appropriate to the occasion. Possessing this enviable institution, the island added to it the inestimable blessing of a local parliament, called the House of Keys, an assembly far in advance of the other parliament belonging to the neighbouring island, in this respect – that the members dispensed with the people, and solemnly elected each other. With these, and many more local particulars, extracted from all sorts and conditions of men, in and about the hotel, Allan wiled away the weary time in his own essentially desultory manner, until the gossip died out of itself, and Midwinter (who had been speaking apart with the landlord) quietly recalled him to the matter in hand. The finest coast scenery in the island was said to be to the westward and the southward, and there was a fishing town in those regions called Port St Mary, with an hotel at which travellers could sleep. If Allan's impressions of Castletown still inclined him to try an excursion to some other place, he had only to say so, and a carriage would be produced immediately. Allan jumped at the proposal, and in ten minutes more, he and Midwinter were on their way to the western wilds of the island.

With trifling incidents, the day of Mr Brock's departure had worn on thus far. With trifling incidents, in which not even Midwinter's nervous watchfulness could see anything to distrust, it was still to proceed, until the night came − a night which one at least of the two companions was destined to remember to the end of his life.

Before the travellers had advanced two miles on their road, an accident happened. The horse fell, and the driver reported that the animal had seriously injured himself. There was no alternative but to send for another carriage to Castletown, or to get on to Port St Mary on foot. Deciding to walk, Midwinter and Allan had not gone far before they were overtaken by a gentleman driving alone in an open chaise. He civilly introduced himself as a medical man, living close to Port St Mary, and offered seats in his carriage. Always ready to make new acquaintances, Allan at once accepted the proposal. He and the doctor (whose name was ascertained to be Hawbury) became friendly and familiar before they had been five minutes in the chaise together; Midwinter sitting behind them, reserved and silent, on the back seat. They separated just outside Port St Mary, before Mr Hawbury's house, Allan boisterously admiring the doctor's neat French windows, and pretty flower-garden and lawn; and wringing his hand at parting, as if they had known each other from boyhood upwards. Arrived in Port St Mary, the two friends found themselves in a second Castletown on a smaller scale. But the country round, wild, open, and hilly, deserved its reputation. A walk brought them well enough on with the day − still the harmless, idle day that it had been from the first − to see the evening near at hand. After waiting a little to admire the sun, setting grandly over hill, and heath, and crag, and talking, while they waited, of Mr Brock and his long journey home − they returned to the hotel to order their early supper. Nearer and nearer, the night, and the adventure which the night was to bring with it, came to the two friends; and still the only incidents that happened were incidents to be laughed at, if they were noticed at all. The supper was badly cooked; the waiting-maid was impenetrably stupid; the old-fashioned bell-rope in the coffee-room had come down in Allan's hands, and striking in its descent a painted china shepherdess on the chimney-piece, had laid the figure in fragments on the floor. Events as trifling as these were still the only events that had happened, when the twilight faded, and the lighted candles were brought into the room.

Finding Midwinter, after the double fatigue of a sleepless night and a restless day, but little inclined for conversation, Allan left him resting on the sofa, and lounged into the passage of the hotel, on the chance of discovering somebody to talk to. Here, another of the trivial incidents of the day brought Allan and Mr Hawbury together again, and helped – whether happily, or not, yet remained to be seen – to strengthen the acquaintance between them on either side.

The 'bar' of the hotel was situated at one end of the passage, and the landlady was in attendance there, mixing a glass of liquor for the doctor, who had just looked in for a little gossip. On Allan's asking permission to make a third in the drinking and the gossiping, Mr Hawbury civilly handed him the glass which the landlady had just filled. It contained cold brandy-and-water. A marked change in Allan's face, as he suddenly drew back and asked for whisky instead, caught the doctor's medical eye. 'A case of nervous antipathy,' said Mr Hawbury, quietly taking the glass away again. The remark obliged Allan to acknowledge that he had an insurmountable loathing (which he was foolish enough to be a little ashamed of mentioning) to the smell and taste of brandy. No matter with what diluting liquid the spirit was mixed, the presence of it – instantly detected by his organs of taste and smell – turned him sick and faint, if the drink touched his lips. Starting from this personal confession, the talk turned on anti-pathies in general; and the doctor acknowledged, on his side, that he took a professional interest in the subject, and that he possessed a collection of curious cases at home, which his new acquaintance was welcome to look at, if Allan had nothing else to do that evening, and if he would call, when the medical work of the day was over, in an hour's time.

Cordially accepting the invitation (which was extended to Midwinter also, if he cared to profit by it), Allan returned to the coffee-room to look after his friend. Half asleep and half awake, Midwinter was still stretched on the sofa, with the local newspaper just dropping out of his languid hand.

'I heard your voice in the passage,' he said drowsily. 'Who were you talking to?'

'The doctor,' replied Allan. 'I am going to smoke a cigar with him, in an hour's time. Will you come too?'

Midwinter assented with a weary sigh. Always shyly unwilling to make new acquaintances, fatigue increased the reluctance he now felt to become Mr Hawbury's guest. As matters stood, however, there was no alternative but to go – for, with Allan's constitutional imprudence, there was no safely trusting him alone anywhere, and more especially in a stranger's house. Mr Brock would certainly not have left his pupil to visit the doctor alone; and Midwinter was still nervously conscious that he occupied Mr Brock's place.

'What shall we do till it's time to go?' asked Allan, looking about him. 'Anything in this?' he added, observing the fallen newspaper, and picking it up from the floor.

'I'm too tired to look. If you find anything interesting, read it out,' said Midwinter – thinking that the reading might help to keep him awake.

Part of the newspaper, and no small part of it, was devoted to extracts from books recently published in London. One of the works most largely laid under contribution in this manner, was of the sort to interest Allan: it was a highly-spiced narrative of Travelling Adventures in the wilds of Australia.[4] Pouncing on an extract which described the sufferings of the travelling-party, lost in a trackless wilderness, and in danger of dying by thirst, Allan announced that he had found something to make his friend's flesh creep, and began eagerly to read the passage aloud. Resolute not to sleep, Midwinter followed the progress of the adventure, sentence by sentence, without missing a word. The consultation of the lost travellers, with death by thirst staring them in the face; the resolution to press on while their strength lasted; the fall of a heavy shower, the vain efforts made to catch the rain-water, the transient relief experienced by sucking their wet clothes; the sufferings renewed a few hours after; the night-advance of the strongest of the party, leaving the weakest behind; the following a flight of birds, when morning dawned; the discovery by the lost men of the broad pool of water that saved their lives – all this, Midwinter's fast failing attention mastered painfully; Allan's voice growing fainter and fainter on his ear, with every sentence that was read. Soon, the next words seemed to drop away gently, and nothing but the slowly-sinking sound of the voice was left. Then, the light in the room darkened gradually; the sound dwindled into delicious silence; and the last waking impressions of the weary Midwinter came peacefully to an end.

The next event of which he was conscious, was a sharp ringing at the closed door of the hotel. He started to his feet, with the ready alacrity of a man whose life has accustomed him to wake at the shortest notice. An instant's look round showed him that the room was empty; and a glance at his watch told him that it was close on midnight. The noise made by the sleepy servant in opening the door, and the tread the next moment of quick footsteps in the passage, filled him with a sudden foreboding of something wrong. As he hurriedly stepped forward to go out and make inquiry, the door of the coffee-room opened, and the doctor stood before him.

'I am sorry to disturb you,' said Mr Hawbury. 'Don't be alarmed; there's nothing wrong.'

'Where is my friend?' asked Midwinter.

'At the pier-head,' answered the doctor. 'I am, to a certain extent, responsible for what he is doing now; and I think some careful person, like yourself, ought to be with him.'

The hint was enough for Midwinter. He and the doctor set out for the pier immediately – Mr Hawbury mentioning, on the way, the circumstances under which he had come to the hotel.

Punctual to the appointed hour, Allan had made his appearance at the doctor's house; explaining that he had left his weary friend so fast asleep on the sofa that he had not had the heart to wake him. The evening had passed pleasantly, and the conversation had turned on many subjects – until, in an evil hour, Mr Hawbury had dropped a hint which showed that he was fond of sailing, and that he possessed a pleasure-boat of his own in the harbour. Excited on the instant by his favourite topic, Allan had left his host no hospitable alternative but to take him to the pier-head and show him the boat. The beauty of the night and the softness of the breeze had done the rest of the mischief – they had filled Allan with irresistible longings for a sail by moonlight. Prevented from accompanying his guest by professional hindrances which obliged him to remain on shore, the doctor, not knowing what else to do, had ventured on disturbing Midwinter, rather than take the responsibility of allowing Mr Armadale (no matter how well he might be accustomed to the sea) to set off on a sailing trip at midnight entirely by himself.

The time taken to make this explanation brought Midwinter and the doctor to the pier-head. There, sure enough, was young Armadale in the boat, hoisting the sail, and singing the sailor's 'Yo-heave-ho!' at the top of his voice.

'Come along, old boy!' cried Allan. 'You're just in time for a frolic by moonlight!'

Midwinter suggested a frolic by daylight, and an adjournment to bed in the meantime.

'Bed!' cried Allan, on whose harum-scarum high spirits Mr Hawbury's hospitality had certainly not produced a sedative effect. 'Hear him, doctor! one would think he was ninety! Bed, you drowsy old dormouse! Look at that – and think of bed, if you can!'

He pointed to the sea. The moon was shining in the cloudless heaven; the night-breeze blew soft and steady from the land; the peaceful waters rippled joyfully in the silence and the glory of the night. Midwinter turned to the doctor, with a wise resignation to circumstances: he had seen enough to satisfy him that all words of remonstrance would be words simply thrown away.

'How is the tide?' he asked.

Mr Hawbury told him.

'Are the oars in the boat?'

'Yes.'

'I am well used to the sea,' said Midwinter, descending the pier-steps. 'You may trust me to take care of my friend, and to take care of the boat.'

'Good-night, doctor!' shouted Allan. 'Your whisky-and-water is delicious – your boat's a little beauty – and you're the best fellow I ever met in my life!'

The doctor laughed, and waved his hand; and the boat glided out from the harbour, with Midwinter at the helm.

As the breeze then blew, they were soon abreast of the westward headland, bounding the bay of Poolvash; and the question was started whether they should run out to sea, or keep along the shore. The wisest proceeding, in the event of the wind failing them, was to keep by the land. Midwinter altered the course of the boat, and they sailed on smoothly in a south-westerly direction, abreast of the coast.

Little by little the cliffs rose in height, and the rocks, massed wild and jagged, showed rifted black chasms yawning deep in their seaward sides. Off the bold promontory called Spanish Head, Midwinter looked ominously at his watch. But Allan pleaded hard for half-an-hour more, and for a glance at the famous channel of the Sound, which they were now fast nearing, and of which he had heard some startling stories from the workmen employed on his yacht. The new change which Midwinter's compliance with this request rendered it necessary to make in the course of the boat, brought her close to the wind; and revealed, on one side, the grand view of the southernmost shores of the Isle of Man, and, on the other, the black precipices of the islet called the Calf, separated from the mainland by the dark and dangerous channel of the Sound.

Once more Midwinter looked at his watch. 'We have gone far enough,' he said. 'Stand by the sheet!'

'Stop!' cried Allan, from the bows of the boat. 'Good God! here's a wrecked ship right ahead of us!'

Midwinter let the boat fall off a little, and looked where the other pointed.

There, stranded midway between the rocky boundaries on either side of the Sound – there, never again to rise on the living waters from her grave on the sunken rock; lost and lonely in the quiet night; high, and dark, and ghostly in the yellow moonshine, lay the Wrecked Ship.

'I know the vessel,' said Allan, in great excitement. 'I heard my workmen talking of her yesterday. She drifted in here, on a pitch dark night, when they couldn't see the lights. A poor old worn-out merchant-man, Midwinter, that the shipbrokers have bought to break up. Let's run in, and have a look at her.'

Midwinter hesitated. All the old sympathies of his sea-life strongly inclined him to follow Allan's suggestion – but the wind was falling light; and he distrusted the broken water and the swirling currents of the channel ahead. 'This is an ugly place to take a boat into, when you know nothing about it,' he said.

'Nonsense!' returned Allan. 'It's as light as day, and we float in two feet of water.'

Before Midwinter could answer, the current caught the boat, and swept them onward through the channel, straight towards the Wreck.

'Lower the sail,' said Midwinter quietly, 'and ship the oars. We are running down on her fast enough now; whether we like it or not.'

Both well accustomed to the use of the oar, they brought the course of the boat under sufficient control to keep her on the smoothest side of the channel – the side which was nearest to the Islet of the Calf. As they came swiftly up with the wreck, Midwinter resigned his oar to Allan; and, watching his opportunity, caught a hold with the boat-hook on the forechains of the vessel. The next moment they had the boat safely in hand, under the lee of the Wreck.

The ship's ladder used by the workmen hung over the forechains. Mounting it, with the boat's rope in his teeth, Midwinter secured one end, and lowered the other to Allan in the boat. 'Make that fast,' he said, 'and wait till I see if it's safe on board.' With those words, he disappeared behind the bulwark.

'Wait?' repeated Allan, in the blankest astonishment at his friend's excessive caution. 'What on earth does he mean? I'll be hanged if I wait – where one of us goes, the other goes too!'

He hitched the loose end of the rope round the forward thwart of the boat; and, swinging himself up the ladder, stood the next moment on the deck. 'Anything very dreadful on board?' he inquired sarcastically, as he and his friend met.

Midwinter smiled. 'Nothing whatever,' he replied. 'But I couldn't be sure that we were to have the whole ship to ourselves, till I got over the bulwark, and looked about me.'

Allan took a turn on the deck, and surveyed the wreck critically from stem to stern.

'Not much of a vessel,' he said; 'the Frenchmen generally build better ships than this.'

Midwinter crossed the deck, and eyed Allan in a momentary silence.

'Frenchmen?' he repeated, after an interval. 'Is this vessel French?'

'Yes.'

'How do you know?'

'The men I have got at work on the yacht told me. They know all about her.'

Midwinter came a little nearer. His swarthy face began to look, to Allan's eyes, unaccountably pale in the moonlight.

'Did they mention what trade she was engaged in?'

'Yes. – The timber-trade.'

As Allan gave that answer, Midwinter's lean brown hand clutched him fast by the shoulder; and Midwinter's teeth chattered in his head, like the teeth of a man struck by a sudden chill.

'Did they tell you her name?' he asked, in a voice that dropped suddenly to a whisper.

'They did, I think. But it has slipped my memory. – Gently, old fellow; those long claws of yours are rather tight on my shoulder.'

'Was the name—?' he stopped; removed his hand; and dashed away the great drops that were gathering on his forehead – 'Was the name *La Grace de Dieu*?'

'How the deuce did you come to know it? That's the name, sure enough. *La Grace de Dieu*.'

At one bound, Midwinter leapt on the bulwark of the wreck.

'The boat!!!' he cried, with a scream of horror that rang far and wide through the stillness of the night, and brought Allan instantly to his side.

The lower end of the carelessly-hitched rope was loose on the water; and, a-head, in the track of the moonlight, a small black object was floating out of view. The boat was adrift.

CHAPTER IV

THE SHADOW OF THE PAST

One stepping back under the dark shelter of the bulwark, and one standing out boldly in the yellow light of the moon, the two friends turned face to face on the deck of the timber-ship, and looked at each other in silence. The next moment Allan's inveterate recklessness seized on the grotesque side of the situation by main force. He seated himself astride on the bulwark, and burst out boisterously into his loudest and heartiest laugh.

'All my fault,' he said; 'but there's no help for it now. Here we are, hard and fast in a trap of our own setting – and there goes the last of the doctor's boat! Come out of the dark, Midwinter; I can't half see you there, and I want to know what's to be done next.'

Midwinter neither answered nor moved. Allan left the bulwark, and, mounting the forecastle, looked down attentively at the waters of the Sound.

'One thing is pretty certain,' he said. 'With the current on that side, and the sunken rocks on this, we can't find our way out of the scrape by swimming, at any rate. So much for the prospect at this end of the wreck. Let's try how things look at the other. Rouse up, messmate!' he called out cheerfully, as he passed Midwinter. 'Come and see what the old tub of a timber-ship has got to show us, astern.' He sauntered on, with his hands in his pockets, humming the chorus of a comic song.

His voice had produced no apparent effect on his friend; but, at the light touch of his hand, in passing, Midwinter started, and moved out slowly from the shadow of the bulwark. 'Come along!' cried Allan, suspending his singing for a moment, and glancing back. Still, without a word of answer, the other followed. Thrice he stopped before he reached the stern end of the wreck: the first time, to throw aside his hat, and push back his hair from his forehead and temples; the second time, reeling giddily, to hold for a moment by a ring-bolt close at hand; the last time (though Allan was plainly visible a few yards a-head), to look stealthily behind him, with the furtive scrutiny of a man who believes that other footsteps are following him in the dark. 'Not yet!' he whispered to himself, with eyes that searched the empty air. 'I shall see him astern, with his hand on the lock of the cabin door.'

The stern end of the wreck was clear of the ship-breaker's lumber, accumulated in the other parts of the vessel. Here, the one object that rose visible on the smooth surface of the deck, was the low wooden structure which held the cabin door, and roofed in the cabin stairs. The wheel-house had been removed, the binnacle had been removed; but the cabin entrance, and all that belonged to it, had been left untouched. The scuttle was on, and the door was closed.

On gaining the after-part of the vessel, Allan walked straight to the stern, and looked out to sea over the taffrail. No such thing as a boat was in view anywhere on the quiet moon-brightened waters. Knowing Midwinter's sight to be better than his own, he called out, 'Come up here, and see if there's a fisherman within hail of us.' Hearing no reply, he looked back. Midwinter had followed him as far as the cabin, and had stopped there. He called again, in a louder voice, and beckoned impatiently. Midwinter had heard the call, for he looked up – but still he never stirred from his place. There he stood, as if he had reached the utmost limits of the ship and could go no further.

Allan went back and joined him. It was not easy to discover what he was looking at, for he kept his face turned away from the moonlight; but it seemed as if his eyes were fixed, with a strange expression of inquiry, on the cabin door. 'What is there to look at there?' Allan asked. 'Let's see if it's locked.' As he took a step forward to open the door, Midwinter's hand seized him suddenly by the coat-collar and forced him back. The moment after, the hand relaxed, without losing its grasp, and trembled violently, like the hand of a man completely unnerved.

'Am I to consider myself in custody?' asked Allan, half astonished and half amused. 'Why, in the name of wonder, do you keep staring at the cabin door? Any suspicious noises below? It's no use disturbing the rats – if that's what you mean – we haven't got a dog with us. Men? Living men they can't be; for they would have heard us and come on deck. Dead men? Quite impossible! No ship's crew could be drowned in a landlocked place like this, unless the vessel broke up under them – and here's the vessel as steady as a church to speak for herself. Man alive, how your hand trembles! What is there to scare you in that rotten old cabin? What are you shaking and shivering about? Any company of the supernatural sort on board? Mercy preserve us! (as the old women say,) do you see a ghost?'

'*I see two!*' answered the other, driven headlong into speech and action by a maddening temptation to reveal the truth. 'Two!' he repeated, his breath bursting from him in deep, heavy gasps, as he tried vainly to force back the horrible words. 'The ghost of a man like you, drowning in the cabin! And the ghost of a man like me, turning the lock of the door on him!'

Once more, young Armadale's hearty laughter rang out loud and long through the stillness of the night.

'Turning the lock of the door, is he?' said Allan, as soon as his merriment left him breath enough to speak. 'That's a devilish unhandsome action, Master Midwinter, on the part of your ghost. The least I can do, after that, is to let mine out of the cabin, and give him the run of the ship.'

With no more than a momentary exertion of his superior strength, he freed himself easily from Midwinter's hold. 'Below there!' he called out gaily, as he laid his strong hand on the crazy lock, and tore open the cabin door. 'Ghost of Allan Armadale, come on deck!' In his terrible ignorance of the truth, he put his head into the doorway, and looked down, laughing, at the place where his murdered father had died. 'Pah!' he exclaimed, stepping back suddenly, with a shudder of disgust. 'The air is foul already – and the cabin is full of water.'

It was true. The sunken rocks on which the vessel lay wrecked had burst their way through her lower timbers astern, and the water had welled up through the rifted wood. Here, where the deed had been done, the fatal parallel between past and present was complete. What the cabin had been in the time of the fathers, that the cabin was now in the time of the sons.

Allan pushed the door to again with his foot, a little surprised at the sudden silence which appeared to have fallen on his friend, from the moment when he had laid his hand on the cabin lock. When he turned to look, the reason of the silence was instantly revealed. Midwinter had dropped on the deck. He lay senseless before the cabin door; his face turned up, white and still, to the moonlight, like the face of a dead man.

In a moment, Allan was at his side. He looked uselessly round the lonely limits of the wreck, as he lifted Midwinter's head on his knee, for a chance of help, where all chance was ruthlessly cut off. 'What am I to do?' he said to himself, in the first impulse of alarm. 'Not a drop of water near, but the foul water in the cabin.' A sudden recollection crossed his memory; the florid colour rushed back over his face; and he drew from his pocket a wicker-covered flask. 'God bless the doctor for giving me this before we sailed!' he broke out fervently, as he poured down Midwinter's throat some drops of the raw whiskey which the flask contained. The stimulant acted instantly on the sensitive system of the swooning man. He sighed faintly, and slowly opened his eyes. 'Have I been dreaming?' he asked, looking up vacantly in Allan's face. His eyes wandered higher, and encountered the dismantled masts of the wreck rising weird and black against the night sky. He shuddered at the sight of them, and hid his face on Allan's knee. 'No dream!' he murmured to himself, mournfully. 'Oh me, no dream!'

'You have been over-tired all day,' said Allan; 'and this infernal adventure of ours has upset you. Take some more whiskey – it's sure to do you good. Can you sit by yourself, if I put you against the bulwark, so?'

'Why by myself? Why do you leave me?' asked Midwinter.

Allan pointed to the mizen shrouds of the wreck, which were still left standing. 'You are not well enough to rough it here till the workmen come off in the morning,' he said. 'We must find our way on shore at once, if we can. I am going up to get a good view all round, and see if there's a house within hail of us.'

Even in the moment that passed while those few words were spoken, Midwinter's eyes wandered back distrustfully to the fatal cabin door. 'Don't go near it!' he whispered. 'Don't try to open it, for God's sake!'

'No, no,' returned Allan, humouring him. 'When I come down from the rigging, I'll come back here.' He said the words a little constrainedly; noticing, for the first time while he now spoke, an underlying distress in Midwinter's face, which grieved and perplexed him. 'You're not angry with me?' he said, in his simple, sweet-tempered way. 'All this is my fault, I know – and I was a brute and a fool to laugh at you, when I ought to have seen you were ill. I am so sorry, Midwinter. Don't be angry with me!'

Midwinter slowly raised his head. His eyes rested with a mournful interest, long and tenderly on Allan's anxious face.

'Angry?' he repeated, in his lowest, gentlest tones. 'Angry with *you*? – Oh, my poor boy, were you to blame for being kind to me when I was ill in the old west-country inn? And was I to blame for feeling your kindness thankfully? Was it our fault that we never doubted each other, and never knew that we were travelling together blindfold on the way that was to lead us here? The cruel time is coming, Allan, when we shall rue the day we ever met. Shake hands, brother, on the edge of the precipice – shake hands while we are brothers still?'[1]

Allan turned away quickly, convinced that his mind had not yet recovered the shock of the fainting fit. 'Don't forget the whiskey!' he said cheerfully, as he sprang into the rigging, and mounted to the mizen-top.

It was past two; the moon was waning; and the darkness that comes before dawn was beginning to gather round the wreck. Behind Allan, as he now stood looking out from the elevation of the mizen-top, spread the broad and lonely sea. Before him, were the low, black, lurking rocks, and the broken waters of the Channel, pouring white and angry into the vast calm of the westward ocean beyond. On the right hand, heaved back grandly from the waterside, were the rocks and precipices, with their little table-lands of grass between; the sloping downs, and upward-rolling heath solitudes of the Isle of Man. On the left hand, rose the craggy sides of the Islet of the Calf – here, rent wildly into deep black chasms; there, lying low under long sweeping acclivities of grass and heath. No sound rose, no light was visible, on either shore. The black lines of the topmost masts of the wreck looked shadowy and faint in the darkening mystery of the sky; the land-breeze had dropped; the small shoreward waves fell noiseless: far or near, no sound was audible but the cheerless bubbling of the broken water ahead, pouring through the awful hush of silence in which earth and ocean waited for the coming day.

Even Allan's careless nature felt the solemn influence of the time. The sound of his own voice startled him, when he looked down and hailed his friend on deck.

'I think I see one house,' he said. 'Hereaway, on the mainland to the right.' He looked again, to make sure, at a dim little patch of white, with faint white lines behind it, nestling low in a grassy hollow, on the main island. 'It looks like a stone house and enclosure,' he resumed. 'I'll hail it, on the chance.' He passed his arm round a rope to steady himself; made a speaking-trumpet of his hands – and suddenly dropped them again without uttering a sound. 'It's so awfully quiet,' he whispered to himself. 'I'm half afraid to call out.' He looked down again on deck. 'I shan't startle you, Midwinter – shall I?' he said, with an uneasy laugh. He looked once more at the faint white object in the grassy hollow. 'It won't do to have come up here for nothing,' he thought – and made a speaking-trumpet of his hands again. This time he gave the hail with the whole power of his lungs. 'On shore there!' he shouted, turning his face to the main island. 'Ahoy-hoy-hoy!'

The last echoes of his voice died away and were lost. No sound answered him but the cheerless bubbling of the broken water ahead.

He looked down again at his friend, and saw the dark figure of Midwinter rise erect, and pace the deck backwards and forwards – never disappearing out of sight of the cabin, when it retired towards the bows of the wreck; and never passing beyond the cabin, when it returned towards the stern. 'He is impatient to get away,' thought

Allan; 'I'll try again.' He hailed the land once more; and, taught by previous experience, pitched his voice in its highest key.

This time, another sound than the sound of the bubbling water answered him. The lowing of frightened cattle rose from the building in the grassy hollow, and travelled far and drearily through the stillness of the morning air. Allan waited and listened. If the building was a farmhouse, the disturbance among the beasts would rouse the men. If it was only a cattle-stable, nothing more would happen. The lowing of the frightened brutes rose and fell drearily; the minutes passed – and nothing happened.

'Once more!' said Allan, looking down at the restless figure pacing beneath him. For the third time he hailed the land. For the third time he waited and listened.

In a pause of silence among the cattle, he heard behind him, on the opposite shore of the channel – faint and far among the solitudes of the Islet of the Calf – a sharp, sudden sound, like the distant clash of a heavy doorbolt drawn back. Turning at once in the new direction, he strained his eyes to look for a house. The last faint rays of the waning moonlight trembled here and there on the higher rocks, and on the steeper pinnacles of ground – but great strips of darkness lay dense and black over all the land between; and in that darkness the house, if house there were, was lost to view.

'I have roused somebody at last,' Allan called out encouragingly to Midwinter, still walking to and fro on the deck, strangely indifferent to all that was passing above and beyond him. 'Look out for the answering hail!' And with his face set towards the Islet, Allan shouted for help.

The shout was not answered, but mimicked with a shrill, shrieking derision – with wilder and wilder cries, rising out of the deep distant darkness, and mingling horribly the expression of a human voice with the sound of a brute's. A sudden suspicion crossed Allan's mind, which made his head swim and turned his hand cold as it held the rigging. In breathless silence he looked towards the quarter from which the first mimicry of his cry for help had come. After a moment's pause the shrieks were renewed, and the sound of them came nearer. Suddenly a figure, which seemed the figure of a man, leapt up black on a pinnacle of rock, and capered and shrieked in the waning gleam of the moonlight. The screams of a terrified woman mingled with the cries of the capering creature on the rock. A red spark flashed out in the darkness from a light kindled in an invisible window. The hoarse shouting of a man's voice in anger, was heard through the noise. A second black figure leapt up on the rock, struggled with the first figure, and disappeared with it in the darkness. The cries grew fainter and fainter – the screams of the woman were stilled – the hoarse voice of the man was heard again for a moment, hailing the wreck in words made unintelligible by the distance, but in tones plainly expressive of rage and fear combined. Another moment, and the clang of the door-bolt was heard again; the red spark of light was quenched in darkness; and all the islet lay quiet in the shadows once more. The lowing of the cattle on the mainland ceased – rose again – stopped. Then, cold and cheerless as ever, the eternal bubbling of the broken water welled up through the great gap of silence – the one sound left, as the mysterious stillness of the hour fell like a mantle from the heavens, and closed over the wreck.

Allan descended from his place in the mizen-top, and joined his friend again on deck.

'We must wait till the ship-breakers come off to their work,' he said, meeting Midwinter half way in the course of his restless walk. 'After what has happened, I don't mind confessing that I've had enough of hailing the land. Only think of there being a madman in that house ashore, and of my waking him! Horrible, wasn't it?'[2]

Midwinter stood still for a moment, and looked at Allan, with the perplexed air of a man who hears circumstances familiarly mentioned, to which he is himself a total stranger. He appeared, if such a thing had been possible, to have passed over entirely without notice, all that had just happened on the Islet of the Calf.

'Nothing is horrible *out* of this ship,' he said. 'Everything is horrible *in* it.'

Answering in those strange words, he turned away again, and went on with his walk.

Allan picked up the flask of whiskey lying on the deck near him, and revived his spirits with a dram. 'Here's one thing on board that isn't horrible,' he retorted briskly, as he screwed on the stopper of the flask; 'and here's another,' he added, as he took a cigar from his case and lit it. 'Three o'clock!' he went on, looking at his watch, and settling himself comfortably on deck, with his back against the bulwark. 'Daybreak isn't far off – we shall have the piping of the birds to cheer us up before long. I say, Midwinter, you seem to have quite got over that unlucky fainting fit. How you do keep walking! Come here and have a cigar, and make yourself comfortable. What's the good of tramping backwards and forwards in that restless way?'

'I am waiting,' said Midwinter.

'Waiting! What for?'

'For what is to happen to you or to me – or to both of us – before we are out of this ship.'

'With submission to your superior judgment, my dear fellow, I think quite enough has happened already. The adventure will do very well as it stands now; more of it is more than I want.' He took another dram of whiskey, and rambled on, between the puffs of his cigar, in his usual easy way. 'I've not got your fine imagination, old boy; and I hope the next thing that happens will be the appearance of the workmen's boat. I suspect that queer fancy of yours has been running away with you, while you were down here all by yourself. Come now! what were you thinking of while I was up in the mizen-top frightening the cows?'

Midwinter suddenly stopped. 'Suppose I tell you?' he said.

'Suppose you do?'

The torturing temptation to reveal the truth, roused once already by his companion's merciless gaiety of spirit, possessed itself of Midwinter for the second time. He leaned back in the dark against the high side of the ship, and looked down in silence at Allan's figure, stretched comfortably on the deck. 'Rouse him,' the fiend whispered subtly, 'from that ignorant self-possession, and that pitiless repose. Show him the place where the deed was done; let him know it with your knowledge, and fear it with your dread. Tell him of the letter you burnt, and of the words no fire can destroy, which are living in your memory now. Let him see your mind as it was yesterday, when it roused your sinking faith in your own convictions, to look back on your life at sea, and to cherish the comforting remembrance that, in all your voyages, you had never fallen in with this ship. Let him see your mind as it is now, when the ship has got you at the turning-point of your new life, at the outset of your friendship with the one man of all men whom your father warned you to avoid. Think of those death-bed words, and whisper them in his ear, that he may think of them too: "Hide yourself from him under an assumed name. Put the mountains and the seas between you; be ungrateful, be unforgiving; be all that is most repellent to your own gentler nature, rather than live under the same roof and breathe the same air with that man."' So the tempter counselled. So, like a noisome exhalation from the father's grave, the father's influence rose and poisoned the mind of the son.

The sudden silence surprised Allan; he looked back drowsily over his shoulder. 'Thinking again!' he exclaimed, with a weary yawn.

Midwinter stepped out from the shadow, and came nearer to Allan than he had come yet. 'Yes,' he said, 'thinking of the past and the future.'

'The past and the future?' repeated Allan, shifting himself comfortably into a new position. 'For my part I'm dumb about the past. It's a sore subject with me – the past means the loss of the doctor's boat. Let's talk about the future. Have you been taking a practical view? as dear old Brock calls it. Have you been considering the next serious question that concerns us both when we get back to the hotel – the question of breakfast?'

After an instant's hesitation, Midwinter took a step nearer. 'I have been thinking of your future and mine,' he said; 'I have been thinking of the time when your way in life, and my way in life, will be two ways instead of one.'

'Here's the daybreak!' cried Allan. 'Look up at the masts; they're beginning to get clear again already. I beg your pardon. What were you saying?'

Midwinter made no reply. The struggle between the hereditary superstition that was driving him on, and the unconquerable affection for Allan that was holding him back, suspended the next words on his lips. He turned aside his face in speechless suffering. 'Oh, my father!' he thought, 'better have killed me on that day when I lay on your bosom, than have let me live for this!'

'What's that about the future?' persisted Allan. 'I was looking for the daylight; I didn't hear.'

Midwinter controlled himself, and answered, 'You have treated me with your usual kindness,' he said, 'in planning to take me with you to Thorpe-Ambrose. I think, on reflection, I had better not intrude myself where I am not known, and not expected.' His voice faltered, and he stopped again. The more he shrank from it, the clearer the picture of the happy life that he was resigning rose on his mind.

Allan's thoughts instantly reverted to the mystification about the new steward, which he had practised on his friend when they were consulting together in the cabin of the yacht. 'Has he been turning it over in his mind?' wondered Allan; 'and is he beginning at last to suspect the truth? I'll try him. – Talk as much nonsense, my dear fellow, as you like,' he rejoined, 'but don't forget that you are engaged to see me established at Thorpe-Ambrose, and to give me your opinion of the new steward.'

Midwinter suddenly stepped forward again, close to Allan.

'I am not talking about your steward or your estate,' he burst out passionately; 'I am talking about myself. Do you hear? Myself! I am not a fit companion for you. You don't know who I am.' He drew back into the shadowy shelter of the bulwark as suddenly as he had come out from it. 'O God! I can't tell him,' he said to himself, in a whisper.

For a moment, and for a moment only, Allan was surprised. 'Not know who you are?' Even as he repeated the words, his easy good-humour got the upper hand again. He took up the whiskey-flask, and shook it significantly. 'I say,' he resumed, 'how much of the doctor's medicine did you take while I was up in the mizen-top?'

The light tone which he persisted in adopting, stung Midwinter to the last pitch of exasperation. He came out again into the light, and stamped his foot angrily on the deck. 'Listen to me!' he said. 'You don't know half the low things I have done in my life-time. I have been a tradesman's drudge; I have swept out the shop and put up the shutters; I have carried parcels through the street, and waited for my master's money at his customers' doors.'

'I have never done anything half as useful,' returned Allan, compos-edly. 'Dear old boy, what an industrious fellow you have been in your time!'

'I've been a vagabond and a blackguard in my time,' returned the other, fiercely; 'I've been a street-tumbler, a tramp, a gipsy's boy! I've sung for halfpence with dancing dogs on the high-road! I've worn a footboy's livery, and waited at table! I've been a common sailors' cook, and a starving fisherman's Jack-of-all-trades! What has a gentleman in your position in common with a man in mine? Can you take *me* into the society at Thorpe-Ambrose? Why, my very name would be a reproach to you. Fancy the faces of your new neighbours when their footmen announce Ozias Midwinter and Allan Armadale in the same breath!' He burst into a harsh laugh, and repeated the two names again, with a scornful bitterness of emphasis which insisted pitilessly on the marked contrast between them.

Something in the sound of his laughter jarred painfully, even on Allan's easy nature. He raised himself on the deck, and spoke seriously for the first time. 'A joke's a joke, Midwinter,' he said, 'as long as you don't carry it too far. I remember your saying something of the same sort to me once before, when I was nursing you in Somersetshire. You forced me to ask you if I deserved to be kept at arm's length by *you* of all the people in the world. Don't force me to say so again. Make as much fun of me as you please, old fellow, in any other way. *That* way hurts me.'[3]

Simple as the words were, and simply as they had been spoken, they appeared to work an instant revolution in Midwinter's mind. His impressible nature recoiled as from some sudden shock. Without a word of reply, he walked away by himself to the forward part of the ship. He sat down on some piled planks between the masts, and passed his hand over his head in a vacant, bewildered way. Though his father's belief in Fatality was his own belief once more – though there was no longer the shadow of a doubt in his mind that the woman whom Mr Brock had met in Somersetshire, and the woman who had tried to destroy herself in London, were one and the same – though all the horror that mastered him when he first read the letter from Wildbad, had now mastered him again, Allan's appeal to their past experience of each other had come home to his heart, with a force more irresistible than the force of his superstition itself. In the strength of that very superstition, he now sought the pretext which might encourage him to sacrifice every less generous feeling to the one predominant dread of wounding the sympathies of his friend. 'Why distress him?' he whispered to himself. 'We are not at the end here – there is the Woman behind us in the dark. Why resist him when the mischief's done, and the caution comes too late? What *is* to be *will* be. What have I to do with the future? and what has he?'

He went back to Allan, sat down by his side, and took his hand. 'Forgive me,' he said, gently; 'I have hurt you for the last time.' Before it was possible to reply, he snatched up the whiskey-flask from the deck. 'Come!' he exclaimed, with a sudden effort to match his friend's cheerfulness; 'you have been trying the doctor's medicine, why shouldn't I?'

Allan was delighted. 'This is something like a change for the better,' he said; 'Midwinter is himself again. Hark! there are the birds. Hail, smiling morn! smiling morn!' He sang the words of the glee, in his old cheerful voice, and clapped Midwinter on the shoulder in his old hearty way. 'How did you manage to clear your head of those confounded meagrims? Do you know you were quite alarming about something happening to one or other of us before we were out of this ship?'

'Sheer nonsense!' returned Midwinter, contemptuously. 'I don't think my head has ever been quite right since that fever; I've got a bee in my bonnet, as they say in the North. Let's talk of something else. About those people you have let the cottage to? I wonder whether the agent's account of Major Milroy's family is to be depended on? There might be another lady in the household besides his wife and his daughter.'

'Oho!' cried Allan, '*you're* beginning to think of nymphs among the trees, and flirtations in the fruit-garden, are you? Another lady – eh? Suppose the major's family circle won't supply another? We shall have to spin that half-crown again, and toss up for which is to have the first chance with Miss Milroy.'

For once Midwinter spoke as lightly and carelessly as Allan himself. 'No, no,' he said; 'the major's landlord has the first claim to the notice of the major's daughter. I'll retire into the background and wait for the next lady who makes her appearance at Thorpe-Ambrose.'

'Very good. I'll have an Address to the women of Norfolk posted in the park[4] to that effect,' said Allan. 'Are you particular to a shade about size or complexion? What's your favourite age?'

Midwinter trifled with his own superstition, as a man trifles with the loaded gun that may kill him, or with the savage animal that may maim him for life. He mentioned the age (as he had reckoned it himself) of the woman in the black gown and the red Paisley shawl.

'Five-and-thirty,' he said.

As the words passed his lips, his factitious spirits deserted him. He left his seat, impenetrably deaf to all Allan's efforts at rallying him on his extraordinary answer; and resumed his restless pacing of the deck in dead silence. Once more the haunting thought which had gone to and fro with him now in the hour of darkness, went to and fro with him now in the hour of daylight. Once more the conviction possessed itself of his mind that something was to happen to Allan or to himself before they left the wreck.

Minute by minute the light strengthened in the eastern sky; and the shadowy places on the deck of the timber-ship revealed their barren emptiness under the eye of day. As the breeze rose again, the sea began to murmur wakefully in the morning light. Even the cold bubbling of the broken water changed its cheerless note, and softened on the ear as the mellowing flood of daylight poured warm over it from the rising sun. Midwinter paused near the forward part of the ship, and recalled his wandering attention to the passing time. The cheering influences of the hour were round him, look where he might. The happy morning smile of the summer sky, so brightly merciful to the old and weary earth, lavished its all-embracing beauty even on the wreck! The dew that lay glittering on the inland fields, lay glittering on the deck; and the worn and rusted rigging was gemmed as brightly as the fresh green leaves on shore. Insensibly, as he looked round, Midwinter's thoughts reverted to the comrade who had shared with him the adventure of the night. He returned to the after-part of the ship and spoke to Allan as he advanced. Receiving no answer, he approached the recumbent figure and looked closer at it. Left to his own resources, Allan had let the fatigues of the night take their own way with him. His head had sunk back; his hat had fallen off; he lay stretched at full length on the deck of the timber-ship, deeply and peacefully asleep.

Midwinter resumed his walk; his mind lost in doubt; his own past thoughts seeming suddenly to have grown strange to him. How darkly his forebodings had distrusted the coming time – and how harmlessly that time had come! The sun was mounting in the heavens, the hour of release was drawing nearer and nearer; and of the two Armadales imprisoned in the fatal ship, one was sleeping away the weary time, and the other was quietly watching the growth of the new day.

The sun climbed higher; the hour wore on. With the latent distrust of the wreck which still clung to him, Midwinter looked inquiringly on either shore for signs of awakening human life. The land was still lonely. The smoke-wreaths that were soon to rise from cottage chimneys, had not risen yet.

After a moment's thought he went back again to the after-part of the vessel, to see if there might be a fisherman's boat within hail, astern of them. Absorbed, for the moment, by the new idea, he passed Allan hastily, after barely noticing that he still lay asleep. One step more would have brought him to the taffrail – when that step was suspended by a sound behind him, a sound like a faint groan. He turned, and looked at the sleeper on the deck. He knelt softly, and looked closer.

'It has come!' he whispered to himself. 'Not to *me* – but to *him*.'

It had come, in the bright freshness of the morning; it had come, in the mystery and terror of a Dream. The face which Midwinter had last seen in perfect repose, was now the distorted face of a suffering man. The perspiration stood thick on Allan's forehead, and matted his curling hair. His partially-opened eyes showed nothing but the white of the eyeball gleaming blindly. His outstretched hands scratched and struggled on the deck. From moment to moment he moaned and muttered helplessly; but the words that escaped him were lost in the grinding and gnashing of his teeth. There he lay – so near in the body to the friend who bent over him; so far away in the spirit, that the two might have been in different worlds – there he lay, with the morning sunshine on his face, in the torture of his dream.

One question, and one only, rose in the mind of the man who was looking at him. What had the Fatality which had imprisoned him in the Wreck decreed that he should see?

Had the treachery of Sleep opened the gates of the grave to that one of the two Armadales whom the other had kept in ignorance of the truth? Was the murder of the father revealing itself to the son – there, on the very spot where the crime had been committed – in the vision of a dream?

With that question over-shadowing all else in his mind, the son of the homicide knelt on the deck, and looked at the son of the man whom his father's hand had slain.

The conflict between the sleeping body and the waking mind was strengthening every moment. The dreamer's helpless groaning for deliverance grew louder; his hands raised themselves, and clutched at the empty air. Struggling with the all-mastering dread that still held him, Midwinter laid his hand gently on Allan's forehead. Light as the touch was, there were mysterious sympathies in the dreaming man that answered it. His groaning ceased, and his hands dropped slowly. There was an instant of suspense, and Midwinter looked closer. His breath just fluttered over the sleeper's face. Before the next breath had risen to his lips, Allan suddenly sprang up on his knees – sprang up, as if the call of a trumpet had rung on his ear, awake in an instant.

'You have been dreaming,' said Midwinter, as the other looked at him wildly, in the first bewilderment of waking.

Allan's eyes began to wander about the wreck – at first vacantly; then with a look of angry surprise. 'Are we here still?' he said, as Midwinter helped him to his feet. 'Whatever else I do on board this infernal ship,' he added, after a moment, 'I won't go to sleep again!'

As he said those words, his friend's eyes searched his face in silent inquiry. They took a turn together on the deck.

'Tell me your dream,' said Midwinter, with a strange tone of suspicion in his voice, and a strange appearance of abruptness in his manner.

'I can't tell it yet,' returned Allan. 'Wait a little till I'm my own man again.'

They took another turn on the deck. Midwinter stopped, and spoke once more.

'Look at me for a moment, Allan,' he said.

There was something of the trouble left by the dream, and something of natural surprise at the strange request just addressed to him, in Allan's face, as he turned it full on the speaker; but no shadow of ill-will, no lurking lines of distrust anywhere. Midwinter turned aside quickly, and hid, as he best might, an irrepressible outburst of relief.

'Do I look a little upset?' asked Allan, taking his arm, and leading him on again. 'Don't make yourself nervous about me if I do. My head feels wild and giddy – but I shall soon get over it.'

For the next few minutes, they walked backwards and forwards in silence – the one, bent on dismissing the terror of the dream from his thoughts; the other, bent on discovering what the terror of the dream might be. Relieved of the dread that had oppressed it, the superstitious nature of Midwinter had leapt to its next conclusion at a bound. What, if the sleeper had been visited by another revelation than the revelation of the Past? What, if the dream had opened those unturned pages in the book of the Future, which told the story of his life to come? The bare doubt that it might be so, strengthened tenfold Midwinter's longing to penetrate the mystery which Allan's silence still kept a secret from him.

'Is your head more composed?' he asked. 'Can you tell me your dream now?'

While he put the question, a last memorable moment in the Adventure of the Wreck was at hand.

They had reached the stern, and were just turning again when Midwinter spoke. As Allan opened his lips to answer, he looked out mechanically to sea. Instead of replying, he suddenly ran to the taffrail, and waved his hat over his head, with a shout of exultation.

Midwinter joined him, and saw a large six-oared boat pulling straight for the channel of the Sound. A figure, which they both thought they recognized, rose eagerly in the stern-sheets, and returned the waving of Allan's hat. The boat came nearer; the steersman called to them cheerfully; and they recognized the doctor's voice.

'Thank God you're both above water?' said Mr Hawbury, as they met him on the deck of the timber-ship. 'Of all the winds of heaven, which wind blew you here?'

He looked at Midwinter, as he made the inquiry – but it was Allan who told him the story of the night; and Allan who asked the doctor for information in return. The one absorbing interest in Midwinter's mind – the interest of penetrating the mystery of the dream – kept him silent throughout. Heedless of all that was said or done about him, he watched Allan, and followed Allan, like a dog, until the time came for getting down into the boat. Mr Hawbury's professional eye rested on him curiously, noting his varying colour, and the incessant restlessness of his hands. 'I wouldn't change nervous systems with that man, for the largest fortune that could be offered me,' thought the doctor as he took the boat's tiller, and gave the oarsmen their order to push off from the wreck.

Having reserved all explanations on his side until they were on their way back to Port St Mary, Mr Hawbury next addressed himself to the gratification of Allan's curiosity. The circumstances which had brought him to the rescue of his two guests of the previous evening were simple enough. The lost boat had been met with at sea, by some fishermen of Port Erin, on the western side of the island, who at once recognized it as the doctor's property, and at once sent a messenger to make inquiry at the doctor's house. The man's statement of what had happened had naturally alarmed Mr Hawbury for the safety of Allan and his friend. He had immediately secured assistance; and guided by the boatmen's advice, had made first for the most dangerous place on the coast – the only place, in that calm weather, in which an accident could have happened to a boat sailed by experienced men – the channel of the Sound. After thus accounting for his welcome appearance on the scene, the doctor hospitably insisted that his guests of the evening should be his guests of the morning as well. It would still be too early when they got back for the people at the hotel to receive them, and they would find bed and breakfast at Mr Hawbury's house.

At the first pause in the conversation between Allan and the doctor, Midwinter – who had neither joined in the talk, nor listened to the talk – touched his friend on the arm. 'Are you better?' he asked in a whisper. 'Shall you soon be composed enough to tell me what I want to know?'

Allan's eyebrows contracted impatiently; the subject of the dream, and Midwinter's obstinacy in returning to it, seemed to be alike distasteful to him. He hardly answered with his usual good-humour. 'I suppose I shall have no peace till I tell you,' he said, 'so I may as well get it over at once.'

'No!' returned Midwinter, with a look at the doctor and his oarsmen. 'Not where other people can hear it – not till you and I are alone.'

'If you wish to see the last, gentlemen, of your quarters for the night,' interposed the doctor, 'now is your time! the coast will shut the vessel out, in a minute more.'

In silence on the one side and on the other, the two Armadales looked their last at the fatal ship. Lonely and lost they had found the Wreck in the mystery of the summer night. Lonely and lost they left the Wreck in the radiant beauty of the summer morning.

An hour later the doctor had seen his guests established in their bedrooms, and had left them to take their rest until the breakfast hour arrived.

Almost as soon as his back was turned, the doors of both rooms opened softly, and Allan and Midwinter met in the passage.

'Can you sleep after what has happened?' asked Allan.

Midwinter shook his head. 'You were coming to my room, were you not?' he said. 'What for?'

'To ask you to keep me company. What were *you* coming to *my* room for?'

'To ask you to tell me your dream.'

'Damn the dream! I want to forget all about it.'

'And *I* want to know all about it.'

Both paused; both refrained instinctively from saying more. For the

138

first time since the beginning of their friendship they were on the verge of a disagreement – and that on the subject of the dream. Allan's good temper just stopped them on the brink.

'You are the most obstinate fellow alive,' he said, 'but if you will know all about it, you must know all about it, I suppose. Come into my room, and I'll tell you.'

He led the way, and Midwinter followed. The door closed, and shut them in together.

CHAPTER V

THE SHADOW OF THE FUTURE

When Mr Hawbury joined his guests in the breakfast-room, the strange contrast of character between them which he had noticed already, was impressed on his mind more strongly than ever. One of them sat at the well-spread table, hungry and happy; ranging from dish to dish, and declaring that he had never made such a breakfast in his life. The other sat apart at the window; his cup thanklessly deserted before it was empty, his meat left ungraciously half eaten on his plate. The doctor's morning greeting to the two, accurately expressed the differing impressions which they had produced on his mind. He clapped Allan on the shoulder, and saluted him with a joke. He bowed constrainedly to Midwinter, and said, 'I am afraid you have not recovered the fatigues of the night.'

'It's not the night, doctor, that has damped his spirits,' said Allan. 'It's something I have been telling him. It is not my fault, mind. If I had only known beforehand that he believed in dreams, I wouldn't have opened my lips.'

'Dreams?' repeated the doctor, looking at Midwinter directly, and addressing him under a mistaken impression of the meaning of Allan's words. 'With your constitution, you ought to be well used to dreaming by this time.'

'This way, doctor; you have taken the wrong turning!' cried Allan. 'I'm the dreamer – not he. Don't look astonished; it wasn't in this comfortable house – it was on board that confounded timber-ship. The fact is, I fell asleep just before you took us off the wreck; and it's not to be denied that I had a very ugly dream. Well, when we got back here—'

'Why do you trouble Mr Hawbury about a matter that cannot possibly interest him?' asked Midwinter, speaking for the first time, and speaking very impatiently.

'I beg your pardon,' returned the doctor, rather sharply; 'so far as I have heard, the matter does interest me.'

'That's right, doctor!' said Allan. 'Be interested, I beg and pray; I want you to clear his head of the nonsense he has got in it now. What do you think? – he will have it that my dream is a warning to me to avoid certain people; and he actually persists in saying that one of those people is – himself! Did you ever hear the like of it? I took great pains; I explained the whole thing to him. I said, warning be hanged – it's all indigestion! You don't know what I ate and drank at the doctor's supper-table – I do. Do you think he would listen to me? Not he. You try him next; you're a professional man, and he must listen to you. Be a good fellow, doctor; and give me a certificate of indigestion; I'll show you my tongue with pleasure.'

'The sight of your face is quite enough,' said Mr Hawbury. 'I certify, on the spot, that you never had such a thing as an indigestion in your life. Let's hear about the dream, and see what we can make of it – if you have no objection, that is to say.'

Allan pointed at Midwinter with his fork.

'Apply to my friend, there,' he said; 'he has got a much better account of it than I can give you. If you'll believe me, he took it all down in writing from my own lips; and he made me sign it at the end, as if it was my "last dying speech and confession", before I went to the gallows. Out with it, old boy – I saw you put it in your pocket-book – out with it!'

'Are you really in earnest?' asked Midwinter, producing his pocket-book with a reluctance which was almost offensive under the circumstances, for it implied distrust of the doctor in the doctor's own house.

Mr Hawbury's colour rose. 'Pray don't show it to me, if you feel the least unwillingness,' he said, with the elaborate politeness of an offended man.

'Stuff and nonsense!' cried Allan. 'Throw it over here!'

Instead of complying with that characteristic request, Midwinter took the paper from the pocket-book, and, leaving his place, approached Mr Hawbury. 'I beg your pardon,' he said, as he offered the doctor the manuscript with his own hand. His eyes dropped to the ground, and his face darkened, while he made the apology. 'A secret, sullen fellow,' thought the doctor, thanking him with formal civility – 'his friend is worth ten thousand of him.' Midwinter went back to the window, and sat down again in silence, with the old impenetrable resignation which had once puzzled Mr Brock.

'Read that, doctor,' said Allan, as Mr Hawbury opened the written paper. 'It's not told in my roundabout way; but there's nothing added to it, and nothing taken away. It's exactly what I dreamed, and exactly what I should have written myself, if I had thought the thing worth putting down on paper, and if I had had the knack of writing – which,' concluded Allan, composedly stirring his coffee, 'I haven't, except it's letters; and I rattle *them* off in no time.'

Mr Hawbury spread the manuscript before him on the breakfast-table, and read these lines:

ALLAN ARMADALE'S DREAM

Early on the morning of June the first, eighteen hundred and fifty-one, I found myself (through circumstances which it is not important to mention in this place) left alone with a friend of mine – a young man about my own age – on board the French timber-ship named *La Grâce de Dieu*, which ship then lay wrecked in the channel of the Sound, between the mainland of the Isle of Man and the islet called the Calf. Having not been in bed the previous night, and feeling overcome by fatigue, I fell asleep on the deck of the vessel. I was in my usual good health at the time, and the morning was far enough advanced for the sun to have risen. Under these circumstances, and at that period of the day, I passed from sleeping to dreaming. As clearly as I can recollect it, after the lapse of a few hours, this was the succession of events presented to me by the dream:

1. The first event of which I was conscious, was the appearance of my father. He took me silently by the hand; and we found ourselves in the cabin of a ship.

2. Water rose slowly over us in the cabin; and I and my father sank through the water together.

3. An interval of oblivion followed; and then the sense came to me of being left alone in the darkness.

4. I waited.

5. The darkness opened, and showed me the vision – as in a picture – of a broad, lonely pool, surrounded by open ground. Above the farther margin of the pool, I saw the cloudless western sky, red with the light of sunset.

6. On the near margin of the pool, there stood the Shadow of a Woman.

7. It was the shadow only. No indication was visible to me by which I could identify it, or compare it with any living creature. The long robe showed me that it was the shadow of a woman, and showed me nothing more.

8. The darkness closed again – remained with me for an interval – and opened for the second time.

9. I found myself in a room, standing before a long window. The only object of furniture or of ornament that I saw (or that I can now remember having seen), was a little statue placed near me. The statue was on my left hand, and the window was on my right. The window opened on a lawn and flower-garden; and the rain was pattering heavily against the glass.

10. I was not alone in the room. Standing opposite to me at the window was the Shadow of a Man.

11. I saw no more of it – I knew no more of it than I saw and knew of the shadow of the woman. But the shadow of the man moved. It stretched out its arm towards the statue; and the statue fell in fragments on the floor.

12. With a confused sensation in me, which was partly anger and partly distress, I stooped to look at the fragments. When I rose again, the Shadow had vanished, and I saw no more.

13. The darkness opened for the third time, and showed me the Shadow of the Woman and the Shadow of the Man, together.

14. No surrounding scene (or none that I can now call to mind) was visible to me.

15. The Man-Shadow was the nearest; the Woman-Shadow stood back. From where she stood, there came a sound as of the pouring of a liquid softly. I saw her touch the shadow of the man with one hand, and with the other give him a glass. He took the glass, and gave it to me. In the moment when I put it to my lips, a deadly faintness mastered me from head to foot. When I came to my senses again, the Shadow had vanished, and the third vision was at an end.

16. The darkness closed over me again; and the interval of oblivion followed.[1]

17. I was conscious of nothing more, till I felt the morning sunshine on my face, and heard my friend tell me that I had awakened from a dream.

After reading the narrative attentively to the last line (under which appeared Allan's signature) the doctor looked across the breakfast-table at Midwinter, and tapped his fingers on the manuscript with a satirical smile.

'Many men, many opinions,' he said. 'I don't agree with either of you about this dream. Your theory,' he added, looking at Allan, with a smile, 'we have disposed of already: the supper that *you* can't digest, is a supper which has yet to be discovered. My theory we will come to presently; your friend's theory claims attention first.' He turned again to Midwinter, with his anticipated triumph over a man whom he disliked a little too plainly visible in his face and manner. 'If I understand rightly,' he went on, 'you believe that this dream is a warning, supernaturally addressed to Mr Armadale, of dangerous events that are threatening him, and of dangerous people connected with those events, whom he would do wisely to avoid. May I inquire whether you have arrived at this conclusion, as an habitual believer in dreams? – or, as having reasons of your own for attaching especial importance to this one dream in particular?'

'You have stated what my conviction is quite accurately,' returned Midwinter, chafing under the doctor's looks and tones. 'Excuse me if I ask you to be satisfied with that admission, and to let me keep my reasons to myself.'

'That's exactly what he said to me,' interposed Allan. 'I don't believe he has got any reasons at all.'

'Gently! gently!' said Mr Hawbury. 'We can discuss the subject, without intruding ourselves into anybody's secrets. Let us come to my own method of dealing with the dream next. Mr Midwinter will probably not be surprised to hear that I look at this matter from an essentially practical point of view.'

'I shall not be at all surprised,' retorted Midwinter. 'The view of a medical man, when he has a problem in humanity to solve, seldom ranges beyond the point of his dissecting-knife.'

The doctor was a little nettled on his side. 'Our limits are not quite so narrow as that,' he said; 'but I willingly grant you that there are some articles of your faith in which we doctors don't believe. For example, we don't believe that a reasonable man is justified in attaching a supernatural interpretation to any phenomenon which comes within the range of his senses, until he has certainly ascertained that there is no such thing as a natural explanation of it to be found in the first instance.'

'Come! that's fair enough, I'm sure,' exclaimed Allan. 'He hit you hard with the "dissecting-knife", doctor; and now you have hit him back again with your "natural explanation". Let's have it.'

'By all means,' said Mr Hawbury; 'here it is. There is nothing at all extraordinary in my theory of dreams:[2] it is the theory accepted by the great mass of my profession. A Dream is the reproduction, in the sleeping state of the brain, of images and impressions produced on it in the waking state; and this reproduction is more or less involved, imperfect, or contradictory, as the action of certain faculties in the dreamer is controlled more or less completely by the influence of sleep. Without inquiring farther into this latter part of the subject – a very curious and interesting part of it – let us take the theory, roughly and generally, as I have just stated it, and apply it at once to the dream now under consideration.' He took up the written paper from the table, and dropped the formal tone (as of a lecturer addressing an audience) into which he had insensibly fallen. 'I see one event already in this dream,' he resumed, 'which I know to be the reproduction of a waking impression produced on Mr Armadale in my own presence. If he will only help me by exerting his memory, I don't despair of tracing back the whole succession of events set down here, to something that he has said or thought, or seen or done, in the four-and-twenty hours, or less, which preceded his falling asleep on the deck of the timber-ship.'

'I'll exert my memory with the greatest pleasure,' said Allan. 'Where shall we start from?'

'Start by telling me what you did yesterday, before I met you and your friend on the road to this place,' replied Mr Hawbury. 'We will say, you got up and had your breakfast. What next?'

'We took a carriage next,' said Allan, 'and drove from Castletown to Douglas to see my old friend, Mr Brock, off by the steamer to Liverpool. We came back to Castletown, and separated at the hotel door. Midwinter went into the house, and I went on to my yacht in the harbour. – By the by, doctor, remember you have promised to go cruising with us before we leave the Isle of Man.'

'Many thanks – but suppose we keep to the matter in hand. What next?'

Allan hesitated. In both senses of the word his mind was at sea already.

'What did you do on board the yacht?'

'Oh, I know! I put the cabin to rights – thoroughly to rights. I give you my word of honour, I turned every blessed thing topsy-turvy. And my friend there came off in a shore-boat and helped me. – Talking of boats, I have never asked you yet whether your boat came to any harm last night. If there's any damage done, I insist on being allowed to repair it.'

The doctor abandoned all futher attempts at the cultivation of Allan's memory in despair.

'I doubt if we shall be able to reach our object conveniently in this way,' he said. 'It will be better to take the events of the dream in their regular order, and to ask the questions that naturally suggest themselves as we go on. Here are the first two events to begin with. You dream that your father appears to you – that you and he find yourselves in the cabin of a ship – that the water rises over you, and that you sink in it together. Were you down in the cabin of the wreck, may I ask?'

'I couldn't be down there,' replied Allan, 'as the cabin was full of water. I looked in and saw it, and shut the door again.'

'Very good,' said Mr Hawbury. 'Here are the waking impressions clear enough, so far. You have had the cabin in your mind, and you have had the water in your mind; and the sound of the channel current (as I well know without asking) was the last sound in your ears when you went to sleep. The idea of drowning comes too naturally out of such impressions as these to need dwelling on. Is there anything else before we go on? Yes; there is one more circumstance left to account for.'

'The most important circumstance of all,' remarked Midwinter, joining in the conversation, without stirring from his place at the window.

'You mean the appearance of Mr Armadale's father? I was just coming to that,' answered Mr Hawbury. 'Is your father alive?' he added, addressing himself to Allan once more.

'My father died before I was born.'

The doctor started. 'This complicates it a little,' he said. 'How did you know that the figure appearing to you in the dream was the figure of your father?'

Allan hesitated again. Midwinter drew his chair a little away from the window, and looked at the doctor attentively for the first time.

'Was your father in your thoughts before you went to sleep?' pursued Mr Hawbury. 'Was there any description of him – any portrait of him at home – in your mind?'

'Of course there was!' cried Allan, suddenly seizing the lost recollection. 'Midwinter! you remember the miniature you found on the floor of the cabin when we were putting the yacht to rights? You said I didn't seem to value it; and I told you I did, because it was a portrait of my father—'

'And was the face in the dream like the face in the miniature?' asked Mr Hawbury.

'Exactly like! I say, doctor, this is beginning to get interesting!'

'What do you say now?' asked Mr Hawbury, turning towards the window again.

Midwinter hurriedly left his chair, and placed himself at the table with Allan. Just as he had once already taken refuge from the tyranny of his own superstition in the comfortable common sense of Mr Brock – so, with the same headlong eagerness, with the same straightforward sincerity of purpose, he now took refuge in the doctor's theory of dreams. 'I say what my friend says,' he answered, flushing with a sudden enthusiasm; 'this is beginning to get interesting. Go on – pray go on.'

The doctor looked at his strange guest more indulgently than he had looked yet. 'You are the only mystic I have met with,' he said, 'who is willing to give fair evidence fair play. I don't despair of converting you before our inquiry comes to an end. Let us get on to the next set of events,' he resumed, after referring for a moment to the manuscript. 'The interval of oblivion which is described as succeeding the first of the appearances in the dream, may be easily disposed of. It means, in plain English, the momentary cessation of the brain's intellectual action, while a deeper wave of sleep flows over it, just as the sense of being alone in the darkness, which follows, indicates the renewal of that action, previous to the reproduction of another set of impressions. Let us see what they are. A lonely pool, surrounded by an open country; a sunset sky on the farther side of the pool; and the shadow of a woman on the near side. Very good; now for it, Mr Armadale! How did that pool get into your head? The open country you saw on your way from Castletown to this place. But we have no pools or lakes hereabouts; and you can have seen none recently elsewhere, for you came here after a cruise at sea. Must we fall back on a picture, or a book, or a conversation with your friend?'

Allan looked at Midwinter. 'I don't remember talking about pools, or lakes,' he said. 'Do you?'

Instead of answering the question, Midwinter suddenly appealed to the doctor.

'Have you got the last number of the Manx newspaper?' he asked.

The doctor produced it from the sideboard. Midwinter turned to the page containing those extracts from the recently published Travels in Australia, which had roused Allan's interest on the previous evening, and the reading of which had ended by sending his friend to sleep. There – in the passage describing the sufferings of the travellers from thirst, and the subsequent discovery which saved their lives – there, appearing at the climax of the narrative, was the broad pool of water which had figured in Allan's dream!

'Don't put away the paper,' said the doctor, when Midwinter had shown it to him, with the necessary explanation. 'Before we are at the end of the inquiry, it is quite possible we may want that extract again. We have got at the pool. How about the sunset? Nothing of that sort is referred to in the newspaper extract. Search your memory again, Mr Armadale; we want your waking impression of a sunset, if you please.'

Once more, Allan was at a loss for an answer; and, once more, Midwinter's ready memory helped him through the difficulty.

'I think I can trace our way back to this impression, as I traced our way back to the other,' he said, addressing the doctor. 'After we got here yesterday afternoon, my friend and I took a long walk over the hills—'

'That's it!' interposed Allan. 'I remember. The sun was setting as we came back to the hotel for supper – and it was such a splendid red sky, we both stopped to look at it. And then we talked about Mr Brock, and wondered how far he had got on his journey home. My memory may be a slow one at starting, doctor; but when it's once set going, stop it if you can! I haven't half done yet.'

'Wait one minute, in mercy to Mr Midwinter's memory and mine,' said the doctor. 'We have traced back to your waking impressions, the vision of the open country, the pool, and the sunset. But the Shadow of the Woman has not been accounted for yet. Can you find us the original of this mysterious figure in the dream-landscape?'

Allan relapsed into his former perplexity, and Midwinter waited for what was to come, with his eyes fixed in breathless interest on the doctor's face. For the first time there was unbroken silence in the room. Mr Hawbury looked interrogatively from Allan to Allan's friend. Neither of them answered him. Between the shadow and the shadow's substance there was a great gulph of mystery, impenetrable alike to all three of them.

'Patience,' said the doctor, composedly. 'Let us leave the figure by the pool for the present, and try if we can't pick her up again as we go on. Allow me to observe, Mr Midwinter, that it is not very easy to identify a shadow; but we won't despair. This impalpable lady of the lake may take some consistency when we next meet with her.'

Midwinter made no reply. From that moment his interest in the inquiry began to flag.

'What is the next scene in the dream?' pursued Mr Hawbury, referring to the manuscript. 'Mr Armadale finds himself in a room. He is standing before a long window opening on a lawn and flower-garden, and the rain is pattering against the glass. The only thing he sees in the room is a little statue; and the only company he has is the Shadow of a Man standing opposite to him. The Shadow stretches out its arm, and the statue falls in fragments on the floor; and the dreamer, in anger and distress at the catastrophe (observe, gentlemen, that here the sleeper's reasoning faculty wakes up a little, and the dream passes rationally, for a moment, from cause to effect), stoops to look at the broken pieces. When he looks up again the scene has vanished. That is to say, in the ebb and flow of sleep, it is the turn of the flow now, and the brain rests a little. What's the matter, Mr Armadale? Has that restive memory of yours run away with you again?'

'Yes,' said Allan. 'I'm off at full gallop. I've run the broken statue to earth; it's nothing more nor less than a china shepherdess I knocked off the mantelpiece in the hotel coffee-room, when I rang the bell for supper last night. I say, how well we get on; don't we? It's like guessing a riddle. Now then, Midwinter! your turn next.'

'No!' said the doctor. 'My turn, if you please. I claim the long window, the garden, and the lawn, as my property. You will find the long window, Mr Armadale, in the next room. If you look out, you'll see the garden and lawn in front of it – and, if you'll exert that wonderful memory of yours, you will recollect that you were good enough to take special and complimentary notice of my smart French window and my neat garden, when I drove you and your friend to Port St Mary yesterday.'

'Quite right,' rejoined Allan, 'so I did. But what about the rain that fell in the dream? I haven't seen a drop of rain for the last week.'

Mr Hawbury hesitated. The Manx newspaper which had been left on the table caught his eye. 'If we can think of nothing else,' he said, 'let us try if we can't find the idea of the rain where we found the idea of the pool.' He looked through the extract carefully. 'I have got it!' he exclaimed. 'Here is rain described as having fallen on these thirsty Australian travellers, before they discovered the pool. Behold the shower, Mr Armadale, which got into your mind when you read the extract to your friend last night! And behold the dream, Mr Midwinter, mixing up separate waking impressions just as usual!'

'Can you find the waking impression which accounts for the human figure at the window?' asked Midwinter; 'or, are we to pass over the Shadow of the Man as we have passed over the Shadow of the Woman already?'

He put the question with scrupulous courtesy of manner, but with a tone of sarcasm in his voice which caught the doctor's ear, and set up the doctor's controversial bristles on the instant.

'When you are picking up shells on the beach, Mr Midwinter, you usually begin with the shells that lie nearest at hand,' he rejoined. 'We are picking up facts now; and those that are easiest to get at are the facts we will take first. Let the Shadow of the Man and the Shadow of the Woman pair off together for the present – we won't lose sight of them, I promise you. All in good time, my dear sir; all in good time!'

He too was polite, and he too was sarcastic. The short truce between the opponents was at an end already. Midwinter returned significantly to his former place by the window. The doctor instantly turned his back on the window more significantly still. Allan, who never quarrelled with anybody's opinion, and never looked below the surface of anybody's conduct, drummed, cheerfully on the table with the handle of his knife. 'Go on, doctor!' he called out; 'my wonderful memory is as fresh as ever.'

'Is it?' said Mr Hawbury, referring again to the narrative of the dream. 'Do you remember what happened, when you and I were gossiping with the landlady at the bar of the hotel last night?'

'Of course I do! You were kind enough to hand me a glass of brandy-and-water, which the landlady had just mixed for your own drinking. And I was obliged to refuse it because, as I told you, the taste of brandy always turns me sick and faint, mix it how you please.'

'Exactly so,' returned the doctor. 'And here is the incident reproduced in the dream. You see the man's shadow and the woman's shadow together this time. You hear the pouring out of liquid (brandy from the hotel bottle, and water from the hotel jug); the glass is handed by the woman-shadow (the landlady) to the man-shadow (myself); the man-shadow hands it to you (exactly what I did); and the faintness (which you had previously described to me) follows in due course. I am shocked to identify these mysterious Appearances, Mr Midwinter, with such miserably unromantic originals as a woman who keeps an hotel, and a man who physics a country district. But your friend himself will tell you that the glass of brandy-and-water was prepared by the landlady, and it reached him by passing from her hand to mine. We have picked up the shadows, exactly as I anticipated; and we have only to account now – which may be done in two words – for the manner of their appearance in the dream. After having tried to introduce the waking impression of the doctor and the landlady separately, in connection with the wrong set of circumstances, the dreaming mind comes right at the third trial, and introduces the doctor and the landlady together, in connection with the right set of circumstances. There it is in a nutshell! – Permit me to hand you back the manuscript, with my best thanks for your very complete and striking confirmation of the rational theory of dreams.' Saying those words, Mr Hawbury returned the written paper to Midwinter, with the pitiless politeness of a conquering man.

'Wonderful! not a point missed anywhere from beginning to end! By Jupiter!' cried Allan, with the ready reverence of intense ignorance. 'What a thing science is!'

'Not a point missed, as you say,' remarked the doctor, complacently. 'And yet I doubt if we have succeeded in convincing your friend.'

'You have *not* convinced me,' said Midwinter. 'But I don't presume on that account to say that you are wrong.'

He spoke quietly, almost sadly. The terrible conviction of the supernatural origin of the dream, from which he had tried to escape, had possessed itself of him again. All his interest in the argument was at an end; all his sensitiveness to its irritating influences was gone. In the case of any other man, Mr Hawbury would have been mollified by such a concession as his adversary had now made to him; but he disliked Midwinter too cordially to leave him in the peaceable enjoyment of an opinion of his own.

'Do you admit,' asked the doctor, more pugnaciously than ever, 'that I have traced back every event of the dream to a waking impression which preceded it in Mr Armadale's mind?'

'I have no wish to deny that you have done so,' said Midwinter, resignedly.

'Have I identified the Shadows with their living originals?'

'You have identified them to your own satisfaction, and to my friend's satisfaction. Not to mine.'

'Not to yours? Can *you* identify them?'

'No. I can only wait till the living originals stand revealed in the future.'

'Spoken like an oracle, Mr Midwinter! Have you any idea at present of who those living originals may be?'

'I have. I believe that coming events will identify the Shadow of the Woman with a person whom my friend has not met with yet; and the Shadow of the Man with myself.'

Allan attempted to speak. The doctor stopped him.

'Let us clearly understand this,' he said to Midwinter. 'Leaving your own case out of the question for the moment, may I ask how a shadow, which has no distinguishing mark about it, is to be identified with a living woman whom your friend doesn't know?'

Midwinter's colour rose a little. He began to feel the lash of the doctor's logic.

'The landscape-picture of the dream has its distinguishing marks,' he replied. 'And, in that landscape, the living woman will appear when the living woman is first seen.'

'The same thing will happen, I suppose,' pursued the doctor, 'with the man-shadow which you persist in identifying with yourself. You will be associated in the future with a statue broken in your friend's presence, with a long window looking out on a garden, and with a shower of rain pattering against the glass? Do you say that?'

'I say that.'

'And so again, I presume, with the next vision? You and the mysterious woman will be brought together in some place now unknown, and will present to Mr Armadale some liquid yet unnamed, which will turn him faint? – Do you seriously tell me you believe this?'

'I seriously tell you I believe it.'

'And, according to your view, these fulfilments of the dream will mark the progress of certain coming events, in which Mr Armadale's happiness, or Mr Armadale's safety, will be dangerously involved?'

'That is my firm conviction.'

The doctor rose – laid aside his moral dissecting-knife – considered for a moment – and took it up again.

'One last question,' he said. 'Have you any reason to give[3] for going out of your way to adopt such a mystical view as this, when an unanswerably rational explanation of the dream lies straight before you?'

'No reason,' replied Midwinter, 'that I can give, either to you or to my friend.'

The doctor looked at his watch with the air of a man who is suddenly reminded that he has been wasting his time.

'We have no common ground to start from,' he said; 'and if we talked till doomsday, we should not agree. Excuse my leaving you rather abruptly. It is later than I thought; and my morning's batch of sick people are waiting for me in the surgery. I have convinced *your* mind, Mr Armadale, at any rate; so the time we have given to this discussion has not been altogether lost. Pray stop here, and smoke your cigar. I shall be at your service again in less than an hour.' He nodded cordially to Allan, bowed formally to Midwinter, and quitted the room.

As soon as the doctor's back was turned, Allan left his place at the table, and appealed to his friend, with that irresistible heartiness of manner which had always found its way to Midwinter's sympathies, from the first day when they met at the Somersetshire inn.

'Now the sparring-match between you and the doctor is over,' said Allan, 'I have got two words to say on my side. Will you do something for my sake which you won't do for your own?'

Midwinter's face brightened instantly. 'I will do anything you ask me,' he said.

'Very well. Will you let the subject of the dream drop out of our talk altogether, from this time forth?'

'Yes, if you wish it.'

'Will you go a step further? Will you leave off thinking about the dream?'

'It's hard to leave off thinking about it, Allan. But I will try.'

'That's a good fellow! Now give me that trumpery bit of paper, and let's tear it up, and have done with it.'

He tried to snatch the manuscript out of his friend's hand; but Midwinter was too quick for him, and kept it beyond his reach.

'Come! come!' pleaded Allan. 'I've set my heart on lighting my cigar with it.'

Midwinter hesitated painfully. It was hard to resist Allan; but he did resist him. 'I'll wait a little,' he said, 'before you light your cigar with it.'

'How long? Till to-morrow?'

'Longer.'

'Till we leave the Isle of Man?'

'Longer.'

'Hang it – give me a plain answer to a plain question! How long *will* you wait?'

Midwinter carefully restored the paper to its place in his pocket-book.

'I'll wait,' he said, 'till we get to Thorpe-Am' ..se.'

THE END OF THE SECOND BOOK

BOOK THE THIRD

CHAPTER I

LURKING MISCHIEF

1. – *From Ozias Midwinter to Mr Brock*

Thorpe-Ambrose, June 15th, 1851.

DEAR MR BROCK, – Only an hour since, we reached this house, just as the servants were locking up for the night. Allan has gone to bed, worn out by our long day's journey, and has left me in the room they call the library, to tell you the story of our journey to Norfolk. Being better seasoned than he is to fatigues of all kinds, my eyes are quite wakeful enough for writing a letter, though the clock on the chimneypiece points to midnight, and we have been travelling since ten in the morning.

The last news you had of us was news sent by Allan from the Isle of Man. If I am not mistaken, he wrote to tell you of the night we passed on board the wrecked ship. Forgive me, dear Mr Brock, if I say nothing on that subject until time has helped me to think of it with a quieter mind. The hard fight against myself must all be fought over again; but I will win it yet, please God; I will indeed.

There is no need to trouble you with any account of our journeyings about the northern and western districts of the island; or of the short cruises we took when the repairs of the yacht were at last complete. It will be better if I get on at once to the morning of yesterday – the fourteenth. We had come in with the night-tide to Douglas harbour; and, as soon as the post-office was open, Allan, by my advice, sent on shore for letters. The messenger returned with one letter only; and the writer of it proved to be the former mistress of Thorpe-Ambrose – Mrs Blanchard.

You ought to be informed, I think, of the contents of this letter; for it has seriously influenced Allan's plans. He loses everything, sooner or later, as you know, and he has lost the letter already. So I must give you the substance of what Mrs Blanchard wrote to him, as plainly as I can.

The first page announced the departure of the ladies from Thorpe-Ambrose. They left on the day before yesterday – the thirteenth – having, after much hesitation, finally decided on going abroad, to visit some old friends settled in Italy, in the neighbourhood of Florence. It appears to be quite possible that Mrs Blanchard and her niece may settle there too, if they can find a suitable house and grounds to let. They both like the Italian country and the Italian people, and they are well enough off to please themselves. The elder lady has her jointure, and the younger is in possession of all her father's fortune.

The next page of the letter was, in Allan's opinion, far from a pleasant page to read. After referring, in the most grateful terms, to the kindness which had left her niece and herself free to leave their old home at their own time, Mrs Blanchard added that Allan's considerate conduct had produced such a strongly favourable impression among the friends and dependants of the family, that they were desirous of giving him a public reception on his arrival among them. A preliminary meeting of the tenants on the estate and the principal persons in the neighbouring town, had already been held to discuss the arrangements; and a letter might be expected shortly from the clergyman, inquiring when it would suit Mr Armadale's convenience to take possession personally and publicly of his estates in Norfolk.

You will now be able to guess the cause of our sudden departure from the Isle of Man. The first and foremost idea in your old pupil's mind, as soon as he had read Mrs Blanchard's account of the proceedings at the meeting, was the idea of escaping the public reception; and the one certain way he could see of avoiding it, was to start for Thorpe-Ambrose before the clergyman's letter could reach him. I tried hard to make him think a little before he acted on his first impulse in this matter; but he only went on packing his portmanteau in his own impenetrably good-humoured way. In ten minutes his luggage was ready; and in five minutes more he had given the crew their directions for taking the yacht back to Somersetshire. The steamer to Liverpool was alongside of us in the harbour, and I had really no choice but to go on board with him, or to let him go by himself. I spare you the account of our stormy voyage, of our detention at Liverpool, and of the trains we missed on our journey across the country. You know that we have got here safely, and that is enough. What the servants think of the new squire's sudden appearance among them, without a word of warning, is of no great consequence. What the committee for arranging the public reception may think of it, when the news flies abroad to-morrow, is, I am afraid, a more serious matter.

Having already mentioned the servants, I may proceed to tell you that the latter part of Mrs Blanchard's letter was entirely devoted to instructing Allan on the subject of the domestic establishment which she has left behind her. It seems that all the servants, indoors and out (with three exceptions), are waiting here, on the chance that Allan will continue them in their places. Two of these exceptions are readily accounted for: Mrs Blanchard's maid and Miss Blanchard's maid go abroad with their mistresses. The third exceptional case is the case of the upper housemaid: and here there is a little hitch. In plain words, the housemaid has been sent away at a moment's notice, for what Mrs Blanchard rather mysteriously describes as 'levity of conduct with a stranger'.

I am afraid you will laugh at me, but I must confess the truth. I have been made so distrustful (after what happened to us in the Isle of Man) of even the most trifling misadventures which connect themselves in any way with Allan's introduction to his new life and prospects, that I have already questioned one of the men-servants here about this apparently unimportant matter of the housemaid's going away in disgrace. All I can learn is, that a strange man had been noticed hanging suspiciously about the grounds; that the housemaid was so ugly a woman as to render it next to a certainty that he had some underhand purpose to serve in making himself agreeable to her; and that he has not as yet been seen again in the neighbourhood since the day of her dismissal. So much for the one servant who has been turned out at Thorpe-Ambrose. I can only hope there is no trouble for Allan brewing in that quarter. As for the other servants who remain, Mrs Blanchard describes them, both men and women, as perfectly trustworthy; and they will all, no doubt, continue to occupy their present places.

Having now done with Mrs Blanchard's letter, my next duty is to beg you, in Allan's name and with Allan's love, to come here and stay with him at the earliest moment when you can leave Somersetshire. Although I cannot presume to think that my own wishes will have any special influence in determining you to accept this invitation, I must nevertheless acknowledge that I have a reason of my own for earnestly desiring to see you here.

Allan has innocently caused me a new anxiety about my future relations with him; and I sorely need your advice to show me the right way of setting that anxiety at rest.

The difficulty which now perplexes me relates to the steward's place at Thorpe-Ambrose. Before to-day, I only knew that Allan had hit on some plan of his own for dealing with this matter; rather strangely involving, among other results, the letting of the cottage which was the old steward's place of abode, in consequence of the new steward's contemplated residence in the great house. A chance word in our conversation on the journey here, led Allan into speaking out more plainly than he had spoken yet; and I heard, to my unutterable astonishment, that the person who was at the bottom of the whole arrangement about the steward was no other than myself!

It is needless to tell you how I felt this new instance of Allan's kindness. The first pleasure of hearing from his own lips that I had deserved the strongest proof he could give of his confidence in me, was soon dashed by the pain which mixes itself with all pleasure – at least, with all that I have ever known. Never has my past life seemed so dreary to look back on as it seems now, when I feel how entirely it has unfitted me to take the place of all others that I should have liked to occupy in my friend's service. I mustered courage to tell him that I had none of the business knowledge and business experience which his steward ought to possess. He generously met the objection by telling me that I could learn; and he promised to send to London for the person who had already been employed for the time being in the steward's office, and who would, therefore, be perfectly competent to teach me. Do you, too, think I can learn? If you do, I will work day and night to instruct myself. But if (as I am afraid) the steward's duties are of far too serious a kind to be learnt off-hand by a man so young and so inexperienced as I am – then, pray hasten your journey to Thorpe-Ambrose, and exert your influence over Allan personally. Nothing less will induce him to pass me over, and to employ a steward who is really fit to take the place. Pray, pray, act in this matter as you think best for Allan's interests. Whatever disappointment I may feel, *he* shall not see it.

Believe me, dear Mr Brock,

Gratefully yours,

OZIAS MIDWINTER

P.S. – I open the envelope again, to add one word more. If you have heard or seen anything since your return to Somersetshire of the woman in the black dress and the red shawl, I hope you will not forget, when you write, to let me know it. – O. M.

2. – *From Mrs Oldershaw to Miss Gwilt*

Ladies' Toilette Repository, Diana Street,
Pimlico: Wednesday.

MY DEAR LYDIA, – To save the post, I write to you, after a long day's worry at my place of business, on the business letter-paper, having news since we last met, which it seems advisable to send you at the earliest opportunity.

To begin at the beginning. After carefully considering the thing, I am quite sure you will do wisely with young Armadale if you hold your tongue about Madeira and all that happened there. Your position was, no doubt, a very strong one with his mother. You had privately helped her in playing a trick on her own father – you had been ungratefully dismissed, at a pitiably tender age, as soon as you had served her purpose – and when you came upon her suddenly, after a separation of more than twenty years, you found her in failing health, with a grown-up son, whom she had kept in total ignorance of the true story of her marriage. Have you any such advantages as these with the young gentleman who has survived her? If he is not a born idiot, he will decline to believe your shocking aspersions on the memory of his mother; and – seeing that you have no proofs at this distance of time to meet him with – there is an end of your money-grubbing in the golden Armadale diggings. Mind! I don't dispute that the old lady's heavy debt of obligation, after what you did for her in Madeira, is not paid yet; and that the son is the next person to settle with you, now the mother has slipped through your fingers. Only squeeze him the right way, my dear, that's what I venture to suggest – squeeze him the right way.

And which is the right way? This brings me to my news. Have you thought again of that other notion of yours of trying your hand on this lucky young gentleman, with nothing but your own good looks and your own quick wits to help you? The idea hung on my mind so strangely after you were gone, that it ended in my sending a little note to my lawyer, to have the will under which young Armadale has got his fortune, examined at Doctors' Commons.[1] The result turns out to be something infinitely more encouraging than either you or I could possibly have hoped for. After the lawyer's report to me, there cannot be a moment's doubt of what you ought to do. In two words, Lydia, take the bull by the horns – and marry him!!!

I am quite serious. He is much better worth the venture than you suppose. Only persuade him to make you Mrs Armadale, and you may set all after-discoveries at flat defiance. As long as he lives, you can make your own terms with him; and, if he dies, the will entitles you, in spite of anything he can say or do – with children, or without them – to an income chargeable on his estate, of *twelve hundred a year for life*. There is no doubt about this – the lawyer himself has looked at the will. Of course Mr Blanchard had his son, and his son's widow in his eye, when he made the provision. But, as it is not limited to any one heir by name, and not revoked anywhere, it now holds as good with young Armadale as it would have held under other circumstances with Mr Blanchard's son. What a chance for you, after all the miseries and the dangers you have gone through, to be mistress of Thorpe-Ambrose, if he lives; to have an income for life, if he dies! Hook him, my poor dear; hook him at any sacrifice.

I dare say you will make the same objection when you read this, which you made when we were talking about it the other day – I mean the objection of your age. Now, my good creature, just listen to me. The question is – not whether you were five-and-thirty last birthday; we will own the dreadful truth, and say you were – but whether you do look, or don't look, your real age. My opinion on this matter ought to be, and is, one of the best opinions in London. I have had twenty years' experience among our charming sex in making up battered old faces and worn-out old figures to look like new – and I say positively you don't look a day over thirty, if as much. If you will follow my advice about dressing, and use one or two of my applications privately, I guarantee to put you back three years more. I will forfeit all the money I shall have to advance for you in this matter, if, when I have ground you young again in my wonderful mill, you look more than seven-and-twenty in any man's eyes living – except, of course, when you wake anxious in the small hours of the morning; and then, my dear, you will be old and ugly in the retirement of your own room, and it won't matter.

'But,' you may say, 'supposing all this, here I am, at my very best, a good sixteen years older than he is;[2] and that is against me at starting.' Is it? Just think again. Surely, your own experience must have shown you that the commonest of all common weaknesses, in young fellows of this Armadale's age, is to fall in love with women older than themselves? Who are the men who really appreciate us in the bloom of our youth (I'm sure I have cause to speak well of the bloom of youth; I made fifty guineas to-day by putting it on the spotted shoulders of a woman old enough to be your mother), – who are the men, I say, who are ready to worship us when we are mere babies of seventeen? The gay young gentlemen in the bloom of their own youth? No! The cunning old wretches who are on the wrong side of forty.

And what is the moral of this, as the story-books say? The moral is that the chances, with such a head as you have got on your shoulders, are all in your favour. If you feel your present forlorn position, as I believe you do; if you know what a charming woman (in the men's eyes) you can still be, when you please; and if all your old resolution has really come back, after that shocking outbreak of desperation on board the steamer (natural enough, I own, under the dreadful provocation laid on you), you will want no further persuasion from me to try this experiment. Only to think of how things turn out! If the other young booby had not jumped into the river after you, *this* young booby would never have had the estate. It really looks as if fate had determined that you were to be Mrs Armadale, of Thorpe-Ambrose – and who can control his fate, as the poet says?

Send me one line to say Yes or No; and believe me

Your attached old friend
MARIA OLDERSHAW.

3. – *From Miss Gwilt to Mrs Oldershaw*

Richmond, Thursday.

YOU OLD WRETCH, – I won't say Yes or No till I have had a long, long look at my glass first. If you had any real regard for anybody but your wicked old self, you would know that the bare idea of marrying again (after what I have gone through) is an idea that makes my flesh creep.

But there can be no harm in your sending me a little more information, while I am making up my mind. You have got twenty pounds of mine still left out of those things you sold for me: send ten pounds here for my expenses, in a post-office order, and use the other ten for making private inquiries at Thorpe-Ambrose. I want to know when the two Blanchard women go away, and when young Armadale stirs up the dead ashes in the family fireplace. Are you quite sure he will turn out as easy to manage as you think? If he takes after his hypocrite of a mother, I can tell you this – Judas Iscariot has come to life again.

I am very comfortable in this lodging. There are lovely flowers in the garden, and the birds wake me in the morning delightfully. I have hired a reasonably good piano. The only man I care two straws about – don't be alarmed; he was laid in his grave many a long year ago, under the name of BEETHOVEN – keeps me company in my lonely hours. The landlady would keep me company, too, if I would only let her. I hate women. The new curate paid a visit to the other lodger yesterday, and passed me on the lawn as he came out. My eyes have lost nothing yet, at any rate, though I *am* five-and-thirty; the poor man actually blushed when I looked at him! What sort of colour do you think he would have turned, if one of the little birds in the garden had whispered in his ear, and told him the true story of the charming Miss Gwilt?

Good-by, Mother Oldershaw. I rather doubt whether I am yours, or anybody's, affectionately; but we all tell lies at the bottoms of our letters, don't we? If you are my attached old friend, I must of course be

Yours affectionately,
LYDIA GWILT.

P. S. – Keep your odious powders[3] and paints and washes for the spotted shoulders of your customers; not one of them shall touch my skin, I promise you. If you really want to be useful, try and find out some quieting draught to keep me from grinding my teeth in my sleep. I shall break them one of these nights; and then what will become of my beauty, I wonder?

4. – *From Mrs Oldershaw to Miss Gwilt*

Ladies' Toilette Repository, Tuesday.

MY DEAR LYDIA, – It is a thousand pities your letter was not addressed to Mr Armadale; your graceful audacity would have charmed him. It doesn't affect me; I am so well used to it, you know. Why waste your sparkling wit, my love, on your own impenetrable Oldershaw? – it only splutters and goes out. Will you try and be serious, this next time? I have news for you from Thorpe-Ambrose, which is beyond a joke, and which must not be trifled with.

An hour after I got your letter, I set the inquiries on foot. Not knowing what consequences they might lead to, I thought it safest to begin in the dark. Instead of employing any of the people whom I have at my own disposal (who know you and know me), I went to the Private Inquiry Office in Shadyside Place, and put the matter in the inspector's hands, in the character of a perfect stranger, and without mentioning you at all. This was not the cheapest way of going to work, I own; but it was the safest way, which is of much greater consequence.

The inspector and I understood each other in ten minutes; and the right person for the purpose – the most harmless-looking young man you ever saw in your life – was produced immediately. He left for Thorpe-Ambrose an hour after I saw him. I arranged to call at the office on the afternoons of Saturday, Monday, and to-day, for news. There was no news till to-day – and there I found our Confidential Agent just returned to town, and waiting to favour me with a full account of his trip to Norfolk.

First of all, let me quiet your mind about those two questions of yours; I have got answers to both the one and the other. The Blanchard women go away to foreign parts on the thirteenth; and young Armadale is at this moment cruising somewhere at sea in his yacht. There is talk at Thorpe-Ambrose of giving him a public reception, and of calling a meeting of the local grandees to settle it all. The speechifying and fuss on these occasions generally wastes plenty of time; and the public reception is not thought likely to meet the new Squire much before the end of the month.

If our messenger had done no more for us than this, I think he would have earned his money. But the harmless young man is a

regular Jesuit at a private inquiry – with this great advantage
over all the Popish priests I have ever seen, that he has not got his
slyness written in his face. Having to get his information through
the female servants, in the usual way, he addressed himself, with
admirable discretion, to the ugliest woman in the house. 'When
they are nice-looking, and can pick and choose,' as he neatly
expressed it to me, 'they waste a great deal of valuable time in
deciding on a sweetheart. When they are ugly, and haven't got
the ghost of a chance of choosing, they snap at a sweetheart, if he
comes their way, like a starved dog at a bone.' Acting on these
excellent principles, our Confidential Agent succeeded, after certain
unavoidable delays, in addressing himself to the upper housemaid at
Thorpe-Ambrose, and took full possession of her confidence at the
first interview. Bearing his instructions carefully in mind, he
encouraged the woman to chatter, and was favoured, of course, with
all the gossip of the servants' hall. The greater part of it (as repeated
to me) was of no earthly importance. But I listened patiently, and
was rewarded by a valuable discovery at last. Here it is.

It seems there is an ornamental cottage in the grounds at
Thorpe-Ambrose. For some reason unknown, young Armadale
has chosen to let it; and a tenant has come in already. He is a
poor half-pay major in the army, named Milroy – a meek sort of
man, by all accounts, with a turn for occupying himself in
mechanical pursuits, and with a domestic incumbrance in the
shape of a bedridden wife, who has not been seen by anybody.
Well, and what of all this? you will ask, with that sparkling
impatience which becomes you so well. My dear Lydia, don't
sparkle! The man's family affairs seriously concern us both – for,
as ill-luck will have it, the man has got a daughter!

You may imagine how I questioned our agent, and how our
agent ransacked his memory, when I stumbled, in due course, on
such a discovery as this. If heaven is responsible for women's
chattering tongues, heaven be praised! From Miss Blanchard to
Miss Blanchard's maid; from Miss Blanchard's maid to Miss
Blanchard's aunt's maid; from Miss Blanchard's aunt's maid, to
the ugly housemaid; from the ugly housemaid to the harmless-
looking young man – so the stream of gossip trickled into the right
reservoir at last, and thirsty Mother Oldershaw has drunk it all
up. In plain English, my dear, this is how it stands. The major's
daughter is a minx just turned sixteen; lively and nice-looking
(hateful little wretch!), dowdy in her dress (thank heaven!), and

deficient in her manners (thank heaven, again!). She has been brought up at home. The governess who last had charge of her, left before her father moved to Thorpe-Ambrose. Her education stands wofully in want of a finishing touch, and the major doesn't quite know what to do next. None of his friends can recommend him a new governess, and he doesn't like the notion of sending the girl to school. So matters rest at present, on the major's own showing – for so the major expressed himself at a morning call which the father and daughter paid to the ladies at the great house.

You have now got my promised news, and you will have little difficulty, I think, in agreeing with me, that the Armadale business must be settled at once, one way or the other. If – with your hopeless prospects, and with what I may call your family claim on this young fellow – you decide on giving him up, I shall have the pleasure of sending you the balance of your account with me (seven-and-twenty shillings), and shall then be free to devote myself entirely to my own proper business. If, on the contrary, you decide to try your luck at Thorpe-Ambrose, then (there being no kind of doubt that the major's minx will set her cap at the young squire) I should be glad to hear how you mean to meet the double difficulty of inflaming Mr Armadale and extinguishing Miss Milroy.

Affectionately yours,
MARIA OLDERSHAW.

5. – *From Miss Gwilt to Mrs Oldershaw (First Answer)*

Richmond, Wednesday Morning.

MRS OLDERSHAW, – Send me my seven-and-twenty shillings, and devote yourself to your own proper business.

Yours,
L. G.

6. – *From Miss Gwilt to Mrs Oldershaw (Second Answer)*

Richmond, Wednesday Night.

DEAR OLD LOVE, – Keep the seven-and-twenty shillings, and burn my other letter. I have changed my mind.

165

I wrote the first time, after a horrible night. I write, this time, after a ride on horseback, a tumbler of claret, and the breast of a chicken. Is that explanation enough? Please say Yes – for I want to go back to my piano.

No; I can't go back yet – I must answer your question first. But are you really so very simple as to suppose that I don't see straight through you and your letter? You know that the major's difficulty is our opportunity as well as I do – but you want me to take the responsibility of making the first proposal; don't you? Suppose I take it in your own roundabout way? Suppose I say – 'Pray don't ask me how I propose inflaming Mr Armadale and extinguishing Miss Milroy; the question is so shockingly abrupt I really can't answer it. Ask me instead, if it is the modest ambition of my life to become Miss Milroy's governess?' Yes, if you please, Mrs Oldershaw – and if you will assist me by becoming my reference.

There it is for you! If some serious disaster happens (which is quite possible), what a comfort it will be to remember that it was all my fault!

Now I have done this for you, will you do something for me? I want to dream away the little time I am likely to have left here, in my own way. Be a merciful Mother Oldershaw, and spare me the worry of looking at the Ins and Outs, and adding up the chances For and Against, in this new venture of mine. Think for me, in short, until I am obliged to think for myself.

I had better not write any more, or I shall say something savage that you won't like. I am in one of my tempers to-night. I want a husband to vex, or a child to beat, or something of that sort. Do you ever like to see the summer insects kill themselves in the candle? I do, sometimes. Good-night, Mrs Jezebel. The longer you can leave me here the better. The air agrees with me, and I am looking charmingly.

L. G.

7. – *From Mrs Oldershaw to Miss Gwilt*

Thursday.

MY DEAR LYDIA, – Some persons in my situation might be a little offended at the tone of your last letter. But I am so fondly attached to you! And when I love a person, it is so very hard, my dear, for that person to offend me! Don't ride quite so far, and only drink half a tumblerful of claret next time. I say no more.

Shall we leave off our fencing-match and come to serious matters now? How curiously hard it always seems to be for women to understand each other – especially when they have got their pens in their hands! But suppose we try.

Well, then, to begin with – I gather from your letter that you have wisely decided to try the Thorpe-Ambrose experiment – and to secure, if you can, an excellent position at starting, by becoming a member of Major Milroy's household. If the circumstances turn against you, and some other woman gets the governess's place (about which I shall have something more to say presently), you will then have no choice but to make Mr Armadale's acquaintance in some other character. In any case, you will want my assistance; and the first question therefore to set at rest between us, is the question of what I am willing to do, and what I can do, to help you.

A woman, my dear Lydia, with your appearance, your manners, your abilities, and your education, can make almost any excursions into society that she pleases, if she only has money in her pocket and a respectable reference to appeal to in cases of emergency. As to the money, in the first place. I will engage to find it, on condition of your remembering my assistance with adequate pecuniary gratitude, if you win the Armadale prize. Your promise so to remember me, embodying the terms in plain figures, shall be drawn out on paper by my own lawyer; so that we can sign and settle at once when I see you in London.

Next, as to the reference. Here, again, my services are at your disposal – on another condition. It is this: that you present yourself at Thorpe-Ambrose, under the name to which you have returned, ever since the dreadful business of your marriage – I mean your own maiden name of Gwilt. I have only one motive in insisting on this; I wish to run no needless risks. My experience, as confidential adviser of my customers, in various romantic cases of private embarrassment, has shown me that an assumed name is, nine times out of ten, a very unnecessary and a very dangerous form of deception. Nothing could justify your assuming a name but the fear of young Armadale's detecting you – a fear from which we are fortunately relieved by his mother's own conduct in keeping your early connection with her a profound secret from her son, and from everybody.

The next, and last, perplexity to settle, relates, my dear, to the chances for and against your finding your way, in the capacity of governess, into Major Milroy's house. Once inside the door, with your knowledge of music and languages, if you can keep your temper, you may be sure of keeping the place. The only doubt, as things are now, is whether you can get it.

In the major's present difficulty about his daughter's education, the chances are, I think, in favour of his advertising for a governess. Say he does advertise, what address will he give for applicants to write to? There is the real pinch of the matter. If he gives an address in London, good-by to all chances in your favour at once; for this plain reason, that we shall not be able to pick out his advertisement from the advertisements of other people who want governesses, and who will give them addresses in London as well. If, on the other hand, our luck helps us, and he refers his correspondents to a shop, post-office, or what not, *at Thorpe-Ambrose*, there we have our advertiser as plainly picked out for us as we can wish. In this last case, I have little or no doubt – with me for your reference – of your finding your way into the major's family circle. We have one great advantage over the other women who will answer the advertisement. Thanks to my inquiries on the spot, I know Major Milroy to be a poor man; and we will fix the salary you ask at a figure that is sure to tempt him. As for the style of the letter, if you and I together can't write a modest and interesting application for the vacant place, I should like to know who can?

All this, however, is still in the future. For the present, my advice is – stay where you are, and dream to your heart's content, till you hear from me again. I take in *The Times* regularly; and you may trust my wary eye not to miss the right advertisement. We can luckily give the major time, without doing any injury to our own interests; for there is no fear, just yet, of the girl's getting the start of you. The public reception, as we know, won't be ready till near the end of the month; and we may safely trust young Armadale's vanity to keep him out of his new house until his flatterers are all assembled to welcome him. Let us wait another ten days at least before we give up the governess notion, and lay our heads together to try some other plan.

It's odd, isn't it, to think how much depends on this half-pay officer's decision? For my part, I shall wake every morning, now, with the same question in my mind. If the major's advertisement appears, which will the major say – Thorpe-Ambrose, or London?

Ever, my dear Lydia,

Affectionately yours,

MARIA OLDERSHAW.

CHAPTER II

ALLAN AS A LANDED GENTLEMAN

Early on the morning after his first night's rest at Thorpe-Ambrose, Allan rose and surveyed the prospect from his bedroom window, lost in the dense mental bewilderment of feeling himself to be a stranger in his own house.

The bedroom looked out over the great front door, with its portico, its terrace and flight of steps beyond, and, farther still, the broad sweep of the well-timbered park to close the view. The morning mist nestled lightly about the distant trees; and the cows were feeding sociably, close to the iron fence which railed off the park from the drive in front of the house. 'All mine!' thought Allan, staring in blank amazement at the prospect of his own possessions. 'Hang me if I can beat it into my head yet. All mine!'

He dressed, left his room, and walked along the corridor which led to the staircase and hall; opening the doors in succession as he passed them. The rooms in this part of the house were bedrooms and dressing-rooms – light, spacious, perfectly furnished; and all empty, except the one bedchamber next to Allan's, which had been appropriated to Midwinter. He was still sleeping when his friend looked in on him, having sat late into the night writing his letter to Mr Brock. Allan went on to the end of the first corridor, turned at right angles into a second, and, that passed, gained the head of the great staircase. 'No romance here,' he said to himself, looking down the handsomely-carpeted stone stairs into the bright modern hall. 'Nothing to startle Midwinter's fidgety nerves in this house.' There was nothing indeed; Allan's essentially superficial observation had not misled him for once. The mansion of Thorpe-Ambrose (built after the pulling down of the dilapidated old manor-house) was barely fifty years old. Nothing picturesque, nothing in the slightest degree suggestive of mystery and romance, appeared in any part of it. It was a purely conventional country-house – the product of the classical idea filtered judiciously through the commercial English mind. Viewed on the outer side, it presented the spectacle of a modern manufactory trying to look like an ancient temple. Viewed on the inner side, it was a marvel of luxurious comfort in every part of it, from basement to roof. 'And quite right, too,' thought Allan, sauntering contentedly down the broad, gently graduated stairs. 'Deuce take all mystery and romance! Let's be clean and comfortable – that's what I say.'

Arrived in the hall, the new master of Thorpe-Ambrose hesitated, and looked about him, uncertain which way to turn next. The four reception-rooms on the ground floor opened into the hall, two on either side. Allan tried the nearest door on his right hand at a venture, and found himself in the drawing-room. Here the first sign of life appeared, under life's most attractive form. A young girl was in solitary possession of the drawing-room. The duster in her hand appeared to associate her with the domestic duties of the house; but at that particular moment she was occupied in asserting the rights of nature over the obligations of service. In other words, she was attentively contemplating her own face in the glass over the mantelpiece.

'There! there! don't let me frighten you,' said Allan, as the girl started away from the glass, and stared at him in unutterable confusion. 'I quite agree with you, my dear: your face is well worth looking at. Who are you? – oh, the housemaid. And what's your name? Susan, eh? Come! I like your name to begin with. Do you know who I am, Susan? I'm your master, though you may not think it. Your character? Oh, yes! Mrs Blanchard gave you a capital character. You shall stop here; don't be afraid. And you'll be a good girl, Susan, and wear smart little caps and aprons and bright ribbons, and you'll look nice and pretty, and dust the furniture, won't you?'

With this summary of a housemaid's duties, Allan sauntered back into the hall, and found more signs of life in that quarter. A man-servant appeared on this occasion, and bowed, as became a vassal in a linen jacket, before his liege lord in a wide-awake hat.[1]

'And who may you be?' asked Allan. 'Not the man who let us in last night? Ah, I thought not. The second footman, eh? Character? Oh, yes; capital character. Stop here, of course. You can valet me, can you? Bother valeting me! I like to put on my own clothes, and brush them, too, when they *are* on; and, if I only knew how to black my own boots, by George I should like to do it! What room's this? Morning-room, eh? And here's the dining-room, of course. Good heavens, what a table! it's as long as my yacht, and longer. I say – by-the-by, what's your name? Richard, is it? – well, Richard, the vessel I sail in is a vessel of my own building. What do you think of that? You look to me just the right sort of man to be my steward on board. If you're not sick at sea – oh, you *are* sick at sea? Well, then, we'll say nothing more about it. And what room is this? Ah, yes; the library, of course – more in Mr Midwinter's way than mine. Mr Midwinter is the gentleman who came here with me last night; and mind this, Richard, you're all to show him as much attention as you show me. Where are we now? What's this door at the back? Billiard-room and smoking-room, eh? Jolly. Another door! and more stairs! Where do they go to? and who's this coming up? Take your time, ma'am; you're not quite so young as you were once – take your time.'

The object of Allan's humane caution was a corpulent elderly woman, of the type called 'motherly'. Fourteen stairs were all that separated her from the master of the house: she ascended them with fourteen stoppages and fourteen sighs. Nature, various in all things, is infinitely various in the female sex. There are some women whose personal qualities reveal the Loves and the Graces; and there are other women whose personal qualities suggest the Perquisites and the Grease Pot. This was one of the other women.

'Glad to see you looking so well, ma'am,' said Allan, when the cook, in the majesty of her office, stood proclaimed before him. 'Your name is Gripper, is it? I consider you, Mrs Gripper, the most valuable person in the house. For this reason, that nobody in the house eats a heartier dinner every day than I do. Directions? Oh, no; I've no directions to give. I leave all that to you. Lots of strong soup, and joints done with the gravy in them – there's my notion of good feeding, in two words. Steady! Here's somebody else. Oh, to be sure – the butler! Another valuable person. We'll go right through all the wine in the cellar, Mr butler; and if I can't give you a sound opinion after that, we'll persevere boldly, and go right through it again. Talking of wine – hullo! here are more of them coming upstairs. There! there! don't trouble yourselves. You've all got capital characters, and you shall all stop here along with me. What was I saying just now? Something about wine; so it was. I'll tell you what, Mr butler, it isn't every day that a new master comes to Thorpe-Ambrose; and it's my wish that we should all start together on the best possible terms. Let the servants have a grand jollification downstairs, to celebrate my arrival; and give them what they like to drink my health in. It's a poor heart, Mrs Gripper, that never rejoices, isn't it? No; I won't look at the cellar now: I want to go out, and get a breath of fresh air before breakfast. Where's Richard? I say, have I got a garden here? Which side of the house is it! That side, eh? You needn't show me round. I'll go alone, Richard, and lose myself, if I can, in my own property.'

With those words Allan descended the terrace-steps in front of the house, whistling cheerfully. He had met the serious responsibility of settling his domestic establishment to his own entire satisfaction. 'People talk of the difficulty of managing their servants,' thought Allan. 'What on earth do they mean? I don't see any difficulty at all.' He opened an ornamental gate leading out of the drive at the side of the house; and, following the footman's directions, entered the shrubbery that sheltered the Thorpe-Ambrose gardens. 'Nice shady sort of place for a cigar,' said Allan, as he sauntered along, with his hands in his pockets. 'I wish I could beat it into my head that it really belongs to *me*.'

The shrubbery opened on the broad expanse of a flower-garden, flooded bright in its summer glory by the light of the morning sun. On one side an archway, broken through a wall, led into the fruit-garden. On the other, a terrace of turf led to ground on a lower level, laid out as an Italian garden. Wandering past the fountains and statues, Allan reached another shrubbery, winding its way apparently to some remote part of the grounds. Thus far, not a human creature had been visible or audible anywhere; but, as he approached the end of the second shrubbery, it struck him that he heard something on the other side of the foliage. He stopped and listened. There were two voices speaking distinctly – an old voice that sounded very obstinate, and a young voice that sounded very angry.

'It's no use, Miss,' said the old voice. 'I mustn't allow it, and I won't allow it. What would Mr Armadale say?'

'If Mr Armadale is the gentleman I take him for, you old brute!' replied the young voice, 'he would say, "Come into my garden, Miss Milroy, as often as you like, and take as many nosegays as you please."'

Allan's bright blue eyes twinkled mischievously. Inspired by a sudden idea, he stole softly to the end of the shrubbery, darted round the corner of it, and, vaulting over a low ring-fence, found himself in a trim little paddock, crossed by a gravel walk. At a short distance down the walk stood a young lady, with her back towards him, trying to force her way past an impenetrable old man, with a rake in his hand, who stood obstinately in front of her, shaking his head.

'Come into my garden, Miss Milroy, as often as you like, and take as many nosegays as you please,' cried Allan, remorselessly repeating her own words.

The young lady turned round, with a scream; her muslin dress, which she was holding up in front, dropped from her hand, and a prodigious lapful of flowers rolled out on the gravel walk.

Before another word could be said, the impenetrable old man stepped forward, with the utmost composure, and entered on the question of his own personal interests, as if nothing whatever had happened, and nobody was present but his new master and himself.

'I bid you humbly welcome to Thorpe-Ambrose, sir,' said this ancient of the gardens. 'My name is Abraham Sage. I've been employed in the grounds for more than forty years; and I hope you'll be pleased to continue me in my place.'

So, with vision inexorably limited to the horizon of his own prospects, spoke the gardener – and spoke in vain. Allan was down on his knees on the gravel walk, collecting the fallen flowers, and forming his first impressions of Miss Milroy from the feet upwards. She was pretty; she was not pretty – she charmed, she disappointed, she charmed again. Tried by recognized line and rule, she was too short, and too well-developed for her age. And yet few men's eyes would have wished her figure other than it was. Her hands were so prettily plump and dimpled, that it was hard to see how red they were with the blessed exuberance of youth and health. Her feet apologized gracefully for her old and ill-fitting shoes; and her shoulders made ample amends for the misdemeanor in muslin which covered them in the shape of a dress. Her dark grey eyes were lovely in their clear softness of colour, in their spirit, tenderness, and sweet good humour of expression; and her hair (where a shabby old garden hat allowed it to be seen) was of just that lighter shade of brown which gave value by contrast to the darker beauty of her eyes. But these attractions passed, the little attendant blemishes and imperfections of this self-contradictory girl began again. Her nose was too short, her mouth was too large, her face was too round, and too rosy. The dreadful justice of photography would have had no mercy on her;[2] and the sculptors of classical Greece would have bowed her regretfully out of their studios. Admitting all this, and more, the girdle round Miss Milroy's waist was the girdle of Venus, nevertheless – and the pass-key that opens the general heart was the key she carried, if ever a girl possessed it yet. Before Allan had picked up his second handful of flowers, Allan was in love with her.

'Don't! pray don't, Mr Armadale!' she said, receiving the flowers under protest, as Allan vigorously showered them back into the lap of her dress. 'I am so ashamed! I didn't mean to invite myself in that bold way into your garden; my tongue ran away with me – it did indeed! What can I say to excuse myself? Oh, Mr Armadale, what must you think of me!'

Allan suddenly saw his way to a compliment, and tossed it up to her forthwith, with the third handful of flowers.

'I'll tell you what I think, Miss Milroy,' he said, in his blunt, boyish way. 'I think the luckiest walk I ever took in my life was the walk this morning that brought me here.'

He looked eager and handsome. He was not addressing a woman worn out with admiration, but a girl just beginning a woman's life – and it did him no harm, at any rate, to speak in the character of master of Thorpe-Ambrose. The penitential expression on Miss Milroy's face gently melted away: she looked down, demure and smiling, at the flowers in her lap.

'I deserve a good scolding,' she said. 'I don't deserve compliments, Mr Armadale – least of all from *you*.'

'Oh, yes, you do!' cried the headlong Allan, getting briskly on his legs. 'Besides, it isn't a compliment; it's true. You are the prettiest – I beg your pardon, Miss Milroy! *my* tongue ran away with me that time.'

Among the heavy burdens that are laid on female human nature, perhaps the heaviest, at the age of sixteen, is the burden of gravity. Miss Milroy struggled – tittered – struggled again – and composed herself for the time being.

The gardener, who still stood where he had stood from the first, immovably waiting for his next opportunity, saw it now, and gently pushed his personal interests into the first gap of silence that had opened within his reach since Allan's appearance on the scene.

'I humbly bid you welcome to Thorpe-Ambrose, sir,' said Abraham Sage; beginning obstinately with his little introductory speech for the second time. 'My name—'

Before he could deliver himself of his name, Miss Milroy looked accidentally in the horticulturist's pertinacious face – and instantly lost her hold on her gravity beyond recall. Allan, never backward in following a boisterous example of any sort, joined in her laughter with right goodwill. The wise man of the gardens showed no surprise, and took no offence. He waited for another gap of silence, and walked in again gently with his personal interests, the moment the two young people stopped to take breath.

'I have been employed in the grounds,' proceeded Abraham Sage, irrepressibly, 'for more than forty years—'

'You shall be employed in the grounds for forty more, if you'll only hold your tongue and take yourself off!' cried Allan, as soon as he could speak.

'Thank you kindly, sir,' said the gardener, with the utmost politeness, but with no present signs either of holding his tongue or of taking himself off.

'Well?' said Allan.

Abraham Sage carefully cleared his throat, and shifted his rake from one hand to the other. He looked down the length of his own invaluable implement, with a grave interest and attention; seeing apparently, not the long handle of a rake, but the long perspective of a vista, with a supplementary personal interest established at the end of it. 'When more convenient, sir,' resumed this immovable man, 'I should wish respectfully to speak to you about my son. Perhaps it may be more convenient in the course of the day? My humble duty, sir, and my best thanks. My son is strictly sober. He is accustomed to the stables, and he belongs to the Church of England – without encumbrances.' Having thus planted his offspring provisionally in his master's estimation, Abraham Sage shouldered his invaluable rake, and hobbled slowly out of view.

'If that's a specimen of a trustworthy old servant,' said Allan, 'I think I'd rather take my chance of being cheated by a new one. *You* shall not be troubled with him again, Miss Milroy, at any rate. All the flower-beds in the garden are at your disposal – and all the fruit in the fruit-season, if you'll only come here and eat it.'

'Oh, Mr Armadale, how very, very kind you are. How can I thank you?'

Allan saw his way to another compliment – an elaborate compliment, in the shape of a trap, this time.

'You can do me the greatest possible favour,' he said. 'You can assist me in forming an agreeable impression of my own grounds.'

'Dear me! how?' asked Miss Milroy, innocently.

Allan judiciously closed the trap on the spot in these words: 'By taking me with you, Miss Milroy, on your morning walk.' He spoke – smiled – and offered his arm.

She saw the way, on her side, to a little flirtation. She rested her hand on his arm – blushed – hesitated – and suddenly took it away again.

'I don't think it's quite right, Mr Armadale,' she said, devoting herself with the deepest attention to her collection of flowers. 'Oughtn't we to have some old lady here? Isn't it improper to take your arm until I know you a little better than I do now? I am obliged to ask; I have had so little instruction; I have seen so little of society – and one of papa's friends once said my manners were too bold for my age. What do *you* think?'

'I think it's a very good thing your papa's friend is not here now,' answered the outspoken Allan; 'I should quarrel with him to a dead certainty. As for society, Miss Milroy, nobody knows less about it than I do; but if we *had* an old lady here, I must say, myself, I think she would be uncommonly in the way. Won't you?' concluded Allan, imploringly offering his arm for the second time. 'Do!'

Miss Milroy looked up at him sidelong from her flowers. 'You are as bad as the gardener, Mr Armadale!' She looked down again in a flutter of indecision. 'I'm sure it's wrong,' she said, and took his arm the instant afterwards, without the slightest hesitation.

They moved away together over the daisied turf of the paddock, young and bright and happy, with the sunlight of the summer morning shining cloudless over their flowery path.

'And where are we going to, now?' asked Allan. 'Into another garden?'

She laughed gaily. 'How very odd of you, Mr Armadale, not to know, when it all belongs to you! Are you really seeing Thorpe-Ambrose this morning for the first time? How indescribably strange it must feel! No, no; don't say any more complimentary things to me just yet. You may turn my head if you do. We haven't got the old lady with us; and I really must take care of myself. Let me be useful; let me tell you all about your own grounds. We are going out at that little gate, across one of the drives in the park, and then over the rustic bridge, and then round the corner of the plantation – where do you think? To where I live, Mr Armadale; to the lovely little cottage that you have let to papa. Oh, if you only knew how lucky we thought ourselves to get it!'

She paused, looked up at her companion, and stopped another compliment on the incorrigible Allan's lips.

'I'll drop your arm,' she said coquettishly, 'if you do! We *were* lucky to get the cottage, Mr Armadale. Papa said he felt under an obligation to you for letting it, the day we got in. And *I* said I felt under an obligation, no longer ago than last week.'

'You, Miss Milroy!' exclaimed Allan.

'Yes. It may surprise you to hear it; but if you hadn't let the cottage to papa, I believe I should have suffered the indignity and misery of being sent to school.'

Allan's memory reverted to the half-crown that he had spun on the cabin-table of the yacht, at Castletown. 'If she only knew that I had tossed up for it!' he thought, guiltily.

'I daresay you don't understand why I should feel such a horror of going to school,' pursued Miss Milroy, misinterpreting the momentary silence on her companion's side. 'If I had gone to school in early life – I mean at the age when other girls go – I shouldn't have minded it now. But I had no such chance at the time. It was the time of mamma's illness and of papa's unfortunate speculations; and as papa had nobody to comfort him but me, of course I stayed at home. You needn't laugh; I was of some use, I can tell you. I helped papa over his troubles, by sitting on his knee after dinner, and asking him to tell me stories of all the remarkable people he had known when he was about in the great world, at home and abroad. Without me to amuse him in the evening, and his clock to occupy him in the daytime—'

'His clock?' repeated Allan.

'Oh, yes! I ought to have told you. Papa is an extraordinary mechanical genius. You will say so, too, when you see his clock. It's nothing like so large, of course, but it's on the model of the famous clock at Strasbourg.[3] Only think, he began it when I was eight years old; and (though I was sixteen last birthday) it isn't finished yet! Some of our friends were quite surprised he should take to such a thing when his troubles began. But papa himself set that right in no time; he reminded them that Louis the Sixteenth[4] took to lock-making when *his* troubles began – and then everybody was perfectly satisfied.' She stopped, and changed colour confusedly. 'Oh, Mr Armadale,' she said, in genuine embarrassment this time, 'here is my unlucky tongue running away with me again! I am talking to you already as if I had known you for years! This is what papa's friend meant when he said my manners were too bold. It's quite true; I have a dreadful way of getting familiar with people, if—' She checked herself suddenly, on the brink of ending the sentence by saying, 'if I like them.'

'No, no; do go on!' pleaded Allan. 'It's a fault of mine to be familiar, too. Besides, we *must* be familiar; we are such near neighbours. I'm rather an uncultivated sort of fellow, and I don't know quite how to say it; but I want your cottage to be jolly and friendly with my house, and my house to be jolly and friendly with your cottage. There's my meaning, all in the wrong words. Do go on, Miss Milroy; pray go on!'

She smiled and hesitated. 'I don't exactly remember where I was,' she replied. 'I only remember I had something I wanted to tell you. This comes, Mr Armadale, of my taking your arm. I should get on so much better, if you would only consent to walk separately. You won't?

177

Well, then, will you tell me what it was I wanted to say? Where was I before I went wandering off to papa's troubles and papa's clock?'

'At school!' replied Allan, with a prodigious effort of memory.

'*Not* at school, you mean,' said Miss Milroy; 'and all through *you*. Now I can go on again, which is a great comfort. I am quite serious, Mr Armadale, in saying that I should have been sent to school, if you had said No when papa proposed for the cottage. This is how it happened. When we began moving in, Mrs Blanchard sent us a most kind message from the great house, to say that her servants were at our disposal, if we wanted any assistance. The least papa and I could do, after that, was to call and thank her. We saw Mrs Blanchard and Miss Blanchard. Mrs was charming, and Miss looked perfectly lovely in her mourning. I'm sure you admire her? She's tall and pale and graceful – quite your idea of beauty, I should think?'

'Nothing like it,' began Allan. 'My idea of beauty at the present moment—'

Miss Milroy felt it coming, and instantly took her hand off his arm.

'I mean I have never seen either Mrs Blanchard or her niece,' added Allan, precipitately correcting himself.

Miss Milroy tempered justice with mercy, and put her hand back again.

'How extraordinary that you should never have seen them!' she went on. 'Why, you are a perfect stranger to everything and everybody at Thorpe-Ambrose! Well, after Miss Blanchard and I had sat and talked a little while, I heard my name on Mrs Blanchard's lips, and instantly held my breath. She was asking papa if I had finished my education. Out came papa's great grievance directly. My old governess, you must know, left us to be married just before we came here, and none of our friends could produce a new one whose terms were reasonable. "I'm told, Mrs Blanchard, by people who understand it better than I do," says papa, "that advertising is a risk. It all falls on me, in Mrs Milroy's state of health, and I suppose I must end in sending my little girl to school. Do you happen to know of a school within the means of a poor man?" Mrs Blanchard shook her head – I could have kissed her on the spot for doing it. "All my experience, Major Milroy," says this perfect angel of a woman, "is in favour of advertising. My niece's governess was originally obtained by an advertisement, and you may imagine her value to us when I tell you that she lived in our family for more than ten years." I could have gone down on both my knees and worshipped Mrs Blanchard then and there – and I only wonder I didn't! Papa was struck at the time – I could see that – and he referred to it again on the way home. "Though I have been long out of the world, my dear," says papa, "I know a highly-bred woman and a sensible woman when I see her. Mrs Blanchard's experience puts advertising in a new light — I must think about it." He *has* thought about it, and (though he hasn't openly confessed it to me) I know that he decided to advertise, no later than last night. So, if papa thanks you for letting the cottage, Mr Armadale, I thank you, too. But for you, we should never have known darling Mrs Blanchard; and but for darling Mrs Blanchard, I should have been sent to school.'

Before Allan could reply, they turned the corner of the plantation, and came in sight of the cottage. Description of it is needless; the civilized universe knows it already. It was the typical cottage of the drawing-master's early lessons in neat shading and the broad pencil touch — with the trim thatch, the luxuriant creepers, the modest lattice-windows, the rustic porch, and the wicker birdcage, all complete.

'Isn't it lovely?' said Miss Milroy. 'Do come in!'

'May I?' asked Allan. 'Won't the major think it too early?'

'Early or late, I'm sure papa will be only too glad to see you.'

She led the way briskly up the garden path, and opened the parlour door. As Allan followed her into the little room, he saw, at the further end of it, a gentleman sitting alone at an old-fashioned writing-table, with his back turned to his visitor.

'Papa! a surprise for you!' said Miss Milroy, rousing him from his occupation; 'Mr Armadale has come to Thorpe-Ambrose; and I have brought him here to see you.'

The major started — rose, bewildered for the moment — recovered himself immediately, and advanced to welcome his young landlord, with hospitable outstretched hand.

A man with a larger experience of the world, and a finer observation of humanity than Allan possessed, would have seen the story of Major Milroy's life written in Major Milroy's face. The home-troubles that had struck him were plainly betrayed in his stooping figure, and his wan, deeply-wrinkled cheeks, when he first showed himself on rising from his chair. The changeless influence of one monotonous pursuit and one monotonous habit of thought was next expressed in the dull, dreamy self-absorption of his manner and his look while his daughter was speaking to him. The moment after, when he had roused himself to welcome his guest, was the moment which made the self-revelation complete. Then there flickered in the major's weary eyes a faint reflec-tion of the spirit of his happier youth. Then there passed over the major's dull and dreamy manner a change which told unmistakably of social graces and accomplishments, learned at some past time in no ignoble social school. A man who had long since taken his patient refuge from trouble in his one mechanical pursuit; a man only roused at intervals to know himself again for what he once had been. So revealed, to all eyes that could read him aright, Major Milroy now stood before Allan, on the first morning of an acquaintance which was destined to be an event in Allan's life.

'I am heartily glad to see you, Mr Armadale,' he said, speaking in the changelessly quiet subdued tone peculiar to most men whose occupations are of the solitary and monotonous kind. 'You have done me one favour already, by taking me as your tenant, and you now do me another by paying this friendly visit. If you have not breakfasted already, let me waive all ceremony on my side, and ask you to take your place at our little table.'

'With the greatest pleasure, Major Milroy, if I am not in the way,' replied Allan, delighted at his reception. 'I was sorry to hear from Miss Milroy that Mrs Milroy is an invalid. Perhaps, my being here unexpectedly; perhaps the sight of a strange face—'

'I understand your hesitation, Mr Armadale,' said the major; 'but it is quite unnecessary. Mrs Milroy's illness keeps her entirely confined to her own room.[5] – Have we got everything we want on the table, my love?' he went on, changing the subject so abruptly, that a closer observer than Allan might have suspected it was distasteful to him. 'Will you come and make tea?'

Miss Milroy's attention appeared to be already pre-engaged: she made no reply. While her father and Allan had been exchanging civilities, she had been putting the writing-table in order, and examining the various objects scattered on it with the unrestrained curiosity of a spoilt child. The moment after the major had spoken to her, she discovered a morsel of paper hidden between the leaves of the blotting-book, snatched it up, looked at it, and turned round instantly, with an exclamation of surprise.

'Do my eyes deceive me, papa?' she asked. 'Or were you really and truly writing *the* advertisement when I came in?'

'I had just finished it,' replied her father. 'But, my dear, Mr Armadale is here – we are waiting for breakfast.'

'Mr Armadale knows all about it,' rejoined Miss Milroy. 'I told him in the garden.'

'Oh, yes!' said Allan. 'Pray, don't make a stranger of me, major! If it's about the governess, I've got something (in an indirect sort of way) to do with it too.'

Major Milroy smiled. Before he could answer, his daughter, who had been reading the advertisement, appealed to him eagerly, for the second time.

'Oh, papa,' she said, 'there's one thing here I don't like at all! Why do you put grandmamma's initials at the end? Why do you tell them to write to grandmamma's house in London?'

'My dear! your mother can do nothing in this matter, as you know. And as for me (even if I went to London), questioning strange ladies about their characters and accomplishments is the last thing in the world that I am fit to do. Your grandmamma is on the spot; and your grandmamma is the proper person to receive the letters, and to make all the necessary inquiries.'

'But I want to see the letters myself,' persisted the spoilt child. 'Some of them are sure to be amusing—'

'I don't apologize for this very unceremonious reception of you, Mr Armadale,' said the major, turning to Allan, with a quaint and quiet humour. 'It may be useful as a warning, if you ever chance to marry and have a daughter – not to begin, as I have done, by letting her have her own way.'

Allan laughed, and Miss Milroy persisted.

'Besides,' she went on, 'I should like to help in choosing which letters we answer, and which we don't. I think I ought to have some voice in the selection of my own governess. Why not tell them, papa, to send their letters down here – to the post-office or the stationer's, or anywhere you like? When you and I have read them, we can send up the letters we prefer to grandmamma; and she can ask all the questions, and pick out the best governess, just as you have arranged already, without leaving ME entirely in the dark, which I consider (don't you, Mr Armadale?) to be quite inhuman. Let me alter the address, papa – do, there's a darling!'

'We shall get no breakfast, Mr Armadale, if I don't say Yes,' said the major, good-humouredly. 'Do as you like, my dear,' he added, turning to his daughter. 'As long as it ends in your grandmamma's managing the matter for us, the rest is of very little consequence.'

Miss Milroy took up her father's pen, drew it through the last line of the advertisement, and wrote the altered address with her own hand as follows:

Apply, by letter, to M., Post-office, Thorpe-Ambrose, Norfolk.

'There!' she said, bustling to her place at the breakfast-table. 'The advertisement may go to London now; and, if a governess *does* come of it, oh, papa, who, in the name of wonder, will she be? – Tea or coffee, Mr Armadale? I'm really ashamed of having kept you waiting. But it is such a comfort,' she added, saucily, 'to get all one's business off one's mind before breakfast!'

Father, daughter, and guest sat down together sociably at the little round table – the best of good neighbours and good friends already.

Three days later, one of the London news-boys got *his* business off his mind before breakfast. His district was Diana Street, Pimlico; and the last of the morning's newspapers which he disposed of, was the newspaper he left at Mrs Oldershaw's door.

CHAPTER III

THE CLAIMS OF SOCIETY

More than an hour after Allan had set forth on his exploring expedition through his own grounds, Midwinter rose, and enjoyed, in his turn, a full view by daylight of the magnificence of the new house.

Refreshed by his long night's rest, he descended the great staircase as cheerfully as Allan himself. One after another, he, too, looked into the spacious rooms on the ground-floor in breathless astonishment at the beauty and the luxury which surrounded him. 'The house where I lived in service when I was a boy was a fine one,' he thought, gaily; 'but it was nothing to this! I wonder if Allan is as surprised and delighted as I am?' The beauty of the summer morning drew him out through the open hall-door, as it had drawn his friend out before him. He ran briskly down the steps, humming the burden of one of the old vagabond tunes which he had danced to long since, in the old vagabond time. Even the memories of his wretched childhood took their colour, on that happy morning, from the bright medium through which he looked back at them. 'If I was not out of practice,' he thought to himself, as he leant on the fence and looked over at the park, 'I could try some of my old tumbling tricks on that delicious grass.' He turned; noticed two of the servants talking together near the shrubbery, and asked for news of the master of the house. The men pointed with a smile in the direction of the gardens; Mr Armadale had gone that way more than an hour since, and had met (as had been reported) with Miss Milroy in the grounds. Midwinter followed the path through the shrubbery, but, on reaching the flower-garden, stopped, considered a little, and retraced his steps. 'If Allan has met with the young lady,' he said to himself, 'Allan doesn't want me.' He laughed as he drew that inevitable inference, and turned considerately to explore the beauties of Thorpe-Ambrose on the other side of the house.

Passing the angle of the front wall of the building, he descended some steps, advanced along a paved walk, turned another angle, and found himself in a strip of garden ground at the back of the house. Behind him was a row of small rooms situated on the level of the servants' offices. In front of him, on the farther side of the little garden, rose a wall, screened by a laurel hedge, and having a door at one end of it, leading past the stables to a gate that opened on the high road. Perceiving that he had only discovered, thus far, the shorter way to the house, used by the servants and tradespeople, Midwinter turned back again, and looked in at the window of one of the rooms on the basement story as he passed it. Were these the servants' offices? No; the offices were apparently in some other part of the ground-floor; the window he had looked in at was the window of a lumber-room. The next two rooms in the row were both empty. The fourth window, when he approached it, presented a little variety. It served also as a door; and it stood open to the garden at that moment.

Attracted by the book-shelves which he noticed on one of the walls, Midwinter stepped into the room. The books, few in number, did not detain him long; a glance at their backs was enough, without taking them down. The Waverley Novels, Tales by Miss Edgeworth, and by Miss Edgeworth's many followers, the Poems of Mrs Hemans,[1] with a few odd volumes of the illustrated gift-books of the period, composed the bulk of the little library. Midwinter turned to leave the room, when an object on one side of the window, which he had not previously noticed, caught his attention and stopped him. It was a statuette standing on a bracket – a reduced copy of the famous Niobe of the Florence Museum. He glanced from the statuette to the window, with a sudden doubt which set his heart throbbing fast. It was a French window; and the statuette was on his left hand as he stood before it. He looked out with a suspicion which he had not felt yet. The view before him was the view of a lawn and garden. For a moment his mind struggled blindly to escape the conclusion which had seized it – and struggled in vain. Here, close round him and close before him; here, forcing him mercilessly back from the happy present to the horrible past, was the room that Allan had seen in the Second Vision of the Dream.[2]

He waited, thinking and looking round him while he thought. There was wonderfully little disturbance in his face and manner; he looked steadily from one to the other of the few objects in the room, as if the discovery of it had saddened rather than surprised him. Matting of some foreign sort covered the floor. Two cane chairs and a plain table comprised the whole of the furniture. The walls were plainly papered, and bare – broken to the eye in one place by a door leading into the interior of the house; in another, by a small stove; in a third, by the book-shelves which Midwinter had already noticed. He returned to the books; and, this time, he took some of them down from the shelves.

The first that he opened contained lines in a woman's handwriting, traced in ink that had faded with time. He read the inscription – 'Jane Armadale, from her beloved father. Thorpe-Ambrose, October, 1828.' In the second, third, and fourth volumes that he opened, the same inscription reappeared. His previous knowledge of dates and persons helped him to draw the true inference from what he saw. The books must have belonged to Allan's mother; and she must have inscribed them with her name, in the interval of time between her return to Thorpe-Ambrose from Madeira, and the birth of her son. Midwinter passed on to a volume on another shelf – one of a series containing the writings of Mrs Hemans. In this case, the blank leaf at the beginning of the book was filled on both sides with a copy of verses, the writing being still in Mrs Armadale's hand. The verses were headed, 'Farewell to Thorpe-Ambrose,' and were dated 'March, 1829' – two months only after Allan had been born.

Entirely without merit in itself, the only interest of the little poem was in the domestic story that it told. The very room in which Midwinter then stood was described – with the view on the garden, the window made to open on it, the book-shelves, the Niobe, and other more perishable ornaments which Time had destroyed. Here, at variance with her brothers, shrinking from her friends, the widow of the murdered man had, on her own acknowledgment, secluded herself, without other comfort than the love and forgiveness of her father, until her child was born. The father's mercy and the father's recent death filled many verses – happily too vague in their commonplace expression of penitence and despair, to give any hint of the marriage-story in Madeira to any reader who looked at them ignorant of the truth. A passing reference to the writer's estrangement from her surviving relatives, and to her approaching departure from Thorpe-Ambrose, followed. Last came the assertion of the mother's resolution to separate herself from all her old associations; to leave behind her every possession, even to the most trifling thing she had, that could remind her of the miserable past; and to date her new life in the future from the birthday of the child who had been spared to console her – who was now the one earthly object that could still speak to her of love and hope. So the old story of passionate feeling that finds comfort in phrases rather than not find comfort at all, was told once again. So the poem in the faded ink faded away to its end.

Midwinter put the book back with a heavy sigh, and opened no other volume on the shelves. 'Here in the country-house, or there on board the Wreck,' he said bitterly, 'the traces of my father's crime follow me, go where I may.' He advanced towards the window – stopped and looked back into the lonely neglected little room. 'Is *this* chance?' he asked himself. 'The place where his mother suffered is the place he sees in the Dream; and the first morning in the new house is the morning that reveals it, not to *him*, but to *me*. Oh, Allan! Allan! how will it end?'

The thought had barely passed through his mind before he heard Allan's voice, from the paved walk at the side of the house, calling to him by his name. He hastily stepped out into the garden. At the same moment Allan came running round the corner, full of voluble apologies for having forgotten, in the society of his new neighbours, what was due to the laws of hospitality and the claims of his friend.

'I really haven't missed you,' said Midwinter; 'and I am very, very glad to hear that the new neighbours have produced such a pleasant impression on you already.'

He tried, as he spoke, to lead the way back by the outside of the house; but Allan's flighty attention had been caught by the open window and the lonely little room. He stepped in immediately. Midwinter followed, and watched him in breathless anxiety, as he looked round. Not the slightest recollection of the Dream troubled Allan's easy mind. Not the slightest reference to it fell from the silent lips of his friend.

'Exactly the sort of place I should have expected you to hit on!' exclaimed Allan gaily. 'Small and snug and unpretending. I know you, Master Midwinter! You'll be slipping off here, when the county families come visiting – and I rather think, on those dreadful occasions you won't find me far behind you. What's the matter? You look ill and out of spirits. Hungry? Of course you are! unpardonable of me to have kept you waiting – this door leads somewhere, I suppose; let's try a short cut into the house. Don't be afraid of my not keeping you company at breakfast. I didn't eat much at the cottage – I feasted my eyes on Miss Milroy, as the poets say. Oh, the darling! the darling! she turns you topsy-turvy the moment you look at her. As for her father; wait till you see his wonderful clock! It's twice the size of the famous clock at Strasbourg, and the most tremendous striker ever heard yet in the memory of man!'

Singing the praises of his new friends in this strain, at the top of his voice, Allan hurried Midwinter along the stone passages on the basement floor which led, as he had rightly guessed, to a staircase communicating with the hall. They passed the servants' offices on the way. At the sight of the cook and the roaring fire, disclosed through the open kitchen door, Allan's mind went off at a tangent, and Allan's dignity scattered itself to the four winds of heaven, as usual.

'Aha, Mrs Gripper; there you are with your pots and pans, and your burning fiery furnace! One had need be Shadrach, Meshech, and the other fellow,[3] to stand over that. Breakfast as soon as ever you like. Eggs, sausages, bacon, kidneys, marmalade, watercresses, coffee, and so forth. My friend and I belong to the select few whom it's a perfect privilege to cook for. Voluptuaries, Mrs Gripper, voluptuaries, both of us. You'll see,' continued Allan, as they went on towards the stairs, 'I shall make that worthy creature young again; I'm better than a doctor for Mrs Gripper. When she laughs she shakes her fat sides; and when she shakes her fat sides she exerts her muscular system; and when she exerts her muscular system – Ha! here's Susan again. Don't squeeze yourself flat against the banisters, my dear; if you don't mind hustling *me* on the stairs, I rather like hustling *you*. She looks like a full-blown rose when she blushes, doesn't she? Stop, Susan! I've some orders to give. Be very particular with Mr Midwinter's room: shake up his bed like mad, and dust his furniture till those nice round arms of yours ache again. Nonsense, my dear fellow! I'm not too familiar with them; I'm only keeping them up to their work. Now then, Richard! where do we breakfast? Oh, here. Between ourselves, Midwinter, these splendid rooms of mine are a size too large for me; I don't feel as if I should ever be on intimate terms with my own furniture. My views in life are of the snug and slovenly sort – a kitchen chair, you know, and a low ceiling. Man wants but little here below, and wants that little long.[4] That's not exactly the right quotation; but it expresses my meaning, and we'll let alone correcting it till the next opportunity.'

'I beg your pardon,' interposed Midwinter, 'here is something waiting for you which you have not noticed yet.'

As he spoke, he pointed a little impatiently to a letter lying on the breakfast-table. He could conceal the ominous discovery which he had made that morning, from Allan's knowledge; but he could not conquer the latent distrust of circumstances which was now roused again in his superstitious nature – the instinctive suspicion of everything that happened, no matter how common or how trifling the event, on the first memorable day when the new life began in the new house.

Allan ran his eye over the letter, and tossed it across the table to his friend. 'I can't make head or tail of it,' he said; 'can you?'

Midwinter read the letter slowly, aloud. 'Sir, – I trust you will pardon the liberty I take in sending these few lines to wait your arrival at Thorpe-Ambrose. In the event of circumstances not disposing you to place your law-business in the hands of Mr Darch—' He suddenly stopped at that point, and considered a little.

'Darch is our friend the lawyer,'⁵ said Allan, supposing Midwinter had forgotten the name. 'Don't you remember our spinning the half-crown on the cabin table, when I got the two offers for the cottage? Heads, the major; tails, the lawyer. This is the lawyer.'

Without making any reply, Midwinter resumed reading the letter.

In the event of circumstances not disposing you to place your law-business in the hands of Mr Darch, I beg to say that I shall be happy to take charge of your interests, if you feel willing to honour me with your confidence. Enclosing a reference (should you desire it) to my agents in London, and again apologizing for this intrusion, I beg to remain, Sir, respectfully yours, A. PED-GIFT, SENR.

'Circumstances?' repeated Midwinter, as he laid the letter down. 'What circumstances can possibly indispose you to give your law-business to Mr Darch?'

'Nothing can indispose me,' said Allan. 'Besides being the family lawyer here, Darch was the first to write me word at Paris of my coming in for my fortune; and, if I have got any business to give, of course he ought to have it.'

Midwinter still looked distrustfully at the open letter on the table. 'I am sadly afraid, Allan, there is something wrong already,' he said. 'This man would never have ventured on the application he has made to you, unless he had some good reason for believing it would succeed. If you wish to put yourself right at starting, you will send to Mr Darch this morning, to tell him you are here, and you will take no notice for the present of Mr Pedgift's letter.'

Before more could be said on either side, the footman made his appearance with the breakfast tray. He was followed, after an interval, by the butler – a man of the essentially confidential kind, with a modulated voice, a courtly manner, and a bulbous nose. Anybody but Allan would have seen in his face that he had come into the room having a special communication to make to his master. Allan, who saw nothing under the surface, and whose head was running on the lawyer's letter, stopped him bluntly with the point-blank question: 'Who's Mr Pedgift?'

The butler's sources of local knowledge opened confidentially on the instant. Mr Pedgift was the second of the two lawyers in the town. Not so long-established, not so wealthy, not so universally looked-up-to as old Mr Darch. Not doing the business of the highest people in the county, and not mixing freely with the best society, like old Mr Darch. A very sufficient man, in his way, nevertheless. Known as a perfectly competent and respectable practitioner all round the neighbourhood. In short, professionally next best to Mr Darch; and personally superior to him (if the expression might be permitted) in this respect − that Darch was a Crusty One, and Pedgift wasn't.

Having imparted this information, the butler, taking a wise advantage of his position, glided without a moment's stoppage, from Mr Pedgift's character to the business that had brought him into the breakfast-room. The Midsummer Audit was near at hand; and the tenants were accustomed to have a week's notice of the rent-day dinner. With this necessity pressing, and with no orders given as yet, and no steward in office at Thorpe-Ambrose, it appeared desirable that some confidential person should bring the matter forward. The butler was that confidential person; and he now ventured accordingly to trouble his master on the subject.

At this point, Allan opened his lips to interrupt, and was himself interrupted before he could utter a word.

'Wait!' interposed Midwinter, seeing in Allan's face that he was in danger of being publicly announced in the capacity of steward. 'Wait!' he repeated eagerly, 'till I can speak to you first.'

The butler's courtly manner remained alike unruffled by Midwinter's sudden interference and his own dismissal from the scene. Nothing but the mounting colour in by his bulbous nose betrayed the sense of injury that animated him as he withdrew. Mr Armadale's chance of regaling his friend and himself that day with the best wine in the cellar, trembled in the balance, as the butler took his way back to the basement story.

'This is beyond a joke, Allan,' said Midwinter, when they were alone. 'Somebody must meet your tenants on the rent-day who is really fit to take the steward's place. With the best will in the world to learn, it is impossible for *me* to master the business at a week's notice. Don't, pray don't let your anxiety for my welfare put you in a false position with other people! I should never forgive myself if I was the unlucky cause—'

'Gently, gently!' cried Allan, amazed at his friend's extraordinary earnestness. 'If I write to London by to-night's post for the man who came down here before, will that satisfy you?'

Midwinter shook his head. 'Our time is short,' he said; 'and the man may not be at liberty. Why not try in the neighbourhood first? You were going to write to Mr Darch. Send at once, and see if he can't help us between this and post-time.'

Allan withdrew to a side-table on which writing materials were placed. 'You shall breakfast in peace, you old fidget,' he replied – and addressed himself forthwith to Mr Darch, with his usual Spartan brevity of epistolary expression. 'Dear Sir, – Here I am, bag and baggage. Will you kindly oblige me by being my lawyer? I ask this, because I want to consult you at once. Please look in in the course of the day, and stop to dinner if you possibly can. Yours truly, ALLAN ARMADALE.' Having read this composition aloud with unconcealed admiration of his own rapidity of literary execution, Allan addressed the letter to Mr Darch, and rang the bell. 'Here, Richard, take this at once, and wait for an answer. And, I say, if there's any news stirring in the town, pick it up and bring it back with you. See how I manage my servants!' continued Allan, joining his friend at the breakfast-table. 'See how I adapt myself to my new duties! I haven't been down here one clear day yet, and I'm taking an interest in the neighbourhood already.'

Breakfast over, the two friends went out to idle away the morning under the shade of a tree in the park. Noon came, and Richard never appeared. One o'clock struck, and still there were no signs of an answer from Mr Darch. Midwinter's patience was not proof against the delay. He left Allan dozing on the grass, and went to the house to make inquiries. The town was described as little more than two miles distant; but the day of the week happened to be market-day, and Richard was being detained no doubt by some of the many acquaintances whom he would be sure to meet with on that occasion.

Half an hour later, the truant messenger returned, and was sent out to report himself to his master under the tree in the park.

'Any answer from Mr Darch?' asked Midwinter, seeing that Allan was too lazy to put the question for himself.

'Mr Darch was engaged, sir. I was desired to say that he would send an answer.'

'Any news in the town?' inquired Allan, drowsily, without troubling himself to open his eyes.

'No, sir; nothing in particular.'

Observing the man suspiciously as he made that reply, Midwinter detected in his face that he was not speaking the truth. He was plainly embarrassed, and plainly relieved when his master's silence allowed him to withdraw. After a little consideration, Midwinter followed, and overtook the retreating servant on the drive before the house.

'Richard,' he said quietly, 'if I was to guess that there *is* some news in the town, and that you don't like telling it to your master, should I be guessing the truth?'

The man started and changed colour. 'I don't know how you have found it out, sir,' he said; 'but I can't deny you have guessed right.'

'If you will let me hear what the news is, I will take the responsibility on myself of telling Mr Armadale.'

After some little hesitation, and some distrustful consideration on his side, of Midwinter's face, Richard at last prevailed on himself to repeat what he had heard that day in the town.

The news of Allan's sudden appearance at Thorpe-Ambrose had preceded the servant's arrival at his destination by some hours. Wherever he went, he found his master the subject of public discussion. The opinion of Allan's conduct among the leading townspeople, the resident gentry of the neighbourhood, and the principal tenants on the estate, was unanimously unfavourable. Only the day before, the committee for managing the public reception of the new squire had sketched the progress of the procession; had settled the serious question of the triumphal arches; and had appointed a competent person to solicit subscriptions for the flags, the flowers, the feasting, the fireworks, and the band. In less than a week more, the money could have been collected, and the rector would have written to Mr Armadale to fix the day. And now, by Allan's own act, the public welcome waiting to honour him, had been cast back contemptuously in the public teeth! Everybody took for granted (what was unfortunately true) that he had received private information of the contemplated proceedings. Everybody declared that he had purposely stolen into his own house like a thief in the night (so the phrase ran), to escape accepting the offered civilities of his neighbours. In brief, the sensitive self-importance of the little town was wounded to the quick; and of Allan's once enviable position in the estimation of the neighbourhood not a vestige remained.

For a moment, Midwinter faced the messenger of evil tidings in silent distress. That moment past, the sense of Allan's critical position roused him, now the evil was known, to seek the remedy.

'Has the little you have seen of your master, Richard, inclined you to like him?' he asked.

This time, the man answered without hesitation. 'A pleasanter and kinder gentleman than Mr Armadale no one could wish to serve.'

'If you think that,' pursued Midwinter, 'you won't object to give me some information which will help your master to set himself right with his neighbours. Come into the house.'

He led the way into the library, and, after asking the necessary questions, took down in writing a list of the names and addresses of the most influential persons living in the town and its neighbourhood. This done, he rang the bell for the head footman, having previously sent Richard with a message to the stables, directing an open carriage to be ready in an hour's time.

'When the late Mr Blanchard went out to make calls in the neighbourhood, it was your place to go with him, was it not?' he asked, when the upper servant appeared. 'Very well. Be ready in an hour's time, if you please, to go out with Mr Armadale.' Having given that order, he left the house again on his way back to Allan, with the visiting list in his hand. He smiled a little sadly as he descended the steps. 'Who would have imagined,' he thought, 'that my footboy's experience of the ways of gentlefolks, would be worth looking back at one day for Allan's sake?'

The object of the popular odium lay innocently slumbering on the grass, with his garden hat over his nose, his waistcoat unbuttoned, and his trousers wrinkled half way up his outstretched legs. Midwinter roused him without hesitation, and remorselessly repeated the servant's news.

Allan accepted the disclosure thus forced on him without the slightest disturbance of temper. 'Oh, hang 'em!' was all he said. 'Let's have another cigar.' Midwinter took the cigar out of his hand, and, insisting on his treating the matter seriously, told him in plain words that he must set himself right with his offended neighbours by calling on them personally to make his apologies. Allan sat up on the grass in astonishment; his eyes opened wide in incredulous dismay. Did Midwinter positively meditate forcing him into a 'chimney-pot hat',[6] a nicely brushed frock-coat, and a clean pair of gloves? Was it actually in contemplation to shut him up in a carriage, with his footman on the box and his card-case in his hand, and send him round from house to house, to tell a pack of fools that he begged their pardon for not letting them make a public show of him? If anything so outrageously absurd as this was really to be done, it could not be done that day, at any rate. He had promised to go back to the charming Milroy at the cottage and to take

Midwinter with him. What earthly need had he of the good opinion of the resident gentry? The only friends he wanted were the friends he had got already. Let the whole neighbourhood turn its back on him if it liked – back or face the Squire of Thorpe-Ambrose didn't care two straws about it.

After allowing him to run on in this way until his whole stock of objections was exhausted, Midwinter wisely tried his personal influence next.[7] He took Allan affectionately by the hand. 'I am going to ask a great favour,' he said. 'If you won't call on these people for your own sake, will you call on them to please *me*?'

Allan delivered himself of a groan of despair, stared in mute surprise at the anxious face of his friend, and good-humouredly gave way. As Midwinter took his arm, and led him back to the house, he looked round with rueful eyes at the cattle hard by, placidly whisking their tails in the pleasant shade. 'Don't mention it in the neighbourhood,' he said; 'I should like to change places with one of my own cows.'

Midwinter left him to dress, engaging to return when the carriage was at the door. Allan's toilette did not promise to be a speedy one. He began it by reading his own visiting cards; and he advanced it a second stage by looking into his wardrobe, and devoting the resident gentry to the infernal regions. Before he could discover any third means of delaying his own proceedings, the necessary pretext was unexpectedly supplied by Richard's appearance with a note in his hand. The messenger had just called with Mr Darch's answer. Allan briskly shut up the wardrobe, and gave his whole attention to the lawyer's letter. The lawyer's letter rewarded him by the following lines:

Sir, – I beg to acknowledge the receipt of your favour of to-day's date, honouring me with two proposals, namely, ONE inviting me to act as your legal adviser, and ONE inviting me to pay you a visit at your house. In reference to the first proposal, I beg permission to decline it with thanks. With regard to the second proposal, I have to inform you that circumstances have come to my knowledge relating to the letting of the cottage at Thorpe-Ambrose, which render it impossible for me (in justice to myself) to accept your invitation. I have ascertained, sir, that my offer reached you at the same time as Major Milroy's; and that, with both proposals thus before you, you gave the preference to a total stranger, who addressed you through a house-agent, over a man who had faithfully served your relatives for two generations, and who had been the first person to inform you of the most important event in your life. After this specimen of your estimate of what is due to the claims of common courtesy and common justice, I cannot flatter myself that I possess any of the qualities which would fit me to take my place on the list of your friends. — I remain, sir, your obedient servant, JAMES DARCH.

'Stop the messenger!' cried Allan, leaping to his feet, his ruddy face aflame with indignation. 'Give me pen, ink and paper! By the Lord Harry, they're a nice set of people in these parts; the whole neighbourhood is in a conspiracy to bully me!' He snatched up the pen in a fine frenzy of epistolary inspiration. 'Sir, — I despise you and your letter.—' At that point the pen made a blot, and the writer was seized with a momentary hesitation. 'Too strong,' he thought; 'I'll give it to the lawyer in his own cool and cutting style.' He began again on a clean sheet of paper. 'Sir, — You remind me of an Irish bull. I mean that story in Joe Miller,[8] where Pat remarked, in the hearing of a wag hard by, that "the reciprocity was all on one side". *Your* reciprocity is all on one side. You take the privilege of refusing to be my lawyer, and then you complain of my taking the privilege of refusing to be your landlord.' He paused fondly over those last words. 'Neat!' he thought. 'Argument and hard hitting both in one. I wonder where my knack of writing comes from?' He went on, and finished the letter in two more sentences. 'As for your casting my invitation back in my teeth, I beg to inform you my teeth are none the worse for it. I am equally glad to have nothing to say to you, either in the capacity of a friend or a tenant. — ALLAN ARMADALE.' He nodded exultingly at his own composition, as he addressed it and sent it down to the messenger. 'Darch's hide must be a thick one,' he said, 'if he doesn't feel *that*!'

The sound of wheels outside suddenly recalled him to the business of the day. There was the carriage waiting to take him on his round of visits; and there was Midwinter at his post, pacing to and fro on the drive. 'Read that,' cried Allan, throwing out the lawyer's letter; 'I've written him back a smasher.'

He bustled away to the wardrobe to get his coat. There was a wonderful change in him; he felt little or no reluctance to pay the visits now. The pleasurable excitement of answering Mr Darch had put him in a fine aggressive frame of mind for asserting himself in the neighbourhood. 'Whatever else they may say of me, they shan't say I was afraid to face them.' Heated red-hot with that idea, he seized his hat and gloves, and, hurrying out of the room, met Midwinter in the corridor with the lawyer's letter in his hand.

'Keep up your spirits!' cried Allan, seeing the anxiety in his friend's face, and misinterpreting the motive of it immediately. 'If Darch can't be counted on to send us a helping hand into the steward's office, Pedgift can.'

'My dear Allan, I was not thinking of that; I was thinking of Mr Darch's letter. I don't defend this sour-tempered man – but I am afraid we must admit he has some cause for complaint. Pray don't give him another chance of putting you in the wrong. Where is your answer to his letter?'

'Gone!' replied Allan; 'I always strike while the iron's hot – a word and a blow, and the blow first, that's my way. Don't, there's a dear good fellow, don't fidget about the steward's books and the rent-day. Here! here's a bunch of keys they gave me last night: one of them opens the room where the steward's books are; go in and read them till I come back. I give you my sacred word of honour I'll settle it all with Pedgift before you see me again.'

'One moment,' interposed Midwinter, stopping him resolutely on his way out to the carriage. 'I say nothing against Mr Pedgift's fitness to possess your confidence, for I know nothing to justify me in distrusting him. But he has not introduced himself to your notice in a very delicate way; and he has not acknowledged (what is quite clear to my mind) that he knew of Mr Darch's unfriendly feeling towards you when he wrote. Wait a little before you go to this stranger; wait till we can talk it over together to-night.'

'Wait!' replied Allan. 'Haven't I told you that I always strike while the iron's hot? Trust my eye for character, old boy; I'll look Pedgift through and through, and act accordingly. Don't keep me any longer, for heaven's sake. I'm in a fine humour for tackling the resident gentry; and if I don't go at once, I'm afraid it may wear off.'

With that excellent reason for being in a hurry, Allan boisterously broke away. Before it was possible to stop him again, he had jumped into the carriage and had left the house.

CHAPTER IV

THE MARCH OF EVENTS

Midwinter's face darkened when the last trace of the carriage had disappeared from view. 'I have done my best,' he said, as he turned back gloomily into the house. 'If Mr Brock himself were here, Mr Brock could do no more!'

He looked at the bunch of keys which Allan had thrust into his hand, and a sudden longing to put himself to the test over the steward's books took possession of his sensitive self-tormenting nature. Inquiring his way to the room in which the various moveables of the steward's office had been provisionally placed, after the letting of the cottage, he sat down at the desk, and tried how his own unaided capacity would guide him through the business records of the Thorpe-Ambrose estate. The result exposed his own ignorance unanswerably before his own eyes. The Ledgers bewildered him; the Leases, the Plans, and even the Correspondence itself, might have been written, for all he could understand of them, in an unknown tongue. His memory reverted bitterly as he left the room again to his two years' solitary self-instruction in the Shrewsbury bookseller's shop. 'If I could only have worked at a business!' he thought. 'If I could only have known that the company of Poets and Philosophers was company too high for a vagabond like me!'[1]

He sat down alone in the great hall; the silence of it fell heavier and heavier on his sinking spirits; the beauty of it exasperated him, like an insult from a purse-proud man. 'Curse the place!' he said, snatching up his hat and stick. 'I like the bleakest hill-side I ever slept on, better than I like this house!'

He impatiently descended the doorsteps, and stopped on the drive, considering by which direction he should leave the park for the country beyond. If he followed the road taken by the carriage, he might risk unsettling Allan by accidentally meeting him in the town. If he went out by the back gate, he knew his own nature well enough to doubt his ability to pass the room of the dream without entering it again. But one other way remained – the way which he had taken, and then abandoned again, in the morning. There was no fear of disturbing Allan and the major's daughter now. Without further hesitation, Midwinter set forth through the gardens to explore the open country on that side of the estate.

Thrown off its balance by the events of the day, his mind was full of that sourly-savage resistance to the inevitable self-assertion of wealth, so amiably deplored by the prosperous and the rich; so bitterly familiar to the unfortunate and the poor. 'The heather-bell costs nothing!' he thought, looking contemptuously at the masses of rare and beautiful flowers that surrounded him; 'and the buttercups and daisies are as bright as the best of you!' He followed the artfully-contrived ovals and squares of the Italian garden, with a vagabond indifference to the symmetry of their construction and the ingenuity of their design. 'How many pounds a foot did *you* cost?' he said, looking back with scornful eyes at the last path as he left it. 'Wind away over high and low like the sheep-walk on the mountain-side, if you can!'

He entered the shrubbery which Allan had entered before him;

crossed the paddock and the rustic bridge beyond; and reached the major's cottage. His ready mind seized the right conclusion, at the first sight of it; and he stopped before the garden gate, to look at the trim little residence which would never have been empty, and would never have been let, but for Allan's ill-advised resolution to force the steward's situation on his friend.

The summer afternoon was warm; the summer air was faint and still. On the upper and the lower floor of the cottage the windows were all open. From one of them, on the upper story, the sound of voices was startlingly audible in the quiet of the park, as Midwinter paused on the outer side of the garden enclosure. The voice of a woman, harsh, high, and angrily complaining – a voice with all the freshness and the melody gone, and with nothing but the hard power of it left – was the discordantly predominant sound. With it, from moment to moment, there mingled the deeper and quieter tones, soothing and compassionate, of the voice of a man. Although the distance was too great to allow Midwinter to distinguish the words that were spoken, he felt the impropriety of remaining within hearing of the voices, and at once stepped forward to continue his walk. At the same moment, the face of a young girl (easily recognizable as the face of Miss Milroy, from Allan's description of her) appeared at the open window of the room. In spite of himself, Midwinter paused to look at her. The expression of the bright young face, which had smiled so prettily on Allan, was weary and disheartened. After looking out absently over the park she suddenly turned her head back into the room; her attention having been apparently struck by something that had just been said in it. 'Oh, mamma, mamma,' she exclaimed indignantly, 'how *can* you say such things!' The words were spoken close to the window; they reached Midwinter's ears, and hurried him away before he heard more. But the self-disclosure of Major Milroy's domestic position had not reached its end yet. As Midwinter turned the corner of the garden fence, a tradesman's boy was handing a parcel in at the wicket gate to the woman servant. 'Well,' said the boy, with the irrepressible impudence of his class, 'how is the missus?' The woman lifted her hand to box his ears. 'How is the missus?' she repeated, with an angry toss of her head as the boy ran off. 'If it would only please God to take the missus, it would be a blessing to everybody in the house.'

No such ill-omened shadow as this had passed over the bright domestic picture of the inhabitants of the cottage, which Allan's enthusiasm had painted for the contemplation of his friend. It was plain that the secret of the tenants had been kept from the landlord so far. Five minutes more of walking brought Midwinter to the park gates. 'Am I fated to see nothing and hear nothing to-day which can give me heart and hope for the future?' he thought, as he angrily swung back the lodge gate. 'Even the people Allan has let the cottage to, are people whose lives are embittered by a household misery which it is *my* misfortune to have found out!'

He took the first road that lay before him, and walked on, noticing little, immersed in his own thoughts. More than an hour passed before the necessity of turning back entered his mind. As soon as the idea occurred to him, he consulted his watch, and determined to retrace his steps, so as to be at the house in good time to meet Allan on his return. Ten minutes of walking brought him back to a point at which three roads met; and one moment's observation of the place satisfied him that he had entirely failed to notice, at the time, by which of the three roads he had advanced. No sign-post was to be seen; the country on either side was lonely and flat, intersected by broad drains and ditches. Cattle were grazing here and there; and a windmill rose in the distance above the pollard willows that fringed the low horizon. But not a house was to be seen, and not a human creature appeared on the visible perspective of any one of the three roads. Midwinter glanced back in the only direction left to look at – the direction of the road along which he had just been walking. There, to his relief, was the figure of a man, rapidly advancing towards him, of whom he could ask his way.

The figure came on, clad from head to foot in dreary black – a moving blot on the brilliant white surface of the sun-brightened road. He was a lean, elderly, miserably respectable man. He wore a poor old black dress-coat, and a cheap brown wig, which made no pretence of being his own natural hair. Short black trousers clung like attached old servants round his wizen legs; and rusty black gaiters hid all they could of his knobbed ungainly feet. Black crape added its mite to the decayed and dingy wretchedness of his old beaver hat; black mohair in the obsolete form of a stock, drearily encircled his neck and rose as high as his haggard jaws. The one morsel of colour he carried about him, was a lawyer's bag of blue serge as lean and limp as himself. The one attractive feature in his clean-shaven, weary old face, was a neat set of teeth – teeth (as honest as his wig), which said plainly to all inquiring eyes, 'We pass our nights on his looking-glass, and our days in his mouth.'

All the little blood in the man's body faintly reddened his fleshless cheeks as Midwinter advanced to meet him, and asked the way to Thorpe-Ambrose. His weak watery eyes looked hither and thither in a bewilderment painful to see. If he had met with a lion instead of a man, and if the few words addressed to him had been words expressing a threat instead of a question, he could hardly have looked more confused and alarmed than he looked now. For the first time in his life, Midwinter saw his own shy uneasiness in the presence of strangers reflected, with tenfold intensity of nervous suffering, in the face of another man – and that man old enough to be his father.

'Which do you please to mean, sir – the Town or the House? I beg your pardon for asking, but they both go by the same name in these parts.'

He spoke with a timid gentleness of tone, an ingratiatory smile, and an anxious courtesy of manner, all distressingly suggestive of his being accustomed to receive rough answers in exchange for his own politeness, from the persons whom he habitually addressed.

'I was not aware that both the House and the Town went by the same name,' said Midwinter: 'I meant the House.' He instinctively conquered his own shyness as he answered in those words; speaking with a cordiality of manner which was very rare with him in his intercourse with strangers.

The man of miserable-respectability seemed to feel the warm return of his own politeness gratefully: he brightened and took a little courage. His lean forefinger pointed eagerly to the right road. 'That way, sir,' he said, 'and when you come to two roads next, please take the left one of the two. I am sorry I have business the other way – I mean in the town. I should have been happy to go with you, and show you. Fine summer weather, sir, for walking? You can't miss your way if you keep to the left. Oh, don't mention it! I'm afraid I have detained you, sir. I wish you a pleasant walk back, and – good morning.'

By the time he had made an end of speaking (under an impression apparently that the more he talked the more polite he would be) he had lost his courage again. He darted away down his own road, as if Midwinter's attempts to thank him, involved a series of trials too terrible to confront. In two minutes more, his black retreating figure had lessened in the distance till it looked again, what it had once looked already, a moving blot on the brilliant white surface of the sun-brightened road.

The man ran strangely in Midwinter's thoughts while he took his way back to the house. He was at a loss to account for it. It never occurred to him that he might have been insensibly reminded of himself, when he saw the plain traces of past misfortune and present nervous suffering in the poor wretch's face. He blindly resented his own perverse interest in this chance foot-passenger on the high road, as he had resented all else that had happened to him since the beginning of the day. 'Have I made another unlucky discovery?' he asked himself impatiently. 'Shall I see this man again, I wonder? who can he be?'

Time was to answer both those questions before many days more had passed over the inquirer's head.

Allan had not returned when Midwinter reached the house. Nothing had happened but the arrival of a message of apology from the cottage. 'Major Milroy's compliments, and he was sorry that Mrs Milroy's illness would prevent his receiving Mr Armadale that day.' It was plain that Mrs Milroy's occasional fits of suffering (or of ill-temper) created no mere transitory disturbance of the tranquillity of the household. Drawing this natural inference, after what he had himself heard at the cottage nearly three hours since, Midwinter withdrew into the library to wait patiently among the books until his friend came back.

It was past six o'clock, when the well-known hearty voice was heard again in the hall. Allan burst into the library, in a state of irrepressible excitement, and pushed Midwinter back unceremoniously into the chair from which he was just rising, before he could utter a word.

'Here's a riddle for you, old boy!' cried Allan. 'Why am I like the resident manager of the Augean stable, before Hercules was called in to sweep the litter out? Because I have had my place to keep up, and I've gone and made an infernal mess of it! Why don't you laugh? By George, he doesn't see the point! Let's try again. Why am I like the resident manager?—'

'For God's sake, Allan, be serious for a moment!' interposed Midwinter. 'You don't know how anxious I am to hear if you have recovered the good opinion of your neighbours.'

'That's just what the riddle was intended to tell you!' rejoined Allan. 'But if you will have it in so many words, my own impression is that you would have done better not to disturb me under that tree in the park. I've been calculating it to a nicety, and I beg to inform you that I have sunk exactly three degrees lower in the estimation of the resident gentry since I had the pleasure of seeing you last.'

'You *will* have your joke out,' said Midwinter, bitterly. 'Well, if I can't laugh, I can wait.'

'My dear fellow, I'm not joking; I really mean what I say. You shall hear what happened – you shall have a report in full of my first visit. It will do, I can promise you, as a sample for all the rest. Mind this, in the first place, I've gone wrong, with the best possible intentions. When I started for these visits, I own I was angry with that old brute of a lawyer, and I certainly had a notion of carrying things with a high hand. But it wore off somehow on the road; and the first family I called on, I went in as I tell you with the best possible intentions. Oh dear, dear! there was the same spick-and-span reception room for me to wait in, with the neat conservatory beyond, which I saw again and again and again at every other house I went to afterwards. There was the same choice selection of books for me to look at – a religious book, a book about the Duke of Wellington, a book about sporting, and a book about nothing in particular, beautifully illustrated with pictures. Down came papa with his nice white hair, and mamma with her nice lace cap; down came young Mister with the pink face and the straw-coloured whiskers, and young Miss with the plump cheeks and the large petti-coats. Don't suppose there was the least unfriendliness on my side; I always began with them in the same way – I insisted on shaking hands all round. That staggered them to begin with. When I came to the sore subject next – the subject of the public reception – I give you my word of honour I took the greatest possible pains with my apologies. It hadn't the slightest effect; they let my apologies in at one ear and out at the other, and then waited to hear more. Some men would have been disheartened: I tried another way with them; I addressed myself to the master of the house, and put it pleasantly next. "The fact is," I said, "I wanted to escape the speechifying – my getting up, you know, and telling you to your face, you're the best of men, and I beg to propose your health; and you're getting up, and telling me to my face, I'm the best of men, and you beg to thank me; and so on, man after man, praising each other and pestering each other all round the table." That's how I put it, in an easy, light-handed, convincing sort of way. Do you think any of them took it in the same friendly spirit? Not one! It's my belief they had got their speeches ready for the reception, with the flags and the flowers, and that they're secretly angry with me for stopping their open mouths just as they were ready to begin. Anyway, whenever we came to the matter of the speechifying (whether they touched it first or I), down I fell in their estimation the first of those three steps I told you of just now. Don't suppose I made no efforts to get up again! I made desperate efforts. I found they were all anxious to know what sort of life I had led before I came in for the Thorpe-Ambrose property, and I did my best to satisfy them. And what came of that, do you think? Hang me, if I didn't disappoint them for the second time! When they found out that I had actually never been to Eton or Harrow, or Oxford or Cambridge, they were quite dumb with astonish-ment. I fancy they thought me a sort of outlaw. At any rate, they all froze up again – and down I fell the second step in their estimation. Never mind! I wasn't to be beaten; I had promised you to do my best, and I did it. I tried cheerful small-talk about the neighbourhood next. The women said nothing in particular; the men, to my unutterable astonishment, all began to condole with me. I shouldn't be able to find a pack of hounds, they said, within twenty miles of my house; and they thought it only right to prepare me for the disgracefully careless manner in which the Thorpe-Ambrose covers had been preserved. I let them go on condoling with me, and then what do you think I did? I put my foot in it again. "Oh, don't take that to heart!" I said; "I don't care two straws about hunting or shooting, either. When I meet with a bird in my walk, I can't for the life of me feel eager to kill it – I rather like to see the bird flying about and enjoying itself." You should have seen their faces! They had thought me a sort of outlaw before; now they evidently thought me mad. Dead silence fell upon them all; and down I tumbled the third step in the general estimation. It was just the same at the next house, and the next, and the next. The devil possessed us all, I think. It *would* come out, now in one way and now in another, that I couldn't make speeches – that I had been brought up without a university education – and that I could enjoy a ride on horseback without galloping after a wretched stinking fox or a poor distracted little hare. Those three unlucky defects of mine are not excused, it seems, in a country gentleman (especially when he has dodged a public reception to begin with). I think I got on best, upon the whole, with the wives and daughters. The women and I always fell, sooner or later, on the subject of Mrs Blanchard and her niece. We invariably agreed that they had done wisely in going to Florence; and the only reason we had to give for our opinion was – that we thought their minds would be benefited after their sad bereavement, by the contemplation of the masterpieces of Italian Art. Every one of the ladies – I solemnly declare it – at every house I went to, came sooner or later to Mrs and Miss Blanchard's bereavement, and the masterpieces of Italian Art. What we should have done without that bright idea to help us, I really don't know. The one pleasant thing at any of the visits was when we all shook our heads together, and declared that the masterpieces would console them. As for the rest of it, there's only one thing more to be said. What I might be in other places I don't know – I'm the wrong man in the wrong place here. Let me muddle on for the future in my own way, with my own few friends; and ask me anything else in the world, as long as you don't ask me to make any more calls on my neighbours.'

With that characteristic request, Allan's report of his exploring expedition among the resident gentry came to a close. For a moment Midwinter remained silent. He had allowed Allan to run on from first to last without uttering a word on his side. The disastrous result of the visits – coming after what had happened earlier in the day; and threatening Allan, as it did, with exclusion from all local sympathies at the very outset of his local career – had broken down Midwinter's power of resisting the stealthily-depressing influence of his own superstition. It was with an effort that he now looked up at Allan; it was with an effort that he roused himself to answer.

'It shall be as you wish,' he said, quietly. 'I am sorry for what has happened – but I am not the less obliged to you, Allan, for having done what I asked you.'

His head sank on his breast; and the fatalist resignation which had once already quieted him on board the Wreck, now quieted him again. 'What *must* be, *will* be,' he thought once more. 'What have I to do with the future, and what has he?'

'Cheer up!' said Allan. '*Your* affairs are in a thriving condition at any rate. I paid one pleasant visit in the town, which I haven't told you of yet. I've seen Pedgift, and Pedgift's son, who helps him in the office. They're the two jolliest lawyers I ever met with in my life – and what's more, they can produce the very man you want to teach you the steward's business.'

Midwinter looked up quickly. Distrust of Allan's discovery was plainly written in his face already; but he said nothing.

'I thought of you,' Allan proceeded, 'as soon as the two Pedgifts and I had had a glass of wine all round to drink to our friendly connection. The finest sherry I ever tasted in my life; I've ordered some of the same – but that's not the question just now. In two words I told these worthy fellows your difficulty, and in two seconds old Pedgift understood all about it. "I have got the man in my office," he said, "and before the audit-day comes, I'll place him with the greatest pleasure at your friend's disposal." '[2]

At this last announcement, Midwinter's distrust found its expression in words. He questioned Allan unsparingly. The man's name, it appeared, was Bashwood. He had been some time (how long, Allan could not remember) in Mr Pedgift's service. He had been previously steward to a Norfolk gentleman (name forgotten) in the westward district of the county. He had lost the steward's place, through some domestic trouble, in connection with his son, the precise nature of which Allan was not able to specify. Pedgift vouched for him, and Pedgift would send him to Thorpe-Ambrose two or three days before the rent-day dinner. He could not be spared, for office reasons, before that time. There was no need to fidget about it; Pedgift laughed at the idea of there being any difficulty with the tenants. Two or three days' work over the steward's books with a man to help Midwinter who practically understood that sort of thing, would put him all right for the audit; and the other business would keep till afterwards.

'Have you seen this Mr Bashwood yourself, Allan?' asked Midwinter, still obstinately on his guard.

'No,' replied Allan; 'he was out – out with the bag, as young Pedgift called it. They tell me he's a decent elderly man. A little broken by his troubles, and a little apt to be nervous and confused in his manner with strangers; but thoroughly competent and thoroughly to be depended on – those are Pedgift's own words.'

Midwinter paused and considered a little, with a new interest in the subject. The strange man whom he had just heard described, and the strange man of whom he had asked his way where the three roads met, were remarkably like each other. Was this another link in the fast-lengthening chain of events? Midwinter grew doubly determined to be careful, as the bare doubt that it might be so passed through his mind.

'When Mr Bashwood comes,' he said, 'will you let me see him, and speak to him, before anything definite is done?'

'Of course I will!' rejoined Allan. He stopped and looked at his watch. 'And I'll tell you what I'll do for you, old boy, in the meantime,' he added; 'I'll introduce you to the prettiest girl in Norfolk! There's just time to run over to the cottage before dinner. Come along, and be introduced to Miss Milroy.'

'You can't introduce me to Miss Milroy to-day,' replied Midwinter; and he repeated the message of apology which had been brought from the major that afternoon. Allan was surprised and disappointed; but he was not to be foiled in his resolution to advance himself in the good graces of the inhabitants of the cottage. After a little consideration he hit on a means of turning the present adverse circumstances to good account. 'I'll show a proper anxiety for Mrs Milroy's recovery,' he said gravely. 'I'll send her a basket of strawberries, with my best respects, to-morrow morning.'

Nothing more happened to mark the end of that first day in the new house.

The one noticeable event of the next day was another disclosure of Mrs Milroy's infirmity of temper. Half-an-hour after Allan's basket of strawberries had been delivered at the cottage, it was returned to him intact (by the hands of the invalid lady's nurse), with a short and sharp message, shortly and sharply delivered. 'Mrs Milroy's compliments, and thanks. Strawberries invariably disagreed with her.' If this curiously petulant acknowledgment of an act of politeness was intended to irritate Allan, it failed entirely in accomplishing its object. Instead of being offended with the mother, he sympathized with the daughter. 'Poor little thing,' was all he said, 'she must have a hard life of it with such a mother as that!'

He called at the cottage himself later in the day, but Miss Milroy was not to be seen; she was engaged upstairs. The major received his visitor in his working apron – far more deeply immersed in his wonderful clock, and far less readily accessible to outer influences than Allan had seen him at their first interview. His manner was as kind as before; but not a word more could be extracted from him on the subject of his wife, than that Mrs Milroy 'had not improved since yesterday'.[3]

The two next days passed quietly and uneventfully. Allan persisted in making his inquiries at the cottage; but all he saw of the major's daughter was a glimpse of her on one occasion, at a window on the bed-room floor. Nothing more was heard from Mr Pedgift; and Mr Bash-wood's appearance was still delayed. Midwinter declined to move in the matter until time enough had passed to allow of his first hearing from Mr Brock, in answer to the letter which he had addressed to the rector on the night of his arrival at Thorpe-Ambrose. He was unusually silent and quiet, and passed most of his hours in the library among the books. The time wore on wearily. The resident gentry acknowledged Allan's visit by formally leaving their cards. Nobody came near the house afterwards; the weather was monotonously fine. Allan grew a little restless and dissatisfied. He began to resent Mrs Milroy's illness; he began to think regretfully of his deserted yacht.

The next day – the twentieth – brought some news with it from the outer world. A message was delivered from Mr Pedgift, announcing that his clerk, Mr Bashwood, would personally present himself at Thorpe-Ambrose on the following day; and a letter in answer to Midwinter was received from Mr Brock.

The letter was dated the 18th, and the news which it contained raised, not Allan's spirits only, but Midwinter's as well. On the day on which he wrote, Mr Brock announced that he was about to journey to London; having been summoned thither on business connected with the interests of a sick relative, to whom he stood in the position of trustee. The business completed, he had good hope of finding one or other of his clerical friends in the metropolis who would be able and willing to do duty for him at the rectory; and, in that case, he trusted to travel on from London to Thorpe-Ambrose in a week's time or less. Under these circumstances, he would leave the majority of the subjects on which Midwinter had written to him to be discussed when they met. But as time might be of importance, in relation to the stewardship of the Thorpe-Ambrose estate, he would say at once that he saw no reason why Midwinter should not apply his mind to learning the steward's duties, and should not succeed in rendering himself invaluably serviceable in that way to the interests of his friend.

Leaving Midwinter reading and re-reading the rector's cheering letter, as if he was bent on getting every sentence in it by heart, Allan went out rather earlier than usual, to make his daily inquiry at the cottage – or, in plainer words, to make a fourth attempt at improving his acquaintance with Miss Milroy. The day had begun encouragingly, and encouragingly it seemed destined to go on. When Allan turned the corner of the second shrubbery, and entered the little paddock where he and the major's daughter had first met, there was Miss Milroy herself loitering to and fro on the grass, to all appearance on the watch for somebody.[4]

She gave a little start when Allan appeared, and came forward without hesitation to meet him. She was not in her best looks. Her rosy complexion had suffered under confinement to the house, and a marked expression of embarrassment clouded her pretty face.

'I hardly know how to confess it, Mr Armadale,' she said, speaking eagerly, before Allan could utter a word, 'but I certainly ventured here this morning, in the hope of meeting with you. I have been very much distressed – I have only just heard, by accident, of the manner in which mamma received the present of fruit you so kindly sent to her. Will you try to excuse her? She has been miserably ill for years, and she is not always quite herself. After your being so very very kind to me (and to papa), I really could not help stealing out here in the hope of seeing you, and telling you how sorry I was. Pray forgive and forget, Mr Armadale – pray do!' Her voice faltered over the last words, and, in her eagerness to make her mother's peace with him, she laid her hand on his arm.

Allan was himself a little confused. Her earnestness took him by surprise, and her evident conviction that he had been offended, honestly distressed him. Not knowing what else to do, he followed his instincts, and possessed himself of her hand to begin with.

'My dear Miss Milroy, if you say a word more you will distress *me* next,' he rejoined, unconsciously pressing her hand closer and closer, in the embarrassment of the moment. 'I never was in the least offended; I made allowances – upon my honour I did – for poor Mrs Milroy's illness. Offended!' cried Allan, reverting energetically to the old complimentary strain. 'I should like to have my basket of fruit sent back every day – if I could only be sure of its bringing you out into the paddock the first thing in the morning.'

Some of Miss Milroy's missing colour began to appear again in her cheeks. 'Oh, Mr Armadale, there is really no end to your kindness,' she said; 'you don't know how you relieve me!' She paused; her spirits rallied with as happy a readiness of recovery as if they had been the spirits of a child; and her native brightness of temper sparkled again in her eyes, as she looked up, shyly smiling in Allan's face. 'Don't you think,' she asked demurely, 'that it is almost time now to let go of my hand?'

Their eyes met. Allan followed his instincts for the second time. Instead of releasing her hand, he lifted it to his lips and kissed it. All the missing tints of the rosier sort returned to Miss Milroy's complexion on the instant. She snatched away her hand as if Allan had burnt it.

'I'm sure *that's* wrong, Mr Armadale,' she said – and turned her head aside quickly, for she was smiling in spite of herself.

'I meant it as an apology for – for holding your hand too long,' stammered Allan. 'An apology can't be wrong – can it?'

There are occasions (though not many) when the female mind accurately appreciates an appeal to the force of pure reason. This was one of the occasions. An abstract proposition had been presented to Miss Milroy, and Miss Milroy was convinced. If it was meant as an apology, that (she admitted) made all the difference. 'I only hope,' said the little coquette, looking at him slyly, 'you're not misleading me. Not that it matters much now,' she added, with a serious shake of her head. 'If we *have* committed any improprieties, Mr Armadale, we are not likely to have the opportunity of committing many more.'

'You're not going away?' exclaimed Allan in great alarm.

'Worse than that, Mr Armadale. My new governess is coming.'

'Coming?' repeated Allan. 'Coming already?'

'As good as coming, I ought to have said – only I didn't know you wished me to be so very particular. We got the answers to the advertisements this morning. Papa and I opened them and read them together half an hour ago – and we both picked out the same letter from all the rest. I picked it out, because it was so prettily expressed; and papa picked it out, because the terms were so reasonable. He is going to send the letter up to grandmamma in London, by to-day's post; and if she finds everything satisfactory, on inquiry, the governess is to be engaged.

You don't know how dreadfully nervous I am getting about it already – a strange governess is such an awful prospect. But it is not quite so bad as going to school; and I have great hopes of this new lady, because she writes such a nice letter! As I said to papa, it almost reconciles me to her horrid, unromantic name.'

'What is her name?' asked Allan. 'Brown? Grubb? Scraggs? Anything of that sort?'

'Hush! hush! Nothing quite so horrible as that. Her name is Gwilt. Dreadfully unpoetical, isn't it? Her reference must be a respectable person, though; for she lives in the same part of London as grand-mamma. Stop, Mr Armadale! we are going the wrong way. No; I can't wait to look at those lovely flowers of yours this morning – and (many thanks) I can't accept your arm. I have stayed here too long already. Papa is waiting for his breakfast; and I must run back every step of the way. Thank you for making those kind allowances for mamma; thank you again and again – and good-by!'

'Won't you shake hands?' asked Allan.

She gave him her hand. 'No more apologies, if you please, Mr Armadale,' she said saucily. Once more their eyes met; and once more the plump dimpled little hand found its way to Allan's lips. 'It isn't an apology this time!' cried Allan, precipitately defending himself. 'It's – it's a mark of respect.'

She started back a few steps, and burst out laughing. 'You won't find me in your grounds again, Mr Armadale,' she said merrily, 'till I have got Miss Gwilt to take care of me!' With that farewell, she gathered up her skirts, and ran back across the paddock at the top of her speed.

Allan stood watching her in speechless admiration till she was out of sight. His second interview with Miss Milroy had produced an extraordinary effect on him. For the first time since he had become the master of Thorpe-Ambrose, he was absorbed in serious consideration of what he owed to his new position in life. 'The question is,' pondered Allan, 'whether I hadn't better set myself right with my neighbours by becoming a married man? I'll take the day to consider; and if I keep in the same mind about it, I'll consult Midwinter to-morrow morning.'

When the morning came, and when Allan descended to the breakfast-room, resolute to consult his friend on the obligations that he owed to his neighbours in general, and to Miss Milroy in particular, no Midwinter was to be seen. On making inquiry it appeared that he had been observed in the hall; that he had taken from the table a letter which the morning's post had brought to him; and that he had gone back immediately to his own room. Allan at once ascended the stairs again, and knocked at his friend's door.

'May I come in?' he asked.

'Not just now,' was the answer.

'You have got a letter, haven't you?' persisted Allan. 'Any bad news? Anything wrong?'

'Nothing. I'm not very well this morning. Don't wait breakfast for me; I'll come down as soon as I can.'

No more was said on either side. Allan returned to the breakfast-room a little disappointed. He had set his heart on rushing headlong into his consultation with Midwinter, and here was the consultation indefinitely delayed. 'What an odd fellow he is!' thought Allan. 'What on earth can he be doing, locked in there by himself?'

He was doing nothing. He was sitting by the window, with the letter which had reached him that morning, open in his hand. The hand-writing was Mr Brock's, and the words written were these:

> My dear Midwinter, – I have literally only two minutes before post-time to tell you that I have just met (in Kensington Gardens) with the woman, whom we both only know, thus far, as the woman with the red Paisley shawl. I have traced her and her companion (a respectable-looking elderly lady) to their residence – after having distinctly heard Allan's name mentioned between them.[5] Depend on my not losing sight of the woman until I am satisfied that she means no mischief at Thorpe-Ambrose; and expect to hear from me again as soon as I know how this strange discovery is to end. – Very truly yours, DECIMUS BROCK.

After reading the letter for the second time Midwinter folded it up thoughtfully, and placed it in his pocket-book, side by side with the manuscript narrative of Allan's dream.

'Your discovery will not end with *you*, Mr Brock,' he said. 'Do what you will with the woman, when the time comes the woman will be here.'

He looked for a moment in the glass – saw that he had composed himself sufficiently to meet Allan's eye – and went downstairs to take his place at the breakfast table.

CHAPTER V

MOTHER OLDERSHAW ON HER GUARD

I. – *From Mrs Oldershaw (Diana Street, Pimlico) to Miss Gwilt
(West Place, Old Brompton)*

Ladies' Toilette Repository,
June 20th, Eight in the Evening.

MY DEAR LYDIA, – About three hours have passed, as well as I can remember, since I pushed you unceremoniously inside my house in West Place; and, merely telling you to wait till you saw me again, banged the door to between us, and left you alone in the hall. I know your sensitive nature, my dear, and I am afraid you have made up your mind by this time that never yet was a guest treated so abominably by her hostess as I have treated you.

The delay that has prevented me from explaining my strange conduct is, believe me, a delay for which I am not to blame. One of the many delicate little difficulties which beset so essentially confidential a business as mine, occurred here (as I have since discovered) while we were taking the air this afternoon in Kensington Gardens. I see no chance of being able to get back to you for some hours to come, and I have a word of very urgent caution for your private ear, which has been too long delayed already. So I must use the spare minutes as they come, and write.

Here is caution the first. On no account venture outside the door again this evening; and be very careful, while the daylight lasts, not to show yourself at any of the front windows. I have reason to fear that a certain charming person now staying with me may possibly be watched. Don't be alarmed, and don't be impatient; you shall know why.

I can only explain myself by going back to our unlucky meeting in the gardens with that reverend gentleman who was so obliging as to follow us both back to my house.

It crossed my mind, just as we were close to the door, that there might be a motive for the parson's anxiety to trace us home, far less creditable to his taste, and far more dangerous to both of us than the motive you supposed him to have. In plainer words, Lydia, I rather doubted whether you had met with another admirer; and I strongly suspected that you had encountered another enemy instead. There was no time to tell you this. There was only time to see you safe into the house, and to make sure of the parson (in case my suspicions were right) by treating him as he had treated us – I mean, by following him in his turn.

I kept some little distance behind him at first, to turn the thing over in my mind, and to be satisfied that my doubts were not misleading me. We have no concealments from each other; and you shall know what my doubts were. I was not surprised at *your* recognizing *him*; he is not at all a common-looking old man; and you had seen him twice in Somersetshire – once when you asked your way of him to Mrs Armadale's house; and once when you saw him again on your way back to the railroad. But I was a little puzzled (considering that you had your veil down on both those occasions, and your veil down also when we were in the Gardens,) at *his* recognizing *you*. I doubted his remembering your figure, in a summer dress, after he had only seen it in a winter dress; and though we were talking when he met us, and your voice is one among your many charms, I doubted his remembering your voice either. And yet I felt persuaded that he knew you. 'How?' you will ask. My dear, as ill-luck would have it, we were speaking at the time of young Armadale. I firmly believe that the name was the first thing that struck him; and when he heard *that*, your voice certainly, and your figure perhaps, came back to his memory. 'And what if it did?' you may say. Think again, Lydia, and tell me whether the parson of the place where Mrs Armadale lived, was not likely to be Mrs Armadale's friend? If he *was* her friend, the very first person to whom she would apply for advice after the manner in which you frightened her, and after what you most injudiciously said on the subject of appealing to her son, would be the clergyman of the parish – and the magistrate too, as the landlord at the inn himself told you.

You will now understand why I left you in that extremely uncivil manner, and I may go on to what happened next.

I followed the old gentleman till he turned into a quiet street, and then accosted him with respect for the Church written (I flatter myself) in every line of my face.

'Will you excuse me,' I said, 'if I venture to inquire, sir, whether you recognized the lady who was walking with me when you happened to pass us in the Gardens?'

'Will you excuse my asking, ma'am, why you put that question?' was all the answer I got.

'I will endeavour to tell you, sir,' I said. 'If my friend is not an absolute stranger to you, I should wish to request your attention to a very delicate subject, connected with a lady deceased, and with her son who survives her.'

He was staggered; I could see that. But he was sly enough at the same time to hold his tongue and wait till I said something more.

'If I am wrong, sir, in thinking that you recognized my friend,' I went on, 'I beg to apologize. But I could hardly suppose it possible that a gentleman in your profession would follow a lady home who was a total stranger to him.'

There I had him. He coloured up (fancy that, at his age!), and owned the truth, in defence of his own precious character.

'I have met with the lady once before, and I acknowledge that I recognized her in the Gardens,' he said. 'You will excuse me if I decline entering into the question of whether I did, or did not, purposely follow her home. If you wish to be assured that your friend is not an absolute stranger to me, you now have that assurance; and if you have anything particular to say to me, I leave you to decide whether the time has come to say it.'

He waited, and looked about. I waited, and looked about. He said the street was hardly a fit place to speak of a delicate subject in. I said the street was hardly a fit place to speak of a delicate subject in. He didn't offer to take me to where he lived. I didn't offer to take him to where I lived. Have you ever seen two strange cats, my dear, nose to nose on the tiles? If you have, you have seen the parson and me done to the life.

'Well, ma'am,' he said, at last, 'shall we go on with our conversation in spite of circumstances?'

'Yes, sir,' I said; 'we are both of us, fortunately, of an age to set circumstances at defiance' (I had seen the old wretch looking at my grey hair, and satisfying himself that his character was safe if he *was* seen with me).

After all this snapping and snarling, we came to the point at last. I began by telling him that I feared his interest in you was not of the friendly sort. He admitted that much – of course, in defence of his own character once more. I next repeated to him everything you had told me about your proceedings in Somerset-shire, when we first found that he was following us home. Don't be alarmed, my dear – I was acting on principle. If you want to make a dish of lies digestible, always give it a garnish of truth. Well, having appealed to the reverend gentleman's confidence in this manner, I next declared that you had become an altered woman since he had seen you last. I revived that dead wretch, your husband (without mentioning names, of course), established him (the first place I thought of) in business at the Brazils, and described a letter which he had written, offering to forgive his erring wife, if she would repent and go back to him. I assured the parson that your husband's noble conduct had softened your obdurate nature; and then, thinking I had produced the right impression, I came boldly to close quarters with him. I said, 'At the very time when you met us, sir, my unhappy friend was speaking in terms of touching self-reproach of her conduct to the late Mrs Armadale. She confided to me her anxiety to make some atonement, if possible, to Mrs Armadale's son; and it is at her entreaty (for she cannot prevail on herself to face you) that I now beg to inquire whether Mr Armadale is still in Somersetshire, and whether he would consent to take back in small instalments the sum of money which my friend acknowledges that she received by practising on Mrs Armadale's fears.' Those were my very words. A neater story (accounting so nicely for everything) was never told; it was a story to melt a stone. But this Somersetshire parson is harder than stone itself. I blush for *him*, my dear, when I assure you that he was evidently insensible enough to disbelieve every word I said about your reformed character, your husband in the Brazils, and your penitent anxiety to pay the money back. It is really a disgrace that such a man should be in the Church; such cunning as his is in the last degree unbecoming in a member of a sacred profession.

'Does your friend propose to join her husband by the next steamer!' was all he condescended to say, when I had done.

I acknowledge I was angry. I snapped at him. I said – 'Yes, she does.'

'How am I to communicate with her?' he asked.

I snapped at him again. 'By letter – through me.'

'At what address, ma'am?'

There I had him once more. 'You have found my address out for yourself, sir,' I said. 'The directory will tell you my name, if you wish to find that out for yourself also; otherwise, you are welcome to my card.'

'Many thanks, ma'am. If your friend wishes to communicate with Mr Armadale, I will give you *my* card in return.'

'Thank you, sir.'

'Thank you, ma'am.'

'Good afternoon, sir.'

'Good afternoon, ma'am.'

So we parted. I went my way to an appointment at my place of business, and he went his in a hurry; which is of itself suspicious. What I can't get over, is his heartlessness. Heaven help the people who send for *him* to comfort them on their death-beds!

The next consideration is, What are we to do? If we don't find out the right way to keep this old wretch in the dark, he may be the ruin of us at Thorpe-Ambrose just as we are within easy reach of our end in view. Wait up till I come to you, with my mind free, I hope, from the other difficulty which is worrying me here. Was there ever such ill-luck as ours? Only think of that man deserting his congregation, and coming to London just at the very time when we have answered the advertisement, and may expect the inquiries to be made next week! I have no patience with him – his bishop ought to interfere.

> Affectionately yours,
> MARIA OLDERSHAW.

2. – *From Miss Gwilt to Mrs Oldershaw*

West Place, June 20th.

MY POOR OLD DEAR, – How very little you know of my sensitive nature, as you call it! Instead of feeling offended when you left me, I went to your piano, and forgot all about you till your messenger came. Your letter is irresistible; I have been laughing over it till I am quite out of breath. Of all the absurd stories I ever read, the story you addressed to the Somersetshire clergyman is the most ridiculous. And as for your interview with him in the street, it is a perfect sin to keep it to ourselves. The public ought really to enjoy it in the form of a farce at one of the theatres.

Luckily for both of us (to come to serious matters), your messenger is a prudent person. He sent upstairs to know if there was an answer. In the midst of my merriment I had presence of mind enough to send downstairs and say, 'Yes.'

Some brute of a man says in some book which I once read, that no woman can keep two separate trains of ideas in her mind at the same time. I declare you have almost satisfied me that the man is right. What! when you have escaped unnoticed to your place of business, and when you suspect this house to be watched, you propose to come back here, and to put it in the parson's power to recover the lost trace of you! What madness! Stop where you are; and when you have got over your difficulty at Pimlico (it is some woman's business of course; what worries women are!), be so good as to read what I have got to say about our difficulty at Brompton.

In the first place, the house (as you supposed) is watched. Half-an-hour after you left me, loud voices in the street interrupted me at the piano, and I went to the window. There was a cab at the house opposite, where they let lodgings; and an old man, who looked like a respectable servant, was wrangling with the driver about his fare. An elderly gentleman came out of the house, and stopped them. An elderly gentleman returned into the house, and appeared cautiously at the front drawing-room window. You know him, you worthy creature – he had the bad taste, some few hours since, to doubt whether you were telling him the truth. Don't be afraid, he didn't see me. When he looked up, after settling with the cab-driver, I was behind the curtain. I have been behind the curtain once or twice since; and I have seen enough to satisfy me that he and his servant will relieve each other at the window, so as never to lose sight of your house here, night or day. That the parson suspects the real truth is of course impossible. But that he firmly believes I mean some mischief to young Armadale, and that you have entirely confirmed him in that conviction, is as plain as that two and two make four. And this has happened (as you helplessly remind me) just when we have answered the advertisement, and when we may expect the major's inquiries to be made in a few days' time.

Surely, here is a terrible situation for two women to find themselves in? A fiddlestick's end for the situation! We have got an easy way out of it – thanks, Mother Oldershaw, to what I myself forced you to do, not three hours before the Somersetshire clergyman met with us.

Has that venomous little quarrel[1] of ours this morning – after we had pounced on the major's advertisement in the newspaper – quite slipped out of your memory? Have you forgotten how I persisted in my opinion that you were a great deal too well known in London to appear safely as my reference in your own name, or to receive an inquiring lady or gentleman (as you were rash enough to propose) in your own house? Don't you remember what a passion you were in when I brought our dispute to an end by declining to stir a step in the matter, unless I could conclude my application to Major Milroy by referring him to an address at which you were totally unknown, and to a name which might be anything you pleased, as long as it was not yours? What a look you gave me when you found there was nothing for it but to drop the whole speculation, or to let me have my own way! How you fumed over the lodging-hunting on the other side of the Park! and how you groaned when you came back, possessed of Furnished Apartments in respectable Bayswater, over the useless expense I had put you to! What do you think of those Furnished Apartments *now*, you obstinate old woman? Here we are, with discovery threatening us at our very door, and with no hope of escape unless we can contrive to disappear from the parson in the dark. And there are the lodgings in Bayswater, to which no inquisitive strangers have traced either you or me, ready and waiting to swallow us up – the lodgings in which we can escape all further molestation, and answer the major's inquiries at our ease. Can you see, at last, a little farther than your poor old nose? Is there anything in the world to prevent your safe disappearance from Pimlico to-night, and your safe establishment at the new lodgings, in the character of my respectable reference, half-an-hour afterwards? Oh, fie, fie, Mother Oldershaw! Go down on your wicked old knees, and thank your stars that you had a she-devil like me to deal with this morning!

Suppose we come now to the only difficulty worth mentioning – *my* difficulty. Watched as I am in this house, how am I to join you without bringing the parson or the parson's servant with me at my heels?

Being to all intents and purposes a prisoner here, it seems to me that I have no choice but to try the old prison plan of escape – a change of clothes. I have been looking at your housemaid. Except that we are both light, her face and hair and my face and hair are as unlike each other as possible. But she is as nearly as can be my height and size; and (if she only knew how to dress herself, and had smaller feet) her figure is a very much better one than it ought to be for a person in her station in life. My idea is, to dress her in the clothes I wore in the Gardens to-day – to send her out, with our reverend enemy in full pursuit of her – and, as soon the coast is clear, to slip away myself and join you. The thing would be quite impossible, of course, if I had been seen with my veil up; but, as events have turned out, it is one advantage of the horrible exposure which followed my marriage, that I seldom show myself in public, and never of course in such a populous place as London, without wearing a thick veil and keeping that veil down. If the housemaid wears my dress, I don't really see why the housemaid may not be counted on to represent me to the life.

The one question is, can the woman be trusted? If she can, send me a line, telling her, on your authority, that she is to place herself at my disposal. I won't say a word till I have heard from you first.

Let me have my answer to-night. As long as we were only talking about my getting the governess's place, I was careless enough how it ended. But now that we have actually answered Major Milroy's advertisement, I am in earnest at last. I mean to be Mrs Armadale of Thorpe-Ambrose; and woe to the man or woman who tries to stop me!

Yours,

LYDIA GWILT.

P.S. – I open my letter again to say that you need have no fear of your messenger being followed on his return to Pimlico. He will drive to a public-house where he is known, will dismiss the cab at the door, and will go out again by a back way which is only used by the landlord and his friends. – L. G.

3. – *From Mrs Oldershaw to Miss Gwilt*

Diana Street, 10 o'clock.

MY DEAR LYDIA, – You have written me a heartless letter. If you had been in my trying position, harassed as I was when I wrote to you, I should have made allowances for my friend when I found my friend not so sharp as usual. But the vice of the present age is a want of consideration for persons in the decline of life. Your mind is in a sad state, my dear; and you stand much in need of a good example. You shall have a good example – I forgive you.

Having now relieved my mind by the performance of a good action, suppose I show you next (though I protest against the vulgarity of the expression) that I *can* see a little farther than my poor old nose?

I will answer your question about the housemaid first. You may trust her implicitly. She has had her troubles, and has learnt discretion. She also looks your age; though it is only her due to say that, in this particular, she has some years the advantage of you. I enclose the necessary directions which will place her entirely at your disposal.

And what comes next? Your plan for joining me at Bayswater comes next. It is very well, as far as it goes; but it stands sadly in need of a little judicious improvement. There is a serious necessity (you shall know why presently) for deceiving the parson far more completely than you propose to deceive him. I want him to see the housemaid's face under circumstances which will persuade him that it is *your* face. And then, going a step farther, I want him to see the housemaid leave London, under the impression that he has seen *you* start on the first stage of your journey to the Brazils. He didn't believe in that journey when I announced it to him this afternoon in the street. He may believe in it yet, if you follow the directions I am now going to give you.

To-morrow is Saturday. Send the housemaid out in your walking dress of to-day, just as you propose – but don't stir out yourself, and don't go near the window. Desire the woman to keep her veil down; to take half-an-hour's walk (quite unconscious, of course, of the parson or his servant at her heels); and then to come back to you. As soon as she appears, send her instantly to the open window, instructing her to lift her veil carelessly, and look out. Let her go away again after a minute or two, take off her bonnet and shawl, and then appear once more at the window, or, better still, in the balcony outside. She may show herself again occasionally (not too often) later in the day. And to-morrow – as we have a professional gentleman to deal with – by all means send her to church. If these proceedings don't persuade the parson that the housemaid's face is your face, and if they don't make him readier to believe in your reformed character than he was when I spoke to him, I have lived sixty years, my love, in this vale of tears to mighty little purpose.

The next day is Monday. I have looked at the shipping advertisements, and I find that a steamer leaves Liverpool for the Brazils on Tuesday. Nothing could be more convenient; we will start you on your voyage under the parson's own eyes. You may manage it in this way:

At one o'clock send out the man who cleans the knives and forks to get a cab; and when he has brought it up to the door, let him go back and get a second cab, which he is to wait in himself, round the corner, in the square. Let the housemaid (still in your dress) drive off, with the necessary boxes, in the first cab to the North-Western Railway. When she is gone, slip out yourself to the cab waiting round the corner, and come to me at Bayswater. They may be prepared to follow the housemaid's cab, because they have seen it at the door; but they won't be prepared to follow your cab, which has been hidden round the corner. When the housemaid has got to the station, and has done her best to disappear in the crowd (I have chosen the mixed train[2] at 2.10, so as to give her every chance), you will be safe with me; and whether they do or do not find out that she does not really start for Liverpool won't matter by that time. They will have lost all trace of *you*; and they may follow the housemaid half over London, if they like. She has my instructions (enclosed) to leave the empty boxes to find their way to the lost luggage office, and to go to her friends in the City, and stay there till I write word that I want her again.

And what is the object of all this? My dear Lydia, the object is your future security (and mine). We may succeed, or we may fail in persuading the parson that you have actually gone to the Brazils. If we succeed, we are relieved of all fear of him. If we fail, he will warn young Armadale to be careful *of a woman like my housemaid, and not of a woman like you*. This last gain is a very important one; for we don't know that Mrs Armadale may not have told him your maiden name. In that event, the 'Miss Gwilt' whom he will describe as having slipped through his fingers here, will be so entirely unlike the 'Miss Gwilt' established at Thorpe-Ambrose, as to satisfy everybody that it is not a case of similarity of persons, but only a case of similarity of names.

What do you say now to my improvement on your idea? Are my brains not quite so addled as you thought them when you wrote? Don't suppose I'm at all over-boastful about my own ingenuity. Cleverer tricks than this trick of mine are played off on the public by swindlers, and are recorded in the newspapers every week. I only want to show you that my assistance is not less necessary to the success of the Armadale speculation now, than it was when I made our first important discoveries, by means of the harmless-looking young man and the private inquiry-office in Shadyside Place.

There is nothing more to say that I know of, except that I am just going to start for the new lodging, with a box directed in my new name. The last expiring moments of Mother Oldershaw, of the Toilette Repository, are close at hand; and the birth of Miss Gwilt's respectable reference, Mrs Mandeville, will take place in a cab in five minutes' time. I fancy I must be still young at heart, for I am quite in love already with my romantic name; it sounds almost as pretty as Mrs Armadale of Thorpe-Ambrose, doesn't it? Good-night, my dear, and pleasant dreams. If any accident happens between this and Monday, write to me instantly by post. If no accident happens, you will be with me in excellent time for the earliest inquiries that the major can possibly make. My last words are, don't go out, and don't venture near the front windows till Monday comes.

Affectionately yours,

M. O.

CHAPTER VI

MIDWINTER IN DISGUISE

Towards noon, on the day of the twenty-first, Miss Milroy was loitering in the cottage garden – released from duty in the sick-room by an improvement in her mother's health – when her attention was attracted by the sound of voices in the park. One of the voices she instantly recognized as Allan's: the other was strange to her. She put aside the branches of a shrub near the garden palings; and peeping through, saw Allan approaching the cottage gate, in company with a slim, dark, undersized man, who was talking and laughing excitably at the top of his voice. Miss Milroy ran indoors, to warn her father of Mr Armadale's arrival, and to add that he was bringing with him a noisy stranger, who was, in all probability, the friend generally reported to be staying with the squire at the great house.

Had the major's daughter guessed right? Was the squire's loud-talking, loud-laughing companion the shy, sensitive Midwinter of other times? It was even so. In Allan's presence, that morning, an extraordinary change had passed over the ordinarily quiet demeanour of Allan's friend.

When Midwinter had first appeared in the breakfast-room, after putting aside Mr Brock's startling letter, Allan had been too much occupied to pay any special attention to him. The undecided difficulty of choosing the day for the audit-dinner had pressed for a settlement once more, and had been fixed at last (under the butler's advice) for Saturday, the twenty-eighth of the month. It was only on turning round to remind Midwinter of the ample space of time which the new arrangement allowed for mastering the steward's books, that even Allan's flighty attention had been arrested by a marked change in the face that confronted him. He had openly noticed the change in his usual blunt manner, and had been instantly silenced by a fretful, almost an angry, reply. The two had sat down together to breakfast without the usual cordiality; and the meal had proceeded gloomily, till Midwinter himself broke the silence by bursting into the strange outbreak of gaiety which had revealed in Allan's eyes a new side to the character of his friend.

As usual with most of Allan's judgments, here again the conclusion was wrong. It was no new side to Midwinter's character that now presented itself – it was only a new aspect of the one ever-recurring struggle of Midwinter's life.

Irritated by Allan's discovery of the change in him, which he had failed to see reflected in his looking-glass, when he had consulted it on leaving his room; feeling Allan's eyes still fixed inquiringly on his face, and dreading the next questions that Allan's curiosity might put, Midwinter had roused himself to efface, by main force, the impression which his own altered appearance had produced. It was one of those efforts which no men compass so resolutely as the men of his quick temper, and his sensitive feminine organization. With his whole mind still possessed by the firm belief that the Fatality had taken one great step nearer to Allan and himself since the rector's discovery in Kensington Gardens – with his face still betraying what he had suffered, under the renewed conviction that his father's death-bed warning was now, in event after event, asserting its terrible claim to part him, at any sacrifice, from the one human creature whom he loved – with the fear still busy at his heart that the first mysterious Vision of Allan's Dream might be a Vision realized, before the new day that now saw the two Armadales together was a day that had passed over their heads – with these triple bonds, wrought by his own superstition, fettering him at that moment as they had never fettered him yet, he mercilessly spurred his resolution to the desperate effort of rivalling, in Allan's presence, the gaiety and good spirits of Allan himself. He talked, and laughed, and heaped his plate indiscriminately from every dish on the breakfast-table. He made noisily merry with jests that had no humour, and stories that had no point. He first astonished Allan, then amused him, then won his easily-encouraged confidence on the subject of Miss Milroy. He shouted with laughter over the sudden development of Allan's views on marriage, until the servants downstairs began to think that their master's strange friend had gone mad. Lastly, he had accepted Allan's proposal that he should be presented to the major's daughter, and judge of her for himself, as readily – nay, more readily than it would have been accepted by the least diffident man living. There the two now stood at the cottage gate – Midwinter's voice rising louder and louder over Allan's – Midwinter's natural manner disguised (how madly and miserably none but he knew!) in a coarse masquerade of boldness – the outrageous, the unendurable boldness of a shy man.

They were received in the parlour by the major's daughter, pending the arrival of the major himself.

Allan attempted to present his friend in the usual form. To his astonishment, Midwinter took the words flippantly out of his lips, and introduced himself to Miss Milroy with a confident look, a hard laugh, and a clumsy assumption of ease which presented him at his worst. His artificial spirits, lashed continuously into higher and higher effervescence since the morning, were now mounting hysterically beyond his own control. He looked and spoke with that terrible freedom of licence which is the necessary consequence, when a diffident man has thrown off his reserve, of the very effort by which he has broken loose from his own restraints. He involved himself in a confused medley of apologies that were not wanted, and of compliments that might have over-flattered the vanity of a savage. He looked backwards and forwards from Miss Milroy to Allan, and declared jocosely that he understood now why his friend's morning walks were always taken in the same direction. He asked her questions about her mother, and cut short the answers she gave him by remarks on the weather. In one breath, he said she must

feel the day insufferably hot; and, in another, he protested that he quite
envied her in her cool muslin dress.

The major came in. Before he could say two words, Midwinter
overwhelmed him with the same frenzy of familiarity, and the same
feverish fluency of speech. He expressed his interest in Mrs Milroy's
health in terms which would have been exaggerated on the lips of a
friend of the family. He overflowed into a perfect flood of apologies for
disturbing the major at his mechanical pursuits. He quoted Allan's
extravagant account of the clock, and expressed his own anxiety to see
it in terms more extravagant still. He paraded his superficial book-
knowledge of the great clock at Strasbourg, with far-fetched jests on
the extraordinary automaton figures which that clock puts in motion –
on the procession of the twelve apostles, which walks out under the
dial at noon, and on the toy-cock, which crows at St Peter's appearance – and this before a man who had studied every wheel in that
complex machinery, and who had passed whole years of his life in
trying to imitate it. 'I hear you have outnumbered the Strasbourg
apostles, and outcrowed the Strasbourg cock,' he exclaimed, with the
tone and manner of a friend habitually privileged to waive all
ceremony; 'and I am dying, absolutely dying, major, to see your
wonderful clock!'

Major Milroy had entered the room with his mind absorbed in his
own mechanical contrivances as usual. But the sudden shock of Midwinter's familiarity was violent enough to recall him instantly to himself,
and to make him master again, for the time, of his social resources as a
man of the world.

'Excuse me for interrupting you,' he said, stopping Midwinter for
the moment, by a look of steady surprise. 'I happen to have seen the
clock at Strasbourg; and it sounds almost absurd in my ears (if you
will pardon me for saying so) to put my little experiment in any light
of comparison with that wonderful achievement. There is nothing else
of the kind like it in the world!' He paused, to control his own
mounting enthusiasm; the clock at Strasbourg was to Major Milroy
what the name of Michael Angelo was to Sir Joshua Reynolds.[1] 'Mr
Armadale's kindness has led him to exaggerate a little,' pursued the
major, smiling at Allan, and passing over another attempt of Midwinter's to seize on the talk, as if no such attempt had been made. 'But as
there does happen to be this one point of resemblance between the
great clock abroad and the little clock at home, that they both show
what they can do on the stroke of noon, and as it is close on twelve
now, if you still wish to visit my workshop, Mr Midwinter, the sooner

I show you the way to it the better.' He opened the door, and apologized to Midwinter, with marked ceremony, for preceding him out of the room.

'What do you think of my friend?' whispered Allan, as he and Miss Milroy followed.

'Must I tell you the truth, Mr Armadale?' she whispered back.

'Of course!'

'Then I don't like him at all!'

'He's the best and dearest fellow in the world,' rejoined the outspoken Allan. 'You'll like him better when you know him better – I'm sure you will!'

Miss Milroy made a little grimace, implying supreme indifference to Midwinter, and saucy surprise at Allan's earnest advocacy of the merits of his friend. 'Has he got nothing more interesting to say to me than *that*,' she wondered, privately, 'after kissing my hand twice yesterday morning?'

They were all in the major's workroom before Allan had the chance of trying a more attractive subject. There, on the top of a rough wooden case, which evidently contained the machinery, was the wonderful clock. The dial was crowned by a glass pedestal placed on rockwork in carved ebony; and on the top of the pedestal sat the inevitable figure of Time, with his everlasting scythe in his hand. Below the dial was a little platform, and at either end of it rose two miniature sentry-boxes, with closed doors. Externally, this was all that appeared, until the magic moment came when the clock struck twelve at noon.

It wanted then about three minutes to twelve; and Major Milroy seized the opportunity of explaining what the exhibition was to be, before the exhibition began. At the first words, his mind fell back again into its old absorption over the one employment of his life. He turned to Midwinter (who had persisted in talking all the way from the parlour, and who was talking still) without a trace left in his manner of the cool and cutting composure with which he had spoken but a few minutes before. The noisy, familiar man, who had been an ill-bred intruder in the parlour, became a privileged guest in the workshop – for *there* he possessed the all-atoning social advantage of being new to the performances of the wonderful clock.

'At the first stroke of twelve, Mr Midwinter,' said the major, quite eagerly, 'keep your eye on the figure of Time: he will move his scythe, and point it downwards to the glass pedestal. You will next see a little printed card appear behind the glass, which will tell you the day of the

223

month and the day of the week. At the last stroke of the clock, Time will lift his scythe again into its former position, and the chimes will ring a peal. The peal will be succeeded by the playing of a tune – the favourite march of my old regiment – and then the final performance of the clock will follow. The sentry-boxes, which you may observe at each side, will both open at the same moment. In one of them you will see the sentinel appear; and, from the other, a corporal and two privates will march across the platform to relieve the guard, and will then disappear, leaving the new sentinel at his post. I must ask your kind allowances for this last part of the performance. The machinery is a little complicated, and there are defects in it which I am ashamed to say I have not yet succeeded in remedying as I could wish. Sometimes the figures go all wrong, and sometimes they go all right. I hope they may do their best on the occasion of your seeing them for the first time.'

As the major, posted near his clock, said the last words, his little audience of three, assembled at the opposite end of the room, saw the hour-hand and the minute-hand on the dial point together to twelve. The first stroke sounded, and Time, true to the signal, moved his scythe. The day of the month and the day of the week announced themselves in print through the glass pedestal next; Midwinter applauding their appearance with a noisy exaggeration of surprise, which Miss Milroy mistook for coarse sarcasm directed at her father's pursuits, and which Allan (seeing that she was offended) attempted to moderate by touching the elbow of his friend. Meanwhile, the performances of the clock went on. At the last stroke of twelve, Time lifted his scythe again, the chimes rang, the march tune of the major's old regiment followed; and the crowning exhibition of the relief of the guard announced itself in a preliminary trembling of the sentry-boxes, and a sudden disappearance of the major at the back of the clock.

The performance began with the opening of the sentry-box on the right-hand side of the platform, as punctually as could be desired; the door on the other side, however, was less tractable – it remained obstinately closed. Unaware of this hitch in the proceedings, the corporal and his two privates appeared in their places in a state of perfect discipline, tottered out across the platform, all three trembling in every limb, dashed themselves headlong against the closed door on the other side, and failed in producing the smallest impression on the immovable sentry presumed to be within. An intermittent clicking, as of the major's keys and tools at work, was heard in the machinery. The corporal and his two privates suddenly returned, backwards, across the platform, and shut themselves up with a bang inside their own door. Exactly at the same moment, the other door opened for the first time, and the provoking sentry appeared with the utmost deliberation at his post, waiting to be relieved. He was allowed to wait. Nothing happened in the other box but an occasional knocking inside the door, as if the corporal and his privates were impatient to be let out. The clicking of the major's tools was heard again among the machinery; the corporal and his party, suddenly restored to liberty, appeared in a violent hurry, and spun furiously across the platform. Quick as they were, however, the hitherto deliberate sentry on the other side, now perversely showed himself to be quicker still. He disappeared like lightning into his own premises, the door closed smartly after him, the corporal and his privates dashed themselves headlong against it for the second time, and the major appearing again round the corner of the clock, asked his audience innocently, 'if they would be good enough to tell him whether anything had gone wrong?'

The fantastic absurdity of the exhibition, heightened by Major Milroy's grave inquiry at the end of it, was so irresistibly ludicrous that the visitors shouted with laughter; and even Miss Milroy, with all her consideration for her father's sensitive pride in his clock, could not restrain herself from joining in the merriment which the catastrophe of the puppets had provoked. But there are limits even to the licence of laughter; and these limits were ere long so outrageously overstepped by one of the little party as to have the effect of almost instantly silencing the other two. The fever of Midwinter's false spirits flamed out into sheer delirium as the performance of the puppets came to an end. His paroxysms of laughter followed each other with such convulsive violence, that Miss Milroy started back from him in alarm, and even the patient major turned on him with a look which said plainly, Leave the room! Allan, wisely impulsive for once in his life, seized Midwinter by the arm, and dragged him out by main force into the garden, and thence into the park beyond.

'Good heavens! What has come to you!' he exclaimed, shrinking back from the tortured face before him, as he stopped and looked close at it for the first time.

For the moment, Midwinter was incapable of answering. The hysterical paroxysm was passing from one extreme to the other. He leaned against a tree, sobbing and gasping for breath, and stretched out his hand in mute entreaty to Allan to give him time.

'You had better not have nursed me through my fever,' he said faintly, as soon as he could speak. 'I'm mad and miserable, Allan – I have never recovered it. Go back, and ask them to forgive me; I am ashamed to go and ask them myself. I can't tell how it happened – I can only ask your pardon and theirs.' He turned aside his head quickly so as to conceal his face. 'Don't stop here,' he said; 'don't look at me – I shall soon get over it.' Allan still hesitated, and begged hard to be allowed to take him back to the house. It was useless. 'You break my heart with your kindness,' he burst out passionately. 'For God's sake leave me by myself!'

Allan went back to the cottage, and pleaded there for indulgence to Midwinter, with an earnestness and simplicity which raised him immensely in the major's estimation, but which totally failed to produce the same favourable impression on Miss Milroy. Little as she herself suspected it, she was fond enough of Allan already to be jealous of Allan's friend.

'How excessively absurd!' she thought, pettishly. 'As if either papa or I considered such a person of the slightest consequence!'

'You will kindly suspend your opinion, won't you, Major Milroy?' said Allan, in his hearty way, at parting.

'With the greatest pleasure!' replied the major, cordially shaking hands.

'And you, too, Miss Milroy?' added Allan.

Miss Milroy made a mercilessly formal bow. '*My* opinion, Mr Armadale, is not of the slightest consequence.'

Allan left the cottage, sorely puzzled to account for Miss Milroy's sudden coolness towards him. His grand idea of conciliating the whole neighbourhood by becoming a married man, underwent some modification as he closed the garden-gate behind him. The virtue called Prudence and the Squire of Thorpe-Ambrose became personally acquainted with each other, on this occasion, for the first time; and Allan, entering headlong as usual on the high-road to moral improvement, actually decided on doing nothing in a hurry!

A man who is entering on a course of reformation ought, if virtue is its own reward, to be a man engaged in an essentially inspiriting pursuit. But virtue is not always its own reward; and the way that leads to reformation is remarkably ill-lighted for so respectable a thoroughfare. Allan seemed to have caught the infection of his friend's despondency. As he walked home, he, too, began to doubt – in his widely-different way, and for his widely-different reasons – whether the life at Thorpe-Ambrose was promising quite as fairly for the future as it had promised at first.

CHAPTER VII

THE PLOT THICKENS

Two messages were waiting for Allan when he returned to the house. One had been left by Midwinter. 'He had gone out for a long walk, and Mr Armadale was not to be alarmed if he did not get back till late in the day.' The other message had been left by 'a person from Mr Pedgift's office', who had called, according to appointment, while the two gentlemen were away at the major's. 'Mr Bashwood's respects, and he would have the honour of waiting on Mr Armadale again, in the course of the evening.'

Towards five o'clock, Midwinter returned, pale and silent. Allan hastened to assure him that his peace was made at the cottage; and then, to change the subject, mentioned Mr Bashwood's message. Midwinter's mind was so pre-occupied or so languid, that he hardly seemed to remember the name. Allan was obliged to remind him that Bashwood was the elderly clerk, whom Mr Pedgift had sent to be his instructor in the duties of the steward's office. He listened without making any remark, and withdrew to his room, to rest till dinner-time.

Left by himself, Allan went into the library, to try if he could while away the time over a book. He took many volumes off the shelves, and put a few of them back again – and there he ended. Miss Milroy contrived in some mysterious manner to get, in this case, between the reader and the books. Her formal bow, and her merciless parting speech, dwelt, try how he might to forget them, on Allan's mind; he began to grow more and more anxious as the idle hour wore on, to recover his lost place in her favour. To call again that day at the cottage, and ask if he had been so unfortunate as to offend her, was impossible. To put the question in writing with the needful nicety of expression, proved, on trying the experiment, to be a task beyond his literary reach. After a turn or two up and down the room, with his pen in his mouth, he decided on the more diplomatic course (which happened, in this case, to be the easiest course too), of writing to Miss Milroy as cordially as if nothing had happened, and of testing his position in her good graces by the answer that she sent him back. An invitation of some kind (including her father, of course, but addressed directly to herself) was plainly the right thing to oblige her to send a written reply – but here the difficulty occurred of what the invitation was to be. A ball was not to be thought of, in his present position with the resident gentry. A dinner-party, with no indispensable elderly lady on the premises to receive Miss Milroy – except Mrs Gripper, who could only receive her in the kitchen – was equally out of the question. What was the invitation to be? Never backward, when he wanted help, in asking for it right and left in every available direction, Allan, feeling himself at the end of his own resources, coolly rang the bell, and astonished the servant who answered it, by inquiring how the late family at Thorpe-Ambrose used to amuse themselves, and what sort of invitations they were in the habit of sending to their friends.

'The family did what the rest of the gentry did, sir,' said the man, staring at his master in utter bewilderment. 'They gave dinner-parties and balls. And, in fine summer weather, sir, like this, they sometimes had lawn-parties and picnics—'

'That'll do!' shouted Allan. 'A picnic's just the thing to please her. Richard, you're an invaluable man – you may go downstairs again.'

Richard retired wondering, and Richard's master seized his ready pen.

DEAR MISS MILROY, – Since I left you, it has suddenly struck me that we might have a picnic. A little change and amusement (what I should call a good shaking-up, if I wasn't writing to a young lady) is just the thing for you, after being so long indoors lately in Mrs Milroy's room. A picnic is a change, and (when the wine is good) amusement too. Will you ask the major if he will consent to the picnic, and come? And if you have got any friends in the neighbourhood who like a picnic, pray ask them too – for I have got none. It shall be your picnic, but I will provide everything and take everybody. You shall choose the day, and we will picnic where you like. I have set my heart on this picnic.

Believe me, ever yours,

ALLAN ARMADALE.

On reading over his composition, before sealing it up, Allan frankly acknowledged to himself, this time, that it was not quite faultless. '"Picnic" comes in a little too often,' he said. 'Never mind – if she likes the idea, she won't quarrel with that.' He sent off the letter on the spot, with strict instructions to the messenger to wait for a reply.

In half-an-hour the answer came back on scented paper, without an erasure anywhere, fragrant to smell and beautiful to see.

The presentation of the naked truth is one of those exhibitions from which the native delicacy of the female mind seems instinctively to revolt. Never were the tables turned more completely than they were now turned on Allan by his fair correspondent. Machiavelli himself would never have suspected, from Miss Milroy's letter, how heartily she had repented her petulance to the young squire as soon as his back was turned, and how extravagantly delighted she was when his invitation was placed in her hands. Her letter was the composition of a model young lady whose emotions are all kept under parental lock and key, and served out for her judiciously as occasion may require. 'Papa' appeared quite as frequently in Miss Milroy's reply as 'picnic' had appeared in Allan's invitation. 'Papa' had been as considerately kind as Mr Armadale, in wishing to procure her a little change and amusement, and had offered to forego his usual quiet habits, and join the picnic. With 'papa's' sanction, therefore, she accepted, with much pleasure, Mr Armadale's proposal; and, at 'papa's' suggestion, she would presume on Mr Armadale's kindness, to add two friends of theirs, recently settled at Thorpe-Ambrose, to the picnic party – a widow lady and her son; the latter in holy orders, and in delicate health. If Tuesday next would suit Mr Armadale, Tuesday next would suit 'papa' – being the first day he could spare from repairs which were required by his clock. The rest, by 'papa's' advice, she would beg to leave entirely in Mr Armadale's hands; and, in the meantime, she would remain, with 'papa's' compliments, Mr Armadale's truly – 'ELEANOR MILROY.' Who would ever have supposed that the writer of that letter had jumped for joy when Allan's invitation arrived? Who would ever have suspected that there was an entry already in Miss Milroy's diary, under that day's date, to this effect: 'The sweetest, dearest letter from *I-know-who*; I'll never behave unkindly to him again as long as I live'? As for Allan, he was charmed with the success of his manoeuvre. Miss Milroy had accepted his invitation – consequently, Miss Milroy was not offended with him. It was on the tip of his tongue to mention the correspondence to his friend when they met at dinner. But there was something in Midwinter's face and manner (even plain enough for Allan to see) which warned him to wait a little before he said anything to revive the painful subject of their visit to the cottage. By common consent they both avoided all topics connected with Thorpe-Ambrose – not even the visit from Mr Bashwood, which was to come with the evening, being referred to by either of them. All through the dinner they drifted farther and farther back into the old endless talk of past times about ships and sailing. When the butler withdrew from his attendance at table, he came downstairs with a nautical problem on his mind, and asked his fellow-servants if they any of them knew the relative merits 'on a wind', and 'off a wind', of a schooner and a brig.

The two young men had sat longer at table than usual that day. When they went out into the garden, with their cigars, the summer twilight fell grey and dim on lawn and flower-bed, and narrowed round them by slow degrees the softly-fading circle of the distant view. The dew was heavy; and, after a few minutes in the garden, they agreed to go back to the drier ground on the drive in front of the house.

They were close to the turning which led into the shrubbery, when there suddenly glided out on them, from behind the foliage, a softly-stepping black figure – a shadow, moving darkly through the dim evening light. Midwinter started back at the sight of it, and even the less finely-strung nerves of his friend were shaken for the moment.

'Who the devil are you!' cried Allan.

The figure bared its head in the grey light, and came slowly a step nearer. Midwinter advanced a step on his side, and looked closer. It was the man of the timid manners and the mourning garments, of whom he had asked the way to Thorpe-Ambrose where the three roads met.

'Who are you?' repeated Allan.

'I humbly beg your pardon, sir,' faltered the stranger, stepping back again confusedly. 'The servants told me I should find Mr Armadale—'

'What, are you Mr Bashwood?'

'Yes, if you please, sir.'

'I beg your pardon for speaking to you so roughly,' said Allan, 'but the fact is, you rather startled me. My name is Armadale (put on your hat, pray), and this is my friend, Mr Midwinter, who wants your help in the steward's office.'

'We hardly stand in need of an introduction,' said Midwinter. 'I met Mr Bashwood out walking a few days since, and he was kind enough to direct me when I had lost my way.'

'Put on your hat,' reiterated Allan, as Mr Bashwood, still bare-headed, stood bowing speechlessly, now to one of the young men, and now to the other. 'My good sir, put on your hat, and let me show you the way back to the house. Excuse me for noticing it,' added Allan, as the man, in sheer nervous helplessness, let his hat fall, instead of putting it back on his head; 'but you seem a little out of sorts – a glass of good wine will do you no harm before you and my friend come to business. Whereabouts did you meet with Mr Bashwood, Midwinter, when you lost your way?'

'I am too ignorant of the neighbourhood to know. I must refer you to Mr Bashwood.'

'Come, tell us where it was,' said Allan, trying, a little too abruptly, to set the man at his ease, as they all three walked back to the house.

The measure of Mr Bashwood's constitutional timidity seemed to be filled to the brim by the loudness of Allan's voice, and the bluntness of Allan's request. He ran over in the same feeble flow of words with which he had deluged Midwinter on the occasion when they first met.

'It was on the road, sir,' he began, addressing himself alternately to Allan, whom he called 'sir', and to Midwinter, whom he called by his name, 'I mean, if you please, on the road to Little Gill Beck. A singular name, Mr Midwinter, and a singular place; I don't mean the village; I mean the neighbourhood – I beg your pardon, I mean the "Broads", beyond the neighbourhood. Perhaps you may have heard of the Norfolk Broads, sir? What they call lakes in other parts of England, they call Broads here. The Broads are quite numerous; I think they would repay a visit. You would have seen the first of them, Mr Midwinter, if you had walked on a few miles from where I had the honour of meeting you. Remarkably numerous, the Broads, sir – situated between this and the sea. About three miles from the sea, Mr Midwinter, – about three miles. Mostly shallow, sir, with rivers running between them. Beautiful; solitary. Quite a watery country, Mr Midwinter; quite separate as it were, in itself. Parties sometimes visit them, sir, – pleasure-parties in boats. It's quite a little network of lakes, or, perhaps, – yes, perhaps more correctly, pools. There is good sport in the cold weather. The wild-fowl are quite numerous. Yes. The Broads would repay a visit, Mr Midwinter, the next time you are walking that way. The distance from here to Little Gill Beck, and then from Little Gill Beck to Girdler Broad, which is the first you come to, is altogether not more —' In sheer nervous inability to leave off, he would apparently have gone on talking of the Norfolk Broads for the rest of the evening, if one of his two listeners had not unceremoniously cut him short before he could find his way into a new sentence.

'Are the Broads within an easy day's drive there and back, from this house?' asked Allan; feeling, if they were, that the place for the picnic was discovered already.

'Oh, yes, sir; a nice drive – quite a nice easy drive from this beautiful place!'

They were by this time ascending the portico steps; Allan leading the way up, and calling to Midwinter and Mr Bashwood to follow him into the library, where there was a lighted lamp. In the interval which elapsed before the wine made its appearance, Midwinter looked at his chance acquaintance of the high-road with strangely-mingled feelings of compassion and distrust – of compassion that strengthened in spite of him; of distrust that persisted in diminishing, try as he might to encourage it to grow. There, perched comfortless on the edge of his chair, sat the poor broken-down nervous wretch, in his worn black garments, with his watery eyes, his honest old outspoken wig, his miserable mohair stock, and his false teeth that were incapable of deceiving anybody – there he sat, politely ill at ease; now shrinking in the glare of the lamp, now wincing under the shock of Allan's sturdy voice; a man with the wrinkles of sixty years in his face, and the manners of a child in the presence of strangers; an object of pity surely, if ever there was a pitiable object yet!

'Whatever else you're afraid of, Mr Bashwood,' cried Allan, pouring out a glass of wine, 'don't be afraid of that! There isn't a headache in a hogshead of it! Make yourself comfortable; I'll leave you and Mr Midwinter to talk your business over by yourselves. It's all in Mr Midwinter's hands; he acts for me, and settles everything at his own discretion.'

He said those words with a cautious choice of expression very uncharacteristic of him, and without further explanation, made abruptly for the door. Midwinter, sitting near it, noticed his face as he went out. Easy as the way was into Allan's favour, Mr Bashwood, beyond all kind of doubt, had in some unaccountable manner failed to find it!

The two strangely-assorted companions were left together – parted widely, as it seemed on the surface, from any possible interchange of sympathy; drawn invisibly one to the other, nevertheless, by those magnetic similarities of temperament which overleap all difference of age or station, and defy all apparent incongruities of mind and character. From the moment when Allan left the room, the hidden Influence that works in darkness began slowly to draw the two men together, across the great social desert which had lain between them up to this day.

Midwinter was the first to approach the subject of the interview.

'May I ask,' he began, 'if you have been made acquainted with my position here, and if you know why it is that I require your assistance?'

Mr Bashwood – still hesitating and still timid, but manifestly relieved by Allan's departure – sat farther back in his chair, and ventured on fortifying himself with a modest little sip of wine.

'Yes, sir,' he replied; 'Mr Pedgift informed me of all – at least I think I may say so – of all the circumstances. I am to instruct, or perhaps I ought to say to advise—'

'No, Mr Bashwood; the first word was the best word of the two. I am quite ignorant of the duties which Mr Armadale's kindness has induced him to intrust to me. If I understand right, there can be no question of your capacity to instruct me, for you once filled a steward's situation yourself. May I inquire where it was?'

'At Sir John Mellowship's, sir, in West Norfolk. Perhaps you would like – I have got it with me – to see my testimonial? Sir John might have dealt more kindly with me – but I have no complaint to make; it's all done and over now!' His watery eyes looked more watery still, and the trembling in his hands spread to his lips as he produced an old dingy letter from his pocket-book, and laid it open on the table.

The testimonial was very briefly and very coldly expressed, but it was conclusive as far as it went. Sir John considered it only right to say that he had no complaint to make of any want of capacity or integrity in his steward. If Mr Bashwood's domestic position had been compatible with the continued performance of his duties on the estate, Sir John would have been glad to keep him. As it was, embarrassments caused by the state of Mr Bashwood's personal affairs had rendered it undesirable that he should continue in Sir John's service; and on that ground, and that only, his employer and he had parted. Such was Sir John's testimony to Mr Bashwood's character. As Midwinter read the last lines, he thought of another testimonial, still in his own possession – of the written character which they had given him at the school, when they turned their sick usher adrift in the world. His superstition (distrusting all new events and all new faces at Thorpe-Ambrose) still doubted the man before him as obstinately as ever. But when he now tried to put those doubts into words, his heart upbraided him, and he laid the letter on the table in silence.

The sudden pause in the conversation appeared to startle Mr Bashwood. He comforted himself with another little sip of wine, and, leaving the letter untouched, burst irrepressibly into words, as if the silence was quite unendurable to him.

'I am ready to answer any question, sir,' he began. 'Mr Pedgift told me that I must answer questions, because I was applying for a place of trust. Mr Pedgift said, neither you nor Mr Armadale were likely to think the testimonial sufficient of itself. Sir John doesn't say – he might have put it more kindly, but I don't complain – Sir John doesn't say what the troubles were that lost me my place. Perhaps you might wish to know—?' He stopped confusedly, looked at the testimonial, and said no more.

'If no interests but mine were concerned in the matter,' rejoined Midwinter, 'the testimonial would, I assure you, be quite enough to satisfy me. But while I am learning my new duties, the person who teaches me will be really and truly the steward of my friend's estate. I am very unwilling to ask you to speak on what may be a painful subject, but perhaps, in Mr Armadale's interests, I ought to know something more, either from yourself, or from Mr Pedgift, if you prefer it—' He, too, stopped confusedly, looked at the testimonial, and said no more.

There was another moment of silence. The night was warm, and Mr Bashwood, among his other misfortunes, had the deplorable infirmity of perspiring at the palms of the hands. He took out a miserable little cotton pocket-handkerchief, rolled it up into a ball, and softly dabbed it to and fro, from one hand to the other, with the regularity of a pendulum. Performed by other men, under other circumstances, the action might have been ridiculous. Performed by this man, at the crisis of the interview, the action was horrible.

'Mr Pedgift's time is too valuable, sir, to be wasted on me,' he said. 'I will mention what ought to be mentioned myself – if you will please to allow me. I have been unfortunate in my family. It was very hard to bear, though it seems not much to tell. My wife—' One of his hands closed fast on the pocket-handkerchief; he moistened his dry lips, struggled with himself, and went on.

'My wife, sir,' he resumed, 'stood a little in my way; she did me (I am afraid I must confess) some injury with Sir John. Soon after I got the steward's situation she contracted – she took – she fell into habits (I hardly know how to say it) of drinking. I couldn't break her of it, and I couldn't always conceal it from Sir John's knowledge. She broke out, and – and – tried his patience once or twice, when he came to my office on business. Sir John excused it, not very kindly; but still he excused it. I don't complain of Sir John; I – I don't complain, now, of my wife.' He pointed a trembling finger at his miserable crape-covered beaver hat on the floor. 'I'm in mourning for her,' he said, faintly. 'She died nearly a year ago, in the county asylum here.'

His mouth began to work convulsively. He took up the glass of wine at his side, and, instead of sipping it this time, drained it to the bottom. 'I'm not much used to wine, sir,' he said, conscious, apparently, of the flush that flew into his face as he drank, and still observant of the obligations of politeness amid all the misery of the recollections that he was calling up.

'I beg, Mr Bashwood, you will not distress yourself by telling me any more,' said Midwinter, recoiling from any further sanction on his part of a disclosure which had already bared the sorrows of the unhappy man before him to the quick.

'I'm much obliged to you, sir,' replied Mr Bashwood. 'But if I don't detain you too long, and if you will please to remember that Mr Pedgift's directions to me were very particular – and, besides, I only mentioned my late wife because if she hadn't tried Sir John's patience to begin with, things might have turned out differently—' He paused, gave up the disjointed sentence in which he had involved himself, and tried another. 'I had only two children, sir,' he went on, advancing to a new point in his narrative; 'a boy and a girl. The girl died when she was a baby. My son lived to grow up – and it was my son who lost me my place. I did my best for him; I got him into a respectable office in London. They wouldn't take him without security. I'm afraid it was imprudent; but I had no rich friends to help me – and I became security. My boy turned out badly, sir. He – perhaps you will kindly understand what I mean, if I say he behaved dishonestly. His employers consented, at my entreaty, to let him off without prosecuting. I begged very hard – I was fond of my son James – and I took him home, and did my best to reform him. He wouldn't stay with me; he went away again to London; he – I beg your pardon, sir! I'm afraid I'm confusing things; I'm afraid I'm wandering from the point?'

'No, no,' said Midwinter, kindly. 'If you think it right to tell me this sad story, tell it in your own way. Have you seen your son since he left you to go to London?'

'No, sir. He's in London still, for all I know. When I last heard of him, he was getting his bread – not very creditably. He was employed, under the Inspector, at the Private Inquiry Office in Shadyside Place.'

He spoke those words – apparently (as events then stood) the most irrelevant to the matter in hand that had yet escaped him; actually (as events were soon to be) the most vitally important that he had uttered yet – he spoke those words absently, looking about him in confusion, and trying vainly to recover the lost thread of his narrative.

Midwinter compassionately helped him. 'You were telling me,' he said, 'that your son had been the cause of your losing your place. How did that happen?'

'In this way, sir,' said Mr Bashwood, getting back again excitedly into the right train of thought. 'His employers consented to let him off – but they came down on his security; and I was the man. I suppose they were not to blame; the security covered their loss. I couldn't pay it all out of my savings; I had to borrow – on the word of a man, sir, I couldn't help it – I had to borrow. My creditor pressed me; it seemed cruel, but, if he wanted the money, I suppose it was only just. I was sold out of house and home. I daresay other gentlemen would have said what Sir John said; I daresay most people would have refused to keep a steward who had had the bailiffs after him, and his furniture sold in the neighbourhood. That was how it ended, Mr Midwinter. I needn't detain you any longer – here is Sir John's address, if you wish to apply to him.'

Midwinter generously refused to receive the address.

'Thank you kindly, sir,' said Mr Bashwood, getting tremulously on his legs. 'There is nothing more, I think, except – except that Mr Pedgift will speak for me, if you wish to inquire into my conduct in his service. I'm very much indebted to Mr Pedgift; he's a little rough with me sometimes, but if he hadn't taken me into his office, I think I should have gone to the workhouse when I left Sir John, I was so broken-down.' He picked up his dingy old hat from the floor. 'I won't intrude any longer, sir. I shall be happy to call again, if you wish to have time to consider before you decide.'

'I want no time to consider, after what you have told me,' replied Midwinter warmly, his memory busy, while he spoke, with the time when *he* had told *his* story to Mr Brock, and was waiting for a generous word in return, as the man before him was waiting now. 'To-day is Saturday,' he went on. 'Can you come and give me my first lesson on Monday morning? I beg your pardon,' he added, interrupting Mr Bashwood's profuse expressions of acknowledgment, and stopping him on his way out of the room; 'there is one thing we ought to settle, ought we not? We haven't spoken yet about your own interest in this matter – I mean, about the terms.' He referred a little confusedly to the pecuniary part of the subject. Mr Bashwood (getting nearer and nearer to the door) answered him more confusedly still.

'Anything, sir – anything you think right. I won't intrude any longer – I'll leave it to you and Mr Armadale.'

'I will send for Mr Armadale, if you like,' said Midwinter, following him into the hall. 'But I am afraid he has as little experience in matters of this kind as I have. Perhaps, if you see no objection, we might be guided by Mr Pedgift?'

Mr Bashwood caught eagerly at the last suggestion, pushing his retreat, while he spoke, as far as the front door. 'Yes, sir – oh, yes, yes! nobody better than Mr Pedgift. Don't – pray don't, disturb Mr Armadale!' His watery eyes looked quite wild with nervous alarm as he turned round for a moment in the light of the hall-lamp, to make that polite request. If sending for Allan had been equivalent to unchaining a ferocious watch-dog, Mr Bashwood could hardly have been more anxious to stop the proceeding. 'I wish you kindly good evening, sir,' he went on, getting out to the steps. 'I'm much obliged to you. I will be scrupulously punctual on Monday morning – I hope – I think – I'm sure you will soon learn everything I can teach you. It's not difficult – oh, dear, no – not difficult at all! I wish you kindly good evening, sir. A beautiful night; yes, indeed, a beautiful night for a walk home.'

With those words, all dropping out of his lips one on the top of the other, and without noticing, in his agony of embarrassment at effecting his departure, Midwinter's outstretched hand, he went noiselessly down the steps, and was lost in the darkness of the night.

As Midwinter turned to re-enter the house, the dining-room door opened, and his friend met him in the hall.

'Has Mr Bashwood gone?' asked Allan.

'He has gone,' replied Midwinter, 'after telling me a very sad story, and leaving me a little ashamed of myself for having doubted him without any just cause. I have arranged that he is to give me my first lesson in the steward's office on Monday morning.'

'All right,' said Allan. 'You needn't be afraid, old boy, of my interrupting you over your studies. I daresay I'm wrong – but I don't like Mr Bashwood.'

'I daresay *I'm* wrong,' retorted the other, a little petulantly. 'I do.'

The Sunday morning found Midwinter in the park, waiting to intercept the postman, on the chance of his bringing more news from Mr Brock.

At the customary hour the man made his appearance, and placed the expected letter in Midwinter's hands. He opened it, far away from all fear of observation this time, and read these lines:

MY DEAR MIDWINTER, – I write more for the purpose of quieting your anxiety than because I have anything definite to say. In my last hurried letter I had no time to tell you that the elder of the two women whom I met in the Gardens had followed me, and spoken to me in the street. I believe I may characterize what she said (without doing her any injustice) as a tissue of falsehoods from beginning to end. At any rate, she confirmed me in the suspicion that some underhand proceeding is on foot, of which Allan is destined to be the victim, and that the prime mover in the conspiracy is the vile woman who helped his mother's marriage and who hastened his mother's death.

Feeling this conviction, I have not hesitated to do, for Allan's sake, what I would have done for no other creature in the world. I have left my hotel, and have installed myself (with my old servant Robert) in a house opposite the house to which I traced the two women. We are alternately on the watch (quite unsuspected, I am certain, by the people opposite) day and night. All my feelings, as a gentleman and a clergyman, revolt from such an occupation as I am now engaged in; but there is no other choice. I must either do this violence to my own self-respect, or I must leave Allan, with his easy nature, and in his assailable position, to defend himself against a wretch who is prepared, I firmly believe, to take the most unscrupulous advantage of his weakness and his youth. His mother's dying entreaty has never left my memory; and God help me, I am now degrading myself in my own eyes in consequence.

There has been some reward already for the sacrifice. This day (Saturday) I have gained an immense advantage – I have at last seen the woman's face. She went out with her veil down as before; and Robert kept her in view, having my instructions, if she returned to the house, not to follow her back to the door. She did return to the house; and the result of my precaution was, as I had expected, to throw her off her guard. I saw her face unveiled at the window, and afterwards again in the balcony. If any occasion should arise for describing her particularly, you shall have the description. At present I need only say that she looks the full age (five-and-thirty) at which you estimated her, and that she is by no means so handsome a woman as I had (I hardly know why) expected to see.

This is all I can now tell you. If nothing more happens by Monday or Tuesday next, I shall have no choice but to apply to my lawyers for assistance; though I am most unwilling to trust this delicate and dangerous matter in other hands than mine.

Setting my own feelings, however, out of the question, the business which has been the cause of my journey to London is too important to be trifled with much longer as I am trifling with it now. In any and every case, depend on my keeping you informed of the progress of events; and believe me

Yours truly,
DECIMUS BROCK

Midwinter secured the letter as he had secured the letter that preceded it – side by side in his pocket-book with the narrative of Allan's Dream.

'How many days more?' he asked himself, as he went back to the house. 'How many days more?'

Not many. The time he was waiting for, was a time close at hand.

Monday came, and brought Mr Bashwood, punctual to the appointed hour. Monday came, and found Allan immersed in his preparations for the picnic. He held a series of interviews, at home and abroad, all through the day. He transacted business with Mrs Gripper, with the butler, and with the coachman, in their three several departments of eating, drinking, and driving. He went to the town to consult his professional advisers on the subject of the Broads, and to invite both the lawyers, father and son (in the absence of anybody else in the neighbourhood whom he could ask), to join the picnic. Pedgift Senior (in his department) supplied general information, but begged to be excused from appearing at the picnic, on the score of business engagements. Pedgift Junior (in his department) added all the details; and, casting business engagements to the winds, accepted the invitation with the greatest pleasure. Returning from the lawyer's office, Allan's next proceeding was to go to the major's cottage and obtain Miss Milroy's approval of the proposed locality for the pleasure-party. This object accomplished, he returned to his own house, to meet the last difficulty now left to encounter – the difficulty of persuading Midwinter to join the expedition to the Broads.

On first broaching the subject, Allan found his friend impenetrably resolute to remain at home. Midwinter's natural reluctance to meet the major and his daughter, after what had happened at the cottage, might probably have been overcome. But Midwinter's determination not to allow Mr Bashwood's course of instruction to be interrupted, was proof against every effort that could be made to shake it. After exerting his influence to the utmost, Allan was obliged to remain contented with a compromise. Midwinter promised, not very willingly, to join the party towards evening, at the place appointed for a gipsy tea-making, which was to close the proceedings of the day. To this extent he would consent to take the opportunity of placing himself on a friendly footing with the Milroys. More he could not concede, even to Allan's persuasion, and for more it would be useless to ask.

The day of the picnic came. The lovely morning, and the cheerful bustle of preparation for the expedition, failed entirely to tempt Midwinter into altering his resolution. At the regular hour he left the breakfast-table to join Mr Bashwood in the steward's office. The two were quietly closeted over the books, at the back of the house, while the packing for the picnic went on in front. Young Pedgift (short in stature, smart in costume, and self-reliant in manner) arrived some little time before the hour for starting, to revise all the arrangements, and to make any final improvements which his local knowledge might suggest. Allan and he were still busy in consultation when the first hitch occurred in the proceedings. The woman-servant from the cottage was reported to be waiting below for an answer to a note from her young mistress, which was placed in Allan's hands.

On this occasion Miss Milroy's emotions had apparently got the better of her sense of propriety. The tone of the letter was feverish, and the handwriting wandered crookedly up and down, in deplorable freedom from all proper restraint.

Oh, Mr Armadale (wrote the major's daughter), such a misfortune! What *are* we to do? Papa has got a letter from grandmamma this morning about the new governess. Her reference has answered all the questions, and she's ready to come at the shortest notice. Grandmamma thinks (how provoking!) the sooner the better; and she says we may expect her – I mean the governess – either to-day or to-morrow. Papa says (he *will* be so absurdly considerate to everybody!) that we can't allow Miss Gwilt to come here (if she comes to-day) and find nobody at home to receive her. What *is* to be done? I am ready to cry with vexation. I have got the worst possible impression (though grandmamma says she is a charming person) of Miss Gwilt. *Can* you suggest something, dear Mr Armadale? I'm sure papa would give way if you could. Don't stop to write – send me a message back. I have got a new hat for the picnic; and, oh, the agony of not knowing whether I am to keep it on or take it off. – Yours truly, E. M.

'The devil take Miss Gwilt!' said Allan, staring at his legal adviser in a state of helpless consternation.

'With all my heart, sir – I don't wish to interfere,' remarked Pedgift Junior. 'May I ask what's the matter?'

Allan told him. Mr Pedgift the Younger might have his faults, but a want of quickness of resource was not among them.

'There's a way out of the difficulty, Mr Armadale,' he said. 'If the governess comes to-day, let's have her at the picnic.'

Allan's eyes opened wide in astonishment.

'All the horses and carriages in the Thorpe-Ambrose stables are not wanted for this small party of ours,' proceeded Pedgift Junior. 'Of course not! Very good. If Miss Gwilt comes to-day, she can't possibly get here before five o'clock. Good again. You order an open carriage to be waiting at the major's door at that time, Mr Armadale; and I'll give the man his directions where to drive to. When the governess comes to the cottage, let her find a nice little note of apology (along with the cold fowl, or whatever else they give her after her journey) begging her to join us at the picnic, and putting a carriage at her own sole disposal to take her there. Gad, sir!' said young Pedgift, gaily, 'she *must* be a Touchy One if she thinks herself neglected after that!'

'Capital!' cried Allan. 'She shall have every attention. I'll give her the pony-chaise and the white harness, and she shall drive herself, if she likes.'

He scribbled a line to relieve Miss Milroy's apprehensions, and gave the necessary orders for the pony-chaise. Ten minutes later, the carriages for the pleasure-party were at the door.

'Now we've taken all this trouble about her,' said Allan, reverting to the governess as they left the house, 'I wonder, if she does come to-day, whether we shall see her at the picnic!'

'Depends entirely on her age, sir,' remarked young Pedgift, pronouncing judgment with the happy confidence in himself which eminently distinguished him. 'If she's an old one, she'll be knocked up with the journey, and she'll stick to the cold fowl and the cottage. If she's a young one, either I know nothing of women, or the pony in the white harness will bring her to the picnic.'

They started for the major's cottage.

CHAPTER VIII

THE NORFOLK BROADS

The little group gathered together in Major Milroy's parlour to wait for the carriages from Thorpe-Ambrose would hardly have conveyed the idea, to any previously uninstructed person introduced among them, of a party assembled in expectation of a picnic. They were almost dull enough, so far as outward appearances went, to have been a party assembled in expectation of a marriage.

Even Miss Milroy herself, though conscious of looking her best in her bright muslin dress and her gaily-feathered new hat, was at this inauspicious moment Miss Milroy under a cloud. Although Allan's note had assured her, in Allan's strongest language, that the one great object of reconciling the governess's arrival with the celebration of the picnic, was an object achieved, the doubt still remained whether the plan proposed – whatever it might be – would meet with her father's approval. In a word, Miss Milroy declined to feel sure of her day's pleasure until the carriage made its appearance and took her from the door. The major, on his side, arrayed for the festive occasion in a tight blue frock-coat which he had not worn for years, and threatened with a whole long day of separation from his old friend and comrade the clock, was a man out of his element, if ever such a man existed yet. As for the friends who had been asked at Allan's request – the widow lady (otherwise Mrs Pentecost) and her son (the Reverend Samuel) in delicate health – two people less capable, apparently, of adding to the hilarity of the day could hardly have been discovered in the length and breadth of all England. A young man who plays his part in society by looking on in green spectacles, and listening with a sickly smile, may be a prodigy of intellect and a mine of virtue, but he is hardly, perhaps, the right sort of man to have at a picnic. An old lady afflicted with deafness, whose one inexhaustible subject of interest is the subject of her son, and who (on the happily rare occasions when that son opens his lips) asks everybody eagerly, 'What does my boy say?' is a person to be pitied in respect of her infirmities, and a person to be admired in respect of her maternal devotedness, but not a person, if the thing could possibly be avoided, to take to a picnic. Such a man, nevertheless, was the Reverend Samuel Pentecost, and such a woman was the Reverend Samuel's mother; and, in the dearth of any other producible guests, there they were, engaged to eat, drink, and be merry for the day at Mr Armadale's pleasure-party to the Norfolk Broads.

The arrival of Allan, with his faithful follower, Pedgift Junior, at his heels, roused the flagging spirits of the party at the cottage. The plan for enabling the governess to join the picnic, if she arrived that day, satisfied even Major Milroy's anxiety to show all proper attention to the lady who was coming into his house. After writing the necessary note of apology and invitation, and addressing it in her very best handwriting to the new governess, Miss Milroy ran upstairs to say good-by to her mother, and returned, with a smiling face and a side-look of relief directed at her father, to announce that there was nothing now to keep any of them a moment longer indoors. The company at once directed their steps to the garden-gate, and were there met face to face by the second great difficulty of the day. How were the six persons of the picnic to be divided between the two open carriages that were in waiting for them?

Here, again, Pedgift Junior exhibited his invaluable faculty of contrivance. This highly-cultivated young man possessed in an eminent degree an accomplishment more or less peculiar to all the young men of the age we live in – he was perfectly capable of taking his pleasure without forgetting his business. Such a client as the Master of Thorpe-Ambrose fell but seldom in his father's way, and to pay special but unobtrusive attention to Allan all through the day, was the business of which young Pedgift, while proving himself to be the life and soul of the picnic, never once lost sight from the beginning of the merrymaking to the end. He had detected the state of affairs between Miss Milroy and Allan at a glance; and he at once provided for his client's inclinations in that quarter, by offering (in virtue of his local knowledge) to lead the way in the first carriage, and by asking Major Milroy and the curate if they would do him the honour of accompanying him. 'We shall pass a very interesting place to a military man, sir,' said young Pedgift, addressing the major, with his happy and unblushing confidence, 'the remains of a Roman encampment. And my father, sir, who is a subscriber,' proceeded this rising lawyer, turning to the curate, 'wished me to ask your opinion of the new Infant School buildings at Little Gill Beck. Would you kindly give it me, as we go along?' He opened the carriage-door, and helped in the major and the curate, before they could either of them start any difficulties. The necessary result followed. Allan and Miss Milroy rode together in the same carriage, with the extra convenience of a deaf old lady in attendance to keep the squire's compliments within the necessary limits.

Never yet had Allan enjoyed such an interview with Miss Milroy as the interview he now obtained on the road to the Broads. The dear old lady, after a little anecdote or two on the subject of her son, did the one thing wanting to secure the perfect felicity of her two youthful companions – she became considerably blind for the occasion, as well as deaf. A quarter of an hour after the carriage left the major's cottage, the poor old soul, reposing on snug cushions, and fanned by a fine summer air, fell peaceably asleep. Allan made love, and Miss Milroy sanctioned the manufacture of that occasionally precious article of human commerce, sublimely indifferent on both sides to a solemn base accompaniment on two notes, played by the curate's mother's unsuspecting nose. The only interruption to the love-making (the snoring being a thing more grave and permanent in its nature, was not interrupted at all) came at intervals from the carriage ahead. Not satisfied with having the major's Roman encampment and the curate's Infant Schools on his mind, Pedgift Junior rose erect from time to time in his place, and, respectfully hailing the hindmost vehicle, directed Allan's attention, in a shrill tenor voice, and with an excellent choice of language, to objects of interest on the road. The only way to quiet him was to answer, which Allan invariably did by shouting back, 'Yes, beautiful' – upon which young Pedgift disappeared again in the recesses of the leading carriage, and took up the Romans and the Infants where he had left them last.

The scene through which the picnic party was now passing, merited far more attention than it received either from Allan or Allan's friends.

An hour's steady driving from the major's cottage had taken young Armadale and his guests beyond the limits of Midwinter's solitary walk, and was now bringing them nearer and nearer to one of the strangest and loveliest aspects of Nature, which the inland landscape, not of Norfolk only, but of all England, can show. Little by little, the face of the country began to change as the carriage approached the remote and lonely district of the Broads. The wheat-fields and turnip-fields became perceptibly fewer; and the fat green grazing-grounds on either side grew wider and wider in their smooth and sweeping range. Heaps of dry rushes and reeds, laid up for the basket-maker and the thatcher, began to appear at the roadside. The old gabled cottages of the early part of the drive dwindled and disappeared, and huts with mud walls rose in their place. With the ancient church towers and the wind and water mills, which had hitherto been the only lofty objects seen over the low marshy flat, there now rose all round the horizon, gliding slow and distant behind fringes of pollard willows, the sails of invisible boats moving on invisible waters. All the strange and startling anomalies presented by an inland agricultural district, isolated from other districts by its intricate surrounding network of pools and streams – holding its communications and carrying its produce by water instead of by land – began to present themselves in closer and closer succession. Nets appeared on cottage palings; little flat-bottomed boats lay strangely at rest among the flowers in cottage gardens; farmers' men passed to and fro clad in composite costume of the coast and the field, in sailors' hats and fishermen's boots, and ploughmen's smocks, – and even yet the low-lying labyrinth of waters, embosomed in its mystery of solitude, was a hidden labyrinth still. A minute more, and the carriages took a sudden turn from the hard high-road into a little weedy lane. The wheels ran noiseless on the damp and spongy ground. A lonely outlying cottage appeared, with its litter of nets and boats. A few yards farther on, and the last morsel of firm earth suddenly ended in a tiny creek and quay. One turn more to the end of the quay – and there, spreading its great sheet of water, far and bright and smooth, on the right hand and the left – there, as pure in its spotless blue, as still in its heavenly peacefulness as the summer sky above it, was the first of the Norfolk Broads.

The carriages stopped, the love-making broke off, and the venerable Mrs Pentecost, recovering the use of her senses at a moment's notice, fixed her eyes sternly on Allan the instant she woke.

'I see in your face, Mr Armadale,' said the old lady, sharply, 'that you think I have been asleep.'

The consciousness of guilt acts differently on the two sexes. In nine cases out of ten, it is a much more manageable consciousness with a woman than with a man. All the confusion, on this occasion, was on the man's side. While Allan reddened and looked embarrassed, the quick-witted Miss Milroy instantly embraced the old lady with a burst of innocent laughter. 'He is quite incapable, dear Mrs Pentecost,' said the little hypocrite, 'of anything so ridiculous as thinking you have been asleep!'

'All I wish Mr Armadale to know,' pursued the old lady, still suspicious of Allan, 'is, that my head being giddy, I am obliged to close my eyes in a carriage. Closing the eyes, Mr Armadale, is one thing, and going to sleep is another. Where is my son?'

The Reverend Samuel appeared silently at the carriage-door with his green spectacles and his sickly smile in perfect working order, and assisted his mother to get out. ('Did you enjoy the drive, Sammy?' asked the old lady. 'Beautiful scenery, my dear, wasn't it?') Young Pedgift, on whom all the arrangements for exploring the Broads devolved, bustled about, giving his orders to the boatmen. Major Milroy, placid and patient, sat apart on an overturned punt, and privately looked at his watch. Was it past noon already? More than an hour past. For the first time, for many a long year, the famous clock at home had struck in an empty workshop. Time had lifted his wonderful scythe, and the corporal and his men had relieved guard, with no master's eye to watch their performances, with no master's hand to encourage them to do their best. The major sighed as he put his watch back in his pocket. 'I'm afraid I'm too old for this sort of thing,' thought the good man, looking about him dreamily. 'I don't find I enjoy it as much as I thought I should. When are we going on the water, I wonder? where's Neelie?'

Neelie – more properly Miss Milroy – was behind one of the carriages with the promoter of the picnic. They were immersed in the interesting subject of their own Christian names, and Allan was as near a point-blank proposal of marriage, as it is well possible for a thoughtless young gentleman of two-and-twenty to be.

'Tell me the truth,' said Miss Milroy, with her eyes modestly riveted on the ground, 'when you first knew what my name was, you didn't like it, did you?'

'I like everything that belongs to you,' rejoined Allan, vigorously. 'I think Eleanor is a beautiful name; and yet, I don't know why, I think the major made an improvement when he changed it to Neelie.'

'I can tell you why, Mr Armadale,' said the major's daughter, with great gravity. 'There are some unfortunate people in this world, whose names are – how can I express it? – whose names are, Misfits. Mine is a Misfit. I don't blame my parents, for of course it was impossible to know when I was a baby how I should grow up. But as things are, I and my name don't fit each other. When you hear a young lady called Eleanor, you think of a tall, beautiful, interesting creature directly – the very opposite of *me*! With my personal appearance Eleanor sounds ridiculous – and Neelie, as you yourself remarked, is just the thing. No! no! don't say any more – I'm tired of the subject; I've got another name in my head, if we must speak of names, which is much better worth talking about than mine.'

She stole a glance at her companion which said plainly enough, 'The name is yours.' Allan advanced a step nearer to her, and lowered his voice (without the slightest necessity,) to a mysterious whisper. Miss Milroy instantly resumed her investigation of the ground. She looked at it with such extraordinary interest that a geologist might have suspected her of scientific flirtation with the superficial strata.

'What name are you thinking of?' asked Allan.

Miss Milroy addressed her answer, in the form of a remark, to the superficial strata – and let them do what they liked with it, in their capacity of conductors of sound, 'If I had been a man,' she said, 'I should so like to have been called Allan!'

She felt his eyes on her as she spoke, and, turning her head aside, became absorbed in the graining of the panel at the back of the carriage. 'How beautiful it is!' she exclaimed with a sudden outburst of interest in the vast subject of varnish. 'I wonder how they do it?'

Man persists, and woman yields. Allan declined to shift the ground from love-making to coach-making. Miss Milroy dropped the subject.

'Call me by my name, if you really like it,' he whispered persuasively. 'Call me "Allan", for once – just to try.'

She hesitated with a heightened colour and a charming smile, and shook her head. 'I couldn't just yet,' she answered softly.

'May I call you Neelie? Is it too soon?'

She looked at him again, with a sudden disturbance about the bosom of her dress, and a sudden flash of tenderness in her dark grey eyes.

'You know best,' she said faintly, in a whisper.

The inevitable answer was on the tip of Allan's tongue. At the very instant, however, when he opened his lips, the abhorrent high tenor of Pedgift Junior, shouting for 'Mr Armadale', rang cheerfully through the quiet air. At the same moment, from the other side of the carriage, the lurid spectacles of the Reverend Samuel showed themselves officiously on the search; and the voice of the Reverend Samuel's mother (who had, with great dexterity, put the two ideas of the presence of water and a sudden movement among the company together) inquired distractedly if anybody was drowned? Sentiment flies and Love shudders at all demonstrations of the noisy kind. Allan said, 'Damn it,' and rejoined young Pedgift. Miss Milroy sighed, and took refuge with her father.

'I've done it, Mr Armadale!' cried young Pedgift, greeting his patron gaily. 'We can all go on the water together; I've got the biggest boat on the Broads. The little skiffs,' he added, in a lower tone, as he led the way to the quay steps, 'besides being ticklish and easily upset, won't hold more than two, with the boatman; and the major told me he should feel it his duty to go with his daughter, if we all separated in different boats. I thought *that* would hardly do, sir,' pursued Pedgift Junior, with a respectfully sly emphasis on the words. 'And, besides, if we had put the old lady into a skiff, with her weight (sixteen stone if she's a pound), we might have had her upside down in the water half her time, which would have occasioned delay, and thrown what you call a damp on the proceedings. Here's the boat, Mr Armadale. What do you think of it?'

The boat added one more to the strangely anomalous objects which appeared at the Broads. It was nothing less than a stout old lifeboat, passing its last declining years on the smooth fresh water, after the stormy days of its youth-time on the wild salt sea. A comfortable little cabin for the use of fowlers in the winter season, had been built amidships, and a mast and sail adapted for inland navigation had been fitted forward. There was room enough and to spare for the guests, the dinner, and the three men in charge. Allan clapped his faithful lieutenant approvingly on the shoulder; and even Mrs Pentecost, when the whole party were comfortably established on board, took a comparatively cheerful view of the prospects of the picnic. 'If anything happens,' said the old lady, addressing the company generally, 'there's one comfort for all of us. My son can swim.'

The boat floated out from the creek into the placid waters of the Broad; and the full beauty of the scene opened on the view.

On the northward and westward, as the boat reached the middle of the lake, the shore lay clear and low in the sunshine, fringed darkly at certain points by rows of dwarf trees; and dotted here and there, in the opener spaces, with windmills and reed-thatched cottages of puddled mud. Southward, the great sheet of water narrowed gradually to a little group of close-nestling islands which closed the prospect; while to the east a long, gently undulating line of reeds followed the windings of the Broad, and shut out all view of the watery wastes beyond. So clear and so light was the summer-air, that the one cloud in the eastern quarter of the heaven was the smoke cloud left by a passing steamer three miles distant and more on the invisible sea. When the voices of the pleasure-party were still, not a sound rose far or near but the faint ripple at the bows, as the men, with slow deliberate strokes of their long poles, pressed the boat forward softly over the shallow water. The world and the world's turmoil seemed left behind for ever on the land; the silence was the silence of enchantment – the delicious inter-flow of the soft purity of the sky and the bright tranquillity of the lake.

Established in perfect comfort in the boat – the major and his daughter on one side, the curate and his mother on the other, and Allan and young Pedgift between the two – the water party floated smoothly towards the little nest of islands at the end of the Broad. Miss Milroy was in raptures; Allan was delighted; and the major for once forgot his clock. Every one felt pleasurably, in their different ways, the quiet and beauty of the scene. Mrs Pentecost, in her way, felt it like a clairvoyante – with closed eyes.

'Look behind you, Mr Armadale,' whispered young Pedgift. 'I think the parson's beginning to enjoy himself.'

An unwonted briskness – portentous apparently of coming speech – did certainly at that moment enliven the curate's manner. He jerked his head from side to side like a bird; he cleared his throat, and clasped his hands, and looked with a gentle interest at the company. Getting into spirits seemed, in the case of this excellent person, to be alarmingly like getting into the pulpit.

'Even in this scene of tranquillity,' said the Reverend Samuel, coming out softly with his first contribution to the society, in the shape of a remark, 'the Christian mind – led, so to speak, from one extreme to another – is forcibly recalled to the unstable nature of all earthly enjoyments. How, if this calm should not last? How, if the winds rose and the waters became agitated?'

'You needn't alarm yourself about that, sir,' said young Pedgift; 'June's the fine season here – and you can swim.'

Mrs Pentecost (mesmerically affected in all probability by the near neighbourhood of her son) opened her eyes suddenly, and asked with her customary eagerness, 'What does my boy say?'

The Reverend Samuel repeated his words in the key that suited his mother's infirmity. The old lady nodded in high approval, and pursued her son's train of thought through the medium of a quotation.

'Ah!' sighed Mrs Pentecost, with infinite relish, 'He rides the whirl-wind,[1] Sammy, and directs the storm!'

'Noble words!' said the Reverend Samuel. 'Noble and consoling words!'

'I say,' whispered Allan, 'if he goes on much longer in that way, what's to be done?'

'I told you, papa, it was a risk to ask them,' added Miss Milroy, in another whisper.

'My dear!' remonstrated the major. 'We knew nobody else in the neighbourhood; and as Mr Armadale kindly suggested our bringing our friends, what could we do?'

'We can't upset the boat,' remarked young Pedgift, with sardonic gravity. 'It's a lifeboat, unfortunately. May I venture to suggest putting something into the reverend gentleman's mouth, Mr Armadale? It's close on three o'clock. What do you say to ringing the dinner-bell, sir?'

Never was the right man more entirely in the right place than Pedgift Junior at the picnic. In ten minutes more the boat was brought to a standstill among the reeds; the Thorpe-Ambrose hampers were unpacked on the roof of the cabin; and the current of the curate's eloquence was checked for the day.

How inestimably important in its moral results – and therefore how praiseworthy in itself – is the act of eating and drinking! The social virtues centre in the stomach. A man who is not a better husband, father, and brother, after dinner than before, is, digestively speaking, an incurably vicious man. What hidden charms of character disclose themselves, what dormant amiabilities awaken when our common humanity gathers together to pour out the gastric juice! At the opening of the hampers from Thorpe-Ambrose, sweet Sociability (offspring of the happy union of Civilization and Mrs Gripper) exhaled among the boating party, and melted in one friendly fusion the discordant elements of which that party had hitherto been composed. Now did the Reverend Samuel Pentecost, whose light had hitherto been hidden under a bushel, prove at last that he could do something, by proving that he could eat. Now did Pedgift Junior shine brighter than ever he had shone yet, in gems of caustic humour and exquisite fertilities of resource. Now did the squire, and the squire's charming guest, prove the triple connection between Champagne that sparkles, Love that grows bolder, and Eyes whose vocabulary is without the word No. Now did cheerful old times come back to the major's memory, and cheerful old stories not told for years find their way to the major's lips. And now did Mrs Pentecost, coming out wakefully in the whole force of her estimable maternal character, seize on a supplementary fork, and ply that useful instrument incessantly between the choicest morsels in the whole round of dishes, and the few vacant places left available on the Reverend Samuel's plate. 'Don't laugh at my son,' cried the old lady, observing the merriment which her proceedings produced among the company. 'It's my fault, poor dear – *I* make him eat!' And there are men in this world who, seeing virtues such as these developed at the table, as they are developed nowhere else, can, nevertheless, rank the glorious privilege of dining with the smallest of the diurnal personal worries which necessity imposes on mankind – with buttoning your waistcoat, for example, or lacing your stays! Trust no such monster as this with your tender secrets, your loves and hatreds, your hopes and fears. His heart is uncorrected by his stomach, and the social virtues are not in him.

The last mellow hours of the day and the first cool breezes of the long summer evening had met, before the dishes were all laid waste, and the bottles as empty as bottles should be. This point in the proceedings attained, the picnic party looked lazily at Pedgift Junior to know what was to be done next. That inexhaustible functionary was equal as ever to all the calls on him. He had a new amusement ready before the quickest of the company could so much as ask him what that amusement was to be.

'Fond of music on the water, Miss Milroy?' he asked in his airiest and pleasantest manner.

Miss Milroy adored music, both on the water and the land – always excepting the one case when she was practising the art herself on the piano at home.

'We'll get out of the reeds first,' said young Pedgift. He gave his orders to the boatmen – dived briskly into the little cabin – and reappeared with a concertina in his hand. 'Neat, Miss Milroy, isn't it?' he observed, pointing to his initials, inlaid on the instrument in mother-of-pearl. 'My name's Augustus, like my father's. Some of my friends knock off the "A", and call me "Gustus Junior". A small joke goes a long way among friends, doesn't it, Mr Armadale? I sing a little, to my own accompaniment, ladies and gentlemen; and, if quite agreeable, I shall be proud and happy to do my best.'

'Stop!' cried Mrs Pentecost; 'I doat on music.'

With this formidable announcement, the old lady opened a prodigious leather-bag, from which she never parted night or day, and took out an ear-trumpet of the old-fashioned kind – something between a key bugle and a French horn. 'I don't care to use the thing generally,' explained Mrs Pentecost, 'because I'm afraid of it's making me deafer than ever. But I can't and won't miss the music. I doat on music. If you'll hold the other end, Sammy, I'll stick it in my ear. Neelie, my dear, tell him to begin.'

Young Pedgift was troubled with no nervous hesitation: he began at once – not with songs of the light and modern kind, such as might have been expected from an amateur of his age and character – but with declamatory and patriotic bursts of poetry, set to the bold and blatant music which the people of England loved dearly at the earlier part of the present century, and which, whenever they can get it, they love dearly still. 'The Death of Marmion', 'The Battle of the Baltic', 'The Bay of Biscay', 'Nelson',[2] under various vocal aspects, as exhibited by the late Braham – these were the songs in which the roaring concertina and strident tenor of Gustus Junior exulted together. 'Tell me when you're tired, ladies and gentlemen,' said the minstrel solicitor. 'There's no conceit about *me*. Will you have a little sentiment by way of variety? Shall I wind up with "The Mistletoe Bough", and "Poor Mary Anne"?'[3]

Having favoured his audience with those two cheerful melodies, young Pedgift respectfully requested the rest of the company to follow his vocal example in turn; offering, in every case, to play 'a running accompaniment' impromptu, if the singer would only be so obliging as to favour him with the key-note.

'Go on, somebody!' cried Mrs Pentecost eagerly. 'I tell you again, I doat on music. We haven't had half enough yet, have we, Sammy?'

The Reverend Samuel made no reply. The unhappy man had reasons of his own – not exactly in his bosom, but a little lower – for remaining silent, in the midst of the general hilarity and the general applause. Alas for humanity! Even maternal love is alloyed with mortal fallibility. Owing much already to his excellent mother, the Reverend Samuel was now additionally indebted to her for a smart indigestion.

Nobody, however, noticed as yet the signs and tokens of internal revolution in the curate's face. Everybody was occupied in entreating everybody else to sing. Miss Milroy appealed to the founder of the feast. 'Do sing something, Mr Armadale,' she said; 'I should so like to hear you!'

'If you once begin, sir,' added the cheerful Pedgift, 'you'll find it get uncommonly easy as you go on. Music is a science which requires to be taken by the throat at starting.'

'With all my heart,' said Allan, in his good-humoured way. 'I know lots of tunes, but the worst of it is the words escape me. I wonder if I can remember one of Moore's Melodies? My poor mother used to be fond of teaching me Moore's Melodies when I was a boy.'

'Whose melodies?' asked Mrs Pentecost. 'Moore's? Aha! I know Tom Moore by heart.'

'Perhaps, in that case, you will be good enough to help me, ma'am, if my memory breaks down,' rejoined Allan. 'I'll take the easiest melody in the whole collection, if you'll allow me. Everybody knows it – "Eveleen's Bower".'[4]

'I'm familiar, in a general sort of way, with the national melodies of England, Scotland, and Ireland,' said Pedgift Junior. 'I'll accompany you, sir, with the greatest pleasure. This is the sort of thing, I think.' He seated himself cross-legged on the roof of the cabin, and burst into a complicated musical improvisation, wonderful to hear – a mixture of instrumental flourishes and groans; a jig corrected by a dirge, and a dirge enlivened by a jig. 'That's the sort of thing,' said young Pedgift, with his smile of supreme confidence. 'Fire away, sir!'

Mrs Pentecost elevated her trumpet, and Allan elevated his voice. '"Oh, weep for the hour when to Eveleen's Bower—"' He stopped; the accompaniment stopped; the audience waited. 'It's a most extraordinary thing,' said Allan; 'I thought I had the next line on the tip of my tongue, and it seems to have escaped me. I'll begin again, if you have no objection. "Oh, weep for the hour when to Eveleen's Bower—"'

'"The lord of the valley with false vows came,"' said Mrs Pentecost.

'Thank you, ma'am,' said Allan. 'Now I shall get on smoothly. "Oh, weep for the hour when to Eveleen's Bower, the lord of the valley with false vows came. The moon was shining bright—"'

'No!' said Mrs Pentecost.

'I beg your pardon, ma'am,' remonstrated Allan. '"The moon was shining bright—"'

'The moon wasn't doing anything of the kind,' said Mrs Pentecost. Pedgift Junior, foreseeing a dispute, persevered *sotto voce* with the accompaniment, in the interests of harmony.

'Moore's own words, ma'am,' said Allan, 'in my mother's copy of the Melodies.'

'Your mother's copy was wrong,' retorted Mrs Pentecost. 'Didn't I tell you just now that I knew Tom Moore by heart?'

Pedgift Junior's peace-making concertina still flourished and groaned, in the minor key.

'Well, what *did* the moon do?' asked Allan, in despair.

'What the moon *ought* to have done, sir, or Tom Moore wouldn't have written it so,' rejoined Mrs Pentecost. '"The moon hid her light from the heaven that night, and wept behind her clouds o'er the maiden's shame!" I wish that young man would leave off playing,' added Mrs Pentecost, venting her rising irritation on Gustus Junior. 'I've had enough of him – he tickles my ears.'

'Proud, I'm sure, ma'am,' said the unblushing Pedgift. 'The whole science of music consists in tickling the ears.'

'We seem to be drifting into a sort of argument,' remarked Major Milroy, placidly. 'Wouldn't it be better if Mr Armadale went on with his song?'

'Do go on, Mr Armadale!' added the major's daughter. 'Do go on, Mr Pedgift!'

'One of them doesn't know the words, and the other doesn't know the music,' said Mrs Pentecost. 'Let them go on, if they can!'

'Sorry to disappoint you, ma'am,' said Pedgift Junior; 'I'm ready to go on, myself, to any extent. Now, Mr Armadale!'

Allan opened his lips to take up the unfinished melody where he had last left it. Before he could utter a note, the curate suddenly rose, with a ghastly face, and a hand pressed convulsively over the middle region of his waistcoat.

'What's the matter?' cried the whole boating party in chorus.

'I am exceedingly unwell,' said the Reverend Samuel Pentecost.

The boat was instantly in a state of confusion. 'Eveleen's Bower' expired on Allan's lips, and even the irrepressible concertina of Pedgift was silenced at last. The alarm proved to be quite needless. Mrs Pentecost's son possessed a mother, and that mother had a bag. In two seconds, the art of medicine occupied the place left vacant in the attention of the company by the art of music.

'Rub it gently, Sammy,' said Mrs Pentecost. 'I'll get out the bottles and give you a dose. It's his poor stomach, major. Hold my trumpet, somebody – and stop the boat. You take that bottle, Neelie, my dear; and you take this one, Mr Armadale; and give them to me as I want them. Ah, poor dear, I know what's the matter with him! Want of power *here*, major – cold, acid, and flabby. Ginger to warm him; soda to correct him; salvolatile to hold him up. There, Sammy! drink it before it settles – and then go and lie down, my dear, in that dog-kennel of a place they call the cabin. No more music!' added Mrs Pentecost, shaking her forefinger at the proprietor of the concertina – unless it's a hymn, and that I don't object to.'

Nobody appearing to be in a fit frame of mind for singing a hymn, the all-accomplished Pedgift drew upon his stores of local knowledge, and produced a new idea. The course of the boat was immediately changed under his direction. In a few minutes more, the company found themselves in a little island-creek, with a lonely cottage at the far end of it, and a perfect forest of reeds closing the view all round them.

'What do you say, ladies and gentlemen, to stepping on shore and seeing what a reed-cutter's cottage looks like?' suggested young Pedgift.

'We say, yes, to be sure,' answered Allan. 'I think our spirits have been a little dashed by Mr Pentecost's illness and Mrs Pentecost's bag,' he added, in a whisper to Miss Milroy. 'A change of this sort is the very thing we want to set us all going again.'

He and young Pedgift handed Miss Milroy out of the boat. The major followed. Mrs Pentecost sat immovable as the Egyptian Sphinx, with her bag on her knees, mounting guard over 'Sammy' in the cabin.

'We must keep the fun going, sir,' said Allan, as he helped the major over the side of the boat. 'We haven't half done yet with the enjoyment of the day.'

His voice seconded his hearty belief in his own prediction to such good purpose, that even Mrs Pentecost heard him, and ominously shook her head.

'Ah!' sighed the curate's mother. 'If you were as old as I am, young gentleman, you wouldn't feel quite so sure of the enjoyment of the day!'

So, in rebuke of the rashness of youth, spoke the caution of age. The negative view is notoriously the safe view, all the world over – and the Pentecost philosophy is, as a necessary consequence, generally in the right.

CHAPTER IX

FATE OR CHANCE?

It was close on six o'clock when Allan and his friends left the boat; and the evening influence was creeping already, in its mystery and its stillness, over the watery solitude of the Broads.

The shore in these wild regions was not like the shore elsewhere. Firm as it looked, the garden-ground in front of the reed-cutter's cottage was floating ground, that rose and fell and oozed into puddles under the pressure of the foot. The boatmen who guided the visitors warned them to keep the path, and pointed through gaps in the reeds and pollards to grassy places, on which strangers would have walked confidently, where the crust of earth was not strong enough to bear the weight of a child over the unfathomed depths of slime and water beneath. The solitary cottage, built of planks pitched black, stood on ground that had been steadied and strengthened by resting it on piles. A little wooden tower rose at one end of the roof, and served as a look-out post in the fowling season. From this elevation the eye ranged far and wide over a wilderness of winding water and lonesome marsh. If the reed-cutter had lost his boat, he would have been as completely isolated from all communication with town or village, as if his place of abode had been a light-vessel instead of a cottage. Neither he nor his family complained of their solitude, or looked in any way the rougher or the worse for it. His wife received the visitors hospitably, in a snug little room, with a raftered ceiling, and windows which looked like windows in a cabin on board ship. His wife's father told stories of the famous days when the smugglers came up from the sea at night, rowing through the network of rivers with muffled oars till they gained the lonely Broads, and sunk their spirit casks in the water, far from the coastguard's reach. His wild little children played at hide-and-seek with the visitors; and the visitors ranged in and out of the cottage, and round and round the morsel of firm earth on which it stood, surprised and delighted by the novelty of all they saw. The one person who noticed the advance of the evening – the one person who thought of the flying time and the stationary Pentecosts in the boat – was young Pedgift. That experienced pilot of the Broads looked askance at his watch, and drew Allan aside at the first opportunity.

'I don't wish to hurry you, Mr Armadale,' said Pedgift Junior; 'but the time is getting on, and there's a lady in the case.'

'A lady?' repeated Allan.

'Yes, sir,' rejoined young Pedgift. 'A lady from London; connected (if you'll allow me to jog your memory) with a pony-chaise and white harness.'

'Good heavens, the governess!' cried Allan; 'why, we have forgotten all about her!'

'Don't be alarmed, sir; there's plenty of time, if we only get into the boat again. This is how it stands, Mr Armadale. We settled, if you remember, to have the gipsy tea-making at the next "Broad" to this – Hurle Mere?'[1]

'Certainly,' said Allan. 'Hurle Mere is the place where my friend Midwinter has promised to come and meet us.'

'Hurle Mere is where the governess will be, sir, if your coachman follows my directions,' pursued young Pedgift. 'We have got nearly an hour's punting to do; along the twists and turns of the narrow waters (which they call The Sounds here) between this and Hurle Mere; and according to my calculations we must get on board again in five minutes, if we are to be in time to meet the governess and to meet your friend.'

'We mustn't miss my friend, on any account,' said Allan; 'or the governess either, of course. I'll tell the major.'

Major Milroy was at that moment preparing to mount the wooden watch-tower of the cottage to see the view. The ever useful Pedgift volunteered to go up with him, and rattle off all the necessary local explanations in half the time which the reed-cutter would occupy in describing his own neighbourhood to a stranger.

Allan remained standing in front of the cottage, more quiet and more thoughtful than usual. His interview with young Pedgift had brought his absent friend to his memory for the first time since the picnic party had started. He was surprised that Midwinter, so much in his thoughts on all other occasions, should have been so long out of his thoughts now. Something troubled him, like a sense of self-reproach, as his mind reverted to the faithful friend at home, toiling hard over the steward's books, in his interests and for his sake. 'Dear old fellow,' thought Allan, 'I shall be so glad to see him at the Mere; the day's pleasure wont be complete till he joins us!'

'Should I be right or wrong, Mr Armadale, if I guessed that you were thinking of somebody?' asked a voice softly behind him.

Allan turned, and found the major's daughter at his side. Miss Milroy (not unmindful of a certain tender interview which had taken place behind a carriage) had noticed her admirer standing thoughtfully by himself, and had determined on giving him another opportunity, while her father and young Pedgift were at the top of the watch-tower.

'You know everything,' said Allan smiling. 'I *was* thinking of somebody.'

Miss Milroy stole a glance at him – a glance of gentle encouragement. There could be but one human creature in Mr Armadale's mind after what had passed between them that morning! It would be only an act of mercy to take him back again at once to the interrupted conversation of a few hours since on the subject of names.

'I have been thinking of somebody too,' she said, half inviting, half repelling the coming avowal. 'If I tell you the first letter of my Somebody's name, will you tell me the first letter of yours?'

'I will tell you anything you like,' rejoined Allan with the utmost enthusiasm.

She still shrank coquettishly from the very subject that she wanted to approach. 'Tell me your letter first,' she said in low tones, looking away from him.

Allan laughed. 'M,' he said, 'is my first letter.'

She started a little. Strange that he should be thinking of her by her surname instead of her Christian name – but it mattered little as long as he *was* thinking of her.

'What is your letter?' asked Allan.

She blushed and smiled. 'A – if you will have it!' she answered in a reluctant little whisper. She stole another look at him, and luxuriously protracted her enjoyment of the coming avowal once more. 'How many syllables is the name in?' she asked, drawing patterns shyly on the ground with the end of her parasol.

No man with the slightest knowledge of the sex would have been rash enough, in Allan's position, to tell her the truth. Allan, who knew nothing whatever of women's natures, and who told the truth right and left in all mortal emergencies, answered as if he had been under examination in a court of justice.

'It's a name in three syllables,' he said.

Miss Milroy's downcast eyes flashed up at him like lightning. 'Three!' she repeated in the blankest astonishment.

Allan was too inveterately straightforward to take the warning even now. 'I'm not strong at my spelling, I know,' he said, with his light-hearted laugh. 'But I don't think I'm wrong in calling Midwinter a name in three syllables. I was thinking of my friend – but never mind my thoughts. Tell me who A is – tell me who *you* were thinking of?'

'Of the first letter of the alphabet, Mr Armadale, and I beg positively to inform you of nothing more!'

With that annihilating answer the major's daughter put up her parasol and walked back by herself to the boat.

Allan stood petrified with amazement. If Miss Milroy had actually boxed his ears (and there is no denying that she had privately longed to devote her hand to that purpose) he could hardly have felt more bewildered than he felt now. 'What on earth have I done?' he asked himself helplessly, as the major and young Pedgift joined him, and the three walked down together to the waterside. 'I wonder what she'll say to me next?'

She said absolutely nothing – she never so much as looked at Allan when he took his place in the boat. There she sat, with her eyes and her complexion both much brighter than usual, taking the deepest interest in the curate's progress towards recovery; in the state of Mrs Pentecost's spirits; in Pedgift Junior (for whom she ostentatiously made room enough to let him sit beside her); in the scenery and the reed-cutter's cottage; in everybody and everything but Allan – whom she would have married with the greatest pleasure five minutes since. 'I'll never forgive him,' thought the major's daughter. 'To be thinking of that ill-bred wretch when I was thinking of *him* – and to make me all but confess it before I found him out! Thank heaven Mr Pedgift is in the boat!'

In this frame of mind Miss Neelie applied herself forthwith to the fascination of Pedgift and the discomfiture of Allan. 'Oh, Mr Pedgift, how extremely clever and kind of you to think of showing us that sweet cottage! Lonely, Mr Armadale? I don't think it's lonely at all; I should like of all things to live there. What would this picnic have been without you, Mr Pedgift; you can't think how I have enjoyed it since we got into the boat. Cool, Mr Armadale? What can you possibly mean by saying it's cool; it's the warmest evening we've had this summer. And the music, Mr Pedgift; how nice it was of you to bring your concertina! I wonder if I could accompany you on the piano? I should so like to try. Oh, yes, Mr Armadale, no doubt you meant to do something musical too, and I daresay you sing very well when you know the words; but, to tell you the truth, I always did, and always shall hate Moore's Melodies!'

Thus, with merciless dexterity of manipulation, did Miss Milroy work that sharpest female weapon of offence, the tongue – and thus she would have used it for some time longer, if Allan had only shown the necessary jealousy, or if Pedgift had only afforded the necessary encouragement. But adverse fortune had decreed that she should select for her victims two men essentially unassailable under existing circumstances. Allan was too innocent of all knowledge of female subtleties and susceptibilities to understand anything, except that the charming Neelie was unreasonably out of temper with him without the slightest cause. The wary Pedgift, as became one of the quick-witted youth of the present generation, submitted to female influence, with his eye fixed immovably all the time on his own interests. Many a young man of the past generation, who was no fool, has sacrificed everything for love. Not one young man in ten thousand of the present generation, *except* the fools, has sacrificed a halfpenny. The daughters of Eve still inherit their mother's merits, and commit their mother's faults. But the sons of Adam, in these latter days, are men who would have handed the famous apple back with a bow, and a 'Thanks, no; it might get me into a scrape.' When Allan – surprised and disappointed – moved away out of Miss Milroy's reach to the forward part of the boat, Pedgift Junior rose and followed him. 'You're a very nice girl,' thought this shrewd and sensible young man; 'but a client's a client – and I am sorry to inform you, Miss, it won't do.' He set himself at once to rouse Allan's spirits by diverting his attention to a new subject. There was to be a regatta that autumn on one of the Broads, and his client's opinion as a yachtsman might be valuable to the committee. 'Something new I should think to you, sir, in a sailing-match on fresh water?' he said in his most ingratiatory manner. And Allan, instantly interested, answered, 'Quite new. Do tell me about it!'

259

As for the rest of the party, at the other end of the boat, they were in a fair way to confirm Mrs Pentecost's doubts whether the hilarity of the picnic would last the day out. Poor Neelie's natural feeling of irritation under the disappointment which Allan's awkwardness had inflicted on her, was now exasperated into silent and settled resentment by her own keen sense of humiliation and defeat. The major had relapsed into his habitually dreamy, absent manner; his mind was turning monotonously with the wheels of his clock. The curate still secluded his indigestion from public view in the innermost recesses of the cabin; and the curate's mother, with a second dose ready at a moment's notice, sat on guard at the door. Women of Mrs Pentecost's age and character generally enjoy their own bad spirits. 'This,' sighed the old lady, wagging her head with a smile of sour satisfaction, 'is what you call a day's pleasure, is it? Ah, what fools we all were to leave our comfortable homes!'

Meanwhile, the boat floated smoothly along the windings of the watery labyrinth which lay between the two Broads. The view on either side was now limited to nothing but interminable rows of reeds. Not a sound was heard, far or near; not so much as a glimpse of cultivated or inhabited land appeared anywhere. 'A trifle dreary hereabouts, Mr Armadale,' said the ever-cheerful Pedgift. 'But we are just out of it now. Look ahead, sir! Here we are at Hurle Mere.'

The reeds opened back on the right hand and the left, and the boat glided suddenly into the wide circle of a pool. Round the nearer half of the circle, the eternal reeds still fringed the margin of the water. Round the farther half, the land appeared again – here, rolling back from the pool in desolate sand-hills; there, rising above it in a sweep of grassy shore. At one point, the ground was occupied by a plantation; and, at another, by the outbuildings of a lonely old red-brick house, with a strip of by-road near, that skirted the garden-wall, and ended at the pool. The sun was sinking in the clear heaven, and the water, where the sun's reflection failed to tinge it, was beginning to look black and cold. The solitude that had been soothing, the silence that had felt like an enchantment on the other Broad, in the day's vigorous prime, was a solitude that saddened here – a silence that struck cold, in the stillness and melancholy of the day's decline.

The course of the boat was directed across the Mere to a creek in the grassy shore. One or two of the little flat-bottomed punts peculiar to the Broads lay in the creek; and the reed-cutters to whom the punts belonged, surprised at the appearance of strangers, came out, staring silently, from behind an angle of the old garden-wall. Not another sign of life was visible anywhere. No pony-chaise had been seen by the reed-cutters; no stranger, either man or woman, had approached the shores of Hurle Mere that day.

Young Pedgift took another look at his watch, and addressed himself to Miss Milroy. 'You may, or may not, see the governess when you get back to Thorpe-Ambrose,' he said; 'but, as the time stands now, you won't see her here. You know best, Mr Armadale,' he added, turning to Allan, 'whether your friend is to be depended on to keep his appointment?'

'I am certain he is to be depended on,' replied Allan, looking about him in unconcealed disappointment at Midwinter's absence.

'Very good,' pursued Pedgift Junior. 'If we light the fire for our gipsy tea-making on the open ground there, your friend may find us out, sir, by the smoke. That's the Indian dodge for picking up a lost man on the prairie, Miss Milroy – and it's pretty nearly wild enough (isn't it?) to be a prairie here!'

There are some temptations – principally those of the smaller kind – which it is not in the defensive capacity of female human nature to resist. The temptation to direct the whole force of her influence, as the one young lady of the party, towards the instant overthrow of Allan's arrangement for meeting his friend, was too much for the major's daughter. She turned on the smiling Pedgift with a look which ought to have overwhelmed him. But who ever overwhelmed a solicitor?

'I think it's the most lonely, dreary, hideous place I ever saw in my life!' said Miss Neelie. 'If you insist on making tea here, Mr Pedgift, don't make any for me. No! I shall stop in the boat; and though I am absolutely dying with thirst, I shall touch nothing till we get back again to the other Broad!'

The major opened his lips to remonstrate. To his daughter's infinite delight, Mrs Pentecost rose from her seat, before he could say a word, and, after surveying the whole landward prospect, and seeing nothing in the shape of a vehicle anywhere, asked indignantly whether they were going all the way back again to the place where they had left the carriages in the middle of the day. On ascertaining that this was, in fact, the arrangement proposed; and that, from the nature of the country, the carriages could not have been ordered round to Hurle Mere without, in the first instance, sending them the whole of the way back to Thorpe-Ambrose, Mrs Pentecost (speaking in her son's interests) instantly declared that no earthly power should induce her to be out on the water after dark. 'Call me a boat!' cried the old lady, in great agitation. 'Wherever there's water, there's a night mist, and wherever there's a night mist, my son Samuel catches cold. Don't talk to *me* about your moonlight and your tea-making – you're all mad! Hi! you two men there!' cried Mrs Pentecost, hailing the silent reed-cutters on shore. 'Sixpence a-piece for you, if you'll take me and my son back in your boat!'

Before young Pedgift could interfere, Allan himself settled the difficulty this time, with perfect patience and good temper.

'I can't think, Mrs Pentecost, of your going back in any boat but the boat you have come out in,' he said. 'There is not the least need (as you and Miss Milroy don't like the place) for anybody to go on shore here, but me. I *must* go on shore. My friend Midwinter never broke his promise to me yet; and I can't consent to leave Hurle Mere, as long as there is a chance of his keeping his appointment. But there's not the least reason in the world why I should stand in the way on that account. You have the major and Mr Pedgift to take care of you; and you can get back to the carriages before dark, if you go at once. I will wait here, and give my friend half-an-hour more – and then I can follow you in one of the reed-cutters' boats.'

'That's the most sensible thing, Mr Armadale, you've said to-day,' remarked Mrs Pentecost, seating herself again in a violent hurry. 'Tell them to be quick!' cried the old lady, shaking her fist at the boatmen. 'Tell them to be quick!'

Allan gave the necessary directions, and stepped on shore. The wary Pedgift (sticking fast to his client,) tried to follow.

'We can't leave you here alone, sir,' he said, protesting eagerly in a whisper. 'Let the major take care of the ladies, and let me keep you company at the Mere.'

'No, no!' said Allan, pressing him back. 'They're all in low spirits on board. If you want to be of service to me, stop like a good fellow where you are, and do your best to keep the thing going.'

He waved his hand, and the men pushed the boat off from the shore. The others all waved their hands in return except the major's daughter, who sat apart from the rest, with her face hidden under her parasol. The tears stood thick in Neelie's eyes. Her last angry feeling against Allan died out, and her heart went back to him penitently, the moment he left the boat. 'How good he is to us all!' she thought, 'and what a wretch I am!' She got up with every generous impulse in her nature urging her to make atonement to him. She got up, reckless of appearances, and looked after him with eager eyes and flushed cheeks, as he stood alone on the shore. 'Don't be long, Mr Armadale!' she said, with a desperate disregard of what the rest of the company thought of her.

The boat was already far out in the water, and with all Neelie's resolution, the words were spoken in a faint little voice, which failed to reach Allan's ears. The one sound he heard, as the boat gained the opposite extremity of the Mere, and disappeared slowly among the reeds, was the sound of the concertina. The indefatigable Pedgift was keeping things going – evidently under the auspices of Mrs Pentecost – by performing a sacred melody.

Left by himself, Allan lit a cigar, and took a turn backwards and forwards on the shore. 'She might have said a word to me at parting!' he thought. 'I've done everything for the best; I've as good as told her how fond of her I am, and this is the way she treats me!' He stopped, and stood looking absently at the sinking sun, and the fast-darkening waters of the Mere. Some inscrutable influence in the scene forced its way stealthily into his mind, and diverted his thoughts from Miss Milroy to his absent friend. He started, and looked about him.

The reed-cutters had gone back to their retreat behind the angle of the wall, not a living creature was visible, not a sound rose anywhere along the dreary shore. Even Allan's spirits began to get depressed. It was nearly an hour after the time when Midwinter had promised to be at Hurle Mere. He had himself arranged to walk to the pool (with a stable-boy from Thorpe-Ambrose, as his guide), by lanes and footpaths which shortened the distance by the road. The boy knew the country well, and Midwinter was habitually punctual at all his appointments. Had anything gone wrong at Thorpe-Ambrose? Had some accident happened on the way? Determined to remain no longer doubting and idling by himself, Allan made up his mind to walk inland from the Mere, on the chance of meeting his friend. He went round at once to the angle in the wall, and asked one of the reed-cutters to show him the footpath to Thorpe-Ambrose.

The man led him away from the road, and pointed to a barely-perceptible break in the outer trees of the plantation. After pausing for one more useless look round him, Allan turned his back on the Mere, and made for the trees.

For a few paces, the path ran straight through the plantation. Thence, it took a sudden turn – and the water and the open country became both lost to view. Allan steadily followed the grassy track before him, seeing nothing and hearing nothing, until he came to another winding of the path. Turning in the new direction, he saw dimly a human figure sitting alone at the foot of one of the trees. Two steps nearer were enough to make the figure familiar to him. 'Midwinter!' he exclaimed, in astonishment. 'This is not the place where I was to meet you! What are you waiting for here?'

Midwinter rose, without answering. The evening dimness among the trees, which obscured his face, made his silence doubly perplexing.

Allan went on eagerly questioning him. 'Did you come here by yourself?' he asked. 'I thought the boy was to guide you?'

This time Midwinter answered. 'When we got as far as these trees,' he said, 'I sent the boy back. He told me I was close to the place, and couldn't miss it.'

'What made you stop here, when he left you?' reiterated Allan. 'Why didn't you walk on?'

'Don't despise me,' answered the other, 'I hadn't the courage!'

'Not the courage?' repeated Allan. He paused a moment. 'Oh, I know!' he resumed, putting his hand gaily on Midwinter's shoulder. 'You're still shy of the Milroys. What nonsense, when I told you myself that your peace was made at the cottage!'

'I wasn't thinking, Allan, of your friends at the cottage. The truth is, I'm hardly myself to-day. I am ill and unnerved; trifles startle me.' He stopped, and shrunk away, under the anxious scrutiny of Allan's eyes. 'If you *will* have it,' he burst out abruptly, 'the horror of that night on board the Wreck has got me again; there's a dreadful oppression on my head; there's a dreadful sinking at my heart – I am afraid of something happening to us, if we don't part before the day is out. I can't break my promise to you; for God's sake, release me from it, and let me go back?'

Remonstrance, to any one who knew Midwinter, was plainly useless at that moment. Allan humoured him. 'Come out of this dark airless place,' he said; 'and we'll talk about it. The water and the open sky are within a stone's throw of us. I hate a wood in the evening – it even gives *me* the horrors. You have been working too hard over the steward's books. Come and breathe freely in the blessed open air.'

Midwinter stopped, considered for a moment, and suddenly submitted.

'You're right,' he said, 'and I'm wrong, as usual. I'm wasting time and distressing you to no purpose. What folly to ask you to let me go back! Suppose you had said yes?'

'Well?' asked Allan.

'Well,' repeated Midwinter, 'something would have happened at the first step to stop me – that's all. Come on.'

They walked together in silence on the way to the Mere.

At the last turn in the path Allan's cigar went out. While he stopped to light it again, Midwinter walked on before him, and was the first to come in sight of the open ground.

Allan had just kindled the match, when, to his surprise, his friend came back to him round the turn in the path. There was light enough to show objects more clearly in this part of the plantation. The match, as Midwinter faced him, dropped on the instant from Allan's hand.

'Good God!' he cried, starting back, 'you look as you looked on board the Wreck!'

Midwinter held up his hand for silence. He spoke with his wild eyes riveted on Allan's face, with his white lips close at Allan's ear.

'You remember how I *looked*,' he answered, in a whisper. 'Do you remember what I *said*, when you and the doctor were talking of the Dream?'

'I have forgotten the Dream,' said Allan.

As he made that answer, Midwinter took his hand, and led him round the last turn in the path.

'Do you remember it now?' he asked, and pointed to the Mere.

The sun was sinking in the cloudless westward heaven. The waters of the Mere lay beneath, tinged red by the dying light. The open country stretched away, darkening drearily already on the right hand and the left. And on the near margin of the pool, where all had been solitude before, there now stood, fronting the sunset, the figure of a Woman.

The two Armadales stood together in silence, and looked at the lonely figure and the dreary view.

Midwinter was the first to speak.

'Your own eyes have seen it,' he said. 'Now look at your own words.'

He opened the narrative of the Dream, and held it under Allan's eyes. His finger pointed to the lines which recorded the first Vision; his voice sinking lower and lower, repeated the words:

'The sense came to me of being left alone in the darkness.

'I waited.

'The darkness opened and showed me the vision – as in a picture – of a broad, lonely pool, surrounded by open ground. Above the farther margin of the pool I saw the cloudless western sky, red with the light of sunset.

'On the near margin of the pool there stood the Shadow of a Woman.'

He ceased, and let the hand which held the manuscript drop to his side. The other hand pointed to the lonely figure, standing with its back turned on them, fronting the setting sun.

'There,' he said, 'stands the living Woman, in the Shadow's place! There speaks the first of the dream-warnings to you and to me! Let the future time find us still together – and the second figure that stands in the Shadow's place will be Mine.'

Even Allan was silenced by the terrible certainty of conviction with which he spoke.

In the pause that followed, the figure at the pool moved, and walked slowly away round the margin of the shore. Allan stepped out beyond the last of the trees, and gained a wider view of the open ground. The first object that met his eyes was the pony-chaise from Thorpe-Ambrose.

He turned back to Midwinter with a laugh of relief. 'What nonsense have you been talking!' he said. 'And what nonsense have I been listening to! It's the governess at last.'

Midwinter made no reply. Allan took him by the arm, and tried to lead him on. He released himself suddenly, and seized Allan with both hands – holding him back from the figure at the pool, as he had held him back from the cabin-door on the deck of the timber-ship. Once again, the effort was in vain. Once again, Allan broke away as easily as he had broken away in the past time.

'One of us must speak to her,' he said. 'And if you won't, I will.'

He had only advanced a few steps towards the Mere, when he heard, or thought he heard, a voice faintly calling after him, once and once only, the word Farewell. He stopped, with a feeling of uneasy surprise, and looked round.

'Was that you, Midwinter?' he asked.

There was no answer. After hesitating a moment more, Allan returned to the plantation. Midwinter was gone.

He looked back at the pool; doubtful in the new emergency, what to do next. The lonely figure had altered its course in the interval: it had turned and was advancing towards the trees. Allan had been evidently either heard or seen. It was impossible to leave a woman unbefriended in that helpless position and in that solitary place. For the second time Allan went out from the trees to meet her.

As he came within sight of her face, he stopped in ungovernable astonishment. The sudden revelation of her beauty, as she smiled and looked at him inquiringly, suspended the movement in his limbs and the words on his lips. A vague doubt beset him whether it was the governess, after all.

He roused himself; and, advancing a few paces, mentioned his name. 'May I ask,' he added, 'if I have the pleasure—'

The lady met him easily and gracefully half way.

'Major Milroy's governess,' she said. 'Miss Gwilt.'

CHAPTER X

THE HOUSEMAID'S FACE

All was quiet at Thorpe-Ambrose. The hall was solitary, the rooms were dark. The servants, waiting for the supper-hour in the garden at the back of the house, looked up at the clear heaven and the rising moon, and agreed that there was little prospect of the return of the picnic party until later in the night. The general opinion, led by the high authority of the cook, predicted that they might all sit down to supper without the least fear of being disturbed by the bell. Having arrived at this conclusion, the servants assembled round the table; and exactly at the moment when they sat down, the bell rang.

The footman, wondering, went upstairs to open the door, and found to his astonishment Midwinter waiting alone on the threshold, and looking (in the servant's opinion) miserably ill. He asked for a light, and, saying he wanted nothing else, withdrew at once to his room. The footman went back to his fellow-servants, and reported that something had certainly happened to his master's friend.

On entering his room, Midwinter closed the door, and hurriedly filled a bag with the necessaries for travelling. This done, he took from a locked drawer, and placed in the breast-pocket of his coat, some little presents which Allan had given to him – a cigar-case, a purse, and a set of studs in plain gold. Having possessed himself of these memorials, he snatched up the bag, and laid his hand on the door. There, for the first time, he paused. There, the headlong haste of all his actions thus far suddenly ceased, and the hard despair in his face began to soften: he waited, with the door in his hand.

Up to that moment he had been conscious of but one motive that animated him, but one purpose that he was resolute to achieve. 'For Allan's sake!' he had said to himself, when he looked back towards the fatal landscape and saw his friend leaving him to meet the woman at the pool. 'For Allan's sake!' he had said again, when he crossed the open country beyond the wood, and saw afar, in the grey twilight, the long line of embankment and the distant glimmer of the railway lamps beckoning him away already to the iron road.

It was only when he now paused before he closed the door behind him – it was only when his own impetuous rapidity of action came for the first time to a check – that the nobler nature of the man rose in protest against the superstitious despair which was hurrying him from all that he held dear. His conviction of the terrible necessity of leaving Allan for Allan's good, had not been shaken for an instant since he had seen the first vision of the Dream realized on the shores of the Mere. But now, for the first time, his own heart rose against him in unanswerable rebuke. 'Go, if you must and will! but remember the time when you were ill, and he sat by your bedside; friendless, and he opened his heart to you – and write, if you fear to speak; write and ask him to forgive you, before you leave him for ever!'

The half-opened door closed again softly. Midwinter sat down at the writing-table and took up the pen. He tried again and again, and yet again, to write the farewell words; he tried, till the floor all round him was littered with torn sheets of paper. Turn from them which way he would, the old times still came back and faced him reproachfully. The spacious bedchamber in which he sat, narrowed, in spite of him, to the sick usher's garret at the West-country inn. The kind hand that had once patted him on the shoulder, touched him again; the kind voice that had cheered him, spoke unchangeably in the old friendly tones. He flung his arms on the table, and dropped his head on them in tearless despair. The parting words that his tongue was powerless to utter, his pen was powerless to write. Mercilessly in earnest, his superstition pointed to him to go while the time was his own; mercilessly in earnest, his love for Allan held him back till the farewell plea for pardon and pity was written.

He rose with a sudden resolution, and rang for the servant. 'When Mr Armadale returns,' he said, 'ask him to excuse my coming down-stairs, and say that I am trying to get to sleep.' He locked the door and put out the light, and sat down alone in the darkness. 'The night will keep us apart,' he said; 'and time may help me to write. I may go in the early morning; I may go while—' The thought died in him uncompleted; and the sharp agony of the struggle forced to his lips the first cry of suffering that had escaped him yet.

He waited in the darkness. As the time stole on, his senses remained mechanically awake, but his mind began to sink slowly under the heavy strain that had now been laid on it for some hours past. A dull vacancy possessed him; he made no attempt to kindle the light and write once more. He never started; he never moved to the open window, when the first sound of approaching wheels broke in on the silence of the night. He heard the carriages draw up at the door; he heard the horses champing their bits; he heard the voices of Allan and young Pedgift on the steps – and still he sat quiet in the darkness, and still no interest was roused in him by the sounds that reached his ear from outside.

The voices remained audible after the carriages had been driven away; the two young men were evidently lingering on the steps before they took leave of each other. Every word they said reached Midwinter through the open window. Their one subject of conversation was the new governess. Allan's voice was loud in her praise. He had never passed such an hour of delight in his life as the hour he had spent with Miss Gwilt in the boat, on the way from Hurle Mere to the picnic party waiting at the other Broad. Agreeing, on his side, with all that his client said in praise of the charming stranger, young Pedgift appeared to treat the subject, when it fell into his hands, from a different point of view. Miss Gwilt's attractions had not so entirely absorbed his attention as to prevent him from noticing the impression which the new governess had produced on her employer and her pupil.

'There's a screw loose somewhere, sir, in Major Milroy's family,' said the voice of young Pedgift.[1] 'Did you notice how the major and his daughter looked when Miss Gwilt made her excuses for being late at the Mere? You don't remember? Do you remember what Miss Gwilt said?'

'Something about Mrs Milroy, wasn't it?' Allan rejoined.

Young Pedgift's voice dropped mysteriously a note lower.

'Miss Gwilt reached the cottage this afternoon, sir, at the time when I told you she would reach it, and she would have joined us at the time I told you she would come, but for Mrs Milroy. Mrs Milroy sent for her upstairs as soon as she entered the house, and kept her upstairs a good half hour and more. That was Miss Gwilt's excuse, Mr Armadale, for being late at the Mere.'

'Well, and what then?'

'You seem to forget, sir, what the whole neighbourhood has heard about Mrs Milroy ever since the major first settled among us. We have all been told, on the doctor's own authority, that she is too great a sufferer to see strangers. Isn't it a little odd that she should have suddenly turned out well enough to see Miss Gwilt (in her husband's absence) the moment Miss Gwilt entered the house?'

'Not a bit of it! Of course she was anxious to make acquaintance with her daughter's governess.'

'Likely enough Mr Armadale. But the major and Miss Neelie don't see it in that light, at any rate. I had my eye on them both when the governess told them that Mrs Milroy had sent for her. If ever I saw a girl look thoroughly frightened, Miss Milroy was that girl; and (if I may be allowed, in the strictest confidence, to libel a gallant soldier) I should say that the major himself was much in the same condition. Take my word for it, sir, there's something wrong upstairs in that pretty cottage of yours; and Miss Gwilt is mixed up in it already.'

There was a minute of silence. When the voices were next heard by Midwinter, they were farther away from the house – Allan was probably accompanying young Pedgift a few steps on his way back.

After a while, Allan's voice was audible once more under the portico, making inquiries after his friend; answered by the servant's voice giving Midwinter's message. This brief interruption over, the silence was not broken again till the time came for shutting up the house. The servants' footsteps passing to and fro, the clang of closing doors, the barking of a disturbed dog in the stable-yard – these sounds warned Midwinter that it was getting late. He rose mechanically to kindle a light. But his head was giddy, his hand trembled – he laid aside the match-box, and returned to his chair. The conversation between Allan and young Pedgift had ceased to occupy his attention the instant he ceased to hear it; and now again, the sense that the precious time was failing him became a lost sense, as soon as the house noises which had awakened it had passed away. His energies of body and mind were both alike worn out; he waited with a stolid resignation for the trouble that was to come to him with the coming day.

An interval passed, and the silence was once more disturbed by voices outside; the voices of a man and a woman this time. The first few words exchanged between them indicated plainly enough a meeting of the clandestine kind; and revealed the man as one of the servants at Thorpe-Ambrose, and the woman as one of the servants at the cottage.

Here again, after the first greetings were over, the subject of the new governess became the all-absorbing subject of conversation. The woman was brimful of forebodings (inspired solely by Miss Gwilt's good looks), which she poured out irrepressibly on the man, try as he might to divert her to other topics. Sooner or later, let him mark her words, there would be an awful 'upset' at the cottage. Her master, it might be mentioned in confidence, led a dreadful life with her mistress. The major was the best of men; he hadn't a thought in his heart beyond his daughter and his everlasting clock. But only let a nice-looking woman come near the place, and Mrs Milroy was jealous of her – raging jealous, like a woman possessed, on that miserable sick-bed of hers. If Miss Gwilt (who was certainly good-looking, in spite of her hideous hair) didn't blow the fire into a flame before many days more were over their heads, the mistress was the mistress no longer, but somebody else. Whatever happened, the fault, this time, would lie at the door of the major's mother. The old lady and the mistress had had a dreadful quarrel two years since; and the old lady had gone away in a fury, telling her son, before all the servants, that if he had a spark of spirit in him, he would never submit to his wife's temper as he did. It would be too much perhaps to accuse the major's mother of purposely picking out a handsome governess to spite the major's wife. But it might be safely said that the old lady was the last person in the world to humour the mistress's jealousy, by declining to engage a capable and respectable governess for her granddaughter, because that governess happened to be blessed with good looks. How it was all to end (except that it was certain to end badly) no human creature could say. Things were looking as black already as things well could. Miss Neelie was crying, after the day's pleasure (which was one bad sign); the mistress had found fault with nobody (which was another); the master had wished her good-night through the door (which was a third); and the governess had locked herself up in her room (which was the worst sign of all, for it looked as if she distrusted the servants). Thus the stream of the woman's gossip ran on, and thus it reached Midwinter's ears through the window, till the clock in the stable-yard struck, and stopped the talking. When the last vibrations of the bell had died away, the voices were not audible again, and the silence was broken no more.

Another interval passed, and Midwinter made a new effort to rouse himself. This time he kindled the light without hesitation, and took the pen in hand.

He wrote at the first trial with a sudden facility of expression, which, surprising him as he went on, ended in rousing in him some vague suspicion of himself. He left the table, and bathed his head and face in water, and came back to read what he had written. The language was barely intelligible – sentences were left unfinished; words were misplaced one for the other – every line recorded the protest of the weary brain against the merciless will that had forced it into action. Midwinter tore up the sheet of paper as he had torn up the other sheets before it – and sinking under the struggle at last, laid his weary head on the pillow.

Almost on the instant, exhaustion overcame him; and before he could put the light out he fell asleep.

He was roused by a noise at the door. The sunlight was pouring into the room; the candle had burnt down into the socket; and the servant was waiting outside with a letter which had come for him by the morning's post.

'I ventured to disturb you, sir,' said the man, when Midwinter opened the door, 'because the letter is marked "Immediate", and I didn't know but it might be of some consequence.'

Midwinter thanked him, and looked at the letter. It *was* of some consequence – the handwriting was Mr Brock's.

He paused to collect his faculties. The torn sheets of paper on the floor recalled to him in a moment the position in which he stood. He locked the door again, in the fear that Allan might rise earlier than usual and come in to make inquiries. Then – feeling strangely little interest in anything that the rector could write to him now – he opened Mr Brock's letter, and read these lines:

Tuesday.

MY DEAR MIDWINTER, – It is sometimes best to tell bad news plainly, in few words. Let me tell mine at once, in one sentence. My precautions have all been defeated: the woman has escaped me.

This misfortune – for it is nothing less – happened yesterday (Monday). Between eleven and twelve in the forenoon of that day, the business which originally brought me to London obliged me to go to Doctors' Commons, and to leave my servant Robert to watch the house opposite our lodging until my return. About an hour and a half after my departure he observed an empty cab drawn up at the door of the house. Boxes and bags made their appearance first; they were followed by the woman herself, in the dress I had first seen her in. Having previously secured a cab, Robert traced her to the terminus of the North-Western Railway – saw her pass through the ticket-office – kept her in view till she reached the platform – and there, in the crowd and confusion caused by the starting of a large mixed train, lost her. I must do him the justice to say that he at once took the right course in this emergency. Instead of wasting time in searching for her on the platform, he looked along the line of carriages; and he positively declares that he failed to see her in any one of them. He admits, at the same time, that his search (conducted between two o'clock,

272

when he lost sight of her, and ten minutes past, when the train started) was, in the confusion of the moment, necessarily an imperfect one. But this latter circumstance, in my opinion, matters little. I as firmly disbelieve in the woman's actual departure by that train as if I had searched every one of the carriages myself; and you, I have no doubt, will entirely agree with me.

You now know how the disaster happened. Let us not waste time and words in lamenting it. The evil is done — and you and I together must find the way to remedy it.

What I have accomplished already, on my side, may be told in two words. Any hesitation I might have previously felt at trusting this delicate business in strangers' hands, was at an end the moment I heard Robert's news. I went back at once to the city, and placed the whole matter confidentially before my lawyers. The conference was a long one; and when I left the office it was past the post-hour, or I should have written to you on Monday instead of writing to-day. My interview with the lawyers was not very encouraging. They warn me plainly that serious difficulties stand in the way of our recovering the lost trace. But they have promised to do their best; and we have decided on the course to be taken — excepting one point on which we totally differ. I must tell you what this difference is; for while business keeps me away from Thorpe-Ambrose, you are the only person whom I can trust to put my convictions to the test.

The lawyers are of opinion, then, that the woman has been aware from the first that I was watching her; that there is, consequently, no present hope of her being rash enough to appear personally at Thorpe-Ambrose; that any mischief she may have it in contemplation to do, will be done in the first instance by deputy; and that the only wise course for Allan's friends and guardians to take, is to wait passively till events enlighten them. My own idea is diametrically opposed to this. After what has happened at the railway, I cannot deny that the woman must have discovered that I was watching her. But she has no reason to suppose that she has not succeeded in deceiving me; and I firmly believe she is bold enough to take us by surprise, and to win, or force her way into Allan's confidence before we are prepared to prevent her. You and you only (while I am detained in London) can decide whether I am right or wrong — and you can do it in this way. Ascertain at once whether any woman who is a stranger in the neighbourhood has appeared since Monday last, at, or near, Thorpe-Ambrose. If any such person has been observed (and nobody escapes observation in the country), take the first opportunity you can get of seeing her, and ask yourself if her face does, or does not, answer certain plain questions which I am now about to write down for you. You may depend on my accuracy. I saw the woman unveiled on more than one occasion – and the last time through an excellent glass.

1. Is her hair light brown, and (apparently) not very plentiful? 2. Is her forehead high, narrow, and sloping backward from the brow? 3. Are her eyebrows very faintly marked, and are her eyes small, and nearer dark than light – either grey or hazel (I have not seen her close enough to be certain which)? 4. Is her nose aquiline? 5. Are her lips thin, and is the upper lip long? 6. Does her complexion look like an originally fair complexion, which has deteriorated into a dull, sickly paleness? 7 (and lastly). Has she a retreating chin, and is there, on the left side of it, a mark of some kind – a mole or a scar, I can't say which?

I add nothing about her expression, for you may see her under circumstances which may partially alter it as seen by me. Test her by her features, which no circumstances can change. If there is a stranger in the neighbourhood, and if her face answers my seven questions – *you have found the woman! Go instantly, in that case, to* the nearest lawyer, and pledge my name and credit for whatever expenses may be incurred in keeping her under inspection night and day. Having done this, take the speediest means of communicating with me; and whether my business is finished or not, I will start for Norfolk by the first train.[2]

In any event – whether you succeed or whether you fail in confirming my suspicions – write to me by return of post. If it is only to tell me that you have received my letter, write! I am suffering under anxiety and suspense, separated as I am from Allan, which you alone can relieve. Having said this, I know you well enough to feel sure that I need say no more.

Always your friend,
DECIMUS BROCK.

Hardened by the fatalist conviction that now possessed him, Midwinter read the rector's confession of defeat from the first line to the last, without the slightest betrayal either of interest or surprise. The one part of the letter at which he looked back was the closing part of it. He read the last paragraph for the second time; and then waited for a moment, reflecting on it. 'I owe much to Mr Brock's kindness,' he thought; 'and I shall never see Mr Brock again. It is useless and hopeless – but he asks me to do it, and it shall be done. A moment's look at her will be enough – a moment's look at her with his letter in my hand – and a line to tell him that the woman is here!'

Again he stood hesitating at the half-opened door; again, the cruel necessity of writing his farewell to Allan stopped him, and stared him in the face.

He looked aside doubtingly at the rector's letter. 'I will write the two together,' he said. 'One may help the other.' His face flushed deep as the words escaped him. He was conscious of doing, what he had not done yet – of voluntarily putting off the evil hour; of making Mr Brock the pretext for gaining the last respite left, the respite of time.

The only sound that reached him through the open door was the sound of Allan stirring noisily in the next room. He stepped at once into the empty corridor; and, meeting no one on the stairs, made his way out of the house. The dread that his resolution to leave Allan might fail him, if he saw Allan again, was as vividly present to his mind in the morning as it had been all through the night. He drew a deep breath of relief as he descended the house steps – relief at having escaped the friendly greeting of the morning from the one human creature whom he loved!

He entered the shrubbery with Mr Brock's letter in his hand, and took the nearest way that led to the major's cottage. Not the slightest recollection was in his mind of the talk which had found its way to his ears during the night. His one reason for determining to see the woman, was the reason which the rector had put in his mind. The one remembrance that now guided him to the place in which she lived, was the remembrance of Allan's exclamation when he first identified the governess with the figure at the pool.

Arrived at the gate of the cottage, he stopped. The thought struck him that he might defeat his own object if he looked at the rector's questions in the woman's presence. Her suspicions would be probably roused, in the first instance, by his asking to see her (as he had determined to ask, with or without an excuse); and the appearance of the letter in his hand might confirm them. She might defeat him by instantly leaving the room. Determined to fix the description in his mind first, and then to confront her, he opened the letter; and, turning away slowly by the side of the house, read the seven questions which he felt absolutely assured beforehand the woman's face would answer.

In the morning quiet of the park, slight noises travelled far. A slight noise disturbed Midwinter over the letter.

He looked up and found himself on the brink of a broad grassy trench, having the park on one side and the high laurel hedge of an enclosure on the other. The enclosure evidently surrounded the back garden of the cottage; and the trench was intended to protect it from being damaged by the cattle grazing in the park. Listening carefully as the slight sound which had disturbed him grew fainter, he recognized in it the rustling of women's dresses. A few paces ahead, the trench was crossed by a bridge (closed by a wicket-gate) which connected the garden with the park. He passed through the gate, crossed the bridge, and, opening a door at the other end, found himself in a summer-house, thickly covered with creepers, and commanding a full view of the garden from end to end.

He looked, and saw the figures of two ladies walking slowly away from him towards the cottage. The shorter of the two failed to occupy his attention for an instant – he never stopped to think whether she was, or was not, the major's daughter. His eyes were riveted on the other figure; the figure that moved over the garden walk with the long lightly-falling dress, and the easy seductive grace. There, presented exactly as he had seen her once already – there, with her back again turned on him, was the Woman at the pool!

There was a chance that they might take another turn in the garden – a turn back towards the summer-house. On that chance Midwinter waited. No consciousness of the intrusion that he was committing had stopped him at the door of the summer-house; and no consciousness of it troubled him even now. Every finer sensibility in his nature, sinking under the cruel laceration of the past night, had ceased to feel. The dogged resolution to do what he had come to do, was the one animating influence left alive in him. He acted, he even looked, as the most stolid man living might have acted and looked in his place. He was self-possessed enough, in the interval of expectation, before governess and pupil reached the end of the walk, to open Mr Brock's letter, and to fortify his memory by a last look at the paragraph which described her face.

He was still absorbed over the description, when he heard the smooth rustle of the dresses travelling towards him again. Standing in the shadow of the summer-house, he waited while she lessened the distance between them. With her written portrait vividly impressed on his mind, and with the clear light of the morning to help him, his eyes questioned her as she came on; and these were the answers that her face gave him back.

The hair in the rector's description was light brown and not plentiful. This woman's hair, superbly luxuriant in its growth, was of the one unpardonably remarkable shade of colour which the prejudice of the Northern nations never entirely forgives – it was *red*![3] The forehead in the rector's description was high, narrow, and sloping backward from the brow; the eyebrows were faintly marked, and the eyes small, and in colour either grey or hazel. This woman's forehead was low, upright, and broad towards the temples; her eyebrows, at once strongly and delicately marked, were a shade darker than her hair; her eyes, large, bright, and well-opened, were of that purely blue colour, without a tinge in it of grey or green, so often presented to our admiration in pictures and books, so rarely met with in the living face. The nose in the rector's description was aquiline. The line of this woman's nose bent neither outward nor inward: it was the straight delicately-moulded nose (with the short upper lip beneath) of the ancient statues and busts. The lips in the rector's description were thin, and the upper lip long; the complexion was of a dull sickly paleness; the chin retreating, and the mark of a mole or a scar on the left side of it. This woman's lips were full, rich, and sensual. Her complexion was the lovely complexion which accompanies such hair as hers – so delicately bright in its rosier tints, so warmly and softly white in its gentler gradations of colour on the forehead and the neck. Her chin, round and dimpled, was pure of the slightest blemish in every part of it, and perfectly in line with her forehead to the end. Nearer and nearer, and fairer and fairer she came, in the glow of the morning light – the most startling, the most unanswerable contradiction that eye could see, or mind conceive, to the description in the rector's letter.

Both governess and pupil were close to the summer-house before they looked that way, and noticed Midwinter standing inside. The governess saw him first.

'A friend of yours, Miss Milroy?' she asked quietly, without starting, or betraying any sign of surprise.

Neelie recognized him instantly. Prejudiced against Midwinter by his conduct when his friend had introduced him at the cottage, she now fairly detested him as the unlucky first cause of her misunderstanding with Allan at the picnic. Her face flushed, and she drew back from the summer-house with an expression of merciless surprise.

'He is a friend of Mr Armadale's,' she replied sharply. 'I don't know what he wants, or why he is here.'

'A friend of Mr Armadale's!' The governess's face lit up with a suddenly-roused interest as she repeated the words. She returned

Midwinter's look, still steadily fixed on her, with equal steadiness on her side.

'For my part,' pursued Neelie, resenting Midwinter's insensibility to her presence on the scene, 'I think it a great liberty to treat papa's garden as if it was the open park!'

The governess turned round, and gently interposed.

'My dear Miss Milroy,' she remonstrated, 'there are certain distinctions to be observed. This gentleman is a friend of Mr Armadale's. You could hardly express yourself more strongly, if he was a perfect stranger.'

'I express my opinion,' retorted Neelie, chafing under the satirically indulgent tone in which the governess addressed her. 'It's a matter of taste, Miss Gwilt; and tastes differ.' She turned away petulantly, and walked back by herself to the cottage.

'She is very young,' said Miss Gwilt, appealing with a smile to Midwinter's forbearance; 'and, as you must see for yourself, sir, she is a spoilt child.' She paused – showed, for an instant only, her surprise at Midwinter's strange silence and strange persistency in keeping his eyes still fixed on her – then set herself, with a charming grace and readiness, to help him out of the false position in which he stood. 'As you have extended your walk thus far,' she resumed, 'perhaps you will kindly favour me, on your return, by taking a message to your friend? Mr Armadale has been so good as to invite me to see the Thorpe-Ambrose gardens this morning. Will you say that Major Milroy permits me to accept the invitation (in company with Miss Milroy) between ten and eleven o'clock?' For a moment her eyes rested, with a renewed look of interest, on Midwinter's face. She waited, still in vain, for an answering word from him – smiled, as if his extraordinary silence amused rather than angered her – and followed her pupil back to the cottage.

It was only when the last trace of her had disappeared that Midwinter roused himself, and attempted to realize the position in which he stood. The revelation of her beauty was in no respect answerable for the breathless astonishment which had held him spell-bound up to this moment. The one clear impression she had produced on him thus far, began and ended with his discovery of the astounding contradiction that her face offered, in one feature after another, to the description in Mr Brock's letter. All beyond this was vague and misty – a dim consciousness of a tall, elegant woman, and of kind words, modestly and gracefully spoken to him, and nothing more.

He advanced a few steps into the garden, without knowing why –

stopped, glancing hither and thither like a man lost – recognized the summer-house by an effort, as if years had elapsed since he had seen it – and made his way out again, at last, into the park. Even here, he wandered first in one direction, then in another. His mind was still reeling under the shock that had fallen on it; his perceptions were all confused. Something kept him mechanically in action, walking eagerly without a motive, walking he knew not where.

A far less sensitively organized man might have been overwhelmed, as he was overwhelmed now, by the immense, the instantaneous revulsion of feeling which the event of the last few minutes had wrought in his mind.

At the memorable instant when he had opened the door of the summer-house, no confusing influence troubled his faculties. Right or wrong, in all that related to his position towards his friend, he had reached an absolutely definite conclusion, by an absolutely definite process of thought. The whole strength of the motive which had driven him into the resolution to part from Allan, rooted itself in the belief that he had seen at Hurle Mere the fatal fulfilment of the first Vision of the Dream. And this belief, in its turn, rested, necessarily, on the conviction that the woman who was the one survivor of the tragedy in Madeira, must be also inevitably the woman whom he had seen standing in the Shadow's place at the pool. Firm in that persuasion, he had himself compared the object of his distrust and of the rector's distrust with the description written by the rector himself – a description, carefully minute, by a man entirely trustworthy – and his own eyes had informed him that the woman whom he had seen at the Mere, and the woman whom Mr Brock had identified in London, were not one, but Two. In the place of the Dream-Shadow, there had stood, on the evidence of the rector's letter, not the instrument of the Fatality – but a stranger!

No such doubts as might have troubled a less superstitious man, were started in *his* mind by the discovery that had now opened on him.

It never occurred to him to ask himself, whether a stranger might not be the appointed instrument of the Fatality, now when the letter had persuaded him that a stranger had been revealed as the figure in the dream-landscape. No such idea entered, or could enter, his mind. The one woman, whom *his* superstition dreaded, was the woman who had entwined herself with the lives of the two Armadales in the first generation, and with the fortunes of the two Armadales in the second – who was at once the marked object of his father's death-bed warning, and the first cause of the family calamities which had opened Allan's way to the Thorpe-Ambrose estate[4] – the woman, in a word, whom he would have known instinctively, but for Mr Brock's letter, to be the woman whom he had now actually seen.

Looking at events as they had just happened, under the influence of the misapprehension into which the rector had innocently misled him, his mind saw and seized its new conclusion instantaneously; acting precisely as it had acted in the past time of his interview with Mr Brock at the Isle of Man.

Exactly as he had once declared it to be an all-sufficient refutation of the idea of the Fatality; that he had never met with the timber-ship in any of his voyages at sea – so he now seized on the similarly derived conclusion, that the whole claim of the Dream to a supernatural origin stood self-refuted by the disclosure of a stranger in the Shadow's place. Once started from this point – once encouraged to let his love for Allan influence him undividedly again – his mind hurried along the whole resulting chain of thought at lightning speed. If the Dream was proved to be no longer a warning from the other world, it followed, inevitably, that accident and not fate had led the way to the night on the Wreck, and that all the events which had happened since Allan and he had parted from Mr Brock, were events in themselves harmless, which his superstition had distorted from their proper shape. In less than a moment, his mobile imagination had taken him back to the morning at Castletown when he had revealed to the rector the secret of his name; when he had declared to the rector, with his father's letter before his eyes, the better faith that was in him. Now once more, he felt his heart holding firmly by the bond of brotherhood between Allan and himself; now once more he could say with the eager sincerity of the old time, 'If the thought of leaving him breaks my heart, the thought of leaving him is wrong!' As that nobler conviction possessed itself again of his mind – quieting the tumult, clearing the confusion within him – the house at Thorpe-Ambrose, with Allan on the steps, waiting and looking for him, opened on his eyes through the trees. A sense of illimitable relief lifted his eager spirit high above the cares, and doubts, and fears that had oppressed it so long; and showed him once more the better and brighter future of his early dreams. His eyes filled with tears, and he pressed the rector's letter, in his wild passionate way to his lips, as he looked at Allan through the vista of the trees. 'But for this morsel of paper,' he thought, 'my life might have been one long sorrow to me, and my father's crime might have parted us for ever!'

*

Such was the result of the stratagem which had shown the housemaid's face to Mr Brock as the face of Miss Gwilt. And so – by shaking Midwinter's trust in his own superstition, in the one case in which that superstition pointed to the truth – did Mother Oldershaw's cunning triumph over difficulties and dangers, which had never been contemplated by Mother Oldershaw herself.

CHAPTER XI

MISS GWILT AMONG THE QUICKSANDS[1]

1. – *From the Reverend Decimus Brock to Ozias Midwinter*

Thursday.

MY DEAR MIDWINTER, – No words can tell what a relief it was to me to get your letter this morning, and what a happiness I honestly feel in having been, thus far, proved to be in the wrong. The precautions you have taken in case the woman should still confirm my apprehensions by venturing herself at Thorpe-Ambrose, seem to me to be all that can be desired. You are no doubt sure to hear of her from one or other of the people in the lawyer's office, whom you have asked to inform you of the appearance of a stranger in the town.

I am the more pleased at finding how entirely I can trust you in this matter – for I am likely to be obliged to leave Allan's interests longer than I supposed solely in your hands. My visit to Thorpe-Ambrose must, I regret to say, be deferred for two months. The only-one of my brother-clegymen in London, who is able to take my duty for me, cannot make it convenient to remove with his family to Somersetshire before that time. I have no alternative but to finish my business here, and be back at my rectory on Saturday next. If anything happens, you will of course instantly communicate with me – and, in that case, be the inconvenience what it may, I must leave home for Thorpe-Ambrose. If, on the other hand, all goes more smoothly than my own obstinate apprehensions will allow me to suppose, then Allan (to whom I have written) must not expect to see me till this day two months.

No result has, up to this time, rewarded our exertions to recover the trace lost at the railway. I will keep my letter open, however, until post-time, in case the next few hours bring any news.

Always truly yours,
DECIMUS BROCK.

P.S. – I have just heard from the lawyers. They have found out the name the woman passed by in London. If this discovery (not a very important one, I am afraid,) suggests any new course of proceeding to you, pray act on it at once. The name is – Miss Gwilt.

2. – *From Miss Gwilt to Mrs Oldershaw*

The Cottage, Thorpe-Ambrose,
Saturday, June 28th.

IF you will promise not to be alarmed, Mamma Oldershaw, I will begin this letter in a very odd way, by copying a page of a letter written by somebody else. You have an excellent memory, and you may not have forgotten that I received a note from Major Milroy's mother (after she engaged me as governess), on Monday last. It was dated and signed; and here it is, as far as the first page: 'June 23rd, 1851. Dear Madam, – Pray excuse my troubling you, before you go to Thorpe-Ambrose, with a word more about the habits observed in my son's household. When I had the pleasure of seeing you at two o'clock to-day, in Kingsdown Crescent, I had another appointment in a distant part of London at three; and, in the hurry of the moment, one or two little matters escaped me, which I think I ought to impress on your attention.' The rest of the letter is not of the slightest importance, but the lines that I have just copied, are well worthy of all the attention you can bestow on them. They have saved me from discovery, my dear, before I have been a week in Major Milroy's service!

It happened no later than yesterday evening, and it began and ended in this manner, –

There is a gentleman here (of whom I shall have more to say presently), who is an intimate friend of young Armadale's, and who bears the strange name of Midwinter. He contrived yesterday to speak to me alone in the park. Almost as soon as he opened his lips, I found that my name had been discovered in London (no doubt by the Somersetshire clergyman); and that Mr Midwinter had been chosen (evidently by the same person) to identify the Miss Gwilt who had vanished from Brompton, with the Miss Gwilt who had appeared at Thorpe-Ambrose. You foresaw this danger, I remember; but you could scarcely have imagined that the exposure would threaten me so soon.

I spare you the details of our conversation, to come to the end. Mr Midwinter put the matter very delicately, declaring, to my great surprise, that he felt quite certain himself, that I was not the Miss Gwilt of whom his friend was in search; and that he only acted as he did out of regard to the anxiety of a person whose wishes he was bound to respect. Would I assist him, in setting that anxiety completely at rest, so far as I was concerned, by kindly answering one plain question – which he had no other right to ask me than the right my indulgence might give him? The lost 'Miss Gwilt' had been missed on Monday last, at two o'clock, in the crowd on the platform of the North-Western Railway, in Euston Square. Would I authorize him to say, that on that day, and at that hour, the Miss Gwilt who was Major Milroy's governess, had never been near the place?

I need hardly tell you that I seized the fine opportunity he had given me of disarming all future suspicion. I took a high tone on the spot, and met him with the old lady's letter. He politely refused to look at it. I insisted on his looking at it. 'I don't choose to be mistaken,' I said, 'for a woman who may be a bad character, because she happens to bear, or to have assumed, the same name as mine. I insist on your reading the first part of this letter for my satisfaction, if not for your own.' He was obliged to comply – and there was the proof, in the old lady's own handwriting, that at two o'clock on Monday last, she and I were together in Kingsdown Crescent, which any directory would tell him is a 'crescent' in Bayswater! I leave you to imagine his apologies, and the perfect sweetness with which I received them.

I might, of course, if I had not preserved the letter, have referred him to you, or to the major's mother with similar results. As it is, the object has been gained without trouble or delay. *I have*

been proved not to be myself;[2] and one of the many dangers that
threatened me at Thorpe-Ambrose, is a danger blown over from
this moment. Your housemaid's face may not be a very handsome
one; but there is no denying that it has done us excellent service.

So much for the past; now for the future. You shall hear how I get
on with the people about me; and you shall judge for yourself
what the chances are, for and against my becoming mistress of
Thorpe-Ambrose.

Let me begin with young Armadale – because it is beginning
with good news. I have produced the right impression on him
already, and heaven knows *that* is nothing to boast of! Any
moderately good-looking woman who chose to take the trouble,
could make him fall in love with her. He is a rattle-pated young
fool – one of those noisy, rosy, light-haired, good-tempered men,
whom I particularly detest. I had a whole hour alone with him in
a boat, the first day I came here, and I have made good use of my
time, I can tell you, from that day to this. The only difficulty with
him is the difficulty of concealing my own feelings – especially
when he turns my dislike of him into downright hatred, by
sometimes reminding me of his mother. I really never saw a man
whom I could use so ill, if I had the opportunity. He will give me
the opportunity, I believe, if no accident happens, sooner than we
calculated on. I have just returned from a party at the great
house, in celebration of the rent-day dinner, and the squire's
attentions to me, and my modest reluctance to receive them, have
already excited general remark.

My pupil, Miss Milroy, comes next. She too is rosy and foolish;
and, what is more, awkward and squat and freckled and ill-
tempered and ill-dressed. No fear of *her*, though she hates me like
poison, which is a great comfort, for I get rid of her out of lesson-
time and walking-time. It is perfectly easy to see that she has
made the most of her opportunities with young Armadale (opportunities, by-the-by, which we never calculated on); and that she
has been stupid enough to let him slip through her fingers. When
I tell you that she is obliged, for the sake of appearances, to go
with her father and me to the little entertainments at Thorpe-
Ambrose, and to see how young Armadale admires me, you will
understand the kind of place I hold in her affections. She would
try me past all endurance, if I didn't see that I aggravate her by
keeping my temper – so of course I keep it. If I do break out, it

will be over our lessons – not over our French, our grammar, history, and globes – but over our music. No words can say how I feel for her poor piano. Half the musical girls in England ought to have their fingers chopped off, in the interests of society – and if I had my way, Miss Milroy's fingers should be executed first.

As for the major, I can hardly stand higher in his estimation than I stand already. I am always ready to make his breakfast – and his daughter is not. I can always find things for him when he loses them – and his daughter can't. I never yawn when he proses – and his daughter does. I like the poor dear harmless old gentleman; so I won't say a word more about him.

Well, here is a fair prospect for the future surely? My good Oldershaw, there never was a prospect yet, without an ugly place in it. *My* prospect has two ugly places in it. The name of one of them is, Mrs Milroy; and the name of the other is, Mr Midwinter.

Mrs Milroy first. Before I had been five minutes in the cottage, on the day of my arrival, what do you think she did? She sent down stairs, and asked to see me. The message startled me a little – after hearing from the old lady, in London, that her daughter-in-law was too great a sufferer to see anybody – but of course when I got her message, I had no choice but to go upstairs to the sick-room. I found her bedridden with an incurable spinal complaint, and a really horrible object to look at – but with all her wits about her; and, if I am not greatly mistaken, as deceitful a woman, with as vile a temper, as you could find anywhere, in all your long experience. Her excessive politeness, and her keeping her own face in the shade of the bed-curtains while she contrived to keep mine in the light, put me on my guard the moment I entered the room. We were more than half an hour together, without my stepping into any one of the many clever little traps she laid for me. The only mystery in her behaviour, which I failed to see through at the time, was her perpetually asking me to bring her things (things she evidently did not want) from different parts of the room.

Since then, events have enlightened me. My first suspicions were raised by overhearing some of the servants' gossip; and I have been confirmed in my opinion by the conduct of Mrs Milroy's nurse. On the few occasions when I have happened to be alone with the major, the nurse has also happened to want something of her master, and has invariably forgotten to announce her appearance by knocking at the door. Do you understand now, why Mrs Milroy sent for me the moment I got into the house, and what she wanted, when she kept me going backwards and forwards, first for one thing and then for another? There is hardly an attractive light in which my face and figure can be seen, in which that woman's jealous eyes have not studied them already. I am no longer puzzled to know why the father and daughter started, and looked at each other, when I was first presented to them – or why the servants still stare at me with a mischievous expectation in their eyes, when I ring the bell and ask them to do anything. It is useless to disguise the truth, Mother Oldershaw, between you and me. When I went upstairs into that sickroom, I marched blindfold into the clutches of a jealous woman. If Mrs Milroy *can* turn me out of the house, Mrs Milroy *will* – and, morning and night, she has nothing else to do in that bed-prison of hers but to find out the way.

In this awkward position, my own cautious conduct is admirably seconded by the dear old major's perfect insensibility. His wife's jealousy of him is as monstrous a delusion as any that could be found in a madhouse – it is the growth of her own vile temper, under the aggravation of an incurable illness. The poor man hasn't a thought beyond his mechanical pursuits; and I don't believe he knows at this moment, whether I am a handsome woman or not. With this chance to help me, I may hope to set the nurse's intrusions and the mistress's contrivances at defiance – for a time, at any rate. But you know what a jealous woman is, and I think I know what Mrs Milroy is; and I own I shall breathe more freely, on the day when young Armadale opens his foolish lips to some purpose, and sets the major advertising for a new governess.

Armadale's name reminds me of Armadale's friend. There is more danger threatening in that quarter; and, what is worse, I don't feel half as well armed beforehand against Mr Midwinter, as I do against Mrs Milroy.

Everything about this man is more or less mysterious, which I don't like to begin with. How does he come to be in the confidence of the Somersetshire clergyman? How much has that clergyman told him? How is it that he was so firmly persuaded, when he spoke to me in the park, that I was not the Miss Gwilt of whom his friend was in search? I haven't the ghost of an answer to give to any of those three questions. I can't even discover who he is, or how he and young Armadale first became acquainted. I hate him. No, I don't; I only want to find out about him. He is very young

– little and lean, and active and dark, with bright black eyes which say to me plainly, 'We belong to a man with brains in his head and a will of his own; a man who hasn't always been hanging about a country house, in attendance on a fool.' Yes; I am positively certain Mr Midwinter has done something or suffered something, in his past life, young as he is; and I would give I don't know what to get at it. Don't resent my taking up so much space in writing about him. He has influence enough over young Armadale to be a very awkward obstacle in my way, unless I can secure his good opinion at starting.

Well, you may ask, and what is to prevent your securing his good opinion? I am sadly afraid, Mother Oldershaw, I have got it on terms I never bargained for. I am sadly afraid the man is in love with me already.

Don't toss your head, and say, 'Just like her vanity!' After the horrors I have gone through, I have no vanity left; and a man who admires me, is a man who makes me shudder. There was a time, I own – Pooh! what am I writing? Sentiment, I declare! Sentiment to *you*! Laugh away, my dear. As for me, I neither laugh nor cry; I mend my pen, and get on with my – what do the men call it? – my report.

The only thing worth inquiring is, whether I am right or wrong in my idea of the impression I have made on him. Let me see – I have been four times in his company. The first time was in the major's garden, where we met unexpectedly, face to face. He stood looking at me, like a man petrified, without speaking a word. The effect of my horrid red hair, perhaps? Quite likely – let us lay it on my hair. The second time was in going over the Thorpe-Ambrose grounds, with young Armadale on one side of me, and my pupil (in the sulks) on the other. Out comes Mr Midwinter to join us – though he had work to do in the steward's office, which he had never been known to neglect on any other occasion. Laziness, possibly? or an attachment to Miss Milroy? I can't say; we will lay it on Miss Milroy, if you like – I only know he did nothing but look at *me*. The third time was at the private interview in the park, which I have told you of already. I never saw a man so agitated at putting a delicate question to a woman in my life. But *that* might have been only awkwardness; and his perpetually looking back after me when we had parted, might have been only looking back at the view. Lay it on the view; by all means lay it on the view! The fourth time was this very evening, at the little party. They made me play; and, as the piano was a good one, I did my best. All the company crowded round me, and paid me their compliments (my charming pupil paid hers, with a face like a cat's, just before she spits), except Mr Midwinter. *He* waited till it was time to go, and then he caught me alone for a moment in the hall. There was just time for him to take my hand, and say two words. Shall I tell you *how* he took my hand, and what his voice sounded like when he spoke? Quite needless! You have always told me that the late Mr Oldershaw doated on you. Just recall the first time he took your hand, and whispered a word or two addressed to your private ear. To what did you attribute his behaviour on that occasion? I have no doubt, if you had been playing on the piano in the course of the evening, you would have attributed it entirely to the music!

No! you may take my word for it, the harm is done. *This* man is no rattle-pated fool, who changes his fancies as readily as he changes his clothes – the fire that lights those big black eyes of his, is not an easy fire, when a woman has once kindled it, for that woman to put out. I don't wish to discourage you; I don't say the chances are against us. But with Mrs Milroy threatening me on one side, and Mr Midwinter on the other, the worst of all risks to run, is the risk of losing time. Young Armadale has hinted already, as well as such a lout can hint, at a private interview! Miss Milroy's eyes are sharp, and the nurse's eyes are sharper; and I shall lose my place if they either of them find me out. No matter! I must take my chance, and give him the interview. Only let me get him alone, only let me escape the prying eyes of the women, and – if his friend doesn't come between us – I answer for the result!

In the meantime, have I anything more to tell you? Are there any other people in our way at Thorpe-Ambrose? Not another creature! None of the resident families call here, young Armadale being, most fortunately, in bad odour in the neighbourhood. There are no handsome highly-bred women to come to the house, and no persons of consequence to protest against his attentions to a governess. The only guests he could collect at his party to-night were the lawyer and his family (a wife, a son, and two daughters), and a deaf old woman, and *her* son – all perfectly unimportant people, and all obedient humble servants of the stupid young squire.

Talking of obedient humble servants, there is one other person established here, who is employed in the steward's office – a miserable, shabby, dilapidated old man, named Bashwood. He is a perfect stranger to me, and I am evidently a perfect stranger to him; for he has been asking the housemaid at the cottage who I am. It is paying no great compliment to myself to confess it; but it is not the less true that I produced the most extraordinary impression on this feeble old creature the first time he saw me. He turned all manner of colours, and stood trembling and staring at me, as if there was something perfectly frightful in my face. I felt quite startled for the moment – for of all the ways in which men have looked at me, no man ever looked at me in that way before. Did you ever see the boa-constrictor fed at the Zoological Gardens?³ They put a live rabbit into his cage, and there is a moment when the two creatures look at each other. I declare Mr Bashwood reminded me of the rabbit!

Why do I mention this? I don't know why. Perhaps I have been writing too long, and my head is beginning to fail me. Perhaps Mr Bashwood's manner of admiring me strikes my fancy by its novelty. Absurd! I am exciting myself, and troubling you about nothing. Oh, what a weary, long letter I have written! and how brightly the stars look at me through the window – and how awfully quiet the night is! Send me some more of those sleeping drops, and write me one of your nice, wicked, amusing letters. You shall hear from me again as soon as I know a little better how it is all likely to end. Good night, and keep a corner in your stony old heart for

L. G.

3. – *From Mrs Oldershaw to Miss Gwilt*

Diana Street, Pimlico, Monday.

MY DEAR LYDIA, – I am in no state of mind to write you an amusing letter. Your news is very discouraging and the recklessness of your tone quite alarms me. Consider the money I have already advanced, and the interests we both have at stake. Whatever else you are, don't be reckless, for heaven's sake!

What can I do? – I ask myself, as a woman of business, what can I do to help you? I can't give you advice, for I am not on the spot, and I don't know how circumstances may alter from one day to another. Situated as we are now, I can only be useful in one way; I can discover a new obstacle that threatens you, and I think I can remove it.

You say, with great truth, that there never was a prospect yet without an ugly place in it, and that there are two ugly places in your prospect. My dear, there may be *three* ugly places, if I don't bestir myself to prevent it; and the name of the third place will be – Brock! Is it possible you can refer, as you have done, to the Somersetshire clergyman, and not see that the progress you make with young Armadale will be sooner or later, reported to him by young Armadale's friend? Why, now I think of it, you are doubly at the parson's mercy! You are at the mercy of any fresh suspicion which may bring him into the neighbourhood himself at a day's notice; and you are at the mercy of his interference the moment he hears that the squire is committing himself with a neighbour's governess. If I can do nothing else, I can keep this additional difficulty out of your way. And, oh, Lydia, with what alacrity I shall exert myself, after the manner in which the old wretch insulted me when I told him that pitiable story in the street! I declare I tingle with pleasure at this new prospect of making a fool of Mr Brock.

And how is it to be done? Just as we have done it already, to be sure. He has lost 'Miss Gwilt' (otherwise my housemaid), hasn't he? Very well. He shall find her again, wherever he is now, suddenly settled within easy reach of him. As long as *she* stops in the place, *he* will stop in it; and as we know he is not at Thorpe-Ambrose, there you are free of him! The old gentleman's suspicions have given us a great deal of trouble so far. Let us turn them to some profitable account at last; let us tie him, by his suspicions, to my housemaid's apron-string. Most refreshing. Quite a moral retribution, isn't it?

The only help I need trouble you for, is help you can easily give. Find out from Mr Midwinter where the parson is now, and let me know by return of post. If he is in London, I will personally assist my housemaid in the necessary mystification of him. If he is anywhere else, I will send her after him, accompanied by a person on whose discretion I can implicitly rely.

You shall have the sleeping-drops to-morrow. In the meantime, I say at the end what I said at the beginning – no recklessness! Don't encourage poetical feelings by looking at the stars; and don't talk about the night being awfully quiet. There are people (in Observatories) paid to look at the stars for you – leave it to them. And as for the night, do what Providence intended you to do with the night when Providence provided you with eyelids – go to sleep in it.

Affectionately yours,
MARIA OLDERSHAW.

4. – *From the Reverend Decimus Brock to Ozias Midwinter*

Boscombe Rectory, West Somerset,
Thursday, July 3rd.

MY DEAR MIDWINTER, – One line before the post goes out, to relieve you of all sense of responsibility at Thorpe-Ambrose, and to make my apologies to the lady who lives as governess in Major Milroy's family.

The Miss Gwilt – or perhaps I ought to say, the woman calling herself by that name – has, to my unspeakable astonishment, openly made her appearance here, in my own parish! She is staying at the inn, accompanied by a plausible-looking man, who passes as her brother. What this audacious proceeding really means – unless it marks a new step in the conspiracy against Allan, taken under new advice – is, of course, more than I can yet find out.

My own idea is, that they have recognized the impossibility of getting at Allan, without finding me (or you) as an obstacle in their way; and that they are going to make a virtue of necessity by boldly trying to open their communications through me. The man looks capable of any stretch of audacity; and both he and the woman had the impudence to bow when I met them in the village half an hour since. They have been making inquiries already about Allan's mother – here, where her exemplary life may set their closest scrutiny at defiance. If they will only attempt to extort money, as the price of the woman's silence on the subject of poor Mrs Armadale's conduct in Madeira at the time of her marriage, they will find me well prepared for them beforehand. I have written by this post to my lawyers, to send a competent man to assist me; and he will stay at the rectory, in any character which he thinks it safest to assume under present circumstances.

You shall hear what happens in the next day or two.

Always truly yours,
DECIMUS BROCK.

CHAPTER XII

THE CLOUDING OF THE SKY

Nine days had passed, and the tenth day was nearly at an end, since Miss Gwilt and her pupil had taken their morning walk in the cottage garden.

The night was overcast. Since sunset, there had been signs in the sky from which the popular forecast had predicted rain. The reception-rooms at the great house were all empty and dark. Allan was away, passing the evening with the Milroys; and Midwinter was waiting his return – not where Midwinter usually waited, among the books in the library – but in the little back room which Allan's mother had inhabited in the last days of her residence at Thorpe-Ambrose.[1]

Nothing had been taken away, but much had been added to the room, since Midwinter had first seen it. The books which Mrs Armadale had left behind her, the furniture, the old matting on the floor, the old paper on the walls, were all undisturbed. The statuette of Niobe still stood on its bracket, and the French window still opened on the garden. But, now, to the relics left by the mother, were added the personal possessions belonging to the son. The wall, bare hitherto, was decorated with water-colour drawings – with a portrait of Mrs Armadale, supported on one side by a view of the old house in Somersetshire, and on the other by a picture of the yacht. Among the books which bore in faded ink Mrs Armadale's inscription, 'From my father,' were other books inscribed in the same handwriting, in brighter ink, 'To my son.' Hanging to the wall, ranged on the chimney-piece, scattered over the table, were a host of little objects, some associated with Allan's past life, others necessary to his daily pleasures and pursuits, and all plainly testifying that the room which he habitually occupied at Thorpe-Ambrose was the very room which had once recalled to Midwinter the second vision of the dream. Here, strangely unmoved by the scene around him, so lately the object of his superstitious distrust, Allan's friend now waited composedly for Allan's return – and here, more strangely still, he looked on a change in the household arrangements, due in the first instance entirely to himself. His own lips had revealed the discovery which he had made on the first morning in the new house; his own voluntary act had induced the son to establish himself in the mother's room.

Under what motives had he spoken the words? Under no motives which were not the natural growth of the new interests and the new hopes that now animated him.

The entire change wrought in his convictions by the memorable event that had brought him face to face with Miss Gwilt, was a change which it was not in his nature to hide from Allan's knowledge. He had spoken openly, and had spoken as it was in his character to speak. The merit of conquering his superstition was a merit which he shrank from claiming, until he had first unsparingly exposed that superstition in its worst and weakest aspects to view. It was only after he had unreservedly acknowledged the impulse under which he had left Allan at the Mere, that he had taken credit to himself for the new point of view from which he could now look at the Dream. Then, and not till then, he had spoken of the fulfilment of the first Vision, as the doctor at the Isle of Man might have spoken of it – he had asked, as the doctor might have asked, Where was the wonder of their seeing a pool at sunset, when they had a whole network of pools within a few hours' drive of them? and what was there extraordinary in discovering a woman at the Mere, when there were roads that led to it, and villages in its neighbourhood, and boats employed on it, and pleasure parties visiting it? So again, he had waited to vindicate the firmer resolution with which he looked to the future, until he had first revealed all that he now saw himself of the errors of the past. The abandonment of his friend's interests, the unworthiness of the confidence that had given him the steward's place, the forgetfulness of the trust that Mr Brock had reposed in him, all implied in the one idea of leaving Allan, were all pointed out. The glaring self-contradictions betrayed in accepting the Dream as the revelation of a fatality, and in attempting to escape that fatality by an exertion of free will – in toiling to store up knowledge of the steward's duties for the future, and in shrinking from letting the future find him in Allan's house – were, in their turn, unsparingly exposed. To every error, to every inconsistency, he resolutely confessed, before he attempted to assert the clearer and better mind that was in him – before he ventured on the last simple appeal which closed all, 'Will you trust me in the future? will you forgive and forget the past?'

A man who could thus open his whole heart, without one lurking reserve inspired by consideration for himself, was not a man to forget any minor act of concealment of which his weakness might have led him to be guilty towards his friend. It lay heavy on Midwinter's conscience that he had kept secret from Allan a discovery which he ought in

Allan's dearest interests to have revealed – the discovery of his mother's room.

But one doubt had closed his lips – the doubt whether Mrs Armadale's conduct in Madeira had been kept secret on her return to England. Careful inquiry, first among the servants, then among the tenantry, careful consideration of the few reports current at the time, as repeated to him by the few persons left who remembered them, convinced him at last that the family secret had been successfully kept within the family limits. Once satisfied that whatever inquiries the son might make would lead to no disclosure which could shake his respect for his mother's memory, Midwinter had hesitated no longer. He had taken Allan into the room, and had shown him the books on the shelves, and all that the writing in the books disclosed. He had said plainly, 'My one motive for not telling you this before, sprang from my dread of interesting you in the room which I looked at with horror as the second of the scenes pointed at in the Dream. Forgive me this also, and you will have forgiven me all.'

With Allan's love for his mother's memory, but one result could follow such an avowal as this. He had liked the little room from the first as a pleasant contrast to the oppressive grandeur of the other rooms at Thorpe-Ambrose – and now that he knew what associations were connected with it, his resolution was at once taken to make it especially his own. The same day, all his personal possessions were collected and arranged in his mother's room – in Midwinter's presence, and with Midwinter's assistance given to the work.

Under those circumstances had the change now wrought in the household arrangements been produced; and in this way had Midwinter's victory over his own fatalism – by making Allan the daily occupant of a room which he might otherwise hardly ever have entered – actually favoured the fulfilment of the Second Vision of the Dream.

The hour wore on quietly as Allan's friend sat waiting for Allan's return. Sometimes reading, sometimes thinking placidly, he wiled away the time. No vexing cares, no boding doubts troubled him now. The rent-day, which he had once dreaded, had come and gone harmlessly. A friendlier understanding had been established between Allan and his tenants; Mr Bashwood had proved himself to be worthy of the confidence reposed in him; the Pedgifts, father and son, had amply justified their client's good opinion of them. Wherever Midwinter looked, the prospect was bright, the future was without a cloud.

He trimmed the lamp on the table beside him, and looked out at the night. The stable-clock was chiming the half-hour past eleven as he walked to the window, and the first raindrops were beginning to fall. He had his hand on the bell, to summon the servant, and send him over to the cottage with an umbrella, when he was stopped by hearing the familiar footstep on the walk outside.

'How late you are!' said Midwinter, as Allan entered through the open French window. 'Was there a party at the cottage?'

'No! only ourselves. The time slipped away somehow.'

He answered in lower tones than usual, and sighed as he took his chair.

'You seem to be out of spirits?' pursued Midwinter. 'What's the matter?'

Allan hesitated. 'I may as well tell you,' he said, after a moment. 'It's nothing to be ashamed of; I only wonder you haven't noticed it before! There's a woman in it as usual – I'm in love.'

Midwinter laughed. 'Has Miss Milroy been more charming to-night than ever?' he asked, gaily.

'Miss Milroy!' repeated Allan. 'What are you thinking of! I'm not in love with Miss Milroy.'

'Who is it, then?'

'Who is it? What a question to ask! Who *can* it be but Miss Gwilt?'

There was a sudden silence. Allan sat listlessly, with his hands in his pockets, looking out through the open window at the falling rain. If he had turned towards his friend when he mentioned Miss Gwilt's name, he might possibly have been a little startled by the change he would have seen in Midwinter's face.

'I suppose you don't approve of it?' he said, after waiting a little.

There was no answer.

'It's too late to make objections,' proceeded Allan. 'I really mean it when I tell you I'm in love with her.'

'A fortnight since you were in love with Miss Milroy,' said the other in quiet, measured tones.

'Pooh! a mere flirtation. It's different this time. I'm in earnest about Miss Gwilt.'

He looked round as he spoke. Midwinter turned his face aside on the instant, and bent it over a book.

'I see you don't approve of the thing,' Allan went on. 'Do you object to her being only a governess? You can't do that, I'm sure. If you were in my place, her being only a governess wouldn't stand in the way with *you?*'

'No,' said Midwinter; 'I can't honestly say it would stand in the way

295

with me.' He gave the answer reluctantly, and pushed his chair back out of the light of the lamp.

'A governess is a lady who is not rich,' said Allan, in an oracular manner; 'and a duchess is a lady who is not poor. And that's all the difference I acknowledge between them. Miss Gwilt is older than I am – I don't deny that. What age do you guess her at, Midwinter? I say, seven or eight and twenty. What do you say?'

'Nothing. I agree with you.'

'Do you think seven or eight and twenty is too old for me? If you were in love with a woman yourself, you wouldn't think seven or eight and twenty too old – would you?'

'I can't say I should think it too old, if—'

'If you were really fond of her?'

Once more there was no answer.

'Well,' resumed Allan, 'if there's no harm in her being only a governess, and no harm in her being a little older than I am, what's the objection to Miss Gwilt?'

'I have made no objection.'

'I don't say you have. But you don't seem to like the notion of it, for all that.'

There was another pause. Midwinter was the first to break the silence this time.

'Are you sure of yourself, Allan?' he asked, with his face bent once more over the book; 'are you really attached to this lady? Have you thought seriously already of asking her to be your wife?'

'I am thinking seriously of it at this moment,' said Allan. 'I can't be happy – I can't live without her. Upon my soul, I worship the very ground she treads on.'

'How long—?' His voice faltered, and he stopped. 'How long,' he reiterated, 'have you worshipped the very ground she treads on?'

'Longer than you think for. I know I can trust you with all my secrets—'

'Don't trust me!'

'Nonsense! I *will* trust you. There is a little difficulty in the way, which I haven't mentioned yet. It's a matter of some delicacy, and I want to consult you about it. Between ourselves, I have had private opportunities with Miss Gwilt—'

Midwinter suddenly started to his feet, and opened the door.

'We'll talk of this to-morrow,' he said. 'Good-night.'

Allan looked round in astonishment. The door was closed again, and he was alone in the room.

'He has never shaken hands with me!' exclaimed Allan, looking bewildered at the empty chair.

As the words passed his lips the door opened, and Midwinter appeared again.

'We haven't shaken hands,' he said, abruptly. 'God bless you, Allan! We'll talk of it to-morrow. Good-night.'

Allan stood alone at the window, looking out at the pouring rain. He felt ill at ease, without knowing why.[2] 'Midwinter's ways get stranger and stranger,' he thought. 'What can he mean by putting me off till to-morrow, when I wanted to speak to him to-night?' He took up his bedroom candle a little impatiently − put it down again − and, walking back to the open window, stood looking out in the direction of the cottage. 'I wonder if she's thinking of me?' he said to himself softly.

She *was* thinking of him. She had just opened her desk to write to Mrs Oldershaw; and her pen had that moment traced the opening line: 'Make your mind easy. I have got him!'

CHAPTER XIII

EXIT

It rained all through the night; and when the morning came, it was raining still.

Contrary to his ordinary habit, Midwinter was waiting in the breakfast-room when Allan entered it. He looked worn and weary, but his smile was gentler, and his manner more composed than usual. To Allan's surprise he approached the subject of the previous night's conversation of his own accord as soon as the servant was out of the room.

'I am afraid you thought me very impatient and very abrupt with you last night,' he said. 'I will try to make amends for it this morning. I will hear everything you wish to say to me on the subject of Miss Gwilt.'

'I hardly like to worry you,' said Allan. 'You look as if you had had a bad night's rest.'

'I have not slept well for some time past,' replied Midwinter quietly. 'Something has been wrong with me. But I believe I have found out the way to put myself right again without troubling the doctors. Later in the morning I shall have something to say to you about this. Let us get back first to what you were talking of last night. You were speaking of some difficulty—' He hesitated, and finished the sentence in a tone so low that Allan failed to hear him. 'Perhaps it would be better,' he went on, 'if, instead of speaking to me, you spoke to Mr Brock?'

'I would rather speak to *you*,' said Allan. 'But tell me first, was I right or wrong last night in thinking you disapproved of my falling in love with Miss Gwilt?'

Midwinter's lean nervous fingers began to crumble the bread in his plate. His eyes looked away from Allan for the first time.

'If you have any objection,' persisted Allan, 'I should like to hear it.'

Midwinter suddenly looked up again, his cheeks turning ashy pale, and his glittering black eyes fixed full on Allan's face.

'You love her,' he said. 'Does *she* love *you*?'

'You won't think me vain?' returned Allan. 'I told you yesterday I had had private opportunities with her—'

Midwinter's eyes dropped again to the crumbs on his plate. 'I understand,' he interposed quickly. 'You were wrong last night. I had no objections to make.'

'Don't you congratulate me?' asked Allan, a little uneasily. 'Such a beautiful woman! such a clever woman!'

Midwinter held out his hand. 'I owe you more than mere congratulations,' he said. 'In anything which is for your happiness I owe you help.' He took Allan's hand, and wrung it hard. 'Can I help you?' he asked, growing paler and paler as he spoke.

'My dear fellow!' exclaimed Allan, 'what *is* the matter with you? Your hand is as cold as ice.'

Midwinter smiled faintly. 'I am always in extremes,' he said; 'my hand was as hot as fire the first time you took it at the old West-country inn. Come to that difficulty which you have not come to yet. You are young, rich, your own master – and she loves you. What difficulty can there be?'

Allan hesitated. 'I hardly know how to put it,' he replied. 'As you said just now, I love her, and she loves me – and yet there is a sort of strangeness between us. One talks a good deal about one's self, when one is in love – at least, I do. I've told her all about myself, and my mother, and how I came in for this place, and the rest of it. Well – though it doesn't strike me when we are together – it comes across me now and then, when I'm away from her, that she doesn't say much on her side. In fact, I know no more about her than you do.'

'Do you mean that you know nothing about Miss Gwilt's family and friends?'

'That's it, exactly.'

'Have you never asked her about them?'

'I said something of the sort the other day,' returned Allan; 'and I'm afraid, as usual, I said it in the wrong way. She looked – I can't quite tell you how; not exactly displeased, but – oh, what things words are! I'd give the world, Midwinter, if I could only find the right word when I want it, as well as you do.'

'Did Miss Gwilt say anything to you in the way of a reply?'

'That's just what I was coming to. She said, "I shall have a melancholy story to tell you one of these days, Mr Armadale, about myself and my family; but you look so happy, and the circumstances are so distressing, that I have hardly the heart to speak of it now." Ah, *she* can express herself – with the tears in her eyes, my dear fellow, with the tears in her eyes! Of course I changed the subject directly. And now the difficulty is how to get back to it, delicately, without making her cry again. We *must* get back to it, you know. Not on my account; I am quite content to marry her first and hear of her family misfortunes, poor thing, afterwards. But I know Mr Brock. If I can't satisfy him about her family when I write to tell him of this (which of course I must do), he will be dead against the whole thing. I'm my own master of course, and I can do as I like about it. But dear old Brock was such a good friend to my poor mother, and he has been such a good friend to me – you see what I mean, don't you?'

'Certainly, Allan; Mr Brock has been your second father. Any disagreement between you about such a serious matter as this, would be the saddest thing that could happen. You ought to satisfy him that Miss Gwilt is (what I am sure Miss Gwilt will prove to be) worthy, in every way worthy—' His voice sank in spite of him, and he left the sentence unfinished.

'Just my feeling in the matter!' Allan struck in glibly. 'Now we can come to what I particularly wanted to consult you about. If this was your case, Midwinter, you would be able to say the right words to her – you would put it delicately, even though you were putting it quite in the dark. I can't do that. I'm a blundering sort of fellow; and I'm horribly afraid, if I can't get some hint at the truth to help me at starting, of saying something to distress her. Family misfortunes are such tender subjects to touch on – especially with such a refined woman, such a tender-hearted woman, as Miss Gwilt. There may have been some dreadful death in the family – some relation who has disgraced himself – some infernal cruelty which has forced the poor thing out on the world as a governess. Well, turning it over in my mind, it struck me that the major might be able to put me on the right tack. It is quite possible that he might have been informed of Miss Gwilt's family circumstances before he engaged her – isn't it?'

'It is possible, Allan, certainly.'

'Just my feeling again! My notion is, to speak to the major. If I could only get the story from him first, I should know so much better how to speak to Miss Gwilt about it afterwards. You advise me to try the major, don't you?'

There was a pause before Midwinter replied. When he did answer it was a little reluctantly.

'I hardly know how to advise you, Allan,' he said. 'This is a very delicate matter.'

'I believe you would try the major, if you were in my place,' returned Allan reverting to his inveterately personal way of putting the question.

'Perhaps I might,' said Midwinter, more and more unwillingly.

'But if I did speak to the major, I should be very careful, in your place, not to put myself in a false position – I should be very careful to let no one suspect me of the meanness of prying into a woman's secrets behind her back.'

Allan's face flushed. 'Good heavens, Midwinter,' he exclaimed, 'who could suspect me of that?'

'Nobody, Allan, who really knows you.'

'The major knows me. The major is the last man in the world to misunderstand me. All I want him to do, is to help me (if he can) to speak about a delicate subject to Miss Gwilt, without hurting her feelings. Can anything be simpler between two gentlemen?'

Instead of replying, Midwinter, still speaking as constrainedly as ever, asked a question on his side. 'Do you mean to tell Major Milroy,' he said, 'what your intentions really are towards Miss Gwilt?'

Allan's manner altered. He hesitated and looked confused.

'I have been thinking of that,' he replied; 'and I mean to feel my way first, and then tell him or not afterwards, as matters turn out.'

A proceeding so cautious as this, was too strikingly inconsistent with Allan's character not to surprise any one who knew him. Midwinter showed his surprise plainly.

'You forget that foolish flirtation of mine with Miss Milroy,' Allan went on, more and more confusedly. 'The major may have noticed it, and may have thought I meant—well, what I didn't mean. It might be rather awkward, mightn't it, to propose to his face for his governess instead of his daughter?'

He waited for a word of answer, but none came. Midwinter opened his lips to speak, and suddenly checked himself. Allan, uneasy at his silence, doubly uneasy under certain recollections of the major's daughter which the conversation had called up, rose from the table, and shortened the interview a little impatiently.

'Come! come!' he said, 'don't sit there looking unutterable things − don't make mountains out of molehills. You have such an old, old head, Midwinter, on those young shoulders of yours. Let's have done with all these pros and cons. Do you mean to tell me in plain words, that it won't do to speak to the major?'

'I can't take the responsibility, Allan, of telling you that. To be plainer still, I can't feel confident of the soundness of any advice I may give you, in − in our present position towards each other. All I am sure of is, that I cannot possibly be wrong in entreating you to do two things.'

'What are they?'

'If you speak to Major Milroy, pray remember the caution I have given you! Pray think of what you say, before you say it!'

'I'll think − never fear! What next?'

'Before you take any serious step in this matter, write and tell Mr Brock. Will you promise me to do that?'

'With all my heart. Anything more?'

'Nothing more. I have said my last words.'

Allan led the way to the door. 'Come into my room,' he said, 'and I'll give you a cigar. The servants will be in here directly, to clear away; and I want to go on talking about Miss Gwilt.'

'Don't wait for me,' said Midwinter; 'I'll follow you in a minute or two.'

He remained seated until Allan had closed the door − then rose, and took from a corner of the room, where it lay hidden behind one of the curtains, a knapsack ready packed for travelling. As he stood at the window thinking, with the knapsack in his hand, a strangely old, careworn look stole over his face: he seemed to lose the last of his youth in an instant.

What the woman's quicker insight had discovered days since, the man's slower perception had only realized in the past night. The pang that had wrung him when he heard Allan's avowal, had set the truth self-revealed before Midwinter for the first time. He had been conscious of looking at Miss Gwilt with new eyes and a new mind, on the next occasion when they met after the memorable interview in Major Milroy's garden; he had been conscious of his growing interest thenceforth in her society, and his growing admiration of her beauty – but he had never until now known the passion that she had roused in him for what it really was. Knowing it at last, feeling it consciously in full possession of him, he had the courage which no man with a happier experience of life would have possessed – the courage to recall what Allan had said to him, and to look resolutely at the future through his own grateful remembrances of the past.

Steadfastly, through the sleepless hours of the night, he had contemplated the sacrifice of himself to the dearest interest of his friend, as part of the great debt of gratitude that he owed to Allan. Steadfastly he had bent his mind to the conviction that he must conquer the passion which had taken possession of him, for Allan's sake; and that the one way to conquer it was – to go. No after-doubt as to sacrifice had troubled him when morning came; and no after-doubt troubled him now. The one question that kept him hesitating was the question of leaving Thorpe-Ambrose. Though Mr Brock's letter relieved him from all necessity of keeping watch in Norfolk for a woman who was known to be in Somersetshire; though the duties of the steward's office were duties which might be safely left in Mr Bashwood's tried and trustworthy hands – still, admitting these considerations, his mind was not easy at the thought of leaving Allan, at a time when a crisis was approaching in Allan's life.

He slung the knapsack loosely over his shoulder, and put the question to his conscience for the last time. 'Can you trust yourself to see her, day by day, as you must see her – can you trust yourself to hear him talk of her, hour by hour, as you must hear him – if you stay in this house?' Again the answer came, as it had come all through the night. Again his heart warned him, in the very interests of the friendship that he held sacred, to go while the time was his own; to go before the woman who had possessed herself of his love had possessed herself of his power of self-sacrifice and his sense of gratitude as well.

He looked round the room mechanically, before he turned to leave it. Every remembrance of the conversation that had just taken place between Allan and himself pointed to the same conclusion, and warned him, as his own conscience had warned him, to go. Had he honestly mentioned any one of the objections which he, or any man, must have seen to Allan's attachment? Had he – as his knowledge of his friend's facile character bound him to do – warned Allan to distrust his own hasty impulses, and to test himself by time and absence, before he made sure that the happiness of his whole life was bound up in Miss Gwilt? No. The bare doubt whether, in speaking of these things, he could feel that he was speaking disinterestedly, had closed his lips, and would close his lips for the future, till the time for speaking had gone by. Was the right man to restrain Allan, the man who would have given the world, if he had it, to stand in Allan's place? There was but one plain course of action that an honest man and a grateful man could follow in the position in which he stood. Far removed from all chance of seeing her, and from all chance of hearing of her – alone with his own faithful recollection of what he owed to his friend – he might hope to fight it down, as he had fought down the tears in his childhood, under his gipsy master's stick; as he had fought down the misery of his lonely youth-time in the country bookseller's shop. 'I must go,' he said, as he turned wearily from the window, 'before she comes to the house again. I must go before another hour is over my head.'

With that resolution he left the room; and, in leaving it, took the irrevocable step from Present to Future.

The rain was still falling. The sullen sky, all round the horizon, still lowered watery and dark, when Midwinter, equipped for travelling, appeared in Allan's room.

'Good heavens!' cried Allan, pointing to the knapsack, 'what does *that* mean?'

'Nothing very extraordinary,' said Midwinter. 'It only means – good-by.'

'Good-by!' repeated Allan, starting to his feet in astonishment.

Midwinter put him back gently into his chair, and drew a seat near to it for himself.

'When you noticed that I looked ill this morning,' he said, 'I told you that I had been thinking of a way to recover my health, and that I meant to speak to you about it later in the day. That later time has come. I have been out of sorts, as the phrase is, for some time past. You have remarked it yourself, Allan, more than once; and, with your usual kindness, you have allowed it to excuse many things in my conduct which would have been otherwise unpardonable, even in your friendly eyes.'

'My dear fellow,' interposed Allan, 'you don't mean to say you are going out on a walking tour in this pouring rain!'

'Never mind the rain,' rejoined Midwinter. 'The rain and I are old friends. You know something, Allan, of the life I led before you met with me. From the time when I was a child, I have been used to hardship and exposure. Night and day, sometimes for months together, I never had my head under a roof. For years and years, the life of a wild animal – perhaps I ought to say, the life of a savage – was the life I led, while you were at home and happy. I have the leaven of the vagabond – the vagabond animal, or the vagabond man, I hardly know which – in me still. Does it distress you to hear me talk of myself in this way? I won't distress you. I will only say that the comfort and the luxury of our life here are, at times, I think, a little too much for a man to whom comforts and luxuries come as strange things. I want nothing to put me right again but more air and exercise; fewer good breakfasts and dinners, my dear friend, than I get here. Let me go back to some of the hardships which this comfortable house is expressly made to shut out. Let me meet the wind and weather as I used to meet them when I was a boy; let me feel weary again for a little while, without a carriage near to pick me up; and hungry when the night falls, with miles of walking between my supper and me. Give me a week or two away, Allan – up northward, on foot, to the Yorkshire moors – and I promise to return to Thorpe-Ambrose, better company for you and for your friends. I shall be back before you have time to miss me. Mr Bashwood will take care of the business in the office; it is only for a fortnight, and it is for my own good – let me go!'

'I don't like it,' said Allan. 'I don't like your leaving me in this sudden manner. There's something so strange and dreary about it. Why not try riding, if you want more exercise; all the horses in the stables are at your disposal. At all events, you can't possibly go to-day. Look at the rain!'

Midwinter looked towards the window, and gently shook his head.

'I thought nothing of the rain,' he said, 'when I was a mere child, getting my living with the dancing dogs – why should I think anything of it now? *My* getting wet, and *your* getting wet, Allan, are two very different things. When I was a fisherman's boy in the Hebrides, I hadn't a dry thread on me for weeks together.'

'But you're not in the Hebrides now,' persisted Allan; 'and I expect our friends from the cottage to-morrow evening. You can't start till after to-morrow. Miss Gwilt is going to give us some more music, and you know you like Miss Gwilt's playing.'

Midwinter turned aside to buckle the straps of his knapsack. 'Give me another chance of hearing Miss Gwilt when I come back,' he said, with his head down, and his fingers busy at the straps.

'You have one fault, my dear fellow, and it grows on you,' remonstrated Allan; 'when you have once taken a thing into your head, you're the most obstinate man alive. There's no persuading you to listen to reason. If you *will* go,' added Allan, suddenly rising as Midwinter took up his hat and stick in silence, 'I have half a mind to go with you, and try a little roughing it too!'

'Go with *me!*' repeated Midwinter, with a momentary bitterness in his tone, 'and leave Miss Gwilt!'

Allan sat down again, and admitted the force of the objection in significant silence. Without a word more on his side, Midwinter held out his hand to take leave. They were both deeply moved, and each was anxious to hide his agitation from the other. Allan took the last refuge which his friend's firmness left to him, he tried to lighten the farewell moment by a joke.

'I'll tell you what,' he said, 'I begin to doubt if you're quite cured yet of your belief in the Dream. I suspect you're running away from me, after all!'

Midwinter looked at him, uncertain whether he was in jest or earnest. 'What do you mean?' he asked.

'What did you tell me,' retorted Allan, 'when you took me in here the other day, and made a clean breast of it? What did you say about this room and the second vision of the dream? By Jupiter!' he exclaimed, starting to his feet once more, 'now I look again, here *is* the Second Vision! There's the rain pattering against the window — there's the lawn and the garden outside — here am I where I stood in the Dream — and there are you where the Shadow stood. The whole scene complete, out of doors and in; and *I've* discovered it this time!'

A moment's life stirred again in the dead remains of Midwinter's superstition. His colour changed; and he eagerly, almost fiercely, disputed Allan's conclusion.

'No!' he said, pointing to the little marble figure on the bracket, 'the scene is *not* complete — you have forgotten something as usual. The Dream is wrong this time, thank God — utterly wrong! In the vision you saw, the statue was lying in fragments on the floor; and you were stooping over them with a troubled and an angry mind. There stands the statue safe and sound! — and you haven't the vestige of an angry feeling in your mind, have you?' He seized Allan impulsively by the hand. At the same moment the consciousness came to him that he was speaking and acting as earnestly as if he still believed in the Dream. The colour rushed back over his face, and he turned away in confused silence.

'What did I tell you?' said Allan, laughing a little uneasily. 'That night on the Wreck is hanging on your mind as heavily as ever.'

'Nothing hangs heavy on me,' retorted Midwinter, with a sudden outburst of impatience, 'but the knapsack on my back, and the time I'm wasting here. I'll go out, and see if it's likely to clear up.'

'You'll come back?' interposed Allan.

Midwinter opened the French window, and stepped out into the garden.

'Yes,' he said, answering with all his former gentleness of manner, 'I'll come back in a fortnight. Good-by, Allan; and good luck with Miss Gwilt!'

He pushed the window to, and was away across the garden before his friend could open it again and follow him.

Allan rose, and took one step into the garden; then checked himself at the window, and returned to his chair. He knew Midwinter well enough to feel the total uselessness of attempting to follow him, or to call him back. He was gone, and for two weeks to come there was no hope of seeing him again. An hour or more passed, the rain still fell, and the sky still threatened. A heavier and heavier sense of loneliness and despondency – the sense of all others which his previous life had least fitted him to understand and endure – possessed itself of Allan's mind. In sheer horror of his own uninhabitably solitary house, he rang for his hat and umbrella, and resolved to take refuge in the major's cottage.

'I might have gone a little way with him,' thought Allan, his mind still running on Midwinter as he put on his hat. 'I should like to have seen the dear old fellow fairly started on his journey.'

He took his umbrella. If he had noticed the face of the servant who gave it to him, he might possibly have asked some questions, and might have heard some news to interest him in his present frame of mind. As it was, he went out without looking at the man, and without suspecting that his servants knew more of Midwinter's last moments at Thorpe-Ambrose than he knew himself. Not ten minutes since, the grocer and the butcher had called in to receive payment of their bills – and the grocer and the butcher had seen how Midwinter started on his journey.

The grocer had met him first, not far from the house, stopping on his way, in the pouring rain, to speak to a little ragged imp of a boy, the pest of the neighbourhood. The boy's customary impudence had broken out even more unrestrainedly than usual at the sight of the gentleman's knapsack. And what had the gentleman done in return? He had stopped and looked distressed, and had put his two hands gently on the boy's shoulders. The grocer's own eyes had seen that; and the grocer's own ears had heard him say, 'Poor little chap! I know how the wind gnaws and the rain wets through a ragged jacket, better than most people who have got a good coat on their backs.' And with those words he had put his hand in his pocket, and had rewarded the boy's impudence with a present of a shilling. 'Wrong hereabouts,' said the grocer, touching his forehead. 'That's my opinion of Mr Armadale's friend!'

The butcher had seen him farther on in the journey, at the other end of the town. He had stopped – again in the pouring rain – and this time to look at nothing more remarkable than a half-starved cur, shivering on a doorstep. 'I had my eye on him,' said the butcher; 'and what do you think he did? He crossed the road over to my shop, and bought a bit of meat fit for a Christian. Very well. He says good-morning, and crosses back again; and, on the word of a man, down he goes on his knees on the wet doorstep, and out he takes his knife, and cuts up the meat, and gives it to the dog. Meat, I tell you again, fit for a Christian! I'm not a hard man, ma'am,' concluded the butcher, addressing the cook, 'but meat's meat; and it will serve your master's friend right if he lives to want it.'

With those old unforgotten sympathies of the old unforgotten time to keep him company on his lonely road, he had left the town behind him, and had been lost to view in the misty rain. The grocer and the butcher had seen the last of him, and had judged a great nature, as all great natures *are* judged from the grocer and the butcher point of view.

THE END OF THE THIRD BOOK

BOOK THE FOURTH

CHAPTER I

MRS MILROY

Two days after Midwinter's departure from Thorpe-Ambrose, Mrs Milroy, having completed her morning toilette, and having dismissed her nurse, rang the bell again five minutes afterwards, and on the woman's reappearance, asked impatiently, if the post had come in.

'Post?' echoed the nurse. 'Haven't you got your watch? Don't you know that it's a good half-hour too soon to ask for your letters?' She spoke with the confident insolence of a servant long accustomed to presume on her mistress's weakness, and her mistress's necessities. Mrs Milroy, on her side, appeared to be well used to her nurse's manner; she gave her orders composedly, without noticing it.

'When the postman does come,' she said, 'see him yourself. I am expecting a letter which I ought to have had two days since. I don't understand it. I'm beginning to suspect the servants.'

The nurse smiled contemptuously. 'Who will you suspect next?' she asked. 'There! don't put yourself out. I'll answer the gate-bell this morning; and we'll see if I can't bring you a letter when the postman comes.' Saying those words, with the tone and manner of a woman who is quieting a fractious child, the nurse, without waiting to be dismissed, left the room.

Mrs Milroy turned slowly and wearily on her bed, when she was left by herself again, and let the light from the window fall on her face.

It was the face of a woman who had once been handsome, and who was still, so far as years went, in the prime of her life. Long-continued suffering of body, and long-continued irritation of mind, had worn her away – in the roughly-expressive popular phrase – to skin and bone. The utter wreck of her beauty was made a wreck horrible to behold, by her desperate efforts to conceal the sight of it from her own eyes, from the eyes of her husband and her child, from the eyes even of the doctor who attended her, and whose business it was to penetrate to the truth. Her head, from which the greater part of the hair had fallen off, would have been less shocking to see than the hideously youthful wig, by which she tried to hide the loss. No deterioration of her complexion, no wrinkling of her skin, could have been so dreadful to look at as the rouge that lay thick on her cheeks, and the white enamel plastered on her forehead. The delicate lace, and the bright trimming on her dressing-gown, the ribbons in her cap, and the rings on her bony fingers, all intended to draw the eye away from the change that had passed over her, directed the eye to it on the contrary; emphasized it; made it by sheer force of contrast more hopeless and more horrible than it really was. An illustrated book of the fashions, in which women were represented exhibiting their finery by means of the free use of their limbs, lay on the bed from which she had not moved for years, without being lifted by her nurse. A hand-glass was placed with the book so that she could reach it easily. She took up the glass after her attendant had left the room, and looked at her face with an unblushing interest and attention which she would have been ashamed of herself at the age of eighteen.

'Older and older, and thinner and thinner!' she said. 'The major will soon be a free man – but I'll have that red-haired hussy out of the house first!'

She dropped the looking-glass on the counterpane, and clenched the hand that had held it. Her eyes suddenly riveted themselves on a little crayon portrait of her husband hanging on the opposite wall; they looked at the likeness with the hard and cruel brightness of the eyes of a bird of prey. 'Red is your taste in your old age, is it?' she said to the portrait. 'Red hair and a scrofulous complexion and a padded figure, a ballet-girl's walk, and a pickpocket's light fingers. *Miss* Gwilt! *Miss*, with those eyes, and that walk!' She turned her head suddenly on the pillow, and burst into a harsh, jeering laugh. '*Miss!*' she repeated over and over again, with the venomously-pointed emphasis of the most merciless of all human forms of contempt – the contempt of one woman for another.

The age we live in is an age which finds no human creature inexcusable. Is there an excuse for Mrs Milroy? Let the story of her life answer the question.

She had married the major at an unusually early age; and, in marrying him, had taken a man for her husband who was old enough to be her father – a man who, at that time, had the reputation, and not unjustly, of having made the freest use of his social gifts, and his advantages of personal appearance in the society of women. Indifferently educated, and below her husband in station, she had begun by accepting his addresses under the influence of her own flattered vanity, and had ended by feeling the fascination which Major Milroy had exercised over women infinitely her mental superiors, in his earlier life. He had been touched, on his side, by her devotion, and had felt, in his turn, the attraction of her beauty, her freshness, and her youth. Up to the time when their little daughter and only child had reached the age of eight years, their married life had been an unusually happy one. At that period, the double misfortune fell on the household, of the failure of the wife's health, and the almost total loss of the husband's fortune; and from that moment, the domestic happiness of the married pair was virtually at an end.

Having reached the age when men in general are readier, under the pressure of calamity, to resign themselves than to resist, the major had secured the little relics of his property, had retired into the country, and had patiently taken refuge in his mechanical pursuits. A woman nearer to him in age, or a woman with a better training and more patience of disposition than his wife possessed, would have understood the major's conduct, and have found consolation in the major's submission. Mrs Milroy found consolation in nothing. Neither nature nor training helped her to meet resignedly the cruel calamity which had struck at her in the bloom of womanhood and the prime of beauty. The curse of incurable sickness blighted her at once and for life.

Suffering can, and does, develop the latent evil that there is in humanity, as well as the latent good. The good that was in Mrs Milroy's nature shrank up under that subtly-deteriorating influence in which the evil grew and flourished. Month by month as she became the weaker woman physically, she became the worse woman morally. All that was mean, cruel, and false in her, expanded in steady proportion to the contraction of all that had once been generous, gentle, and true. Old suspicions of her husband's readiness to relapse into the irregularities of his bachelor life, which, in her healthier days of mind and body, she had openly confessed to him – which she had always sooner or later seen to be suspicions that he had not deserved – came back, now that sickness had divorced her from him, in the form of that baser conjugal distrust which keeps itself cunningly secret; which gathers together its inflammatory particles atom by atom into a heap, and sets the slowly-burning frenzy of jealousy alight in the mind. No proof of her husband's blameless and patient life that could now be shown to Mrs Milroy; no appeal that could be made to her respect for herself, or for her child growing up to womanhood, availed to dissipate the terrible delusion born of her hopeless illness, and growing steadily with its growth. Like all other madness it had its ebb and flow, its time of spasmodic outburst, and its time of deceitful repose – but active or passive, it was always in her. It had injured innocent servants, and insulted blameless strangers.

It had brought the first tears of shame and sorrow into her daughter's eyes, and had set the deepest lines that scored it in her husband's face. It had made the secret misery of the little household for years – and it was now to pass beyond the family limits, and to influence coming events at Thorpe-Ambrose, in which the future interests of Allan and Allan's friend were vitally concerned.

A moment's glance at the posture of domestic affairs in the cottage, prior to the engagement of the new governess, is necessary to the due appreciation of the serious consequences that followed Miss Gwilt's appearance on the scene.

On the marriage of the governess who had lived in his service for many years (a woman of an age and an appearance to set even Mrs Milroy's jealousy at defiance), the major had considered the question of sending his daughter away from home, far more seriously than his wife supposed. On the one hand, he was conscious that scenes took place in the house at which no young girl should be present. On the other, he felt an invincible reluctance to apply the one efficient remedy – the keeping his daughter away from home in school-time and holiday-time alike. The struggle thus raised in his mind once set at rest, by the resolution to advertise for a new governess, Major Milroy's natural tendency to avoid trouble rather than to meet it, had declared itself in its customary manner. He had closed his eyes again on his home anxieties as quietly as usual, and had gone back, as he had gone back on hundreds of previous occasions, to the consoling society of his old friend the clock.

It was far otherwise with the major's wife. The chance which her husband had entirely overlooked, that the new governess who was to come might be a younger and a more attractive woman than the old governess who had gone, was the first chance that presented itself as possible to Mrs Milroy's mind. She had said nothing. Secretly waiting, and secretly nursing her inveterate distrust, she had encouraged her husband and her daughter to leave her on the occasion of the picnic, with the express purpose of making an opportunity for seeing the new governess alone. The governess had shown herself; and the smouldering fire of Mrs Milroy's jealousy had burst into flame, in the moment when she and the handsome stranger first set eyes on each other.

The interview over, Mrs Milroy's suspicions fastened at once and immovably on her husband's mother. She was well aware that there was no one else in London on whom the major could depend to make the necessary inquiries; she was well aware that Miss Gwilt had applied for the situation, in the first instance, as a stranger answering an advertisement published in a newspaper. Yet knowing this, she had obstinately closed her eyes, with the blind frenzy of the blindest of all the passions, to the facts straight before her; and, looking back to the last of many quarrels between them which had ended in separating the elder lady and herself, had seized on the conclusion that Miss Gwilt's engagement was due to her mother-in-law's vindictive enjoyment of making mischief in her household. The inference which the very servants themselves, witnesses of the family scandal, had correctly drawn – that the major's mother, in securing the services of a well-recommended governess for her son, had thought it not part of her duty to consider that governess's looks in the purely fanciful interests of the major's wife – was an inference which it was simply impossible to convey into Mrs Milroy's mind. The resolution which her jealousy of her husband would, in any case, have led her to take after seeing Miss Gwilt, was a resolution doubly confirmed by the conviction that now possessed her. Miss Gwilt had barely closed the sick-room door when the whispered words hissed out of Mrs Milroy's lips, 'Before another week is over your head, my lady, you go!'

From that moment, through the wakeful night and the weary day, the one object of the bedridden woman's life was to procure the new governess's dismissal from the house.

The assistance of the nurse, in the capacity of spy, was secured – as Mrs Milroy had been accustomed to secure other extra services which her attendant was not bound to render her – by a present of a dress from the mistress's wardrobe. One after another, articles of wearing apparel which were now useless to Mrs Milroy, had ministered in this way to feed the nurse's greed – the insatiable greed of an ugly woman for fine clothes. Bribed with the smartest dress she had secured yet, the household spy took her secret orders, and applied herself with a vile enjoyment of it to her secret work.

The days passed, the work went on – but nothing came of it. Mistress and servant had a woman to deal with who was a match for both of them. Repeated intrusions on the major, when the governess happened to be in the same room with him, failed to discover the slightest impropriety of word, look, or action, on either side. Stealthy watching and listening at the governess's bedroom door, detected that she kept a light in her room at late hours of the night, and that she groaned and ground her teeth in her sleep – and detected nothing more. Careful superintendence in the day-time, proved that she regularly posted her own letters, instead of giving them to the servant; and that on certain occasions when the occupation of her hours out of lesson-time and walking-time was left at her own disposal, she had been suddenly missed from the garden, and then caught coming back alone to it from the park. Once, and once only, the nurse had found an opportunity of following her out of the garden – had been detected immediately in the park – and had been asked with the most exasperating politeness, if she wished to join Miss Gwilt in a walk. Small circumstances of this kind, which were sufficiently suspicious to the mind of a jealous woman, were discovered in abundance. But circumstances, on which to found a valid ground of complaint that might be laid before the major, proved to be utterly wanting. Day followed day, and Miss Gwilt remained persistently correct in her conduct, and persistently irreproachable in her relations towards her employer and her pupil.

Foiled in this direction, Mrs Milroy tried next to find an assailable place in the statement which the governess's reference had made on the subject of the governess's character.

Obtaining from the major the minutely careful report which his mother had addressed to him on this topic, Mrs Milroy read and re-read it, and failed to find the weak point of which she was in search in any part of the letter. All the customary questions on such occasions had been asked, and all had been scrupulously and plainly answered. The one sole opening for an attack which it was possible to discover, was an opening which showed itself, after more practical matters had been all disposed of, in the closing sentences of the letter.

'I was so struck' (the passage ran) 'by the grace and distinction of Miss Gwilt's manners, that I took an opportunity, when she was out of the room, of asking how she first came to be a governess. "In the usual way," I was told. "A sad family misfortune, in which she behaved nobly. She is a very sensitive person, and shrinks from speaking of it among strangers – a natural reluctance which I have always felt it a matter of delicacy to respect." Hearing this, of course I felt the same delicacy on my side. It was no part of my duty to intrude on the poor thing's private sorrows; my only business was to do, what I have now done, to make sure that I was engaging a capable and respectable governess to instruct my grandchild.'

After careful consideration of these lines, Mrs Milroy having a strong desire to find the circumstances suspicious, found them suspicious accordingly. She determined to sift the mystery of Miss Gwilt's family misfortunes to the bottom, on the chance of extracting from it something useful to her purpose. There were two ways of doing this. She might begin by questioning the governess herself, or she might begin by questioning the governess's reference. Experience of Miss Gwilt's quickness of resource in dealing with awkward questions at their introductory interview, decided her on taking the latter course. 'I'll get the particulars from the reference first,' thought Mrs Milroy, 'and then question the creature herself, and see if the two stories agree.'

The letter of inquiry was short and scrupulously to the point. Mrs Milroy began by informing her correspondent that the state of her health necessitated leaving her daughter entirely under the governess's influence and control. On that account she was more anxious than most mothers to be thoroughly informed in every respect about the person to whom she confided the entire charge of an only child; and, feeling this anxiety, she might perhaps be excused for putting what might be thought, after the excellent character Miss Gwilt had received, a somewhat unnecessary question. With that preface, Mrs Milroy came to the point, and requested to be informed of the circumstances which had obliged Miss Gwilt to go out as a governess.

The letter, expressed in these terms, was posted the same day. On the morning when the answer was due, no answer appeared. The next morning arrived, and still there was no reply. When the third morning came, Mrs Milroy's impatience had broken loose from all restraint. She had rung for the nurse in the manner which has been already recorded, and had ordered the woman to be in waiting to receive the letters of the morning with her own hands. In this position matters now stood; and in these domestic circumstances the new series of events at Thorpe-Ambrose took their rise.

Mrs Milroy had just looked at her watch, and had just put her hand once more to the bell-pull, when the door opened and the nurse entered the room.

'Has the postman come?' asked Mrs Milroy.

The nurse laid a letter on the bed without answering, and waited, with unconcealed curiosity, to watch the effect which it produced on her mistress.

Mrs Milroy tore open the envelope the instant it was in her hand. A printed paper appeared (which she threw aside), surrounding a letter (which she looked at) in her own handwriting! She snatched up the printed paper. It was the customary Post-Office circular, informing her that her letter had been duly presented at the right address, and that the person whom she had written to was not to be found.

'Something wrong?' asked the nurse, detecting a change in her mistress's face.

The question passed unheeded. Mrs Milroy's writing-desk was on the table at the bedside. She took from it the letter which the major's mother had written to her son, and turned to the page containing the name and address of Miss Gwilt's reference. 'Mrs Mandeville, 18, Kingsdown Crescent, Bayswater,' she read eagerly to herself, and then looked at the address on her own returned letter. No error had been committed: the directions were identically the same.

'Something wrong?' reiterated the nurse, advancing a step nearer to the bed.

'Thank God – yes!' cried Mrs Milroy, with a sudden outburst of exultation. She tossed the Post-Office circular to the nurse, and beat her bony hands on the bed-clothes, in an ecstasy of anticipated triumph. 'Miss Gwilt's an impostor! Miss Gwilt's an impostor! If I die for it, Rachel, I'll be carried to the window to see the police take her away!'

'It's one thing to say she's an impostor behind her back, and another thing to prove it to her face,' remarked the nurse. She put her hand as she spoke into her apron pocket, and, with a significant look at her mistress, silently produced a second letter.

'For me?' asked Mrs Milroy.

'No,' said the nurse, 'for Miss Gwilt.'

The two women eyed each other, and understood each other without another word.

'Where is she?' said Mrs Milroy.

The nurse pointed in the direction of the park. 'Out again, for another walk before breakfast – by herself.'

Mrs Milroy beckoned to the nurse to stoop close over her. 'Can you open it, Rachel?' she whispered.

Rachel nodded.

'Can you close it again, so that nobody would know?'

'Can you spare the scarf that matches your pearl-grey dress?' asked Rachel.

'Take it!' said Mrs Milroy, impatiently.

The nurse opened the wardrobe in silence; took the scarf in silence; and left the room in silence. In less than five minutes she came back with the envelope of Miss Gwilt's letter open in her hand.

'Thank you, ma'am, for the scarf,' said Rachel, putting the opened letter composedly on the counterpane of the bed.

Mrs Milroy looked at the envelope. It had been closed as usual by means of adhesive gum, which had been made to give way by the application of steam. As Mrs Milroy took out the letter, her hand trembled violently, and the white enamel parted into cracks over the wrinkles on her forehead. 'My drops,' she said. 'I'm dreadfully excited, Rachel. My drops!'

Rachel produced the drops, and then went to the window to keep watch on the park. 'Don't hurry,' she said. 'No signs of her yet.'

Mrs Milroy still paused, keeping the all-important morsel of paper folded in her hand. She could have taken Miss Gwilt's life – but she hesitated at reading Miss Gwilt's letter.

'Are you troubled with scruples?' asked the nurse, with a sneer. 'Consider it a duty you owe to your daughter.'

'You wretch!' said Mrs Milroy. With that expression of opinion, she opened the letter.

It was evidently written in great haste – was undated – and was signed in initials only. Thus it ran:

> Diana Street.
>
> MY DEAR LYDIA, – The cab is waiting at the door, and I have only a moment to tell you that I am obliged to leave London, on business, for three or four days, or a week at longest. My letters will be forwarded if you write. I got yours yesterday, and I agree with you that it is very important to put him off the awkward subject of yourself and your family as long as you safely can. The better you know him, the better you will be able to make up the sort of story that will do. Once told, you will have to stick to it – and, *having* to stick to it, beware of making it complicated, and beware of making it in a hurry. I will write again about this, and give you my own ideas. In the meantime, don't risk meeting him too often in the park. – Yours, M. O.

'Well?' asked the nurse, returning to the bedside. 'Have you done with it?'

'Meeting him in the park?' repeated Mrs Milroy, with her eyes still fastened on the letter. '*Him*! Rachel, where is the major?'

'In his own room.'

'I don't believe it!'

'Have your own way. I want the letter and the envelope.'

'Can you close it again so that she won't know?'

'What I can open I can shut. Anything more?'

'Nothing more.'

Mrs Milroy was left alone again, to review her plan of attack by the new light that had now been thrown on Miss Gwilt.

The information that had been gained, by opening the governess's letter, pointed plainly to the conclusion that an adventuress had stolen her way into the house by means of a false reference. But having been obtained by an act of treachery which it was impossible to acknowledge, it was not information that could be used either for warning the major or for exposing Miss Gwilt. The one available weapon in Mrs Milroy's hands was the weapon furnished by her own returned letter – and the one question to decide was how to make the best and speediest use of it.

The longer she turned the matter over in her mind, the more hasty and premature seemed the exultation which she had felt at the first sight of the Post-Office circular. That a lady acting as reference to a governess should have quitted her residence without leaving any trace behind her, and without even mentioning an address to which her letters could be forwarded, was a circumstance in itself sufficiently suspicious to be mentioned to the major. But Mrs Milroy, however perverted her estimate of her husband might be in some respects, knew enough of his character to be assured that, if she told him what had happened, he would frankly appeal to the governess herself for an explanation. Miss Gwilt's quickness and cunning would, in that case, produce some plausible answer on the spot, which the major's partiality would be only too ready to accept; and she would at the same time, no doubt, place matters in train, by means of the post, for the due arrival of all needful confirmation on the part of her accomplice in London. To keep strict silence for the present, and to institute (without the governess's knowledge) such inquiries as might be necessary to the discovery of undeniable evidence, was plainly the only safe course to take with such a man as the major, and with such a woman as Miss Gwilt. Helpless herself, to whom could Mrs Milroy commit the difficult and dangerous task of investigation? The nurse, even if she was to be trusted, could not be spared at a day's notice, and could not be sent away without the risk of exciting remark. Was there any other competent and reliable person to employ, either at Thorpe-Ambrose or in London? Mrs Milroy turned from side to side of the bed, searching every corner of her mind for the needful discovery, and searching in vain. 'Oh, if I could only lay my hand on some man I could trust!' she thought, despairingly. 'If I only knew where to look for somebody to help me!'

As the idea passed through her mind, the sound of her daughter's voice startled her from the other side of the door.

'May I come in?' asked Neelie.

'What do you want?' returned Mrs Milroy, impatiently.

'I have brought up your breakfast, mamma.'

'My breakfast?' repeated Mrs Milroy, in surprise. 'Why doesn't

Rachel bring it up as usual?' She considered a moment, and then called out sharply, 'Come in!'

CHAPTER II

THE MAN IS FOUND

Neelie entered the room, carrying the tray with the tea, the dry toast, and the pat of butter which composed the invalid's invariable breakfast.

'What does this mean?' asked Mrs Milroy, speaking and looking as she might have spoken and looked if the wrong servant had come into the room.

Neelie put the tray down on the bedside table. 'I thought I should like to bring you up your breakfast, mamma, for once in a way,' she replied, 'and I asked Rachel to let me.'

'Come here,' said Mrs Milroy, 'and wish me good-morning.'

Neelie obeyed. As she stooped to kiss her mother, Mrs Milroy caught her by the arm, and turned her roughly to the light. There were plain signs of disturbance and distress in her daughter's face. A deadly thrill of terror ran through Mrs Milroy on the instant. She suspected that the opening of the letter had been discovered by Miss Gwilt, and that the nurse was keeping out of the way in consequence.

'Let me go, mamma,' said Neelie, shrinking under her mother's grasp. 'You hurt me.'

'Tell me why you have brought up my breakfast this morning,' persisted Mrs Milroy.

'I have told you, mamma.'

'You have *not*! You have made an excuse – I see it in your face. Come! what is it?'

Neelie's resolution gave way before her mother's. She looked aside uneasily at the things in the tray. 'I have been vexed,' she said with an effort; 'and I didn't want to stop in the breakfast-room. I wanted to come up here, and speak to you.'

'Vexed? Who has vexed you? What has happened? Has Miss Gwilt anything to do with it?'

Neelie looked round again at her mother in sudden curiosity and alarm. 'Mamma!' she said, 'you read my thoughts – I declare you frighten me. It *was* Miss Gwilt.'

Before Mrs Milroy could say a word more on her side, the door opened, and the nurse looked in.

'Have you got what you want?' she asked as composedly as usual. 'Miss, there, insisted on taking your tray up this morning. Has she broken anything?'

'Go to the window – I want to speak to Rachel,' said Mrs Milroy. As soon as her daughter's back was turned, she beckoned eagerly to the nurse. 'Anything wrong?' she asked in a whisper. 'Do you think she suspects us?'

The nurse turned away, with her hard sneering smile. 'I told you it should be done,' she said, 'and it *has* been done. She hasn't the ghost of a suspicion. I waited in the room – and I saw her take up the letter, and open it.'

Mrs Milroy drew a deep breath of relief. 'Thank you,' she said, loud enough for her daughter to hear. 'I want nothing more.'

The nurse withdrew; and Neelie came back from the window. Mrs Milroy took her by the hand, and looked at her more attentively and more kindly than usual. Her daughter interested her that morning – for her daughter had something to say on the subject of Miss Gwilt.

'I used to think you promised to be pretty, child,' she said, cautiously resuming the interrupted conversation in the least direct way. 'But you don't seem to be keeping your promise. You look out of health and out of spirits – what is the matter with you?'

If there had been any sympathy between mother and child, Neelie might have owned the truth. She might have said frankly, 'I am looking ill, because my life is miserable to me. I am fond of Mr Armadale, and Mr Armadale was once fond of me. We had one little disagreement, only one, in which I was to blame. I wanted to tell him so at the time, and I have wanted to tell him so ever since – and Miss Gwilt stands between us and prevents me. She has made us like strangers; she has altered him, and taken him away from me. He doesn't look at me as he did; he doesn't speak to me as he did; he is never alone with me as he used to be; I can't say the words to him that I long to say; and I can't write to him, for it would look as if I wanted to get him back. It is all over between me and Mr Armadale, – and it is that woman's fault. There is ill-blood between Miss Gwilt and me the whole day long; and say what I may, and do what I may, she always gets the better of me, and always puts me in the wrong. Everything I saw at Thorpe-Ambrose pleased me, everything I did at Thorpe-Ambrose made me happy, before she came. Nothing pleases me, and nothing makes me happy now!' If Neelie had ever been accustomed to ask her mother's advice and to trust herself to her mother's love, she might have said such words as these. As it was, the tears came into her eyes, and she hung her head in silence.

'Come!' said Mrs Milroy, beginning to lose patience. 'You have something to say to me about Miss Gwilt. What is it?'

Neelie forced back the tears, and made an effort to answer.

'She aggravates me beyond endurance, mamma; I can't bear her; I shall do something—' Neelie stopped, and stamped her foot angrily on the floor. 'I shall throw something at her head, if we go on much longer like this! I should have thrown something this morning if I hadn't left the room. Oh, do speak to papa about it! do find out some reason for sending her away! I'll go to school – I'll do anything in the world to get rid of Miss Gwilt!'

To get rid of Miss Gwilt! At those words – at that echo from her daughter's lips of the one dominant desire kept secret in her own heart – Mrs Milroy slowly raised herself in the bed. What did it mean? Was the help she wanted coming from the very last of all quarters in which she could have thought of looking for it?

'Why do you want to get rid of Miss Gwilt,' she asked. 'What have you got to complain of?'

'Nothing!' said Neelie. 'That's the aggravation of it. Miss Gwilt won't let me have anything to complain of. She is perfectly detestable; she is driving me mad; and she is the pink of propriety all the time. I daresay it's wrong, but, I don't care – I hate her!'

Mrs Milroy's eyes questioned her daughter's face as they had never questioned it yet. There was something under the surface, evidently – something which it might be of vital importance to her own purpose to discover – which had not risen into view. She went on probing her way gently deeper and deeper into Neelie's mind, with a warmer and warmer interest in Neelie's secret.

'Pour me out a cup of tea,' she said; 'and don't excite yourself, my dear. Why do you speak to *me* about this? Why don't you speak to your father?'

'I have tried to speak to papa,' said Neelie. 'But it is no use; he is too good to know what a wretch she is. She is always on her best behaviour with him; she is always contriving to be useful to him. I can't make him understand why I dislike Miss Gwilt – I can't make *you* understand – I only understand it myself.' She tried to pour out the tea, and in trying upset the cup. 'I'll go downstairs again!' exclaimed Neelie, with a burst of tears. 'I'm not fit for anything – I can't even pour out a cup of tea!'

Mrs Milroy seized her hand, and stopped her. Trifling as it was,

Neelie's reference to the relations between the major and Miss Gwilt had roused her mother's ready jealousy. The restraints which Mrs Milroy had laid on herself thus far, vanished in a moment – vanished, even in the presence of a girl of sixteen, and that girl her own child!

'Wait here!' she said, eagerly. 'You have come to the right place and the right person. Go on abusing Miss Gwilt. I like to hear you – I hate her too!'

'You, mamma!' exclaimed Neelie, looking at her mother in astonishment.

For a moment, Mrs Milroy hesitated before she said more. Some last-left instinct of her married life in its earlier and happier time, pleaded hard with her to respect the youth and the sex of her child. But jealousy respects nothing; in the heaven above and on the earth beneath, nothing but itself. The slow fire of self-torment burning night and day in the miserable woman's breast, flashed its deadly light into her eyes, as the next words dropped slowly and venomously from her lips.

'If you had had eyes in your head you would never have gone to your father,' she said. 'Your father had reasons of his own for hearing nothing that you can say, or that anybody can say, against Miss Gwilt.'

Many girls at Neelie's age would have failed to see the meaning hidden under those words. It was the daughter's misfortune, in this instance to have had experience enough of the mother to understand her. Neelie started back from the bedside, with her face in a glow. 'Mamma!' she said, 'you are talking horribly! Papa is the best and dearest and kindest – oh, I won't hear it! – I won't hear it!'

Mrs Milroy's fierce temper broke out in an instant – broke out all the more violently from her feeling herself, in spite of herself, to have been in the wrong.

'You impudent little fool!' she retorted furiously, 'do you think I want *you* to remind me of what I owe to your father? Am I to learn how to speak of your father, and how to think of your father, and how to love and honour your father, from a forward little minx like you! I was finely disappointed, I can tell you, when you were born – I wished for a boy, you impudent hussy! If you ever find a man who is fool enough to marry you, he will be a lucky man if you only love him half as well, a quarter as well, a hundred-thousandth part as well, as I loved your father. Ah, you can cry when it's too late; you can come creeping back to beg your mother's pardon after you have insulted her. You little dowdy, half-grown creature! I was handsomer than ever you will be when I married your father – I would have gone through fire and water to serve your father! If he had asked me to cut off one of my arms, I would have done it – I would have done it to please him!' She turned suddenly with her face to the wall – forgetting her daughter, forgetting her husband, forgetting everything but the torturing remembrance of her lost beauty. 'My arms!' she repeated to herself, faintly. 'What arms I had when I was young!' She snatched up the sleeve of her dressing-gown furtively, with a shudder. 'Oh, look at it now! look at it now!'

Neelie fell on her knees at the bedside, and hid her face. In sheer despair of finding comfort and help anywhere else, she had cast herself impulsively on her mother's mercy – and this was how it had ended! 'Oh, mamma,' she pleaded, 'you know I didn't mean to offend you! I couldn't help it when you spoke so of my father. Oh, do, do, forgive me.'

Mrs Milroy turned again on her pillow, and looked at her daughter vacantly. 'Forgive you?' she repeated, with her mind still in the past, groping its way back darkly to the present.

'I beg your pardon, mamma – I beg your pardon on my knees. I am so unhappy; I do so want a little kindness! Won't you forgive me?'

'Wait a little,' rejoined Mrs Milroy. 'Ah,' she said, after an interval, 'now I know! Forgive you? Yes – I'll forgive you on one condition.' She lifted Neelie's head, and looked her searchingly in the face. 'Tell me why you hate Miss Gwilt! You've a reason of your own for hating her, and you haven't confessed it yet.'

Neelie's head dropped again. The burning colour that she was hiding by hiding her face, showed itself on her neck. Her mother saw it, and gave her time.

'Tell me,' reiterated Mrs Milroy, more gently, 'why do you hate her?'

The answer came reluctantly, a word at a time, in fragments.

'Because she is trying—'

'Trying what?'

'Trying to make somebody who is much—'

'Much what?'

'Much too young for her—'

'Marry her?'

'Yes, mamma.'

Breathlessly interested, Mrs Milroy leaned forward, and twined her hand caressingly in her daughter's hair.

'Who is it, Neelie?' she asked, in a whisper.

'You will never say I told you, mamma?'

'Never! Who is it?'

'Mr Armadale.'

Mrs Milroy leaned back on her pillow in dead silence. The plain betrayal of her daughter's first love, by her daughter's own lips, which would have absorbed the whole attention of other mothers, failed to occupy her for a moment. Her jealousy, distorting all things to fit its own conclusions, was busied in distorting what she had just heard. 'A blind,' she thought, 'which has deceived my girl. It doesn't deceive *me*. Is Miss Gwilt likely to succeed?' she asked aloud. 'Does Mr Armadale show any sort of interest in her?'

Neelie looked up at her mother for the first time. The hardest part of the confession was over now – she had revealed the truth about Miss Gwilt, and she had openly mentioned Allan's name.

'He shows the most unaccountable interest,' she said. 'It's impossible to understand it. It's downright infatuation – I haven't patience to talk about it!'

'How do *you* come to be in Mr Armadale's secrets?' inquired Mrs Milroy. 'Has he informed *you*, of all the people in the world, of his interest in Miss Gwilt?'

'Me!' exclaimed Neelie, indignantly. 'It's quite bad enough that he should have told papa.'

At the reappearance of the major in the narrative, Mrs Milroy's interest in the conversation rose to its climax. She raised herself again from the pillow. 'Get a chair,' she said. 'Sit down, child, and tell me all about it. Every word, mind – every word!'

'I can only tell you, mamma, what papa told me.'

'When?'

'Saturday.¹ I went in with papa's lunch to the workshop, and he said, "I have just had a visit from Mr Armadale; and I want to give you a caution, while I think of it." I didn't say anything, mamma – I only waited. Papa went on, and told me that Mr Armadale had been speaking to him on the subject of Miss Gwilt, and that he had been asking a question about her which nobody in his position had a right to ask. Papa said he had been obliged, good-humouredly, to warn Mr Armadale to be a little more delicate, and a little more careful next time. I didn't feel much interested, mamma – it didn't matter to *me* what Mr Armadale said or did. Why should I care about it?'

'Never mind yourself,' interposed Mrs Milroy, sharply. 'Go on with what your father said. What was he doing when he was talking about Miss Gwilt? How did he look?'

'Much as usual, mamma. He was walking up and down the workshop; and I took his arm and walked up and down with him.'

'I don't care what _you_ were doing,' said Mrs Milroy, more and more irritably. 'Did your father tell you what Mr Armadale's question was – or did he not?'

'Yes, mamma. He said Mr Armadale began by mentioning that he was very much interested in Miss Gwilt, and he then went on to ask whether papa could tell him anything about her family misfortunes—'

'What!!!' cried Mrs Milroy. The word burst from her almost in a scream, and the white enamel on her face cracked in all directions. 'Mr Armadale said _that?_' she went on, leaning out farther and farther over the side of the bed.

Neelie started up, and tried to put her mother back on the pillow.

'Mamma!' she exclaimed, 'are you in pain? are you ill? You frighten me!'

'Nothing, nothing, nothing,' said Mrs Milroy. She was too violently agitated to make any other than the commonest excuse. 'My nerves are bad this morning – don't notice it. I'll try the other side of the pillow. Go on! go on! I'm listening, though I'm not looking at you.' She turned her face to the wall, and clenched her trembling hands convulsively beneath the bed-clothes. 'I've got her!' she whispered to herself, under her breath. 'I've got her at last!'

'I'm afraid I've been talking too much,' said Neelie; 'I'm afraid I've been stopping here too long. Shall I go downstairs, mamma, and come back later in the day?'

'Go on,' repeated Mrs Milroy, mechanically. 'What did your father say next? Anything more about Mr Armadale?'

'Nothing more, except how papa answered him,' replied Neelie. 'Papa repeated his own words when he told me about it. He said, "In the absence of any confidence volunteered by the lady herself, Mr Armadale, all I know or wish to know – and you must excuse me for saying, all any one else need know or wish to know – is, that Miss Gwilt gave me a perfectly satisfactory reference before she entered my house." Severe, mamma, wasn't it? I don't pity him in the least – he richly deserved it. The next thing was papa's caution to _me_. He told me to check Mr Armadale's curiosity if he applied to me next. As if he was likely to apply to me! and as if I should listen to him if he did! That's all, mamma. You won't suppose, will you, that I have told you this because I want to hinder Mr Armadale from marrying Miss Gwilt? Let him marry her if he pleases – I don't care!' said Neelie, in a voice that faltered a little, and with a face which was hardly composed enough to be in perfect harmony with a declaration of indifference. 'All I want is to be relieved from the misery of having Miss Gwilt for my governess. I'd rather go to school. I should like to go to school. My mind's quite changed about all that – only I haven't the heart to tell papa. I don't know what's come to me – I don't seem to have heart enough for anything now – and when papa takes me on his knee in the evening, and says, "Let's have a talk, Neelie," he makes me cry. Would you mind breaking it to him, mamma, that I've changed my mind, and I want to go to school?' The tears rose thickly in her eyes, and she failed to see that her mother never even turned on the pillow to look round at her.

'Yes, yes,' said Mrs Milroy, vacantly. 'You're a good girl; you shall go to school.'

The cruel brevity of the reply, and the tone in which it was spoken, told Neelie plainly that her mother's attention had been wandering far away from her, and that it was useless and needless to prolong the interview. She turned aside quietly, without a word of remonstrance. It was nothing new, in her experience, to find herself shut out from her mother's sympathies. She looked at her eyes in the glass, and, pouring out some cold water, bathed her face. 'Miss Gwilt shan't see I've been crying!' thought Neelie, as she went back to the bedside to take her leave. 'I've tired you out, mamma,' she said gently. 'Let me go now; and let me come back a little later when you have had some rest.'

'Yes,' repeated her mother, as mechanically as ever; 'a little later, when I have had some rest.'

Neelie left the room. The minute after the door had closed on her, Mrs Milroy rang the bell for her nurse. In the face of the narrative she had just heard, in the face of every reasonable estimate of probabilities, she held to her own jealous conclusions as firmly as ever. 'Mr Armadale may believe her, and my daughter may believe her,' thought the furious woman. 'But I know the major – and she can't deceive *me!*'

The nurse came in. 'Prop me up,' said Mrs Milroy. 'And give me my desk. I want to write.'

'You're excited,' replied the nurse. 'You're not fit to write.'

'Give me the desk,' reiterated Mrs Milroy.

'Anything more?' asked Rachel, repeating her invariable formula as she placed the desk on the bed.

'Yes. Come back in half-an-hour. I shall want you to take a letter to the great house.'

The nurse's sardonic composure deserted her for once. 'Mercy on us!' she exclaimed, with an accent of genuine surprise. 'What next? You don't mean to say you're going to write—?'

'I am going to write to Mr Armadale,' interposed Mrs Milroy; 'and you are going to take the letter to him, and wait for an answer – and, mind this, not a living soul but our two selves must know of it in the house.'

'Why are you writing to Mr Armadale?' asked Rachel. 'And why is nobody to know of it but our two selves?'

'Wait,' rejoined Mrs Milroy; 'and you will see.'

The nurse's curiosity, being a woman's curiosity, declined to wait.

'I'll help you, with my eyes open,' she said. 'But I won't help you blindfold.'

'Oh, if I only had the use of my limbs!' groaned Mrs Milroy. 'You wretch, if I could only do without you!'

'You have the use of your head,' retorted the impenetrable nurse. 'And you ought to know better than to trust me by halves, at this time of day.'

It was brutally put; but it was true – doubly true, after the opening of Miss Gwilt's letter. Mrs Milroy gave way.

'What do you want to know?' she asked. 'Tell me – and leave me.'

'I want to know what you are writing to Mr Armadale about?'

'About Miss Gwilt.'

'What has Mr Armadale to do with you and Miss Gwilt?'

Mrs Milroy held up the letter which had been returned to her by the authorities at the Post-Office.

'Stoop,' she said. 'Miss Gwilt may be listening at the door. I'll whisper.'

The nurse stooped, with her eye on the door.

'You know that the postman went with this letter to Kingsdown Crescent?' said Mrs Milroy. 'And you know that he found Mrs Mandeville gone away, nobody could tell where?'

'Well,' whispered Rachel, 'what next?'

'This, next. When Mr Armadale gets the letter that I am going to write to him, he will follow the same road as the postman – and we'll see what happens when *he* knocks at Mrs Mandeville's door.'

'How do you get him to the door?'

'I tell him to go to Miss Gwilt's reference.'

'Is he sweet on Miss Gwilt?'

'Yes.'

'Ah!' said the nurse. 'I see!'

CHAPTER III

THE BRINK OF DISCOVERY

The morning of the interview between Mrs Milroy and her daughter, at the cottage, was a morning of serious reflection for the squire, at the great house.

Even Allan's easy-tempered nature had not been proof against the disturbing influence exercised on it by the events of the last three days. Midwinter's abrupt departure had vexed him; and Major Milroy's reception of his inquiries relating to Miss Gwilt weighed unpleasantly on his mind. Since his visit to the cottage, he had felt impatient and ill at ease, for the first time in his life, with everybody who came near him. Impatient with Pedgift Junior, who had called on the previous evening, to announce his departure for London on business the next day, and to place his services at the disposal of his client; ill at ease with Miss Gwilt, at a secret meeting with her in the park that morning; and ill at ease in his own company, as he now sat moodily smoking, in the solitude of his room. 'I can't live this sort of life much longer,' thought Allan. 'If nobody will help me to put the awkward question to Miss Gwilt, I must stumble on some way of putting it for myself.'

What way? The answer to that question was as hard to find as ever. Allan tried to stimulate his sluggish invention by walking up and down the room, and was disturbed by the appearance of the footman at the first turn.

'Now then! what is it?' he asked impatiently.

'A letter, sir; and the person waits for an answer.'

Allan looked at the address. It was in a strange handwriting. He opened the letter; and a little note enclosed in it dropped to the ground. The note was directed, still in the strange handwriting, to 'Mrs Mandeville, 18, Kingsdown Crescent, Bayswater. Favoured by Mr Armadale.' More and more surprised, Allan turned for information to the signature at the end of the letter. It was 'Anne Milroy'.

'Anne Milroy?' he repeated. 'It must be the major's wife. What can she possibly want with me?'

By way of discovering what she wanted, Allan did at last what he might more wisely have done at first. He sat down to read the letter.

[Private.]

The Cottage, Monday.

DEAR SIR, – The name at the end of these lines will, I fear, recall to you a very rude return made on my part, some time since, for an act of neighbourly kindness on yours. I can only say in excuse, that I am a great sufferer, and that if I was ill-tempered enough, in a moment of irritation under severe pain, to send back your present of fruit, I have regretted doing so ever since. Attribute this letter, if you please, to my desire to make you some atonement, and to my wish to be of service to our good friend and landlord if I possibly can.

I have been informed of the question which you addressed to my husband the day before yesterday, on the subject of Miss Gwilt. From all I have heard of you, I am quite sure that your anxiety to know more of this charming person than you know now, is an anxiety proceeding from the most honourable motives. Believing this, I feel a woman's interest – incurable invalid as I am – in assisting you. If you are desirous of becoming acquainted with Miss Gwilt's family circumstances without directly appealing to Miss Gwilt herself, it rests with you to make the discovery – and I will tell you how.

It so happens that some few days since, I wrote privately to Miss Gwilt's reference on this very subject. I had long observed that my governess was singularly reluctant to speak of her family and her friends; and without attributing her silence to other than perfectly proper motives, I felt it my duty to my daughter to make some inquiry on the subject. The answer that I have received is satisfactory as far as it goes. My correspondent informs me that Miss Gwilt's story is a very sad one, and that her own conduct throughout has been praiseworthy in the extreme. The circumstances (of a domestic nature, as I gather,) are all plainly stated in a collection of letters now in the possession of Miss Gwilt's reference. This lady is perfectly willing to let me see the letters – but, not possessing copies of them, and being personally responsible for their security, she is reluctant, if it can be avoided, to trust them to the post; and she begs me to wait until she or I can find some reliable person who can be employed to transmit the packet from her hands to mine.

Under these circumstances, it has struck me that you might possibly, with your interest in the matter, be not unwilling to take charge of the papers. If I am wrong in this idea, and if you are not disposed, after what I have told you, to go to the trouble and expense of a journey to London, you have only to burn my letter and enclosure, and to think no more about it. If you decide on becoming my envoy, I gladly provide you with the necessary introduction to Mrs Mandeville. You have only, on presenting it, to receive the letters in a sealed packet, to send them here on your return to Thorpe-Ambrose, and to wait an early communication from me acquainting you with the result.

In conclusion, I have only to add that I see no impropriety in your taking (if you feel so inclined) the course that I propose to you. Miss Gwilt's manner of receiving such allusions as I have made to her family circumstances, has rendered it unpleasant for me (and would render it quite impossible for you) to seek information in the first instance from herself. I am certainly justified in applying to her reference; and you are certainly not to blame for being the medium of safely transmitting a sealed communication from one lady to another. If I find in that communication family secrets which cannot honourably be mentioned to any third person, I shall of course be obliged to keep you waiting until I have first appealed to Miss Gwilt. If I find nothing recorded but what is to her honour, and what is sure to raise her still higher in your estimation, I am undeniably doing her a service by taking you into my confidence. This is how I look at the matter – but pray don't allow me to influence *you*.

In any case, I have one condition to make, which I am sure you will understand to be indispensable. The most innocent actions are liable, in this wicked world, to the worst possible interpretation. I must, therefore, request that you will consider this communication as *strictly private*. I write to you in a confidence which is on no account (until circumstances may, in my opinion, justify the revelation of it) to extend beyond our two selves.

Believe me, dear sir, truly yours,
ANNE MILROY.

In this tempting form the unscrupulous ingenuity of the major's wife had set the trap. Without a moment's hesitation, Allan followed his impulses as usual, and walked straight into it – writing his answer, and pursuing his own reflections simultaneously, in a highly characteristic state of mental confusion.

'By Jupiter, this *is* kind of Mrs Milroy!' ('My dear madam.') 'Just the thing I wanted, at the time when I needed it most!' ('I don't know how to express my sense of your kindness, except by saying that I will go to London and fetch the letters with the greatest pleasure.') 'She shall have a basket of fruit regularly every day, all through the season.' ('I will go at once, dear madam, and be back to-morrow.') 'Ah, nothing like the women for helping one when one is in love! This is just what my poor mother would have done in Mrs Milroy's place.' ('On my word of honour as a gentleman, I will take the utmost care of the letters – and keep the thing strictly private, as you request.') 'I would have given five hundred pounds to anybody who would have put me up to the right way to speak to Miss Gwilt – and here is this blessed woman does it for nothing.' ('Believe me, my dear madam, gratefully yours, Allan Armadale.')

Having sent his reply out to Mrs Milroy's messenger, Allan paused in a momentary perplexity. He had an appointment with Miss Gwilt in the park for the next morning. It was absolutely necessary to let her know that he would be unable to keep it; she had forbidden him to write, and he had no chance that day of seeing her alone. In this difficulty, he determined to let the necessary intimation reach her through the medium of a message to the major, announcing his departure for London on business, and asking if he could be of service to any member of the family. Having thus removed the only obstacle to his departure, Allan consulted the time-table, and found, to his disappointment, that there was a good hour to spare before it would be necessary to drive to the railway-station. In his existing frame of mind, he would infinitely have preferred starting for London in a violent hurry.

When the time came at last, Allan, on passing the steward's office, drummed at the door, and called through it, to Mr Bashwood, 'I'm going to town – back to-morrow.' There was no answer from within; and the servant interposing, informed his master that Mr Bashwood, having no business to attend to that day, had locked up the office, and had left some hours since.

On reaching the station, the first person whom Allan encountered was Pedgift Junior, going to London on the legal business which he had mentioned on the previous evening, at the great house. The necessary explanations exchanged, it was decided that the two should travel in the same carriage. Allan was glad to have a companion; and Pedgift, enchanted as usual to make himself useful to his client, bustled away to get the tickets and see to the luggage. Sauntering to and fro on the platform until his faithful follower returned, Allan came suddenly upon no less a person than Mr Bashwood himself – standing back in a corner with the guard of the train, and putting a letter (accompanied, to all appearance, by a fee) privately into the man's hand.

'Hullo!' cried Allan in his hearty way. 'Something important there, Mr Bashwood – eh?'

If Mr Bashwood had been caught in the act of committing murder, he could hardly have shown greater alarm than he now testified at Allan's sudden discovery of him. Snatching off his dingy old hat, he bowed bareheaded, in a palsy of nervous trembling from head to foot. 'No, sir, no, sir; only a little letter, a little letter,' said the deputy-steward, taking refuge in reiteration, and bowing himself swiftly back-wards out of his employer's sight.

Allan turned carelessly on his heel. 'I wish I could take to that fellow,' he thought – 'but I can't; he's such a sneak! What the deuce was there to tremble about? Does he think I want to pry into his secrets?'

Mr Bashwood's secret on this occasion concerned Allan more nearly than Allan supposed. The letter which he had just placed in charge of the guard was nothing less than a word of warning addressed to Mrs Oldershaw, and written by Miss Gwilt.

If you can hurry your business (wrote the major's governess) do so, and come back to London immediately. Things are going wrong here, and Miss Milroy is at the bottom of the mischief. This morning she insisted on taking up her mother's breakfast, always on other occasions taken up by the nurse. They had a long confabulation in private; and half an hour later I saw the nurse slip out with a letter, and take the path that leads to the great house. The sending of the letter has been followed by young Armadale's sudden departure for London – in the face of an appointment which he had with me for to-morrow morning. This looks serious. The girl is evidently bold enough to make a fight of it for the position of Mrs Armadale of Thorpe-Ambrose, and she has found out some way of getting her mother to help her. Don't suppose I am in the least nervous or discouraged; and don't do anything till you hear from me again. Only get back to London – for I may have serious need of your assistance in the course of the next day or two.

I send this letter to town (to save a post) by the mid-day train, in charge of the guard. As you insist on knowing every step I take at Thorpe-Ambrose, I may as well tell you that my messenger (for I can't go to the station myself) is that curious old creature whom I mentioned to you in my first letter. Ever since that time, he has been perpetually hanging about here for a look at me. I am not sure whether I frighten him or fascinate him – perhaps I do both together. All you need care to know is, that I can trust him with my trifling errands, and possibly, as time goes on, with something more.

L. G.

Meanwhile the train had started from the Thorpe-Ambrose station, and the squire and his travelling companion were on their way to London.

Some men, finding themselves in Allan's company under present circumstances, might have felt curious to know the nature of his business in the metropolis. Young Pedgift's unerring instinct as a man of the world penetrated the secret without the slightest difficulty. 'The old story,' thought his wary old head, wagging privately on its lusty young shoulders. 'There's a woman in the case, as usual. Any other business would have been turned over to *me*.' Perfectly satisfied with this conclusion, Mr Pedgift the younger proceeded, with an eye to his professional interest, to make himself as agreeable to his client as usual. He seized on the whole administrative business of the journey to London, as he had seized on the whole administrative business of the picnic at the Broads. On reaching the terminus, Allan was ready to go to any hotel that might be recommended. His invaluable solicitor straightway drove him to an hotel at which the Pedgift family had been accustomed to put up for three generations.

'You don't object to vegetables, sir?' said the cheerful Pedgift, as the cab stopped at an hotel in Covent Garden Market. 'Very good, you may leave the rest to my grandfather, my father, and me. I don't know which of the three is most beloved and respected in this house. How-d'ye-do, William? (Our head-waiter, Mr Armadale.) Is your wife's rheumatism better, and does the little boy get on nicely at school? Your master's out, is he? Never mind, you'll do. This, William, is Mr Armadale of Thorpe-Ambrose. I have prevailed on Mr Armadale to try our house. Have you got the bedroom I wrote for? Very good. Let Mr Armadale have it, instead of me (my grandfather's favourite bedroom, sir; number five, on the second floor;) pray take it – I can sleep anywhere. Will you have the mattress on the top of the feather-bed? You hear, William? Tell Matilda, the mattress on the top of the feather-bed. How is Matilda? Has she got the tooth-ache, as usual? The head-chambermaid, Mr Armadale, and a most extraordinary woman;

she will *not* part with a hollow tooth in her lower jaw. My grandfather says, "have it out" – my father says, "have it out" – I say, "have it out," and Matilda turns a deaf ear to all three of us. Yes, William, yes; if Mr Armadale approves, this sitting-room will do. About dinner, sir? You would prefer getting your business over first, and coming back to dinner? Shall we say, in that case, half-past seven? William, half-past seven. Not the least need to order anything, Mr Armadale. The head-waiter has only to give my compliments to the cook, and the best dinner in London will be sent up, punctual to the minute, as a necessary consequence. Say Mr Pedgift, junior, if you please, William – otherwise, sir, we might get my grandfather's dinner or my father's dinner, and they *might* turn out a little too heavy and old-fashioned in their way of feeding for you and me. As to the wine, William. At dinner, *my* champagne, and the sherry that my father thinks nasty. After dinner, the claret with the blue seal – the wine my innocent grandfather said wasn't worth sixpence a bottle. Ha! ha! poor old boy! You will send up the evening papers and the playbills, just as usual, and – that will do, I think, William, for the present. An invaluable servant, Mr Armadale; they're all invaluable servants in this house. We may not be fashionable here, sir, but by the Lord Harry we are snug! A cab? you would like a cab? Don't stir! I've rung the bell twice – that means, Cab wanted in a hurry. Might I ask, Mr Armadale, which way your business takes you? Towards Bayswater? Would you mind dropping me in the park? It's a habit of mine when I'm in London to air myself among the aristocracy. Yours truly, sir, has an eye for a fine woman and a fine horse; and when he's in Hyde Park he's quite in his native element.' Thus the all-accomplished Pedgift ran on; and by these little arts did he recommend himself to the good opinion of his client.

When the dinner-hour united the travelling companions again in their sitting-room at the hotel, a far less acute observer than young Pedgift must have noticed the marked change that appeared in Allan's manner. He looked vexed and puzzled, and sat drumming with his fingers on the dining-table without uttering a word.

'I'm afraid something has happened to annoy you, sir, since we parted company in the Park?' said Pedgift Junior. 'Excuse the question – I only ask it in case I can be of any use.'

'Something that I never expected has happened,' returned Allan; 'I don't know what to make of it. I should like to have your opinion,' he added, after a little hesitation; 'that is to say, if you will excuse my not entering into any particulars?'

'Certainly!' assented young Pedgift. 'Sketch it in outline, sir. The merest hint will do; I wasn't born yesterday.' ('Oh, these women!' thought the youthful philosopher, in parenthesis.)

'Well,' began Allan, 'you know what I said when we got to this hotel; I said I had a place to go to in Bayswater' (Pedgift mentally checked off the first point – Case in the suburbs, Bayswater); 'and a person – that is to say – no – as I said before, a person to inquire after.' (Pedgift checked off the next point: Person in the case. She-person, or he-person? She-person unquestionably!) 'Well, I went to the house, and when I asked for her – I mean the person – she – that is to say, the person – oh, confound it!' cried Allan, 'I shall drive myself mad, and you too, if I try to tell my story in this roundabout way. Here it is in two words. I went to number eighteen Kingsdown Crescent, to see a lady named Mandeville; and when I asked for her, the servant said Mrs Mandeville had gone away, without telling anybody where, and without even leaving an address at which letters could be sent to her. There! it's out at last, and what do you think of it now?'

'Tell me first, sir,' said the wary Pedgift, 'what inquiries you made, when you found this lady had vanished?'

'Inquiries?' repeated Allan, 'I was utterly staggered; I didn't say anything. What inquiries ought I to have made?'

Pedgift Junior cleared his throat, and crossed his legs in a strictly professional manner.

'I have no wish, Mr Armadale,' he began, 'to inquire into your business with Mrs Mandeville—'

'No,' interposed Allan, bluntly, 'I hope you won't inquire into that. My business with Mrs Mandeville must remain a secret.'

'But,' pursued Pedgift, laying down the law with the forefinger of one hand on the outstretched palm of the other, 'I may, perhaps, be allowed to ask generally, whether your business with Mrs Mandeville is of a nature to interest you in tracing her from Kingsdown Crescent to her present residence?'

'Certainly!' said Allan. 'I have a very particular reason for wishing to see her.'

'In that case, sir,' returned Pedgift Junior, 'there were two obvious questions which you ought to have asked, to begin with – namely, on what date Mrs Mandeville left, and how she left. Having discovered this, you should have ascertained next, under what domestic circumstances she went away – whether there was a misunderstanding with anybody; say a difficulty about money-matters. Also, whether she went away alone, or with somebody else. Also, whether the house was her own, or whether she only lodged in it. Also, in the latter event—'

337

'Stop! stop! you're making my head swim,' cried Allan. 'I don't understand all these ins and outs – I'm not used to this sort of thing.'

'I've been used to it myself from my childhood upwards, sir,' remarked Pedgift. 'And if I can be of any assistance, say the word.'

'You're very kind,' returned Allan. 'If you could only help me to find Mrs Mandeville; and if you wouldn't mind leaving the thing afterwards entirely in my hands—?'

'I'll leave it in your hands, sir, with all the pleasure in life,' said Pedgift Junior. ('And I'll lay five to one,' he added mentally, 'when the time comes, you'll leave it in mine!') 'We'll go to Bayswater together, Mr Armadale, to-morrow morning. In the meantime here's the soup. The case now before the court is – Pleasure *versus* Business. I don't know what you say, sir; I say, without a moment's hesitation, Verdict for the plaintiff. Let us gather our rosebuds while we may. Excuse my high spirits, Mr Armadale. Though buried in the country, I was made for a London life; the very air of the metropolis intoxicates me.' With that avowal the irresistible Pedgift placed a chair for his patron, and issued his orders cheerfully to his viceroy, the head-waiter. 'Iced punch, William, after the soup. I answer for the punch, Mr Armadale – it's made after a receipt of my great-uncle's. He kept a tavern, and founded the fortunes of the family. I don't mind telling you the Pedgifts have had a publican among them; there's no false pride about me. "Worth makes the man (as Pope says), and want of it the fellow; the rest is all but leather and prunella."[1] I cultivate poetry as well as music, sir, in my leisure hours; in fact, I'm more or less on familiar terms with the whole of the nine Muses. Aha! here's the punch! The memory of my great-uncle, the publican, Mr Armadale – drunk in solemn silence!'

Allan tried hard to emulate his companion's gaiety and good humour, but with very indifferent success. His visit to Kingsdown Crescent recurred ominously again and again to his memory, all through the dinner, and all through the public amusements to which he and his legal adviser repaired at a later hour of the evening. When Pedgift Junior put out his candle that night, he shook his wary head, and regretfully apostrophized 'the women' for the second time.

By ten o'clock the next morning, the indefatigable Pedgift was on the scene of action. To Allan's great relief, he proposed making the necessary inquiries at Kingsdown Crescent, in his own person, while his patron waited near at hand, in the cab which had brought them from the hotel. After a delay of little more than five minutes, he re-appeared, in full possession of all attainable particulars. His first proceeding was to request Allan to step out of the cab, and to pay the driver. Next, he politely offered his arm, and led the way round the corner of the crescent, across a square, and into a by-street, which was rendered exceptionally lively by the presence of the local cab-stand. Here he stopped, and asked jocosely, whether Mr Armadale saw his way now, or whether it would be necessary to test his patience by making an explanation.

'See my way?' repeated Allan in bewilderment. 'I see nothing but a cab-stand.'

Pedgift Junior smiled compassionately, and entered on his explanation. It was a lodging-house at Kingsdown Crescent, he begged to state to begin with. He had insisted on seeing the landlady. A very nice person, with all the remains of having been a fine girl about fifty years ago; quite in Pedgift's style – if he had only been alive at the beginning of the present century – quite in Pedgift's style. But perhaps Mr Armadale would prefer hearing about Mrs Mandeville? Unfortunately, there was nothing to tell. There had been no quarrelling, and not a farthing left unpaid: the lodger had gone, and there wasn't an explanatory circumstance to lay hold of anywhere. It was either Mrs Mandeville's way to vanish, or there was something under the rose, quite undiscoverable so far. Pedgift had got the date on which she left, and the time of day at which she left, and the means by which she left. The means might help to trace her. She had gone away in a cab which the servant had fetched from the nearest stand. The stand was now before their eyes; and the waterman was the first person to apply to – going to the waterman for information, being clearly (if Mr Armadale would excuse the joke) going to the fountain-head. Treating the subject in this airy manner, and telling Allan that he would be back in a moment, Pedgift Junior sauntered down the street, and beckoned the waterman confidentially into the nearest public-house.

In a little while the two reappeared; the waterman taking Pedgift in succession to the first, third, fourth and sixth of the cabmen whose vehicles were on the stand. The longest conference was held with the sixth man; and it ended in the sudden approach of the sixth cab to the part of the street where Allan was waiting.

'Get in, sir,' said Pedgift, opening the door, 'I've found the man. He remembers the lady; and, though he has forgotten the name of the street, he believes he can find the place he drove her to when he once gets back into the neighbourhood. I am charmed to inform you, Mr Armadale, that we are in luck's way so far. I asked the waterman to show me the regular men on the stand – and it turns out that one of the regular men drove Mrs Mandeville. The waterman vouches for him;

he's quite an anomaly – a respectable cabman; drives his own horse, and has never been in any trouble. These are the sort of men, sir, who sustain one's belief in human nature. I've had a look at our friend; and I agree with the waterman – I think we can depend on him.'

The investigation required some exercise of patience at the outset. It was not till the cab had traversed the distance between Bayswater and Pimlico, that the driver began to slacken his pace and look about him. After once or twice retracing its course, the vehicle entered a quiet by-street, ending in a dead wall, with a door in it; and stopped at the last house on the left-hand side, the house next to the wall.

'Here it is, gentlemen,' said the man, opening the cab-door.

Allan and Allan's adviser both got out, and both looked at the house, with the same feeling of instinctive distrust. Buildings have their physiognomy – especially buildings in great cities – and the face of this house was essentially furtive in its expression. The front windows were all shut, and the front blinds were all drawn down. It looked no larger than the other houses in the street, seen in front; but it ran back deceitfully, and gained its greater accommodation by means of its greater depth. It affected to be a shop on the ground-floor – but it exhibited absolutely nothing in the space that intervened between the window and an inner row of red curtains, which hid the interior entirely from view. At one side was the shop-door, having more red curtains behind the glazed part of it, and bearing a brass plate on the wooden part of it, inscribed with the name of 'Oldershaw'. On the other side was the private door, with a bell marked Professional; and another brass plate, indicating a medical occupant on this side of the house, for the name on it was 'Doctor Downward'. If ever brick and mortar spoke yet, the brick and mortar here said plainly, 'We have got our secrets inside, and we mean to keep them.'

'This can't be the place,' said Allan; 'there must be some mistake.'

'You know best, sir,' remarked Pedgift Junior, with his sardonic gravity. 'You know Mrs Mandeville's habits.'

'I!' exclaimed Allan. 'You may be surprised to hear it – but Mrs Mandeville is a total stranger to me.'

'I'm not in the least surprised to hear it, sir – the landlady at Kingsdown Crescent informed me that Mrs Mandeville was an old woman. Suppose we inquire?' added the impenetrable Pedgift, looking at the red curtains in the shop-window with a strong suspicion that Mrs Mandeville's grand-daughter might possibly be behind them.

They tried the shop-door first. It was locked. They rang. A lean and yellow young woman, with a tattered French novel in her hand, opened it.

'Good morning, miss,' said Pedgift. 'Is Mrs Mandeville at home?'

The yellow young woman stared at him in astonishment. 'No person of that name is known here,' she answered sharply, in a foreign accent.

'Perhaps they know her at the private door?' suggested Pedgift Junior.

'Perhaps they do,' said the yellow young woman, and shut the door in his face.

'Rather a quick-tempered young person that, sir,' said Pedgift. 'I congratulate Mrs Mandeville on not being acquainted with her.' He led the way, as he spoke, to Doctor Downward's side of the premises, and rang the bell.

The door was opened this time by a man in a shabby livery. He, too, stared when Mrs Mandeville's name was mentioned; and he, too, knew of no such person in the house.

'Very odd,' said Pedgift, appealing to Allan.

'What is odd?' asked a softly-speaking gentleman in black, suddenly appearing on the threshold of the parlour-door.

Pedgift Junior politely explained the circumstances, and begged to know whether he had the pleasure of speaking to Doctor Downward.

The doctor bowed. If the expression may be pardoned, he was one of those carefully-constructed physicians, in whom the public – especially the female public – implicitly trust. He had the necessary bald head, the necessary double eyeglass, the necessary black clothes, and the necessary blandness of manner, all complete. His voice was soothing, his ways were deliberate, his smile was confidential. What particular branch of his profession Doctor Downward followed, was not indicated on his door-plate – but he had utterly mistaken his vocation, if he was not a ladies' medical man.[2]

'Are you quite sure there is no mistake about the name?' asked the doctor, with a strong underlying anxiety in his manner. 'I have known very serious inconvenience to arise sometimes from mistakes about names. No? There is really no mistake? In that case, gentlemen, I can only repeat what my servant has already told you. Don't apologize, pray. Good morning.' The doctor withdrew as noiselessly as he had appeared; the man in the shabby livery silently opened the door; and Allan and his companion found themselves in the street again.

'Mr Armadale,' said Pedgift, 'I don't know how you feel – I feel puzzled.'

'That's awkward,' returned Allan; 'I was just going to ask you what we ought to do next.'

'I don't like the look of the place, the look of the shopwoman, or the look of the doctor,' pursued the other. 'And yet I can't say I think they are deceiving us – I can't say I think they really do know Mrs Mandeville's name.'

The impressions of Pedgift Junior seldom misled him; and they had not misled him in this case. The caution which had dictated Mrs Oldershaw's private removal from Bayswater, was the caution which frequently over-reaches itself. It had warned her to trust nobody at Pimlico with the secret of the name she had assumed as Miss Gwilt's reference; but it had entirely failed to prepare her for the emergency that had really happened. In a word, Mrs Oldershaw had provided for everything, except for the unimaginable contingency of an after-inquiry into the character of Miss Gwilt.

'We must do something,' said Allan; 'it seems useless to stop here.'

Nobody had ever yet caught Pedgift Junior at the end of his resources; and Allan failed to catch him at the end of them now. 'I quite agree with you, sir,' he said; 'we must do something. We'll cross-examine the cabman.'

The cabman proved to be immovable. Charged with mistaking the place, he pointed to the empty shop-window. 'I don't know what you may have seen, gentlemen,' he remarked; 'but there's the only shop-window I ever saw with nothing at all inside it. *That* fixed the place in my mind at the time, and I know it again when I see it.' Charged with mistaking the person, or the day, or the house at which he had taken the person up, the cabman proved to be still unassailable. The servant who fetched him was marked as a girl well known on the stand. The day was marked, as the unluckiest working day he had had since the first of the year; and the lady was marked, as having had her money ready at the right moment (which not one elderly lady in a hundred usually had), and having paid him his fare on demand without disputing it (which not one elderly lady in a hundred usually did). 'Take my number, gentlemen,' concluded the cabman, 'and pay me for my time; and what I've said to you, I'll swear to anywhere.'

Pedgift made a note in his pocket-book of the man's number. Having added to it the name of the street, and the names on the two brass plates, he quietly opened the cab-door. 'We are quite in the dark, thus far,' he said. 'Suppose we grope our way back to the hotel?'

He spoke and looked more seriously than usual. The mere fact of 'Mrs Mandeville's' having changed her lodging without telling any one where she was going, and without leaving any address at which letters could be forwarded to her – which the jealous malignity of Mrs Milroy had interpreted as being undeniably suspicious in itself – had produced no great impression on the more impartial judgment of Allan's solicitor. People frequently left their lodgings in a private manner, with perfectly producible reasons for doing so. But the appearance of the place to which the cabman persisted in declaring that he had driven 'Mrs Mandeville', set the character and proceedings of that mysterious lady before Pedgift Junior in a new light. His personal interest in the inquiry suddenly strengthened, and he began to feel a curiosity to know the real nature of Allan's business which he had not felt yet.

'Our next move, Mr Armadale, is not a very easy move to see,' he said, as they drove back to the hotel. 'Do you think you could put me in possession of any further particulars?'

Allan hesitated; and Pedgift Junior saw that he had advanced a little too far. 'I mustn't force it,' he thought; 'I must give it time, and let it come of its own accord.' 'In the absence of any other information, sir,' he resumed,[3] 'what do you say, to my making some inquiry about that queer shop, and about those two names on the door-plate? My business in London, when I leave you, is of a professional nature; and I am going into the right quarter for getting information, if it is to be got.'

'There can't be any harm, I suppose, in making inquiries,' replied Allan.

He, too, spoke more seriously than usual; he, too, was beginning to feel an all-mastering curiosity to know more. Some vague connection, not to be distinctly realized or traced out, began to establish itself in his mind between the difficulty of approaching Miss Gwilt's family circumstances, and the difficulty of approaching Miss Gwilt's reference. 'I'll get down and walk, and leave you to go on to your business,' he said. 'I want to consider a little about this; and a walk and a cigar will help me.'

'My business will be done, sir, between one and two,' said Pedgift, when the cab had been stopped, and Allan had got out. 'Shall we meet again at two o'clock, at the hotel?'

Allan nodded, and the cab drove off.

CHAPTER IV

ALLAN AT BAY

Two o'clock came; and Pedgift Junior, punctual to his time, came with it. His vivacity of the morning had all sparkled out; he greeted Allan with his customary politeness, but without his customary smile; and when the head-waiter came in for orders, his dismissal was instantly pronounced in words never yet heard to issue from the lips of Pedgift in that hotel: 'Nothing at present.'

'You seem to be in low spirits,' said Allan. 'Can't we get our information? Can nobody tell you anything about the house in Pimlico?'

'Three different people have told me about it, Mr Armadale; and they have all three said the same thing.'

Allan eagerly drew his chair nearer to the place occupied by his travelling companion. His reflections in the interval since they had last seen each other, had not tended to compose him. That strange connection, so easy to feel, so hard to trace, between the difficulty of approaching Miss Gwilt's family circumstances, and the difficulty of approaching Miss Gwilt's reference, which had already established itself in his thoughts, had by this time stealthily taken a firmer and firmer hold on his mind. Doubts troubled him which he could neither understand nor express. Curiosity filled him, which he half-longed and half-dreaded to satisfy.

'I am afraid I must trouble you with a question or two, sir, before I can come to the point,' said Pedgift Junior. 'I don't want to force myself into your confidence; I only want to see my way, in what looks to me like a very awkward business. Do you mind telling me whether others beside yourself are interested in this inquiry of ours?'

'Other people *are* interested in it,' replied Allan. 'There's no objection to telling you that.'

'Is there any other person who is the object of the inquiry besides Mrs Mandeville herself?' pursued Pedgift, winding his way a little deeper into the secret.

'Yes; there is another person,' said Allan, answering rather unwillingly.

'Is the person a young woman, Mr Armadale?'

Allan started. 'How do you come to guess that?' he began – then checked himself, when it was too late. 'Don't ask me any more questions,' he resumed. 'I'm a bad hand at defending myself against a sharp fellow like you; and I'm bound in honour towards other people to keep the particulars of this business to myself.'

Pedgift Junior had apparently heard enough for his purpose. He drew his chair, in his turn, nearer to Allan. He was evidently anxious and embarrassed – but his professional manner began to show itself again from sheer force of habit.

'I've done with my questions, sir,' he said; 'and I have something to say now, on my side. In my father's absence, perhaps you may be kindly disposed to consider me as your legal adviser. If you will take my advice, you will not stir another step in this inquiry.'

'What do you mean?' interposed Allan.

'It is just possible, Mr Armadale, that the cabman, positive as he is, may have been mistaken. I strongly recommend you to take it for granted that he *is* mistaken – and to drop it there.'

The caution was kindly intended; but it came too late. Allan did what ninety-nine men out of a hundred in his position would have done – he declined to take his lawyer's advice.

'Very well, sir,' said Pedgift Junior; 'if you will have it, you must have it.'

He leaned forward close to Allan's ear, and whispered what he had heard of the house in Pimlico, and of the people who occupied it.

'Don't blame me, Mr Armadale,' he added, when the irrevocable words had been spoken. 'I tried to spare you.'

Allan suffered the shock, as all great shocks are suffered, in silence. His first impulse would have driven him headlong for refuge to that very view of the cabman's assertion which had just been recommended to him, but for one damning circumstance which placed itself inexorably in his way. Miss Gwilt's marked reluctance to approach the story of her past life, rose irrepressibly on his memory, in indirect but horrible confirmation of the evidence which connected Miss Gwilt's reference with the house in Pimlico. One conclusion, and one only – the conclusion which any man must have drawn, hearing what he had just heard, and knowing no more than he knew – forced itself into his mind. A miserable, fallen woman, who had abandoned herself in her extremity to the help of wretches skilled in criminal concealment – who had stolen her way back to decent society and a reputable employment, by means of a false character – and whose position now imposed on her the dreadful necessity of perpetual secrecy and perpetual deceit in relation to her past life – such was the aspect in which the beautiful governess at Thorpe-Ambrose now stood revealed to Allan's eyes!

Falsely revealed, or truly revealed? Had she stolen her way back to decent society, and a reputable employment, by means of a false character? She had. Did her position impose on her the dreadful necessity of perpetual secrecy and perpetual deceit, in relation to her past life? It did. Was she some such pitiable victim to the treachery of a man unknown as Allan had supposed? *She was no such pitiable victim.* The conclusion which Allan had drawn – the conclusion literally forced into his mind by the facts before him – was, nevertheless, the conclusion of all others that was farthest even from touching on the truth. The true story of Miss Gwilt's connection with the house in Pimlico and the people who inhabited it – a house rightly described as filled with wicked secrets, and people rightly represented as perpetually in danger of feeling the grasp of the law – was a story which coming events were yet to disclose: a story infinitely less revolting, and yet infinitely more terrible, than Allan or Allan's companion had either of them supposed.

'I tried to spare you, Mr Armadale,' repeated Pedgift. 'I was anxious, if I could possibly avoid it, not to distress you.'

Allan looked up, and made an effort to control himself. 'You have distressed me dreadfully,' he said. 'You have quite crushed me down. But it is not your fault. I ought to feel you have done me a service – and what I ought to do I will do, when I am my own man again. There is one thing,' Allan added, after a moment's painful consideration, 'which ought to be understood between us at once. The advice you offered me just now was very kindly meant, and it was the best advice that could be given. I will take it gratefully. We will never talk of this again, if you please; and I beg and entreat you will never speak about it to any other person. Will you promise me that?'

Pedgift gave the promise with very evident sincerity, but without his professional confidence of manner. The distress in Allan's face seemed to daunt him. After a moment of very uncharacteristic hesitation, he considerately quitted the room.

Left by himself, Allan rang for writing materials, and took out of his pocket-book the fatal letter of introduction to 'Mrs Mandeville', which he had received from the major's wife.

A man accustomed to consider consequences and to prepare himself for action by previous thought would, in Allan's present circumstances, have felt some difficulty as to the course which it might now be least embarrassing and least dangerous to pursue. Accustomed to let his impulses direct him on all other occasions, Allan acted on impulse in the serious emergency that now confronted him. Though his attachment to Miss Gwilt was nothing like the deeply-rooted feeling which he had himself honestly believed it to be, she had taken no common place in his admiration, and she filled him with no common grief when he thought of her now. His one dominant desire, at that critical moment in his life, was a man's merciful desire to protect from exposure and ruin the unhappy woman who had lost her place in his estimation, without losing her claim to the forbearance that could spare and to the compassion that could shield her. 'I can't go back to Thorpe-Ambrose; I can't trust myself to speak to her, or to see her again. But I can keep her miserable secret – and I will!' With that thought in his heart, Allan set himself to perform the first and foremost duty which now claimed him – the duty of communicating with Mrs Milroy. If he had possessed a higher mental capacity and a clearer mental view, he might have found

the letter no easy one to write. As it was, he calculated no consequences, and felt no difficulty. His instinct warned him to withdraw
at once from the position in which he now stood towards the major's
wife, and he wrote what his instinct counselled him to write under
those circumstances, as rapidly as the pen could travel over the
paper:

Dunn's Hotel, Covent Garden, Tuesday.

DEAR MADAM, – Pray excuse my not returning to Thorpe-
Ambrose to-day, as I said I would. Unforeseen circumstances
oblige me to stop in London. I am sorry to say I have not
succeeded in seeing Mrs Mandeville, for which reason I cannot
perform your errand; and I beg, therefore, with many apologies,
to return the letter of introduction. I hope you will allow me to
conclude by saying that I am very much obliged to you for your
kindness, and that I will not venture to trespass on it any further.

I remain, dear madam, yours truly,
ALLAN ARMADALE.

In those artless words, still entirely unsuspicious of the character of
the woman he had to deal with, Allan put the weapon she wanted into
Mrs Milroy's hands.

The letter and its enclosure once sealed up, and addressed, he was
free to think of himself and his future. As he sat idly drawing lines with
his pen on the blotting-paper, the tears came into his eyes for the first
time – tears in which the woman who had deceived him had no share.
His heart had gone back to his dead mother. 'If she had been alive,' he
thought, 'I might have trusted *her*, and she would have comforted me.'
It was useless to dwell on it – he dashed away the tears, and turned his
thoughts with the heart-sick resignation that we all know, to living and
present things.

He wrote a line to Mr Bashwood, briefly informing the deputy-
steward that his absence from Thorpe-Ambrose was likely to be prolonged for some little time, and that any further instructions which
might be necessary, under those circumstances, would reach him
through Mr Pedgift the elder. This done, and the letters sent to the
post, his thoughts were forced back once more on himself. Again the
blank future waited before him to be filled up; and again his heart
shrank from it to the refuge of the past.

This time, other images than the image of his mother filled his mind.
The one all-absorbing interest of his earlier days stirred living and eager

in him again. He thought of the sea; he thought of his yacht lying idle in the fishing harbour at his West-country home. The old longing got possession of him to hear the wash of the waves; to see the filling of the sails; to feel the vessel that his own hands had helped to build, bounding under him once more. He rose in his impetuous way, to call for the time-table, and to start for Somersetshire by the first train – when the dread of the questions which Mr Brock might ask, the suspicion of the change which Mr Brock might see in him, drew him back to his chair. 'I'll write,' he thought, 'to have the yacht rigged and refitted, and I'll wait to go to Somersetshire myself till Midwinter can go with me.' He sighed as his memory reverted to his absent friend. Never had he felt the void made in his life by Midwinter's departure so painfully as he felt it now, in the dreariest of all social solitudes – the solitude of a stranger in London, left by himself at an hotel.

Before long, Pedgift Junior looked in, with an apology for his intrusion. Allan felt too lonely and too friendless not to welcome his companion's reappearance gratefully. 'I'm not going back to Thorpe-Ambrose,' he said: 'I'm going to stay a little while in London. I hope you will be able to stay with me?' To do him justice, Pedgift was touched, by the solitary position in which the owner of the great Thorpe-Ambrose estate now appeared before him. He had never, in his relations with Allan, so entirely forgotten his business-interests as he forgot them now.

'You are quite right, sir, to stop here – London's the place to divert your mind,' said Pedgift cheerfully. 'All business is more or less elastic in its nature, Mr Armadale; I'll spin *my* business out, and keep you company with the greatest pleasure. We are both of us on the right side of thirty, sir – let's enjoy ourselves. What do you say to dining early, and going to the play, and trying the Great Exhibition in Hyde Park[1] to-morrow morning, after breakfast? If we only live like fighting-cocks, and go in perpetually for public amusements, we shall arrive in no time at the *mens sana in corpore sano* of the ancients. Don't be alarmed at the quotation, sir. I dabble a little in Latin after business hours, and enlarge my sympathies by occasional perusal of the Pagan writers, assisted by a crib. William, dinner at five; and, as it's particularly important to-day, I'll see the cook myself.'

The evening passed – the next day passed – Thursday morning came, and brought with it a letter for Allan. The direction was in Mrs Milroy's handwriting; and the form of address adopted in the letter warned Allan the moment he opened it that something had gone wrong.

[Private.]

The Cottage, Thorpe-Ambrose, Wednesday.

SIR, – I have just received your mysterious letter. It has more than surprised, it has really alarmed me. After having made the friendliest advances to you on my side, I find myself suddenly shut out from your confidence in the most unintelligible, and, I must add, the most discourteous manner. It is quite impossible that I can allow the matter to rest where you have left it. The only conclusion I can draw from your letter is, that my confidence must have been abused in some way, and that you know a great deal more than you are willing to tell me. Speaking in the interest of my daughter's welfare, I request that you will inform me what the circumstances are which have prevented your seeing Mrs Mandeville, and which have led to the withdrawal of the assistance that you unconditionally promised me in your letter of Monday last.

In my state of health, I cannot involve myself in a lengthened correspondence. I must endeavour to anticipate any objections you may make, and I must say all that I have to say in my present letter. In the event (which I am most unwilling to consider possible) of your declining to accede to the request that I have just addressed to you, I beg to say that I shall consider it my duty to my daughter to have this very unpleasant matter cleared up. If I don't hear from you to my full satisfaction by return of post, I shall be obliged to tell my husband that circumstances have happened which justify us in immediately testing the respectability of Miss Gwilt's reference. And when he asks me for my authority, I will refer him to you.

Your obedient servant,
ANNE MILROY.

In those terms the major's wife threw off the mask, and left her victim to survey at his leisure the trap in which she had caught him. Allan's belief in Mrs Milroy's good faith had been so implicitly sincere, that her letter simply bewildered him. He saw vaguely that he had been deceived in some way, and that Mrs Milroy's neighbourly interest in him was not what it had looked on the surface; and he saw no more. The threat of appealing to the major – on which, with a woman's ignorance of the natures of men, Mrs Milroy had relied for producing its effect – was the only part of the letter to which Allan reverted with any satisfaction: it relieved instead of alarming him. 'If there *is* to be a quarrel,' he thought, 'it will be a comfort, at any rate, to have it out with a man.'

Firm in his resolution to shield the unhappy woman whose secret he wrongly believed himself to have surprised, Allan sat down to write his apologies to the major's wife. After setting up three polite declarations, in close marching order, he retired from the field. 'He was extremely sorry to have offended Mrs Milroy. He was innocent of all intention to offend Mrs Milroy. And he begged to remain Mrs Milroy's truly.' Never had Allan's habitual brevity as a letter-writer done him better service than it did him now. With a little more skilfulness in the use of his pen, he might have given his enemy even a stronger hold on him than the hold she had got already.

The interval-day passed, and with the next morning's post Mrs Milroy's threat came realized in the shape of a letter from her husband. The major wrote less formally than his wife had written, but his questions were mercilessly to the point.

The Cottage, Thorpe-Ambrose,
Friday, July 11th, 1851.

[Private.]

DEAR SIR, – When you did me the favour of calling here a few days since, you asked a question relating to my governess, Miss Gwilt, which I thought rather a strange one at the time, and which caused, as you may remember, a momentary embarrassment between us.

This morning, the subject of Miss Gwilt has been brought to my notice again in a manner which has caused me the utmost astonishment. In plain words, Mrs Milroy has informed me that Miss Gwilt has exposed herself to the suspicion of having deceived us by a false reference. On my expressing the surprise which such an extraordinary statement caused me, and requesting that it might be instantly substantiated, I was still further astonished by being told to apply for all particulars to no less a person than Mr Armadale. I have vainly requested some further explanation from Mrs Milroy; she persists in maintaining silence, and in referring me to yourself.

Under these extraordinary circumstances I am compelled, in justice to all parties, to ask you certain questions, which I will endeavour to put as plainly as possible, and which I am quite ready to believe (from my previous experience of you) that you will answer frankly on your side.

I beg to inquire in the first place, whether you admit or deny

Mrs Milroy's assertion that you have made yourself acquainted with particulars relating either to Miss Gwilt or to Miss Gwilt's reference, of which I am entirely ignorant? In the second place, if you admit the truth of Mrs Milroy's statement, I request to know how you became acquainted with those particulars? Thirdly, and lastly, I beg to ask you what the particulars are?

If any special justification for putting these questions be needed – which, purely as a matter of courtesy towards yourself, I am willing to admit – I beg to remind you that the most precious charge in my house, the charge of my daughter, is confided to Miss Gwilt; and that Mrs Milroy's statement places you, to all appearance, in the position of being competent to tell me whether that charge is properly bestowed or not.

I have only to add that, as nothing has thus far occurred to justify me in entertaining the slightest suspicion either of my governess or her reference, I shall wait before I make any appeal to Miss Gwilt until I have received your answer – which I shall expect by return of post.

Believe me, dear sir, faithfully yours,
DAVID MILROY.

This transparently straightforward letter at once dissipated the confusion which had thus far existed in Allan's mind: he saw the snare in which he had been caught, as he had not seen it yet. Mrs Milroy had clearly placed him between two alternatives – the alternative of putting himself in the wrong, by declining to answer her husband's questions; or the alternative of meanly sheltering his responsibility behind the responsibility of a woman, by acknowledging to the major's own face that the major's wife had deceived him. In this difficulty Allan acted, as usual, without hesitation. His pledge to Mrs Milroy to consider their correspondence private still bound him, disgracefully as she had abused it. And his resolution was as immovable as ever to let no earthly consideration tempt him into betraying Miss Gwilt. 'I may have behaved like a fool,' he thought, 'but I won't break my word; and I won't be the means of turning that miserable woman adrift in the world again.'

He wrote to the major as artlessly and briefly as he had written to the major's wife. He declared his unwillingness to cause a friend and neighbour any disappointment, if he could possibly help it. On this occasion he had no other choice. The questions the major asked him were questions which he could not consent to answer. He was not very clever at explaining himself, and he hoped he might be excused for putting it in that way, and saying no more.

Monday's post brought with it Major Milroy's rejoinder, and closed the correspondence.

The Cottage, Thorpe-Ambrose, Sunday.

Sir, – Your refusal to answer my questions, unaccompanied as it is by even the shadow of an excuse for such a proceeding, can be interpreted but in one way. Besides being an implied acknowledgment of the correctness of Mrs Milroy's statement, it is also an implied reflection on my governess's character. As an act of justice towards a lady who lives under the protection of my roof, and who has given me no reason whatever to distrust her, I shall now show our correspondence to Miss Gwilt: and I shall repeat to her the conversation which I had with Mrs Milroy on this subject, in Mrs Milroy's presence.

One word more respecting the future relations between us, and I have done. My ideas on certain subjects are, I daresay, the ideas of an old-fashioned man. In my time, we had a code of honour by which we regulated our actions. According to that code, if a man made private inquiries into a lady's affairs, without being either her husband, her father, or her brother, he subjected himself to the responsibility of justifying his conduct in the estimation of others; and if he evaded that responsibility, he abdicated the position of a gentleman. It is quite possible that this antiquated way of thinking exists no longer; but it is too late for me, at my time of life, to adopt more modern views. I am scrupulously anxious, seeing that we live in a country and a time in which the only court of honour is a police-court, to express myself with the utmost moderation of language upon this the last occasion that I shall have to communicate with you. Allow me, therefore, merely to remark, that our ideas of the conduct which is becoming in a gentleman, differ seriously; and permit me on this account to request that you will consider yourself for the future as a stranger to my family and to myself.

Your obedient servant,
DAVID MILROY.

The Monday morning on which his client received the major's letter, was the blackest Monday that had yet been marked in Pedgift's calendar. When Allan's first angry sense of the tone of contempt in which his friend and neighbour pronounced sentence on him had subsided, it left him sunk in a state of depression from which no efforts made by his travelling companion could rouse him for the rest of the day. Reverting naturally, now that his sentence of banishment had been pronounced, to his early intercourse with the cottage, his memory went back to Neelie, more regretfully and more penitently than it had gone back to her yet. 'If *she* had shut the door on me, instead of her father,' was the bitter reflection with which Allan now reviewed the past, 'I shouldn't have had a word to say against it; I should have felt it served me right.'

The next day brought another letter – a welcome letter this time, from Mr Brock. Allan had written to Somersetshire on the subject of refitting the yacht some days since. The letter had found the rector engaged, as he innocently supposed, in protecting his old pupil against the woman whom he had watched in London, and whom he now believed to have followed him back to his own home. Acting under the directions sent to her, Mrs Oldershaw's housemaid had completed the mystification of Mr Brock. She had tranquillized all further anxiety on the rector's part, by giving him a written undertaking (in the character of Miss Gwilt), engaging never to approach Mr Armadale, either personally or by letter! Firmly persuaded that he had won the victory at last, poor Mr Brock answered Allan's note in the highest spirits, expressing some natural surprise at his leaving Thorpe-Ambrose, but readily promising that the yacht should be refitted, and offering the hospitality of the rectory in the heartiest manner.

This letter did wonders in raising Allan's spirits. It gave him a new interest to look to, entirely disassociated from his past life in Norfolk. He began to count the days that were still to pass before the return of his absent friend. It was then Tuesday. If Midwinter came back from his walking-trip, as he had engaged to come back, in a fortnight, Saturday would find him at Thorpe-Ambrose. A note sent to meet the traveller might bring him to London the same night; and, if all went well, before another week was over, they might be afloat together in the yacht.

The next day passed, to Allan's relief, without bringing any letters. The spirits of Pedgift rose sympathetically with the spirits of his client. Towards dinner-time he reverted to the *mens sana in corpore sano* of the ancients, and issued his orders to the head-waiter more royally than ever.

Thursday came, and brought the fatal postman with more news from Norfolk. A letter-writer now stepped on the scene who had not appeared there yet; and the total overthrow of all Allan's plans for a visit to Somersetshire was accomplished on the spot.

Pedgift Junior happened that morning to be first at the breakfast-table. When Allan came in, he relapsed into his professional manner, and offered a letter to his patron with a bow performed in dreary silence.

'For me?' inquired Allan, shrinking instinctively from a new correspondent.

'For you, sir — from my father,' replied Pedgift, 'enclosed in one to myself. Perhaps you will allow me to suggest, by way of preparing you for — for something a little unpleasant, — that we shall want a particularly good dinner to-day; and (if they're not performing any modern German music to-night,) I think we should do well to finish the evening melodiously at the Opera.'

'Something wrong at Thorpe-Ambrose?' asked Allan.

'Yes, Mr Armadale; something wrong at Thorpe-Ambrose.'

Allan sat down resignedly, and opened the letter.

High Street, Thorpe-Ambrose,
17th July, 1851.

[Private and confidential.]

DEAR SIR, — I cannot reconcile it with my sense of duty to your interests, to leave you any longer in ignorance of reports current in this town and its neighbourhood, which, I regret to say, are reports affecting yourself.

The first intimation of anything unpleasant reached me on Monday last. It was widely rumoured in the town that something had gone wrong at Major Milroy's with the new governess, and that Mr Armadale was mixed up in it. I paid no heed to this, believing it to be one of the many trumpery pieces of scandal perpetually set going here; and as necessary as the air they breathe, to the comfort of the inhabitants of this highly respectable place.

Tuesday, however, put the matter in a new light. The most interesting particulars were circulated on the highest authority. On Wednesday, the gentry in the neighbourhood took the matter up, and universally sanctioned the view adopted by the town. To-day, the public feeling has reached its climax, and I find myself under the necessity of making you acquainted with what has happened.

To begin at the beginning. It is asserted that a correspondence took place last week between Major Milroy and yourself; in which you cast a very serious suspicion on Miss Gwilt's respectability, without defining your accusation, and without (on being applied to) producing your proofs. Upon this, the major appears to have felt it his duty (while assuring his governess of his own firm belief in her respectability) to inform her of what had happened, in order that she might have no future reason to complain of his having had any concealments from her in a matter affecting her character. Very magnanimous on the major's part; but you will see directly that Miss Gwilt was more magnanimous still. After expressing her thanks in a most becoming manner, she requested permission to withdraw herself from Major Milroy's service.

Various reports are in circulation as to the governess's reason for taking this step.

The authorized version (as sanctioned by the resident gentry) represents Miss Gwilt to have said that she could not condescend – in justice to herself, and in justice to her highly respectable reference – to defend her reputation against undefined imputations cast on it by a comparative stranger. At the same time it was impossible for her to pursue such a course of conduct as this, unless she possessed a freedom of action which was quite incompatible with her continuing to occupy the dependent position of a governess. For that reason she felt it incumbent on her to leave her situation. But while doing this, she was equally determined not to lead to any mis-interpretation of her motives, by leaving the neighbourhood. No matter at what inconvenience to herself, she would remain long enough at Thorpe-Ambrose to await any more definitely-expressed imputations that might be made on her character, and to repel them publicly the instant they assumed a tangible form.

Such is the position which this high-minded lady has taken up, with an excellent effect on the public mind in these parts. It is clearly her interest, for some reason, to leave her situation, without leaving the neighbourhood. On Monday last she established herself in a cheap lodging on the outskirts of the town. And on the same day, she probably wrote to her reference, for yesterday there came a letter from that lady to Major Milroy, full of virtuous indignation, and courting the fullest inquiry. The letter has been shown publicly, and has immensely strengthened Miss Gwilt's position. She is now considered to be quite a heroine. The *Thorpe-Ambrose Mercury* has got a leading article about her, comparing her to Joan of Arc. It is considered probable that she will be referred to in the sermon next Sunday. We reckon five strong-minded single ladies in this neighbourhood – and all five have called on her. A testimonial was suggested; but it has been given up at Miss Gwilt's own request, and a general movement is now on foot to get her employment as a teacher of music. Lastly, I have had the honour of a visit from the lady herself, in her capacity of martyr, to tell me, in the sweetest manner, that she doesn't blame Mr Armadale; and that she considers him to be an innocent instrument in the hands of other and more designing people. I was carefully on my guard with her; for I don't altogether believe in Miss Gwilt, and I have my lawyer's suspicions of the motive that is at the bottom of her present proceedings.

I have written thus far, my dear sir, with little hesitation or embarrassment. But there is unfortunately a serious side to this business as well as a ridiculous side; and I must unwillingly come to it before I close my letter.

It is, I think, quite impossible that you can permit yourself to be spoken of as you are spoken of now, without stirring personally in the matter. You have unluckily made many enemies here, and foremost among them is my colleague, Mr Darch. He has been showing everywhere a somewhat rashly-expressed letter you wrote to him, on the subject of letting the cottage to Major Milroy instead of to himself; and it has helped to exasperate the feeling against you. It is roundly stated in so many words, that you have been prying into Miss Gwilt's family affairs, with the most dishonourable motives; that you have tried, for a profligate purpose of your own, to damage her reputation, and to deprive her of the protection of Major Milroy's roof; and that, after having been asked to substantiate by proof the suspicions that you have cast on the reputation of a defenceless woman, you have maintained a silence which condemns you in the estimation of all honourable men.

I hope it is quite unnecessary for me to say that I don't attach the smallest particle of credit to these infamous reports. But they are too widely spread and too widely believed to be treated with contempt. I strongly urge you to return at once to this place, and to take the necessary measures for defending your character, in concert with me, as your legal adviser. I have formed, since my interview with Miss Gwilt, a very strong opinion of my own on the subject of that lady, which it is not necessary to commit to paper. Suffice it to say here, that I shall have a means to propose to you for silencing the slanderous tongues of your neighbours, on the success of which I stake my professional reputation, if you will only back me by your presence and authority.

It may, perhaps, help to show you the necessity there is for your return, if I mention one other assertion respecting yourself, which is in everybody's mouth. Your absence is, I blush to tell you, attributed to the meanest of all motives. It is said that you are remaining in London because you are afraid to show your face at Thorpe-Ambrose.

Believe me, dear sir, your faithful servant,

A. PEDGIFT Sen[r].

Allan was of an age to feel the sting contained in the last sentence of his lawyer's letter. He started to his feet in a paroxysm of indignation, which revealed his character to Pedgift Junior in an entirely new light.

'Where's the time-table?' cried Allan. 'I must go back to Thorpe-Ambrose by the next train! If it doesn't start directly, I'll have a special engine. I must and will go back instantly, and I don't care two straws for the expense!'

'Suppose we telegraph to my father, sir?' suggested the judicious Pedgift. 'It's the quickest way of expressing your feelings, and the cheapest.'

'So it is,' said Allan. 'Thank you for reminding me of it. Telegraph to them! Tell your father to give every man in Thorpe-Ambrose the lie direct, in my name. Put it in capital letters, Pedgift – put it in capital letters!'

Pedgift smiled and shook his head. If he was acquainted with no other variety of human nature, he thoroughly knew the variety that exists in country towns.

'It won't have the least effect on them, Mr Armadale,' he remarked quietly. 'They'll only go on lying harder than ever. If you want to upset the whole town, one line will do it. With five shillingsworth of human labour and electric fluid,[2] sir (I dabble a little in science after business hours), we'll explode a bombshell in Thorpe-Ambrose!' He produced the bombshell on a slip of paper as he spoke: 'A. Pedgift Junior, to A. Pedgift Senior. – Spread it all over the place that Mr Armadale is coming down by the next train.'

'More words,' suggested Allan, looking over his shoulder. 'Make it stronger.'

'Leave my father to make it stronger, sir,' returned the judicious Pedgift. 'My father is on the spot – and his command of language is something quite extraordinary.' He rang the bell, and despatched the telegram.

Now that something had been done, Allan subsided gradually into a state of composure. He looked back again at Mr Pedgift's letter, and then handed it to Mr Pedgift's son.

'Can you guess your father's plan for setting me right in the neighbourhood?' he asked.

Pedgift the younger shook his wise head. 'His plan appears to be connected in some way, sir, with his opinion of Miss Gwilt.'

'I wonder what he thinks of her?' said Allan.

'I shouldn't be surprised, Mr Armadale,' returned Pedgift Junior, 'if his opinion staggers you a little, when you come to hear it. My father has had a large legal experience of the shady side of the sex – and he learnt his profession at the Old Bailey.'[3]

Allan made no further inquiries. He seemed to shrink from pursuing the subject, after having started it himself. 'Let's be doing something to kill the time,' he said. 'Let's pack up, and pay the bill.'

They packed up, and paid the bill. The hour came, and the train left for Norfolk at last.

While the travellers were on their way back, a somewhat longer telegraphic message than Allan's was flashing its way past them along the wires, in the reverse direction – from Thorpe-Ambrose to London. The message was in cypher, and signs being interpreted, it ran thus:

'From Lydia Gwilt to Maria Oldershaw – Good news! He is coming back. I mean to have an interview with him. Everything looks well. Now I have left the cottage, I have no women's prying eyes to dread, and I can come and go as I please. Mr Midwinter is luckily out of the way. I don't despair of becoming Mrs Armadale yet. Whatever happens, depend on my keeping away from London, until I am certain of not taking any spies after me to your place. I am in no hurry to leave Thorpe-Ambrose. I mean to be even with Miss Milroy first.'

Shortly after that message was received in London, Allan was back again in his own house. It was evening – Pedgift Junior had just left him – and Pedgift Senior was expected to call on business in half an hour's time.

CHAPTER V

PEDGIFT'S REMEDY

After waiting to hold a preliminary consultation with his son, Mr Pedgift the elder set forth alone for his interview with Allan at the great house.

Allowing for the difference in their ages, the son was, in this instance, so accurately the reflection of the father, that an acquaintance with either of the two Pedgifts was almost equivalent to an acquaintance with both. Add some little height and size to the figure of Pedgift Junior; give some additional breadth and boldness to his humour, and some additional solidity and composure to his confidence in himself – and the presence and character of Pedgift Senior stood for all general purposes revealed before you.

The lawyer's conveyance to Thorpe-Ambrose was his own smart gig, drawn by his famous fast-trotting mare. It was his habit to drive himself; and it was one among the trifling external peculiarities in which he and his son differed a little, to affect something of a sporting character in his dress. The drab trousers of Pedgift the elder fitted close to his legs; his boots in dry weather and wet alike, were equally thick in the sole; his coat pockets overlapped his hips, and his favourite summer cravat was of light spotted muslin, tied in the neatest and smallest of bows. He used tobacco like his son, but in a different form. While the younger man smoked, the elder took snuff copiously; and it was noticed among his intimates that he always held his 'pinch' in a state of suspense between his box and his nose, when he was going to clinch a good bargain, or to say a good thing. The art of diplomacy enters largely into the practice of all successful men in the lower branch of the law. Mr Pedgift's form of diplomatic practice had been the same throughout his life, on every occasion when he found his arts of persuasion required at an interview with another man. He invariably kept his strongest argument, or his boldest proposal, to the last, and invariably remembered it at the door (after previously taking his leave), as if it was a purely accidental consideration which had that instant occurred to him. Jocular friends, acquainted by previous experience with this form of proceeding, had given it the name of 'Pedgift's postscript'. There were few people in Thorpe-Ambrose who did not know what it meant, when the lawyer suddenly checked his exit at the opened door; came back softly to his chair, with his pinch of snuff suspended between his box and his nose; said, 'By-the-by, there's a point occurs to me;' and settled the question off-hand, after having given it up in despair not a minute before.

This was the man whom the march of events at Thorpe-Ambrose had now thrust capriciously into a foremost place. This was the one friend at hand to whom Allan in his social isolation could turn for counsel in the hour of need.

'Good evening, Mr Armadale. Many thanks for your prompt attention to my very disagreeable letter,' said Pedgift Senior, opening the conversation cheerfully the moment he entered his client's house. 'I hope you understand, sir, that I had really no choice under the circumstances, but to write as I did?'

'I have very few friends, Mr Pedgift,' returned Allan simply. 'And I am sure you are one of the few.'

'Much obliged, Mr Armadale. I have always tried to deserve your good opinion, and I mean, if I can, to deserve it now. You found yourself comfortable I hope, sir, at the hotel in London? We call it Our hotel. Some rare old wine in the cellar, which I should have introduced to your notice if I had had the honour of being with you. My son unfortunately knows nothing about wine.'

Allan felt his false position in the neighbourhood far too acutely to be capable of talking of anything but the main business of the evening. His lawyer's politely roundabout method of approaching the painful subject to be discussed between them, rather irritated than composed him. He came at once to the point, in his own bluntly straightforward way.

'The hotel was very comfortable, Mr Pedgift, and your son was very kind to me. But we are not in London now; and I want to talk to you about how I am to meet the lies that are being told of me in this place. Only point me out any one man,' cried Allan with a rising voice and a mounting colour, – 'any one man who says I am afraid to show my face in the neighbourhood; and I'll horsewhip him publicly before another day is over his head!'

Pedgift Senior helped himself to a pinch of snuff, and held it calmly in suspense midway between his box and his nose.

'You can horsewhip a man, sir; but you can't horsewhip a neighbourhood,' said the lawyer in his politely epigrammatic manner. 'We will fight our battle, if you please, without borrowing our weapons of the coachman yet awhile, at any rate.'

'But how are we to begin?' asked Allan impatiently. 'How am I to contradict the infamous things they say of me?'

'There are two ways of stepping out of your present awkward position, sir – a short way, and a long way,' replied Pedgift Senior. 'The short way (which is always the best) has occurred to me since I have heard of your proceedings in London from my son. I understand that you permitted him, after you received my letter, to take me into your confidence. I have drawn various conclusions from what he has told me, which I may find it necessary to trouble you with presently. In the meantime I should be glad to know under what circumstances you went to London to make these unfortunate inquiries about Miss Gwilt? Was it your own notion to pay that visit to Mrs Mandeville? or were you acting under the influence of some other person?'

Allan hesitated. 'I can't honestly tell you it was my own notion,' he replied – and said no more.

'I thought as much!' remarked Pedgift Senior in high triumph. 'The short way out of our present difficulty, Mr Armadale, lies straight through that other person, under whose influence you acted. That other person must be presented forthwith to public notice, and must stand in that other person's proper place. The name if you please, sir, to begin with – we'll come to the circumstances directly.'

'I am sorry to say, Mr Pedgift, that we must try the longest way, if you have no objection,' replied Allan quietly. 'The short way happens to be a way I can't take on this occasion.'

The men who rise in the law are the men who decline to take No for an answer. Mr Pedgift the elder had risen in the law; and Mr Pedgift the elder now declined to take No for an answer. But all pertinacity – even professional pertinacity included – sooner or later finds its limits; and the lawyer, doubly fortified as he was by long experience and copious pinches of snuff, found his limits at the very outset of the interview. It was impossible that Allan could respect the confidence which Mrs Milroy had treacherously affected to place in him. But he had an honest man's regard for his own pledged word – the regard which looks straightforward at the fact, and which never glances sidelong at the circumstances – and the utmost persistency of Pedgift Senior failed to move him a hair's breadth from the position which he had taken up. 'No' is the strongest word in the English language, in the mouth of any man who has the courage to repeat it often enough – and Allan had the courage to repeat it often enough on this occasion.

'Very good, sir,' said the lawyer, accepting his defeat without the slightest loss of temper. 'The choice rests with you, and you have chosen. We will go the long way. It starts (allow me to inform you) from my office; and it leads (as I strongly suspect) through a very miry road to – Miss Gwilt.'

Allan looked at his legal adviser in speechless astonishment.

'If you won't expose the person who is responsible, in the first instance, sir, for the inquiries to which you unfortunately lent yourself,' proceeded Mr Pedgift the elder, 'the only other alternative, in your present position, is to justify the inquiries themselves.'

'And how is that to be done?' inquired Allan.

'By proving to the whole neighbourhood, Mr Armadale, what I firmly believe to be the truth – that the pet object of the public protection is an adventuress of the worst class; an undeniably worthless and dangerous woman. In plainer English still, sir, by employing time enough and money enough to discover the truth about Miss Gwilt.'

Before Allan could say a word in answer, there was an interruption at the door. After the usual preliminary knock, one of the servants came in.

'I told you I was not to be interrupted,' said Allan irritably. 'Good heavens! am I never to have done with them? another letter!'

'Yes, sir,' said the man, holding it out. 'And,' he added, speaking words of evil omen in his master's ears, 'the person waits for an answer.'

Allan looked at the address of the letter with a natural expectation of encountering the handwriting of the major's wife. The anticipation was not realized. His correspondent was plainly a lady, but the lady was not Mrs Milroy.

'Who can it be?' he said, looking mechanically at Pedgift Senior as he opened the envelope.

Pedgift Senior gently tapped his snuff-box, and said without a moment's hesitation – 'Miss Gwilt.'

Allan opened the letter. The first two words in it were the echo of the two words the lawyer had just pronounced. It *was* Miss Gwilt!

Once more, Allan looked at his legal adviser in speechless astonishment.

'I have known a good many of them in my time, sir,' explained Pedgift Senior, with a modesty equally rare and becoming in a man of his age. 'Not as handsome as Miss Gwilt, I admit. But quite as bad, I dare say. Read your letter, Mr Armadale – read your letter.'

Allan read these lines:

'Miss Gwilt presents her compliments to Mr Armadale, and begs to know if it will be convenient to him to favour her with an interview, either this evening or to-morrow morning. Miss Gwilt offers no apology for making her present request. She believes Mr Armadale will grant it as an act of justice towards a friendless woman whom he has been innocently the means of injuring, and who is earnestly desirous to set herself right in his estimation.'

Allan handed the letter to his lawyer in silent perplexity and distress.

The face of Mr Pedgift the elder expressed but one feeling when he had read the letter in his turn and had handed it back – a feeling of profound admiration. 'What a lawyer she would have made,' he exclaimed, fervently, 'if she had only been a man!'

'I can't treat this as lightly as you do, Mr Pedgift,' said Allan. 'It's dreadfully distressing to me. I was so fond of her,' he added, in a lower tone, – 'I was so fond of her once.'

Mr Pedgift Senior suddenly became serious on his side.

'Do you mean to say, sir, that you actually contemplate seeing Miss Gwilt?' he asked, with an expression of genuine dismay.

'I can't treat her cruelly,' returned Allan. 'I have been the means of injuring her – without intending it, God knows! – I can't treat her cruelly after that!'

'Mr Armadale,' said the lawyer, 'you did me the honour, a little while since, to say that you considered me your friend. May I presume on that position to ask you a question or two, before you go straight to your own ruin?'

'Any questions you like,' said Allan, looking back at the letter – the only letter he had ever received from Miss Gwilt.

'You have had one trap set for you already, sir, and you have fallen into it. Do you want to fall into another?'

'You know the answer to that question, Mr Pedgift, as well as I do.'

'I'll try again, Mr Armadale; we lawyers are not easily discouraged. Do you think that any statement Miss Gwilt might make to you, if you do see her, would be a statement to be relied on, after what you and my son discovered in London?'

'She might explain what we discovered in London,' suggested Allan, still looking at the writing, and thinking of the hand that had traced it.

'*Might* explain it? My dear sir, she is quite certain to explain it! I will do her justice: I believe she would make out a case without a single flaw in it from beginning to end.'

That last answer forced Allan's attention away from the letter. The lawyer's pitiless common sense showed him no mercy.

'If you see that woman again, sir,' proceeded Pedgift Senior, 'you will commit the rashest act of folly I ever heard of in all my experience. She can have but one object in coming here – to practise on your weakness for her. Nobody can say into what false step she may not lead you, if you once give her the opportunity. You admit yourself that you have been fond of her – your attentions to her have been the subject of general remark – if you haven't actually offered her the chance of becoming Mrs Armadale, you have done the next thing to it – and knowing all this, you propose to see her and to let her work on you with her devilish beauty and her devilish cleverness, in the character of your interesting victim! You, who are one of the best matches in England! You who are the natural prey of all the hungry single women in the community! I never heard the like of it; I never, in all my professional experience, heard the like of it! If you must positively put yourself in a dangerous position, Mr Armadale,' concluded Pedgift the elder, with the everlasting pinch of snuff held in suspense between his box and his nose, 'there's a wild-beast show coming to our town next week. Let in the tigress, sir, – don't let in Miss Gwilt!'

For the third time Allan looked at his lawyer. And for the third time his lawyer looked back at him quite unabashed.

'You seem to have a very bad opinion of Miss Gwilt,' said Allan.

'The worst possible opinion, Mr Armadale,' retorted Pedgift Senior, coolly. 'We will return to that, when we have sent the lady's messenger about his business. Will you take my advice? Will you decline to see her?'

'I would willingly decline – it would be so dreadfully distressing to both of us,' said Allan. 'I would willingly decline, if I only knew how.'

'Bless my soul, Mr Armadale, it's easy enough! Don't commit yourself in writing. Send out to the messenger, and say there's no answer.'

The short course thus suggested, was a course which Allan positively declined to take. 'It's treating her brutally,' he said; 'I can't and won't do it.'

Once more, the pertinacity of Pedgift the elder found its limits – and once more that wise man yielded gracefully to a compromise. On receiving his client's promise not to see Miss Gwilt, he consented to Allan's committing himself in writing – under his lawyer's dictation. The letter thus produced was modelled on Allan's own style; it began and ended in one sentence. 'Mr Armadale presents his compliments to Miss Gwilt and regrets that he cannot have the pleasure of seeing her at Thorpe-Ambrose.' Allan had pleaded hard for a second sentence, explaining that he only declined Miss Gwilt's request from a conviction that an interview would be needlessly distressing on both sides. But his legal adviser firmly rejected the proposed addition to the letter. 'When you say No to a woman, sir,' remarked Pedgift Senior, 'always say it in one word. If you give her your reasons, she invariably believes that you mean Yes.'

Producing that little gem of wisdom from the rich mine of his professional experience, Mr Pedgift the elder sent out the answer to Miss Gwilt's messenger, and recommended the servant to 'see the fellow, whoever he was, well clear of the house.'

'Now, sir,' said the lawyer, 'we will come back, if you like, to my opinion of Miss Gwilt. It doesn't at all agree with yours, I'm afraid. You think her an object for pity – quite natural at your age. I think her an object for the inside of a prison – quite natural at mine. You shall hear the grounds on which I have formed my opinion directly. Let me show you that I am in earnest by putting the opinion itself, in the first place, to a practical test. Do you think Miss Gwilt is likely to persist in paying you a visit, Mr Armadale, after the answer you have just sent to her?'

'Quite impossible!' cried Allan, warmly. 'Miss Gwilt is a lady; after the letter I have sent to her, she will never come near me again.'

'There we join issue, sir,' cried Pedgift Senior. 'I say she will snap her fingers at your letter (which was one of the reasons why I objected to your writing it). I say, she is in all probability waiting her messenger's return, in or near your grounds at this moment. I say, she will try to force her way in here, before four-and-twenty hours more are over your head. Egad, sir!' cried Mr Pedgift, looking at his watch, 'it's only seven o'clock now. She's bold enough and clever enough to catch you unawares this very evening. Permit me to ring for the servant – permit me to request that you will give him orders immediately to say you are not at home. You needn't hesitate, Mr Armadale! If you're right about Miss Gwilt, it's a mere formality. If I'm right, it's a wise precaution. Back your opinion, sir,' said Mr Pedgift, ringing the bell, 'I back mine!'

Allan was sufficiently nettled when the bell rang, to feel ready to give the order. But when the servant came in, past remembrances got the better of him, and the words stuck in his throat. 'You give the order,' he said to Mr Pedgift – and walked away abruptly to the window. 'You're a good fellow!' thought the old lawyer, looking after him, and penetrating his motive on the instant. 'The claws of that she-devil shan't scratch you if I can help it.'

The servant waited inexorably for his orders.

'If Miss Gwilt calls here, either this evening, or at any other time,' said Pedgift Senior, 'Mr Armadale is not at home. Wait! If she asks when Mr Armadale will be back, you don't know. Wait! If she proposes coming in and sitting down, you have a general order that nobody is to come in and sit down, unless they have a previous appointment with Mr Armadale. Come!' cried old Pedgift, rubbing his hands cheerfully when the servant had left the room, 'I've stopped her out now, at any rate! The orders are all given, Mr Armadale. We may go on with our conversation.'

Allan came back from the window. 'The conversation is not a very pleasant one,' he said. 'No offence to you, but I wish it was over.'

'We will get it over as soon as possible, sir,' said Pedgift Senior, still persisting as only lawyers and women *can* persist, in forcing his way little by little nearer and nearer to his own object. 'Let us go back, if you please, to the practical suggestion which I offered to you when the servant came in with Miss Gwilt's note. There is, I repeat, only one way left for you, Mr Armadale, out of your present awkward position. You must pursue your inquiries about this woman to an end – on the chance (which I consider next to a certainty) that the end will justify you in the estimation of the neighbourhood.'

'I wish to God I had never made any inquiries at all!' said Allan. 'Nothing will induce me, Mr Pedgift, to make any more.'

'Why?' asked the lawyer.

'Can you ask me why,' retorted Allan, hotly, 'after your son has told you what we found out in London? Even if I had less cause to be – to be sorry for Miss Gwilt than I have; even if it was some other woman, do you think I would inquire any further into the secret of a poor betrayed creature – much less expose it to the neighbourhood? I should think myself as great a scoundrel as the man who has cast her out helpless on the world, if I did anything of the kind. I wonder you can ask me the question – upon my soul, I wonder you can ask me the question!'

'Give me your hand, Mr Armadale!' cried Pedgift Senior, warmly; 'I honour you for being so angry with me. The neighbourhood may say what it pleases; you're a gentleman, sir, in the best sense of the word. Now,' pursued the lawyer, dropping Allan's hand, and lapsing back instantly from sentiment to business, 'just hear what I have got to say in my own defence. Suppose Miss Gwilt's real position happens to be nothing like what you are generously determined to believe it to be?'

'We have no reason to suppose that,' said Allan resolutely.

'Such is your opinion, sir,' persisted Pedgift. 'Mine, founded on what is publicly known of Miss Gwilt's proceedings here, and on what I have seen of Miss Gwilt herself, is that she is as far as I am from being the sentimental victim you are inclined to make her out. Gently, Mr

Armadale! remember that I have put my opinion to a practical test, and wait to condemn it off-hand until events have justified you. Let me put my points, sir, – make allowances for me as a lawyer – and let me put my points. You and my son are young men; and I don't deny that the circumstances, on the surface, appear to justify the interpretation which, as young men, you have placed on them. I am an old man – I know that circumstances are not always to be taken as they appear on the surface – and I possess the great advantage, in the present case, of having had years of professional experience among some of the wickedest women who ever walked this earth.'

Allan opened his lips to protest, and checked himself, in despair of producing the slightest effect. Pedgift Senior bowed in polite acknowledgment of his client's self-restraint, and took instant advantage of it to go on.

'All Miss Gwilt's proceedings,' he resumed, 'since your unfortunate correspondence with the major, show me that she is an old hand at deceit. The moment she is threatened with exposure – exposure of some kind, there can be no doubt, after what you discovered in London – she turns your honourable silence to the best possible account, and leaves the major's service in the character of a martyr. Once out of the house, what does she do next? She boldly stops in the neighbourhood, and serves three excellent purposes by doing so. In the first place, she shows everybody that she is not afraid of facing another attack on her reputation. In the second place, she is close at hand to twist you round her little finger, and to become Mrs Armadale in spite of circumstances, if you (and I) allow her the opportunity. In the third place, if you (and I) are wise enough to distrust her, she is equally wise on her side, and doesn't give us the first great chance of following her to London, and associating her with her accomplices. Is this the conduct of an unhappy woman who has lost her character in a moment of weakness, and who has been driven unwillingly into a deception to get it back again?'

'You put it cleverly,' said Allan, answering with marked reluctance; 'I can't deny that you put it cleverly.'

'Your own common sense, Mr Armadale, is beginning to tell you that I put it justly,' said Pedgift Senior. 'I don't presume to say yet what this woman's connection may be with those people at Pimlico. All I assert is, that it is not the connection you suppose. Having stated the facts so far, I have only to add my own personal impression of Miss Gwilt. I won't shock you, if I can help it – I'll try if I can't put it cleverly again. She came to my office (as I told you in my letter), no doubt to make friends with your lawyer, if she could – she came to tell me in the most forgiving and Christian manner, that she didn't blame *you*.'

'Do you ever believe in anybody, Mr Pedgift?' interposed Allan.

'Sometimes, Mr Armadale,' returned Pedgift the elder, as unabashed as ever. 'I believe as often as a lawyer can. To proceed, sir. When I was in the criminal branch of practice, it fell to my lot to take instructions for the defence of women committed for trial, from the women's own lips. Whatever other difference there might be among them, I got, in time, to notice, among those who were particularly wicked and unquestionably guilty, one point in which they all resembled each other. Tall and short, old and young, handsome and ugly, they all had a secret self-possession that nothing could shake. On the surface they were as different as possible. Some of them were in the state of indignation; some of them were drowned in tears; some of them were full of pious confidence; and some of them were resolved to commit suicide before the night was out. But only put your finger suddenly on the weak point in the story told by any one of them, and there was an end of her rage, or her tears, or her piety, or her despair – and out came the genuine woman, in full possession of all her resources, with a neat little lie that exactly suited the circumstance of the case. Miss Gwilt was in tears, sir – becoming tears that didn't make her nose red, – and I put my finger suddenly on the weak point in *her* story. Down dropped her pathetic pocket-handkerchief from her beautiful blue eyes, and out came the genuine woman with the neat little lie that exactly suited the circumstances! I felt twenty years younger, Mr Armadale, on the spot. I declare I thought I was in Newgate again with my note-book in my hand, taking my instruction for the defence!'

'The next thing, you'll say, Mr Pedgift,' cried Allan, angrily, 'is that Miss Gwilt has been in prison!'

Pedgift Senior calmly rapped his snuff-box, and had his answer ready at a moment's notice.

'She may have richly deserved to see the inside of a prison, Mr Armadale; but, in the age we live in, that is one excellent reason for her never having been near any place of the kind. A prison, in the present tender state of public feeling,[1] for a charming woman like Miss Gwilt! My dear sir, if she had attempted to murder you or me, and if an inhuman judge and jury had decided on sending her to a prison, the first object of modern society would be to prevent her going into it; and, if that couldn't be done, the next object would be to let her out again as soon as possible. Read your newspaper, Mr Armadale, and you'll find we live in piping times for the black sheep of the community – if they are only black enough. I insist on asserting, sir, that we have got one of the blackest of the lot to deal with in this case. I insist on asserting that you have had the rare luck, in these unfortunate inquiries, to pitch on a woman who happens to be a fit object for inquiry, in the interests of the public protection. Differ with me as strongly as you please – but don't make up your mind finally about Miss Gwilt, until events have put those two opposite opinions of ours to the test that I have proposed. A fairer test there can't be. I agree with you, that no lady worthy of the name could attempt to force her way in here, after receiving your letter. But I deny that Miss Gwilt *is* worthy of the name; and I say she will try to force her way in here in spite of you.'

'And I say she won't!' retorted Allan, firmly.

Pedgift Senior leaned back in his chair and smiled. There was a momentary silence – and in that silence, the door-bell rang.

The lawyer and the client both looked expectantly in the direction of the hall.

'No!' cried Allan, more angrily than ever.

'Yes!' said Pedgift Senior, contradicting him with the utmost politeness.

They waited the event. The opening of the house-door was audible, but the room was too far from it for the sound of voices to reach the ear as well. After a long interval of expectation, the closing of the door was heard at last. Allan rose impetuously, and rang the bell. Mr Pedgift the elder sat sublimely calm, and enjoyed, with a gentle zest, the largest pinch of snuff he had taken yet.

'Anybody for me?' asked Allan, when the servant came in.

The man looked at Pedgift Senior, with an expression of unutterable reverence, and answered – 'Miss Gwilt.'

'I don't want to crow over you, sir,' said Mr Pedgift the elder, when the servant had withdrawn. 'But what do you think of Miss Gwilt *now*?'

Allan shook his head in silent discouragement and distress.

'Time is of some importance, Mr Armadale. After what has just happened, do you still object to taking the course I have had the honour of suggesting to you?'

'I can't, Mr Pedgift,' said Allan. 'I can't be the means of disgracing her in the neighbourhood. I would rather be disgraced myself – as I am.'

'Let me put it in another way, sir. Excuse my persisting. You have been very kind to me and my family; and I have a personal interest, as well as a professional interest in you. If you can't prevail on yourself to show this woman's character in its true light, will you take common precautions to prevent her doing any more harm? Will you consent to having her privately watched, as long as she remains in this neighbourhood?'

For the second time, Allan shook his head.

'Is that your final resolution, sir?'

'It is, Mr Pedgift; but I am much obliged to you for your advice, all the same.'

Pedgift Senior rose in a state of gentle resignation, and took up his hat. 'Good evening, sir,' he said, and made sorrowfully for the door. Allan rose on his side, innocently supposing that the interview was at an end. Persons better acquainted with the diplomatic habits of his legal adviser, would have recommended him to keep his seat. The time was ripe for 'Pedgift's postscript', and the lawyer's indicative snuff-box was at that moment in one of his hands, as he opened the door with the other.

'Good evening,' said Allan.

Pedgift Senior opened the door – stopped – considered – closed the door again – came back mysteriously with his pinch of snuff in suspense between his box and his nose – and repeating his invariable formula, 'By-the-by, there's a point occurs to me,' quietly resumed possession of his empty chair.

Allan, wondering, took the seat, in his turn, which he had just left. Lawyer and client looked at each other once more, and the inexhaustible interview began again.

CHAPTER VI

PEDGIFT'S POSTSCRIPT

'I mentioned that a point had occurred to me, sir,' remarked Pedgift Senior.

'You did,' said Allan.

'Would you like to hear what it is, Mr Armadale?'

'If you please,' said Allan.

'With all my heart, sir! This is the point. I attach considerable importance – if nothing else can be done – to having Miss Gwilt privately looked after, as long as she stops at Thorpe-Ambrose. It struck me just now at the door, Mr Armadale, that what you are not willing to

370

do for your own security, you might be willing to do for the security of another person.'

'What other person?' inquired Allan.

'A young lady who is a near neighbour of yours, sir. Shall I mention the name, in confidence? Miss Milroy.'

Allan started, and changed colour.

'Miss Milroy!' he repeated. 'Can *she* be concerned in this miserable business? I hope not, Mr Pedgift; I sincerely hope not.'

'I paid a visit, in your interests, sir, at the cottage, this morning,' proceeded Pedgift Senior. 'You shall hear what happened there, and judge for yourself. Major Milroy has been expressing his opinion of you pretty freely; and I thought it highly desirable to give him a caution. It's always the way with those quiet addle-headed men – when they do once wake up, there's no reasoning with their obstinacy, and no quieting their violence. Well, sir, this morning I went to the cottage. The major and Miss Neelie were both in the parlour – miss not looking so pretty as usual; pale, I thought, pale, and worn, and anxious. Up jumps the addle-headed major (I wouldn't give *that*, Mr Armadale, for the brains of a man who can occupy himself for half his lifetime in making a clock!) – up jumps the addle-headed major, in the loftiest manner, and actually tries to look me down. Ha! ha! the idea of anybody looking *me* down, at my time of life. I behaved like a Christian; I nodded kindly to old What's-o'clock. "Fine morning, major," says I. "Have you any business with me?" says he. "Just a word," says I. Miss Neelie, like the sensible girl she is, gets up to leave the room; and what does her ridiculous father do? He stops her. "You needn't go, my dear; I have nothing to say to Mr Pedgift," says this old military idiot, and turns my way, and tries to look me down again. "You are Mr Armadale's lawyer," says he; "if you come on any business relating to Mr Armadale, I refer you to my solicitor." (His solicitor is Darch; and Darch has had enough of *me* in business, I can tell you!) "My errand here, major, does certainly relate to Mr Armadale," says I; "but it doesn't concern your lawyer – at any rate, just yet. I wish to caution you to suspend your opinion of my client, or, if you won't do that, to be careful how you express it in public. I warn you that our turn is to come, and that you are not at the end yet of this scandal about Miss Gwilt." It struck me as likely that he would lose his temper when he found himself tackled in that way, and he amply fulfilled my expectations. He was quite violent in his language – the poor weak creature – actually violent with *me*! I behaved like a Christian again; I nodded kindly, and wished him good morning. When I looked round to wish Miss Neelie good morning too, she was gone. You seem restless, Mr Armadale,' remarked Pedgift Senior, as Allan, feeling the sting of old recollections, suddenly started out of his chair, and began pacing up and down the room. 'I won't try your patience much longer, sir; I am coming to the point.'

'I beg your pardon, Mr Pedgift,' said Allan, returning to his seat, and trying to look composedly at the lawyer through the intervening image of Neelie which the lawyer had called up.

'Well, sir, I left the cottage,' resumed Pedgift Senior. 'Just as I turned the corner from the garden into the park, who should I stumble on but Miss Neelie herself, evidently on the look-out for me. "I want to speak to you for one moment, Mr Pedgift!" says she. "Does Mr Armadale think *me* mixed up in this matter?" She was violently agitated – tears in her eyes, sir, of the sort which my legal experience has *not* accustomed me to see. I quite forgot myself; I actually gave her my arm, and led her away gently among the trees. (A nice position to find me in, if any of the scandal-mongers of the town had happened to be walking in that direction!) "My dear Miss Milroy," says I, "why should Mr Armadale think *you* mixed up in it?" '

'You ought to have told her at once that I thought nothing of the kind!' exclaimed Allan, indignantly. 'Why did you leave her a moment in doubt about it?'

'Because I am a lawyer, Mr Armadale,' rejoined Pedgift Senior, drily. 'Even in moments of sentiment, under convenient trees, with a pretty girl on my arm, I can't entirely divest myself of my professional caution. Don't look distressed, sir, pray! I set things right in due course of time. Before I left Miss Milroy, I told her, in the plainest terms, no such idea had ever entered your head.'

'Did she seem relieved?' asked Allan.

'She was able to dispense with the use of my arm, sir,' replied old Pedgift, as drily as ever, 'and to pledge me to inviolable secresy on the subject of our interview. She was particularly desirous that *you* should hear nothing about it. If you are at all anxious on your side, to know why I am now betraying her confidence, I beg to inform you that her confidence related to no less a person than the lady who favoured you with a call just now – Miss Gwilt.'

Allan, who had been once more restlessly pacing the room, stopped, and returned to his chair.

'Is this serious?' he asked.

'Most serious, sir,' returned Pedgift Senior. 'I am betraying Miss Neelie's secret, in Miss Neelie's own interest. Let us go back to that cautious question I put to her. She found some little difficulty in answering it – for the reply involved her in a narrative of the parting interview between her governess and herself. This is the substance of it. The two were alone when Miss Gwilt took leave of her pupil; and the words she used (as reported to me by Miss Neelie) were these. She said, "Your mother has declined to allow me to take leave of her. Do you decline too?" Miss Neelie's answer was a remarkably sensible one for a girl of her age. "We have not been good friends," she said, "and I believe we are equally glad to part with each other. But I have no wish to decline taking leave of you." Saying that, she held out her hand. Miss Gwilt stood looking at her steadily, without taking it, and addressed her in these words: "*You are not Mrs Armadale yet.*" Gently, sir! Keep your temper. It's not at all wonderful that a woman conscious of having her own mercenary designs on you, should attribute similar designs to a young lady who happens to be your near neighbour. Let me go on. Miss Neelie, by her own confession (and quite naturally, I think), was excessively indignant. She owns to having answered, "You shameless creature, how dare you say that to me!" Miss Gwilt's rejoinder was rather a remarkable one – the anger, on her side, appears to have been of the cool, still, venomous kind. "Nobody ever yet injured me, Miss Milroy," she said, "without sooner or later bitterly repenting it. *You* will bitterly repent it." She stood looking at her pupil for a moment in dead silence, and then left the room. Miss Neelie appears to have felt the imputation fastened on her, in connection with you, far more sensitively than she felt the threat. She had previously known, as everybody had known in the house, that some unacknowledged proceedings of yours in London had led to Miss Gwilt's voluntary withdrawal from her situation. And she now inferred, from the language addressed to her, that she was actually believed by Miss Gwilt to have set those proceedings on foot, to advance herself, and to injure her governess, in your estimation. Gently, sir, gently! I haven't quite done yet. As soon as Miss Neelie had recovered herself, she went upstairs to speak to Mrs Milroy. Miss Gwilt's abominable imputation had taken her by surprise; and she went to her mother first for enlightenment and advice. She got neither the one nor the other. Mrs Milroy declared she was too ill to enter on the subject, and she has remained too ill to enter on it ever since. Miss Neelie applied next to her father. The major stopped her the moment your name passed her lips: he declared he would never hear you mentioned again by any member of his family. She has been left in the dark from that time to this – not knowing how she might have been misrepresented by Miss Gwilt, or what falsehoods you might have been led to believe of her. At my age and in my profession, I don't profess to have any extraordinary softness of heart. But I do think, Mr Armadale, that Miss Neelie's position deserves our sympathy.'

'I'll do anything to help her!' cried Allan, impulsively. 'You don't know, Mr Pedgift, what reason I have—' He checked himself, and confusedly repeated his first words. 'I'll do anything,' he reiterated earnestly – 'anything in the world to help her!'

'Do you really mean that, Mr Armadale? Excuse my asking – but you can very materially help Miss Neelie if you choose!'

'How?' asked Allan. 'Only tell me how!'

'By giving me your authority, sir, to protect her from Miss Gwilt.'

Having fired that shot point-blank at his client, the wise lawyer waited a little to let it take its effect before he said any more.

Allan's face clouded, and he shifted uneasily from side to side of his chair.

'Your son is hard enough to deal with, Mr Pedgift,' he said. 'And you are harder than your son.'

'Thank you, sir,' rejoined the ready Pedgift, 'in my son's name and my own, for a handsome compliment to the firm. If you really wish to be of assistance to Miss Neelie,' he went on more seriously, 'I have shown you the way. You can do nothing to quiet her anxiety, which I have not done already. As soon as I had assured her that no misconception of her conduct existed in your mind, she went away satisfied. Her governess's parting threat doesn't seem to have dwelt on her memory. I can tell you, Mr Armadale, it dwells on mine! You know my opinion of Miss Gwilt; and you know what Miss Gwilt herself has done this very evening, to justify that opinion even in your eyes. May I ask, after all that has passed, whether you think she is the sort of woman who can be trusted to confine herself to empty threats?'

The question was a formidable one to answer. Forced steadily back from the position which he had occupied at the outset of the interview, by the irresistible pressure of plain facts, Allan began for the first time to show symptoms of yielding on the subject of Miss Gwilt. 'Is there no other way of protecting Miss Milroy but the way you have mentioned?' he asked uneasily.

'Do you think the major would listen to you, sir, if you spoke to him?' asked Pedgift Senior sarcastically; 'I'm rather afraid he wouldn't honour *me* with his attention. Or perhaps you would prefer alarming Miss Neelie by telling her in plain words that we both think her in danger? Or, suppose you send me to Miss Gwilt, with instructions to inform her that she has done her pupil a cruel injustice? Women are so proverbially ready to listen to reason; and they are so universally disposed to alter their opinions of each other on application – especially when one woman thinks that another woman has destroyed her prospect of making a good marriage. Don't mind *me*, Mr Armadale – I'm only a lawyer, and I can sit waterproof under another shower of Miss Gwilt's tears!'

'Damn it, Mr Pedgift, tell me in plain words what you want to do!' cried Allan, losing his temper at last.

'In plain words, Mr Armadale, I want to keep Miss Gwilt's proceedings privately under view, as long as she stops in this neighbourhood. I answer for finding a person who will look after her delicately and discreetly. And I agree to discontinue even this harmless superintendence of her actions, if there isn't good reason shown for continuing it, to your entire satisfaction, in a week's time. I make that moderate proposal, sir, in what I sincerely believe to be Miss Milroy's interest, and I wait your answer, Yes or No.'

'Can't I have time to consider?' asked Allan, driven to the last helpless expedient of taking refuge in delay.

'Certainly, Mr Armadale. But don't forget, while you are considering, that Miss Milroy is in the habit of walking out alone in your park, innocent of all apprehension of danger – and that Miss Gwilt is perfectly free to take any advantage of that circumstance that Miss Gwilt pleases.'

'Do as you like!' exclaimed Allan in despair. 'And, for God's sake, don't torment me any longer!'

Popular prejudice may deny it – but the profession of the law is a practically Christian profession in one respect at least. Of all the large collection of ready answers lying in wait for mankind on a lawyer's lips, none is kept in better working order than 'the soft answer which turneth away wrath'. Pedgift Senior rose with the alacrity of youth in his legs, and the wise moderation of age on his tongue. 'Many thanks, sir,' he said, 'for the attention you have bestowed on me. I congratulate you on your decision, and I wish you good evening.' This time, his indicative snuff-box was not in his hand, when he opened the door, and he actually disappeared, without coming back for a second postscript.

Allan's head sank on his breast, when he was left alone. 'If it was only the end of the week!' he thought longingly. 'If I only had Midwinter back again!'

As that aspiration escaped the client's lips, the lawyer got gaily into his gig. 'Hie away, old girl!' cried Pedgift Senior, patting the fast-trotting mare with the end of his whip. 'I never keep a lady waiting – and I've got business to-night with one of your own sex!'

CHAPTER VII

THE MARTYRDOM OF MISS GWILT

The outskirts of the little town of Thorpe-Ambrose, on the side nearest to 'the great house', have earned some local celebrity as exhibiting the prettiest suburb of the kind to be found in East Norfolk. Here, the villas and gardens are for the most part built and laid out in excellent taste; the trees are in the prime of their growth; and the heathy common beyond the houses, rises and falls in picturesque and delightful variety of broken ground. The rank, fashion, and beauty of the town make this place their evening promenade; and when a stranger goes out for a drive, if he leaves it to the coachman, the coachman starts by way of the common as a matter of course.

On the opposite side, that is to say, on the side farthest from 'the great house', the suburbs (in the year eighteen hundred and fifty-one) were universally regarded as a sore subject by all persons zealous for the reputation of the town.

Here, Nature was uninviting; man was poor; and social progress, as exhibited under the form of building, halted miserably. The streets dwindled feebly as they receded from the centre of the town, into smaller and smaller houses, and died away on the barren open ground into an atrophy of skeleton cottages. Builders hereabouts appeared to have universally abandoned their work in the first stage of its creation. Land-holders set up poles on lost patches of ground; and, plaintively advertising that they were to let for building, raised sickly little crops meanwhile, in despair of finding a purchaser to deal with them. All the waste paper of the town seemed to float congenially to this neglected spot; and all the fretful children came and cried here, in charge of all the slatternly nurses who disgraced the place. If there was any intention in Thorpe-Ambrose of sending a worn-out horse to the knackers, that horse was sure to be found waiting his doom in a field on this side of the town. No growth flourished in these desert regions, but the arid growth of rubbish; and no human creatures rejoiced but the creatures of the night – the vermin here and there in the beds, and the cats everywhere on the tiles.

The sun had set, and the summer twilight was darkening. The fretful children were crying in their cradles; the horse destined for the knacker dozed forlorn in the field of his imprisonment; the cats waited stealthily in corners for the coming night. But one living figure appeared in the lonely suburb – the figure of Mr Bashwood. But one faint sound disturbed the dreadful silence – the sound of Mr Bashwood's softly-stepping feet.

Moving slowly past the heaps of bricks rising at intervals along the road; coasting carefully round the old iron, and the broken tiles scattered here and there in his path, Mr Bashwood advanced from the direction of the country towards one of the unfinished streets of the suburb. His personal appearance had been apparently made the object of some special attention. His false teeth were brilliantly white; his wig was carefully brushed; his mourning garments, renewed throughout, gleamed with the hideous and slimy gloss of cheap black cloth. He moved with a nervous jauntiness, and looked about him with a vacant smile. Having reached the first of the skeleton cottages, his watery eyes settled steadily for the first time on the view of the street before him. The next instant he started; his breath quickened; he leaned trembling and flushing against the unfinished wall at his side. A lady, still at some distance, was advancing towards him down the length of the street. 'She's coming!' he whispered, with a strange mixture of rapture and fear, of alternating colour and paleness, showing itself in his haggard face. 'I wish I was the ground she treads on! I wish I was the glove she's got on her hand!' He burst ecstatically into those extravagant words, with a concentrated intensity of delight in uttering them that actually shook his feeble figure from head to foot.

Smoothly and gracefully the lady glided nearer and nearer, until she revealed to Mr Bashwood's eyes, what Mr Bashwood's instincts had recognized in the first instance – the face of Miss Gwilt.

She was dressed with an exquisitely expressive economy of outlay. The plainest straw bonnet procurable, trimmed sparingly with the cheapest white ribbon, was on her head. Modest and tasteful poverty expressed itself in the speckless cleanliness and the modestly-proportioned skirts of her light 'print' gown, and in the scanty little mantilla of cheap black silk which she wore over it, edged with a simple frilling of the same material. The lustre of her terrible red hair showed itself unshrinkingly in a plaited coronet above her forehead, and escaped in one vagrant lovelock, perfectly curled, that dropped over her left shoulder. Her gloves, fitting her like a second skin, were of the sober brown hue which is slowest to show signs of use. One hand lifted her dress daintily above the impurities of the road; the other held a little nosegay of the commonest garden flowers. Noiselessly and smoothly she came on, with a gentle and regular undulation of the print gown; with the lovelock softly lifted from moment to moment in the evening breeze; with her head a little drooped, and her eyes on the ground – in walk, and look, and manner, in every casual movement that escaped her, expressing that subtle mixture of the voluptuous and the modest which, of the many attractive extremes that meet in women, is in a man's eyes the most irresistible of all.

'Mr Bashwood!' she exclaimed, in loud clear tones indicative of the utmost astonishment, 'what a surprise to find you here! I thought none but the wretched inhabitants ever ventured near this side of the town. Hush!' she added quickly in a whisper. – 'You heard right, when you heard that Mr Armadale was going to have me followed and watched. There's a man behind one of the houses. We must talk out loud of indifferent things, and look as if we had met by accident. Ask me what I am doing. Out loud! Directly! You shall never see me again, if you don't instantly leave off trembling, and do what I tell you!'

She spoke with a merciless tyranny of eye and voice – with a merciless use of her power over the feeble creature whom she addressed. Mr Bashwood obeyed her in tones that quavered with agitation, and with eyes that devoured her beauty in a strange fascination of terror and delight.

'I am trying to earn a little money by teaching music,' she said, in the voice intended to reach the spy's ears. 'If you are able to recommend me any pupils, Mr Bashwood, your good word will oblige me. Have you been in the grounds to-day?' she went on, dropping her voice again to a whisper. 'Has Mr Armadale been near the cottage? Has Miss Milroy been out of the garden? No? Are you sure? Look out for them to-morrow, and next day, and next day. They are certain to meet and make it up again, and I must and will know of it. Hush! Ask me my terms for teaching music. What are you frightened about? It's me the man's after – not you. Louder than when you asked me what I was doing, just now; louder, or I won't trust you any more; I'll go to somebody else!'

Once more Mr Bashwood obeyed. 'Don't be angry with me,' he murmured faintly, when he had spoken the necessary words. 'My heart beats so – you'll kill me!'

'You poor old dear!' she whispered back, with a sudden change in her manner – with an easy satirical tenderness. 'What business have you with a heart at your age? Be here to-morrow at the same time, and tell me what you have seen in the grounds. My terms are only five shillings a lesson,' she went on, in her louder tone; 'I'm sure that's not much, Mr Bashwood – I give such long lessons, and I get all my pupils' music half-price.' She suddenly dropped her voice again, and looked him brightly into instant subjection. 'Don't let Mr Armadale out of your sight to-morrow! If that girl manages to speak to him, and if I don't hear of it, I'll frighten you to death. If I *do* hear of it, I'll kiss you! Hush! Wish me good-night, and go on to the town, and leave me to go the other way. I don't want you – I'm not afraid of the man behind the houses; I can deal with him by myself. Say good-night, and I'll let you shake hands. Say it louder, and I'll give you one of my flowers, if you'll promise not to fall in love with it.' She raised her voice again. 'Good-night, Mr Bashwood! Don't forget my terms. Five shillings a lesson, and the lessons last an hour at a time, and I get all my pupils' music half-price, which is an immense advantage, isn't it?' She slipped a flower into his hand – frowned him into obedience, and smiled to reward him for obeying, at the same moment – lifted her dress again above the impurities of the road – and went on her way with a dainty and indolent deliberation, as a cat goes on her way when she has exhausted the enjoyment of frightening a mouse.

Left alone, Mr Bashwood turned to the low cottage wall near which he had been standing, and, resting himself on it wearily, looked at the flower in his hand. His past existence had disciplined him to bear disaster and insult, as few happier men could have borne them – but it had not prepared him to feel the master-passion of humanity, for the first time, at the dreary end of his life, in the hopeless decay of a manhood that had withered under the double blight of conjugal disappointment and parental sorrow. 'Oh, if I was only young again!' murmured the poor wretch, resting his arms on the wall, and touching the flower with his dry fevered lips, in a stealthy rapture of tenderness. 'She might have liked me when I was twenty!' He suddenly started back into an erect position, and stared about him in vacant bewilderment and terror. 'She told me to go home,' he said, with a startled look. 'Why am I stopping here?' He turned, and hurried on to the town – in such dread of her anger, if she looked round and saw him, that he never so much as ventured on a backward glance at the road by which she had retired, and never detected the spy dogging her footsteps, under cover of the empty houses and the brick-heaps by the road-side.

Smoothly and gracefully, carefully preserving the speckless integrity of her dress, never hastening her pace, and never looking aside to the right hand or the left, Miss Gwilt pursued her way towards the open country. The suburban road branched off at its end in two directions. On the left, the path wound through a ragged little coppice, to the grazing grounds of a neighbouring farm. On the right, it led across a hillock of waste land to the high road. Stopping a moment to consider, but not showing the spy that she suspected him, by glancing behind her, while there was a hiding-place within his reach, Miss Gwilt took the path across the hillock. 'I'll catch him there,' she said to herself, looking up quietly at the long straight line of the empty high road. Once on the ground that she had chosen for her purpose, she met the difficulties of the position with perfect tact and self-possession. After walking some thirty yards along the road, she let her nosegay drop – half turned round, in stooping to pick it up – saw the man stopping at the same moment behind her – and instantly went on again, quickening her pace, little by little, until she was walking at the top of her speed. The spy fell into the snare laid for him. Seeing the night coming, and fearing that he might lose sight of her in the darkness, he rapidly lessened the distance between them. Miss Gwilt went on faster and faster, till she plainly heard his footsteps behind her – then stopped – turned – and met the man face to face the next moment.

'My compliments to Mr Armadale,' she said, 'and tell him I've caught you watching me.'

'I'm not watching you, miss,' retorted the spy, thrown off his guard by the daring plainness of the language in which she had spoken to him.

Miss Gwilt's eyes measured him contemptuously from head to foot. He was a weakly, undersized man. She was the taller, and (quite possibly) the stronger of the two.

'Take your hat off, you blackguard, when you speak to a lady,' she said – and tossed his hat in an instant across a ditch by which they were standing, into a pool on the other side.

This time the spy was on his guard. He knew, as well as Miss Gwilt knew, the use which might be made of the precious minutes, if he turned his back on her, and crossed the ditch to recover his hat. 'It's well for you you're a woman,' he said, standing scowling at her bareheaded in the fast-darkening light.

Miss Gwilt glanced sidelong down the onward vista of the road, and saw, through the gathering obscurity, the solitary figure of a man, rapidly advancing towards her. Some women would have noticed the approach of a stranger at that hour and in that lonely place with a certain anxiety. Miss Gwilt was too confident in her own powers of persuasion not to count on the man's assistance beforehand, whoever he might be, *because* he was a man. She looked back at the spy with redoubled confidence in herself, and measured him contemptuously from head to foot for the second time.

'I wonder whether I'm strong enough to throw you after your hat?' she said. 'I'll take a turn and consider it.'

She sauntered on a few steps towards the figure advancing along the road. The spy followed her close. 'Try it,' he said brutally. 'You're a fine woman – you're welcome to put your arms round me if you like.' As the words escaped him, he too saw the stranger for the first time. He drew back a step and waited. Miss Gwilt, on her side, advanced a step and waited too.

The stranger came on, with the lithe light step of a practised walker, swinging a stick in his hand, and carrying a knapsack on his shoulders. A few paces nearer, and his face became visible. He was a dark man, his black hair was powdered with dust, and his black eyes were looking steadfastly forward along the road before him.

Miss Gwilt advanced with the first signs of agitation she had shown yet. 'Is it possible?' she said softly. 'Can it really be you!'

It was Midwinter, on his way back to Thorpe-Ambrose, after his fortnight among the Yorkshire moors.

He stopped and looked at her, in breathless surprise. The image of the woman had been in his thoughts, at the moment when the woman herself spoke to him. 'Miss Gwilt!' he exclaimed, and mechanically held out his hand.

She took it, and pressed it gently. 'I should have been glad to see you at any time,' she said. 'You don't know how glad I am to see you now. May I trouble you to speak to that man? He has been following me, and annoying me, all the way from the town.'

Midwinter stepped past her, without uttering a word. Faint as the light was, the spy saw what was coming in his face, and turning instantly, leapt the ditch by the roadside. Before Midwinter could follow, Miss Gwilt's hand was on his shoulder.

'No,' she said. 'You don't know who his employer is.'

Midwinter stopped, and looked at her.

'Strange things have happened since you left us,' she went on. 'I have been forced to give up my situation, and I am followed and watched by a paid spy. Don't ask who forced me out of my situation, and who pays the spy – at least not just yet. I can't make up my mind to tell you till I am a little more composed. Let the wretch go. Do you mind seeing me safe back to my lodging? It's in your way home. May I – may I ask for the support of your arm? My little stock of courage is quite exhausted.' She took his arm and clung close to it. The woman who had tyrannized over Mr Bashwood was gone, and the woman who had tossed the spy's hat into the pool was gone. A timid, shrinking, interesting creature filled the fair skin, and trembled on the symmetrical limbs of Miss Gwilt. She put her handkerchief to her eyes. 'They say necessity has no law,' she murmured faintly. 'I am treating you like an old friend. God knows I want one!'

They went on towards the town. She recovered herself with a touching fortitude – she put her handkerchief back in her pocket, and persisted in turning the conversation on Midwinter's walking tour. 'It is bad enough to be a burden on you,' she said, gently pressing on his arm as she spoke. 'I mustn't distress you as well. Tell me where you have been, and what you have seen. Interest me in your journey; help me to escape from myself.'

They reached the modest little lodging, in the miserable little suburb. Miss Gwilt sighed, and removed her glove before she took Midwinter's hand. 'I have taken refuge here,' she said, simply. 'It is clean and quiet – I am too poor to want or expect more. We must say good-by, I suppose, unless—' she hesitated modestly, and satisfied herself by a quick look round that they were unobserved – 'unless you would like to come in and rest a little? I feel so gratefully towards you, Mr Midwinter! Is there any harm, do you think, in my offering you a cup of tea?'

The magnetic influence of her touch was thrilling through him while she spoke. Change and absence to which he had trusted to weaken her hold on him, had treacherously strengthened it instead. A man exceptionally sensitive, a man exceptionally pure in his past life, he stood hand in hand in the tempting secrecy of the night, with the first woman who had exercised over him the all-absorbing influence of her sex. At his age and in his position, who could have left her? The man (with a man's temperament) doesn't live who could have left her. Midwinter went in.

A stupid, sleepy lad opened the house-door. Even he, being a male creature, brightened under the influence of Miss Gwilt. 'The urn, John,' she said, kindly, 'and another cup and saucer. I'll borrow your candle to light my candles upstairs – and then I won't trouble you any more tonight.' John was wakeful and active in an instant. 'No trouble, miss,' he said, with awkward civility. Miss Gwilt took his candle with a smile. 'How good people are to me!' she whispered innocently to Midwinter, as she led the way upstairs to the little drawing-room on the first floor.

She lit the candles, and, turning quickly on her guest, stopped him at the first attempt he made to remove the knapsack from his shoulders. 'No,' she said, gently. 'In the good old times, there were occasions when the ladies unarmed their knights. I claim the privilege of unarming *my* knight.' Her dexterous fingers intercepted his at the straps and buckles;

and she had the dusty knapsack off, before he could protest against her touching it.

They sat down at the one little table in the room. It was very poorly furnished – but there was something of the dainty neatness of the woman who inhabited it in the arrangement of the few poor ornaments on the chimney-piece, in the one or two prettily-bound volumes on the cheffonier, in the flowers on the table, and the modest little work-basket in the window. 'Women are not all coquettes,' she said, as she took off her bonnet and mantilla, and laid them carefully on a chair. 'I won't go into my room, and look in my glass, and make myself smart – you shall take me just as I am.' Her hands moved about among the tea-things with a smooth, noiseless activity. Her magnificent hair flashed crimson in the candle-light, as she turned her head hither and thither, searching, with an easy grace, for the things she wanted in the tray. Exercise had heightened the brilliancy of her complexion, and had quickened the rapid alternations of expression in her eyes – the delicious languor that stole over them when she was listening or thinking, the bright intelligence that flashed from them softly when she spoke. In the lightest word she said, in the least thing she did, there was something that gently solicited the heart of the man who sat with her. Perfectly modest in her manner, possessed to perfection of the graceful restraints and refinements of a lady, she had all the allurements that feast the eye, all the Siren-invitations that seduce the sense – a subtle suggestiveness in her silence, and a sexual sorcery in her smile.

'Should I be wrong,' she asked, suddenly suspending the conversation which she had thus far persistently restricted to the subject of Midwinter's walking tour, 'if I guessed that you have something on your mind – something which neither my tea nor my talk can charm away? Are men as curious as women? Is the something – Me?'

Midwinter struggled against the fascination of looking at her and listening to her. 'I am very anxious to hear what has happened since I have been away,' he said. 'But I am still more anxious, Miss Gwilt, not to distress you by speaking of a painful subject.'

She looked at him gratefully. 'It is for your sake that I have avoided the painful subject,' she said, toying with her spoon among the dregs in her empty cup. 'But you will hear about it from others, if you don't hear about it from me; and you ought to know why you found me in that strange situation, and why you see me here. Pray remember one thing to begin with. I don't blame your friend Mr Armadale – I blame the people whose instrument he is.'

Midwinter started. 'Is it possible,' he began, 'that Allan can be in any way answerable—?' He stopped, and looked at Miss Gwilt in silent astonishment.

She gently laid her hand on his. 'Don't be angry with me for only telling the truth,' she said. 'Your friend is answerable for everything that has happened to me – innocently answerable, Mr Midwinter, I firmly believe. We are both victims. *He* is the victim of his position as the richest single man in the neighbourhood; and *I* am the victim of Miss Milroy's determination to marry him.'

'Miss Milroy?' repeated Midwinter, more and more astonished. 'Why, Allan himself told me—' He stopped again.

'He told you that I was the object of his admiration? Poor fellow, he admires everybody – his head is almost as empty as this,' said Miss Gwilt, smiling indicatively into the hollow of her cup. She dropped the spoon, sighed, and became serious again. 'I am guilty of the vanity of having let him admire me,' she went on penitently, 'without the excuse of being able, on my side, to reciprocate even the passing interest that he felt in me. I don't undervalue his many admirable qualities, or the excellent position he can offer to his wife. But a woman's heart is not to be commanded – no, Mr Midwinter, not even by the fortunate master of Thorpe-Ambrose who commands everything else.'

She looked him full in the face as she uttered that magnanimous sentiment. His eyes dropped before hers, and his dark colour deepened. He had felt his heart leap in him at the declaration of her indifference to Allan. For the first time since they had known each other, his interests now stood self-revealed before him as openly adverse to the interests of his friend.

'I have been guilty of the vanity of letting Mr Armadale admire me, and I have suffered for it,' resumed Miss Gwilt. 'If there had been any confidence between my pupil and me, I might have easily satisfied her that she might become Mrs Armadale – if she could – without having any rivalry to fear on my part. But Miss Milroy disliked and distrusted me from the first. She took her own jealous view, no doubt, of Mr Armadale's thoughtless attentions to me. It was her interest to destroy the position, such as it was, that I held in his estimation; and it is quite likely her mother assisted her. Mrs Milroy had her motive also (which I am really ashamed to mention) for wishing to drive me out of the house. Anyhow, the conspiracy has succeeded. I have been forced (with Mr Armadale's help) to leave the major's service. Don't be angry, Mr Midwinter! don't form a hasty opinion! I dare say Miss Milroy has some good qualities, though I have not found them out; and I assure you again and again that I don't blame Mr Armadale – I only blame the people whose instrument he is.'

'How is he their instrument? How can he be the instrument of any enemy of yours?' asked Midwinter. 'Pray excuse my anxiety, Miss Gwilt – Allan's good name is as dear to me as my own!'

Miss Gwilt's eyes turned full on him again, and Miss Gwilt's heart abandoned itself innocently to an outburst of enthusiasm. 'How I admire your earnestness!' she said. 'How I like your anxiety for your friend! Oh, if women could only form such friendships! Oh, you happy, happy men!' Her voice faltered, and her convenient teacup absorbed her for the third time. 'I would give all the little beauty I possess,' she said, 'if I could only find such a friend as Mr Armadale has found in *you*. I never shall, Mr Midwinter, I never shall. Let us go back to what we were talking about. I can only tell you how your friend is concerned in my misfortunes, by telling you something first about myself. I am like many other governesses; I am the victim of sad domestic circumstances. It may be weak of me, but I have a horror of alluding to them among strangers. My silence about my family and my friends exposes me to misinterpretation in my dependent position. Does it do me any harm, Mr Midwinter, in your estimation?'

'God forbid!' said Midwinter, fervently. 'There is no man living,' he went on, thinking of his own family story, 'who has better reason to understand and respect your silence than I have.'

Miss Gwilt seized his hand impulsively. 'Oh,' she said, 'I knew it, the first moment I saw you! I knew that you, too, had suffered, that you too had sorrows which you kept sacred! Strange, strange sympathy! I believe in mesmerism[1] – do you?' She suddenly recollected herself and shuddered. 'Oh, what have I done? what must you think of me?' she exclaimed, as he yielded to the magnetic fascination of her touch, and forgetting everything but the hand that lay warm in his own, bent over it and kissed it. 'Spare me!' she said, faintly, as she felt the burning touch of his lips. 'I am so friendless, I am so completely at your mercy!'

He turned away from her, and hid his face in his hands – he was trembling, and she saw it. She looked at him, while his face was hidden from her – she looked at him with a furtive interest and surprise. 'How that man loves me!' she thought. 'I wonder whether there was a time once when I might have loved *him*?'

The silence between them remained unbroken for some minutes. He had felt her appeal to his consideration as she had never expected or intended him to feel it – he shrank from looking at her or from speaking to her again.

'Shall I go on with my story?' she asked. 'Shall we forget and forgive on both sides?' A woman's inveterate indulgence for every expression of a man's admiration which keeps within the limits of personal respect, curved her lips gently into a charming smile. She looked down meditatively at her dress, and brushed a crumb off her lap with a little fluttering sigh. 'I was telling you,' she went on, 'of my reluctance to speak to strangers of my sad family story. It was in that way, as I afterwards found out, that I laid myself open to Miss Milroy's malice and Miss Milroy's suspicion. Private inquiries about me were addressed to the lady who was my reference – at Miss Milroy's suggestion, in the first instance, I have no doubt. I am sorry to say, this is not the worst of it. By some underhand means of which I am quite ignorant, Mr Armadale's simplicity was imposed on – and when application was made secretly to my reference in London, it was made, Mr Midwinter, through your friend.'

Midwinter suddenly rose from his chair and looked at her. The fascination that she exercised over him, powerful as it was, became a suspended influence, now that the plain disclosure came plainly at last from her lips. He looked at her, and sat down again like a man bewildered, without uttering a word.

'Remember how weak he is,' pleaded Miss Gwilt gently, 'and make allowances for him as I do. The trifling accident of his failing to find my reference at the address given him seems, I can't imagine why, to have excited Mr Armadale's suspicion. At any rate, he remained in London. What he did there, it is impossible for me to say. I was quite in the dark; I knew nothing; I distrusted nobody; I was as happy in my little round of duties as I could be with a pupil whose affections I had failed to win – when, one morning, to my indescribable astonishment, Major Milroy showed me a correspondence between Mr Armadale and himself. He spoke to me in his wife's presence. Poor creature, I make no complaint of her – such affliction as she suffers excuses everything. I wish I could give you some idea of the letters between Major Milroy and Mr Armadale – but my head is only a woman's head, and I was so confused and distressed at the time! All I can tell you is, that Mr Armadale chose to preserve silence about his proceedings in London, under circumstances which made that silence a reflection on my character. The major was most kind; his confidence in me remained unshaken – but could his confidence protect me against his wife's prejudice and his daughter's ill-will? Oh, the hardness of women to each other! Oh, the humiliation if men only knew some of us as we really are! What could I do? I couldn't defend myself against mere imputations; and I couldn't remain in my situation after a slur had been cast on me. My pride (Heaven help me. I was brought up like a gentlewoman, and I have sensibilities that are not blunted even yet!) – my pride got the better of me, and I left my place. Don't let it distress you, Mr Midwinter! There's a bright side to the picture. The ladies in the neighbourhood have overwhelmed me with kindness; I have the prospect of getting pupils to teach; I am spared the mortification of going back to be a burden on my friends. The only complaint I have to make is I think a just one? Mr Armadale has been back at Thorpe-Ambrose for some days. I have entreated him, by letter, to grant me an interview; to tell me what dreadful suspicions he has of me, and to let me set myself right in his estimation. Would you believe it? he has declined to see me – under the influence of others; not of his own free will, I am sure! Cruel, isn't it? But he has even used me more cruelly still – he persists in suspecting me – it is he who is having me watched. Oh, Mr Midwinter, don't hate me for telling you what you *must* know! The man you found persecuting me and frightening me to-night was only earning his money after all as Mr Armadale's spy.'

Once more Midwinter started to his feet; and this time the thoughts that were in him found their way into words.

'I can't believe it; I won't believe it!' he exclaimed indignantly. 'If the man told you that, the man lied. I beg your pardon, Miss Gwilt; I beg your pardon from the bottom of my heart. Don't, pray don't think I doubt *you*; I only say there is some dreadful mistake. I am not sure that I understand as I ought all that you have told me. But this last infamous meanness of which you think Allan guilty, I *do* understand. I swear to you, he is incapable of it! Some scoundrel has been taking advantage of him; some scoundrel has been using his name. I'll prove it to you if you will only give me time. Let me go and clear it up at once. I can't rest; I can't bear to think of it; I can't even enjoy the pleasure of being here. Oh,' he burst out desperately, 'I'm sure you feel for me, after what you have said – I feel so for *you*!'

He stopped in confusion. Miss Gwilt's eyes were looking at him again; and Miss Gwilt's hand had found its way once more into his own.

'You are the most generous of living men,' she said softly; 'I will believe what you tell me to believe. Go,' she added in a whisper, suddenly releasing his hand and turning away from him. 'For both our sakes, go!'

His heart beat fast; he looked at her as she dropped into a chair and put her handkerchief to her eyes. For one moment he hesitated – the next, he snatched up his knapsack from the floor, and left her precipitately without a backward look, or a parting word.

She rose when the door closed on him. A change came over her the instant she was alone. The colour faded out of her cheeks; the beauty died out of her eyes; her face hardened horribly with a silent despair. 'It's even baser work than I bargained for,' she said, 'to deceive *him*.' After pacing to and fro in the room for some minutes, she stopped wearily before the glass over the fireplace. 'You strange creature!' she murmured, leaning her elbows on the mantel-piece, and languidly addressing the reflection of herself in the glass. 'Have you got any conscience left? And has that man roused it?'

The reflection of her face changed slowly. The colour returned to her cheeks, the delicious languor began to suffuse her eyes again. Her lips parted gently, and her quickening breath began to dim the surface of the glass. She drew back from it, after a moment's absorption in her own thoughts, with a start of terror. 'What am I doing?' she asked herself in a sudden panic of astonishment. 'Am I mad enough to be thinking of him in *that* way?'

She burst into a mocking laugh, and opened her desk on the table recklessly with a bang. 'It's high time I had some talk with mother Jezebel,' she said, and sat down to write to Mrs Oldershaw.

'I have met with Mr Midwinter,' she began, 'under very lucky circumstances; and I have made the most of my opportunity. He has just left me for his friend Armadale; and one of two good things will happen to-morrow. If they don't quarrel, the doors of Thorpe-Ambrose will be opened to me again at Mr Midwinter's intercession. If they do quarrel, I shall be the unhappy cause of it, and I shall find my way in for myself, on the purely Christian errand of reconciling them.'

She hesitated at the next sentence, wrote the first few words of it, scratched them out again, and petulantly tore the letter into fragments and threw the pen to the other end of the room. Turning quickly on her chair, she looked at the seat which Midwinter had occupied; her foot restlessly tapping the floor, and her handkerchief thrust like a gag between her clenched teeth. 'Young as you are,' she thought, with her mind reviving the image of him in the empty chair, – 'there has been something out of the common in *your* life – and I must and will know it!'

The house-clock struck the hour and roused her. She sighed, and walking back to the glass, wearily loosened the fastenings of her dress; wearily removed the studs from the chemisette beneath it, and put them on the chimney-piece. She looked indolently at the reflected beauties of her neck and bosom, as she unplaited her hair and threw it back in one great mass over her shoulders. 'Fancy,' she thought, 'if he saw me now!' She turned back to the table, and sighed again as she extinguished one of the candles and took the other in her hand. 'Midwinter?' she said, as she passed through the folding-doors of the room to her bedchamber. 'I don't believe in his name, to begin with!'

The night had advanced by more than an hour before Midwinter was back again at the great house.

Twice, well as the homeward way was known to him, he had strayed out of the right road. The events of the evening — the interview with Miss Gwilt herself, after his fortnight's solitary thinking of her; the extraordinary change that had taken place in her position since he had seen her last; and the startling assertion of Allan's connection with it — had all conspired to throw his mind into a state of ungovernable confusion. The darkness of the cloudy night added to his bewilderment. Even the familiar gates of Thorpe-Ambrose seemed strange to him. When he tried to think of it, it was a mystery to him how he had reached the place.

The front of the house was dark and closed for the night. Midwinter went round to the back. The sound of men's voices, as he advanced, caught his ear. They were soon distinguishable as the voices of the first and second footman, and the subject of conversation between them was their master.

'I'll bet you an even half-crown he's driven out of the neighbourhood before another week is over his head,' said the first footman.

'Done.' said the second. 'He isn't as easy driven as you think.'

'Isn't he?' retorted the other. 'He'll be mobbed if he stops here! I tell you again, he's not satisfied with the mess he's got into already. I know it for certain he's having the governess watched.'

At those words, Midwinter mechanically checked himself before he turned the corner of the house. His first doubt of the result of his meditated appeal to Allan ran through him like a sudden chill. The influence exercised by the voice of public scandal is a force which acts in opposition to the ordinary law of mechanics. It is strongest, not by concentration, but by distribution. To the primary sound we may shut our ears; but the reverberation of it in echoes is irresistible. On his way back, Midwinter's one desire had been to find Allan up, and to speak to him immediately. His one hope now was to gain time to contend with the new doubts and to silence the new misgivings — his one present anxiety was to hear that Allan had gone to bed. He turned the corner of the house, and presented himself before the men smoking their pipes in the back garden. As soon as their astonishment allowed them to speak, they offered to rouse their master. Allan had given his friend up for that night, and had gone to bed about half an hour since.

'It was my master's particular order, sir,' said the head footman, 'that he was to be told of it if you came back.'

'It is *my* particular request,' returned Midwinter, 'that you won't disturb him.'

The men looked at each other wonderingly, as he took his candle and left them.[2]

CHAPTER VIII

SHE COMES BETWEEN THEM

Appointed hours for the various domestic events of the day were things unknown at Thorpe-Ambrose. Irregular in all his habits, Allan accommodated himself to no stated times (with the solitary exception of dinner-time) at any hour of the day or night. He retired to rest early or late, and he rose early or late, exactly as he felt inclined. The servants were forbidden to call him; and Mrs Gripper was accustomed to improvise the breakfast as she best might, from the time when the kitchen fire was first lighted, to the time when the clock stood on the stroke of noon.

Towards nine o'clock on the morning after his return, Midwinter knocked at Allan's door; and, on entering the room, found it empty. After inquiry among the servants, it appeared that Allan had risen that morning before the man who usually attended on him was up, and that his hot water had been brought to the door by one of the housemaids, who was then still in ignorance of Midwinter's return. Nobody had chanced to see the master, either on the stairs or in the hall; nobody had heard him ring the bell for breakfast as usual. In brief, nobody knew anything about him, except what was obviously clear to all – that he was not in the house.

Midwinter went out under the great portico. He stood at the head of the flight of steps considering in which direction he should set forth to look for his friend. Allan's unexpected absence added one more to the disquieting influences which still perplexed his mind. He was in the mood in which trifles irritate a man, and fancies are all-powerful to exalt or depress his spirits.

The sky was cloudy; and the wind blew in puffs from the south — there was every prospect, to weather-wise eyes, of coming rain. While Midwinter was still hesitating, one of the grooms passed him on the drive below. The man proved, on being questioned, to be better informed about his master's movements than the servants indoors. He had seen Allan pass the stables more than an hour since, going out by the back way into the park, with a nosegay in his hand.

A nosegay in his hand? The nosegay hung incomprehensibly on Midwinter's mind as he walked round, on the chance of meeting Allan, to the back of the house. 'What does the nosegay mean?' he asked himself with an unintelligible sense of irritation, and a petulant kick at a stone that stood in his way.

It meant that Allan had been following his impulses as usual. The one pleasant impression left on his mind after his interview with Pedgift Senior, was the impression made by the lawyer's account of his conversation with Neelie in the park. The anxiety that he should not misjudge her, which the major's daughter had so earnestly expressed, placed her before Allan's eyes, in an irresistibly attractive character — the character of the one person among all his neighbours who had some respect still left for his good opinion. Acutely sensible of his social isolation, now that there was no Midwinter to keep him company in the empty house; hungering and thirsting in his solitude for a kind word and a friendly look, he began to think more and more regretfully and more and more longingly of the bright young face, so pleasantly associated with his first happiest days at Thorpe-Ambrose. To be conscious of such a feeling as this, was with a character like Allan's, to act on it headlong, lead him where it might. He had gone out on the previous morning to look for Neelie with a peace-offering of flowers, but with no very distinct idea of what he should say to her if they met; and failing to find her on the scene of her customary walks, he had characteristically persisted the next morning in making a second attempt with another peace-offering on a larger scale. Still ignorant of his friend's return, he was now at some distance from the house, searching the park in a direction which he had not tried yet.

After walking out a few hundred yards beyond the stables, and failing to discover any signs of Allan, Midwinter retraced his steps, and waited for his friend's return, pacing slowly to and fro on the little strip of garden ground at the back of the house.

From time to time, as he passed it, he looked in absently at the room which had formerly been Mrs Armadale's, which was now (through his interposition) habitually occupied by her son — the room with the

Statuette on the bracket, and the French windows opening to the ground, which had once recalled to him the Second Vision of the Dream. The Shadow of the Man, which Allan had seen standing opposite to him at the long window; the view over a lawn and flower-garden; the pattering of the rain against the glass; the stretching out of the Shadow's arm, and the fall of the statue in fragments on the floor – these objects and events of the visionary scene, so vividly present to his memory once, were all superseded by later remembrances now, were all left to fade as they might in the dim background of time. He could pass the room again and again, alone and anxious, and never once think of the boat drifting away in the moonlight, and the night's imprisonment on the Wrecked Ship!

Towards ten o'clock the well-remembered sound of Allan's voice became suddenly audible in the direction of the stables. In a moment more, he was visible from the garden. His second morning's search for Neelie had ended to all appearance in a second defeat of his object. The nosegay was still in his hand; and he was resignedly making a present of it to one of the coachman's children.

Midwinter impulsively took a step forward towards the stables, and abruptly checked his further progress. Conscious that his position towards his friend was altered already in relation to Miss Gwilt, the first sight of Allan filled his mind with a sudden distrust of the governess's influence over him, which was almost a distrust of himself. He knew that he had set forth from the moors on his return to Thorpe-Ambrose with the resolution of acknowledging the passion that had mastered him, and of insisting, if necessary, on a second and a longer absence in the interests of the sacrifice which he was bent on making to the happiness of his friend. What had become of that resolution now? The discovery of Miss Gwilt's altered position, and the declaration that she had voluntarily made of her indifference to Allan, had scattered it to the winds. The first words with which he would have met his friend, if nothing had happened to him on the homeward way, were words already dismissed from his lips. He drew back as he felt it, and struggled with an instinctive loyalty towards Allan, to free himself at the last moment from the influence of Miss Gwilt.

Having disposed of his useless nosegay, Allan passed on into the garden, and the instant he entered it, recognized Midwinter with a loud cry of surprise and delight.

'Am I awake, or dreaming?' he exclaimed, seizing his friend excitably by both hands. 'You dear old Midwinter, have you sprung up out of the ground, or have you dropped from the clouds?'

It was not till Midwinter had explained the mystery of his unexpected appearance in every particular, that Allan could be prevailed on to say a word about himself. When he did speak, he shook his head ruefully, and subdued the hearty loudness of his voice, with a preliminary look round to see if the servants were within hearing.

'I've learnt to be cautious since you went away and left me,' said Allan. 'My dear fellow, you haven't the least notion what things have happened, and what an awful scrape I'm in at this very moment!'

'You are mistaken, Allan. I have heard more of what has happened than you suppose.'

'What! the dreadful mess I'm in with Miss Gwilt? the row with the major? the infernal scandal-mongering in the neighbourhood? You don't mean to say—?'

'Yes,' interposed Midwinter quietly, 'I have heard of it all.'

'Good heavens! how? Did you stop at Thorpe-Ambrose on your way back? Have you been in the coffee-room at the hotel? Have you met Pedgift? Have you dropped into the Reading Rooms, and seen what they call the freedom of the press in the town newspaper?'

Midwinter paused before he answered, and looked up at the sky. The clouds had been gathering unnoticed over their heads, and the first rain-drops were beginning to fall.

'Come in here,' said Allen. 'We'll go up to breakfast this way.' He led Midwinter through the open French window into his own sitting-room. The wind blew towards that side of the house, and the rain followed them in. Midwinter, who was last, turned and closed the window.

Allan was too eager for the answer which the weather had interrupted, to wait for it till they reached the breakfast-room. He stopped close at the window, and added two more to his string of questions.

'How can you possibly have heard about me and Miss Gwilt?' he asked. 'Who told you?'

'Miss Gwilt herself,' replied Midwinter gravely.

Allan's manner changed the moment the governess's name passed his friend's lips.

'I wish you had heard my story first,' he said. 'Where did you meet with Miss Gwilt?'

There was a momentary pause. They both stood still at the window, absorbed in the interest of the moment. They both forgot that their contemplated place of shelter from the rain had been the breakfast-room upstairs.

'Before I answer your question,' said Midwinter a little constrainedly,

'I want to ask you something, Allan, on my side. Is it really true that you are in some way concerned in Miss Gwilt's leaving Major Milroy's service?'

There was another pause. The disturbance which had begun to appear in Allan's manner palpably increased.

'It's rather a long story,' he began. 'I have been taken in, Midwinter. I've been imposed on by a person, who – I can't help saying it – who cheated me into promising what I oughtn't to have promised, and doing what I had better not have done. It isn't breaking my promise to tell *you*. I can trust in your discretion, can't I? You will never say a word, will you?'

'Stop!' said Midwinter. 'Don't trust me with any secrets which are not your own. If you have given a promise, don't trifle with it, even in speaking to such an intimate friend as I am.' He laid his hand gently and kindly on Allan's shoulder. 'I can't help seeing that I have made you a little uncomfortable,' he went on. 'I can't help seeing that my question is not so easy a one to answer as I had hoped and supposed. Shall we wait a little? shall we go upstairs and breakfast first?'

Allan was far too earnestly bent on presenting his conduct to his friend in the right aspect, to heed Midwinter's suggestion. He spoke eagerly on the instant, without moving from the window.

'My dear fellow, it's a perfectly easy question to answer. Only—' He hesitated. 'Only it requires what I'm a bad hand at – it requires an explanation.'

'Do you mean,' asked Midwinter more seriously, but not less gently than before, 'that you must first justify yourself, and then answer my question?'

'That's it!' said Allan, with an air of relief. 'You've hit the right nail on the head, just as usual.'

Midwinter's face darkened for the first time. 'I am sorry to hear it,' he said; his voice sinking low, and his eyes dropping to the ground as he spoke.

The rain was beginning to fall thickly. It swept across the garden, straight on the closed windows, and pattered heavily against the glass.

'Sorry!' repeated Allan. 'My dear fellow, you haven't heard the particulars yet. Wait till I explain the thing first.'

'You are a bad hand at explanations,' said Midwinter, repeating Allan's own words. 'Don't place yourself at a disadvantage. Don't explain it.'

Allan looked at him, in silent perplexity and surprise.

'You are my friend – my best and dearest friend,' Midwinter went on. 'I can't bear to let you justify yourself to me as if I was your judge, or as if I doubted you.' He looked up again at Allan frankly and kindly as he said those words. 'Besides,' he resumed, 'I think if I look into my memory, I can anticipate your explanation. We had a moment's talk, before I went away, about some very delicate questions, which you proposed putting to Major Milroy. I remember I warned you; I remember I had my misgivings. Should I be guessing right if I guessed that those questions have been in some way the means of leading you into a false position? If it is true that you have been concerned in Miss Gwilt's leaving her situation, is it also true – is it only doing you justice to believe – that any mischief for which you are responsible, has been mischief innocently done?'

'Yes,' said Allan, speaking for the first time a little constrainedly on his side. 'It is only doing me justice to say that.' He stopped and began drawing lines absently with his finger on the blurred surface of the window-pane. 'You're not like other people, Midwinter,' he resumed suddenly, with an effort; 'and I should have liked you to have heard the particulars all the same.'

'I will hear them if you desire it,' returned Midwinter. 'But I am satisfied without another word, that you have not willingly been the means of depriving Miss Gwilt of her situation. If that is understood between you and me, I think we need say no more. Besides, I have another question to ask, of much greater importance: a question that has been forced on me by what I saw with my own eyes, and heard with my own ears, last night.'

He stopped, recoiling in spite of himself. 'Shall we go upstairs first?' he asked abruptly, leading the way to the door, and trying to gain time.

It was useless. Once again, the room which they were both free to leave, the room which one of them had twice tried to leave already, held them as if they were prisoners.

Without answering, without even appearing to have heard Midwinter's proposal to go upstairs, Allan followed him mechanically as far as the opposite side of the window. There he stopped. 'Midwinter!' he burst out, in a sudden panic of astonishment and alarm, 'there seems to be something strange between us! you're not like yourself. What is it?'

With his hand on the lock of the door, Midwinter turned, and looked back into the room. The moment had come. His haunting fear of doing his friend an injustice had shown itself in a restraint of word, look, and action, which had been marked enough to force its way to Allan's notice. The one course left now, in the dearest interests of the friendship that united them, was to speak at once, and to speak boldly.

'There's something strange between us,' reiterated Allan. 'For God's sake what is it?'

Midwinter took his hand from the door, and came down again to the window, fronting Allan. He occupied the place, of necessity, which Allan had just left. It was the side of the window on which the Statuette stood. The little figure, placed on its projecting bracket, was close behind him on his right hand. No signs of change appeared in the stormy sky. The rain still swept slanting across the garden, and pattered heavily against the glass.

'Give me your hand, Allan.'

Allan gave it, and Midwinter held it firmly while he spoke.

'There *is* something strange between us,' he said. 'There is something to be set right which touches you nearly; and it has not been set right yet. You asked me just now where I met with Miss Gwilt. I met with her on my way back here, upon the high road on the farther side of the town. She entreated me to protect her from a man who was following, and frightening her. I saw the scoundrel with my own eyes, and I should have laid hands on him, if Miss Gwilt herself had not stopped me. She gave a very strange reason for stopping me. She said I didn't know who his employer was.'

Allan's ruddy colour suddenly deepened; he looked aside quickly through the window at the pouring rain. At the same moment their hands fell apart, and there was a pause of silence on either side. Midwinter was the first to speak again.

'Later in the evening,' he went on, 'Miss Gwilt explained herself. She told me two things. She declared that the man whom I had seen following her was a hired spy. I was surprised, but I could not dispute it. She told me next, Allan – what I believe with my whole heart and soul to be a falsehood which has been imposed on her as the truth – she told me that the spy was in *your* employment!'

Allan turned instantly from the window, and looked Midwinter full in the face again. 'I *must* explain myself this time,' he said resolutely.

The ashy paleness, peculiar to him in moments of strong emotion, began to show itself on Midwinter's cheeks.

'More explanations!' he said, and drew back a step, with his eyes fixed in a sudden terror of inquiry on Allan's face.

'You don't know what I know, Midwinter. You don't know that what I have done has been done with a good reason. And what is more, I have not trusted to myself – I have had good advice.'

'Did you hear what I said just now?' asked Midwinter, incredulously; 'you can't – surely, you can't have been attending to me?'

'I haven't missed a word,' rejoined Allan. 'I tell you again, you don't know what I know of Miss Gwilt. She has threatened Miss Milroy. Miss Milroy is in danger while her governess stops in this neighbourhood.'

Midwinter dismissed the major's daughter from the conversation with a contemptuous gesture of his hand.

'I don't want to hear about Miss Milroy,' he said. 'Don't mix up Miss Milroy – Good God, Allan, am I to understand that the spy set to watch Miss Gwilt was doing his vile work with your approval?'

'Once for all, my dear fellow, will you, or will you not, let me explain?'

'Explain!' cried Midwinter, his eyes aflame, and his hot Creole blood rushing crimson into his face. 'Explain the employment of a spy? What! after having driven Miss Gwilt out of her situation, by meddling with her private affairs, you meddle again, by the vilest of all means – the means of a paid spy? You set a watch on the woman whom you yourself told me you loved, only a fortnight since! the woman you were thinking of as your wife! I don't believe it; I won't believe it. Is my head failing me? Is it Allan Armadale I am speaking to? Is it Allan Armadale's face looking at me? Stop! you are acting under some mistaken scruple. Some low fellow has crept into your confidence, and has done this in your name without telling you first.'

Allan controlled himself with admirable patience and admirable consideration for the temper of his friend. 'If you persist in refusing to hear me,' he said, 'I must wait as well as I can till my turn comes.'

'Tell me you are a stranger to the employment of that man, and I will hear you willingly.'

'Suppose there should be a necessity, that you know nothing about, for employing him?'

'I acknowledge no necessity for the cowardly persecution of a helpless woman.'

A momentary flush of irritation – momentary, and no more – passed over Allan's face. 'You mightn't think her quite so helpless,' he said, 'if you knew the truth.'

'Are *you* the man to tell me the truth?' retorted the other. 'You who have refused to hear her in her own defence! You, who have closed the doors of this house against her!'

Allan still controlled himself, but the effort began at last to be visible.

'I know your temper is a hot one,' he said. 'But for all that, your violence quite takes me by surprise. I can't account for it, unless—' he hesitated a moment, and then finished the sentence in his usual frank, outspoken way – 'unless you are sweet yourself on Miss Gwilt.'

Those last words heaped fuel on the fire. They stripped the truth instantly of all concealments and disguises, and laid it bare to view. Allan's instinct had guessed, and the guiding influence stood revealed of Midwinter's interest in Miss Gwilt.

'What right have you to say that?' he asked, with raised voice and threatening eyes.

'I told *you*,' said Allan, simply, 'when I thought I was sweet on her myself. Come! come! it's a little hard, I think, even if you *are* in love with her, to believe everything she tells you, and not to let me say a word. Is *that* the way you decide between us?'

'Yes, it is!' cried the other, infuriated by Allan's second allusion to Miss Gwilt. 'When I am asked to choose between the employer of a spy, and the victim of a spy, I side with the victim!'

'Don't try me too hard, Midwinter; I have a temper to lose as well as you.'

He stopped, struggling with himself. The torture of passion in Midwinter's face, from which a less simple and less generous nature might have recoiled in horror, touched Allan suddenly with an artless distress, which, at that moment, was little less than sublime. He advanced, with his eyes moistening, and his hand held out. 'You asked me for my hand just now,' he said, 'and I gave it you. Will you remember old times, and give me yours, before it's too late?'

'No!' retorted Midwinter, furiously. 'I may meet Miss Gwilt again, and I may want my hand free to deal with your spy!'

He had drawn back along the wall, as Allan advanced, until the bracket which supported the Statuette was before instead of behind him. In the madness of his passion, he saw nothing but Allan's face confronting him. In the madness of his passion, he stretched out his right hand as he answered and shook it threateningly in the air. It struck the forgotten projection of the bracket – and the next instant the Statuette lay in fragments on the floor.

The rain drove slanting over flower-bed and lawn, and pattered heavily against the glass; and the two Armadales stood by the window, as the two Shadows had stood in the second Vision of the Dream, with the wreck of the image between them.

Allan stooped over the fragments of the little figure, and lifted them one by one from the floor. 'Leave me,' he said, without looking up, 'or we shall both repent it.'

Without a word, Midwinter moved back slowly. He stood for the second time with his hand on the door, and looked his last at the room. The horror of the night on the Wreck had got him once more, and the flame of his passion was quenched in an instant.

'The Dream!' he whispered, under his breath. 'The Dream again!'

The door was tried from the outside, and a servant appeared with a trivial message about the breakfast.

Midwinter looked at the man with a blank, dreadful helplessness in his face. 'Show me the way out,' he said. 'The place is dark, and the room turns round with me.'

The servant took him by the arm, and silently led him out.

As the door closed on them, Allan picked up the last fragment of the broken figure. He sat down alone at the table, and hid his face in his hands. The self-control which he had bravely preserved under exasperation renewed again and again, now failed him at last in the friendless solitude of his room; and in the first bitterness of feeling that Midwinter had turned against him like the rest, he burst into tears.

The moments followed each other, the slow time wore on. Little by little the signs of a new elemental disturbance began to show themselves in the summer storm. The shadow of a swiftly-deepening darkness swept over the sky. The pattering of the rain lessened with the lessening wind. There was a momentary hush of stillness. Then on a sudden, the rain poured down again like a cataract, and the low roll of thunder came up solemnly on the dying air.

CHAPTER IX

SHE KNOWS THE TRUTH

1. – *From Mr Bashwood to Miss Gwilt*

Thorpe-Ambrose, July 20th, 1851.

DEAR MADAM, – I received yesterday, by private messenger, your obliging note, in which you direct me to communicate with you, through the post only, as long as there is reason to believe that any visitors who may come to you are likely to be observed. May I be permitted to say, that I look forward with respectful anxiety to the time when I shall again enjoy the only real happiness I have ever experienced – the happiness of personally addressing you?

In compliance with your desire that I should not allow this day (the Sunday) to pass without privately noticing what went on at the great house, I took the keys, and went this morning to the steward's office. I accounted for my appearance to the servants, by informing them that I had work to do which it was important to complete in the shortest possible time. The same excuse would have done for Mr Armadale, if we had met, but no such meeting happened.

Although I was at Thorpe-Ambrose, in what I thought good time, I was too late to see or hear anything myself of a serious quarrel which appeared to have taken place, just before I arrived, between Mr Armadale and Mr Midwinter.

All the little information I can give you in this matter is derived from one of the servants. The man told me that he heard the voices of the two gentlemen loud, in Mr Armadale's sitting-room. He went in to announce breakfast shortly afterwards, and found Mr Midwinter in such a dreadful state of agitation, that he had to be helped out of the room. The servant tried to take him upstairs to lie down and compose himself. He declined, saying he would wait a little first in one of the lower rooms, and begging that he might be left alone. The man had hardly got downstairs again, when he heard the front door opened and closed. He ran back, and found that Mr Midwinter was gone. The rain was pouring at the time, and thunder and lightning came soon afterwards. Dreadful weather, certainly, to go out in. The servant thinks Mr Midwinter's mind was unsettled. I sincerely hope not. Mr Midwinter is one of the few people I have met with in the course of my life who have treated me kindly.

Hearing that Mr Armadale still remained in his sitting-room, I went into the steward's office (which, as you may remember, is on the same side of the house), and left the door ajar, and set the window open, waiting and listening for anything that might happen. Dear madam, there was a time when I might have thought such a position in the house of my employer not a very becoming one. Let me hasten to assure you that this is far from being my feeling now. I glory in any position which makes me serviceable to *you*.

The state of the weather seemed hopelessly adverse to that renewal of intercourse between Mr Armadale and Miss Milroy, which you so confidently anticipate, and of which you are so anxious to be made aware. Strangely enough, however, it is actually in consequence of the state of the weather, that I am now in a position to give you the very information you require. Mr Armadale and Miss Milroy met about an hour since. The circumstances were as follows:

Just at the beginning of the thunderstorm, I saw one of the grooms run across from the stables, and heard him tap at his master's window. Mr Armadale opened the window, and asked what was the matter. The groom said he came with a message from the coachman's wife. She had seen from her room over the stables (which looks on to the park,) Miss Milroy quite alone, standing for shelter under one of the trees. As that part of the park was at some distance from the major's cottage, she had thought that her master might wish to send and ask the young lady into the house – especially as she had placed herself, with a thunderstorm coming on, in what might turn out to be a very dangerous position.

The moment Mr Armadale understood the man's message, he called for the waterproof things and the umbrellas, and ran out himself, instead of leaving it to the servants. In a little time, he and the groom came back with Miss Milroy between them, as well protected as could be from the rain.

I ascertained from one of the women-servants, who had taken the young lady into a bedroom, and had supplied her with such dry things as she wanted, that Miss Milroy had been afterwards shown into the drawing-room, and that Mr Armadale was there with her. The only way of following your instructions, and finding out what passed between them, was to go round the house in the pelting rain, and get into the conservatory (which opens into the drawing-room) by the outer door. I hesitate at nothing, dear madam, in your service; I would cheerfully get wet every day, to please you. Besides, though I may at first sight be thought rather an elderly man, a wetting is of no very serious consequence to me. I assure you I am not so old as I look, and I am of a stronger constitution than appears.

It was impossible for me to get near enough in the conservatory to see what went on in the drawing-room, without the risk of being discovered. But most of the conversation reached me, except when they dropped their voices. This is the substance of what I heard:

I gathered that Miss Milroy had been prevailed on, against her will, to take refuge from the thunderstorm in Mr Armadale's house. She said so at least, and she gave two reasons. The first was, that her father had forbidden all intercourse between the cottage and the great house. Mr Armadale met this objection by declaring that her father had issued his orders under a total misconception of the truth, and by entreating her not to treat him as cruelly as the major had treated him. He entered, I suspect, into some explanations at this point, but as he dropped his voice, I am unable to say what they were. His language, when I did hear it, was confused and ungrammatical. It seemed, however, to be quite intelligible enough to persuade Miss Milroy that her father had been acting under a mistaken impression of the circumstances. At least, I infer this; for, when I next heard the conversation, the young lady was driven back to her second objection to being in the house – which was, that Mr Armadale had behaved very badly to her, and that he richly deserved that she should never speak to him again.

In this latter case, Mr Armadale attempted no defence of any kind. He agreed with her that he had behaved badly; he agreed with her that he richly deserved she should never speak to him again. At the same time he implored her to remember that he had suffered his punishment already. He was disgraced in the neighbourhood; and his dearest friend, his one intimate friend in the world, had that very morning turned against him like the rest. Far or near, there was not a living creature whom he was fond of, to comfort him, or to say a friendly word to him. He was lonely and miserable, and his heart ached for a little kindness – and that was his only excuse for asking Miss Milroy to forget and forgive the past.

I must leave you, I fear, to judge for yourself of the effect of this on the young lady; for though I tried hard, I failed to catch what she said. I am almost certain I heard her crying, and Mr Armadale entreating her not to break his heart. They whispered a great deal, which aggravated me. I was afterwards alarmed by Mr Armadale coming out into the conservatory to pick some flowers. He did not come as far, fortunately, as the place where I was hidden; and he went in again into the drawing-room, and there was more talking (I suspect at close quarters), which to my great regret I again failed to catch. Pray forgive me for having so little to tell you. I can only add, that when the storm cleared off, Miss

Milroy went away with the flowers in her hand, and with Mr Armadale escorting her from the house. My own humble opinion is that he had a powerful friend at court, all through the interview, in the young lady's own liking for him.

This is all I can say at present, with the exception of one other thing I heard, which I blush to mention. But your word is law, and you have ordered me to have no concealments from you.

Their talk turned once, dear madam, on yourself. I think I heard the word 'Creature' from Miss Milroy; and I am certain that Mr Armadale, while acknowledging that he had once admired you, added that circumstances had since satisfied him of 'his folly'. I quote his own expression – it made me quite tremble with indignation. If I may be permitted to say so, the man who admires Miss Gwilt lives in paradise. Respect, if nothing else, ought to have closed Mr Armadale's lips. He is my employer, I know – but, after his calling it an act of folly to admire you (though I *am* his deputy steward), I utterly despise him.

Trusting that I may have been so happy as to give you satisfaction thus far, and earnestly desirous to deserve the honour of your continued confidence in me, I remain, dear madam,

> Your grateful and devoted servant,
> FELIX BASHWOOD.

2. – *From Mrs Oldershaw to Miss Gwilt*

Diana Street, Monday, July 21st.

MY DEAR LYDIA, – I trouble you with a few lines. They are written under a sense of the duty which I owe to myself, in our present position towards each other.

I am not at all satisfied with the tone of your two last letters; and I am still less pleased at your leaving me this morning without any letter at all – and this when we had arranged, in the doubtful state of our prospects, that I was to hear from you every day. I can only interpret your conduct in one way. I can only infer that matters at Thorpe-Ambrose, having been all mismanaged, are all going wrong.

It is not my present object to reproach you, for why should I waste time, language, and paper? I merely wish to recall to your memory certain considerations which you appear to be disposed to overlook. Shall I put them in the plainest English? Yes – for with all my faults, I am frankness personified.

In the first place, then, I have an interest in your becoming Mrs Armadale of Thorpe-Ambrose as well as you. Secondly, I have provided you (to say nothing of good advice) with all the money needed to accomplish our object. Thirdly, I hold your notes-of-hand,[1] at short dates, for every farthing so advanced. Fourthly and lastly, though I am indulgent to a fault in the capacity of a friend – in the capacity of a woman of business, my dear, I am not to be trifled with. That is all, Lydia, at least for the present.

Pray don't suppose I write in anger; I am only sorry and disheartened. My state of mind resembles David's. If I had the wings of a dove,[2] I would flee away and be at rest.

Affectionately yours,
MARIA OLDERSHAW.

3. – *From Mr Bashwood to Miss Gwilt*

Thorpe-Ambrose, July 21st.

DEAR MADAM, – You will probably receive these lines a few hours after my yesterday's communication reaches you. I posted my first letter last night, and I shall post this before noon to-day.

My present object in writing is to give you some more news from this house. I have the inexpressible happiness of announcing that Mr Armadale's disgraceful intrusion on your privacy is at an end. The watch set on your actions is to be withdrawn this day. I write, dear madam, with the tears in my eyes – tears of joy, caused by feelings which I ventured to express in my previous letter (see first paragraph towards the end). Pardon me this personal reference. I can speak to you (I don't know why) so much more readily with my pen than with my tongue.

Let me try to compose myself, and proceed with my narrative.

I had just arrived at the steward's office this morning, when Mr Pedgift the elder followed me to the great house to see Mr Armadale by special appointment. It is needless to say that I at once suspended any little business there was to do, feeling that your interests might possibly be concerned. It is also most gratifying to add that this time circumstances favoured me. I was able to stand under the open window, and to hear the whole interview.

Mr Armadale explained himself at once in the plainest terms. He gave orders that the person who had been hired to watch you should be instantly dismissed. On being asked to explain this sudden change of purpose, he did not conceal that it was owing to the effect produced on his mind by what had passed between Mr Midwinter and himself on the previous day. Mr Midwinter's language, cruelly unjust as it was, had nevertheless convinced him that no necessity whatever could excuse any proceeding so essentially base in itself as the employment of a spy, and on that conviction he was now determined to act.

But for your own positive directions to me to conceal nothing that passes here in which your name is concerned, I should really be ashamed to report what Mr Pedgift said on his side. He has behaved kindly to me, I know. But if he was my own brother, I could never forgive him the tone in which he spoke of you, and the obstinacy with which he tried to make Mr Armadale change his mind.

He began by attacking Mr Midwinter. He declared that Mr Midwinter's opinion was the very worst opinion that could be taken; for it was quite plain that you, dear madam, had twisted him round your finger. Producing no effect by this coarse suggestion (which nobody who knows you could for a moment believe), Mr Pedgift next referred to Miss Milroy, and asked Mr Armadale if he had given up all idea of protecting her. What this meant I cannot imagine. I can only report it for your private consideration. Mr Armadale briefly answered that he had his own plan for protecting Miss Milroy, and that the circumstances were altered in that quarter, or words to a similar effect. Still Mr Pedgift persisted. He went on (I blush to mention) from bad to worse. He tried to persuade Mr Armadale next to bring an action at law against one or other of the persons who had been most strongly condemning his conduct in the neighbourhood, for the purpose – I really hardly know how to write it – of getting you into the witness-box. And worse yet: when Mr Armadale still said No, Mr Pedgift, after having, as I suspected by the sound of his voice, been on the point of leaving the room, artfully came back, and proposed sending for a detective officer from London, simply to look at you. 'The whole of this mystery about Miss Gwilt's true character,' he said, 'may turn on a question of identity. It won't cost much to have a man down from London; and it's worth trying whether her face is or is not known at head-quarters to the police.' I again and again assure you, dearest lady, that I only repeat those abominable words from a sense of duty towards yourself. I shook – I declare I shook from head to foot when I heard them.

To resume, for there is more to tell you.

Mr Armadale (to his credit – I don't deny it, though I don't like him) still said No. He appeared to be getting irritated under Mr Pedgift's persistence, and he spoke in a somewhat hasty way. 'You persuaded me on the last occasion when we talked about this,' he said, 'to do something that I have been since heartily ashamed of. You won't succeed in persuading me, Mr Pedgift, a second time.' Those were his words. Mr Pedgift took him up short; Mr Pedgift seemed to be nettled on his side.

'If that is the light in which you see my advice, sir,' he said, 'the less you have of it for the future, the better. Your character and position are publicly involved in this matter between yourself and Miss Gwilt; and you persist, at a most critical moment, in taking a course of your own, which I believe will end badly. After what I have already said and done in this very serious case, I can't consent to go on with it with both my hands tied; and I can't drop it with credit to myself, while I remain publicly known as your solicitor. You leave me no alternative, sir, but to resign the honour of acting as your legal adviser.' 'I am sorry to hear it,' says Mr Armadale, 'but I have suffered enough already through interfering with Miss Gwilt. I can't and won't stir any further in the matter.' '*You* may not stir any further in it, sir,' says Mr Pedgift, 'and *I* shall not stir any further in it, for it has ceased to be a question of professional interest to me. But mark my words, Mr Armadale, you are not at the end of this business yet. Some other person's curiosity may go on from the point where you (and I) have stopped, and some other person's hand may let the broad daylight in yet on Miss Gwilt.'

I report their language, dear madam, almost word for word, I believe, as I heard it. It produced an indescribable impression on me; it filled me, I hardly know why, with quite a panic of alarm. I don't at all understand it, and I understand still less what happened immediately afterwards.

Mr Pedgift's voice, when he said those last words, sounded dreadfully close to me. He must have been speaking at the open window, and he must, I fear, have seen me under it. I had time, before he left the house, to get out quietly from among the laurels, but not to get back to the office. Accordingly I walked away along the drive towards the lodge, as if I was going on some errand connected with the steward's business.

Before long, Mr Pedgift overtook me in his gig, and stopped. 'So *you* feel some curiosity about Miss Gwilt, do you?' he said. 'Gratify your curiosity by all means – *I* don't object to it.' I felt naturally nervous, but I managed to ask him what he meant. He didn't answer; he only looked down at me from the gig in a very odd manner, and laughed. 'I have known stranger things happen even than *that*!' he said to himself suddenly, and drove off.

I have ventured to trouble you with this last incident, though it may seem of no importance in your eyes, in the hope that your superior ability may be able to explain it. My own poor faculties, I confess, are quite unable to penetrate Mr Pedgift's meaning. All I know is, that he has no right to accuse me of any such impertinent feeling as curiosity in relation to a lady whom I ardently esteem and admire. I dare not put it in warmer words.

I have only to add that I am in a position to be of continued service to you here if you wish it. Mr Armadale has just been into the office, and has told me briefly that, in Mr Midwinter's continued absence, I am still to act as steward's deputy till further notice. Believe me, dear madam, anxiously and devotedly yours,

FELIX BASHWOOD.

4. – *From Allan Armadale to the Rev. Decimus Brock*

Thorpe-Ambrose, Tuesday.

MY DEAR MR BROCK, – I am in sad trouble. Midwinter has quarrelled with me and left me; and my lawyer has quarrelled with me and left me; and (except dear little Miss Milroy, who has forgiven me) all the neighbours have turned their backs on me.

There is a good deal about '*me*' in this, but I can't help it. I am very miserable alone in my own house. Do pray come and see me! You are the only old friend I have left, and I do long so to tell you about it. N.B. – On my word of honour as a gentleman, I am not to blame. Yours affectionately,

ALLAN ARMADALE.

P.S. – I would come to you (for this place is grown quite hateful to me), but I have a reason for not going too far away from Miss Milroy just at present.

5. – *From Robert Stapleton to Allan Armadale, Esq.*

Boscombe Rectory, Thursday Morning.

RESPECTED SIR, – I see a letter in your writing, on the table along with the others, which I am sorry to say my master is not well enough to open. He is down with a sort of low fever. The doctor says it has been brought on with worry and anxiety, which master was not strong enough to bear. This seems likely; for I was with him when he went to London last month, and what with his own business, and the business of looking after that person who afterwards gave us the slip, he was worried and anxious all the time; and for the matter of that, so was I.

My master was talking of you a day or two since. He seemed unwilling that you should know of his illness, unless he got worse. But I think you ought to know of it. At the same time he is not worse – perhaps a trifle better. The doctor says he must be kept very quiet, and not agitated on any account. So be pleased to take no notice of this – I mean in the way of coming to the rectory. I have the doctor's orders to say it is not needful, and it would only upset my master in the state he is in now.

I will write again if you wish it. Please accept of my duty, and believe me to remain, sir, your humble servant,

ROBERT STAPLETON.

P.S. – The yacht has been rigged and repainted, waiting your orders. She looks beautiful.

6. – *From Mrs Oldershaw to Miss Gwilt*

Diana Street, July 24th.

MISS GWILT, – The post-hour has passed for three mornings following, and has brought me no answer to my letter. Are you purposely bent on insulting me? or have you left Thorpe-Ambrose? In either case, I won't put up with your conduct any longer. The law shall bring you to book, if I can't.

Your first note-of-hand (for thirty pounds) falls due on Tuesday next, the 29th. If you had behaved with common consideration towards me, I would have let you renew it with pleasure. As things are, I shall have the note presented; and, if it is not paid, I shall instruct my man of business to take the usual course.

Yours,
MARIA OLDERSHAW.

7. – *From Miss Gwilt to Mrs Oldershaw*

5, Paradise Place, Thorpe-Ambrose, July 25th.

MRS OLDERSHAW, – The time of your man of business being, no doubt, of some value, I write a line to assist him when he takes the usual course. He will find me waiting to be arrested in the first-floor apartments, at the above address. In my present situation, and with my present thoughts, the best service you can possibly render me is to lock me up.

L. G.

8. – *From Mrs Oldershaw to Miss Gwilt*

Diana Street, July 26th.

MY DARLING LYDIA, – The longer I live in this wicked world the more plainly I see that women's own tempers are the worst enemies women have to contend with. What a truly regrettable style of correspondence we have fallen into! What a sad want of self-restraint, my dear, on your side and on mine!

Let me, as the oldest in years, be the first to make the needful excuses, the first to blush for my own want of self-control. Your cruel neglect Lydia, stung me into writing as I did. I am so sensitive to ill-treatment, when it is inflicted on me by a person whom I love and admire – and, though turned sixty, I am still (unfortunately for myself) so young at heart. Accept my apologies for having made use of my pen, when I ought to have been content to take refuge in my pocket-handkerchief. Forgive your attached Maria for being still young at heart!

But oh, my dear – though I own I threatened you – how hard of you to take me at my word! How cruel of you, if your debt had been ten times what it is, to suppose me capable (whatever I might say) of the odious inhumanity of arresting my bosom friend! Heavens! have I deserved to be taken at my word in this unmercifully exact way, after the years of tender intimacy that have united us? But I don't complain; I only mourn over the frailty of our common human nature. Let us expect as little of each other as possible, my dear; we are both women, and we can't help it. I declare, when I reflect on the origin of our unfortunate sex – when I remember that we were all originally made of no better material than the rib of a man (and that rib of so little importance to its possessor that he never appears to have missed it afterwards), I am quite astonished at our virtues, and not in the least surprised at our faults.

I am wandering a little; I am losing myself in serious thought, like that sweet character in Shakspeare who was 'fancy free'.[3] One last word, dearest, to say that my longing for an answer to this proceeds entirely from my wish to hear from you again in your old friendly tone, and is quite unconnected with any curiosity to know what you are doing at Thorpe-Ambrose – except such curiosity as you yourself might approve. Need I add that I beg you as a favour to *me*, to renew, on the customary terms? I refer to the little bill due on Tuesday next, and I venture to suggest that day six weeks.

Yours, with a truly motherly feeling,
MARIA OLDERSHAW.

9. – *From Miss Gwilt to Mrs Oldershaw*

Paradise Place, July 27th.

I HAVE just got your last letter. The brazen impudence of it has roused me. I am to be treated like a child, am I? – to be threatened first, and then, if threatening fails, to be coaxed afterwards? You *shall* coax me; you shall know, my motherly friend, the sort of child you have to deal with.

I had a reason, Mrs Oldershaw, for the silence which has so seriously offended you. I was afraid – yes, actually afraid – to let you into the secret of my thoughts. No such fear troubles me now. My only anxiety this morning is to make you my best acknowledgments for the manner in which you have written to me. After carefully considering it, I think the worst turn I can possibly do you, is to tell you what you are burning to know. So here I am at my desk, bent on telling it. You shall hear what has happened at Thorpe-Ambrose – you shall see my thoughts as plainly as I see them myself. If you don't bitterly repent, when you are at the end of this letter, not having held to your first resolution, and locked me up out of harm's way while you had the chance, my name is not Lydia Gwilt.

Where did my last letter end? I don't remember, and don't care. Make it out as you can – I am not going back any further than this day week. That is to say, Sunday last.

There was a thunderstorm in the morning. It began to clear off towards noon. I didn't go out – I waited to see Midwinter or to hear from him. (Are you surprised at my not writing 'Mr' before his name? We have got so familiar, my dear, that 'Mr' would be quite out of place.) He had left me the evening before, under very interesting circumstances. I had told him that his friend, Armadale, was persecuting me by means of a hired spy. He had declined to believe it, and had gone straight to Thorpe-Ambrose to clear the thing up. I had let him kiss my hand before he went. He had promised to come back the next day (the Sunday). I felt I had secured my influence over him; and I believed he would keep his word.

Well, the thunder passed away as I told you. The weather cleared up; the people walked out in their best clothes; the dinners came in from the baker's; I sat dreaming at my wretched

411

little hired piano, nicely dressed and looking my best – and still no Midwinter appeared. It was late in the afternoon, and I was beginning to feel offended, when a letter was brought to me. It had been left by a strange messenger who went away again immediately. I looked at the letter. Midwinter at last – in writing, instead of in person. I began to feel more offended than ever – for, as I told you, I thought I had used my influence over him to better purpose.

The letter, when I read it, set my mind off in a new direction. It surprised, it puzzled, it interested me. I thought, and thought, and thought of him, all the rest of the day.

He began by asking my pardon for having doubted what I told him. Mr Armadale's own lips had confirmed me. They had quarrelled (as I had anticipated they would) – and he, and the man who had once been his dearest friend on earth, had parted for ever. So far, I was not surprised. I was amused by his telling me in his extravagant way that he and his friend were parted for ever; and I rather wondered what he would think when I carried out my plan, and found my way into the great house on pretence of reconciling them.

But the second part of the letter set me thinking. Here it is, in his own words.

'It is only by struggling against myself (and no language can say how hard the struggle has been) that I have decided on writing, instead of speaking to you. A merciless necessity claims my future life. I must leave Thorpe-Ambrose, I must leave England, without hesitating, without stopping to look back. There are reasons – terrible reasons, which I have madly trifled with – for my never letting Mr Armadale set eyes on me, or hear of me again, after what has happened between us. I must go, never more to live under the same roof, never more to breathe the same air with that man. I must hide myself from him, under an assumed name; I must put the mountains and the seas between us. I have been warned as no human creature was ever warned before. I believe – I dare not tell you why – I believe that if the fascination you have for me draws me back to you, fatal consequences will come of it to the man whose life has been so strangely mingled with your life and mine – the man who was once *your* admirer and *my* friend. And yet, feeling this, seeing it in my mind as plainly as I see the sky above my head, there is a weakness in me that still shrinks from the one imperative sacrifice of never seeing you again. I am fighting with it as a man fights with the strength of his despair. I have been near enough, not an hour since, to see the house where you live, and have forced myself away again out of sight of it. Can I force myself away farther still, now that my letter is written – now, when the useless confession escapes me, and I own to loving you with the first love I have ever known, with the last love I shall ever feel? Let the coming time answer the question; I dare not write of it or think of it more.'

Those were the last words. In that strange way the letter ended.

I felt a perfect fever of curiosity to know what he meant. His loving me, of course, was easy enough to understand. But what did he mean by saying he had been warned? Why was he never to live under the same roof, never to breathe the same air again with young Armadale? What sort of quarrel could it be which obliged one man to hide himself from another under an assumed name, and to put the mountains and the seas between them? Above all, if he came back, and let me fascinate him, why should it be fatal to the hateful lout who possesses the noble fortune, and lives in the great house?

I never longed in my life as I longed to see him again, and put these questions to him. I got quite superstitious about it as the day drew on. They gave me a sweetbread and a cherry pudding for dinner. I actually tried if he would come back by the stones in the plate! He will, he won't, he will, he won't – and so on. It ended in 'he won't'. I rang the bell, and had the things taken away. I contradicted Destiny quite fiercely. I said, 'He will!' and I waited at home for him.

You don't know what a pleasure it is to me to give you all these little particulars. Count up – my bosom friend, my second mother – count up the money you have advanced on the chance of my becoming Mrs Armadale, and then think of my feeling this breathless interest in another man. Oh, Mrs Oldershaw, how intensely I enjoy the luxury of irritating you!

The day got on towards evening. I rang again, and sent down to borrow a railway time-table. What trains were there to take him away on Sunday? The national respect for the Sabbath stood my friend. There was only one train, which had started hours before he wrote to me. I went and consulted my glass. It paid me the compliment of contradicting the divination by cherry-stones. My glass said, 'Get behind the window-curtain; he won't pass the long lonely evening without coming back again to look at the house.' I got behind the window-curtain, and waited with his letter in my hand.

The dismal Sunday light faded, and the dismal Sunday quietness in the street grew quieter still. The dusk came, and I heard a step coming with it in the silence. My heart gave a little jump – only think of my having any heart left! I said to myself, 'Midwinter!' And Midwinter it was.

When he came in sight he was walking slowly, stopping and hesitating at every two or three steps. My ugly little drawing-room window seemed to be beckoning him on in spite of himself. After waiting till I saw him come to a standstill, a little aside from the house, but still within view of my irresistible window, I put on my things and slipped out by the back way into the garden. The landlord and his family were at supper, and nobody saw me. I opened the door in the wall, and got round by the lane into the street. At that awkward moment I suddenly remembered, what I had forgotten before, the spy set to watch me, who was, no doubt, waiting somewhere in sight of the house.

It was necessary to get time to think, and it was (in my state of mind) impossible to let Midwinter go without speaking to him. In great difficulties you generally decide at once, if you decide at all. I decided to make an appointment with him for the next evening, and to consider in the interval how to manage the interview so that it might escape observation. This, as I felt at the time, was leaving my own curiosity free to torment me for four-and-twenty mortal hours – but what other choice had I? It was as good as giving up being mistress of Thorpe-Ambrose altogether, to come to a private understanding with Midwinter in the sight and possibly in the hearing of Armadale's spy.

Finding an old letter of yours in my pocket, I drew back into the lane, and wrote on the blank leaf, with the little pencil that hangs at my watch-chain: 'I must and will speak to you. It is impossible to-night, but be in the street to-morrow at this time, and leave me afterwards for ever, if you like. When you have read this, overtake me, and say as you pass, without stopping or looking round, "Yes, I promise."'

I folded up the paper, and came on him suddenly from behind. As he started and turned round, I put the note into his hand, pressed his hand, and passed on. Before I had taken ten steps I heard him behind me. I can't say he didn't look round – I saw his big black eyes, bright and glittering in the dusk, devour me from head to foot in a moment; but otherwise he did what I told him. 'I can deny you nothing,' he whispered; 'I promise.' He went on and left me. I couldn't help thinking at the time how that brute and booby Armadale would have spoilt everything in the same situation.

I tried hard all night to think of a way of making our interview of the next evening safe from discovery, and tried in vain.[4] Even as early as this, I began to feel as if Midwinter's letter had, in some unaccountable manner, stupefied me.

Monday morning made matters worse. News came from my faithful ally, Mr Bashwood, that Miss Milroy and Armadale had met and become friends again. You may fancy the state I was in! An hour or two later there came more news from Mr Bashwood – good news this time. The mischievous idiot at Thorpe-Ambrose had shown sense enough at last to be ashamed of himself. He had decided on withdrawing the spy that very day, and he and his lawyer had quarrelled in consequence.

So here was the obstacle which I was too stupid to remove for myself, obligingly removed for me! No more need to fret about the coming interview with Midwinter – and plenty of time to consider my next proceedings, now that Miss Milroy and her precious swain had come together again. Would you believe it, the letter, or the man himself (I don't know which), had taken such a hold on me that, though I tried and tried, I could think of nothing else – and this, when I had every reason to fear that Miss Milroy was in a fair way of changing her name to Armadale, and when I knew that my heavy debt of obligation to her was not paid yet? Was there ever such perversity? I can't account for it – can you?

The dusk of the evening came at last. I looked out of the window – and there he was!

I joined him at once; the people of the house, as before, being too much absorbed in their eating and drinking to notice anything else. 'We mustn't be seen together here,' I whispered. 'I must go on first, and you must follow me.'

He said nothing in the way of reply. What was going on in his mind I can't pretend to guess – but, after coming to his appointment, he actually hung back as if he was half inclined to go away again.

'You look as if you were afraid of me,' I said.

'I *am* afraid of you,' he answered – 'of you, and of myself.'

It was not encouraging; it was not complimentary. But I was in such a frenzy of curiosity by this time, that if he had been ruder still, I should have taken no notice of it. I led the way a few steps towards the new buildings, and stopped and looked round after him.

'Must I ask it of you as a favour,' I said, 'after your giving me your promise, and after such a letter as you have written to me?'

Something suddenly changed him; he was at my side in an instant. 'I beg your pardon, Miss Gwilt; lead the way where you please.' He dropped back a little after that answer, and I heard him say to himself, 'What *is* to be, *will* be. What have I to do with it, and what has she?'

It could hardly have been the words, for I didn't understand them – it must have been the tone he spoke in, I suppose, that made me feel a momentary tremor. I was half inclined, without the ghost of a reason for it, to wish him good-night, and go in again. Not much like *me*, you will say. Not much, indeed! It didn't last a moment. Your darling Lydia soon came to her senses again.

I led the way towards the unfinished cottages, and the country beyond. It would have been much more to my taste to have had him into the house, and have talked to him in the light of the candles. But I had risked it once already; and in this scandal-mongering place, and in my critical position, I was afraid to risk it again. The garden was not to be thought of either – for the landlord smokes his pipe there after his supper. There was no alternative but to take him away from the town.

From time to time, I looked back as I went on. There he was, always at the same distance, dim and ghostlike in the dusk, silently following me.

I must leave off for a little while. The church bells have broken out, and the jangling of them drives me mad. In these days, when we have all got watches or clocks, why are bells wanted to remind us when the service begins? We don't require to be rung into the theatre. How excessively discreditable to the clergy to be obliged to ring us into the church!

They have rung the congregation in at last – and I can take up my pen, and go on again.

I was a little in doubt where to lead him to. The high-road was on one side of me – but, empty as it looked, somebody might be passing when we least expected it. The other way was through the coppice. I led him through the coppice.

At the outskirts of the trees, on the other side, there was a dip in the ground, with some felled timber lying in it, and a little pool beyond, still and white and shining in the twilight. The long grazing-grounds rose over its farther shore, with the mist thickening on them, and a dim black line far away of cattle in slow procession going home. There wasn't a living creature near; there wasn't a sound to be heard. I sat down on one of the felled trees, and looked back for him. 'Come,' I said softly, 'come and sit by me here.'

Why am I so particular about all this? I hardly know. The place made an unaccountably vivid impression on me, and I can't help writing about it. If I end badly – suppose we say on the scaffold? – I believe the last thing I shall see, before the hangman pulls the drop, will be the little shining pool, and the long misty grazing-grounds, and the cattle winding dimly home in the thickening night. Don't be alarmed, you worthy creature! My fancy plays me strange tricks sometimes – and there is a little of last night's laudanum,[5] I dare say, in this part of my letter.

He came – in the strangest silent way, like a man walking in his sleep – he came and sat down by me. Either the night was very close, or I was by this time literally in a fever – I couldn't bear my bonnet on; I couldn't bear my gloves. The want to look at him, and see what his singular silence meant, and the impossibility of doing it in the darkening light, irritated my nerves till I thought I should have screamed. I took his hand, to try if that would help me. It was burning hot; and it closed instantly on mine – you know how. Silence, after *that*, was not to be thought of. The one safe way was to begin talking to him at once.

'Don't despise me,' I said. 'I am obliged to bring you to this lonely place; I should lose my character if we were seen together.'

I waited a little. His hand warned me once more not to let the silence continue. I determined to *make* him speak to me this time.

'You have interested me, and frightened me,' I went on. 'You have written me a very strange letter. I must know what it means.'

'It is too late to ask. *You* have taken the way, and *I* have taken the way, from which there is no turning back.' He made that strange answer in a tone that was quite new to me – a tone that made me even more uneasy than his silence had made me the moment before. 'Too late,' he repeated, 'too late! There is only one question to ask me now.'

'What is it?'

As I said the words, a sudden trembling passed from his hand to mine, and told me instantly that I had better have held my tongue. Before I could move, before I could think, he had me in his arms. 'Ask me if I love you,' he whispered. At the same moment his head sank on my bosom; and some unutterable torture that was in him burst its way out, as it does with *us*, in a passion of sobs and tears.

My first impulse was the impulse of a fool. I was on the point of making our usual protest and defending myself in our usual way. Luckily or unluckily, I don't know which, I have lost the fine edge of the sensitiveness of youth; and I checked the first movement of my hands, and the first word on my lips. Oh, dear, how old I felt, while he was sobbing his heart out on my breast! How I thought of the time when he might have possessed himself of my love! All he had possessed himself of now was – my waist.

I wonder whether I pitied him? It doesn't matter if I did. At any rate, my hand lifted itself somehow, and my fingers twined themselves softly in his hair. Horrible recollections came back to me of other times, and made me shudder as I touched him. And yet I did it. What fools women are!

'I won't reproach you,' I said gently; 'I won't say this is a cruel advantage to take of me, in such a position as mine. You are dreadfully agitated – I will let you wait a little, and compose yourself.'

Having got as far as that, I stopped to consider how I should put the questions to him that I was burning to ask. But I was too confused, I suppose, or perhaps too impatient to consider. I let out what was uppermost in my mind, in the words that came first.

'I don't believe you love me,' I said. 'You write strange things to me; you frighten me with mysteries. What did you mean by saying in your letter that it would be fatal to Mr Armadale if you came back to me? What danger can there be to Mr Armadale—?'

Before I could finish the question, he suddenly lifted his head and unclasped his arms. I had apparently touched some painful subject which recalled him to himself. Instead of my shrinking from *him*, it was he who shrank from *me*. I felt offended with him; why, I don't know — but offended I was; and I thanked him with my bitterest emphasis, for remembering what was due to me, *at last*!

'Do you believe in Dreams?' he burst out in the most strangely abrupt manner, without taking the slightest notice of what I had said to him. 'Tell me,' he went on, without allowing me time to answer, 'were you, or was any relation of yours, ever connected with Allan Armadale's father or mother? Were you, or was anybody belonging to you, ever in the island of Madeira?'

Conceive my astonishment, if you can. I turned cold. In an instant I turned cold all over. He was plainly in the secret of what had happened when I was in Mrs Armadale's service in Madeira — in all probability before he was born! That was startling enough of itself. And he had evidently some reason of his own for trying to connect *me* with those events — which was more startling still.

'No,' I said, as soon as I could trust myself to speak. 'I know nothing of his father or mother.'

'And nothing of the island of Madeira?'

'Nothing of the island of Madeira.'

He turned his head away; and began talking to himself.

'Strange!' he said. 'As certainly as I was in the Shadow's place at the window, *she* was in the Shadow's place at the pool!'

Under other circumstances, his extraordinary behaviour might have alarmed me. But after his question about Madeira, there was some greater fear in me which kept all common alarm at a distance. I don't think I ever determined on anything in my life as I determined on finding out how he had got his information, and who he really was. It was quite plain to me that I had roused some hidden feeling in him by my question about Armadale, which was as strong in its way as his feeling for *me*. What had become of my influence over him?

I couldn't imagine what had become of it; but I could and did set to work to make him feel it again.

'Don't treat me cruelly,' I said; 'I didn't treat *you* cruelly just now. Oh, Mr Midwinter, it's so lonely, it's so dark – don't frighten me!'

'Frighten you!' He was close to me again in a moment. 'Frighten you!' He repeated the word with as much astonishment as if I had woke him from a dream, and charged him with something that he had said in his sleep.

It was on the tip of my tongue, finding how I had surprised him, to take him while he was off his guard, and to ask why my question about Armadale had produced such a change in his behaviour to me. But after what had happened already, I was afraid to risk returning to the subject too soon. Something or other – what they call an instinct, I daresay – warned me to let Armadale alone for the present, and to talk to him first about himself. As I told you in one of my early letters, I had noticed signs and tokens in his manner and appearance which convinced me, young as he was, that he had done something or suffered something out of the common in his past life. I had asked myself more and more suspiciously every time I saw him, whether he was what he appeared to be; and first and foremost among my other doubts was a doubt whether he was passing among us by his real name. Having secrets to keep about my own past life, and having gone myself in other days by more than one assumed name, I suppose I am all the readier to suspect other people when I find something mysterious about them. Any way, having the suspicion in my mind, I determined to startle him, as he had startled me, by an unexpected question on my side – a question about his name.

While I was thinking, he was thinking – and, as it soon appeared, of what I had just said to him. 'I am so grieved to have frightened you,' he whispered, with that gentleness and humility which we all so heartily despise in a man when he speaks to other women, and which we all so dearly like when he speaks to ourselves. 'I hardly know what I have been saying,' he went on; 'my mind is miserably disturbed. Pray forgive me, if you can – I am not myself to-night.'

'I am not angry,' I said; 'I have nothing to forgive. We are both imprudent – we are both unhappy.' I laid my head on his shoulder. 'Do you really love me?' I asked him softly, in a whisper.

His arm stole round me again; and I felt the quick beat of his heart get quicker and quicker. 'If you only knew!' he whispered back; 'if you only knew—' He could say no more. I felt his face bending towards mine, and dropped my head lower, and stopped him in the very act of kissing me. 'No,' I said; 'I am only a woman who has taken your fancy. You are treating me as if I was your promised wife.'

'*Be* my promised wife!' he whispered eagerly, and tried to raise my head. I kept it down. The horror of those old remembrances that you know of, came back, and made me tremble a little when he asked me to be his wife. I don't think I was actually faint; but something like faintness made me close my eyes. The moment I shut them, the darkness seemed to open as if lightning had split it: and the ghosts of *those other men* rose in the horrid gap, and looked at me.

'Speak to me!' he whispered, tenderly. 'My darling, my angel, speak to me!'

His voice helped me to recover myself. I had just sense enough left to remember that the time was passing, and that I had not put my question to him yet about his name.

'Suppose I felt for you as you feel for me?' I said. 'Suppose I loved you dearly enough to trust you with the happiness of all my life to come?'

I paused a moment to get my breath. It was unbearably still and close – the air seemed to have died when the night came.

'Would you be marrying me honourably,' I went on, 'if you married me in your present name?'

His arm dropped from my waist, and I felt him give one great start. After that he sat by me, still, and cold, and silent, as if my question had struck him dumb. I put my arm round his neck, and lifted my head again on his shoulder. Whatever the spell was I had laid on him, my coming closer in that way seemed to break it.

'Who told you?' – he stopped. 'No,' he went on, 'nobody can have told you. What made you suspect—?' He stopped again.

'Nobody told me,' I said; 'and I don't know what made me suspect. Women have strange fancies sometimes. Is Midwinter really your name?'

'I can't deceive you,' he answered, after another interval of silence, 'Midwinter is *not* really my name.'

I nestled a little closer to him.

'What *is* your name?' I asked.

He hesitated.

I lifted my face till my cheek just touched his. I persisted, with my lips close at his ear, –

'What, no confidence in me even yet! No confidence in the woman who has almost confessed she loves you – who has almost consented to be your wife!'

He turned his face to mine. For the second time he tried to kiss me, and for the second time I stopped him.

'If I tell you my name,' he said, 'I must tell you more.'

I let my cheek touch his cheek again.

'Why not?' I said. 'How can I love a man – much less marry him – if he keeps himself a stranger to me?'

There was no answering that, as I thought. But he did answer it.

'It is a dreadful story,' he said. 'It may darken all your life, if you know it, as it has darkened mine.'

I put my other arm round him, and persisted. 'Tell it me; I'm not afraid; tell it me.'

He began to yield to my other arm.

'Will you keep it a sacred secret?' he said. 'Never to be breathed – never to be known but to you and me?'

I promised him it should be a secret. I waited in a perfect frenzy of expectation. Twice he tried to begin, and twice his courage failed him.

'I can't!' he broke out in a wild helpless way. 'I can't tell it!'

My curiosity, or more likely my temper, got beyond all control. He had irritated me till I was reckless what I said or what I did. I suddenly clasped him close, and pressed my lips to his. 'I love you!' I whispered in a kiss. '*Now* will you tell me?'

For the moment he was speechless. I don't know whether I did it purposely to drive him wild. I don't know whether I did it involuntarily in a burst of rage. Nothing is certain but that I interpreted his silence the wrong way. I pushed him back from me in a fury the instant after I had kissed him. 'I hate you!' I said. 'You have maddened me into forgetting myself. Leave me! I don't care for the darkness. Leave me instantly, and never see me again!'

He caught me by the hand and stopped me. He spoke in a new voice – he suddenly *commanded*, as only men can.

'Sit down,' he said. 'You have given me back my courage – you shall know who I am.'

In the silence and the darkness all round us, I obeyed him, and sat down.

In the silence and the darkness all round us, he took me in his arms again, and told me who he was.

Shall I trust you with his story? Shall I tell you his real name? Shall I show you, as I threatened, the thoughts that have grown out of my interview with him, and out of all that has happened to me since that time?

Or shall I keep his secret as I promised? and keep my own secret too, by bringing this weary long letter to an end at the very moment when you are burning to hear more!'

Those are serious questions, Mrs Oldershaw – more serious than you suppose.[6] I have had time to calm down, and I begin to see what I failed to see when I first took up my pen to write to you – the wisdom of looking at consequences. Have I frightened myself in trying to frighten *you*? It is possible – strange as it may seem, it is really possible.

I have been at the window for the last minute or two, thinking. There is plenty of time for thinking before the post leaves. The people are only now coming out of church.

I have settled to put my letter on one side, and to take a look at my diary. In plainer words I must see what I risk if I decide on trusting you; and my diary will show me what my head is too weary to calculate without help. I have written the story of my days (and sometimes the story of my nights) much more regularly than usual for the last week, having reasons of my own for being particularly careful in this respect under present circumstances. If I end in doing what it is now in my mind to do, it would be madness to trust to my memory. The smallest forgetfulness of the slightest event that has happened from the night of my interview with Midwinter to the present time, might be utter ruin to me.

'Utter ruin to her!' you will say. 'What kind of ruin does she mean?'

Wait a little, till I have asked my diary whether I can safely tell you?

CHAPTER X

MISS GWILT'S DIARY

July 21st, Monday night, eleven o'clock. – He has just left me. We parted by my desire at the path out of the coppice; he going his way to the hotel, and I going mine to my lodgings.

I have managed to avoid making another appointment with him, by arranging to write to him to-morrow morning. This gives me the night's interval to compose myself, and to coax my mind back (if I can) to my own affairs. I say, 'if I can', for I feel as if his story had taken possession of me, never to leave me again. Will the night pass, and the morning find me still thinking of the Letter that came to him from his father's death-bed? of the night he watched through, on the Wrecked Ship; and, more than all, of the first breathless moment when he told me his real Name?

Would it help me to shake off these impressions, I wonder, if I made the effort of writing them down? There would be no danger, in that case, of my forgetting anything important. And perhaps, after all, it may be the fear of forgetting something which I ought to remember that keeps this story of Midwinter's weighing as it does on my mind. At any rate, the experiment is worth trying. In my present situation I *must* be free to think of other things, or I shall never find my way through all the difficulties at Thorpe-Ambrose that are still to come.

Let me think. What *haunts* me, to begin with?

The Names haunt me. I keep saying and saying to myself: Both alike! – Christian name and surname, both alike! A light-haired Allan Armadale, whom I have long since known of, and who is the son of my old mistress. A dark-haired Allan Armadale, whom I only know of now, and who is only known to others under the name of Ozias Midwinter. Stranger still; it is not relationship, it is not chance, that has made them namesakes. The father of the light Armadale was the man who was *born* to the family name, and who lost the family inheritance. The father of the dark Armadale was the man who *took* the name, on condition of getting the inheritance – and who got it.

So there are two of them – I can't help thinking of it – both unmarried. The light-haired Armadale, who offers to the woman who can secure him, eight thousand a year while he lives; who leaves her twelve hundred a year when he dies; who must and shall marry me for those two golden reasons; and whom I hate and loathe as I never hated and loathed a man yet. And the dark-haired Armadale, who has a poor little income which might perhaps pay his wife's milliner, if his wife was careful; who has just left me, persuaded that I mean to marry him; and whom – well, whom I *might* have loved once, before I was the woman I am now.

And Allan the Fair doesn't know he has a namesake. And Allan the Dark has kept the secret from everybody but the Somersetshire clergyman (whose discretion he can depend on), and myself.

And there are two Allan Armadales – two Allan Armadales – two Allan Armadales. There! three is a lucky number. Haunt me again, after that, if you can!

What next? The murder in the timber-ship? No; the murder is a good reason why the dark Armadale, whose father committed it, should keep his secret from the fair Armadale, whose father was killed; but it doesn't concern *me*. I remember that there was a suspicion in Madeira at the time of something wrong. *Was* it wrong? Was the man who had been tricked out of his wife, to blame for shutting the cabin-door, and leaving the man who had tricked him, to drown in the wreck? Yes, – the woman wasn't worth it.

What am I sure of that really concerns myself?

I am sure of one very important thing. I am sure that Midwinter – I must call him by his ugly false name, or I may confuse the two Armadales before I have done – I am sure that Midwinter is perfectly ignorant that I and the little imp of twelve years old who waited on Mrs Armadale in Madeira, and copied the letters that were supposed to arrive from the West Indies, are one and the same. There are not many girls of twelve who could have imitated a man's handwriting, and held their tongues about it afterwards, as I did – but that doesn't matter now. What does matter is, that Midwinter's belief in the Dream is Midwinter's only reason for trying to connect me with Allan Armadale, by associating me with Allan Armadale's father and mother. I asked him if he actually thought me old enough to have known either of them. And he said No, poor fellow, in the most innocent bewildered way. Would he say No, if he saw me now? Shall I turn to the glass and see if I look my five-and-thirty years? or shall I go on writing? I will go on writing.

There is one thing more that haunts me almost as obstinately as the Names.

I wonder whether I am right in relying on Midwinter's superstition (as I do) to help me in keeping him at arm's length. After having let the excitement of the moment hurry me into saying more than I need have said, he is certain to press me; he is certain to come back, with a man's hateful selfishness and impatience in such things, to the question of marrying me. Will the Dream help me to check him? After alternately believing and disbelieving in it, he has got, by his own confession, to believing in it again. Can I say I believe in it, too? I have better reasons for doing so than he knows of. I am not only the person who helped Mrs Armadale's marriage by helping her to impose on her own father, – I am the woman who tried to drown herself; the woman who started the series of accidents which put young Armadale in possession of his fortune; the woman who has come to Thorpe-Ambrose to marry him for his fortune now he has got it; and more extraordinary still, the woman who stood in the Shadow's place at the pool! These may be coincidences, but they are strange coincidences. I declare I begin to fancy that *I* believe in the Dream too!

Suppose I say to him, 'I think as you think. I say, what you said in your letter to me, Let us part before the harm is done. Leave me before the third Vision of the Dream comes true. Leave me; and put the mountains and the seas between you and the man who bears your name!'

Suppose, on the other side, that his love for me makes him reckless of everything else? Suppose he says those desperate words again, which I understand now: 'What *is* to be, *will* be. What have I to do with it, and what has she?' Suppose – suppose –

I won't write any more. I hate writing! It doesn't relieve me – it makes me worse. I'm farther from being able to think of all that I *must* think of, than I was when I sat down. It is past midnight. To-morrow has come already – and here I am as helpless as the stupidest woman living! Bed is the only fit place for me.

Bed? If it was ten years since, instead of to-day; and if I had married Midwinter for love, I might be going to bed now with nothing heavier on my mind than a visit on tiptoe to the nursery, and a last look at night to see if my children were sleeping quietly in their cribs. I wonder whether I should have loved my children if I had ever had any? Perhaps, yes – perhaps, no. It doesn't matter.

Tuesday morning, ten o'clock. – Who was the man who invented laudanum? I thank him from the bottom of my heart, whoever he was. If all the miserable wretches in pain of body and mind, whose comforter he has been, could meet together to sing his praises, what a chorus it would be! I have had six delicious hours of oblivion; I have woke up with my mind composed; I have written a perfect little letter to Midwinter; I have drunk my nice cup of tea, with a real relish of it; I have dawdled over my morning toilet with an exquisite sense of relief – and all through the modest little bottle of Drops which I see on my bedroom chimney-piece at this moment. 'Drops', you are a darling! If I love nothing else, I love *you*.

My letter to Midwinter has been sent through the post; and I have told him to reply to me in the same manner.

I feel no anxiety about his answer – he can only answer in one way. I have asked for a little time to consider, because my family circumstances require some consideration, in his interests as well as in mine. I have engaged to tell him what those circumstances are (what shall I say, I wonder?) when we next meet; and I have requested him in the meantime to keep all that has passed between us a secret for the present. As to what he is to do himself in the interval while I am supposed to be considering, I have left it to his own discretion – merely reminding him that, in our present situation, his remaining at Thorpe-Ambrose might lead to inquiry into his motives, and that his attempting to see me again (while our positions towards each other cannot be openly avowed) might injure my reputation. I have offered to write to him if he wishes it; and I have ended by promising to make the interval of our necessary separation as short as I can.

This sort of plain unaffected letter – which I might have written to him last night, if his story had not been running in my head as it did – has one defect, I know. It certainly keeps him out of the way, while I am casting my net, and catching my gold fish at the great house for the second time – but it also leaves an awkward day of reckoning to come with Midwinter if I succeed. How am I to manage him? What am I to do? I ought to face those two questions as boldly as usual – but somehow my courage seems to fail me; and I don't quite fancy meeting *that* difficulty, till the time comes when it *must* be met. Shall I confess to my diary that I am sorry for Midwinter, and that I shrink a little from thinking of the day when he hears that I am going to be mistress at the great house?

But I am not mistress yet – and I can't take a step in the direction of the great house till I have got the answer to my letter, and till I know that Midwinter is out of the way. Patience! patience! I must go and forget myself at my piano. There is the 'Moonlight Sonata' open, and tempting me, on the music-stand. Have I nerve enough to play it, I wonder? Or will it set me shuddering with the mystery and terror of it, as it did the other day?

Five o'clock. – I have got his answer. The slightest request I can make is a command to him. He has gone – and he sends me his address in London. 'There are two considerations,' (he says,) 'which help to reconcile me to leaving you. The first is, that *you* wish it, and that it is only to be for a little while. The second is, that I think I can make some arrangements in London for adding to my income by my own labour. I have never cared for money for myself – but you don't know how I am beginning already to prize the luxuries and refinements that money can provide, for my wife's sake.' Poor fellow! I almost wish I had not written to him as I did; I almost wish I had not sent him away from me.

Fancy, if Mother Oldershaw saw this page in my diary! I have had a letter from her this morning – a letter to remind me of my obligations, and to tell me she suspects things are all going wrong. Let her suspect! I shan't trouble myself to answer – I can't be worried with that old wretch in the state I am in now.

It is a lovely afternoon – I want a walk – I mustn't think of Midwinter. Suppose I put on my bonnet, and try my experiment at once at the great house? Everything is in my favour. There is no spy to follow me, and no lawyer to keep me out, this time. Am I handsome enough, to-day? Well, yes – handsome enough to be a match for a little dowdy, awkward, freckled creature, who ought to be perched on a form at school, and strapped to a back-board to straighten her crooked shoulders.

> The nursery lisps out in all they utter;
> Besides, they always smell of bread and butter.

How admirably Byron has described girls in their teens![1]

Eight o'clock. – I have just got back from Armadale's house. I have seen him, and spoken to him; and the end of it may be set down in three plain words. I have failed. There is no more chance of my being Mrs Armadale of Thorpe-Ambrose than there is of my being Queen of England.

Shall I write and tell Oldershaw? Shall I go back to London? Not till I have had time to think a little. Not just yet.

Let me think; I have failed completely – failed, with all the circumstances in favour of success. I caught him alone on the drive in front of the house. He was excessively disconcerted, but at the same time quite willing to hear me. I tried him, first quietly – then with tears, and the rest of it. I introduced myself in the character of the poor innocent woman whom he had been the means of injuring. I confused, I interested, I convinced him. I went on to the purely Christian part of my errand, and spoke with such feeling of his separation from his friend, for which I was innocently responsible, that I turned his odious rosy face quite pale, and made him beg me at last not to distress him. But, whatever other feelings I roused in him, I never once roused his old feeling for *me*. I saw it in his eyes when he looked at me; I felt it in his fingers when we shook hands. We parted friends and nothing more.

It is for this, is it, Miss Milroy, that I resisted temptation,[2] morning after morning, when I knew you were out alone in the park? I have just left you time to slip in, and take my place in Armadale's good graces, have I? I never resisted temptation yet without suffering for it in some such way as this! If I had only followed my first thoughts, on the day when I took leave of you, my young lady – well, well, never mind that now. I have got the future before me; you are not Mrs Armadale yet! And I can tell you one other thing – whoever else he marries, he will never marry *you*. If I am even with you in no other way, trust me, whatever comes of it, to be even with you there!

I am not, to my own surprise, in one of my furious passions. The last time I was in this perfectly cool state, under serious provocation, something came of it, which I daren't write down, even in my own private diary. I shouldn't be surprised if something comes of it now.

On my way back, I called at Mr Bashwood's lodgings in the town. He was not at home, and I left a message telling him to come here to-night and speak to me. I mean to relieve him at once of the duty of looking after Armadale and Miss Milroy. I may not see my way yet to ruining her prospects at Thorpe-Ambrose as completely as she has ruined mine. But when the time comes, and I do see it, I don't know to what lengths my sense of injury may take me; and there may be inconvenience, and possibly danger, in having such a chicken-hearted creature as Mr Bashwood in my confidence.

I suspect I am more upset by all this than I supposed. Midwinter's story is beginning to haunt me again, without rhyme or reason.

A soft, quick, trembling knock at the street door! I know who it is. No hand but old Bashwood's could knock in that way.

*

Nine o'clock. – I have just got rid of him. He has surprised me by coming out in a new character.

It seems (though I didn't detect him) that he was at the great house while I was in company with Armadale. He saw us talking on the drive; and he afterwards heard what the servants said, who saw us too. The wise opinion below stairs is that we have 'made it up', and that the master is likely to marry me after all. 'He's sweet on her red hair,' was the elegant expression they used in the kitchen. 'Little Missie can't match her there – and little Missie will get the worst of it.' How I hate the coarse ways of the lower orders!

While old Bashwood was telling me this, I thought he looked even more confused and nervous than usual. But I failed to see what was really the matter until after I had told him that he was to leave all further observation of Mr Armadale and Miss Milroy to me. Every drop of the little blood there is in the feeble old creature's body seemed to fly up into his face. He made quite an overpowering effort; he really looked as if he would drop down dead of fright at his own boldness; but he forced out the question, for all that, stammering, and stuttering, and kneading desperately with both hands at the brim of his hideous great hat. 'I beg your pardon, Miss Gwi-Gwi-Gwilt! You are not really go go-going to marry Mr Armadale, are you?' Jealous – if ever I saw it in a man's face yet, I saw it in his – actually jealous of Armadale, at his age![3] If I had been in the humour for it, I should have burst out laughing in his face. As it was, I was angry, and lost all patience with him. I told him he was an old fool, and ordered him to go on quietly with his usual business until I sent him word that he was wanted again. He submitted as usual; but there was an indescribable something in his watery old eyes, when he took leave of me, which I have never noticed in them before. Love has the credit of working all sorts of strange transformations. Can it be really possible that Love has made Mr Bashwood man enough to be angry with me?

Wednesday. – My experience of Miss Milroy's habits suggested a suspicion to me last night, which I thought it desirable to clear up this morning.

It was always her way, when I was at the cottage, to take a walk early in the morning before breakfast. Considering that I used often to choose that very time for *my* private meetings with Armadale, it struck me as likely that my former pupil might be taking a leaf out of my book, and that I might make some desirable discoveries if I turned my steps in the direction of the major's garden at the right hour. I deprived myself of my Drops, to make sure of waking; passed a miserable night in consequence; and was ready enough to get up at six o'clock, and walk the distance from my lodgings to the cottage in the fresh morning air.

I had not been five minutes on the park-side of the garden enclosure before I saw her come out. *She* seemed to have had a bad night too; her eyes were heavy and red, and her lips and cheeks looked swollen as if she had been crying. There was something on her mind, evidently; something, as it soon appeared, to take her out of the garden into the park. She walked (if one can call it walking, with such legs as hers!) straight to the summer-house, and opened the door, and crossed the bridge, and went on quicker and quicker towards the low ground in the park, where the trees are thickest. I followed her over the open space with perfect impunity, in the preoccupied state she was in; and when she began to slacken her pace among the trees, I was among the trees too, and was not afraid of her seeing me.

Before long, there was a crackling and trampling of heavy feet coming up towards us through the underwood in a deep dip of the ground. I knew that step as well as she knew it. 'Here I am,' she said, in a faint little voice. I kept behind the trees a few yards off, in some doubt on which side Armadale would come out of the underwood to join her. He came out, up the side of the dell opposite to the tree behind which I was standing. They sat down together on the bank. I sat down behind the tree, and looked at them through the underwood, and heard without the slightest difficulty every word that they said.

The talk began by his noticing that she looked out of spirits, and asking if anything had gone wrong at the cottage. The artful little minx lost no time in making the necessary impression on him; she began to cry. He took her hand, of course, and tried, in his brutishly straight-forward way, to comfort her. No: she was not to be comforted. A miserable prospect was before her; she had not slept the whole night for thinking of it. Her father had called her into his room the previous evening, had spoken about the state of her education, and had told her, in so many words, that she was to go to school. The place had been found, and the terms had been settled; and as soon as her clothes could be got ready, Miss was to go. 'While that hateful Miss Gwilt was in the house,' says this model young person, 'I would have gone to school willingly – I wanted to go. But it's all different now; I don't think of it in the same way; I feel too old for school. I'm quite heart-broken, Mr Armadale.' There she stopped, as if she had meant to say more, and gave him a look which finished the sentence plainly – 'I'm quite heart-broken, Mr Armadale, now we are friendly again, at going away from *you*!' For downright brazen impudence, which a grown woman would be ashamed of, give me the young girls whose 'modesty' is so pertinaciously insisted on by the nauseous domestic sentimentalists of the present day![4]

Even Armadale, booby as he is, understood her. After bewildering himself in a labyrinth of words that led nowhere, he took her – one can hardly say round the waist, for she hasn't got one – he took her round the last hook-and-eye of her dress, and, by way of offering her a refuge from the indignity of being sent to school at her age, made her a proposal of marriage in so many words.

If I could have killed them both at that moment by lifting up my little finger, I have not the least doubt I should have lifted it. As things were, I only waited to see what Miss Milroy would do.

She appeared to think it necessary – feeling, I suppose, that she had met him without her father's knowledge, and not forgetting that I had had the start of her as the favoured object of Mr Armadale's good opinion – to assert herself by an explosion of virtuous indignation. She wondered how he could think of such a thing after his conduct with Miss Gwilt, and after her father had forbidden him the house! Did he want to make her feel how inexcusably she had forgotten what was due to herself? Was it worthy of a gentleman to propose what he knew as well as she did, was impossible? and so on, and so on. Any man with brains in his head would have known what all this rodomontade really meant. Armadale took it so seriously that he actually attempted to justify himself. He declared, in his headlong blundering way, that he was quite in earnest; he and her father might make it up, and be friends again; and if the major persisted in treating him as a stranger, young ladies and gentlemen in their situation had made runaway marriages before now, and fathers and mothers who wouldn't forgive them before, had forgiven them afterwards. Such outrageously straightforward love-making as this, left Miss Milroy, of course, but two alternatives – to confess that she had been saying No, when she meant Yes, or to take refuge in another explosion. She was hypocrite enough to prefer another explosion. 'How dare you, Mr Armadale? Go away directly! It's inconsiderate, it's heartless, it's perfectly disgraceful to say such things to me!' and so on, and so on. It seems incredible, but it is not the less true, that he was positively fool enough to take her at her word. He begged her pardon, and went away like a child that is put in the corner – the most contemptible object in the form of man that eyes ever looked on!

She waited, after he had gone, to compose herself, and I waited behind the trees to see how she would succeed. Her eyes wandered round slily to the path by which he had left her. She smiled (grinned would be the truer way of putting it, with such a mouth as hers); took a few steps on tiptoe to look after him; turned back again, and suddenly burst into a violent fit of crying. I am not quite so easily taken in as Armadale, and I saw what it all meant plainly enough.

'To-morrow,' I thought to myself, 'you will be in the park again, miss, by pure accident. The next day, you will lead him on into proposing to you for the second time. The day after, he will venture back to the subject of runaway marriages, and you will only be becomingly confused. And the day after that, if he has got a plan to propose, and if your clothes are ready to be packed for school, you will listen to him.' Yes, yes; Time is always on the man's side, where a woman is concerned, if the man is only patient enough to let Time help him.

I let her leave the place and go back to the cottage, quite unconscious that I had been looking at her. I waited among the trees thinking. The truth is, I was impressed by what I had heard and seen, in a manner that it is not very easy to describe. It put the whole thing before me in a new light. It showed me – what I had never even suspected till this morning – that she is really fond of him.

Heavy as my debt of obligation is to her, there is no fear *now*, of my failing to pay it to the last farthing. It would have been no small triumph for me to stand between Miss Milroy and her ambition to be one of the leading ladies of the county. But it is infinitely more, where her first love is concerned, to stand between Miss Milroy and her heart's desire. Shall I remember my own youth and spare her? No! She has deprived me of the one chance I had of breaking the chain that binds me to a past life too horrible to be thought of. I am thrown back into a position, compared to which the position of an outcast who walks the streets is endurable and enviable. No, Miss Milroy – no, Mr Armadale; I will spare neither of you.

I have been back some hours. I have been thinking, and nothing has come of it. Ever since I got that strange letter of Midwinter's last Sunday, my usual readiness in emergencies has deserted me. When I am not thinking of him or of his story, my mind feels quite stupefied. I who have always known what to do on other occasions, don't know what to do now. It would be easy enough, of course, to warn Major Milroy of his daughter's proceedings. But the major is fond of his daughter; Armadale is anxious to be reconciled with him; Armadale

433

is rich and prosperous, and ready to submit to the elder man – and sooner or later they will be friends again, and the marriage will follow. Warning Major Milroy is only the way to embarrass them for the present; it is not the way to part them for good and all.

What *is* the way? I can't see it. I could tear my own hair off my head! I could burn the house down! If there was a train of gunpowder under the whole world, I could light it, and blow the whole world to destruction – I am in such a rage, such a frenzy with myself for not seeing it!

Poor dear Midwinter! Yes, '*dear*'. I don't care. I'm lonely and helpless. I want somebody who is gentle and loving, to make much of me; I wish I had his head on my bosom again; I have a good mind to go to London, and marry him. Am I mad? Yes; all people who are as miserable as I am, are mad. I must go to the window and get some air. Shall I jump out? No; it disfigures one so, and the coroner's inquest lets so many people see it.

The air has revived me. I begin to remember that I have Time on my side, at any rate. Nobody knows but me, of their secret meetings in the park the first thing in the morning. If jealous old Bashwood, who is slinking and sly enough for anything, tries to look privately after Armadale, in his own interests, he will try at the usual time when he goes to the steward's office. He knows nothing of Miss Milroy's early habits; and he won't be on the spot till Armadale has got back to the house. For another week to come, I may wait and watch them, and choose my own time and way of interfering the moment I see a chance of his getting the better of her hesitation, and making her say, Yes.

So here I wait, without knowing how things will end with Midwinter in London; with my purse getting emptier and emptier, and no appearance so far of any new pupils to fill it; with Mother Oldershaw certain to insist on having her money back the moment she knows I have failed, without prospects, friends, or hopes of any kind – a lost woman, if ever there was a lost woman yet. Well! I say it again and again and again – I don't care! Here I stop, if I sell the clothes off my back, if I hire myself at the public-house to play to the brutes in the tap-room; here I stop till the time comes, and I see the way to parting Armadale and Miss Milroy for ever!

Seven o'clock. – Any signs that the time is coming yet? I hardly know – there are signs of a change, at any rate, in my position in the neighbourhood.

Two of the oldest and ugliest of the many old and ugly ladies who took up my case when I left Major Milroy's service, have just called, announcing themselves with the insufferable impudence of charitable Englishwomen, as a deputation from my patronesses. It seems, that the news of my reconciliation with Armadale has spread from the servants' offices at the great house, and has reached the town, with this result. It is the unanimous opinion of my 'patronesses' (and the opinion of Major Milroy also, who has been consulted,) that I have acted with the most inexcusable imprudence in going to Armadale's house, and in there speaking on friendly terms with a man whose conduct towards myself has made his name a by-word in the neighbourhood. My total want of self-respect in this matter, has given rise to a report that I am trading as cleverly as ever on my good looks, and that I am as likely as not to end in making Armadale marry me after all. My 'patronesses' are of course too charitable to believe this. They merely feel it necessary to remonstrate with me in a Christian spirit, and to warn me that any second and similar imprudence on my part would force all my best friends in the place to withdraw the countenance and protection which I now enjoy.

Having addressed me, turn and turn about, in these terms (evidently all rehearsed beforehand), my two Gorgon-visitors straightened themselves in their chairs, and looked at me as much as to say, 'You may often have heard of Virtue, Miss Gwilt, but we don't believe you ever really saw it in full bloom till we came and called on you.'

Seeing they were bent on provoking me, I kept my temper, and answered them in my smoothest, sweetest, and most ladylike manner. I have noticed that the Christianity of a certain class of respectable people begins when they open their prayer-books at eleven o'clock on Sunday morning, and ends when they shut them up again at one o'clock on Sunday afternoon. Nothing so astonishes and insults Christians of this sort as reminding them of their Christianity on a week-day. On this hint, as the man says in the play, I spoke.[5]

'What have I done that is wrong?' I asked, innocently. 'Mr Armadale has injured me; and I have been to his house and forgiven him the injury. Surely there must be some mistake, ladies? You can't have really come here to remonstrate with me in a Christian spirit for performing an act of Christianity?'

The two Gorgons got up. I firmly believe some women have cats' tails as well as cats' faces. I firmly believe the tails of those two particular cats wagged slowly under their petticoats, and swelled to four times their proper size.

'Temper we were prepared for, Miss Gwilt,' they said, 'but not Profanity. We wish you good evening.'

So they left me, and so 'Miss Gwilt' sinks out of the patronizing notice of the neighbourhood.

I wonder what will come of this trumpery little quarrel? One thing will come of it which I can see already. The report will reach Miss Milroy's ears. She will insist on Armadale's justifying himself – and Armadale will end in satisfying her of his innocence by making another proposal. This will be quite likely to hasten matters between them – at least it would with me. If I was in her place, I should say to myself, 'I will make sure of him while I can.' Supposing it doesn't rain to-morrow morning, I think I will take another early walk in the direction of the park.

Midnight. – As I can't take my drops, with a morning walk before me, I may as well give up all hope of sleeping, and go on with my diary. Even *with* my drops, I doubt if my head would be very quiet on my pillow to-night. Since the little excitement of the scene with my 'lady-patronesses' has worn off, I have been troubled with misgivings which would leave me but a poor chance, under any circumstances, of getting much rest.

I can't imagine why, but the parting words spoken to Armadale by that old brute of a lawyer, have come back to my mind! Here they are, as reported in Mr Bashwood's letter: 'Some other person's curiosity may go on from the point where you (and I) have stopped, and some other person's hand may let the broad daylight in yet on Miss Gwilt.'

What does he mean by that? And what did he mean afterwards when he overtook old Bashwood in the drive, by telling him to gratify his curiosity? Does this hateful Pedgift actually suppose there is any chance—? Ridiculous! Why, I have only to *look* at the feeble old creature, and he daren't lift his little finger unless I tell him. *He* try to pry into my past life indeed! Why, people with ten times his brains, and a hundred times his courage, have tried – and have left off as wise as they began.

I don't know though – it might have been better if I had kept my temper when Bashwood was here the other night. And it might be better still if I saw him to-morrow, and took him back into my good graces by giving him something to do for me. Suppose I tell him to look after the two Pedgifts, and to discover whether there is any chance of their attempting to renew their connection with Armadale? No such thing is at all likely – but if I gave old Bashwood this commission, it would flatter his sense of his own importance to me, and would at the same time serve the excellent purpose of keeping him out of my way.

*

Thursday morning, nine o'clock. – I have just got back from the park.

For once, I have proved a true prophet. There they were together, at the same early hour, in the same secluded situation among the trees; and there was Miss in full possession of the report of my visit to the great house, and taking her tone accordingly.

After saying one or two things about me, which I promise him not to forget, Armadale took the way to convince her of his constancy which I felt beforehand he would be driven to take. He repeated his proposal of marriage, with excellent effect this time. Tears and kisses and protestations followed; and my late pupil opened her heart at last, in the most innocent manner. Home, she confessed, was getting so miserable to her now, that it was only less miserable than going to school. Her mother's temper was becoming more violent and unmanageable every day. The nurse, who was the only person with any influence over her, had gone away in disgust. Her father was becoming more and more immersed in his clock, and was made more and more resolute to send her away from home, by the distressing scenes which now took place with her mother, almost day by day. I waited through these domestic disclosures on the chance of hearing any plans they might have for the future discussed between them; and my patience, after no small exercise of it, was rewarded at last.

The first suggestion (as was only natural where such a fool as Armadale was concerned) came from the girl. She started an idea, which I own I had not anticipated. She proposed that Armadale should write to her father; and, cleverer still, she prevented all fear of his blundering by telling him what he was to say. He was to express himself as deeply distressed at his estrangement from the major, and to request permission to call at the cottage, and say a few words in his own justification. That was all. The letter was not to be sent that day, for the applicants for the vacant place of Mrs Milroy's nurse were coming, and seeing them and questioning them would put her father, with his dislike of such things, in no humour to receive Armadale's application indulgently. The Friday would be the day to send the letter, and on the Saturday morning, if the answer was unfortunately not favourable, they might meet again. 'I don't like deceiving my father; he has always been so kind to me. And there will be no need to deceive him, Allan, if we can only make you friends again.' Those were the last words the little hypocrite said, when I left them.

What will the major do? Saturday morning will show. I won't think of it till Saturday morning has come and gone. They are not man and wife yet; and again and again I say it, though my brains are still as helpless as ever, man and wife they shall never be.

On my way home again, I caught Bashwood at his breakfast, with his poor old black teapot, and his little penny loaf, and his one cheap morsel of oily butter, and his darned dirty table-cloth. It sickens me to think of it.

I coaxed and comforted the miserable old creature till the tears stood in his eyes, and he quite blushed with pleasure. He undertakes to look after the Pedgifts with the utmost alacrity. Pedgift the elder, he describes, when once roused, as the most obstinate man living; nothing will induce him to give way, unless Armadale gives way also on his side. Pedgift the younger is much the more likely of the two to make attempts at a reconciliation. Such at least is Bashwood's opinion. It is of very little consequence now what happens either way. The only important thing is to tie my elderly admirer safely again to my apron-string. And this is done.

The post is late this morning. It has only just come in, and has brought me a letter from Midwinter.

It is a charming letter; it flatters me and flutters me as if I was a young girl again. No reproaches for my never having written to him; no hateful hurrying of me, in plain words, to marry him. He only writes to tell me a piece of news. He has obtained, through his lawyers, a prospect of being employed as occasional correspondent to a newspaper which is about to be started in London.[6] The employment will require him to leave England for the Continent, which would exactly meet his own wishes for the future, but he cannot consider the proposal seriously until he has first ascertained whether it would meet my wishes too. He knows no will but mine, and he leaves me to decide, after first mentioning the time allowed him before his answer must be sent in. It is the time of course (if I agree to his going abroad) in which I must marry him. But there is not a word about this in his letter. He asks for nothing but a sight of my handwriting to help him through the interval, while we are separated from each other.

That is the letter; not very long, but so prettily expressed.

I think I can penetrate the secret of his fancy for going abroad. That wild idea of putting the mountains and the seas between Armadale and himself is still in his mind. As if either he or I could escape doing what we are fated to do – supposing we really are fated – by putting a few hundred, or a few thousand miles, between Armadale and ourselves! What strange absurdity and inconsistency! And yet how I like him for being absurd and inconsistent; for don't I see plainly that I am at the bottom of it all? Who leads this clever man astray in spite of himself?

438

Who makes him too blind to see the contradiction in his own conduct, which he would see plainly in the conduct of another person? How interested I do feel in him! How dangerously near I am to shutting my eyes on the past, and letting myself love him! Was Eve fonder of Adam than ever, I wonder, after she had coaxed him into eating the apple? I should have quite doated on him if I had been in her place. (Memorandum: To write Midwinter a charming little letter on my side, with a kiss in it; and as time is allowed him before he sends in his answer, to ask for time too, before I tell him whether I will or will not go abroad.)[7]

Five o'clock.[8] – A tiresome visit from my landlady; eager for a little gossip, and full of news, which she thinks will interest me.

She is acquainted, I find, with Mrs Milroy's late nurse; and she has been seeing her friend off, at the station, this afternoon. They talked of course of affairs at the cottage, and my name turned up in the course of conversation. I am quite wrong, it seems, if the nurse's authority is to be trusted, in believing Miss Milroy to be responsible for sending Mr Armadale to my reference in London. Miss Milroy really knew nothing about it, and it all originated in her mother's mad jealousy of me. The present wretched state of things at the cottage is due entirely to the same cause. Mrs Milroy is firmly persuaded that my remaining at Thorpe-Ambrose is referable to my having some private means of communicating with the major which it is impossible for her to discover. With this conviction in her mind, she has become so unmanageable that no person, with any chance of bettering herself, could possibly remain in attendance on her; and, sooner or later, the major, object to it as he may, will be obliged to place her under proper medical care.

That is the sum and substance of what the wearisome landlady had to tell me. Unnecessary to say that I was not in the least interested by it. Even if the nurse's assertion is to be depended on – which I persist in doubting – it is of no importance now. I know that Miss Milroy, and nobody *but* Miss Milroy, has utterly ruined my prospect of becoming Mrs Armadale of Thorpe-Ambrose – and I care to know nothing more. If her mother was really alone in the attempt to expose my false reference, her mother seems to be suffering for it, at any rate. And so good-by to Mrs Milroy – and heaven defend me from any more last glimpses at the cottage, seen through the medium of my landlady's spectacles!

Nine o'clock. – Bashwood has just left me, having come with news from the great house. Pedgift the younger has made his attempt at bringing about a reconciliation this very day, and has failed. I am the sole cause of the failure. Armadale is quite willing to be reconciled, if Pedgift the elder will avoid all future occasion of disagreement between them, by never recurring to the subject of Miss Gwilt. This, however, happens to be exactly the condition which Pedgift's father – with his opinion of me and my doings – would consider it his duty to Armadale *not* to accept. So lawyer and client remain as far apart as ever, and the obstacle of the Pedgifts is cleared out of my way.

It might have been a very awkward obstacle, so far as Pedgift the elder is concerned, if one of his suggestions had been carried out – I mean, if an officer of the London police had been brought down here to look at me. It is a question, even now, whether I had better not take to the thick veil again, which I always wear in London and other large places. The only difficulty is, that it would excite remark in this inquisitive little town to see me wearing a thick veil, for the first time, in the summer weather.

It is close on ten o'clock – I have been dawdling over my diary longer than I supposed. No words can describe how weary and languid I feel. Why don't I take my sleeping drops and go to bed? There is no meeting between Armadale and Miss Milroy to force me into early rising to-morrow morning. Am I trying, for the hundredth time, to see my way clearly into the future – trying, in my present state of fatigue, to be the quick-witted woman I once was, before all these anxieties came together and overpowered me? or am I perversely afraid of my bed when I want it most? I don't know – I am tired and miserable; I am looking wretchedly haggard and old. With a little encouragement, I might be fool enough to burst out crying. Luckily, there is no one to encourage me. What sort of night is it, I wonder?

A cloudy night, with the moon showing at intervals, and the wind rising. I can just hear it moaning among the ins and outs of the unfinished cottages at the end of the street. My nerves must be a little shaken, I think. I was startled just now by a shadow on the wall. It was only after a moment or two that I mustered sense enough to notice where the candle was, and to see that the shadow was my own.

Shadows remind me of Midwinter – or, if the shadows don't, something else does. I must have another look at his letter, and then I will positively go to bed.

I shall end in getting fond of him. If I remain much longer in this lonely uncertain state – so irresolute, so unlike my usual self – I shall end in getting fond of him. What madness! As if *I* could ever be really fond of a man again!

Suppose I took one of my sudden resolutions, and married him. Poor as he is, he would give me a name and a position, if I became his wife. Let me see how the name – his own name – would look, if I really did consent to take it for mine.

'Mrs Armadale!' Pretty.

'Mrs Allan Armadale!' Prettier still.

My nerves *must* be shaken. Here is my own handwriting startling me now! It is so strange – it is enough to startle anybody. The similarity in the two names never struck me in this light before. Marry which of the two I might, my name would of course be the same. I should have been Mrs Armadale, if I had married the light-haired Allan at the great house. And I can be Mrs Armadale still, if I marry the dark-haired Allan in London. It's almost maddening to write it down – to feel that something ought to come of it – and to find nothing come.

How *can* anything come of it? If I did go to London, and marry him (as of course I must marry him) under his real name, would he let me be known by it afterwards? With all his reasons for concealing his real name, he would insist – no, he is too fond of me to do that – he would entreat me to take the name which he has assumed. Mrs Midwinter. Hideous! Ozias, too, when I wanted to address him familiarly as his wife should. Worse than hideous!

And yet, there would be some reason for humouring him in this, if he asked me. Suppose the brute at the great house happened to leave this neighbourhood as a single man; and suppose, in his absence, any of the people who know him heard of a Mrs Allan Armadale, they would set her down at once as his wife. Even if they actually saw me – if I actually came among them with that name, and if he was not present to contradict it – his own servants would be the first to say, 'We knew she would marry him after all!' And my lady-patronesses, who will be ready to believe anything of me now we have quarrelled, would join the chorus *sotto voce*: 'Only think, my dear, the report that so shocked us, actually turns out to be true!' No. If I marry Midwinter, I must either be perpetually putting my husband and myself in a false position – or I must leave his real name, his pretty, romantic name, behind me at the church door.

My husband! As if I was really going to marry him! I am *not* going to marry him, and there's an end of it.

Half-past ten. – Oh dear! oh dear! how my temples throb, and how hot my weary eyes feel! There is the moon looking at me through the window. How fast the little scattered clouds are flying before the wind! Now they let the moon in; and now they shut the moon out. What strange shapes the patches of yellow light take, and lose again, all in a moment! No peace and quiet for me, look where I may. The candle keeps flickering, and the very sky itself is restless to-night.

'To bed! to bed!' as Lady Macbeth says. I wonder by-the-by what Lady Macbeth would have done in my position? She would have killed somebody when her difficulties first began. Probably Armadale.

Friday morning. – A night's rest, thanks again to my Drops. I went to breakfast in better spirits, and received a morning welcome in the shape of a letter from Mrs Oldershaw.

My silence has produced its effect on Mother Jezebel. She attributes it to the right cause, and she shows her claws at last. If I am not in a position to pay my note-of-hand for thirty pounds, which is due on Tuesday next, her lawyer is instructed to 'take the usual course'. *If* I am not in a position to pay it! Why, when I have settled to-day with my landlord, I shall have barely five pounds left! There is not the shadow of a prospect between now and Tuesday of my earning any money; and I don't possess a friend in this place who would trust me with sixpence. The difficulties that are swarming round me wanted but one more to complete them, and that one has come.

Midwinter would assist me, of course, if I could bring myself to ask him for assistance. But *that* means marrying him. Am I really desperate enough and helpless enough to end it in that way? No; not yet.

My head feels heavy; I must get out into the fresh air, and think about it.

Two o'clock. – I believe I have caught the infection of Midwinter's superstition. I begin to think that events are forcing me nearer and nearer to some end which I don't see yet, but which I am firmly persuaded is now not far off.

I have been insulted – deliberately insulted before witnesses – by Miss Milroy.

After walking, as usual, in the most unfrequented place I could pick out, and after trying not very successfully to think to some good purpose of what I am to do next, I remembered that I needed some note-paper and pens, and went back to the town, to the stationer's shop. It might have been wiser to have sent for what I wanted. But I was weary of myself, and weary of my lonely rooms; and I did my own errand, for no better reason than that it was something to do.

I had just got into the shop, and was asking for what I wanted, when another customer came in. We both looked up, and recognized each other at the same moment: Miss Milroy.

A woman and a lad were behind the counter, besides the man who was serving me. The woman civilly addressed the new customer. 'What can we have the pleasure of doing for you, Miss?' After pointing it first, by looking me straight in the face, she answered, 'Nothing, thank you, at present. I'll come back when the shop is empty.'

She went out. The three people in the shop looked at me in silence. In silence, on my side, I paid for my purchases, and left the place. I don't know how I might have felt if I had been in my usual spirits. In the anxious unsettled state I am in now, I can't deny it, the girl stung me.

In the weakness of the moment (for it was nothing else) I was on the point of matching her petty spitefulness by spitefulness quite as petty on my side. I had actually got as far as the whole length of the street, on my way to the major's cottage, bent on telling him the secret of his daughter's morning walks, before my better sense came back to me. When I did cool down, I turned round at once, and took the way home. No, no, Miss Milroy: mere temporary mischief-making at the cottage, which would only end in your father forgiving you, and in Armadale profiting by his indulgence, will nothing like pay the debt I owe you. I don't forget that your heart is set on Armadale; and that the major, however he may talk, has always ended hitherto in giving you your own way. My head *may* be getting duller and duller, but it has not quite failed me yet.

In the meantime, there is Mother Oldershaw's letter waiting obstinately to be answered; and here am I, not knowing what to do about it yet. Shall I answer it or not? It doesn't matter for the present; there are some hours still to spare before the post goes out.

Suppose I asked Armadale to lend me the money? I should enjoy getting *something* out of him; and I believe, in his present situation with Miss Milroy, he would do anything to be rid of me. Mean enough this, on my part. Pooh! When you hate and despise a man, as I hate and despise Armadale, who cares for looking mean in *his* eyes?

And yet my pride – or my something else, I don't know what – shrinks from it.

Half-past two – only half-past two. Oh, the dreadful weariness of these long summer days! I can't keep thinking and thinking any longer; I must do something to relieve my mind. Can I go to my piano? No; I'm not fit for it. Work? No; I shall get thinking again, if I take to my needle. A man, in my place, would find refuge in drink. I'm not a man, and I can't drink. I'll dawdle over my dresses, and put my things tidy.

Has an hour passed? More than an hour. It seems like a minute.

I can't look back through these leaves, but I know I wrote the words somewhere. I know I felt myself getting nearer and nearer to some end that was still hidden from me. The end is hidden no longer. The cloud is off my mind, the blindness has gone from my eyes. I see it! I see it![9]

It came to me – I never sought it. If I was lying on my death-bed, I could swear, with a safe conscience, I never sought it.

I was only looking over my things; I was as idly and as frivolously employed as the most idle and most frivolous woman living. I went through my dresses and my linen. What could be more innocent? Children go through their dresses and their linen.

It was such a long summer day, and I was so tired of myself. I went to my boxes next. I looked over the large box first, which I usually leave open; and then I tried the small box, which I always keep locked.

From one thing to the other, I came at last to the bundle of letters at the bottom – the letters of the man for whom I once sacrificed and suffered everything; the man who has made me what I am. A hundred times I have determined to burn his letters; but I have never burnt them. This time, all I said was, 'I won't read his letters!' And I did read them.

The villain – the false, cowardly, heartless villain – what have I to do with his letters now? Oh, the misery of being a woman! Oh, the meanness that our memory of a man can tempt us to, when our love for him is dead and gone! I read the letters – I was so lonely and so miserable, I read the letters.[10]

I came to the last – the letter he wrote to encourage me, when I hesitated as the terrible time came nearer and nearer; the letter that revived me when my resolution failed at the eleventh hour. I read on, line after line, till I came to these words:

> . . . I really have no patience with such absurdities as you have written to me. You say I am driving you on to do what is beyond a woman's courage. Am I? I might refer you to any collection of Trials, English or foreign, to show that you were utterly wrong. But such collections may be beyond your reach; and I will only refer you to a case in yesterday's newspaper. The circumstances are totally different from *our* circumstances; but the example of resolution in a woman is an example worth your notice.

You will find, among the law reports, a married woman charged with fraudulently representing herself to be the missing widow of an officer in the merchant service, who was supposed to have been drowned.[11] The name of the prisoner's husband (living), and the name of the officer (a very common one, both as to Christian and surname), happened to be identically the same. There was money to be got by it (sorely wanted by the prisoner's husband, to whom she was devotedly attached), if the fraud had succeeded. The woman took it all on herself. Her husband was helpless and ill, and the bailiffs were after him. The circumstances, as you may read for yourself, were all in her favour, and were so well managed by her that the lawyers themselves acknowledged she might have succeeded, if the supposed drowned man had not turned up alive and well in the nick of time to confront her. The scene took place at the lawyers' office, and came out in the evidence at the police-court. The woman was handsome, and the sailor was a good-natured man. He wanted, at first, if the lawyers would have allowed him, to let her off. He said to her, among other things, 'You didn't count on the drowned man coming back, alive and hearty, did you, ma'am?' 'It's lucky for you,' she said, 'I didn't count on it. You have escaped the sea, but you wouldn't have escaped *me*.' 'Why, what would you have done, if you *had* known I was coming back?' says the sailor. She looked him steadily in the face, and answered: 'I would have killed you.' There! Do you think such a woman as that would have written to tell me I was pressing her farther than she had courage to go? A handsome woman, too, like yourself! You would drive some men in my position to wish they had her now in your place.[12]

I read no farther. When I had got on, line by line, to those words, it burst on me like a flash of lightning. In an instant I saw it as plainly as I see it now. It is horrible, it is unheard-of, it out-dares all daring; but, if I can only nerve myself to face one terrible necessity, it is to be done. *I may personate the richly-provided widow of Allan Armadale of Thorpe-Ambrose, if I can count on Allan Armadale's death in a given time.*

There, in plain words, is the frightful temptation under which I now feel myself sinking. It is frightful in more ways than one – for it has come straight out of that other temptation to which I yielded in the bygone time.

Yes; there the letter has been waiting for me in my box, to serve a purpose never thought of by the villain who wrote it. There is the Case, as he calls it – only quoted to taunt me; utterly unlike my own case at the time – there it has been, waiting and lurking for me through all the changes in my life, till it has come to be like *my* case at last.

It might startle any woman to see this, and even this is not the worst. The whole thing has been in my Diary, for days past, without my knowing it! Every idle fancy that escaped me, has been tending secretly that one way! And I never saw, never suspected it, till the reading of the letter put my own thoughts before me in a new light – till I saw the shadow of my own circumstances suddenly reflected in one special circumstance of that other woman's case!

It is to be done, if I can but look the necessity in the face. It is to be done, *if I can count on Allan Armadale's death in a given time*.

All but his death is easy. The whole series of events under which I have been blindly chafing and fretting for more than a week past, have been one and all – though I was too stupid to see it – events in my favour; events paving the way smoothly and more smoothly straight to the end.

In three bold steps – only three! – that end might be reached. Let Midwinter marry me privately, under his real name – step the first! Let Armadale leave Thorpe-Ambrose a single man, and die in some distant place among strangers – step the second!

Why am I hesitating? Why not go on to step the third, and last?

I *will* go on. Step the third, and last, is my appearance, after the announcement of Armadale's death has reached this neighbourhood, in the character of Armadale's widow, with my marriage certificate in my hand to prove my claim. It is as clear as the sun at noonday. Thanks to the exact similarity between the two names, and thanks to the careful manner in which the secret of that similarity has been kept, I may be the wife of the dark Allan Armadale, known as such to nobody but my husband and myself; and I may, out of that very position, claim the character of widow of the light Allan Armadale, with proof to support me (in the shape of my marriage certificate) which would be proof in the estimation of the most incredulous person living.

To think of my having put all this in my Diary! To think of my having actually contemplated this very situation, and having seen nothing more in it, at the time, than a reason (if I married Midwinter) for consenting to appear in the world under my husband's assumed name!

What is it daunts me? The dread of obstacles? The fear of discovery?

Where are the obstacles? where is the fear of discovery?

I am actually suspected all over the neighbourhood, of intriguing to be mistress of Thorpe-Ambrose. I am the only person who knows the real turn that Armadale's inclinations have taken. Not a creature but myself is as yet aware of his early morning meetings with Miss Milroy. If it is necessary to part them, I can do it at any moment, by an anonymous line to the major. If it is necessary to remove Armadale from Thorpe-Ambrose, I can get him away at three days' notice. His own lips informed me, when I last spoke to him, that he would go to the ends of the earth to be friends again with Midwinter, if Midwinter would let him. I have only to tell Midwinter to write from London, and ask to be reconciled; and Midwinter would obey me – and to London Armadale would go. Every difficulty, at starting, is smoothed over ready to my hand. Every after-difficulty I could manage for myself. In the whole venture – desperate as it looks to pass myself off for the widow of one man, while I am all the while the wife of the other – there is absolutely no necessity that wants twice considering, but the one terrible necessity of Armadale's death.

His death! it might be a terrible necessity to any other woman – but is it, ought it to be terrible to Me?

I hate him for his mother's sake. I hate him for his own sake. I hate him for going to London behind my back, and making inquiries about me. I hate him for forcing me out of my situation before I wanted to go. I hate him for destroying all my hopes of marrying him, and throwing me back helpless on my own miserable life. But, oh, after what I have done already in the past time, how can I? how can I?

The girl, too – the girl who has come between us; who has taken him away from me; who has openly insulted me this very day – how the girl whose heart is set on him would feel it, if he died! What a vengeance on *her*, if I did it! And when I was received as Armadale's widow, what a triumph for *me*. Triumph! It is more than triumph – it is the salvation of me. A name that can't be assailed, a station that can't be assailed, to hide myself in from my past life! Comfort, luxury, wealth! An income of twelve hundred a year secured to me – secured by a will which has been looked at by a lawyer; secured independently of anything he can say or do himself! I never had twelve hundred a year. At my luckiest time, I never had half as much, really my own. What have I got now? Just five pounds left in the world – and the prospect next week of a debtors' prison.

But, oh, after what I have done already in the past time, how can I? how can I?

Some women – in my place, and with my recollections to look back on – would feel it differently. Some women would say – 'It's easier the second time than the first.' Why can't I? why can't I?

Oh, you Devil tempting me, is there no Angel near, to raise some timely obstacle between this and to-morrow, which might help me to give it up?

I shall sink under it – I shall sink, if I write or think of it any more! I'll shut up these leaves and go out again. I'll get some common person to come with me, and we will talk of common things. I'll take out the woman of the house, and her children. We will go and see something. There is a show of some kind in the town – I'll treat them to it. I'm not such an ill-natured woman when I try; and the landlady has really been kind to me. Surely I might occupy my mind a little, in seeing her and her children enjoying themselves.

A minute since, I shut up these leaves as I said I would; and now I have opened them again, I don't know why. I think my brain is turned. I feel as if something was lost out of my mind; I feel as if I ought to find it here.

I have found it! *Midwinter!!!*

Is it possible that I can have been thinking of the reasons For and Against, for an hour past – writing Midwinter's name over and over again – speculating seriously on marrying him – and all the time not once remembering that, even with every other impediment removed, *he* alone, when the time came, would be an insurmountable obstacle in my way? Has the effort to face the consideration of Armadale's death absorbed me to *that* degree? I suppose it has. I can't account for such extraordinary forgetfulness on my part, in any other way.

Shall I stop and think it out, as I have thought out all the rest? Shall I ask myself if the obstacle of Midwinter would after all, when the time came, be the unmanageable obstacle that it looks at present? No! What need is there to think of it? I have made up my mind to get the better of the temptation. I have made up my mind to give my landlady and her children a treat; I have made up my mind to close my Diary. And closed it shall be.

Six o'clock. – The landlady's gossip is unendurable; the landlady's children distract me. I have left them, to run back here before post-time and write a line to Mrs Oldershaw.

The dread that I shall sink under the temptation has grown stronger and stronger on me. I have determined to put it beyond my power to have my own way and follow my own will. Mother Oldershaw shall be the salvation of me for the first time since I have known her. If I can't pay my note-of-hand, she threatens me with an arrest. Well, she *shall* arrest me. In the state my mind is in now, the best thing that can happen to me is to be taken away from Thorpe-Ambrose, whether I like it or not. I will write and say that I am to be found here. I will write and tell her, in so many words, that the best service she can render me is to lock me up!

Seven o'clock. – The letter has gone to the post. I had begun to feel a little easier, when the children came in to thank me for taking them to the show. One of them is a girl, and the girl upset me. She is a forward child, and her hair is nearly the colour of mine. She said, 'I shall be like you when I have grown bigger, shan't I?' Her idiot of a mother said, 'Please to excuse her, miss,' and took her out of the room, laughing. Like me! I don't pretend to be fond of the child – but think of her being like Me!

Saturday morning. – I have done well for once in acting on impulse, and writing as I did to Mrs Oldershaw. The only new circumstance that has happened, is another circumstance in my favour!

Major Milroy has answered Armadale's letter, entreating permission to call at the cottage, and justify himself. His daughter read it in silence, when Armadale handed it to her at their meeting this morning, in the park. But they talked about it afterwards, loud enough for me to hear them. The major persists in the course he has taken. He says his opinion of Armadale's conduct has been formed, not on common report, but on Armadale's own letters; and he sees no reason to alter the conclusion at which he arrived when the correspondence between them was closed.

This little matter had, I confess, slipped out of my memory. It might have ended awkwardly for *me*. If Major Milroy had been less obstinately wedded to his own opinion, Armadale might have justified himself; the marriage engagement might have been acknowledged; and all *my* power of influencing the matter might have been at an end. As it is, they must continue to keep the engagement strictly secret; and Miss Milroy, who has never ventured herself near the great house since the thunderstorm forced her into it for shelter, will be less likely than ever to venture there now. I can part them when I please; with an anonymous line to the major, I can part them when I please!

After having discussed the letter, the talk between them turned on what they were to do next. Major Milroy's severity, as it soon appeared, produced the usual results. Armadale returned to the subject of the elopement – and, this time she listened to him. There is everything to drive her to it. Her outfit of clothes is nearly ready; and the summer holidays, at the school which has been chosen for her, end at the end of next week. When I left them, they had decided to meet again and settle something on Monday.

The last words I heard him address to her, before I went away, shook me a little. He said: 'There is one difficulty, Neelie, that needn't trouble us, at any rate. I have got plenty of money.' And then he kissed her. The way to his life began to look an easier way to me when he talked of his money, and kissed her.

Some hours have passed, and the more I think of it, the more I fear the blank interval between this time and the time when Mrs Oldershaw calls in the law, and protects me against myself. It might have been better if I had stopped at home this morning. But how could I? After the insult she offered me yesterday, I tingled all over to go and look at her.

To-day; Sunday; Monday; Tuesday. They can't arrest me for the money before Wednesday. And my miserable five pounds are dwindling to four! And he told her he had plenty of money! And she blushed and trembled when he kissed her! It might have been better for him, better for her, and better for me, if my debt had fallen due yesterday, and if the bailiffs had their hands on me at this moment.

Suppose I had the means of leaving Thorpe-Ambrose by the next train, and going somewhere abroad, and absorbing myself in some new interest, among new people. Could I do it, rather than look again at that easy way to his life which would smooth the way to everything else?

Perhaps I might. But where is the money to come from? Surely some way of getting it struck me a day or two since? Yes; that mean idea of asking Armadale to help me! Well; I *will* be mean for once. I'll give him the chance of making a generous use of that well-filled purse which it is such a comfort to him to reflect on in his present circumstances. It would soften my heart towards any man if he lent me money in my present extremity; and if Armadale lends me money, it might soften my heart towards *him*. When shall I go? At once! I won't give myself time to feel the degradation of it, and to change my mind.

Three o'clock. – I mark the hour. He has sealed his own doom. He has insulted me.

Yes! I have suffered it once from Miss Milroy. And I have now suffered it a second time from Armadale himself. An insult – a marked, merciless, deliberate insult in the open day!

I had got through the town, and had advanced a few hundred yards along the road that leads to the great house, when I saw Armadale, at a little distance, coming towards me. He was walking fast, evidently, with some errand of his own to take him to the town. The instant he caught sight of me he stopped, coloured up, took off his hat, hesitated, and turned aside down a lane behind him, which I happen to know would take him exactly in the contrary direction to the direction in which he was walking when he first saw me. His conduct said, in so many words, 'Miss Milroy may hear of it; I daren't run the risk of being seen speaking to you.' Men have used me heartlessly; men have done and said hard things to me – but no man living ever yet treated me as if I was plague-struck, and as if the very air about me was infected by my presence!

I say no more. When he walked away from me down that lane, he walked to his death. I have written to Midwinter to expect me in London next week, and to be ready for our marriage soon afterwards.

Four o'clock. – Half-an-hour since, I put on my bonnet to go out and post the letter to Midwinter myself. And here I am, still in my room, with my mind torn by doubts, and my letter on the table.

Armadale counts for nothing in the perplexities that are now torturing me. It is Midwinter who makes me hesitate. Can I take the first of those three steps that lead me to the end, without the common caution of looking at consequences? Can I marry Midwinter, without knowing beforehand how to meet the obstacle of my husband, when the time comes which transforms me from the living Armadale's wife, to the dead Armadale's widow?

Why can't I think of it, when I know I *must* think of it? Why can't I look at it as steadily as I have looked at all the rest? I feel his kisses on my lips; I feel his tears on my bosom; I feel his arms round me again. He is far away in London – and yet, he is here and won't let me think of it!

Why can't I wait a little? Why can't I let Time help me? Time? It's Saturday! What need is there to think of it, unless I like? There is no post to London to-day. I *must* wait. If I posted the letter it wouldn't go. Besides, to-morrow I may hear from Mrs Oldershaw. I ought to wait to hear from Mrs Oldershaw. I can't consider myself a free woman till I know what Mrs Oldershaw means to do. There is a necessity for waiting till to-morrow. I shall take my bonnet off, and lock the letter up in my desk.

Sunday morning. – There is no resisting it! One after another the circumstances crowd on me. They come thicker and thicker, and they all force me one way.

I have got Mother Oldershaw's answer. The wretch fawns on me, and cringes to me. I can see, as plainly as if she had acknowledged it, that she suspects me of seeing my own way to success at Thorpe-Ambrose without her assistance. Having found threatening me useless, she tries coaxing me now. I am her darling Lydia again! She is quite shocked that I could imagine she ever really intended to arrest her bosom friend – and she has only to entreat me, as a favour to herself, to renew the bill!

I say once more, no mortal creature could resist it! Time after time I have tried to escape the temptation; and time after time the circumstances drive me back again. I can struggle no longer. The post that takes the letters to-night shall take my letter to Midwinter among the rest.

To-night! If I give myself till to-night, something else may happen. If I give myself till to-night, I may hesitate again. I'm weary of the torture of hesitating. I must and will have relief in the present, cost what it may in the future. My letter to Midwinter will drive me mad if I see it staring and staring at me in my desk any longer. I can post it in ten minutes' time – and I will!

It is done. The first of the three steps that lead me to the end, is a step taken. My mind is quieter – the letter is in the post.

By to-morrow Midwinter will receive it. Before the end of the week, Armadale must be publicly seen to leave Thorpe-Ambrose; and I must be publicly seen to leave with him.

Have I looked at the consequences of my marriage to Midwinter? No! Do I know how to meet the obstacle of my husband, when the time comes which transforms me from the living Armadale's wife, to the dead Armadale's widow?

No! When the time comes, I must meet the obstacle as I best may. I am going blindfold then – so far as Midwinter is concerned – into this frightful risk? Yes; blindfold. Am I out of my senses? Very likely. Or am I a little too fond of him to look the thing in the face? I daresay. Who cares?

I won't, I won't, I won't think of it! Haven't I a will of my own? And can't I think, if I like, of something else?

Here is Mother Jezebel's cringing letter. *That* is something else to think of. I'll answer it. I am in a fine humour for writing to Mother Jezebel.

Conclusion of Miss Gwilt's Letter to Mrs Oldershaw

... I told you, when I broke off, that I would wait before I finished this, and ask my Diary if I could safely tell you what I have now got it in my mind to do. Well, I have asked; and my Diary says, 'Don't tell her!' Under these circumstances, I close my letter – with my best excuses for leaving you in the dark.

I shall probably be in London before long – and I may tell you by word of mouth what I don't think it safe to write here. Mind, I make no promise! It all depends on how I feel towards you at the time. I don't doubt your discretion – but (under certain circumstances) I am not so sure of your courage.

L. G.

P.S. – My best thanks for your permission to renew the bill. I decline profiting by the proposal. The money will be ready, when the money is due. I have a friend now in London who will pay it, if I ask him. Do you wonder who the friend is? You will wonder at one or two other things, Mrs Oldershaw, before many weeks more are over your head and mine.

CHAPTER XI

LOVE AND LAW

On the morning of Monday, the twenty-eighth of July, Miss Gwilt – once more on the watch for Allan and Neelie – reached her customary post of observation in the park, by the usual roundabout way.

She was a little surprised to find Neelie alone at the place of meeting. She was more seriously astonished, when the tardy Allan made his appearance ten minutes later, to see him mounting the side of the dell, with a large volume under his arm, and to hear him say, as an apology for being late, that 'he had muddled away his time in hunting for the Books; and that he had only found one, after all, which seemed in the least likely to repay either Neelie or himself for the trouble of looking into it.'

If Miss Gwilt had waited long enough in the park, on the previous Saturday, to hear the lovers' parting words on that occasion, she would have been at no loss to explain the mystery of the volume under Allan's arm, and she would have understood the apology which he now offered for being late, as readily as Neelie herself.

There is a certain exceptional occasion in life – the occasion of marriage – on which even girls in their teens sometimes become capable (more or less hysterically) of looking at consequences. At the farewell moment of the interview on Saturday, Neelie's mind had suddenly precipitated itself into the future; and she had utterly confounded Allan by inquiring whether the contemplated elopement was an offence punishable by the Law? Her memory satisfied her that she had certainly read somewhere, at some former period, in some book or other (possibly a novel), of an elopement with a dreadful end – of a bride dragged home in hysterics – and of a bridegroom sentenced to languish in prison, with all his beautiful hair cut off, by Act of Parliament, close to his head. Supposing she could bring herself to consent to the elopement at all – which she positively declined to promise – she must first insist on discovering whether there was any fear of the police being concerned in her marriage as well as the parson and the clerk. Allan being a man, ought to know; and to Allan she looked for information – with this preliminary assurance to assist him in laying down the law, that she would die of a broken heart a thousand times over, rather than be the innocent means of sending him to languish in prison, and of cutting his hair off, by Act of Parliament, close to his head. 'It's no laughing matter,' said Neelie resolutely, in conclusion; 'I decline even to think of our marriage, till my mind is made easy first on the subject of the Law.'

'But I don't know anything about the law, not even as much as you do,' said Allan. 'Hang the law! I don't mind my head being cropped. Let's risk it.'

'Risk it?' repeated Neelie, indignantly. 'Have you no consideration for *me*? I won't risk it! Where there's a will, there's a way. We must find out the law for ourselves.'

'With all my heart,' said Allan. 'How?'

'Out of books, to be sure! There must be quantities of information in that enormous library of yours at the great house. If you really love me, you won't mind going over the backs of a few thousand books, for my sake!'

'I'll go over the backs of ten thousand!' cried Allan, warmly. 'Would you mind telling me what I'm to look for?'

'For "Law", to be sure! When it says "Law" on the back, open it, and look inside for Marriage – read every word of it – and then come here and explain it to me. What? you don't think your head is to be trusted to do such a simple thing as that?'

'I'm certain it isn't,' said Allan. 'Can't you help me?'

'Of course I can, if you can't manage without me! Law may be hard, but it can't be harder than music; and I must, and will, satisfy my mind. Bring me all the books you can find, on Monday morning – in a wheelbarrow, if there are a good many of them, and if you can't manage it in any other way.'

The result of this conversation was Allan's appearance in the park, with a volume of Blackstone's Commentaries under his arm, on the fatal Monday morning, when Miss Gwilt's written engagement of marriage was placed in Midwinter's hands. Here again, in this, as in all other human instances, the widely discordant elements of the grotesque and the terrible were forced together by that subtle law of contrast which is one of the laws of mortal life. Amid all the thickening complications now impending over their heads – with the shadow of meditated murder stealing towards one of them already, from the lurking-place that hid Miss Gwilt – the two sat down, unconscious of the future, with the book between them; and applied themselves to the study of the law of marriage, with a grave resolution to understand it, which, in two such students, was nothing less than a burlesque in itself!

'Find the place,' said Neelie, as soon as they were comfortably established. 'We must manage this, by what they call a division of labour. You shall read – and I'll take notes.'

She produced forthwith a smart little pocket-book and pencil, and opened the book in the middle, where there was a blank page on the right hand and the left. At the top of the right-hand page, she wrote the word, *Good*. At the top of the left-hand page, she wrote the word, *Bad*. '"Good" means where the law is on our side,' she explained; 'and "Bad" means where the law is against us. We will have "Good" and "Bad" opposite each other, all down the two pages; and when we get to the bottom, we'll add them up, and act accordingly. They say girls have no heads for business. Haven't they! Don't look at me – look at Blackstone, and begin.'

'Would you mind giving me a kiss first?' asked Allan.

'I should mind it very much. In our serious situation, when we have both got to exert our intellects, I wonder you can ask for such a thing!'

'That's why I asked for it,' said the unblushing Allan. 'I feel as if it would clear my head.'

'Oh, if it would clear your head, that's quite another thing! I must clear your head, of course, at any sacrifice. Only one, mind,' she whispered coquettishly; 'and pray be careful of Blackstone, or you'll lose the place.'

There was a pause in the conversation. Blackstone and the pocket-book both rolled on the ground together.

'If this happens again,' said Neelie, picking up the pocket-book, with her eyes and her complexion at their brightest and best, 'I shall sit with my back to you for the rest of the morning. *Will* you go on?'

Allan found his place for the second time, and fell headlong into the bottomless abyss of the English Law.

'Page two-hundred-and-eighty,' he began. 'Law of husband and wife. Here's a bit I don't understand, to begin with: "It may be observed generally, that the law considers marriage in the light of a Contract." What does that mean? I thought a contract was the sort of thing a builder signs, when he promises to have the workmen out of the house in a given time, and when the time comes (as my poor mother used to say) the workmen never go.'

'Is there nothing about Love?' asked Neelie. 'Look a little lower down.'

'Not a word. He sticks to his confounded "Contract", all the way through.'

'Then he's a brute! Go on to something else that's more in our way.'

'Here's a bit that's more in our way: "Incapacities. If any persons under legal incapacities come together, it is a meretricious, and not a matrimonial union." (Blackstone's a good one at long words, isn't he? I wonder what he means by meretricious?) "The first of these legal disabilities is a prior marriage, and having another husband or wife living—"'

'Stop!' said Neelie. 'I must make a note of that.' She gravely made her first entry on the page headed 'Good,' as follows: 'I have no husband, and Allan has no wife. We are both entirely unmarried at the present time.'

'All right, so far,' remarked Allan, looking over her shoulder.

'Go on,' said Neelie. 'What next?'

'"The next disability,"' proceeded Allan, '"is want of age. The age for consent to matrimony is, fourteen in males, and twelve in females." Come!' cried Allan cheerfully, 'Blackstone begins early enough at any rate!'

Neelie was too business-like to make any other remark, on her side, than the necessary remark in the pocket-book. She made another entry under the head of 'Good' – '"I am old enough to consent, and so is Allan too." Go on,' resumed Neelie, looking over the reader's shoulder. 'Never mind all that prosing of Blackstone's, about the husband being of years of discretion, and the wife under twelve. Abominable wretch! the wife under twelve! Skip to the third incapacity, if there is one.'

'The third incapacity,' Allan went on, 'is want of reason.'

Neelie immediately made a third entry on the side of 'Good': ' "Allan and I are both perfectly reasonable." – Skip to the next page.'

Allan skipped. 'A fourth incapacity is in respect of proximity of relationship.'

A fourth entry followed instantly on the cheering side of the pocket-book: ' "He loves me and I love him – without our being in the slightest degree related to each other." Any more?' asked Neelie, tapping her chin impatiently with the end of the pencil.

'Plenty more,' rejoined Allan; 'all in hieroglyphics. Look here: "Marriage Acts, 4 Geo. iv. c. 76, and 6 and 7 Will. iv. c. 85 (q)." Blackstone's intellect seems to be wandering here. Shall we take another skip, and see if he picks himself up again on the next page.'

'Wait a little,' said Neelie; 'what's that I see in the middle?' She read for a minute in silence, over Allan's shoulder, and suddenly clasped her hands in despair. 'I knew I was right!' she exclaimed. 'Oh, heavens, here it is!'

'Where?' asked Allan. 'I see nothing about languishing in prison, and cropping a fellow's hair close to his head, unless it's in the hieroglyphics. Is "4 Geo. iv." short for "Lock him up"? and does "c. 85 (q)" mean, "Send for the hair-cutter"?'

'Pray be serious,' remonstrated Neelie. 'We are both sitting on a volcano. There!' she said, pointing to the place. 'Read it! If anything can bring you to a proper sense of our situation, *that* will.'

Allan cleared his throat, and Neelie held the point of her pencil ready on the depressing side of the account – otherwise the 'Bad' page of the pocket-book.

' "And as it is the policy of our law," Allan began, "to prevent the marriage of persons under the age of twenty-one, without the consent of parents and guardians" ' – (Neelie made her first entry on the side of 'Bad.' 'I am only seventeen next birthday, and circumstances forbid me to confide my attachment to papa') – ' "it is provided that in the case of the publication of banns of a person under twenty-one, not being a widower or widow, who are deemed emancipated" ' – (Neelie made another entry on the depressing side. 'Allan is not a widower, and I am not a widow; consequently, we are neither of us emancipated,') – '"if the parent or guardian openly signifies his dissent at the time the banns are published"' – ('which papa would be certain to do') – '"such publication shall be void." I'll take breath here, if you'll allow me,' said Allan. 'Blackstone might put it in shorter sentences, I think, if he can't put it in fewer words. Cheer up, Neelie! there must be other ways of marrying, besides this roundabout way, that ends in a Publication and a Void. Infernal gibberish! I could write better English myself.'

'We are not at the end of it yet,' said Neelie. 'The Void is nothing to what is to come.'

'Whatever it is,' rejoined Allan, 'we'll treat it like a dose of physic – we'll take it at once, and be done with it.' He went on reading: '"And no licence to marry without banns shall be granted, unless oath shall be first made by one of the parties that he or she believes that there is no impediment of kindred or alliance" – well, I can take my oath of that with a safe conscience! What next? "And one of the said parties must, for the space of fifteen days immediately preceding such licence, have had his or her usual place of abode within the parish or chapelry within which such marriage is to be solemnized!" Chapelry! I'd live fifteen days in a dog-kennel with the greatest pleasure. I say, Neelie, all this seems like plain sailing enough. What are you shaking your head about? Go on, and I shall see? Oh, all right; I'll go on. Here we are – "And where one of the said parties, not being a widower or widow, shall be under the age of twenty-one years, oath must first be made that the consent of the person or persons whose consent is required, has been obtained, or that there is no person having authority to give such consent. The consent required by this Act is that of the father—"' At those last formidable words Allan came to a full stop. 'The consent of the father,' he repeated, with all needful seriousness of look and manner. 'I couldn't exactly swear to that, could I?'

Neelie answered in expressive silence. She handed him the pocket-book, with the final entry completed, on the side of 'Bad,' in these terms – 'Our marriage is impossible, unless Allan commits perjury.'

The lovers looked at each other across the insuperable obstacle of Blackstone, in speechless dismay.

'Shut up the book,' said Neelie, resignedly. 'I have no doubt we should find the police, and the prison, and the hair-cutting – all punishments for perjury, exactly as I told you! – if we looked at the next page. But we needn't trouble ourselves to look; we have found out quite enough already. It's all over with us. I must go to school on Saturday, and you must manage to forget me as soon as you can. Perhaps we may meet in after-life, and you may be a widower and I may be a widow, and the cruel law may consider us emancipated, when it's too late to be of the slightest use. By that time no doubt I shall be old and ugly, and you will naturally have ceased to care about me, and it will all end in the grave, and the sooner the better. Good-by,' concluded Neelie, rising mournfully, with the tears in her eyes. 'It's only prolonging our misery to stop here, unless – unless you have anything to propose?'

'I've got something to propose,' cried the headlong Allan. 'It's an entirely new idea. Would you mind trying the blacksmith at Gretna Green?'[1]

'No earthly consideration,' answered Neelie indignantly, 'would induce me to be married by a blacksmith!'

'Don't be offended,' pleaded Allan; 'I meant it for the best. Lots of people in our situation have tried the blacksmith, and found him quite as good as a clergyman, and a most amiable man, I believe, into the bargain. Never mind! We must try another string to our bow.'

'We haven't got another to try,' said Neelie.

'Take my word for it,' persisted Allan stoutly, 'there must be ways and means of circumventing Blackstone (without perjury), if we only knew of them. It's a matter of law, and we must consult somebody in the profession. I daresay it's a risk. But nothing venture, nothing have. What do you say to young Pedgift? He's a thorough good fellow. I'm sure we could trust young Pedgift to keep our secret.'

'Not for worlds!' exclaimed Neelie. 'You may be willing to trust your secrets to the vulgar little wretch, I won't have him trusted with mine. I hate him. No!' she continued, with a mounting colour and a peremptory stamp of her foot on the grass. 'I positively forbid you to take any of the Thorpe-Ambrose people into your confidence. They would instantly suspect *me*, and it would be all over the place in a moment. My attachment may be an unhappy one,' remarked Neelie, with her handkerchief to her eyes, 'and papa may nip it in the bud, but I won't have it profaned by the town-gossip!'

'Hush! hush!' said Allan. 'I won't say a word at Thorpe-Ambrose, I won't indeed!' He paused, and considered for a moment. 'There's another way!' he burst out, brightening up on the instant. 'We've got the whole week before us. I'll tell you what I'll do, I'll go to London!'

There was a sudden rustling – heard neither by one nor the other – among the trees behind them that screened Miss Gwilt. One more of the difficulties in her way (the difficulty of getting Allan to London), now promised to be removed by an act of Allan's own will.

'To London?' repeated Neelie, looking up in astonishment.

'To London!' reiterated Allan. 'That's far enough away from Thorpe-Ambrose, surely? Wait a minute, and don't forget that this is a question of law. Very well, I know some lawyers in London who managed all my business for me when I first came in for this property; they are just the men to consult. And if they decline to be mixed up in it, there's their head clerk, who is one of the best fellows I ever met with in my life. I asked him to go yachting with me, I remember; and though he couldn't go, he said he felt the obligation all the same. That's the man to help us. Blackstone's a mere infant to him. Don't say it's absurd; don't say it's exactly like *me*. Do pray hear me out. I won't breathe your name or your father's. I'll describe you as "a young lady to whom I am devotedly attached". And if my friend the clerk asks where you live, I'll say the north of Scotland, or the west of Ireland, or the Channel Islands, or anywhere else you like. My friend the clerk is a total stranger to Thorpe-Ambrose and everybody in it (which is one recommendation); and in five minutes' time, he'd put me up to what to do (which is another). If you only knew him! He's one of those extraordinary men who appear once or twice in a century – the sort of man who won't allow you to make a mistake if you try. All I have got to say to him (putting it short) is, "My dear fellow, I want to be privately married, without perjury." All he has got to say to me (putting it short) is, "You must do So-and-So, and So-and-So; and you must be careful to avoid This, That, and The other. I have nothing in the world to do but to follow his directions; and you have nothing in the world to do but what the bride always does when the bridegroom is ready and waiting!' His arm stole round Neelie's waist, and his lips pointed the moral of the last sentence with that inarticulate eloquence which is so uniformly successful in persuading a woman against her will.

All Neelie's meditated objections dwindled, in spite of her, to one feeble little question. 'Suppose I allow you to go, Allan?' she whispered, toying nervously with the stud in the bosom of his shirt, 'Shall you be very long away?'

'I'll be off to-day,' said Allan, 'by the eleven o'clock train. And I'll be back to-morrow, if I and my friend the clerk can settle it all in time. If not, by Wednesday at latest.'

'You'll write to me every day?' pleaded Neelie, clinging a little closer to him. 'I shall sink under the suspense, if you don't promise to write to me every day.'

Allan promised to write twice a day, if she liked – letter-writing, which was such an effort to other men, was no effort to *him*!

'And mind, whatever those people may say to you in London,'

proceeded Neelie, 'I insist on your coming back for me. I positively decline to run away, unless you promise to fetch me.'

Allan promised for the second time, on his sacred word of honour, and at the full compass of his voice. But Neelie was not satisfied even yet. She reverted to first principles, and insisted on knowing whether Allan was quite sure he loved her. Allan called heaven to witness how sure he was; and got another question directly for his pains. Could he solemnly declare that he would never regret taking Neelie away from home? Allan called heaven to witness again, louder than ever. All to no purpose! The ravenous female appetite for tender protestations still hungered for more. 'I know what will happen one of these days,' persisted Neelie. 'You will see some other girl who is prettier than I am; and you will wish you had married her instead of Me!'

As Allan opened his lips for a final outburst of asseveration, the stable-clock at the great house was faintly audible in the distance, striking the hour. Neelie started guiltily. It was breakfast-time at the cottage – in other words, time to take leave. At the last moment her heart went back to her father; and her head sank on Allan's bosom as she tried to say, Good-by. 'Papa has always been so kind to me, Allan,' she whispered, holding him back tremulously when he turned to leave her. 'It seems so guilty and so heartless to go away from him and be married in secret. Oh, do, do think before you really go to London; is there no way of making him a little kinder and juster to *you*?' The question was useless; the major's resolutely unfavourable reception of Allan's letter rose in Neelie's memory, and answered her as the words passed her lips. With a girl's impulsiveness, she pushed Allan away before he could speak, and signed to him impatiently to go. The conflict of contending emotions, which she had mastered thus far, burst its way outward in spite of her after he had waved his hand for the last time, and had disappeared in the depths of the dell. When she turned from the place, on her side, her long-restrained tears fell freely at last, and made the lonely way back to the cottage the dimmest prospect that Neelie had seen for many a long day past.

As she hurried homeward, the leaves parted behind her, and Miss Gwilt stepped softly into the open space. She stood there in triumph, tall, beautiful, and resolute. Her lovely colour brightened while she watched Neelie's retreating figure hastening lightly away from her over the grass.

'Cry, you little fool!' she said, with her quiet clear tones, and her steady smile of contempt. 'Cry as you have never cried yet! You have seen the last of your sweetheart.'

CHAPTER XII

A SCANDAL AT THE STATION

An hour later, the landlady at Miss Gwilt's lodgings was lost in astonishment, and the clamorous tongues of the children were in a state of ungovernable revolt. 'Unforeseen circumstances' had suddenly obliged the tenant of the first floor to terminate the occupation of her apartments, and to go to London that day by the eleven o'clock train.

'Please to have a fly at the door, at half-past ten,' said Miss Gwilt, as the amazed landlady followed her upstairs. 'And excuse me, you good creature, if I beg and pray not to be disturbed till the fly comes.'

Once inside her room, she locked the door, and then opened her writing-desk. 'Now for my letter to the major!' she said. 'How shall I word it?'

A moment's consideration apparently decided her. Searching through her collection of pens, she carefully selected the worst that could be found, and began the letter by writing the date of the day on a soiled sheet of note-paper, in crooked clumsy characters, which ended in a blot made purposely with the feather of the pen. Pausing, sometimes to think a little, sometimes to make another blot, she completed the letter in these words:

> HON^D SIR, – It is on my conscience to tell you something, which I think you ought to know. You ought to know of the goings-on of Miss, your daughter, with young Mister Armadale. I wish you to make sure, and what is more, I advise you to be quick about it, if she is going the way you want her to go, when she takes her morning walk before breakfast. I scorn to make mischief, where there is true love on both sides. But I don't think the young man means truly by Miss. What I mean is, I think Miss only has his fancy. Another person, who shall be nameless betwixt us, has his true heart. Please to pardon my not putting my name; I am only an humble person, and it might get me into trouble. This is all at present, dear sir, from yours,
>
> A WELL-WISHER.

'There!' said Miss Gwilt, as she folded the letter up. 'If I had been a professed novelist, I could hardly have written more naturally in the character of a servant than that!' She wrote the necessary address to Major Milroy; looked admiringly for the last time at the coarse and clumsy writing which her own delicate hand had produced; and rose to post the letter herself, before she entered next on the serious business of packing up. 'Curious!' she thought, when the letter had been posted, and she was back again making her travelling preparations in her own room; 'here I am, running headlong into a frightful risk – and I never was in better spirits in my life!'

The boxes were ready when the fly was at the door, and Miss Gwilt was equipped (as becomingly as usual) in her neat travelling costume. The thick veil, which she was accustomed to wear in London, appeared on her country straw-bonnet for the first time. 'One meets such rude men occasionally in the railway,' she said to the landlady. 'And though I dress quietly, my hair is so very remarkable.' She was a little paler than usual; but she had never been so sweet-tempered and engaging, so gracefully cordial and friendly, as now, when the moment of departure had come. The simple people of the house were quite moved at taking leave of her. She insisted on shaking hands with the landlord – on speaking to him in her prettiest way, and sunning him in her brightest smiles. 'Come!' she said to the landlady, 'you have been so kind, you have been so like a mother to me, you must give me a kiss at parting.' She embraced the children all together in the lump, with a mixture of humour and tenderness delightful to see, and left a shilling among them to buy a cake. 'If I was only rich enough to make it a sovereign,' she whispered to the mother, 'how glad I should be!' The awkward lad who ran on errands stood waiting at the fly-door. He was clumsy, he was frowsy, he had a gaping mouth and a turn-up nose – but the ineradicable female delight in being charming, accepted him, for all that, in the character of a last chance. 'You dear dingy John!' she said kindly at the carriage door. 'I am so poor I have only sixpence to give you – with my very best wishes. Take my advice, John – grow to be a fine man, and find yourself a nice sweetheart! Thank you a thousand times!' She gave him a friendly little pat on the cheek with two of her gloved fingers, and smiled, and nodded, and got into the fly.

'Armadale next!' she said to herself as the carriage drove off.

Allan's anxiety not to miss the train had brought him to the station in better time than usual. After taking his ticket and putting his portmanteau under the porter's charge, he was pacing the platform and thinking of Neelie – when he heard the rustling of a lady's dress behind him, and turning round to look, found himself face to face with Miss Gwilt.

There was no escaping her this time. The station wall was on his right hand, and the line was on his left; a tunnel was behind him, and Miss Gwilt was in front, inquiring in her sweetest tones whether Mr Armadale was going to London.

Allan coloured scarlet with vexation and surprise. There he was, obviously waiting for the train; and there was his portmanteau close by, with his name on it, already labelled for London! What answer but the true one could he make after that? Could he let the train go without him, and lose the precious hours so vitally important to Neelie and himself? Impossible! Allan helplessly confirmed the printed statement on his portmanteau, and heartily wished himself at the other end of the world as he said the words.

'How very fortunate!' rejoined Miss Gwilt. 'I am going to London too. Might I ask you, Mr Armadale (as you seem to be quite alone), to be my escort on the journey?'

Allan looked at the little assembly of travellers, and travellers' friends, collected on the platform, near the booking-office door. They were all Thorpe-Ambrose people. He was probably known by sight, and Miss Gwilt was probably known by sight, to every one of them. In sheer desperation, hesitating more awkwardly than ever, he produced his cigar-case. 'I should be delighted,' he said, with an embarrassment which was almost an insult under the circumstances. 'But I – I'm what the people who get sick over a cigar, call a slave to smoking.'

'I delight in smoking!' said Miss Gwilt, with undiminished vivacity and good humour. 'It's one of the privileges of the men which I have always envied. I'm afraid, Mr Armadale, you must think I am forcing myself on you. It certainly looks like it. The real truth is, I want particularly to say a word to you in private about Mr Midwinter.'

The train came up at the same moment. Setting Midwinter out of the question, the common decencies of politeness left Allan no alternative but to submit. After having been the cause of her leaving her situation at Major Milroy's, after having pointedly avoided her only a few days since on the high-road, to have declined going to London in the same carriage with Miss Gwilt would have been an act of downright brutality which it was simply impossible to commit. 'Damn her!' said Allan, internally, as he handed his travelling companion into an empty carriage, officiously placed at his disposal, before all the people at the station, by the guard. 'You shan't be disturbed, sir,' the man whispered confidentially, with a smile, and a touch of his hat. Allan could have knocked him down with the utmost pleasure. 'Stop!' he said, from the window. 'I don't want the carriage—' It was useless; the guard was out of hearing; the whistle blew, and the train started for London.

The select assembly of travellers' friends, left behind on the platform, congregated in a circle on the spot, with the station-master in the centre.

The station-master – otherwise, Mr Mack – was a popular character in the neighbourhood. He possessed two social qualifications which invariably impress the average English mind – he was an old soldier, and he was a man of few words. The conclave on the platform insisted on taking his opinion, before it committed itself positively to an opinion of its own. A brisk fire of remarks exploded, as a matter of course, on all sides; but everybody's view of the subject ended interrogatively, in a question aimed point-blank at the station-master's ears.

'She's got him, hasn't she?' 'She'll come back "Mrs Armadale",' won't she?' 'He'd better have stuck to Miss Milroy, hadn't he?' 'Miss Milroy stuck to *him*. She paid him a visit at the great house, didn't she?' 'Nothing of the sort; it's a shame to take the girl's character away. She was caught in a thunderstorm close by; he was obliged to give her shelter; and she's never been near the place since. Miss Gwilt's been there, if you like, with no thunderstorm to force *her* in; and Miss Gwilt's off with him to London in a carriage all to themselves, eh, Mr Mack?' 'Ah, he's a soft one, that Armadale! with all his money, to take up with a red-haired woman, a good eight or nine years older than he is! She's thirty if she's a day. That's what I say, Mr Mack. What do you say?' 'Older or younger, she'll rule the roost at Thorpe-Ambrose; and I say, for the sake of the place, and for the sake of trade, let's make the best of it; and Mr Mack, as a man of the world, sees it in the same light as I do, don't you, sir?'

'Gentlemen,' said the station-master, with his abrupt military accent, and his impenetrable military manner, 'she's a devilish fine woman. And, when I was Mr Armadale's age, it's my opinion, if her fancy had laid that way, she might have married Me.'

With that expression of opinion the station-master wheeled to the right, and intrenched himself impregnably in the stronghold of his own office.

The citizens of Thorpe-Ambrose looked at the closed door, and gravely shook their heads. Mr Mack had disappointed them. No opinion which openly recognizes the frailty of human nature, is ever a popular opinion with mankind. 'It's as good as saying that any of *us* might have married her, if *we* had been Mr Armadale's age!' Such was the general impression on the minds of the conclave, when the meeting had been adjourned, and the members were leaving the station.

The last of the party to go was a slow old gentleman, with a habit of deliberately looking about him. Pausing at the door, this observant person stared up the platform, and down the platform, and discovered in the latter direction, standing behind an angle of the wall, an elderly man in black, who had escaped the notice of everybody up to that time. 'Why, bless my soul!' said the old gentleman, advancing inquisitively by a step at a time, 'it can't be Mr Bashwood!'

It *was* Mr Bashwood – Mr Bashwood, whose constitutional curiosity had taken him privately to the station, bent on solving the mystery of Allan's sudden journey to London – Mr Bashwood who had seen and heard, behind his angle in the wall, what everybody else had seen and heard, and who appeared to have been impressed by it in no ordinary way. He stood stiffly against the wall, like a man petrified, with one hand pressed on his bare head, and the other holding his hat – he stood, with a dull flush on his face, and a dull stare in his eyes, looking straight into the black depths of the tunnel outside the station, as if the train to London had disappeared in it but the moment before.

'Is your head bad?' asked the old gentleman. 'Take my advice. Go home and lie down.'

Mr Bashwood listened mechanically, with his usual attention, and answered mechanically, with his usual politeness.

'Yes, sir,' he said, in a low lost tone, like a man between dreaming and waking; 'I'll go home and lie down.'

'That's right,' rejoined the old gentleman, making for the door. 'And take a pill, Mr Bashwood – take a pill.'

Five minutes later, the porter charged with the business of locking up the station, found Mr Bashwood, still standing bareheaded against the wall, and still looking straight into the black depths of the tunnel, as if the train to London had disappeared in it but a moment since.

'Come, sir!' said the porter. 'I must lock up. Are you out of sorts? Anything wrong with your inside? Try a drop of gin-and-bitters.'

'Yes,' said Mr Bashwood, answering the porter exactly as he had answered the old gentleman; 'I'll try a drop of gin-and-bitters.'

The porter took him by the arm, and led him out. 'You'll get it there,' said the man, pointing confidentially to a public-house; 'and you'll get it good.'

'I shall get it there,' echoed Mr Bashwood, still mechanically repeating what was said to him; 'and I shall get it good.'

His will seemed to be paralysed; his actions depended absolutely on what other people told him to do. He took a few steps in the direction of the public-house – hesitated; staggered – and caught at the pillar of one of the station lamps near him.

The porter followed, and took him by the arm once more.

'Why, you've been drinking already!' exclaimed the man, with a suddenly-quickened interest in Mr Bashwood's case. 'What was it? Beer?'

Mr Bashwood, in his low lost tones, echoed the last word.

It was close on the porter's dinner-time. But when the lower orders of the English people believe they have discovered an intoxicated man, their sympathy with him is boundless. The porter let his dinner take its chance, and carefully assisted Mr Bashwood to reach the public-house. 'Gin-and-bitters will put you on your legs again,' whispered this Samaritan setter-right of the alcoholic disasters of mankind.

If Mr Bashwood had really been intoxicated, the effect of the porter's remedy would have been marvellous indeed. Almost as soon as the glass was emptied, the stimulant did its work. The long-weakened nervous system of the deputy-steward, prostrated for the moment by the shock that had fallen on it, rallied again like a weary horse under the spur. The dull flush on his cheeks, the dull stare in his eyes, disappeared simultaneously. After a momentary effort, he recovered memory enough of what had passed to thank the porter, and to ask whether he would take something himself. The worthy creature instantly accepted a dose of his own remedy – in the capacity of a preventive – and went home to dinner as only those men can go home who are physically warmed by gin-and-bitters, and morally elevated by the performance of a good action.

Still strangely abstracted (but conscious now of the way by which he went), Mr Bashwood left the public-house a few minutes later, in his turn. He walked on mechanically, in his dreary black garments, moving like a blot on the white surface of the sun-brightened road, as Midwinter had seen him move in the early days at Thorpe-Ambrose when they had first met. Arrived at the point where he had to choose between the way that led into the town, and the way that led to the great house, he stopped, incapable of deciding, and careless, apparently, even of making the attempt. 'I'll be revenged on her!' he whispered to himself, still absorbed in his jealous frenzy of rage against the woman who had deceived him. 'I'll be revenged on her,' he repeated in louder tones, 'if I spend every halfpenny I've got!'

Some women of the disorderly sort, passing on their way to the town, heard him. 'Ah, you old brute,' they called out, with the measureless licence of their class; 'whatever she did, she served you right!'

The coarseness of the voices startled him, whether he comprehended the words or not. He shrank away from more interruption and more insult, into the quieter road that led to the great house.

At a solitary place by the wayside, he stopped and sat down. He took off his hat, and lifted his youthful wig a little from his bald old head, and tried desperately to get beyond the one immovable conviction which lay on his mind like lead – the conviction that Miss Gwilt had been purposely deceiving him from the first. It was useless. No effort would free him from that one dominant impression, and from the one answering idea that it had evoked – the idea of revenge. He got up again, and put on his hat, and walked rapidly forward a little way – then turned without knowing why, and slowly walked back again. 'If I had only dressed a little smarter!' said the poor wretch, helplessly. 'If I had only been a little bolder with her, she might have overlooked my being an old man!' The angry fit returned on him. He clenched his clammy trembling hands, and shook them fiercely in the empty air. 'I'll be revenged on her,' he reiterated. 'I'll be revenged on her, if I spend every halfpenny I've got!' It was terribly suggestive of the hold she had taken on him, that his vindictive sense of injury could not get far enough away from her to reach the man whom he believed to be his rival, even yet. In his rage, as in his love, he was absorbed, body and soul, by Miss Gwilt.

In a moment more, the noise of running wheels approaching from behind startled him. He turned, and looked round. There was Mr Pedgift the elder, rapidly overtaking him in the gig, just as Mr Pedgift had overtaken him once already, on that former occasion when he had listened under the window at the great house, and when the lawyer had bluntly charged him with feeling a curiosity about Miss Gwilt!

In an instant, the inevitable association of ideas burst on his mind. The opinion of Miss Gwilt, which he had heard the lawyer express to Allan, at parting, flashed back into his memory, side by side with Mr Pedgift's sarcastic approval of anything in the way of inquiry which his own curiosity might attempt. 'I may be even with her yet,' he thought, 'if Mr Pedgift will help me! – Stop, sir!' he called out desperately as the gig came up with him. 'If please, sir, I want to speak to you.'

Pedgift Senior slackened the pace of his fast-trotting mare, without pulling up. 'Come to the office in half-an-hour,' he said. 'I'm busy now.' Without waiting for an answer, without noticing Mr Bashwood's bow, he gave the mare the rein again, and was out of sight in another minute.

Mr Bashwood sat down once more in a shady place by the roadside. He appeared to be incapable of feeling any slight but the one unpardonable slight put upon him by Miss Gwilt. He not only declined to resent, he even made the best of Mr Pedgift's unceremonious treatment of him. 'Half-an-hour,' he said, resignedly. 'Time enough to compose myself; and I want time. Very kind of Mr Pedgift, though he mightn't have meant it.'

The sense of oppression on his head forced him once again to remove his hat. He sat with it on his lap, deep in thought; his face bent low, and the wavering fingers of one hand drumming absently on the crown of the hat. If Mr Pedgift the elder, seeing him as he sat now, could only have looked a little beyond him into the future, the monotonously-drumming hand of the deputy-steward might have been strong enough, feeble as it was, to stop the lawyer by the roadside. It was the worn, weary, miserable old hand of a worn, weary, miserable old man – but it was, for all that (to use the language of Mr Pedgift's own parting prediction to Allan), the hand that was now destined to 'let the light in on Miss Gwilt'.

CHAPTER XIII

AN OLD MAN'S HEART

Punctual to the moment, when the half hour's interval had expired, Mr Bashwood was announced at the office, as waiting to see Mr Pedgift by special appointment.

The lawyer looked up from his papers with an air of annoyance: he had totally forgotten the meeting by the roadside. 'See what he wants,' said Pedgift Senior to Pedgift Junior, working in the same room with him. 'And, if it's nothing of importance, put it off to some other time.'

Pedgift Junior swiftly disappeared, and swiftly returned.

'Well?' asked the father.

'Well,' answered the son, 'he is rather more shaky and unintelligible than usual. I can make nothing out of him, except that he persists in wanting to see you. My own idea,' pursued Pedgift Junior, with his usual sardonic gravity, 'is, that he is going to have a fit, and that he wishes to acknowledge your uniform kindness to him, by obliging you with a private view of the whole proceeding.'

Pedgift Senior habitually matched everybody – his son included – with their own weapons. 'Be good enough to remember, Augustus,' he rejoined, 'that My Room is not a Court of Law. A bad joke is not invariably followed by "roars of laughter" *here*. Let Mr Bashwood come in.'

Mr Bashwood was introduced, and Pedgift Junior withdrew. 'You mustn't bleed him, sir,'[1] whispered the incorrigible joker, as he passed the back of his father's chair. 'Hot-water bottles to the soles of his feet, and a mustard plaster on the pit of his stomach – that's the modern treatment.'

'Sit down, Bashwood,' said Pedgift Senior, when they were alone. 'And don't forget that time's money. Out with it, whatever it is, at the quickest possible rate, and in the fewest possible words.'

These preliminary directions, bluntly but not at all unkindly spoken, rather increased than diminished the painful agitation under which Mr Bashwood was suffering. He stammered more helplessly, he trembled more continuously than usual, as he made his little speech of thanks, and added his apologies at the end for intruding on his patron in business hours.

'Everybody in the place, Mr Pedgift, sir, knows your time is valuable. Oh, dear, yes! oh, dear, yes! most valuable, most valuable! Excuse me, sir, I'm coming out with it. Your goodness – or rather your business – no, your goodness gave me half-an-hour to wait – and I have thought of what I had to say, and prepared it, and put it short.' Having got as far as that, he stopped with a pained, bewildered look. He had put it away in his memory, and now, when the time came, he was too confused to find it. And there was Mr Pedgift mutely waiting; his face and manner alike expressive of that silent sense of the value of his own time, which every patient who has visited a great doctor, every client who has consulted a lawyer in large practice, knows so well. 'Have you heard the news, sir?' stammered Mr Bashwood, shifting his ground in despair, and letting the uppermost idea in his mind escape him, simply because it was the one idea in him that was ready to come out.

'Does it concern *me*?' asked Pedgift Senior, mercilessly brief, and mercilessly straight in coming to the point.

'It concerns a lady, sir, – no, not a lady – a young man I ought to say, in whom you used to feel some interest. Oh, Mr Pedgift, sir, what do you think! Mr Armadale and Miss Gwilt have gone up to London together to-day – alone, sir – alone in a carriage reserved for their two selves. Do you think he's going to marry her? Do you really think, like the rest of them, he's going to marry her?'

He put the question with a sudden flush in his face, and a sudden energy in his manner. His sense of the value of the lawyer's time, his conviction of the greatness of the lawyer's condescension, his constitutional shyness and timidity – all yielded together to his one overwhelming interest in hearing Mr Pedgift's answer. He was loud for the first time in his life, in putting the question.

'After my experience of Mr Armadale,' said the lawyer, instantly hardening in look and manner, 'I believe him to be infatuated enough to marry Miss Gwilt a dozen times over, if Miss Gwilt chose to ask him. Your news doesn't surprise me in the least, Bashwood. I'm sorry for him. I can honestly say that, though he *has* set my advice at defiance. And I'm more sorry still,' he continued, softening again as his mind reverted to his interview with Neelie under the trees of the park; 'I'm more sorry still for another person who shall be nameless. But what have I to do with all this? and what on earth is the matter with you?' he resumed, noticing for the first time the abject misery in Mr Bashwood's manner, the blank despair in Mr Bashwood's face, which his answer had produced. 'Are you ill? Is there something behind the curtain that you're afraid to bring out? I don't understand it. Have you come here – here in my private room, in business hours – with nothing to tell me but that young Armadale has been fool enough to ruin his prospects for life? Why, I foresaw it all weeks since, and what is more, I as good as told him so at the last conversation I had with him in the great house.'

At those last words, Mr Bashwood suddenly rallied. The lawyer's passing reference to the great house had led him back in a moment to the purpose that he had in view.

'That's it, sir!' he said eagerly; 'that's what I wanted to speak to you about; that's what I've been preparing in my mind. Mr Pedgift, sir, the last time you were at the great house, when you came away in your gig, you – you overtook me on the drive.'

'I daresay I did,' remarked Pedgift, resignedly. 'My mare happens to be a trifle quicker on her legs than you are on yours, Bashwood. Go on, go on. We shall come in time, I suppose, to what you are driving at.'

'You stopped, and spoke to me, sir,' proceeded Mr Bashwood, advancing more and more eagerly to his end. 'You said you suspected me of feeling some curiosity about Miss Gwilt, and you told me (I remember the exact words, sir) – you told me to gratify my curiosity by all means, for you didn't object to it.'

Pedgift Senior began for the first time to look interested in hearing more.

'I remember something of the sort,' he replied; 'and I also remember thinking it rather remarkable that you should *happen* – we won't put it in any more offensive way – to be exactly under Mr Armadale's open window while I was talking to him. It might have been accident of course; but it looked rather more like curiosity. I could only judge by appearances,' concluded Pedgift, pointing his sarcasm with a pinch of snuff; 'and appearances, Bashwood, were decidedly against you.'

'I don't deny it, sir. I only mentioned the circumstance because I wished to acknowledge that I *was* curious, and *am* curious about Miss Gwilt.'

'Why?' asked Pedgift Senior, seeing something under the surface in Mr Bashwood's face and manner, but utterly in the dark thus far as to what that something might be.

There was silence for a moment. The moment passed, Mr Bashwood took the refuge usually taken by nervous unready men, placed in his circumstances, when they are at a loss for an answer. He simply reiterated the assertion that he had just made. 'I feel some curiosity, sir,' he said, with a strange mixture of doggedness and timidity, 'about Miss Gwilt.'

There was another moment of silence. In spite of his practised acuteness and knowledge of the world, the lawyer was more puzzled than ever. The case of Mr Bashwood presented the one human riddle of all others, which he was least qualified to solve. Though year after year witnesses, in thousands and thousands of cases, the remorseless disinheriting of nearest and dearest relations, the unnatural breaking-up of sacred family ties, the deplorable severance of old and firm friendships, due entirely to the intense self-absorption which the sexual passion can produce when it enters the heart of an old man, the association of love with infirmity and grey hairs arouses, nevertheless, all the world over, no other idea than the idea of extravagant improbability or extravagant absurdity in the general mind. If the interview now taking place in Mr Pedgift's consulting-room had taken place at his dinner-table instead, when wine had opened his mind to humorous influences, it is possible that he might, by this time, have suspected the truth. But, in his business hours, Pedgift Senior was in the habit of investigating men's motives seriously from the business point of view; and he was on that very account simply incapable of conceiving any improbability so startling, any absurdity so enormous, as the absurdity and improbability of Mr Bashwood's being in love.

Some men in the lawyer's position would have tried to force their way to enlightenment by obstinately repeating the unanswered question. Pedgift Senior wisely postponed the question until he had moved the conversation on another step. 'Well,' he resumed, 'let us say you feel a curiosity about Miss Gwilt. What next?'

The palms of Mr Bashwood's hands began to moisten under the influence of his agitation, as they had moistened in the past days when he had told the story of his domestic sorrows to Midwinter at the great house. Once more he rolled his handkerchief into a ball, and dabbed it softly to and fro from one hand to the other.

'May I ask if I am right, sir,' he began, 'in believing that you have a very unfavourable opinion of Miss Gwilt? You are quite convinced, I think—'

'My good fellow,' interrupted Pedgift Senior, 'why need you be in any doubt about it? You were under Mr Armadale's open window all the while I was talking to him; and your ears, I presume, were not absolutely shut.'

Mr Bashwood showed no sense of the interruption. The little sting of the lawyer's sarcasm was lost in the nobler pain that wrung him from the wound inflicted by Miss Gwilt.

'You are quite convinced, I think, sir,' he resumed, 'that there are circumstances in this lady's past life, which would be highly discreditable to her if they were discovered at the present time?'

'The window was open at the great house, Bashwood; and your ears, I presume, were not absolutely shut.'

Still impenetrable to the sting, Mr Bashwood persisted more obstinately than ever.

'Unless I am greatly mistaken,' he said, 'your long experience in such things has even suggested to you, sir, that Miss Gwilt might turn out to be known to the police?'

Pedgift Senior's patience gave way. 'You have been over ten minutes in this room,' he broke out; 'can you, or can you not, tell me in plain English what you want?'

In plain English – with the passion that had transformed him, the passion which (in Miss Gwilt's own words) had made a man of him, burning in his haggard cheeks – Mr Bashwood met the challenge, and faced the lawyer (as the worried sheep faces the dog) on his own ground.

'I wish to say, sir,' he answered, 'that your opinion in this matter is my opinion too. I believe there is something wrong in Miss Gwilt's past life, which she keeps concealed from everybody – and I want to be the man who knows it.'

Pedgift Senior saw his chance, and instantly reverted to the question that he had postponed. 'Why?' he asked for the second time.

For the second time, Mr Bashwood hesitated. Could he acknowledge that he had been mad enough to love her, and mean enough to be a spy for her? Could he say, She has deceived me from the first, and she has deserted me now her object is served. After robbing me of my happiness, robbing me of my honour, robbing me of my last hope left in life, she has gone from me for ever, and left me nothing but my old man's longing, slow and sly, and strong and changeless, for revenge. Revenge that I may have, if I can poison her success by dragging her frailties into the public view. Revenge that I will buy (for what is gold or what is life to me?) with the last farthing of my hoarded money and the last drop of my stagnant blood. Could he say that to the man who sat waiting for his answer? No: he could only crush it down and be silent.

The lawyer's expression began to harden once more.[2]

'One of us must speak out,' he said; 'and, as you evidently won't, I will. I can only account for this extraordinary anxiety of yours to make yourself acquainted with Miss Gwilt's secrets, in one of two ways. Your motive is either an excessively mean one (no offence, Bashwood, I am only putting the case), or an excessively generous one. After my experience of your honest character and your creditable conduct, it is only your due that I should absolve you at once of the mean motive. I believe you are as incapable as I am – I can say no more – of turning to mercenary account any discoveries you might make to Miss Gwilt's prejudice in Miss Gwilt's past life. Shall I go on any further? or would you prefer, on second thoughts, opening your mind frankly to me of your own accord?'

'I should prefer not interrupting you, sir,' said Mr Bashwood.

'As you please,' pursued Pedgift Senior. 'Having absolved you of the mean motive, I come to the generous motive next. It is possible that you are an unusually grateful man; and it is certain that Mr Armadale has been remarkably kind to you. After employing you under Mr Midwinter, in the steward's office, he has had confidence enough in your honesty and your capacity, now his friend has left him, to put his business entirely and unreservedly in your hands. It's not in my experience of human nature – but it may be possible nevertheless – that you are so gratefully sensible of that confidence, and so gratefully interested in your employer's welfare, that you can't see him, in his friendless position, going straight to his own disgrace and ruin, without making an effort to save him. To put it in two words. Is it your idea that Mr Armadale might be prevented from marrying Miss Gwilt, if he could be informed in time of her real character? And do you wish to be the man who opens his eyes to the truth? If that is the case—'

He stopped in astonishment. Acting under some uncontrollable impulse, Mr Bashwood had started to his feet. He stood, with his withered face lit up by a sudden irradiation from within, which made him look younger than his age by a good twenty years – he stood, gasping for breath enough to speak, and gesticulated entreatingly at the lawyer with both hands.

'Say it again, sir!' he burst out eagerly; recovering his breath, before Pedgift Senior had recovered his surprise. 'The question about Mr Armadale, sir! – only once more! – only once more, Mr Pedgift, please!'

With his practised observation closely and distrustfully at work on Mr Bashwood's face, Pedgift Senior motioned to him to sit down again, and put the question for the second time.

'Do I think,' said Mr Bashwood, repeating the sense, but not the words of the question, 'that Mr Armadale might be parted from Miss Gwilt, if she could be shown to him as she really is? Yes, sir! And do I wish to be the man who does it? Yes, sir! yes, sir!! yes, sir!!!'

'It's rather strange,' remarked the lawyer, looking at him more and more distrustfully, 'that you should be so violently agitated, simply because my question happens to have hit the mark.'

The question happened to have hit a mark which Pedgift little dreamed of. It had released Mr Bashwood's mind in an instant, from the dead pressure of his one dominant idea of revenge, and had shown him a purpose to be achieved by the discovery of Miss Gwilt's secrets, which had never occurred to him till that moment. The marriage which he had blindly regarded as inevitable, was a marriage that might be stopped – not in Allan's interests, but in his own – and the woman whom he believed that he had lost, might yet, in spite of circumstances, be a woman won! His brain whirled as he thought of it. His own roused resolution almost daunted him, by its terrible incongruity with all the familiar habits of his mind, and all the customary proceedings of his life.

Finding his last remark unanswered, Pedgift Senior considered a little, before he said anything more.[3]

'One thing is clear,' reasoned the lawyer with himself. 'His true motive in this matter, is a motive which he is afraid to avow. My question evidently offered him a chance of misleading me, and he has accepted it on the spot. That's enough for *me*. If I was Mr Armadale's lawyer, the mystery might be worth investigating. As things are, it's no interest of mine to hunt Mr Bashwood from one lie to another, till I run him to earth at last. I have nothing whatever to do with it; and I shall leave him free to follow his own roundabout courses, in his own roundabout way.' Having arrived at that conclusion, Pedgift Senior pushed back his chair, and rose briskly to terminate the interview.

'Don't be alarmed, Bashwood,' he began. 'The subject of our conversation is a subject exhausted, so far as I am concerned. I have only a few last words to say, and it's a habit of mine, as you know, to say my last words on my legs. Whatever else I may be in the dark about, I have made one discovery, at any rate. I have found out what you really want with me – at last! You want me to help you.'

'If you would be so very, very kind, sir?' stammered Mr Bashwood. 'If you would only give me the great advantage of your opinion and advice—?'

'Wait a bit, Bashwood. We will separate those two things if you please. A lawyer may offer an opinion like any other man; but when a lawyer gives his advice – by the Lord Harry, sir, it's Professional! You're welcome to my opinion in this matter; I have disguised it from nobody. I believe there have been events in Miss Gwilt's career, which (if they could be discovered) would even make Mr Armadale, infatuated as he is, afraid to marry her – supposing, of course, that he really *is* going to marry her; for though the appearances are in favour of it so far, it is only an assumption after all. As to the mode of proceeding by which the blots on this woman's character might or might not be brought to light in time – she may be married by licence in a fortnight if she likes – *that* is a branch of the question on which I positively decline to enter. It implies speaking in my character as a lawyer, and giving you, what I decline positively to give you, my professional advice.'

'Oh, sir, don't say that!' pleaded Mr Bashwood. 'Don't deny me the great favour, the inestimable advantage of your advice! I have such a poor head, Mr Pedgift! I am so old and so slow, sir, and I get so sadly startled and worried when I'm thrown out of my ordinary ways. It's quite natural you should be a little impatient with me for taking up your time – I know that time is money, to a clever man like you. Would you excuse me – would you please excuse me, if I venture to say that I have saved a little something, a few pounds, sir; and being quite lonely, with nobody dependent on me, I'm sure I may spend my savings as I please?' Blind to every consideration but the one consideration of propitiating Mr Pedgift, he took out a dingy, ragged old pocket-book, and tried, with trembling fingers, to open it on the lawyer's table.

'Put your pocket-book back directly,' said Pedgift Senior. 'Richer men than you have tried that argument with me, and have found that there is such a thing (off the stage) as a lawyer who is not to be bribed.

I will have nothing to do with the case, under existing circumstances. If you want to know why, I beg to inform you that Miss Gwilt ceased to be professionally interesting to me on the day when I ceased to be Mr Armadale's lawyer. I may have other reasons besides, which I don't think it necessary to mention. The reason already given is explicit enough. Go your own way, and take your responsibility on your own shoulders. You *may* venture within reach of Miss Gwilt's claws, and come out again without being scratched. Time will show. In the meanwhile, I wish you good-morning – and I own, to my shame, that I never knew till to-day what a hero you were.'

This time, Mr Bashwood felt the sting. Without another word of expostulation or entreaty, without even saying 'Good-morning' on his side, he walked to the door, opened it softly, and left the room.

The parting look in his face, and the sudden silence that had fallen on him, were not lost on Pedgift Senior. 'Bashwood will end badly,' said the lawyer, shuffling his papers, and returning impenetrably to his interrupted work.

The change in Mr Bashwood's face and manner to something dogged and self-contained, was so startlingly uncharacteristic of him, that it even forced itself on the notice of Pedgift Junior and the clerks, as he passed through the outer office. Accustomed to make the old man their butt, they took a boisterously comic view of the marked alteration in him. Deaf to the merciless raillery with which he was assailed on all sides, he stopped opposite young Pedgift; and looking him attentively in the face, said, in a quiet absent manner, like a man thinking aloud, 'I wonder whether *you* would help me?'

'Open an account instantly,' said Pedgift Junior to the clerks, 'in the name of Mr Bashwood. Place a chair for Mr Bashwood, with a footstool close by, in case he wants it. Supply me with a quire of extra doublewove satin paper, and a gross of picked quills to take notes of Mr Bashwood's case; and inform my father instantly that I am going to leave him and set up in business for myself, on the strength of Mr Bashwood's patronage. Take a seat, sir, pray take a seat, and express your feelings freely.'

Still impenetrably deaf to the raillery of which he was the object, Mr Bashwood waited until Pedgift Junior had exhausted himself, and then turned quietly away.

'I ought to have known better,' he said, in the same absent manner as before. 'He is his father's son all over – he would make game of me on my death-bed.' He paused a moment at the door, mechanically brushing his hat with his hand, and went out into the street.

The bright sunshine dazzled his eyes, the passing vehicles and foot-passengers startled and bewildered him. He shrank into a by-street, and put his hand over his eyes. 'I'd better go home,' he thought, 'and shut myself up, and think about it in my own room.'

His lodging was in a small house, in the poor quarter of the town. He let himself in with his key, and stole softly upstairs. The one little room he possessed met him cruelly, look round it where he might, with silent memorials of Miss Gwilt. On the chimney-piece were the flowers she had given him at various times, all withered long since, and all preserved on a little china pedestal, protected by a glass shade. On the wall hung a wretched coloured print of a woman, which he had caused to be nicely framed and glazed, because there was a look in it that reminded him of her face. In his clumsy old mahogany writing-desk were the few letters, brief and peremptory, which she had written to him at the time when he was watching and listening meanly at Thorpe-Ambrose to please *her*. And when, turning his back on these, he sat down wearily on his sofa-bedstead – there, hanging over one end of it, was the gaudy cravat of blue satin, which he had bought because she had told him she liked bright colours, and which he had never yet had the courage to wear, though he had taken it out morning after morning with the resolution to put it on! Habitually quiet in his actions, habitually restrained in his language, he now seized the cravat as if it was a living thing that could feel, and flung it to the other end of the room with an oath.

The time passed; and still, though his resolution to stand between Miss Gwilt and her marriage remained unbroken, he was as far as ever from discovering the means which might lead him to his end. The more he thought and thought of it, the darker and the darker his course in the future looked to him.

He rose again, as wearily as he had sat down, and went to his cupboard. 'I'm feverish and thirsty,' he said; 'a cup of tea may help me.' He opened his canister, and measured out his small allowance of tea, less carefully than usual. 'Even my own hands won't serve me to-day!' he thought, as he scraped together the few grains of tea that he had spilt, and put them carefully back in the canister.

In that fine summer weather, the one fire in the house was the kitchen-fire. He went downstairs for the boiling water, with his teapot in his hand.

Nobody but the landlady was in the kitchen. She was one of the many English matrons whose path through this world is a path of thorns; and who take a dismal pleasure, whenever the opportunity is afforded them, in inspecting the scratched and bleeding feet of other people in a like condition with themselves. Her one vice was of the lighter sort – the vice of curiosity; and among the many counterbalancing virtues she possessed, was the virtue of greatly respecting Mr Bashwood, as a lodger whose rent was regularly paid, and whose ways were always quiet and civil from one year's end to another.

'What did you please to want, sir?' asked the landlady. 'Boiling water, is it? Did you ever know the water boil, Mr Bashwood, when you wanted it? Did you ever see a sulkier fire than that? I'll put a stick or two in, if you'll wait a little, and give me the chance. Dear, dear me, you'll excuse my mentioning it, sir, but how poorly you do look to-day!'

The strain on Mr Bashwood's mind was beginning to tell. Something of the helplessness which he had shown at the station, appeared again in his face and manner as he put his teapot on the kitchen-table, and sat down.

'I'm in trouble, ma'am,' he said quietly; 'and I find trouble gets harder to bear than it used to be.'

'Ah, you may well say that!' groaned the landlady. '*I'm* ready for the undertaker, Mr Bashwood, when *my* time comes, whatever you may be. You're too lonely, sir. When you're in trouble it's some help – though not much – to shift a share of it off on another person's shoulders. If your good lady had only been alive now, sir, what a comfort you would have found her, wouldn't you?'

A momentary spasm of pain passed across Mr Bashwood's face. The landlady had ignorantly recalled him to the misfortunes of his married life. He had been long since forced to quiet her curiosity about his family affairs, by telling her that he was a widower, and that his domestic circumstances had not been happy ones; but he had taken her no further into his confidence than this. The sad story which he had related to Midwinter, of his drunken wife who had ended her miserable life in a lunatic asylum, was a story which he had shrunk from confiding to the talkative woman, who would have confided it in her turn to every one else in the house.

'What I always say to my husband, when he's low, sir,' pursued the landlady, intent on the kettle, 'is, "What would you do *now*, Sam, without Me?" When his temper don't get the better of him (it will boil directly, Mr Bashwood), he says, "Elizabeth, I could do nothing." When his temper does get the better of him, he says, "I should try the public-house, missus; and I'll try it now." Ah, I've got *my* troubles! A man with grown-up sons and daughters, tippling in a public-house! I don't call to mind, Mr Bashwood, whether *you* ever had any sons and daughters? And yet, now I think of it, I seem to fancy you said yes, you had. Daughters, sir, weren't they? – and, ah, dear! dear! to be sure! all dead.'

'I had one daughter, ma'am,' said Mr Bashwood, patiently – 'Only one, who died before she was a year old.'

'Only one!' repeated the sympathizing landlady. 'It's as near boiling as it ever will be, sir; give me the teapot. Only one! Ah, it comes heavier (don't it?) when it's an only child? You said it was an only child, I think, didn't you, sir?'

For a moment, Mr Bashwood looked at the woman with vacant eyes, and without attempting to answer her. After ignorantly recalling the memory of the wife who had disgraced him, she was now, as ignorantly, forcing him back on the miserable remembrance of the son who had ruined and deserted him. For the first time, since he had told his story to Midwinter, at their introductory interview in the great house, his mind reverted once more to the bitter disappointment and disaster of the past. Again, he thought of the bygone days, when he had become security for his son, and when that son's dishonesty had forced him to sell everything he possessed, to pay the forfeit that was exacted when the forfeit was due. 'I have a son, ma'am,' he said, becoming conscious that the landlady was looking at him in mute and melancholy surprise. 'I did my best to help him forward in the world, and he has behaved very badly to me.'

'Did he now?' rejoined the landlady, with an appearance of the greatest interest. 'Behaved badly to you – almost broke your heart, didn't he? Ah, it will come home to him, sooner or later. Don't you fear! Honour your father and mother, wasn't put on Moses's tables of stone for nothing, Mr Bashwood. Where may he be, and what is he doing now, sir?'

The question was in effect almost the same as the question which Midwinter had put when the circumstances had been described to him. As Mr Bashwood had answered it on the former occasion, so (in nearly the same words) he answered it now.

'My son is in London, ma'am, for all I know to the contrary. He was employed, when I last heard of him, in no very creditable way, at the Private Inquiry Office—'

At those words, he suddenly checked himself. His face flushed, his eyes brightened; he pushed away the cup which had just been filled for him, and rose from his seat. The landlady started back a step. There was something in her lodger's face that she had never seen in it before.

'I hope I've not offended you, sir,' said the woman, recovering her self-possession, and looking a little too ready to take offence on her side, at a moment's notice.

'Far from it, ma'am, far from it!' he rejoined in a strangely eager, hurried way. 'I have just remembered something – something very important. I must go upstairs – it's a letter, a letter, a letter. I'll come back to my tea, ma'am. I beg your pardon, I'm much obliged to you, you've been very kind – I'll say good-by, if you'll allow me, for the present.' To the landlady's amazement, he cordially shook hands with her, and made for the door, leaving tea and teapot to take care of themselves.

The moment he reached his own room, he locked himself in. For a little while he stood holding by the chimney-piece, waiting to recover his breath. The moment he could move again, he opened his writing-desk on the table. 'That for you, Mr Pedgift and Son!' he said, with a snap of his fingers as he sat down. 'I've got a son too!'

There was a knock at the door – a knock, soft, considerate, and confidential. The anxious landlady wished to know whether Mr Bash-wood was ill, and begged to intimate for the second time, that she earnestly trusted she had given him no offence.

'No! no!' he called through the door. 'I'm quite well – I'm writing, ma'am, I'm writing – please to excuse me. She's a good woman; she's an excellent woman,' he thought when the landlady had retired. 'I'll make her a little present. My mind's so unsettled, I might never have thought of it but for her. Oh, if my boy is at the office still! Oh, if I can only write a letter that will make him pity me!'

He took up his pen, and sat thinking anxiously, thinking long, before he touched the paper. Slowly, with many patient pauses to think and think again, and with more than ordinary care to make his writing legible, he traced these lines:

MY DEAR JAMES, – You will be surprised, I am afraid, to see my handwriting. Pray don't suppose I am going to ask you for money, or to reproach you for having sold me out of house and home when you forfeited your security, and I had to pay. I am willing, and anxious, to let bygones be bygones, and to forget the past.

It is in your power (if you are still at the Private Inquiry Office) to do me a great service. I am in sore anxiety and trouble, on the subject of a person in whom I am interested. The person is a lady. Please don't make game of me for confessing this, if you can help it. If you knew what I am now suffering, I think you would be more inclined to pity than to make game of me.

I would enter into particulars, only I know your quick temper, and I fear exhausting your patience. Perhaps, it may be enough to say, that I have reason to believe the lady's past life has not been a very creditable one, and that I am interested – more interested than words can tell – in finding out what her life has really been, and in making the discovery within a fortnight from the present time.[4]

Though I know very little about the ways of business in an office like yours, I can understand that, without first having the lady's present address, nothing can be done to help me. Unfortunately, I am not yet acquainted with her present address. I only know that she went to town to-day, accompanied by a gentleman, in whose employment I now am, and who (as I believe) will be likely to write to me for money before many days more are over his head.

Is this circumstance of a nature to help us? I venture to say 'us', because I count already, my dear boy, on your kind assistance and advice. Don't let money stand between us – I have saved a little something, and it is all freely at your disposal. Pray, pray write to me by return of post! If you will only try your best to end the dreadful suspense under which I am now suffering, you will atone for all the grief and disappointment you caused me in times that are past, and you will confer an obligation that he will never forget, on,

Your affectionate Father,
FELIX BASHWOOD.

After waiting a little, to dry his eyes, Mr Bashwood added the date and address, and directed the letter to his son, at 'The Private Inquiry Office, Shadyside Place, London.' That done, he went out at once, and posted his letter with his own hands. It was then Monday; and, if the answer was sent by return of post, the answer would be received on Wednesday morning.

The interval day, the Tuesday, was passed by Mr Bashwood in the steward's office at the great house. He had a double motive for absorbing himself as deeply as might be in the various occupations connected with the management of the estate. In the first place, employment helped him to control the devouring impatience with which he looked for the coming of the next day. In the second place, the more forward he was with the business of the office, the more free he would be to join his son in London, without attracting suspicion to himself by openly neglecting the interests placed under his charge.

Towards the Tuesday afternoon, vague rumours of something wrong at the cottage, found their way (through Major Milroy's servants) to the servants at the great house, and attempted ineffectually through this latter channel to engage the attention of Mr Bashwood, impenetrably fixed on other things. The major and Miss Neelie had been shut up together in mysterious conference; and Miss Neelie's appearance after the close of the interview, plainly showed that she had been crying. This had happened on the Monday afternoon; and on the next day (that present Tuesday) the major had startled the household by announcing briefly that his daughter wanted a change to the air of the sea-side, and that he proposed taking her himself, by the next train, to Lowestoft. The two had gone away together, both very serious and silent, but both, apparently, very good friends, for all that. Opinions at the great house attributed this domestic revolution to the reports current on the subject of Allan and Miss Gwilt. Opinions at the cottage rejected that solution of the difficulty, on practical grounds. Miss Neelie had remained inaccessibly shut up in her own room, from the Monday afternoon to the Tuesday morning when her father took her away. The major, during the same interval, had not been outside the door, and had spoken to nobody. And Mrs Milroy, at the first attempt of her new attendant to inform her of the prevailing scandal in the town, had sealed the servant's lips by flying into one of her terrible passions, the instant Miss Gwilt's name was mentioned. Something must have happened, of course, to take Major Milroy and his daughter so suddenly from home – but that something was certainly not Mr Armadale's scandalous elopement, in broad daylight, with Miss Gwilt.

The afternoon passed, and the evening passed, and no other event happened but the purely private and personal event which had taken place at the cottage. Nothing occurred (for nothing in the nature of things *could* occur) to dissipate the delusion on which Miss Gwilt had counted – the delusion which all Thorpe-Ambrose now shared with Mr Bashwood, that she had gone privately to London with Allan, in the character of Allan's future wife.

On the Wednesday morning, the postman, entering the street in which Mr Bashwood lived, was encountered by Mr Bashwood himself, so eager to know if there was a letter for him, that he had come out without his hat. There *was* a letter for him – the letter that he longed for from his vagabond son.

These were the terms, in which Bashwood the younger answered his father's supplication for help – after having previously ruined his father's prospects for life:

Shadyside Place, Tuesday, July 29.

MY DEAR DAD, – We have some little practice in dealing with mysteries at this office; but the mystery of your letter beats me altogether. Are you speculating on the interesting hidden frailties of some charming woman? Or, after *your* experience of matrimony, are you actually going to give me a stepmother at this time of day? Whichever it is, upon my life your letter interests me.

I am not joking, mind, – though the temptation is not an easy one to resist. On the contrary, I have given you a quarter of an hour of my valuable time already. The place you date from sounded somehow familiar to me. I referred back to the memorandum book, and found that I was sent down to Thorpe-Ambrose to make private inquiries not very long since. My employer was a lively old lady, who was too sly to give us her right name and address. As a matter of course, we set to work at once, and found out who she was. Her name is Mrs Oldershaw – and if you think of *her* for my stepmother, I strongly recommend you to think again before you make her Mrs Bashwood.

If it is not Mrs Oldershaw, then all I can do, so far, is to tell you how you may find out the unknown lady's address. Come to town yourself, as soon as you get the letter you expect from the gentleman who has gone away with her (I hope he is not a handsome young man, for your sake); and call here. I will send somebody to help you in watching his hotel or lodging; and if he communicates with the lady, or the lady with him, you may consider her address discovered from that moment. Once let me identify her, and know where she is, – and you shall see all her charming little secrets as plainly as you see the paper on which your affectionate son is now writing to you.

A word more about the terms. I am as willing as you are to be friends again; but, though I own you were out of pocket by me once, I can't afford to be out of pocket by you. It must be understood that you are answerable for all the expenses of the inquiry. We may have to employ some of the women attached to this office, if your lady is too wide-awake, or too nice-looking, to be dealt with by a man. There will be cab-hire, and postage-stamps – admissions to public amusements, if she is inclined that way – shillings for pew-openers, if she is serious, and takes our people into churches to hear popular preachers, and so on. My own professional services you shall have gratis; but I can't lose by you as well. Only remember that – and you shall have your way. Bygones shall be bygones, and we will forget the past.

Your affectionate Son,
JAMES BASHWOOD.

In the ecstasy of seeing help placed at last within his reach, the father put the son's atrocious letter to his lips. 'My good boy!' he murmured tenderly. 'My dear, good boy!'

He put the letter down, and fell into a new train of thought. The next question to face was the serious question of time. Mr Pedgift had told him Miss Gwilt might be married in a fortnight. One day of the fourteen had passed already, and another was passing. He beat his hand impatiently on the table at his side, wondering how soon the want of money would force Allan to write to him from London. 'To-morrow?' he asked himself. 'Or next day?'

The morrow passed; and nothing happened. The next day came – and the letter arrived! It was on business, as he had anticipated; it asked for money, as he had anticipated – and there, at the end of it, in a post-script, was the address added, concluding with the words, 'You may count on my staying here till further notice.'

He gave one deep gasp of relief; and instantly busied himself – though there were nearly two hours to spare before the train started for London – in packing his bag. The last thing he put in was his blue satin cravat. 'She likes bright colours,' he said, 'and she may see me in it yet!'

CHAPTER XIV

MISS GWILT'S DIARY

All Saints' Terrace, New Road, London, July 28th, Monday night. – I can hardly hold my head up, I am so tired. But, in my situation, I dare not trust anything to memory. Before I go to bed, I must write my customary record of the events of the day.

So far, the turn of luck in my favour (it was long enough before it

485

took the turn!) seems likely to continue. I succeeded in forcing Armadale – the brute required nothing short of forcing – to leave Thorpe-Ambrose for London, alone in the same carriage with me, before all the people in the station. There was a full attendance of dealers in small scandal, all staring hard at us, and all evidently drawing their own conclusions. Either I knew nothing of Thorpe-Ambrose – or the town-gossip is busy enough by this time with Mr Armadale and Miss Gwilt.

I had some difficulty with him for the first half-hour after we left the station. The guard (delightful man! I felt so grateful to him!) had shut us up together in expectation of half-a-crown at the end of the journey. Armadale was suspicious of me, and he showed it plainly. Little by little I tamed my wild beast – partly by taking care to display no curiosity about his journey to town, and partly by interesting him on the subject of his friend Midwinter; dwelling especially on the opportunity that now offered itself for a reconciliation between them. I kept harping on this string till I set his tongue going, and made him amuse me as a gentleman is bound to do when he has the honour of escorting a lady on a long railway journey.

What little mind he has was full, of course, of his own affairs and Miss Milroy's. No words can express the clumsiness he showed in trying to talk about himself, without taking me into his confidence or mentioning Miss Milroy's name. He was going to London, he gravely informed me, on a matter of indescribable interest to him. It was a secret for the present, but he hoped to tell it me soon; it had made a great difference already in the way in which he looked at the slanders spoken of him in Thorpe-Ambrose; he was too happy to care what the scandal-mongers said of him now, and he should soon stop their mouths by appearing in a new character that would surprise them all. So he blundered on, with the firm persuasion that he was keeping me quite in the dark. It was hard not to laugh, when I thought of my anonymous letter on its way to the major; but I managed to control myself – though, I must own, with some difficulty. As the time wore on, I began to feel a terrible excitement: the position was, I think, a little too much for me. There I was, alone with him, talking in the most innocent, easy, familiar manner, and having it in my mind all the time, to brush his life out of my way, when the moment comes, as I might brush a stain off my gown. It made my blood leap, and my cheeks flush. I caught myself laughing once or twice much louder than I ought – and long before we got to London I thought it desirable to put my face in hiding by pulling down my veil.

There was no difficulty, on reaching the terminus, in getting him to come in the cab with me to the hotel where Midwinter is staying. He was all eagerness to be reconciled with his dear friend – principally, I have no doubt, because he wants the dear friend to lend a helping hand to the elopement. The real difficulty lay, of course, with Midwinter. My sudden journey to London had allowed me no opportunity of writing to combat his superstitious conviction that he and his former friend are better apart. I thought it wise to leave Armadale in the cab at the door, and to go into the hotel by myself to pave the way for him.

Fortunately, Midwinter had not gone out. His delight at seeing me some days sooner than he had hoped, had something infectious in it, I suppose. Pooh! I may own the truth to my own diary! There was a moment when *I* forgot everything in the world but our two selves as completely as he did. I felt as if I was back in my 'teens – until I remembered the lout in the cab at the door. And then I was five-and-thirty again in an instant.

His face altered when he heard who was below, and what it was I wanted of him – he looked, not angry but distressed. He yielded, however, before long, not to my reasons, for I gave him none, but to my entreaties. His old fondness for his friend might possibly have had some share in persuading him against his will – but my own opinion is that he acted entirely under the influence of his fondness for Me.

I waited in the sitting-room while he went down to the door; so I knew nothing of what passed between them when they first saw each other again. But, oh, the difference between the two men when the interval had passed, and they came upstairs together and joined me. They were both agitated, but in such different ways! The hateful Armadale, so loud and red and clumsy; the dear, lovable Midwinter, so pale and quiet, with such a gentleness in his voice when he spoke, and such tenderness in his eyes every time they turned my way. Armadale overlooked me as completely as if I had not been in the room. *He* referred to me over and over again in the conversation; *he* constantly looked at me to see what I thought, while I sat in my corner silently watching them; *he* wanted to go with me and see me safe to my lodgings, and spare me all trouble with the cabman and the luggage. When I thanked him and declined, Armadale looked unaffectedly relieved at the prospect of seeing my back turned, and of having his friend all to himself. I left him, with his awkward elbows half over the table, scrawling a letter (no doubt to Miss Milroy), and shouting to the waiter that he wanted a bed at the hotel. I had calculated on his staying as a matter of course where he found his friend staying. It was pleasant to find my anticipations realized, and to know that I have as good as got him now under my own eye.

After promising to let Midwinter know where he could see me to-morrow, I went away in the cab to hunt for lodgings by myself.

With some difficulty I have succeeded in getting an endurable sitting-room and bedroom in this house, where the people are perfect strangers to me. Having paid a week's rent in advance (for I naturally preferred dispensing with a reference), I find myself with exactly three shillings and ninepence left in my purse. It is impossible to ask Midwinter for money, after he has already paid Mrs Oldershaw's note-of-hand. I must borrow something to-morrow on my watch and chain at the pawn-broker's. Enough to keep me going for a fortnight is all, and more than all, that I want. In that time, or in less than that time, Midwinter will have married me.

July 29th. Two o'clock. – Early in the morning I sent a line to Midwinter, telling him that he would find me here at three this afternoon. That done, I devoted the morning to two errands of my own. One is hardly worth mentioning – it was only to raise money on my watch and chain. I got more than I expected; and more (even supposing I buy myself one or two little things in the way of cheap summer dress) than I am at all likely to spend before the wedding-day.

The other errand was of a far more serious kind. It led me into an attorney's office.

I was well aware last night (though I was too weary to put it down in my diary), that I could not possibly see Midwinter this morning – in the position he now occupies towards me – without at least *appearing* to take him into my confidence, on the subject of myself and my circumstances. Excepting one necessary consideration which I must be careful not to overlook, there is not the least difficulty in my drawing on my invention, and telling him any story I please – for thus far I have told no story to anybody. Midwinter went away to London before it was possible to approach the subject. As to the Milroys (having provided them with the customary reference), I could fortunately keep them at arm's length on all questions relating purely to myself. And lastly, when I effected my reconciliation with Armadale on the drive in front of the house, he was fool enough to be too generous to let me defend my character. When I had expressed my regret for having lost my temper and threatened Miss Milroy, and when I had accepted his assurance that my pupil had never done or meant to do me any injury, he was too magnanimous to hear a word on the subject of my private affairs. Thus, I am quite unfettered by any former assertions of my own; and I may tell any story I please – with the one drawback hinted at already in the shape of a restraint. Whatever I may invent in the way of pure fiction, I must preserve the character in which I have appeared at Thorpe-Ambrose – for, with the notoriety that is attached to *my other name*, I have no other choice but to marry Midwinter in my maiden name as 'Miss Gwilt'.[1]

This was the consideration that took me into the lawyer's office. I felt that I must inform myself, before I saw Midwinter later in the day, of any awkward consequences that may follow the marriage of a widow, if she conceals her widow's name.

Knowing of no other professional person whom I could trust, I went boldly to the lawyer who had my interests in his charge, at that terrible past time in my life, which I have more reason than ever to shrink from thinking of now. He was astonished, and, as I could plainly detect, by no means pleased to see me. I had hardly opened my lips, before he said he hoped I was not consulting him *again* (with a strong emphasis on the word) on my own account. I took the hint, and put the question I had come to ask, in the interests of that accommodating personage on such occasions – an absent friend. The lawyer evidently saw through it at once; but he was sharp enough to turn my 'friend' to good account on his side. He said he would answer the question as a matter of courtesy towards a lady represented by myself; but he must make it a condition that this consultation of him by deputy should go no further.[2]

I accepted his terms – for I really respected the clever manner in which he contrived to keep me at arm's length without violating the laws of good breeding. In two minutes I heard what he had to say, mastered it in my own mind, and went out.

Short as it was, the consultation told me everything I wanted to know. I risk nothing by marrying Midwinter in my maiden instead of my widow's name. The marriage is a good marriage in this way: that it can only be set aside if my husband finds out the imposture, and takes proceedings to invalidate our marriage in my lifetime. That is the lawyer's answer in the lawyer's own words. It relieves me at once – in this direction at any rate – of all apprehension about the future. The only imposture my husband will ever discover – and then only if he happens to be on the spot – is the imposture that puts me in the place, and gives me the income, of Armadale's widow; and, by that time, I shall have invalidated my own marriage for ever.

Half-past two! Midwinter will be here in half an hour. I must go and ask my glass how I look. I must rouse my invention, and make up my little domestic romance. Am I feeling nervous about it? Something flutters in the place where my heart used to be. At five and thirty, too! and after such a life as mine!

Six o'clock. – He has just gone. The day for our marriage is a day determined on already.

I have tried to rest, and recover myself. I can't rest. I have come back to these leaves. There is much to be written in them since Midwinter has been here, that concerns me nearly.

Let me begin with what I hate most to remember, and so be the sooner done with it – let me begin with the paltry string of falsehoods I told him about my family troubles.

What *can* be the secret of this man's hold on me? How is it that he alters me so that I hardly know myself again? I was like myself in the railway carriage yesterday with Armadale. It was surely frightful to be talking to the living man, through the whole of that long journey, with the knowledge in me all the while that I meant to be his widow – and yet I was only excited and fevered. Hour after hour I never shrunk once from speaking to Armadale – but the first trumpery falsehood I told Midwinter, turned me cold when I saw that he believed it! I felt a dreadful hysterical choking in the throat when he entreated me not to reveal my troubles. And once – I am horrified when I think of it – once, when he said, 'If I *could* love you more dearly, I should love you more dearly, now,' I was within a hair's breadth of turning traitor to myself. I was on the very point of crying out to him, 'Lies! all lies! I'm a fiend in human shape! Marry the wretchedest creature that prowls the streets, and you will marry a better woman than me!' Yes! the seeing his eyes moisten, the hearing his voice tremble while I was deceiving him, shook me in that way. I have seen handsomer men by hundreds, cleverer men by hundreds. What can this man have roused in me? Is it Love? I thought I *had* loved, never to love again. Does a woman not love, when the man's hardness to her drives her to drown herself? A man drove *me* to that last despair in days gone by. Did all my misery at that time come from something which was not Love? Have I lived to be five and thirty, and am I only feeling, now, what Love really is? – now, when it is too late? Ridiculous! Besides, what is the use of asking? What do I know about it? What does any woman ever know? The more we think of it, the more we deceive ourselves. I wish I had been born an animal. My beauty might have been of some use to me then – it might have got me a good master.

Here is a whole page of my diary filled; and nothing written yet that is of the slightest use to me! My miserable made-up story must be told over again here, while the incidents are fresh in my memory – or how am I to refer to it consistently on after-occasions when I may be obliged to speak of it again?

There was nothing new in what I told him: it was the commonplace rubbish of the circulating libraries. A dead father; a lost fortune; vagabond brothers, whom I dread ever seeing again; a bedridden mother dependent on my exertions – No! I can't write it down! I hate myself, I despise myself, when I remember that *he* believed it because I said it – that *he* was distressed by it, because it was my story! I will face the chances of contradicting myself – I will risk discovery and ruin – anything rather than dwell on that contemptible deception of him a moment longer.

My lies came to an end at last. And then he talked to me of himself, and of his prospects. Oh, what a relief it was to turn to that, at the time! What a relief it is to come to it now!

He has accepted the offer about which he wrote to me at Thorpe-Ambrose; and he is now engaged as occasional foreign correspondent to the new newspaper. His first destination is Naples. I wish it had been some other place, for I have certain past associations with Naples which I am not at all anxious to renew. It has been arranged that he is to leave England not later than the eleventh of next month. By that time, therefore, I, who am to go with him, must go with him as his wife.

There is not the slightest difficulty about the marriage. All this part of it is so easy, that I begin to dread an accident. The proposal to keep the thing strictly private – which it might have embarrassed me to make – comes from him. Marrying me in his own name – the name that he has kept concealed from every living creature but myself and Mr Brock – it is his interest that not a soul who knows him should be present at the ceremony; his friend Armadale least of all. He has been a week in London already. When another week has passed, he proposes to get the Licence, and to be married in the church belonging to the parish in which the hotel is situated. These are the only necessary formalities. I had but to say 'Yes' (he told me), and to feel no further anxiety about the future. I said 'Yes', with such a devouring anxiety about the future, that I was afraid he would see it. What minutes the next few minutes were, when he whispered delicious words to me, while I hid my face on his breast!

I recovered myself first, and led him back to the subject of Armadale; having my own reasons for wanting to know what they said to each other, after I had left them yesterday.

The manner in which Midwinter replied, showed me that he was speaking under the restraint of respecting a confidence placed in him by his friend. Long before he had done, I detected what the confidence was. Armadale had been consulting him (exactly as I anticipated) on the subject of the elopement. Although he appears to have remonstrated against taking the girl secretly away from her home, Midwinter seems to have felt some delicacy about speaking strongly; remembering (widely different as the circumstances are) that he was contemplating a private marriage himself. I gathered, at any rate, that he had produced very little effect by what he had said; and that Armadale had already carried out his absurd intention of consulting the head-clerk in the office of his London lawyers.

Having got as far as this, Midwinter put the question which I felt must come sooner or later. He asked if I objected to our engagement being mentioned in the strictest secresy to his friend.

'I will answer,' he said, 'for Allan's respecting any confidence that I place in him. And I will undertake, when the time comes, so to use my influence over him as to prevent his being present at the marriage, and discovering (what he must never know) that my name is the same as his own. It would help me,' he went on, 'to speak more strongly about the object that has brought him to London, if I can requite the frankness with which he has spoken of his private affairs to me, by the same frankness on my side.'

I had no choice but to give the necessary permission, and I gave it. It is of the utmost importance to me to know what course Major Milroy takes with his daughter and Armadale, after receiving my anonymous letter; and, unless I invite Armadale's confidence in some way, I am nearly certain to be kept in the dark. Let him once be trusted with the knowledge that I am to be Midwinter's wife; and what he tells his friend about his love-affair, he will tell me.[3]

When it had been understood between us that Armadale was to be taken into our confidence, we began to talk about ourselves again. How the time flew! What a sweet enchantment it was to forget everything in his arms! How he loves me! – ah, poor fellow, how he loves me!

I have promised to meet him to-morrow morning in the Regent's Park. The less he is seen here the better. The people in this house are strangers to me certainly – but it may be wise to consult appearances, as if I was still at Thorpe-Ambrose, and not to produce the impression, even on their minds, that Midwinter is engaged to me. If any after-inquiries are made, when I have run my grand risk, the testimony of my London landlady might be testimony worth having.

That wretched old Bashwood! Writing of Thorpe-Ambrose reminds me of him. What will he say when the town-gossip tells him that Armadale has taken me to London, in a carriage reserved for ourselves?

It really is too absurd in a man of Bashwood's age and appearance to presume to be in love! . . .

July 30th. News at last! Armadale has heard from Miss Milroy. My anonymous letter has produced its effect. The girl is removed from Thorpe-Ambrose already; and the whole project of the elopement is blown to the winds at once and for ever. This was the substance of what Midwinter had to tell me, when I met him in the Park. I affected to be excessively astonished, and to feel the necessary feminine longing to know all the particulars. 'Not that I expected to have my curiosity satisfied,' I added, 'for Mr Armadale and I are little better than mere acquaintances, after all.'

'You are far more than a mere acquaintance in Allan's eyes,' said Midwinter. 'Having your permission to trust him, I have already told him how near and dear you are to me.'

Hearing this, I thought it desirable, before I put any questions about Miss Milroy, to attend to my own interests first, and to find out what effect the announcement of my coming marriage had produced on Armadale. It was possible that he might be still suspicious of me, and that the inquiries he made in London, at Mrs Milroy's instigation, might be still hanging on his mind.

'Did Mr Armadale seem surprised,' I asked, 'when you told him of our engagement, and when you said it was to be kept a secret from everybody?'

'He seemed greatly surprised,' said Midwinter, 'to hear that we were going to be married. All he said when I told him it must be kept a secret was, that he supposed there were family reasons on your side for making the marriage a private one.'

'What did you say,' I inquired, 'when he made that remark?'

'I said the family reasons were on my side,' answered Midwinter. 'And I thought it right to add – considering that Allan had allowed himself to be misled by the ignorant distrust of you at Thorpe-Ambrose – that you had confided to me the whole of your sad family story, and that you had amply justified your unwillingness, under any ordinary circumstances, to speak of your private affairs.'

(I breathed freely again. He had said just what was wanted, just in the right way.)

'Thank you,' I said, 'for putting me right in your friend's estimation. Does he wish to see me?' I added, by way of getting back to the other subject of Miss Milroy and the elopement.

'He is longing to see you,' returned Midwinter. 'He is in great distress, poor fellow – distress which I have done my best to soothe, but which I believe would yield far more readily to a woman's sympathy than to mine.'

'Where is he now?' I asked.

He was at the hotel; and to the hotel I instantly proposed that we should go. It is a busy, crowded place; and (with my veil down) I have less fear of compromising myself there than at my quiet lodgings. Besides, it is vitally important to me to know what Armadale does next, under this total change of circumstances, – for I must so control his proceedings as to get him away from England if I can. We took a cab: such was my eagerness to sympathize with the heart-broken lover, that we took a cab!

Anything so ridiculous as Armadale's behaviour under the double shock of discovering that his young lady has been taken away from him, and that I am to be married to Midwinter, I never before witnessed in all my experience. To say that he was like a child is a libel on all children who are not born idiots. He congratulated me on my coming marriage, and execrated the unknown wretch who had written the anonymous letter, little thinking that he was speaking of one and the same person in one and the same breath. Now he submissively acknowledged that Major Milroy had his rights as a father, and now he reviled the major as having no feeling for anything but his mechanics and his clock. At one moment he started up, with the tears in his eyes, and declared that his 'darling Neelie' was an angel on earth. At another he sat down sulkily, and thought that a girl of her spirit might have run away on the spot and joined him in London. After a good half-hour of this absurd exhibition, I succeeded in quieting him; and then a few words of tender inquiry produced what I had expressly come to the hotel to see – Miss Milroy's letter.

It was outrageously long and rambling and confused – in short, the letter of a fool. I had to wade through plenty of vulgar sentiment and lamentation, and to lose time and patience over maudlin outbursts of affection, and nauseous kisses enclosed in circles of ink. However, I contrived to extract the information I wanted at last; and here it is:

The major, on receipt of my anonymous warning, appears to have sent at once for his daughter, and to have shown her the letter. 'You know what a hard life I lead with your mother; don't make it harder still, Neelie, by deceiving me.' That was all the poor old gentleman said. I always did like the major; and, though he was afraid to show it, I know he always liked me. His appeal to his daughter (if *her* account of it is to be believed) cut her to the heart. She burst out crying (let her alone for crying at the right moment!), and confessed everything.

After giving her time to recover herself (if he had given her a good box on the ears it would have been more to the purpose!) the major seems to have put certain questions, and to have become convinced (as I was convinced myself) that his daughter's heart, or fancy, or whatever she calls it, was really and truly set on Armadale. The discovery evidently distressed as well as surprised him. He appears to have hesitated, and to have maintained his own unfavourable opinion of Miss Neelie's lover for some little time. But his daughter's tears and entreaties (so like the weakness of the dear old gentleman!) shook him at last. Though he firmly refused to allow of any marriage engagement at present, he consented to overlook the clandestine meetings in the park, and to put Armadale's fitness to become his son-in-law to the test, on certain conditions.

These conditions are, that for the next six months to come, all communication is to be broken off, both personally and by writing, between Armadale and Miss Milroy. That space of time is to be occupied by the young gentleman as he himself thinks best, and by the young lady in completing her education at school. If, when the six months have passed, they are both still of the same mind, and if Armadale's conduct in the interval has been such as to improve the major's opinion of him, he will be allowed to present himself in the character of Miss Milroy's suitor – and, in six months more, if all goes well, the marriage may take place.

I declare I could kiss the dear old major, if I was only within reach of him! If I had been at his elbow, and had dictated the conditions myself, I could have asked for nothing better than this. Six months of total separation between Armadale and Miss Milroy! In half that time – with all communication cut off between the two – it must go hard with me indeed if I don't find myself dressed in the necessary mourning, and publicly recognized as Armadale's widow.

But I am forgetting the girl's letter. She gives her father's reasons for making his conditions, in her father's own words. The major seems to have spoken so sensibly and so feelingly that he left his daughter no decent alternative – and he leaves Armadale no decent alternative – but to submit. As well as I can remember it, he seems to have expressed himself to Miss Neelie in these, or nearly in these terms:

'Don't think I am behaving cruelly to you, my dear – I am merely asking you to put Mr Armadale to the proof. It is not only right, it is absolutely necessary, that you should hold no communication with him for some time to come; and I will show you why. In the first place, if you go to school, the necessary rules in such places – necessary for the sake of the other girls – would not permit you to see Mr Armadale, or to receive letters from him; and, if you *are* to become mistress of Thorpe-Ambrose, to school you must go, for you would be ashamed, and I should be ashamed, if you occupied the position of a lady of station, without having the accomplishments which all ladies of station are expected to possess. In the second place, I want to see whether Mr Armadale will continue to think of you as he thinks now, without being encouraged in his attachment by seeing you, or reminded of it by hearing from you. If I am wrong in thinking him flighty and unreliable; and if your opinion of him is the right one, this is not putting the young man to an unfair test – true love survives much longer separations than a separation of six months. And when that time is over, and well over; and when I have had him under my own eye for another six months, and have learnt to think as highly of him as you do – even then, my dear, after all that terrible delay, you will still be a married woman before you are eighteen. Think of this, Neelie; and show that you love me and trust me, by accepting my proposal. I will hold no communication with Mr Armadale myself. I will leave it to you to write and tell him what has been decided on. He may write back one letter, and one only, to acquaint you with his decision. After that, for the sake of your reputation, nothing more is to be said, and nothing more is to be done, and the matter is to be kept strictly private until the six months' interval is at an end.'

To this effect the major spoke. His behaviour to that little slut of a girl has produced a stronger impression on me than anything else in the letter. It has set me thinking (me, of all the people in the world!) of what they call 'a moral difficulty'. We are perpetually told that there can be no possible connection between virtue and vice. Can there not? Here is Major Milroy doing exactly what an excellent father, at once kind and prudent, affectionate and firm, would do under the circumstances – and by that very course of conduct, he has now smoothed the way for *me*, as completely as if he had been the chosen accomplice of that abominable creature, Miss Gwilt. Only think of my reasoning in this way! But I am in such good spirits, I can do anything to-day. I have not looked so bright and so young as I look now, for months past!

To return to the letter, for the last time – it is so excessively dull and stupid that I really can't help wandering away from it into reflections of my own, as a mere relief.

After solemnly announcing[4] that she meant to sacrifice herself to her beloved father's wishes (the brazen assurance of her setting up for a martyr after what has happened, exceeds anything I ever heard or read of!), Miss Neelie next mentioned that the major proposed taking her to the seaside for change of air, during the few days that were still to elapse before she went to school. Armadale was to send his answer by return of post, and to address her, under cover to her father, at Lowestoft. With this, and with a last outburst of tender protestation, crammed crookedly into a corner of the page, the letter ended. (N.B. – The major's object in taking her to the seaside is plain enough. He still privately distrusts Armadale, and he is wisely determined to prevent any more clandestine meetings in the park, before the girl is safely disposed of at school.)

When I had done with the letter – I had requested permission to read parts of it which I particularly admired, for the second and third time! – we all consulted together in a friendly way about what Armadale was to do.

He was fool enough, at the outset, to protest against submitting to Major Milroy's conditions. He declared, with his odious red face looking the picture of brute health, that he should never survive a six months' separation from his beloved Neelie. Midwinter (as may easily be imagined) seemed a little ashamed of him, and joined me in bringing him to his senses. We showed him what would have been plain enough to anybody but a booby, that there was no honourable, or even decent, alternative left but to follow the example of submission set by the young lady. 'Wait – and you will have her for your wife,' was what I said. 'Wait – and you will force the major to alter his unjust opinion of you,' was what Midwinter added. With two clever people hammering common sense into his head at that rate, it is needless to say that his head gave way, and he submitted.

Having decided him to accept the major's conditions (I was careful to warn him, before he wrote to Miss Milroy, that my engagement to Midwinter was to be kept as strictly secret from her as from everybody else), the next question we had to settle related to his future proceedings. I was ready with the necessary arguments to stop him, if he had proposed returning to Thorpe-Ambrose. But he proposed nothing of the sort. On the contrary, he declared, of his own accord, that nothing would induce him to go back. The place and the people were associated with everything that was hateful to him. There would be no Miss Milroy now to meet him in the park, and no Midwinter to keep him company in the solitary house. 'I'd rather break stones on the road,' was the sensible and cheerful way in which he put it, 'than go back to Thorpe-Ambrose.'

The first suggestion after this came from Midwinter. The sly old clergyman who gave Mrs Oldershaw and me so much trouble, has it seems been ill; but has been latterly reported better. 'Why not go to Somersetshire,' said Midwinter; 'and see your good friend, and my good friend, Mr Brock?'

Armadale caught at the proposal readily enough. He longed, in the first place, to see 'dear old Brock', and he longed, in the second place, to see his yacht. After staying a few days more in London with Midwinter, he would gladly go to Somersetshire. But what after that?

Seeing my opportunity, *I* came to the rescue this time. 'You have got a yacht, Mr Armadale,' I said; 'and you know that Midwinter is going to Italy. When you are tired of Somersetshire, why not make a voyage to the Mediterranean, and meet your friend, and your friend's wife, at Naples?'

I made the allusion to 'his friend's wife', with the most becoming modesty and confusion. Armadale was enchanted. I had hit on the best of all ways of occupying the weary time. He started up, and wrung my hand in quite an ecstasy of gratitude. How I do hate people who can only express their feelings by hurting other people's hands!

Midwinter was as pleased with my proposal as Armadale; but he saw difficulties in the way of carrying it out. He considered the yacht too small for a cruise to the Mediterranean, and he thought it desirable to hire a larger vessel. His friend thought otherwise. I left them arguing the question. It was quite enough for me to have made sure, in the first place, that Armadale will not return to Thorpe-Ambrose; and to have decided him, in the second place, on going abroad. He may go how he likes. I should prefer the small yacht myself – for there seems to be a chance that the small yacht might do me the inestimable service of drowning him . . .

Five o'clock. – The excitement of feeling that I had got Armadale's future movements completely under my own control, made me so restless, when I returned to my lodgings, that I was obliged to go out again, and do something. A new interest to occupy me being what I wanted, I went to Pimlico to have it out with Mother Oldershaw.

I walked – and made up my mind, on the way, that I would begin by quarrelling with her. One of my notes-of-hand being paid already, and Midwinter being willing to pay the other two when they fall due, my present position with the old wretch is as independent a one as I could desire. I always get the better of her when it comes to a downright battle between us, and find her wonderfully civil and obliging the moment I have made her feel that mine is the strongest will of the two. In my present situation, she might be of use to me in various ways, if I could secure her assistance, without trusting her with secrets which I am now more than ever determined to keep to myself. That was my idea as I walked to Pimlico. Upsetting Mother Oldershaw's nerves, in the first place, and then twisting her round my little finger, in the second, promised me, as I thought, an interesting occupation for the rest of the afternoon.

When I got to Pimlico, a surprise was in store for me. The house was shut up – not only on Mrs Oldershaw's side, but on Doctor Downward's as well. A padlock was on the shop-door; and a man was hanging about on the watch, who might have been an ordinary idler certainly, but who looked, to my mind, like a policeman in disguise.

Knowing the risks the doctor runs in his particular form of practice, I suspected at once that something serious had happened, and that even cunning Mrs Oldershaw was compromised this time. Without stopping, or making any inquiry, therefore, I called the first cab that passed me, and drove to the post-office to which I had desired my letters to be forwarded if any came for me after I left my Thorpe-Ambrose lodging.

On inquiry a letter was produced for 'Miss Gwilt'. It was in Mother Oldershaw's handwriting, and it told me (as I had supposed) that the doctor had got into a serious difficulty – that she was herself most unfortunately mixed up in the matter – and that they were both in hiding for the present. The letter ended with some sufficiently venomous sentences about my conduct at Thorpe-Ambrose, and with a warning that I have not heard the last of Mrs Oldershaw yet. It relieved me to find her writing in this way – for she would have been civil and cringing if she had had any suspicion of what I have really got in view. I burnt the letter as soon as the candles came up. And there, for the present, is an end of the connection between Mother Jezebel and me. I must do all my own dirty work now – and I shall be all the safer, perhaps, for trusting nobody's hands to do it but my own.

July 31st. – More useful information for me. I met Midwinter again in the Park (on the pretext that my reputation might suffer, if he called too often at my lodgings); and heard the last news of Armadale, since I left the hotel yesterday.

After he had written to Miss Milroy, Midwinter took the opportunity of speaking to him about the necessary business arrangements during his absence from the great house. It was decided that the servants should be put on board wages, and that Mr Bashwood should be left in charge. (Somehow, I don't like this reappearance of Mr Bashwood in connection with my present interests, but there is no help for it.) The next question – the question of money – was settled at once by Armadale himself. All his available ready-money (a large sum) is to be lodged by Mr Bashwood in Coutts's Bank, and to be there deposited in Armadale's name. This, he said, would save him the worry of any further letter-writing to his steward, and would enable him to get what he wanted, when he went abroad, at a moment's notice. The plan thus proposed being certainly the simplest and the safest, was adopted with Midwinter's full concurrence; and here the business discussion would have ended, if the everlasting Mr Bashwood had not turned up again in the conversation, and prolonged it in an entirely new direction.

On reflection, it seems to have struck Midwinter that the whole responsibility at Thorpe-Ambrose ought not to rest on Mr Bashwood's shoulders. Without in the least distrusting him, Midwinter felt, nevertheless, that he ought to have somebody set over him, to apply to, in case of emergency. Armadale made no objection to this; he only asked, in his helpless way, who the person was to be?

The answer was not an easy one to arrive at. Either of the two solicitors at Thorpe-Ambrose might have been employed – but Armadale was on bad terms with both of them. Any reconciliation with such a bitter enemy as the elder lawyer, Mr Darch, was out of the question; and reinstating Mr Pedgift in his former position, implied a tacit sanction on Armadale's part, of the lawyer's abominable conduct towards *me*, which was scarcely consistent with the respect and regard that he felt for a lady who was soon to be his friend's wife. After some further discussion, Midwinter hit on a new suggestion which appeared to meet the difficulty. He proposed that Armadale should write to a respectable solicitor at Norwich, stating his position in general terms, and requesting that gentleman to take charge of his affairs, and to act as Mr Bashwood's adviser and superintendent when occasion required. Norwich being within an easy railway ride of Thorpe-Ambrose, Armadale saw no objection to the proposal, and promised to write to the Norwich lawyer. Fearing that he might make some mistake, if he wrote without assistance, Midwinter had drawn him out a draft of the necessary letter, and Armadale was now engaged in copying the draft, and also in writing to Mr Bashwood to lodge the money immediately in Coutts's Bank.

These details are so dry and uninteresting in themselves, that I hesitated at first about putting them down in my diary. But a little reflection has convinced me that they are too important to be passed over. Looked at from my point of view, they mean this – that Armadale's own act is now cutting him off from all communication with Thorpe-Ambrose, even by letter. *He is as good as dead, already, to everybody he leaves behind him.* The causes which have led to such a result as that, are causes which certainly claim the best place I can give them in these pages.

August 1st. – Nothing to record, but that I have had a long quiet, happy day with Midwinter. He hired a carriage, and we drove to Richmond, and dined there. After to-day's experience, it is impossible to deceive myself any longer. Come what may of it, I love him.

I have fallen into low spirits since he left me. A persuasion has taken possession of my mind, that the smooth and prosperous course of my affairs since I have been in London, is too smooth and prosperous to last. There is something oppressing me to-night, which is more than the oppression of the heavy London air.

August 2nd. Three o'clock. – My presentiments, like other people's, have deceived me often enough – but I am almost afraid that my presentiment of last night was really prophetic, for once in a way.

I went after breakfast to a milliner's in this neighbourhood to order a few cheap summer things, and thence to Midwinter's hotel to arrange with him for another day in the country. I drove to the milliner's and to the hotel, and part of the way back. Then, feeling disgusted with the horrid close smell of the cab (somebody had been smoking in it, I suppose), I got out to walk the rest of the way. Before I had been two minutes on my feet, I discovered that I was being followed by a strange man.

This may mean nothing but that an idle fellow has been struck by my figure, and my appearance generally. My face could have made no impression on him – for it was hidden as usual by my veil. Whether he followed me (in a cab of course) from the milliner's, or from the hotel, I cannot say. Nor am I quite certain whether he did or did not track me to this door. I only know that I lost sight of him before I got back. There is no help for it but to wait till events enlighten me. If there is anything serious in what has happened, I shall soon discover it.

Five o'clock. – It *is* serious. Ten minutes since, I was in my bed-room, which communicates with the sitting-room. I was just coming out, when I heard a strange voice on the landing outside – a woman's voice. The next instant the sitting-room door was suddenly opened; the woman's voice said, 'Are these the apartments you have got to let?' –

and though the landlady, behind her, answered, 'No! higher up, ma'am,' the woman came on straight to my bed-room, as if she had not heard. I had just time to slam the door in her face before she saw me. The necessary explanations and apologies followed between the landlady and the stranger in the sitting-room – and then I was left alone again.

'I have no time to write more. It is plain that somebody has an interest in trying to identify me, and that, but for my own quickness, the strange woman would have accomplished this object by taking me by surprise. She and the man who followed me in the street are, I suspect, in league together; and there is probably somebody in the background whose interests they are serving. Is Mother Oldershaw attacking me in the dark? or who else can it be? No matter who it is; my present situation is too critical to be trifled with. I must get away from this house to-night, and leave no trace behind me by which I can be followed to another place.

August 3rd. – Gary Street, Tottenham Court Road. – I got away last night (after writing an excuse to Midwinter, in which 'my invalid mother' figured as the all-sufficient cause of my disappearance); and I have found refuge here. It has cost me some money; but my object is attained! Nobody can possibly have traced me from All Saints' Terrace to this address.

After paying my landlady the necessary forfeit for leaving her without notice, I arranged with her son that he should take my boxes in a cab to the cloak-room at the nearest railway station, and send me the ticket in a letter, to wait my application for it at the post-office. While he went his way in one cab, I went mine in another, with a few things for the night in my little hand-bag. I drove straight to the milliner's shop – which I had observed, when I was there yesterday, had a back entrance into a mews, for the apprentices to go in and out by. I went in at once, leaving the cab waiting for me at the door. 'A man is following me,' I said; 'and I want to get rid of him. Here is my cab-fare; wait ten minutes before you give it to the driver, and let me out at once by the back way!' In a moment I was out in the mews – in another, I was in the next street – in a third, I hailed a passing omnibus, and was a free woman again.[5]

Having now cut off all communication between me and my last lodgings, the next precaution (in case Midwinter or Armadale are watched) is to cut off all communication, for some days to come at least, between me and the hotel. I have written to Midwinter – making my suppositious mother once more the excuse – to say that I am tied to my nursing duties, and that we must communicate by writing only for the present. Doubtful as I still am of who my hidden enemy really is, I can do no more to defend myself than I have done now.

August 4th. – The two friends at the hotel have both written to me. Midwinter expresses his regret at our separation, in the tenderest terms. Armadale writes an entreaty for help under very awkward circumstances. A letter from Major Milroy has been forwarded to him from the great house, and he encloses it in his letter to me.

Having left the seaside, and placed his daughter safely at the school originally chosen for her (in the neighbourhood of Ely), the major appears to have returned to Thorpe-Ambrose at the close of last week; to have heard then, for the first time, the reports about Armadale and me; and to have written instantly to Armadale to tell him so.

The letter is stern and short. Major Milroy dismisses the report as unworthy of credit, because it is impossible for him to believe in such an act of 'cold-blooded treachery', as the scandal would imply, if the scandal were true. He simply writes to warn Armadale that, if he is not more careful in his actions for the future, he must resign all pretensions to Miss Milroy's hand. 'I neither expect, nor wish for, an answer to this' (the letter ends), 'for I desire to receive no mere protestations in words. By your conduct, and by your conduct alone, I shall judge you as time goes on. Let me also add, that I positively forbid you to consider this letter as an excuse for violating the terms agreed on between us, by writing again to my daughter. You have no need to justify yourself in her eyes – for I fortunately removed her from Thorpe-Ambrose before this abominable report had time to reach her; and I shall take good care, for her sake, that she is not agitated and unsettled by hearing it where she is now.'

Armadale's petition to me, under these circumstances, entreats (as I am the innocent cause of the new attack on his character), that I will write to the major to absolve him of all indiscretion in the matter, and to say that he could not, in common politeness, do otherwise than accompany me to London. I forgive the impudence of his request, in consideration of the news that he sends me. It is certainly another circumstance in my favour, that the scandal at Thorpe-Ambrose is not to be allowed to reach Miss Milroy's ears. With her temper (if she did hear it) she might do something desperate in the way of claiming her lover, and might compromise me seriously. As for my own course with Armadale, it is easy enough. I shall quiet him by promising to write to

Major Milroy; and I shall take the liberty, in my own private interests, of not keeping my word.

Nothing in the least suspicious has happened to-day. Whoever my enemies are, they have lost me, and between this and the time when I leave England they shall not find me again. I have been to the post-office, and have got the ticket for my luggage, enclosed to me in a letter from All Saints' Terrace as I directed. The luggage itself I shall still leave at the cloak-room, until I see the way before me more clearly than I see it now.

August 5th. – Two letters again from the hotel. Midwinter writes to remind me, in the prettiest possible manner, that he will have lived long enough in the parish by to-morrow to be able to get our marriage licence, and that he proposes applying for it in the usual way at Doctors' Commons. Now, if I am ever to say it, is the time to say No. I can't say No. There is the plain truth – and there is an end of it!

Armadale's letter is a letter of farewell. He thanks me for my kindness in consenting to write to the major, and bids me good-by till we meet again at Naples. He has learnt from his friend that there are private reasons which will oblige him to forbid himself the pleasure of being present at our marriage. Under these circumstances, there is nothing to keep him in London. He has made all his business arrangements; he goes to Somersetshire by to-night's train; and, after staying some time with Mr Brock, he will sail for the Mediterranean from the Bristol Channel (in spite of Midwinter's objections) in his own yacht.

The letter encloses a jeweller's box, with a ring in it – Armadale's present to me on my marriage. It is a ruby – but rather a small one, and set in the worst possible taste. He would have given Miss Milroy a ring worth ten times the money, if it had been *her* marriage present. There is no more hateful creature, in my opinion, than a miserly young man. I wonder whether his trumpery little yacht will drown him?

I am so excited and fluttered, I hardly know what I am writing. Not that I shrink from what is coming – I only feel as if I was being hurried on faster than I quite like to go. At this rate, if nothing happens, Midwinter will have married me, by the end of the week. And then—!

August 6th. – If anything could startle me now, I should feel startled by the news that has reached me to-day.

On his return to the hotel this morning, after getting the Marriage Licence, Midwinter found a telegram waiting for him. It contained an urgent message from Armadale, announcing that Mr Brock had had a relapse, and that all hope of his recovery was pronounced by the doctors to be at an end. By the dying man's own desire, Midwinter was summoned to take leave of him, and was entreated by Armadale not to lose a moment in starting for the rectory by the first train.

The hurried letter which tells me this, tells me also that, by the time I receive it, Midwinter will be on his way to the west. He promises to write at greater length, after he has seen Mr Brock, by to-night's post.

This news has an interest for me, which Midwinter little suspects. There is but one human creature, besides myself, who knows the secret of his birth and his name – and that one, is the old man who now lies waiting for him at the point of death. What will they say to each other at the last moment? Will some chance word take them back to the time when I was in Mrs Armadale's service at Madeira? Will they speak of Me?

August 7th. – The promised letter has just reached me. No parting words have been exchanged between them – it was all over before Midwinter reached Somersetshire. Armadale met him at the rectory gate with the news that Mr Brock was dead.

I try to struggle against it, but, coming after the strange complication of circumstances that has been closing round me for weeks past, there is something in this latest event of all that shakes my nerves. But one last chance of detection stood in my way when I opened my diary yesterday. When I open it to-day, that chance is removed by Mr Brock's death. It means something; I wish I knew what.

The funeral is to be on Saturday morning. Midwinter will attend it as well as Armadale. But he proposes returning to London first; and he writes word that he will call to-night, in the hope of seeing me on his way from the station to the hotel. Even if there was any risk in it, I should see him, as things are now. But there is no risk if he comes here from the station, instead of coming from the hotel.[6]

Five o'clock. – I was not mistaken in believing that my nerves were all unstrung. Trifles that would not have cost me a second thought at other times, weigh heavily on my mind now.

Two hours since, in despair of knowing how to get through the day, I bethought myself of the milliner who is making my summer dress. I had intended to go and try it on yesterday – but it slipped out of my memory, in the excitement of hearing about Mr Brock. So I went this afternoon, eager to do anything that might help me to get rid of myself. I have returned, feeling more uneasy and more depressed than I felt when I went out – for I have come back, fearing that I may yet have reason to repent not having left my unfinished dress on the milliner's hands.

Nothing happened to me, this time, in the street. It was only in the trying-on room that my suspicions were roused; and, there, it certainly did cross my mind that the attempt to discover me, which I defeated at All Saints' Terrace, was not given up yet, and that some of the shopwomen had been tampered with, if not the mistress herself.

Can I give myself anything in the shape of a reason for this impression? Let me think a little.

I certainly noticed two things which were out of the ordinary routine, under the circumstances. In the first place, there were twice as many women as were needed in the trying-on room. This looked suspicious – and yet, I might have accounted for it in more ways than one. Is it not the slack time now? and don't I know by experience that I am the sort of woman about whom other women are always spitefully curious? I thought again, in the second place, that one of the assistants persisted rather oddly in keeping me turned in a particular direction, with my face towards the glazed and curtained door that led into the work-room. But, after all, she gave a reason, when I asked for it. She said the light fell better on me that way – and, when I looked round, there was the window to prove her right. Still, these trifles produced such an effect on me, at the time, that I purposely found fault with the dress, so as to have an excuse for trying it on again, before I told them where I lived, and had it sent home. Pure fancy, I dare say. Pure fancy, perhaps, at the present moment. I don't care – I shall act on instinct (as they say), and give up the dress. In plainer words still, I won't go back.

Midnight. – Midwinter came to see me as he promised. An hour has passed since we said good-night; and here I still sit, with my pen in my hand, thinking of him. No words of mine can describe what has passed between us. The end of it is all I can write in these pages – and the end of it is, that he has shaken my resolution. For the first time since I saw the easy way to Armadale's life at Thorpe-Ambrose, I feel as if the man whom I have doomed in my own thoughts, had a chance of escaping me.

Is it my love for Midwinter that has altered me? Or is it *his* love for *me* that has taken possession, not only of all I wish to give him, but of all I wish to keep from him as well? I feel as if I had lost myself – lost myself, I mean, in *him* – all through the evening. He was in great agitation about what had happened in Somersetshire – and he made me feel as disheartened and as wretched about it as he did. Though he never confessed it in words, I know that Mr Brock's death has startled him as an ill-omen for our marriage – I know it because I feel Mr Brock's death as an ill-omen too. The superstition – *his* superstition – took so strong a hold on me, that when we grew calmer, and he spoke of the future – when he told me that he must either break his engagement with his new employers, or go abroad, as he is pledged to go, on Monday next – I actually shrank at the thought of our marriage following close on Mr Brock's funeral; I actually said to him, in the impulse of the moment, 'Go, and begin your new life alone! go, and leave me here to wait for happier times.'

He took me in his arms. He sighed, and kissed me with an angelic tenderness. He said – oh, so softly and so sadly! – 'I have no life now, apart from *you*.' As those words passed his lips, the thought seemed to rise in my mind like an echo, 'Why not live out all the days that are left to me, happy and harmless in a love like this!' I can't explain it – I can't realize it. That was the thought in me at the time; and that is the thought in me still. I see my own hand while I write the words – and I ask myself whether it is really the hand of Lydia Gwilt!

Armadale—

No! I will never write, I will never think of Armadale again.

Yes! Let me write once more – let me think once more of him, because it quiets me to know that he is going away, and that the sea will have parted us before I am married. His old home is home to him no longer, now that the loss of his mother has been followed by the loss of his best and earliest friend. When the funeral is over, he has decided to sail the same day for the foreign seas. We may, or we may not, meet at Naples. Shall I be an altered woman, if we do? I wonder! I wonder!

August 8th. – A line from Midwinter. He has gone back to Somersetshire to be in readiness for the funeral to-morrow; and he will return here (after bidding Armadale good-by) to-morrow evening.

The last forms and ceremonies preliminary to our marriage have been complied with. I am to be his wife, on Monday next. The hour must not be later than half-past ten – which will give us just time, when the service is over, to get from the church door to the railway, and to start on our journey to Naples the same day.

To-day – Saturday – Sunday! I am not afraid of the time; the time will pass. I am not afraid of myself, if I can only keep all thoughts but one out of my mind. I love him! Day and night, till Monday comes, I will think of nothing but that. I love him!

Four o'clock. – Other thoughts are forced into my mind in spite of me. My suspicions of yesterday were no mere fancies; the milliner *has* been tampered with. My folly in going back to her house has led to my being traced here. I am absolutely certain that I never gave the woman my address – and yet my new gown was sent home to me at two o'clock to-day!

A man brought it with the bill, and a civil message to say that, as I had not called at the appointed time to try it on again, the dress had been finished and sent to me. He caught me in the passage; I had no choice but to pay the bill, and dismiss him. Any other proceeding, as events have now turned out, would have been pure folly. The messenger (not the man who followed me in the street, but another spy sent to look at me beyond all doubt) would have declared he knew nothing about it, if I had spoken to him. The milliner would tell me to my face, if I went to her, that I had given her my address. The one useful thing to do now, is to set my wits to work in the interests of my own security, and to step out of the false position in which my own rashness has placed me – if I can.

Seven o'clock. – My spirits have risen again. I believe I am in a fair way of extricating myself already.

I have just come back from a long round in a cab. First, to the cloak-room of the Great Western, to get the luggage which I sent there from All Saints' Terrace. Next, to the cloak-room of the South Eastern, to leave my luggage (labelled in Midwinter's name), to wait for me till the starting of the tidal train[7] on Monday. Next, to the General Post Office, to post a letter to Midwinter at the rectory, which he will receive to-morrow morning. Lastly, back again to this house – from which I shall move no more till Monday comes.

My letter to Midwinter will, I have little doubt, lead to his seconding (quite innocently) the precautions that I am taking for my own safety. The shortness of the time at our disposal, on Monday, will oblige him to pay his bill at the hotel and to remove his luggage, before the marriage ceremony takes place. All I ask him to do beyond this, is to take the luggage himself to the South Eastern (so as to make any inquiries useless which may address themselves to the servants at the hotel) – and, that done, to meet me at the church door, instead of calling for me here. The rest concerns nobody but myself. When Sunday night or Monday morning comes, it will be hard indeed – freed as I am now from all encumbrances – if I can't give the people who are watching me the slip for the second time.

It seems needless enough to have written to Midwinter to-day, when he is coming back to me to-morrow night. But it was impossible to ask, what I have been obliged to ask of him, without making my false family circumstances once more the excuse; and having this to do – I must own the truth – I wrote to him because, after what I suffered on the last occasion, I can never again deceive him to his face.

August 9th. – Two o'clock. – I rose early this morning, more depressed in spirits than usual. The re-beginning of one's life, at the re-beginning of every day, has always been something weary and hopeless to me for years past. I dreamt too all through the night – not of Midwinter and of my married life, as I had hoped to dream – but of the wretched conspiracy to discover me, by which I have been driven from one place to another, like a hunted animal. Nothing in the shape of a new revelation enlightened me in my sleep. All I could guess, dreaming, was what I had guessed waking, that Mother Oldershaw is the enemy who is attacking me in the dark. Except old Bashwood (whom it would be ridiculous to think of in such a serious matter as this), who else but Mother Oldershaw can have an object to serve by interfering with my proceedings at the present time?

My restless night has, however, produced one satisfactory result. It has led to my winning the good graces of the servant here, and securing all the assistance she can give me when the time comes for making my escape.

The girl noticed this morning that I looked pale and anxious. I took her into my confidence, to the extent of telling her that I was privately engaged to be married, and that I had enemies who were trying to part me from my sweetheart. This instantly roused her sympathy – and a present of a ten-shilling piece for her kind services to me did the rest. In the intervals of her house-work she has been with me nearly the whole morning; and I have found out, among other things, that *her* sweetheart is a private soldier in the Guards, and that she expects to see him to-morrow. I have got money enough left, little as it is, to turn the head of any Private in the British army – and, if the person appointed to watch me to-morrow is a man, I think it just possible that he may find his attention disagreeably diverted from Miss Gwilt in the course of the evening.

When Midwinter came here last from the railway, he came at half-past eight. How am I to get through the weary, weary hours between this and the evening? I think I shall darken my bedroom, and drink the blessing of oblivion from my bottle of Drops.

Eleven o'clock. – We have parted for the last time before the day comes that makes us man and wife.

He has left me, as he left me before, with an absorbing subject of interest to think of in his absence. I noticed a change in him the moment he entered the room. When he told me of the funeral, and of his parting with Armadale on board the yacht, though he spoke with feelings deeply moved, he spoke with a mastery over himself which is new to me in my experience of him. It was the same when our talk turned next on our own hopes and prospects. He was plainly disappointed when he found that my family embarrassments would prevent our meeting to-morrow, and plainly uneasy at the prospect of leaving me to find my way by myself on Monday to the church. But there was a certain hopefulness and composure of manner underlying it all, which produced so strong an impression on me that I was obliged to notice it. 'You know what odd fancies take possession of me sometimes,' I said. 'Shall I tell you the fancy that has taken possession of me now? I can't help thinking that something has happened since we last saw each other, which you have not told me yet.'

'Something *has* happened,' he answered. 'And it is something which you ought to know.'

With those words he took out his pocket-book, and produced two written papers from it. One he looked at and put back. The other he placed on the table before me. Keeping his hand on it for a moment, he spoke again.

'Before I tell you what this is, and how it came into my possession,' he said, 'I must own something that I have concealed from you. It is no more serious confession than the confession of my own weakness.'

He then acknowledged to me, that the renewal of his friendship with Armadale had been clouded, through the whole period of their intercourse in London, by his own superstitious misgivings. On every occasion when they were alone together, the terrible words of his father's death-bed letter, and the terrible confirmation of them in the warnings of the Dream, were present to his mind. Day after day, the conviction that fatal consequences to Armadale would come of the renewal of their friendship, and of my share in accomplishing it, had grown stronger and stronger in its influence over him. He had obeyed the summons which called him to the rector's bedside, with the firm intention of confiding his previsions of coming trouble to Mr Brock; and he had been doubly confirmed in his superstition, when he found that Death had entered the house before him, and had parted them, in this world, for ever. He had travelled back to be present at the funeral, with a secret sense of relief at the prospect of being parted from Armadale, and with a secret resolution to make the after-meeting agreed on between us three at Naples, a meeting that should never take place. With that purpose in his heart, he had gone up alone to the room prepared for him, on his arrival at the rectory, and had opened a letter which he found waiting for him on the table. The letter had only that day been discovered – dropped and lost – under the bed on which Mr Brock had died. It was in the rector's handwriting throughout; and the person to whom it was addressed, was Midwinter himself.

Having told me this, nearly in the words in which I have written it, he lifted his hand from the written paper that lay on the table between us.

'Read it,' he said; 'and you will not need to be told that my mind is at peace again, and that I took Allan's hand at parting, with a heart that was worthier of Allan's love.'

I read the letter. There was no superstition to be conquered in *my* mind; there were no old feelings of gratitude towards Armadale, to be roused in *my* heart – and yet, the effect which the letter had had on Midwinter, was, I firmly believe, more than matched by the effect that the letter now produced on Me.

It was vain to ask him to leave it, and to let me read it again (as I wished) when I was left by myself. He is determined not to let it out of his own possession; he is determined to keep it side by side with that other paper which I had seen him take out of his pocket-book, and which contains the written narrative of Armadale's Dream. All I could do was to ask his leave to copy it; and this he granted readily. I wrote the copy in his presence; and I now place it here in my diary, to mark a day which is one of the memorable days of my life.

Boscombe Rectory, August 2nd.

MY DEAR MIDWINTER, – For the first time since the beginning of my illness, I found strength enough yesterday to look over my letters. One among them is a letter from Allan, which has been lying unopened on my table for ten days past. He writes to me in great distress, to say that there has been dissension between you, and that you have left him. If you still remember what passed between us, when you first opened your heart to me in the Isle of Man, you will be at no loss to understand how I have thought over this miserable news, through the night that has now passed, and you will not be surprised to hear that I have roused myself this morning to make the effort of writing to you. Although I am far from despairing of myself, I dare not, at my age, trust too confidently to my prospects of recovery. While the time is still my own, I must employ it for Allan's sake and for yours.

I want no explanation of the circumstances which have parted you from your friend. If my estimate of your character is not founded on an entire delusion, the one influence which can have led to your estrangement from Allan, is the influence of that evil spirit of Superstition, which I have once already cast out of your heart – which I will once again conquer, please God, if I have strength enough to make my pen speak my mind to you in this letter.

It is no part of my design to combat the belief which I know you to hold, that mortal creatures may be the objects of super-natural intervention in their pilgrimage through this world. Speaking as a reasonable man, I own that I cannot prove you to be wrong. Speaking as a believer in the Bible, I am bound to go farther, and to admit that you possess a higher than any human warrant for the faith that is in you. The one object which I have it at heart to attain, is to induce you to free yourself from the paralysing fatalism of the heathen and the savage, and to look at the mysteries that perplex, and the por-tents that daunt you, from the Christian's point of view. If I can succeed in this, I shall clear your mind of the ghastly doubts that now oppress it, and I shall re-unite you to your friend, never to be parted from him again.

I have no means of seeing and questioning you. I can only send this letter to Allan to be forwarded, if he knows, or can discover, your present address. Placed in this position towards you, I am bound to assume all that *can* be assumed in your favour. I will take it for granted that something has happened to you or to Allan, which to your mind has not only confirmed the fatalist conviction in which your father died, but has added a new and terrible meaning to the warning which he sent you in his death-bed letter.

On this common ground I meet you. On this common ground I appeal to your higher nature and your better sense.

Preserve your present conviction that the events which have happened (be they what they may) are not to be reconciled with ordinary mortal coincidences and ordinary mortal laws; and view your own position by the best and clearest light that your supersti-tion can throw on it. What are you? You are a helpless instrument in the hands of Fate. You are doomed, beyond all human capacity of resistance, to bring misery and destruction blindfold on a man to whom you have harmlessly and gratefully united yourself in the bonds of a brother's love. All that is morally firmest in your will and morally purest in your aspirations, avails nothing against the hereditary impulsion of you towards evil, caused by a crime which your father committed before you were born. In what does that belief end? It ends in the darkness in which you are now lost; in the self-contradictions in which you are now bewildered – in the stubborn despair by which a man profanes his own soul, and lowers himself to the level of the brutes that perish.

Look up, my poor suffering brother – look up, my hardly-tried, my well-loved friend, higher than this! Meet the doubts that now assail you from the blessed vantage-ground of Christian courage and Christian hope; and your heart will turn again to Allan, and your mind will be at peace. Happen what may, God is all-merciful, God is all-wise: natural or supernatural, it happens through Him. The mystery of Evil that perplexes our feeble minds, the sorrow and the suffering that torture us in this little life, leave the one great truth unshaken that the destiny of man is in the hands of his Creator, and that God's blessed Son died to make us worthier of it. Nothing that is done in unquestioning submission to the wisdom of the Almighty, is done wrong. No evils exists, out of which, in obedience to His laws, Good may not come. Be true to what Christ tells you is true. Encourage in yourself, be the circumstances what they may, all that is loving, all that is grateful, all that is patient, all that is forgiving, towards your fellow-men. And humbly and trustfully leave the rest to the God who made you, and to the Saviour who loved you better than his own life.

This is the faith in which I have lived, by the Divine help and mercy, from my youth upward. I ask you earnestly, I ask you confidently, to make it your faith too. It is the mainspring of all the good I have ever done, of all the happiness I have ever known; it lightens my darkness, it sustains my hope; it comforts and quiets me, lying here, to live or die, I know not which. Let it sustain, comfort, and enlighten you. It will help you in your sorest need, as it has helped me in mine. It will show you another purpose in the events which brought you and Allan together than the purpose which your guilty father foresaw. Strange things, I do not deny it, have happened to you already. Stranger things still may happen before long, which I may not live to see. Remember, if that time comes, that I died firmly disbelieving in your influence over Allan being other than an influence for good. The great sacrifice of the Atonement – I say it reverently – has its mortal reflections, even in this world. If danger ever threatens Allan, you, whose father took his father's life – You, and no other, may be the man whom the providence of God has appointed to save him.

Come to me, if I live. Go back to the friend who loves you, whether I live or die. – Yours affectionately to the last,

DECIMUS BROCK.

'You, and no other, may be the man whom the providence of God has appointed to save him!'

Those are the words which have shaken me to the soul. Those are the words which make me feel as if the dead man had left his grave, and had put his hand on the place in my heart where my terrible secret lies hidden from every living creature but myself. One part of the letter has come true already. The danger that it foresees, threatens Armadale at this moment – and threatens him from Me!

If the favouring circumstances which have driven me thus far, drive me on to the end; and if that old man's last earthly conviction is prophetic of the truth, Armadale will escape me, do what I may. And Midwinter will be the victim who is sacrificed to save his life.

It is horrible! it is impossible! it shall never be! At the thinking of it only, my hand trembles, and my heart sinks. I bless the trembling that unnerves me! I bless the sinking that turns me faint! I bless those words in the letter which have revived the relenting thoughts that first came to me two days since! Is it hard, now that events are taking me, smoothly and safely, nearer and nearer to the End – is it hard to conquer the temptation to go on? No! If there is only a chance of harm coming to Midwinter, the dread of that chance is enough to decide me – enough to strengthen me to conquer the temptation, for his sake. I have never loved him yet, never, never, never as I love him now!

Sunday, August 10th. – The eve of my wedding-day! I close and lock this book, never to write in it, never to open it again.

I have won the great victory; I have trampled my own wickedness under foot. I am innocent; I am happy again. My love! my angel! when to-morrow gives me to you, I will not have a thought in my heart which is not *your* thought, as well as mine!

CHAPTER XV

THE WEDDING DAY

The time was nine o'clock in the morning. The place was a private room in one of the old-fashioned inns, which still remain on the Borough side of the Thames. The date was Monday, the 11th of August. And the person was Mr Bashwood, who had travelled to London on a summons from his son, and had taken up his abode at the inn, on the previous day.

He had never yet looked so pitiably old and helpless as he looked now. The fever and chill of alternating hope and despair, had dried and withered and wasted him. The angles of his figure had sharpened. The outline of his face had shrunk. His dress pointed the melancholy change in him, with a merciless and shocking emphasis. Never, even in his youth, had he worn such clothes as he wore now. With the desperate resolution to leave no chance untried of producing an impression on Miss Gwilt, he had cast aside his dreary black garments; he had even mustered the courage to wear his blue satin cravat. His coat was a riding coat of light grey. He had ordered it, with a vindictive subtlety of purpose, to be made on the pattern of a coat that he had seen Allan wear. His waistcoat was white; his trousers were of the gayest summer pattern, in the largest check. His wig was oiled and scented, and brushed round, on either side, to hide the wrinkles on his temples. He was an object to laugh at – he was an object to weep over. His enemies, if a creature so wretched could have had enemies, would have forgiven him, on seeing him in his new dress. His friends – had any of his friends been left – would have been less distressed if they had looked at him in his coffin, than if they had looked at him as he was now. Incessantly restless, he paced the room from end to end. Now he looked at his watch; now he looked out of window; now he looked at the well-furnished breakfast-table – always with the same wistful uneasy inquiry in his eyes. The waiter coming in, with the urn of boiling water, was addressed for the fiftieth time in the one form of words which the miserable creature seemed to be capable of uttering that morning,

– 'My son is coming to breakfast. My son is very particular. I want everything of the best – hot things, and cold things – and tea and coffee – and all the rest of it, waiter; all the rest of it.' For the fiftieth time, he now reiterated those anxious words. For the fiftieth time, the impenetrable waiter had just returned his one pacifying answer, – 'All right, sir; you may leave it to me' – when the sound of leisurely footsteps was heard on the stairs; the door opened; and the long-expected son sauntered indolently into the room, with a neat little black-leather bag in his hand.

'Well done, old gentleman!' said Bashwood the younger, surveying his father's dress with a smile of sardonic encouragement. 'You're ready to be married to Miss Gwilt at a moment's notice!'

The father took the son's hand, and tried to echo the son's laugh.

'You have such good spirits, Jemmy,' he said, using the name in its familiar form, as he had been accustomed to use it, in happier days. 'You always had good spirits, my dear, from a child. Come and sit down; I've ordered you a nice breakfast. Everything of the best! everything of the best! What a relief it is to see you! Oh, dear, dear, what a relief it is to see you.' He stopped and sat down at the table – his face flushed with the effort to control the impatience that was devouring him. 'Tell me about her!' he burst out, giving up the effort with a sudden self-abandonment. 'I shall die, Jemmy, if I wait for it any longer. Tell me! tell me! tell me!'

'One thing at a time,' said Bashwood the younger, perfectly unmoved by his father's impatience. 'We'll try the breakfast first, and come to the lady afterwards? Gently does it, old gentleman – gently does it!'

He put his leather bag on a chair, and sat down opposite to his father, composed, and smiling, and humming a little tune.

No ordinary observation, applying the ordinary rules of analysis, would have detected the character of Bashwood the younger in his face. His youthful look, aided by his light hair, and his plump beardless cheeks; his easy manner, and his ever ready smile; his eyes which met unshrinkingly the eyes of every one whom he addressed, all combined to make the impression of him a favourable impression in the general mind. No eye for reading character, but such an eye as belongs to one person, perhaps, in ten thousand, could have penetrated the smoothly-deceptive surface of this man, and have seen him for what he really was – the vile creature whom the viler need of Society has fashioned for its own use. There he sat – the Confidential Spy of modern times, whose business is steadily enlarging,[1] whose Private Inquiry Offices are steadily on the increase. There he sat – the necessary Detective attendant on the progress of our national civilization; a man who was in this instance at least, the legitimate and intelligible product of the vocation that employed him; a man professionally ready on the merest suspicion (if the merest suspicion paid him) to get under our beds, and to look through gimlet-holes in our doors; a man who would have been useless to his employers if he could have felt a touch of human sympathy in his father's presence; and who would have deservedly forfeited his situation, if, under any circumstances whatever, he had been personally accessible to a sense of pity or a sense of shame.

'Gently does it, old gentleman,' he repeated, lifting the covers from the dishes, and looking under them one after the other all round the table. 'Gently does it!'

'Don't be angry with me, Jemmy,' pleaded his father. 'Try, if you can, to think how anxious I must be. I got your letter as long ago as yesterday morning. I have had to travel all the way from Thorpe-Ambrose, – I have had to get through the dreadful long evening, and the dreadful long night – with your letter telling me that you had found out who she is, and telling me nothing more. Suspense is very hard to bear, Jemmy, when you come to my age. What was it prevented you, my dear, from coming to me when I got here yesterday evening?'

'A little dinner at Richmond,' said Bashwood the younger. 'Give me some tea.'

Mr Bashwood tried to comply with the request; but the hand with which he lifted the teapot trembled so unmanageably that the tea missed the cup and streamed out on the cloth. 'I'm very sorry; I can't help trembling when I'm anxious,' said the old man, as his son took the teapot out of his hand. 'I'm afraid you bear me malice, Jemmy, for what happened when I was last in town. I own I was obstinate and unreasonable about going back to Thorpe-Ambrose. I'm more sensible now. You were quite right in taking it all on yourself, as soon as I showed you the veiled lady, when we saw her come out of the hotel; and you were quite right to send me back the same day to my business in the steward's office at the Great House.' He watched the effect of these concessions on his son, and ventured doubtfully on another entreaty. 'If you won't tell me anything else just yet,' he said, faintly, 'will you tell me how you found her out? Do, Jemmy, – do!'

Bashwood the younger looked up from his plate. 'I'll tell you that,' he said. 'The reckoning up of Miss Gwilt has cost more money and taken more time than I expected; and the sooner we come to a settlement about it, the sooner we shall get to what you want to know.'

Without a word of expostulation, the father laid his dingy old pocket-book and his purse on the table before the son. Bashwood the younger looked into the purse; observed, with a contemptuous elevation of the eyebrows, that it held no more than a sovereign and some silver; and returned it intact. The pocket-book, on being opened next, proved to contain four five-pound notes. Bashwood the younger transferred three of the notes to his own keeping; and handed the pocket-book back to his father, with a bow expressive of mock gratitude, and sarcastic respect.

'A thousand thanks,' he said. 'Some of it is for the people at our office, and the balance is for myself. One of the few stupid things, my dear sir, that I have done in the course of my life, was to write you word when you first consulted me, that you might have my services gratis. As you see, I hasten to repair the error. An hour or two at odd times, I was ready enough to give you. But this business has taken days, and has got in the way of other jobs. I told you I couldn't be out of pocket by you – I put it in my letter, as plain as words could say it.'

'Yes, yes, Jemmy. I don't complain, my dear, I don't complain. Never mind the money – tell me how you found her out.'

'Besides,' pursued Bashwood the younger, proceeding impenetrably with his justification of himself, 'I have given you the benefit of my experience – I've done it cheap. It would have cost double the money, if another man had taken this in hand. Another man would have kept a watch on Mr Armadale as well as Miss Gwilt. I have saved you that expense. You are certain that Mr Armadale is bent on marrying her. Very good. In that case, while we have our eye on *her*, we have, for all useful purposes, got our eye on *him*. Know where the lady is, and you know that the gentleman can't be far off.'

'Quite true, Jemmy. But how was it Miss Gwilt came to give you so much trouble?'

'She's a devilish clever woman,' said Bashwood the younger; 'that's how it was. She gave us the slip at a milliner's shop. We made it all right with the milliner, and speculated on the chance of her coming back to try on a gown she had ordered. The cleverest women lose the use of their wits in nine cases out of ten, where there's a new dress in the case – and even Miss Gwilt was rash enough to go back. That was all we wanted. One of the women from our office helped to try on her new gown, and put her in the right position to be seen by one of our men behind the door. He instantly suspected who she was, on the strength of what he had been told of her – for she's a famous woman in her way. Of course, we didn't trust to that. We traced her to her new address; and we got a man from Scotland Yard, who was certain to know her, if our own man's idea was the right one. The man from Scotland Yard turned milliner's lad for the occasion, and took her gown home. He saw her in the passage, and identified her in an instant. You're in luck, I can tell you. Miss Gwilt's a public character. If we had had a less notorious woman to deal with, she might have cost us weeks of inquiry, and you might have had to pay hundreds of pounds. A day did it in Miss Gwilt's case; and another day put the whole story of her life, in black and white, into my hands. There it is at the present moment, old gentleman, in my black bag.'

Bashwood the father made straight for the bag with eager eyes, and outstretched hand. Bashwood the son took a little key out of his waistcoat pocket – winked – shook his head – and put the key back again.

'I hav'n't done breakfast yet,' he said. 'Gently does it, my dear sir – gently does it.'

'I can't wait!' cried the old man, struggling vainly to preserve his self-control. 'It's past nine! It's a fortnight to-day, since she went to London with Mr Armadale! She may be married to him in a fortnight! She may be married to him this morning! I can't wait! I can't wait!'

'There's no knowing what you can do till you try,' rejoined Bashwood the younger. 'Try; and you'll find you *can* wait. What has become of your curiosity?' he went on, feeding the fire ingeniously with a stick at a time. 'Why don't you ask me what I mean by calling Miss Gwilt a public character? Why don't you wonder how I came to lay my hand on the story of her life, in black and white? If you'll sit down again, I'll tell you. If you won't, I shall confine myself to my breakfast.'

Mr Bashwood sighed heavily, and went back to his chair.

'I wish you were not so fond of your joke, Jemmy,' he said; 'I wish, my dear, you were not quite so fond of your joke.'

'Joke?' repeated his son. 'It would be serious enough in some people's eyes, I can tell you. Miss Gwilt has been tried for her life; and the papers in that black bag are the lawyer's instructions for the Defence. Do you call that a joke?'

The father started to his feet, and looked straight across the table at the son with a smile of exultation that was terrible to see.

'She's been tried for her life!' he burst out, with a deep gasp of satisfaction. 'She's been tried for her life!' He broke into a low prolonged laugh, and snapped his fingers exultingly. 'Aha-ha-ha! Something to frighten Mr Armadale in *that*!'

Scoundrel as he was, the son was daunted by the explosion of pent-up passion which burst on him in those words.

'Don't excite yourself,' he said, with a sullen suppression of the mocking manner in which he had spoken thus far.

Mr Bashwood sat down again, and passed his handkerchief over his forehead. 'No,' he said, nodding and smiling at his son. 'No, no – no excitement, as you say – I can wait now, Jemmy; I can wait now.'

He waited with immovable patience. At intervals, he nodded, and smiled, and whispered to himself, 'Something to frighten Mr Armadale in *that*!' But he made no further attempt, by word, look, or action to hurry his son.

Bashwood the younger finished his breakfast slowly, out of pure bravado; lit a cigar, with the utmost deliberation; looked at his father, and, seeing him still as immovably patient as ever, opened the black bag at last, and spread the papers on the table.

'How will you have it?' he asked. 'Long or short? I have got her whole life here. The counsel who defended her at the trial was instructed to hammer hard at the sympathies of the jury: he went head over ears into the miseries of her past career, and shocked everybody in court in the most workmanlike manner. Shall I take the same line? Do you want to know all about her, from the time when she was in short frocks and frilled trousers? or do you prefer getting on at once to her first appearance as a prisoner in the dock?'

'I want to know all about her,' said his father eagerly. 'The worst, and the best – the worst, particularly. Don't spare my feelings, Jemmy – whatever you do, don't spare my feelings! Can't I look at the papers myself?'

'No, you can't. They would be all Greek and Hebrew to you. Thank your stars that you have got a sharp son, who can take the pith out of these papers, and give it a smack of the right flavour in serving it up. There are not ten men in England who could tell you this woman's story as I can tell it. It's a gift, old gentleman, of the sort that is given to very few people – and it lodges here.'

He tapped his forehead smartly, and turned to the first page of the manuscript before him, with an unconcealed triumph at the prospect of exhibiting his own cleverness, which was the first expression of a genuine feeling of any sort that had escaped him yet.

'Miss Gwilt's story begins,' said Bashwood the younger, 'in the market-place at Thorpe-Ambrose. One day, something like a quarter of a century ago, a travelling quack-doctor,[2] who dealt in perfumery as well as medicines, came to the town, with his cart, and exhibited, as a living example of the excellence of his washes and hair-oils and so on, a pretty little girl, with a beautiful complexion and wonderful hair. His name was Oldershaw. He had a wife, who helped him in the perfumery part of his business, and who carried it on by herself after his death. She has risen in the world of late years; and she is identical with that sly old lady who employed me professionally a short time since. As for the pretty little girl, you know who she was as well as I do. While the quack was haranguing the mob, and showing them the child's hair, a young lady, driving through the market-place, stopped her carriage to hear what it was all about; saw the little girl; and took a violent fancy to her on the spot. The young lady was the daughter of Mr Blanchard, of Thorpe-Ambrose. She went home, and interested her father in the fate of the innocent little victim of the quack-doctor. The same evening, the Oldershaws were sent for to the great house, and were questioned. They declared themselves to be her uncle and aunt – a lie, of course! – and they were quite willing to let her attend the village school, while they stayed at Thorpe-Ambrose, when the proposal was made to them. The new arrangement was carried out the next day. And the day after that, the Oldershaws had disappeared, and had left the little girl on the squire's hands! She evidently hadn't answered as they expected in the capacity of an advertisement – and that was the way they took of providing for her for life. There is the first act of the play for you! Clear enough, so far, isn't it?'

'Clear enough, Jemmy, to clever people. But I'm old and slow. I don't understand one thing. Whose child was she?'

'A very sensible question. Sorry to inform you that nobody can answer it – Miss Gwilt herself included. These Instructions that I'm referring to are founded, of course, on her own statements, sifted by her attorney. All she could remember, on being questioned, was, that she was beaten and half starved, somewhere in the country, by a woman who took in children at nurse. The woman had a card with her, stating that her name was Lydia Gwilt, and got a yearly allowance for taking care of her (paid through a lawyer), till she was eight years old.[3] At that time, the allowance stopped; the lawyer had no explanation to offer; nobody came to look after her; nobody wrote. The Oldershaws saw her, and thought she might answer to exhibit; and the woman parted with her for a trifle to the Oldershaws; and the Oldershaws parted with her for good and all to the Blanchards. That's the story of her birth, parentage, and education! She may be the daughter of a Duke, or the daughter of a costermonger. The circumstances may be highly romantic, or utterly commonplace. Fancy anything you like – there's nothing to stop you. When you've had your fancy out, say the word, and I'll turn over the leaves and go on.'

'Please to go on, Jemmy – please to go on.'

'The next glimpse of Miss Gwilt,' resumed Bashwood the younger, turning over the papers, 'is a glimpse at a family mystery. The deserted child was in luck's way at last. She had taken the fancy of an amiable young lady with a rich father, and she was petted and made much of at the great house, in the character of Miss Blanchard's last new plaything. Not long afterwards Mr Blanchard and his daughter went abroad, and took the girl with them in the capacity of Miss Blanchard's little maid. When they came back, the daughter had married, and become a widow, in the interval; and the pretty little maid, instead of returning with them to Thorpe-Ambrose, turns up suddenly, all alone, as a pupil at a school in France. There she was, at a first-rate establishment, with her maintenance and education secured until she married and settled in life, on this understanding, – that she never returned to England. Those were all the particulars she could be prevailed on to give the lawyer who drew up these instructions. She declined to say what had happened abroad; she declined even, after all the years that had passed, to mention her mistress's married name. It's quite clear, of course, that she was in possession of some family secret; and that the Blanchards paid for the schooling on the Continent to keep her out of the way. And it's equally plain that she would never have kept her secret as she did, if she had not seen her way to trading on it for her own advantage at some future time. A clever woman, as I've told you already! A devilish clever woman, who hasn't been knocked about in the world, and seen the ups and downs of life abroad and at home for nothing.'

'Yes, yes, Jemmy; quite true. How long did she stop, please, at the school in France?'

Bashwood the younger referred to the papers.

'She stopped at the French school,' he replied, 'till she was seventeen. At that time, something happened at the school which I find mildly described in these papers as "something unpleasant". The plain fact was, that the music-master attached to the establishment fell in love with Miss Gwilt. He was a respectable middle-aged man, with a wife and family – and finding the circumstances entirely hopeless, he took a pistol, and rashly assuming that he had brains in his head, tried to blow them out. The doctors saved his life, but not his reason – he ended, where he had better have begun, in an asylum. Miss Gwilt's beauty having been at the bottom of the scandal, it was of course impossible – though she was proved to have been otherwise quite blameless in the matter – for her to remain at the school after what had happened. Her "friends" (the Blanchards) were communicated with. And her friends transferred her to another school; at Brussels, this time. – What are you sighing about? what's wrong now?'

'I can't help feeling a little for the poor music-master, Jemmy. Go on.'

'According to her own account of it, dad, Miss Gwilt seems to have felt for him too. She took a serious turn; and was "converted" (as they call it) by the lady who had charge of her in the interval before she went to Brussels. The priest at the Belgian school appears to have been a man of some discretion, and to have seen that the girl's sensibilities were getting into a dangerously excited state. Before he could quiet her down, he fell ill, and was succeeded by another priest, who was a fanatic. You will understand the sort of interest he took in the girl, and the way in which he worked on her feelings, when I tell you that she announced it as her decision, after having been nearly two years at the school, to end her days in a convent! You may well stare! Miss Gwilt, in the character of a Nun,[4] is the sort of female phenomenon you don't often set eyes on. Women are queer creatures.'[5]

'Did she go into the convent?' asked Mr Bashwood. 'Did they let her go in, so friendless and so young, with nobody to advise her for the best?'

'The Blanchards were consulted, as a matter of form,' pursued Bashwood the younger. '*They* had no objection to her shutting herself up in a convent, as you may well imagine. The pleasantest letter they ever had from her, I'll answer for it, was the letter in which she solemnly took leave of them in this world for ever. The people at the convent were as careful as usual not to commit themselves. Their rules wouldn't allow her to take the veil till she had tried the life for a year first, and then, if she had any doubt, for another year after that. She tried the life for the first year, accordingly – and doubted. She tried it for the second year – and was wise enough, by that time, to give it up without further hesitation. Her position was rather an awkward one when she found herself at liberty again. The sisters at the convent had lost their interest in her; the mistress at the school declined to take her back as teacher, on the ground that she was too nice-looking for the place; the priest considered her to be possessed by the devil. There was nothing for it but to write to the Blanchards again, and ask them to start her in life as a teacher of music on her own account. She wrote to her former mistress accordingly. Her former mistress had evidently doubted the genuineness of the girl's resolution to be a nun, and had seized the opportunity offered by the farewell letter of three years since to cut off all further communication between her ex-waiting maid and herself. Miss Gwilt's letter was returned by the post-office. She caused inquiries to be made; and found that Mr Blanchard was dead, and that his daughter had left the great house for some place of retirement unknown. The next thing she did, upon this, was to write to the heir in possession of the estate. The letter was answered by his solicitors; who were instructed to put the law in force at the first attempt she made to extort money from any member of the family at Thorpe-Ambrose. The last chance was to get at the address of her mistress's place of retirement. The family bankers, to whom she wrote, wrote back to say that they were instructed not to give the lady's address to any one applying for it, without being previously empowered to do so by the lady herself. That last letter settled the question – Miss Gwilt could do nothing more. With money at her command, she might have gone to England, and made the Blanchards think twice before they carried things with too high a hand. Not having a halfpenny at command, she was helpless. Without money and without friends, you may wonder how she supported herself while the correspondence was going on. She supported herself by playing the pianoforte at a low concert-room in Brussels. The men laid siege to her, of course, in all directions – but they found her insensible as adamant. One of these rejected gentlemen was a Russian; and he was the means of making her acquainted with a countrywoman of his – whose name is unpronounceable by English lips. Let us give her her title, and call her the Baroness. The two women liked each other at their first introduction; and a new scene opened in Miss Gwilt's life. She became reader and companion to the Baroness. Everything was right, everything was smooth on the surface. Everything was rotten and everything was wrong, under it.'

'In what way, Jemmy? Please to wait a little, and tell me in what way.'

'In this way. The Baroness was fond of travelling, and she had a select set of friends about her, who were quite of her way of thinking. They went from one city on the Continent to another, and were such charming people that they picked up acquaintances everywhere. The acquaintances were invited to the Baroness's receptions – and card-tables were invariably a part of the Baroness's furniture. Do you see it now? or must I tell you, in the strictest confidence, that cards were not considered sinful on these festive occasions, and that the luck, at the end of the evening, turned out to be almost invariably on the side of the Baroness and her friends. Swindlers, all of them – and there isn't a doubt on my mind, whatever there may be on yours, that Miss Gwilt's manners and appearance made her a valuable member of the society in the capacity of a decoy. Her own statement is, that she was innocent of all knowledge of what really went on; that she was quite ignorant of card-playing; that she hadn't such a thing as a respectable friend to turn to in the world; and that she honestly liked the Baroness, for the simple reason that the Baroness was a hearty good friend to her from first to last. Believe that or not, as you please. For five years she travelled about all over the Continent, with these card-sharpers in high life, and she might have been among them at this moment, for anything I know to the contrary, if the Baroness had not caught a Tartar at Naples, in the shape of a rich travelling Englishman, named Waldron. Aha! that name startles you, does it? You've read the Trial of the famous Mrs Waldron,[6] like the rest of the world? And you know who Miss Gwilt is now, without my telling you?'

He paused, and looked at his father in sudden perplexity. Far from being overwhelmed by the discovery which had just burst on him, Mr Bashwood, after the first natural movement of surprise, faced his son with a self-possession which was nothing short of extraordinary under the circumstances. There was a new brightness in his eyes, and a new colour in his face. If it had been possible to conceive such a thing of a man in his position, he seemed to be absolutely encouraged instead of depressed by what he had just heard. 'Go on, Jemmy,' he said, quietly; 'I am one of the few people who didn't read the Trial – I only heard of it.'

Still wondering inwardly, Bashwood the younger recovered himself, and went on.

'You always were, and you always will be, behind the age,' he said. 'When we come to the Trial, I can tell you as much about it as you need know. In the meantime, we must go back to the Baroness and Mr Waldron. For a certain number of nights the Englishman let the card-sharpers have it all their own way – in other words, he paid for the privilege of making himself agreeable to Miss Gwilt. When he thought he had produced the necessary impression on her, he exposed the whole confederacy without mercy. The police interfered; the Baroness found herself in prison; and Miss Gwilt was put between the two alternatives of accepting Mr Waldron's protection, or being thrown on the world again. She was amazingly virtuous, or amazingly clever, which you please. To Mr Waldron's astonishment, she told him that she could face the prospect of being thrown on the world; and that he must address her honourably or leave her for ever. The end of it was what the end always is, where the man is infatuated and the woman is determined. To the disgust of his family and friends, Mr Waldron made a virtue of necessity, and married her.'

'How old was he?' asked Bashwood the elder eagerly.

Bashwood the younger burst out laughing. 'He was about old enough, daddy, to be your son, and rich enough to have burst that precious pocket-book of yours with thousand-pound notes! Don't hang your head. It wasn't a happy marriage, though he *was* so young and so rich. They lived abroad, and got on well enough at first. He made a new will, of course, as soon as he was married, and provided handsomely for his wife, under the tender pressure of the honeymoon. But women wear out, like other things, with time; and one fine morning Mr Waldron woke up with a doubt in his mind whether he had not acted like a fool. He was an ill-tempered man; he was discontented with himself; and of course he made his wife feel it. Having begun by quarrelling with her, he got on to suspecting her, and became savagely jealous of every male creature who entered the house. They had no incumbrances in the shape of children, and they moved from one place to another, just as his jealousy inclined him, till they moved back to England at last, after having been married close on four years. He had a lonely old house of his own among the Yorkshire moors, and there he shut his wife and himself up from every living creature, except his servants and his dogs. Only one result could come, of course, of treating a high-spirited young woman in that way. It may be fate, or it may be chance – but, whenever a woman is desperate, there is sure to be a man handy to take advantage of it. The man in this case was rather a 'dark horse', as they say on the turf. He was a certain Captain Manuel, a native of Cuba, and (according to his own account) an ex-officer in the Spanish navy. He had met Mr Waldron's beautiful wife on the journey back to England; had contrived to speak to her in spite of her husband's jealousy; and had followed her to her place of imprisonment in Mr Waldron's house on the moors. The captain is described as a clever, determined fellow – of the daring piratical sort – with the dash of mystery about him that women like—'

'She's not the same as other women!' interposed Mr Bashwood, suddenly interrupting his son. 'Did she—?' His voice failed him, and he stopped without bringing the question to an end.

'Did she like the captain?' suggested Bashwood the younger with another laugh. 'According to her own account of it, she adored him. At the same time her conduct (as represented by herself) was perfectly innocent. Considering how carefully her husband watched her, the statement (incredible as it appears) is probably true. For six weeks or so, they confined themselves to corresponding privately; the Cuban captain (who spoke and wrote English perfectly,) having contrived to make a go-between of one of the female servants in the Yorkshire house. How it might have ended we needn't trouble ourselves to inquire – Mr Waldron himself brought matters to a crisis. Whether he got wind of the clandestine correspondence or not, doesn't appear. But this is certain, that he came home from a ride one day, in a fiercer temper than usual – that his wife showed him a sample of that high spirit of hers which he had never yet been able to break – and that it ended in his striking her across the face with his riding-whip. Ungentlemanly conduct, I am afraid we must admit; but to all outward appearance, the riding-whip produced the most astonishing results. From that moment, the lady submitted as she had never submitted before. For a fortnight afterwards, he did what he liked; and she never thwarted him – he said what he liked; and she never uttered a word of protest. Some men might have suspected this sudden reformation of hiding something dangerous under the surface. Whether Mr Waldron looked at it in that light, I can't tell you. All that is known is, that before the mark of the whip was off his wife's face, he fell ill, and that in two days afterwards, he was a dead man. What do you say to that?'

'I say he deserved it!' answered Mr Bashwood, striking his hand excitedly on the table, as his son paused, and looked at him.

'The doctor who attended the dying man was not of your way of thinking,' remarked Bashwood the younger, drily. 'He called in two other medical men, and they all three refused to certify the death. The usual legal investigation followed. The evidence of the doctors and the evidence of the servants pointed irresistibly in one and the same direction; and Mrs Waldron was committed for trial, on the charge of murdering her husband by poison. A solicitor in first-rate criminal practice was sent for from London, to get up the prisoner's defence – and these "Instructions" took their form and shape accordingly. What's the matter? What do you want now?'

Suddenly rising from his chair, Mr Bashwood stretched across the table, and tried to take the papers from his son. 'I want to look at them,' he burst out eagerly. 'I want to see what they say about the captain from Cuba. He was at the bottom of it, Jemmy – I'll swear he was at the bottom of it!'

'Nobody doubted that, who was in the secret of the case at the time,' rejoined his son. 'But nobody could prove it. Sit down again, dad, and compose yourself. There's nothing here about Captain Manuel but the lawyer's private suspicions of him, for the counsel to act on or not, at the counsel's discretion. From first to last, she persisted in screening the captain. At the outset of the business, she volunteered two statements to the lawyer – both of which he suspected to be false. In the first place, she declared that she was innocent of the crime. He wasn't surprised, of course, so far; his clients were, as a general rule, in the habit of deceiving him in that way. In the second place, while admitting her private correspondence with the Cuban captain, she declared that the letters on both sides related solely to a proposed elopement, to which her husband's barbarous treatment had induced her to consent. The lawyer naturally asked to see the letters. "He has burnt all my letters, and I have burnt all his,' was the only answer he got. It was quite possible that Captain Manuel might have burnt *her* letters, when he heard there was a coroner's inquest in the house. But it was in her solicitor's experience (as it is in my experience too) that when a woman is fond of a man, in ninety-nine cases out of a hundred, risk or no risk, she keeps his letters. Having his suspicions roused in this way, the lawyer privately made some inquiries about the foreign captain – and found that he was as short of money as a foreign captain could be. At the same time, he put some questions to his client about her expectations from her deceased husband. She answered, in high indignation, that a will had been found among her husband's papers, privately executed only a few days before his death, and leaving her no more, out of all his immense fortune, than five thousand pounds. "Was there an older will, then," says the lawyer, "which the new will revoked?" Yes, there was; a will that he had given into her own possession; a will made when they were first married. "Leaving his widow well provided for?" Leaving her just ten times as much as the second will left her. "Had she ever mentioned that first will, now revoked, to Captain Manuel?" She saw the trap set for her – and said, "No, never!" without an instant's hesitation. That reply confirmed the lawyer's suspicions. He tried to frighten her by declaring that her life might pay the forfeit of her deceiving him in this matter. With the usual obstinacy of women, she remained just as immovable as ever. The captain, on his side, behaved in the most exemplary manner. He confessed to planning the elopement; he declared that he had burnt all the lady's letters as they reached him, out of regard for her reputation; he remained in the neighbourhood; and he volunteered to attend before the magistrates. Nothing was discovered that could legally connect him with the crime – or that could put him into court on the day of the Trial, in any other capacity than the capacity of a witness. I don't believe myself that there's any moral doubt (as they call it) that Manuel knew of the will which left her mistress of fifty thousand pounds; and that he was ready and willing, in virtue of that circumstance, to marry her on Mr Waldron's death. If anybody tempted her to effect her own release from her husband by making herself a widow, the captain must have been the man. And unless she contrived, guarded and watched as she was, to get the poison for herself, the poison must have come to her in one of the captain's letters.'

'I don't believe she used it, if it did come to her!' exclaimed Mr Bashwood. 'I believe it was the captain himself who poisoned her husband!'

Bashwood the younger, without noticing the interruption, folded up the Instructions for the Defence, which had now served their purpose; put them back in his bag; and produced a printed pamphlet in their place.

'Here is one of the published Reports of the Trial,' he said, 'which you can read at your leisure, if you like. We needn't waste time now by going into details. I have told you already how cleverly her counsel paved his way for treating the charge of murder, as the crowning calamity of the many that had already fallen on an innocent woman. The two legal points relied on for the defence (after this preliminary flourish) were: First, that there was no evidence to connect her with the possession of poison; and, secondly, that the medical witnesses,[7] while positively declaring that her husband had died by poison, differed in their conclusions as to the particular drug that had killed him. Both good points, and both well worked; but the evidence on the other side bore down everything before it. The prisoner was proved to have had no less than three excellent reasons for killing her husband. He had treated her with almost unexampled barbarity; he had left her in a will (unrevoked so far as she knew) mistress of a fortune on his death; and she was by her own confession contemplating an elopement with another man. Having set forth these motives, the prosecution next showed by evidence, which was never once shaken on any single point, that the one person in the house who could by any human possibility have administered the poison, was the prisoner at the bar. What could the judge and jury do, with such evidence before them as this? The verdict was Guilty, as a matter of course; and the judge declared that he agreed with it. The female part of the audience was in hysterics; and the male part was not much better. The judge sobbed, and the Bar shuddered. She was sentenced to death in such a scene as had never been previously witnessed in an English Court of Justice. And she is alive and hearty at the present moment; free to do any mischief she pleases, and to poison at her own entire convenience, any man, woman, or child that happens to stand in her way. A most interesting woman! Keep on good terms with her, my dear sir, whatever you do – for the Law has said to her in the plainest possible English, "My charming friend, I have no terrors for *you*!"'

'How was she pardoned?' asked Mr Bashwood breathlessly. 'They told me at the time – but I have forgotten. Was it the Home-Secretary? If it was, I respect the Home-Secretary! I say the Home-Secretary was deserving of his place.'

'Quite right, old gentleman!' rejoined Bashwood the younger. 'The Home-Secretary was the obedient humble servant of an enlightened Free Press – and he *was* deserving of his place. Is it possible you don't know how she cheated the gallows? If you don't I must tell you. On the evening of the Trial, two or three of the young Buccaniers of Literature went down to two or three newspaper offices, and wrote two or three heart-rending leading articles on the subject of the proceedings in court. The next morning the public caught light like tinder; and the prisoner was tried over again, before an amateur court of justice, in the columns of the newspapers. All the people who had no personal experience whatever on the subject, seized their pens, and rushed (by kind permission of the editor) into print. Doctors who had *not* attended the sick man, and who had *not* been present at the examination of the body, declared by dozens that he had died a natural death. Barristers without business, who had *not* heard the evidence, attacked the jury who *had* heard it, and judged the Judge, who had sat on the bench before some of them were born. The general public followed the lead of the barristers and the doctors, and the young Buccaniers who had set the thing going. Here was the Law that they all paid to protect them, actually doing its duty in dreadful earnest! Shocking! shocking! The British Public rose to protest as one man against the working of its own machinery; and the Home-Secretary, in a state of distraction, went to the Judge. The Judge held firm. He had said it was the right verdict at the time, and he said so still. "But suppose," says the Home-Secretary, "that the prosecution had tried some other way of proving her guilty at the trial than the way they did try – what would you and the jury have done then?" Of course it was quite impossible for the Judge to say. This comforted the Home-Secretary, to begin with. And, when he got the Judge's consent, after that, to having the conflict of medical evidence submitted to one great doctor; and when the one great doctor took the merciful view, after expressly stating, in the first instance, that he knew nothing practically of the merits of the case, the Home-Secretary was perfectly satisfied. The prisoner's death-warrant went into the waste-paper basket; the verdict of the Law was reversed by general acclamation; and the verdict of the newspapers carried the day. But the best of it is to come. You know what happened when the people found themselves with the pet object of their sympathy suddenly cast loose on their hands? A general impression prevailed directly that she was not quite innocent enough, after all, to be let out of prison then and there! Punish her a little – that was the state of the popular feeling – punish her a little, Mr Home-Secretary, on general moral grounds. A small course of gentle legal medicine, if you love us – and then we shall feel perfectly easy on the subject to the end of our days.'

'Don't joke about it!' cried his father. 'Don't, don't, don't, Jemmy! Did they try her again? They couldn't! they durs'n't! Nobody can be tried twice over for the same offence.'

'Pooh! pooh! she could be tried a second time for a second offence,' retorted Bashwood the younger – 'and tried she was. Luckily for the pacification of the public mind, she had rushed headlong into redressing her own grievances (as women will), when she discovered that her husband had cut her down from a legacy of fifty thousand pounds to a legacy of five thousand, by a stroke of his pen. The day before the Inquest a locked drawer in Mr Waldron's dressing-room table, which contained some valuable jewellery, was discovered to have been opened and emptied – and when the prisoner was committed by the magistrates, the precious stones were found torn out of their settings, and sewn up in her stays. The lady considered it a case of justifiable self-compensation. The Law declared it to be a robbery committed on the executors of the dead man. The lighter offence – which had been passed over, when such a charge as murder was brought against her – was just the thing to revive, to save appearances in the eyes of the public. They had stopped the course of justice, in the case of the prisoner, at one trial; and now all they wanted was to set the course of justice going again, in the case of the prisoner, at another! She was arraigned for the robbery, after having been pardoned for the murder. And, what is more, if her beauty and her misfortunes hadn't made a strong impression on her lawyer, she would not only have had to stand another trial, but would have had even the five thousand pounds, to which she was entitled by the second will, taken away from her, as a felon, by the Crown.'

'I respect her lawyer! I admire her lawyer!' exclaimed Mr Bashwood. 'I should like to take his hand, and tell him so.'

'He wouldn't thank you, if you did,' remarked Bashwood the younger.

'He is under a comfortable impression that nobody knows how he saved Mrs Waldron's legacy for her but himself.'

'I beg your pardon, Jemmy,' interposed his father. 'But don't call her Mrs Waldron. Speak of her, please, by her name when she was innocent and young, and a girl at school. Would you mind, for my sake, calling her Miss Gwilt?'

'Not I! It makes no difference to me what name I give her. Bother your sentiment! let's get on with the facts. This is what the lawyer did before the second trial came off. He told her she would be found guilty *again*, to a dead certainty. "And this time," he said, "the public will let the law take its course. Have you got an old friend whom you can trust?" She hadn't such a thing as an old friend in the world. "Very well, then," says the lawyer, "you must trust me. Sign this paper; and you will have executed a fictitious sale of all your property to myself. When the right time comes, I shall first carefully settle with your husband's executors; and I shall then re-convey the money to you, securing it properly (in case you ever marry again) in your own possession. The Crown, in other transactions of this kind, frequently waives its right of disputing the validity of the sale – and if the Crown is no harder on you than on other people, when you come out of prison you will have your five thousand pounds to begin the world with again." – Neat of the lawyer, when she was going to be tried for robbing the executors, to put her up to a way of robbing the Crown, wasn't it? Ha! ha! what a world it is!'

The last effort of the son's sarcasm passed unheeded by the father. 'In prison!' he said to himself. 'Oh me, after all that misery, in prison again!'

'Yes,' said Bashwood the younger, rising and stretching himself, 'that's how it ended. The verdict was Guilty; and the sentence was imprisonment for two years. She served her time; and came out, as well as I can reckon it, about three years since. If you want to know what she did when she recovered her liberty, and how she went on afterwards, I may be able to tell you something about it – say, on another occasion, when you have got an extra note or two in your pocket-book. For the present, all you need know, you do know. There isn't the shadow of a doubt that this fascinating lady has the double slur on her, of having been found guilty of murder, and of having served her term of imprisonment for theft. There's your moneysworth for your money – with the whole of my wonderful knack at stating a case clearly, thrown in for nothing. If you have any gratitude in you, you ought to do something handsome, one of these days, for your son. But for me, I'll tell you what you would have done, old gentleman. If you could have had your own way, you would have married Miss Gwilt.'

Mr Bashwood rose to his feet; and looked his son steadily in the face.

'If I could have my own way,' he said, 'I would marry her now.'

Bashwood the younger started back a step. 'After all I have told you?' he asked, in the blankest astonishment.

'After all you have told me.'

'With the chance of being poisoned, the first time you happened to offend her?'

'With the chance of being poisoned,' answered Mr Bashwood, 'in four-and-twenty hours.'

The Spy of the Private Inquiry Office dropped back into his chair, cowed by his father's words and his father's looks.

'Mad!' he said to himself. 'Stark mad, by jingo!'

Mr Bashwood looked at his watch, and hurriedly took his hat from a side-table.

'I should like to hear the rest of it,' he said. 'I should like to hear every word you have to tell me about her, to the very last. But the time, the dreadful, galloping time, is getting on. For all I know, they may be on their way to be married at this very moment.'

'What are you going to do?' asked Bashwood the younger, getting between his father and the door.

'I am going to the hotel,' said the old man, trying to pass him. 'I am going to see Mr Armadale.'

'What for?'

'To tell him everything you have told me.' He paused after making that reply. The terrible smile of triumph which had once already appeared on his face, overspread it again. 'Mr Armadale is young; Mr Armadale has all his life before him,' he whispered cunningly, with his trembling fingers clutching his son's arm. 'What doesn't frighten *me* will frighten *him*!'

'Wait a minute,' said Bashwood the younger. 'Are you as certain as ever that Mr Armadale is the man?'

'What man?'

'The man who is going to marry her.'

'Yes! yes! yes! Let me go, Jemmy – let me go.'

The Spy set his back against the door, and considered for a moment. Mr Armadale was rich. Mr Armadale (if *he* was not stark mad, too) might be made to put the right money-value on information that saved him from the disgrace of marrying Miss Gwilt. 'It may be a hundred pounds in my pocket, if I work it myself,' thought Bashwood the younger. 'And it won't be a halfpenny if I leave it to my father.' He took up his hat, and his leather bag. 'Can you carry it all in your own addled old head, daddy?' he asked, with his easiest impudence of manner. 'Not you! I'll go with you, and help you. What do you think of that?'

The father threw his arms in an ecstasy round the son's neck. 'I can't help it, Jemmy,' he said, in broken tones. 'You are so good to me. Take the other note, my dear – I'll manage without it – take the other note.'

The son threw open the door with a flourish; and magnanimously turned his back on the father's offered pocket-book. 'Hang it, old gentleman, I'm not quite so mercenary as *that*!' he said, with an appearance of the deepest feeling. 'Put up your pocket-book, and let's be off. – If I took my respected parent's last five-pound note,' he thought to himself, as he led the way downstairs, 'how do I know he mightn't cry halves when he sees the colour of Mr Armadale's money? – Come along, dad!' he resumed. 'We'll take a cab and catch the happy bridegroom before he starts for the church!'

They hailed a cab in the street, and started for the hotel which had been the residence of Midwinter and Allan during their stay in London. The instant the door of the vehicle had closed, Mr Bashwood returned to the subject of Miss Gwilt.

'Tell me the rest,' he said, taking his son's hand, and patting it tenderly. 'Let's go on talking about her all the way to the hotel. Help me through the time, Jemmy – help me through the time.'

Bashwood the younger was in high spirits at the prospect of seeing the colour of Mr Armadale's money. He trifled with his father's anxiety to the very last.

'Let's see if you remember what I've told you already,' he began. 'There's a character in the story that's dropped out of it without being accounted for. Come! can you tell me who it is?'

He had reckoned on finding his father unable to answer the question. But Mr Bashwood's memory, for anything that related to Miss Gwilt, was as clear and ready as his son's. 'The foreign scoundrel who tempted her, and let her screen him at the risk of her own life,' he said, without an instant's hesitation. 'Don't speak of him, Jemmy, don't speak of him again!'

'I *must* speak of him,' retorted the other. 'You want to know what became of Miss Gwilt, when she got out of prison, don't you? Very good – I'm in a position to tell you. She became Mrs Manuel. It's no use staring at me, old gentleman. I know it officially. At the latter part of last year, a foreign lady came to our place, with evidence to prove that she had been lawfully married to Captain Manuel, at a former period of his career, when he had visited England for the first time. She had only lately discovered that he had been in this country again; and she had reason to believe that he had married another woman in Scotland. Our people were employed to make the necessary inquiries. Comparison of dates showed that the Scotch marriage[8] – if it was a marriage at all, and not a sham – had taken place just about the time when Miss Gwilt was a free woman again. And a little further investigation showed us that the second Mrs Manuel was no other than the heroine of the famous criminal trial – whom we didn't know then, but whom we do know now, to be identical with your fascinating friend, Miss Gwilt.'

Mr Bashwood's head sank on his breast. He clasped his trembling hands fast in each other, and waited in silence to hear the rest.

'Cheer up!' pursued his son. 'She was no more the captain's wife than you are – and what is more, the captain himself is out of your way now. One foggy day in December last, he gave us the slip, and was off to the Continent, nobody knew where. He had spent the whole of the second Mrs Manuel's five thousand pounds, in the time that had elapsed (between two and three years) since she had come out of prison – and the wonder was, where he had got the money to pay his travelling expenses. It turned out that he had got it from the second Mrs Manuel herself. She had filled his empty pockets; and there she was, waiting confidently in a miserable London lodging, to hear from him and join him as soon as he was safely settled in foreign parts! Where had *she* got the money, you may ask naturally enough? Nobody could tell at the time. My own notion is, now, that her former mistress must have been still living, and that she must have turned her knowledge of the Blanchards' family secret to profitable account at last. This is mere guess-work of course; but there's a circumstance that makes it likely guess-work, to my mind. She had an elderly female friend to apply to at the time, who was just the woman to help her in ferreting out her mistress's address. Can you guess the name of the elderly female friend? Not you! Mrs Oldershaw of course!'

Mr Bashwood suddenly looked up. 'Why should she go back,' he asked, 'to the woman who had deserted her when she was a child?'

'I can't say,' rejoined his son, 'unless she went back in the interests of her own magnificent head of hair. The prison-scissors, I needn't tell you, had made short work of it with Miss Gwilt's love-locks, in every sense of the word – and Mrs Oldershaw, I beg to add, is the most eminent woman in England, as Restorer-General of the dilapidated heads and faces of the female sex. Put two and two together; and perhaps you'll agree with me, in this case, that they make four.'

'Yes, yes; two and two make four,' repeated his father, impatiently. 'But I want to know something else. Did she hear from him again? Did he send for her after he had gone away to foreign parts?'

'The captain? Why, what on earth can you be thinking of? Hadn't he spent every farthing of her money? and wasn't he loose on the Continent out of her reach? She waited to hear from him, I daresay, for she persisted in believing in him. But I'll lay you any wager you like, she never saw the sight of *his* handwriting again. We did our best at the office to open her eyes – we told her plainly that he had a first wife living, and that she hadn't the shadow of a claim on him. She wouldn't believe us, though we met her with the evidence. Obstinate, devilish obstinate. I daresay she waited for months together before she gave up the last hope of ever seeing him again.'

Mr Bashwood looked aside quickly out of the cab window. 'Where could she turn for refuge next?' he said, not to his son, but to himself. 'What, in heaven's name, could she do?'

'Judging by my experience of women,' remarked Bashwood the younger, overhearing him, 'I should say she probably tried to drown herself. But that's only guess-work again – it's all guess-work at this part of her story. You catch me at the end of my evidence, dad, when you come to Miss Gwilt's proceedings in the spring and summer of the present year. She might, or she might not, have been desperate enough to attempt suicide; and she might, or she might not, have been at the bottom of those inquiries that I made for Mrs Oldershaw. I daresay you'll see her this morning, and perhaps, if you use your influence, you may be able to make her finish her own story herself.'

Mr Bashwood, still looking out of the cab window, suddenly laid his hand on his son's arm.

'Hush! hush!' he exclaimed, in violent agitation. 'We have got there at last. Oh, Jemmy, feel how my heart beats! Here is the hotel.'

'Bother your heart,' said Bashwood the younger. 'Wait here while I make the inquiries.'

'I'll come with you!' cried his father. 'I can't wait! I tell you, I can't wait!'

They went into the hotel together, and asked for 'Mr Armadale'.

The answer, after some little hesitation and delay, was that Mr Armadale had gone away six days since. A second waiter added, that Mr Armadale's friend – Mr Midwinter – had only left that morning.

Where had Mr Armadale gone? Somewhere into the country. Where had Mr Midwinter gone? Nobody knew.

Mr Bashwood looked at his son in speechless and helpless dismay.

'Stuff and nonsense!' said Bashwood the younger, pushing his father back roughly into the cab. 'He's safe enough. We shall find him at Miss Gwilt's.'

The old man took his son's hand and kissed it. 'Thank you, my dear,' he said, gratefully. 'Thank you for comforting me.'

The cab was driven next to the second lodging which Miss Gwilt had occupied, in the neighbourhood of Tottenham Court Road.

'Stop here,' said the Spy, getting out, and shutting his father into the cab. 'I mean to manage this part of the business myself.'

He knocked at the house door. 'I have got a note for Miss Gwilt,' he said, walking into the passage, the moment the door was opened.

'She's gone,' answered the servant. 'She went away last night.'

Bashwood the younger wasted no more words with the servant. He insisted on seeing the mistress. The mistress confirmed the announcement of Miss Gwilt's departure on the previous evening. Where had she gone to? The woman couldn't say. How had she left? On foot. At what hour? Between nine and ten. What had she done with her luggage? She had no luggage. Had a gentleman been to see her on the previous day? Not a soul, gentle or simple, had come to the house to see Miss Gwilt.

The father's face, pale and wild, was looking out of the cab window, as the son descended the house-steps. 'Isn't she there, Jemmy?' he asked faintly – 'Isn't she there?'

'Hold your tongue,' cried the Spy, with the native coarseness of his nature rising to the surface at last. 'I'm not at the end of my inquiries yet.'

He crossed the road, and entered a coffee-shop situated exactly opposite the house he had just left.

In the box nearest the window two men were sitting talking together anxiously.

'Which of you was on duty yesterday evening, between nine and ten o'clock?' asked Bashwood the younger, suddenly joining them, and putting his question in a quick peremptory whisper.

'I was, sir,' said one of the men, unwillingly.

'Did you lose sight of the house? – Yes! I see you did.'

'Only for a minute, sir. An infernal blackguard of a soldier came in—'

'That will do,' said Bashwood the younger. 'I know what the soldier did, and who sent him to do it. She has given us the slip again. You are the greatest Ass living. Consider yourself dismissed.' With those words, and with an oath to emphasize them, he left the coffee-shop and returned to the cab.

'She's gone!' cried his father. 'Oh, Jemmy, Jemmy, I see it in your face!' He fell back into his own corner of the cab, with a faint wailing cry. 'They're married,' he moaned to himself; his hands falling helplessly on his knees; his hat falling unregarded from his head. 'Stop them!' he exclaimed, suddenly rousing himself, and seizing his son in a frenzy by the collar of the coat.

'Go back to the hotel,' shouted Bashwood the younger, to the cabman. 'Hold your noise!' he added, turning fiercely on his father. 'I want to think.'

The varnish of smoothness was all off him by this time. His temper was roused. His pride – even such a man has his pride! – was wounded to the quick. Twice had he matched his wits against a woman's; and twice the woman had baffled him.

He got out, on reaching the hotel for the second time; and privately tried the servants with the offer of money. The result of the experiment satisfied him that they had, in this instance, really and truly, no information to sell. After a moment's reflection, he stopped, before leaving the hotel, to ask the way to the parish church. 'The chance may be worth trying,' he thought to himself, as he gave the address to the driver. 'Faster!' he called out, looking first at his watch, and then at his father. 'The minutes are precious this morning; and the old one is beginning to give in.'

It was true. Still capable of hearing and of understanding, Mr Bashwood was past speaking by this time. He clung with both hands to his son's grudging arm, and let his head fall helplessly on his son's averted shoulder.

The parish church stood back from the street, protected by gates and railings, and surrounded by a space of open ground. Shaking off his father's hold, Bashwood the younger made straight for the vestry. The clerk, putting away the books, and the clerk's assistant, hanging up a surplice, were the only persons in the room when he entered it, and asked leave to look at the marriage Register for the day.

The clerk gravely opened the book, and stood aside from the desk on which it lay.

The day's register comprised three marriages solemnized that morning – and the first two signatures on the page, were 'Allan Armadale' and 'Lydia Gwilt'!

Even the Spy – ignorant as he was of the truth; unsuspicious as he was of the terrible future consequences to which the act of that morning might lead – even the Spy started, when his eye first fell on the page. It was done! Come what might of it, it was done now. There, in black and white, was the registered evidence of the marriage, which was at once a truth in itself, and a lie in the conclusion to which it led! There – through the fatal similarity in the names – there, in Midwinter's own signature, was the proof to persuade everybody that, not Midwinter, but Allan, was the husband of Miss Gwilt!

Bashwood the younger closed the book and returned it to the clerk. He descended the vestry steps with his hands thrust doggedly into his pockets, and with a serious shock inflicted on his professional self-esteem.

The beadle met him under the church wall. He considered for a moment whether it was worth while to spend a shilling in questioning the man, and decided in the affirmative. If they could be traced and overtaken, there might be a chance of seeing the colour of Mr Armadale's money, even yet.

'How long is it,' he asked, 'since the first couple married here this morning, left the church?'

'About an hour,' said the beadle.

'How did they go away?'

The beadle deferred answering that second question until he had first pocketed his fee. 'You won't trace them from here, sir,' he said, when he had got his shilling. 'They went away on foot.'

'And that is all you know about it?'

'That, sir, is all I know about it.'

Left by himself, even the Detective of the Private Inquiry Office paused for a moment before he returned to his father at the gate. He was roused from his hesitation by the sudden appearance, within the church enclosure, of the driver of the cab.

'I'm afraid the old gentleman is going to be taken ill, sir,' said the man.

Bashwood the younger frowned angrily, and walked back to the cab. As he opened the door and looked in, his father leaned forward and confronted him, with lips that moved speechlessly, and with a white stillness over all the rest of his face.

'She's done us,' said the Spy. 'They were married here this morning.'

The old man's body swayed for a moment from one side to the other. The instant after, his eyes closed, and his head fell forward towards the front seat of the cab. 'Drive to the hospital!' cried his son. 'He's in a fit. This is what comes of putting myself out of my way to please my father,' he muttered, sullenly raising Mr Bashwood's head, and loosening his cravat. 'A nice morning's work. Upon my soul, a nice morning's work!'

The hospital was near, and the house-surgeon was at his post.

'Will he come out of it?' asked Bashwood the younger roughly.

'Who are *you*?' asked the surgeon sharply, on his side.

'I am his son.'

'I shouldn't have thought it,' rejoined the surgeon, taking the restoratives that were handed to him by the nurse, and turning from the son to the father with an air of relief which he was at no pains to conceal. 'Yes,' he added, after a minute or two. 'Your father will come out of it, this time.'

'When can he be moved away from here?'

'He can be moved from the hospital in an hour or two.'

The Spy laid a card on the table. 'I'll come back for him or send for him,' he said. 'I suppose I can go now, if I leave my name and address?' With those words, he put on his hat, and walked out.

'He's a brute!' said the nurse.

'No,' said the surgeon quietly. 'He's a man.'

Between nine and ten o'clock that night, Mr Bashwood awoke in his bed at the inn in the Borough. He had slept for some hours, since he had been brought back from the hospital; and his mind and body were now slowly recovering together.

A light was burning on the bedside-table, and a letter lay on it, waiting for him till he was awake. It was in his son's handwriting, and it contained these words:

MY DEAR DAD, – Having seen you safe out of the hospital, and back at your hotel, I think I may fairly claim to have done my duty by you, and may consider myself free to look after my own affairs. Business will prevent me from seeing you to-night; and I don't think it at all likely I shall be in your neighbourhood to-morrow morning. My advice to you is, to go back to Thorpe-Ambrose, and to stick to your employment in the steward's office. Wherever Mr Armadale may be, he must, sooner or later, write to you on business. I wash my hands of the whole matter, mind, so far as I am concerned, from this time forth. But if *you* like to go on with it, my professional opinion is (though you couldn't hinder his marriage), you may part him from his wife.

Pray take care of yourself.

Your affectionate son,
JAMES BASHWOOD.

The letter dropped from the old man's feeble hands. 'I wish Jemmy could have come to see me to-night,' he thought. 'But it's very kind of him to advise me all the same.'

He turned wearily on the pillow, and read the letter a second time. 'Yes,' he said, 'there's nothing left for me but to go back. I'm too poor and too old to hunt after them all by myself.' He closed his eyes: the tears trickled slowly over his wrinkled cheeks. 'I've been a trouble to Jemmy,' he murmured, faintly; 'I've been a sad trouble, I'm afraid, to poor Jemmy!' In a minute more his weakness overpowered him, and he fell asleep again.

The clock of the neighbouring church struck. It was ten. As the bell tolled the hour, the tidal train – with Midwinter and his wife among the passengers – was speeding nearer and nearer to Paris. As the bell tolled the hour, the watch on board Allan's outward-bound yacht, had sighted the lighthouse off the Land's End, and had set the course of the vessel for Ushant and Finisterre.

THE END OF THE FOURTH BOOK

BOOK THE FIFTH

CHAPTER I

MISS GWILT'S DIARY

Naples, October 10th. – It is two months to-day, since I declared that I had closed my Diary, never to open it again.

Why have I broken my resolution? Why have I gone back to this secret friend of my wretchedest and wickedest hours? Because I am more friendless than ever; because I am more lonely than ever, though my husband is sitting writing in the next room to me. My misery is a woman's misery, and it *will* speak – here, rather than nowhere; to my second self, in this book, if I have no one else to hear me.

How happy I was in the first days that followed our marriage, and how happy I made *him*! Only two months have passed, and that time is a bygone time already! I try to think of anything I might have said or done wrongly, on my side – of anything he might have said or done wrongly, on his – and I can remember nothing unworthy of my husband, nothing unworthy of myself. I cannot even lay my finger on the day when the cloud first rose between us.[1]

I could bear it, if I loved him less dearly than I do. I could conquer the misery of our estrangement if he only showed the change in him as brutally as other men would show it.

But this never has happened, never will happen. It is not in his nature to inflict suffering on others. Not a hard word, not a hard look, escapes him. It is only at night, when I hear him sighing in his sleep; and sometimes when I see him dreaming, in the morning hours, that I know how hopelessly I am losing the love he once felt for me. He hides, or tries to hide it, in the day, for my sake. He is all gentleness, all kindness – but his heart is not on his lips, when he kisses me now; his hand tells me nothing when it touches mine. Day after day, the hours that he gives to his hateful writing grow longer and longer; day after day, he becomes more and more silent, in the hours that he gives to Me.

And, with all this, there is nothing that I can complain of – nothing marked enough to justify me in noticing it. His disappointment shrinks from all open confession; his resignation collects itself by such fine degrees that even my watchfulness fails to see the growth of it. Fifty times a day, I feel the longing in me, to throw my arms round his neck, and say, 'For God's sake, do anything to me, rather than treat me like this!' – and fifty times a day the words are forced back into my heart by the cruel considerateness of his conduct, which gives me no excuse for speaking them. I thought I had suffered the sharpest pain that I could feel, when my first husband laid his whip across my face. I thought I knew the worst that despair could do, on the day when I knew that the other villain, the meaner villain still, had cast me off. Live and learn. There is sharper pain than I felt under Waldron's whip; there is bitterer despair than the despair I knew when Manuel deserted me.

Am I too old for him? Surely not yet! Have I lost my beauty? Not a man passes me in the street but his eyes tell me I am as handsome as ever.

Ah, no! no! the secret lies deeper than *that*! I have thought and thought about it, till a horrible fancy has taken possession of me. He has been noble and good in his past life, and I have been wicked and disgraced. Who can tell what a gap that dreadful difference may make between us, unknown to him and unknown to me? It is folly, it is madness – but when I lie awake by him in the darkness, I ask myself whether any unconscious disclosure of the truth escapes me in the close intimacy that now unites us? Is there an unutterable Something left by the horror of my past life, which clings invisibly to me still? And is *he* feeling the influence of it, sensibly, and yet incomprehensibly to himself? Oh me! is there no purifying power in such love as mine? Are there plague-spots of past wickedness on my heart which no after-repentance can wash out?

Who can tell? There is something wrong in our married life – I can only come back to that. There is some adverse influence that neither he nor I can trace, which is parting us farther and farther from each other, day by day. Well! I suppose I shall be hardened in time, and learn to bear it.

An open carriage has just driven by my window, with a nicely-dressed lady in it. She had her husband by her side, and her children on the seat opposite. At the moment when I saw her she was laughing and talking in high spirits; a sparkling, light-hearted, happy woman, Ah, my lady, when you were a few years younger, if you had been left to yourself, and thrown on the world like me —'

October 11th. – The eleventh day of the month was the day (two months since) when we were married. He said nothing about it to me when we woke, nor I to him. But I thought I would make it the occasion, at breakfast-time, of trying to win him back.

I don't think I ever took such pains with my toilette before; I don't think I ever looked better than I looked when I went downstairs this morning. He had breakfasted by himself, and I found a little slip of paper on the table with an apology written on it. The post to England, he said, went out that day, and his letter to the newspaper must be finished. In his place, I would have let fifty posts go out, rather than breakfast without him. I went into his room. There he was, immersed body and soul in his hateful writing! 'Can't you give me a little time this morning?' I asked. He got up with a start. 'Certainly, if you wish it.' He never even looked at me as he said the words. The very sound of his voice told me that all his interest was centred in the pen that he had just laid down. 'I see you are occupied,' I said; 'I don't wish it.' Before I had closed the door on him he was back at his desk. I have often heard that the wives of authors have been for the most part unhappy women. And now I know why.

I suppose, as I said yesterday, I shall learn to bear it. (What *stuff*, by the by, I seem to have written yesterday! How ashamed I should be if anybody saw it but myself!) I hope the trumpery newspaper he writes for won't succeed! I hope his rubbishing letter will be well cut up by some other newspaper as soon as it gets into print!

What am I to do with myself all the morning? I can't go out, – it's raining. If I open the piano, I shall disturb the industrious journalist who is scribbling in the next room. Oh dear! it was lonely enough in my lodging at Thorpe-Ambrose, but how much lonelier it is here. Shall I read? No; books don't interest me; I hate the whole tribe of authors. I think I shall look back through these pages, and live my life over again when I was plotting and planning, and finding a new excitement to occupy me in every new hour of the day.

He might have looked at me, though he *was* so busy with his writing. He might have said, 'How nicely you are dressed this morning!'

He might have remembered, – never mind what! All he remembers is the newspaper.

Twelve o'clock. – I have been reading and thinking; and, thanks to my Diary, I have got through an hour.

What a time it was, – what a life it was, at Thorpe-Ambrose! I wonder I kept my senses. It makes my heart beat, it makes my face flush, only to read about it now!

The rain still falls, and the journalist still scribbles. I don't want to think the thoughts of that past time over again. And yet, what else can I do?

Supposing – I only say supposing – I felt now, as I felt when I travelled to London with Armadale; and when I saw my way to his life as plainly as I saw the man himself all through the journey . . . ?

I'll go and look out of the window. I'll go and count the people as they pass by.

A funeral has gone by, with the penitents in their black hoods, and the wax torches sputtering in the wet, and the little bell ringing, and the priests droning their monotonous chant. A pleasant sight to meet me at the window! I shall go back to my Diary.

Supposing I was not the altered woman I am – I only say, supposing – how would the Grand Risk that I once thought of running, look now? I have married Midwinter in the name that is really his own. And by doing that, I have taken the first of those three steps which were once to lead me, through Armadale's life, to the fortune and the station of Armadale's widow. No matter how innocent my intentions might have been on the wedding-day – and they *were* innocent – this is one of the unalterable results of the marriage. Well, having taken the first step, then, whether I would or no, how – supposing I meant to take the second step, which I don't – how would present circumstances stand towards me? Would they warn me to draw back, I wonder? or would they encourage me to go on?

It will interest me to calculate the chances; and I can easily tear the leaf out, and destroy it, if the prospect looks too encouraging.

We are living here (for economy's sake), far away from the expensive English quarter, in a suburb of the city, on the Portici side. We have made no travelling acquaintances among our own country-people. Our poverty is against us; Midwinter's shyness is against us; and (with the women) my personal appearance is against us. The men from whom my husband gets his information for the newspaper, meet him at the café, and never come here. I discourage his bringing any strangers to see me; for, though years have passed since I was last at Naples, I cannot be sure that some of the many people I once knew in this place may not be living still. The moral of all this is (as the children's story-books say), that not a single witness has come to this house who could declare, if any after-inquiry took place in England, that Midwinter and I had been living here as man and wife. So much for present circumstances as they affect Me.

Armadale next. Has any unforeseen accident led him to communicate with Thorpe-Ambrose? Has he broken the conditions which the major imposed on him, and asserted himself in the character of Miss Milroy's promised husband since I saw him last?

Nothing of the sort has taken place. No unforeseen accident has altered his position – his tempting position – towards myself. I know all that has happened to him since he left England, through the letters which he writes to Midwinter, and which Midwinter shows to me.

He has been wrecked, to begin with. His trumpery little yacht has actually tried to drown him, after all, and has failed! It happened (as Midwinter warned him it might happen with so small a vessel) in a sudden storm. They were blown ashore on the coast of Portugal. The yacht went to pieces, but the lives, and papers, and so on, were saved. The men have been sent back to Bristol, with recommendations from their master, which have already got them employment on board an outward-bound ship. And the master himself is on his way here, after stopping first at Lisbon, and next at Gibraltar, and trying ineffectually in both places to supply himself with another vessel. His third attempt is to be made at Naples, where there is an English yacht 'laid up', as they call it, to be had for sale or hire. He has had no occasion to write home since the wreck – for he took away from Coutts's the whole of the large sum of money lodged there for him, in circular notes.[2] And he has felt no inclination to go back to England himself – for, with Mr Brock dead, Miss Milroy at school, and Midwinter here, he has not a living creature in whom he is interested, to welcome him if he returned. To see *us*, and to see the new yacht, are the only two present objects he has in view. Midwinter has been expecting him for a week past, and he may walk into this very room in which I am writing, at this very moment, for all I know to the contrary.

Tempting circumstances, these – with all the wrongs I have suffered at his mother's hands and at his, still alive in my memory; with Miss Milroy confidently waiting to take her place at the head of his household; with my dream of living happy and innocent in Midwinter's love, dispelled for ever, and with nothing left in its place to help me against myself. I wish it wasn't raining; I wish I could go out.

Perhaps, something may happen to prevent Armadale from coming to Naples? When he last wrote, he was waiting at Gibraltar for an English steamer in the Mediterranean trade to bring him on here. He may get tired of waiting before the steamer comes, or he may hear of a yacht at some other place than this. A little bird whispers in my ear that it may possibly be the wisest thing he ever did in his life, if he breaks his engagement to join us at Naples.

Shall I tear out the leaf on which all these shocking things have been written? No. My Diary is so nicely bound – it would be positive barbarity to tear out a leaf. Let me occupy myself harmlessly with something else. What shall it be? My dressing-case – I will put my dressing-case tidy, and polish up the few little things in it which my misfortunes have still left in my possession.

I have shut up the dressing-case again. The first thing I found in it was Armadale's shabby present to me on my marriage – the rubbishing little ruby ring. That irritated me to begin with. The second thing that turned up was my bottle of Drops. I caught myself measuring the doses with my eye, and calculating how many of them would be enough to take a living creature over the border-land between sleep and death. Why I should have locked the dressing-case in a fright, before I had quite completed my calculation, I don't know – but I did lock it. And here I am back again at my Diary, with nothing, absolutely nothing, to write about. Oh, the weary day! the weary day! Will nothing happen to excite me a little in this horrible place?

October 12th. – Midwinter's all-important letter to the newspaper was despatched by the post last night. I was foolish enough to suppose that I might be honoured by having some of his spare attention bestowed on me to-day. Nothing of the sort! He had a restless night, after all his writing, and got up with his head aching, and his spirits miserably depressed. When he is in this state, his favourite remedy is to return to his old vagabond habits, and go roaming away by himself nobody knows where. He went through the form, this morning (knowing I had no riding-habit), of offering to hire a little broken-kneed brute of a pony for me, in case I wished to accompany him! I preferred remaining at home. I will have a handsome horse and a handsome habit, or I won't ride at all. He went away, without attempting to persuade me to change my mind. I wouldn't have changed it of course; but he might have tried to persuade me all the same.

I can open the piano, in his absence – that is one comfort. And I am in a fine humour for playing – that is another. There is a sonata of Beethoven's (I forget the number), which always suggests to me the agony of lost spirits in a place of torment. Come, my fingers and thumbs, and take me among the lost spirits, this morning!

October 13th. – Our windows look out on the sea. At noon to-day, we saw a steamer coming in, with the English flag flying. Midwinter has gone to the port, on the chance that this may be the vessel from Gibraltar, with Armadale on board.

Two o'clock. – It *is* the vessel from Gibraltar.[3] Armadale has added one more to the long list of his blunders – he has kept his engagement to join us at Naples.

How will it end, *now?*

Who knows!

MISS GWILT'S DIARY

October 16th. – Two days missed out of my Diary! I can hardly tell why, unless it is that Armadale irritates me beyond all endurance. The mere sight of him takes me back to Thorpe-Ambrose. I fancy I must have been afraid of what I might write about him, in the course of the last two days, if I indulged myself in the dangerous luxury of opening these pages.

This morning, I am afraid of nothing – and I take up my pen again accordingly.

Is there any limit, I wonder, to the brutish stupidity of some men? I thought I had discovered Armadale's limit when I was his neighbour in Norfolk – but my later experience at Naples shows me that I was wrong. He is perpetually in and out of this house (crossing over to us in a boat from the hotel at Santa Lucia, where he sleeps); and he has exactly two subjects of conversation – the yacht for sale in the harbour here, and Miss Milroy. Yes! he selects ME as the confidante of his devoted attachment to the major's daughter! 'It's so nice to talk to a woman about it!' That is all the apology he has thought it necessary to make for appealing to my sympathies – *my* sympathies! – on the subject of 'his darling Neelie', fifty times a day. He is evidently persuaded (if he thinks about it at all) that I have forgotten, as completely as he has forgotten, all that once passed between us, when I was first at Thorpe-Ambrose. Such an utter want of the commonest delicacy and the commonest tact, in a creature who is, to all appearance, possessed of a skin, and not a hide, and who does, unless my ears deceive me, talk, and not bray, is really quite incredible when one comes to think of it. But it is, for all that, quite true. He asked me – he actually asked me, last night – how many hundreds a year the wife of a rich man could spend on her dress. 'Don't put it too low,' the idiot added, with his intolerable grin. 'Neelie shall be one of the best-dressed women in England when I have married her.' And this to me, after having had him at my feet, and then losing him again through Miss Milroy! This to me, with an Alpaca gown on, and a husband whose income must be helped by a newspaper!

I had better not dwell on it any longer. I had better think and write of something else.

The yacht. As a relief from hearing about Miss Milroy, I declare the yacht in the harbour is quite an interesting subject to me! She (the men call a vessel 'She'; and I suppose if the women took an interest in such things, *they* would call a vessel 'He'); she is a beautiful model; and her 'top-sides' (whatever they may be) are especially distinguished by being built of mahogany. But, with these merits, she has the defect, on the other hand, of being old – which is a sad drawback – and the crew and the sailing-master have been 'paid off', and sent home to England – which is additionally distressing. Still, if a new crew and a new sailing-master can be picked up here, such a beautiful creature (with all her drawbacks) is not to be despised. It might answer to hire her for a cruise, and to see how she behaves. (If she is of *my* mind, her behaviour will rather astonish her new master!) The cruise will determine what faults she has, and what repairs, through the unlucky circumstance of her age, she really stands in need of. And then it will be time to settle, whether to buy her outright or not. Such is Armadale's conversation, when he is not talking of 'his darling Neelie'. And Midwinter, who can steal no time from his newspaper work, for his wife, can steal hours for his friend, and can offer them unreservedly to my irresistible rival, the new yacht.

I shall write no more, to-day. If so ladylike a person as I am could feel a tigerish tingling all over her to the very tips of her fingers, I should suspect myself of being in that condition at the present moment. But, with *my* manners and accomplishments, the thing is, of course, out of the question. We all know that a lady has no passions.

October 17th. – A letter for Midwinter this morning, from the slave-owners – I mean the newspaper-people in London – which has set him at work again harder than ever. A visit at luncheon-time, and another visit at dinner-time from Armadale. Conversation at luncheon about the yacht. Conversation at dinner about Miss Milroy. I have been honoured, in regard to that young lady, by an invitation to go with Armadale to-morrow to the Toledo, and help him to buy some presents for the beloved object. I didn't fly out at him – I only made an excuse. Can words express the astonishment I feel at my own patience? No words can express it.

October 18th. – Armadale came to breakfast this morning, by way of catching Midwinter before he shuts himself up over his work.

Conversation the same as yesterday's conversation at lunch. Armadale has made his bargain with the agent for hiring the yacht. The agent (compassionating his total ignorance of the language) has helped him to find an interpreter, but can't help him to find a crew. The interpreter is civil and willing, but doesn't understand the sea. Midwinter's assistance is indispensable; and Midwinter is requested (and consents!) to work harder than ever, so as to make time for helping his friend. When the crew is found, the merits and defects of the vessel are to be tried by a cruise to Sicily, with Midwinter on board to give his opinion. Lastly (in case she should feel lonely), the ladies' cabin is most obligingly placed at the disposal of Midwinter's wife. All this was settled at the breakfast-table; and it ended with one of Armadale's neatly-turned compliments, addressed to myself: 'I mean to take Neelie sailing with me, when we are married. And you have such good taste, you will be able to tell me everything the ladies' cabin wants between that time and this.'

If some women bring such men as this into the world, ought other women to allow them to live? It is a matter of opinion. *I* think not.

What maddens me, is to see, as I do see plainly, that Midwinter finds in Armadale's company, and in Armadale's new yacht, a refuge from *me*. He is always in better spirits when Armadale is here. He forgets me in Armadale almost as completely as he forgets me in his work. And I bear it! What a pattern wife, what an excellent Christian I am!

October 19th. – Nothing new. Yesterday over again.

October 20th. – One piece of news. Midwinter is suffering from nervous headache; and is working in spite of it, to make time for his holiday with his friend.

October 21st. – Midwinter is worse. Angry and wild and unapproachable, after two bad nights, and two uninterrupted days at his desk. Under any other circumstances he would take the warning, and leave off. But nothing warns him now. He is still working as hard as ever, for Armadale's sake. How much longer will my patience last?

October 22nd. – Signs, last night, that Midwinter is taxing his brains beyond what his brains will bear. When he did fall asleep, he was frightfully restless; groaning and talking and grinding his teeth. From some of the words I heard, he seemed at one time to be dreaming of his life when he was a boy, roaming the country with the dancing dogs. At another time he was back again with Armadale, imprisoned all night on the wrecked ship. Towards the early morning hours, he grew quieter. I fell asleep; and, waking after a short interval, found myself alone. My first glance round showed me a light burning in Midwinter's dressing-room. I rose softly, and went to look at him.

He was seated in the great ugly old-fashioned chair, which I ordered to be removed into the dressing-room out of the way, when we first came here. His head lay back, and one of his hands hung listlessly over the arm of the chair. The other hand was on his lap. I stole a little nearer, and saw that exhaustion had overpowered him, while he was either reading or writing – for there were books, pens, ink, and paper on the table before him. What had he got up to do secretly, at that hour of the morning? I looked closer at the papers on the table. They were all neatly folded (as he usually keeps them), with one exception – and that exception, lying open on the rest, was Mr Brock's letter.

I looked round at him again, after making this discovery, and then noticed for the first time another written paper, lying under the hand that rested on his lap. There was no moving it away without the risk of waking him. Part of the open manuscript, however, was not covered by his hand. I looked at it to see what he had secretly stolen away to read, besides Mr Brock's letter – and made out enough to tell me that it was the Narrative of Armadale's Dream.

That second discovery sent me back at once to my bed – with something serious to think of.

Travelling through France, on our way to this place, Midwinter's shyness was conquered for once, by a very pleasant man – an Irish doctor – whom we met in the railway carriage, and who quite insisted on being friendly and sociable with us all through the day's journey. Finding that Midwinter was devoting himself to literary pursuits, our travelling companion warned him not to pass too many hours together at his desk. 'Your face tells me more than you think,' the doctor said. 'If you are ever tempted to overwork your brain, you will feel it sooner than most men. When you find your nerves playing you strange tricks, don't neglect the warning – drop your pen.'[4]

After my last night's discovery in the dressing-room, it looks as if Midwinter's nerves were beginning already to justify the doctor's opinion of them. If one of the tricks they are playing him, is the trick of tormenting him again with his old superstitious terrors, there will be a change in our lives here before long. I shall wait curiously to see whether the conviction that we two are destined to bring fatal danger to

Armadale, takes possession of Midwinter's mind once more. If it does, I know what will happen. He will not stir a step towards helping his friend to find a crew for the yacht; and he will certainly refuse to sail with Armadale, or to let me sail with him, on the trial cruise.

October 23rd. – Mr Brock's letter has, apparently, not lost its influence yet. Midwinter is working again to-day, and is as anxious as ever for the holiday-time that he is to pass with his friend.

Two o'clock. – Armadale here as usual; eager to know when Midwinter will be at his service. No definite answer to be given to the question yet – seeing that it all depends on Midwinter's capacity to continue at his desk. Armadale sat down disappointed – he yawned, and put his great clumsy hands in his pockets. I took up a book. The brute didn't understand that I wanted to be left alone; he began again on the unendurable subject of Miss Milroy, and of all the fine things she was to have when he married her. Her own riding horse; her own pony-carriage; her own beautiful little sitting-room upstairs at the great house, and so on. All that I might have had once, Miss Milroy is to have now – *if I let her.*

Six o'clock. – More of the everlasting Armadale! Half an hour since, Midwinter came in from his writing, giddy and exhausted. I had been pining all day for a little music, and I knew they were giving *Norma* at the theatre here. It struck me that an hour or two at the opera might do Midwinter good, as well as me; and I said, 'Why not take a box at the San Carlo to-night?' He answered in a dull, uninterested manner, that he was not rich enough to take a box. Armadale was present, and flourished his well-filled purse in his usual insufferable way. '*I'm* rich enough, old boy, and it comes to the same thing.' With those words, he took up his hat, and trampled out on his great elephant's feet, to get the box. I looked after him from the window, as he went down the street. 'Your widow, with her twelve hundred a year,' I thought to myself, 'might take a box at the San Carlo whenever she pleased, without being beholden to anybody.' The empty-headed wretch whistled as he went his way to the theatre, and tossed his loose silver magnificently to every beggar who ran after him.

Midnight. – I am alone again at last. Have I nerve enough to write the history of this terrible evening, just as it has passed? I have nerve enough, at any rate, to turn to a new leaf, and try.

CHAPTER II

THE DIARY CONTINUED

We went to the San Carlo. Armadale's stupidity showed itself, even in such a simple matter as taking a box. He had confounded an opera with a play, and had chosen a box close to the stage, with the idea that one's chief object at a musical performance is to see the faces of the singers as plainly as possible! Fortunately for our ears, Bellini's lovely melodies[1] are, for the most part, tenderly and delicately accompanied – or the orchestra might have deafened us.

I sat back in the box at first, well out of sight; for it was impossible to be sure that some of my old friends of former days at Naples might not be in the theatre. But the sweet music gradually tempted me out of my seclusion. I was so charmed and interested that I leaned forward without knowing it, and looked at the stage.

I was made aware of my own imprudence, by a discovery which, for the moment, literally chilled my blood. One of the singers, among the chorus of Druids, was looking at me while he sang with the rest. His head was disguised in the long white hair, and the lower part of his face was completely covered with the flowing white beard, proper to the character. But the eyes with which he looked at me were the eyes of the one man on earth whom I have most reason to dread ever seeing again – Manuel!

If it had not been for my smelling-bottle, I believe I should have lost my senses. As it was, I drew back again into the shadow. Even Armadale noticed the sudden change in me: he, as well as Midwinter, asked if I was ill. I said I felt the heat, but hoped I should be better presently – and then leaned back in the box, and tried to rally my courage. I succeeded in recovering self-possession enough to be able to look again at the stage (without showing myself) the next time the chorus appeared. There was the man again! 'But to my infinite relief, he never looked towards our box a second time. This welcome indifference, on his part, helped to satisfy me that I had seen an extraordinary accidental resemblance, and nothing more. I still hold to this conclusion, after having had leisure to think – but my mind would be more completely at ease than it is, if I had seen the rest of the man's face, without the stage disguises that hid it from all investigation.

When the curtain fell on the first act, there was a tiresome ballet to be performed (according to the absurd Italian custom), before the opera went on. Though I had got over my first fright, I had been far too seriously startled to feel comfortable in the theatre. I dreaded all sorts of impossible accidents – and when Midwinter and Armadale put the question to me, I told them I was not well enough to stay through the rest of the performance.

At the door of the theatre, Armadale proposed to say good night. But Midwinter – evidently dreading the evening with *me* – asked him to come back to supper, if I had no objection. I said the necessary words – and we all three returned together to this house.

Ten minutes' quiet in my own room (assisted by a little dose of Eau-de-Cologne and water) restored me to myself. I joined the men at the supper-table. They received my apologies for taking them away from the opera, with the complimentary assurance that I had not cost either of them the slightest sacrifice of his own pleasure. Midwinter declared that he was too completely worn out to care for anything but the two great blessings, unattainable at the theatre, of quiet and fresh air. Armadale said – with an Englishman's exasperating pride in his own stupidity, wherever a matter of Art is concerned – that he couldn't make head or tail of the performance. The principal disappointment, he was good enough to add, was mine, for I evidently understood foreign music, and enjoyed it. Ladies generally did. His darling little Neelie—

I was in no humour to be persecuted with his 'Darling Neelie' after what I had gone through at the theatre. It might have been the irritated state of my nerves, or it might have been the Eau-de-Cologne flying to my head – but the bare mention of the girl seemed to set me in a flame. I tried to turn Armadale's attention in the direction of the supper-table. He was much obliged, but he had no appetite for more. I offered him wine next – the wine of the country, which is all that our poverty allows us to place on the table. He was much obliged again. The foreign wine was very little more to his taste than the foreign music; but he would take some because I asked him; and he would drink my health in the old-fashioned way – with his best wishes for the happy time when we should all meet again at Thorpe-Ambrose, and when there would be a mistress to welcome me at the great house.

Was he mad to persist in this way? No; his face answered for him. He was under the impression that he was making himself particularly agreeable to me.

I looked at Midwinter. He might have seen some reason for interfering to change the conversation, if he had looked at me in return. But he sat

557

silent in his chair, irritable and overworked, with his eyes on the ground, thinking.

I got up and went to the window. Still impenetrable to a sense of his own clumsiness, Armadale followed me. If I had been strong enough to toss him out of the window into the sea, I should certainly have done it at that moment. Not being strong enough, I looked steadily at the view over the bay, and gave him a hint, the broadest and rudest I could think of, to go.

'A lovely night for a walk,' I said, 'if you are tempted to walk back to the hotel.'

I doubt if he heard me. At any rate I produced no sort of effect on him. He stood staring sentimentally at the moonlight; and – there is really no other word to express it – *blew* a sigh. I felt a presentiment of what was coming, unless I stopped his mouth by speaking first.

'With all your fondness for England,' I said, 'you must own that we have no such moonlight as that at home.'

He looked at me vacantly, and blew another sigh.

'I wonder whether it's as fine to-night in England as it is here?' he said. 'I wonder whether my dear little girl at home is looking at the moonlight, and thinking of Me?'

I could endure it no longer. I flew out at him at last.

'Good heavens, Mr Armadale!' I exclaimed, 'is there only one subject worth mentioning, in the narrow little world you live in? I'm sick to death of Miss Milroy. Do pray talk of something else!'

His great broad stupid face coloured up to the roots of his hideous yellow hair. 'I beg your pardon,' he stammered, with a kind of sulky surprise. 'I didn't suppose—' he stopped confusedly, and looked from me to Midwinter. I understood what the look meant. 'I didn't suppose she could be jealous of Miss Milroy after marrying *you*!' That is what he would have said to Midwinter, if I had left them alone together in the room!

As it was, Midwinter had heard us. Before I could speak again – before Armadale could add another word – he finished his friend's uncompleted sentence, in a tone that I now heard, and with a look that I now saw, for the first time.

'You didn't suppose, Allan,' he said, 'that a lady's temper could be so easily provoked.'

The first bitter word of irony, the first hard look of contempt, I had ever had from him! And Armadale the cause of it!

My anger suddenly left me. Something came in its place, which steadied me in an instant, and took me silently out of the room.

I sat down alone in the bed-room. I had a few minutes of thought with myself, which I don't choose to put into words, even in these secret pages. I got up, and unlocked – never mind what. I went round to Midwinter's side of the bed, and took – no matter what I took. The last thing I did, before I left the room, was to look at my watch. It was half-past ten; Armadale's usual time for leaving us. I went back at once and joined the two men again.

I approached Armadale good-humouredly, and said to him, –

No! On second thoughts, I won't put down what I said to him – or what I did, afterwards. I'm sick of Armadale! he turns up at every second word I write. I shall pass over what happened in the course of the next hour – the hour between half-past ten and half-past eleven – and take up my story again at the time when Armadale had left us. Can I tell what took place, as soon as our visitor's back was turned, between Midwinter and me in our own room? Why not pass over what happened, in that case as well as in the other? Why agitate myself by writing it down? I don't know! Why do I keep a diary at all? Why did the clever thief the other day (in the English newspapers) keep the very thing to convict him, in the shape of a record of every thing he stole? Why are we not perfectly reasonable in all that we do? Why am I not always on my guard and never inconsistent with myself, like a wicked character in a novel? Why? why? why?

I don't care why! I must write down what happened between Midwinter and me to-night, *because* I must. There's a reason that nobody can answer – myself included.

It was half-past eleven. Armadale had gone. I had put on my dressing-gown, and had just sat down to arrange my hair for the night, when I was surprised by a knock at the door – and Midwinter came in.

He was frightfully pale. His eyes looked at me with a terrible despair in them. He never answered when I expressed my surprise at his coming in so much sooner than usual; he wouldn't even tell me, when I asked the question, if he was ill. Pointing peremptorily to the chair from which I had risen on his entering the room, he told me to sit down again; and then after a moment, added these words: 'I have something serious to say to you.'

I thought of what I had done – or, no, of what I had tried to do – in that interval between half past ten and half past eleven, which I have left unnoticed in my diary – and the deadly sickness of terror, which I never felt at the time, came upon me now. I sat down again, as I had been told, without speaking to Midwinter, and without looking at him.

He took a turn up and down the room, and then came and stood over me.

'If Allan comes here to-morrow,' he began, 'and if you see him—'

His voice faltered, and he said no more. There was some dreadful grief at his heart that was trying to master him. But there are times when his will is a will of iron. He took another turn in the room, and crushed it down. He came back, and stood over me again.

'When Allan comes here to-morrow,' he resumed, 'let him come into my room, if he wants to see me. I shall tell him that I find it impossible to finish the work I now have on hand as soon as I had hoped, and that he must, therefore, arrange to find a crew for the yacht, without any assistance on my part. If he comes, in his disappointment, to appeal to you — give him no hope of my being free in time to help him, if he waits. Encourage him to take the best assistance he can get from strangers, and to set about manning the yacht without any further delay. The more occupation he has to keep him away from this house; and the less you encourage him to stay here, if he does come, the better I shall be pleased. Don't forget that, and don't forget one last direction which I have now to give you. When the vessel is ready for sea, and when Allan invites us to sail with him, it is my wish that you should positively decline to go. He will try to make you change your mind — for I shall, of course, decline, on my side, to leave you in this strange house and in this foreign country by yourself. No matter what he says, let nothing persuade you to alter your decision. Refuse, positively and finally! Refuse, I insist on it, to set your foot on the new yacht!'

He ended quietly and firmly — with no faltering in his voice, and no signs of hesitation or relenting in his face. The sense of surprise which I might otherwise have felt at the strange words he had addressed to me, was lost in the sense of relief that they brought to my mind. The dread of *those other words* that I had expected to hear from him, left me as suddenly as it had come. I could look at him, I could speak to him once more.

'You may depend,' I answered, 'on my doing exactly what you order me to do. Must I obey you blindly? Or may I know your reason for the extraordinary directions you have just given to me?'

His face darkened, and he sat down on the other side of my dressing-table, with a heavy, hopeless sigh.

'You may know the reason,' he said, 'if you wish it.' He waited a little, and considered. 'You have a right to know the reason,' he resumed, 'for you yourself are concerned in it.' He waited a little again, and again went on. 'I can only explain the strange request I have just made to you, in one way,' he said. 'I must ask you to recall what happened in the next room, before Allan left us to-night.'

He looked at me with a strange mixture of expressions in his face. At one moment I thought he felt pity for me. At another, it seemed more like horror of me. I began to feel frightened again; I waited for his next words in silence.

'I know that I have been working too hard lately,' he went on, 'and that my nerves are sadly shaken. It is possible, in the state I am in now, that I may have unconsciously misinterpreted, or distorted, the circumstances that really took place. You will do me a favour if you will test my recollection of what has happened by your own. If my fancy has exaggerated anything, if my memory is playing me false anywhere, I entreat you to stop me, and tell me of it.'[2]

I commanded myself sufficiently to ask what the circumstances were to which he referred, and in what way I was personally concerned in them.

'You were personally concerned in them, in this way,' he answered. 'The circumstances to which I refer, began with your speaking to Allan about Miss Milroy, in what I thought, a very inconsiderate and very impatient manner. I am afraid I spoke just as petulantly on my side – and I beg your pardon for what I said to you in the irritation of the moment. You left the room. After a short absence, you came back again, and made a perfectly proper apology to Allan, which he received with his usual kindness, and sweetness of temper. While this went on, you and he were both standing by the supper-table; and Allan resumed some conversation which had already passed between you about the Neapolitan wine. He said he thought he should learn to like it in time, and he asked leave to take another glass of the wine we had on the table. Am I right so far?'

The words almost died on my lips; but I forced them out, and answered him that he was right so far.

'You took the flask out of Allan's hand,' he proceeded. 'You said to him, good-humouredly, "You know you don't really like the wine, Mr Armadale. Let me make you something which may be more to your taste. I have a receipt of my own for lemonade. Will you favour me by trying it?" In those words, you made your proposal to him, and he accepted it. Did he also ask leave to look on, and learn how the lemonade was made? and did you tell him that he would only confuse you, and that you would give him the receipt in writing, if he wanted it?'

This time, the words did really die on my lips. I could only bow my head, and answer 'Yes' mutely in that way. Midwinter went on.

'Allan laughed, and went to the window to look out at the Bay, and I went with him. After a while, Allan remarked, jocosely, that the mere sound of the liquids you were pouring out, made him thirsty. When he said this, I turned round from the window. I approached you, and said the lemonade took a long time to make. You touched me, as I was walking away again, and handed me the tumbler filled to the brim. At the same time, Allan turned round from the window; and I, in my turn, handed the tumbler to *him*. – Is there any mistake so far?'

The quick throbbing of my heart almost choked me. I could just shake my head – I could do no more.

'I saw Allan raise the tumbler to his lips. – Did *you* see it? I saw his face turn white, in an instant. – Did *you*? I saw the glass fall from his hand on the floor. I saw him stagger, and caught him before he fell. Are these things true? For God's sake, search your memory, and tell me – are these things true?'

The throbbing at my heart seemed, for one breathless instant, to stop. The next moment something fiery, something maddening, flew through me. I started to my feet, with my temper in a flame, reckless of all consequences, desperate enough to say anything.

'Your questions are an insult! Your looks are an insult!' I burst out. '*Do you think I tried to poison him?*'

The words rushed out of my lips in spite of me. They were the last words under heaven that any woman, in such a situation as mine, ought to have spoken. And yet I spoke them!

He rose in alarm, and gave me my smelling-bottle. 'Hush! hush!' he said. 'You, too, are overwrought – you, too, are over-excited by all that has happened to-night. You are talking wildly and shockingly. Good God! how can you have so utterly misunderstood me? Compose yourself – pray, compose yourself.'

He might as well have told a wild animal to compose herself. Having been mad enough to say the words, I was mad enough next, to return to the subject of the lemonade, in spite of his entreaties to me to be silent.

'I told you what I had put in the glass, the moment Mr Armadale fainted,' I went on; insisting furiously on defending myself, when no attack was made on me. 'I told you I had taken the flask of brandy which you keep at your bedside, and mixed some of it with the lemonade. How could I know that he had a nervous horror of the smell and taste of brandy? Didn't he say to me himself, when he came to his senses, It's my fault; I ought to have warned you to put no brandy in it? Didn't he remind you, afterwards, of the time when you and he were in the Isle of Man together, and when the Doctor there innocently made the same mistake with him that I made to-night?'

[I laid a great stress on my innocence – and with some reason too. Whatever else I may be, I pride myself on not being a hypocrite. I *was* innocent – so far as the brandy was concerned. I had put it into the lemonade, in pure ignorance of Armadale's nervous peculiarity, to disguise the taste of – never mind what![3] Another of the things I pride myself on is, that I never wander from my subject. What Midwinter said next, is what I ought to be writing about now.]

He looked at me for a moment, as if he thought I had taken leave of my senses. Then he came round to my side of the table, and stood over me again.

'If nothing else will satisfy you that you are entirely misinterpreting my motives,' he said, 'and that I haven't an idea of blaming *you* in the matter – read this.'

He took a paper from the breast-pocket of his coat, and spread it open under my eyes. It was the Narrative of Armadale's Dream.

In an instant the whole weight on my mind was lifted off it. I felt mistress of myself again – I understood him at last.

'Do you know what this is?' he asked. 'Do you remember what I said to you at Thorpe-Ambrose, about Allan's Dream? I told you, then, that two out of the three Visions had already come true. I tell you now, that the third Vision has been fulfilled in this house to-night.'

He turned over the leaves of the manuscript, and pointed to the lines that he wished me to read.[4]

I read these, or nearly these words, from the Narrative of the Dream, as Midwinter had taken it down from Armadale's own lips:

The darkness opened for the third time, and showed me the Shadow of the Man, and the Shadow of the Woman together. The Man-Shadow was the nearest; the Woman-Shadow stood back. From where she stood, I heard a sound like the pouring out of a liquid softly. I saw her touch the Shadow of the Man with one hand, and give him a glass with the other. He took the glass, and handed it to me. At the moment when I put it to my lips, a deadly faintness overcame me. When I recovered my senses again, the Shadows had vanished, and the Vision was at an end.

For the moment, I was as completely staggered by this extraordinary coincidence as Midwinter himself.

He put one hand on the open Narrative, and laid the other heavily on my arm.

'*Now* do you understand my motive in coming here?' he asked. '*Now* do you see that the last hope I had to cling to, was the hope that your memory of the night's events might prove my memory to be wrong? *Now* do you know why I won't help Allan? Why I won't sail with him? Why I am plotting and lying, and making you plot and lie too, to keep my best and dearest friend out of the house?'

'Have you forgotten Mr Brock's letter?' I asked.

He struck his hand passionately on the open manuscript. 'If Mr Brock had lived to see what we have seen to-night, he would have felt what I feel, he would have said what I say!' His voice sank mysteriously, and his great black eyes glittered at me as he made that answer. 'Thrice the Shadows of the Vision warned Allan in his sleep,' he went on; 'and thrice those Shadows have been embodied in the aftertime by You, and by Me! You, and no other, stood in the Woman's place at the pool. I, and no other, stood in the Man's place at the window. And you and I together, when the last Vision showed the Shadows together, stand in the Man's place and the Woman's place still! For *this*, the miserable day dawned when you and I first met. For *this*, your influence drew me to you, when my better angel warned me to fly the sight of your face. There is a curse on our lives! there is a fatality in our footsteps! Allan's future depends on his separation from us at once and for ever. Drive him from the place we live in, and the air we breathe. Force him among strangers – the worst and wickedest of them will be more harmless to him than we are! Let his yacht sail, though he goes on his knees to ask us, without You and without Me – and let him know how I loved him in another world than this, where the wicked cease from troubling and the weary are at rest!'

His grief conquered him – his voice broke into a sob when he spoke those last words. He took the Narrative of the Dream from the table, and left me as abruptly as he had come in.

As I heard his door locked between us, my mind went back to what he had said to me, about myself. In remembering 'the miserable day' when we first saw each other, and 'the better angel' that had warned him to 'fly the sight of my face', I forgot all else. It doesn't matter what I felt. I wouldn't own it, even if I had a friend to speak to. Who cares for the misery of such a woman as I am? who believes in it? Besides, he spoke under the influence of the mad superstition that has got possession of him again. There is every excuse for *him* – there is no excuse for *me*. If I can't help being fond of him, through it all, I must take the consequences and suffer. I deserve to suffer; I deserve neither love nor pity from anybody. – Good heavens, what a fool I am! And how unnatural all this would be, if it was written in a book!

It has struck one. I can hear Midwinter still, pacing to and fro in his room.

He is thinking, I suppose? Well! I can think too. What am I to do next? I shall wait and see. Events take odd turns, sometimes – and events may justify the fatalism of the amiable man in the next room, who curses the day when he first saw my face. He may live to curse it for other reasons than he has now. If I *am* the Woman pointed at in the Dream, there will be another temptation put in my way before long – and there will be no brandy in Armadale's lemonade if I mix it for him a second time.

October 24th. – Barely twelve hours have passed since I wrote my yesterday's entry – and that other temptation has come, tried, and conquered me already!

This time there was no alternative. Instant exposure and ruin stared me in the face – I had no choice but to yield in my own defence. In plainer words still, it was no accidental resemblance that startled me at the theatre last night. The chorus-singer at the opera was Manuel himself!

Not ten minutes after Midwinter had left the sitting-room for his study, the woman of the house came in with a dirty little three-cornered note in her hand. One look at the writing on the address was enough. He had recognized me in the box; and the ballet between the acts of the opera had given him time to trace me home. I drew that plain conclusion in the moment that elapsed before I opened the letter. It informed me, in two lines, that he was waiting in a by-street, leading to the beach; and that, if I failed to make my appearance in ten minutes, he should interpret my absence as an invitation to him to call at the house.

What I went through yesterday, must have hardened me, I suppose. At any rate, after reading the letter, I felt more like the woman I once was than I have felt for months past. I put on my bonnet, and went downstairs, and left the house as if nothing had happened.

He was waiting for me at the entrance to the street.

In the instant when we stood face to face, all my wretched life with him came back to me. I thought of my trust that he had betrayed; I thought of the cruel mockery of a marriage that he had practised on me, when he knew that he had a wife living; I thought of the time when

I had felt despair enough at his desertion of me to attempt my own life. When I recalled all this, and when the comparison between Midwinter and the mean, miserable villain whom I had once believed in, forced itself into my mind, I knew, for the first time, what a woman feels when every atom of respect for herself has left her. If he had personally insulted me, at that moment, I believe I should have submitted to it.

But he had no idea of insulting me, in the more brutal meaning of the word. He had me at his mercy, and his way of making me feel it was to behave with an elaborate mockery of penitence and respect. I let him speak as he pleased, without interrupting him, without looking at him a second time, without even allowing my dress to touch him, as we walked together towards the quieter part of the beach. I had noticed the wretched state of his clothes, and the greedy glitter in his eyes, in my first look at him. And I knew it would end – as it did end – in a demand on me for money.

Yes! After taking from me the last farthing I possessed of my own, and the last farthing I could extort for him from my old mistress, he turned on me as we stood by the margin of the sea, and asked if I could reconcile it to my conscience to let him be wearing such a coat as he then had on his back, and earning his miserable living as a chorussinger at the opera!

My disgust, rather than my indignation, roused me into speaking to him at last.

'You want money,' I said. 'Suppose I am too poor to give it to you?'

'In that case,' he replied, 'I shall be forced to remember that you are a treasure in yourself. And I shall be under the painful necessity of pressing my claim to you on the attention of one of those two gentlemen whom I saw with you at the opera – the gentleman, of course, who is now honoured by your preference, and who lives provisionally in the light of your smiles.'

I made him no answer – for I had no answer to give. Disputing his right to claim me from anybody, would have been a mere waste of words. He knew as well as I did that he had not the shadow of a claim on me. But the mere attempt to raise it would, as he was well aware, lead necessarily to the exposure of my whole past life.

Still keeping silence, I looked out over the sea. I don't know why – except that I instinctively looked anywhere rather than look at *him*.

A little sailing boat was approaching the shore. The man steering was hidden from me by the sail; but the boat was so near that I thought I recognized the flag on the mast. I looked at my watch. Yes! It was

Armadale coming over from Santa Lucia, at his usual time, to visit us in his usual way.

Before I had put my watch back in my belt, the means of extricating myself from the frightful position I was placed in showed themselves to me as plainly as I see them now.

I turned and led the way to the higher part of the beach, where some fishing-boats were drawn up which completely screened us from the view of any one landing on the shore below. Seeing probably that I had a purpose of some kind, Manuel followed me without uttering a word. As soon as we were safely under the shelter of the boats, I forced myself, in my own defence, to look at him again.

'What should you say,' I asked, 'if I was rich, instead of poor? What should you say if I could afford to give you a hundred pounds?'

He started. I saw plainly that he had not expected so much as half the sum I had mentioned. It is needless to add that his tongue lied, while his face spoke the truth; and that when he replied to me, the answer was, 'Nothing like enough.'

'Suppose,' I went on, without taking any notice of what he had said, 'that I could show you a way of helping yourself to twice as much – three times as much – five times as much as a hundred pounds, are you bold enough to put out your hand, and take it?'

The greedy glitter came into his eyes once more. His voice dropped low, in breathless expectation of my next words.

'Who is the person?' he asked. 'And what is the risk?'

I answered him at once, in the plainest terms. I threw Armadale to him, as I might have thrown a piece of meat to a wild beast who was pursuing me.

'The person is a rich young Englishman,' I said. 'He has just hired the yacht called the *Dorothea*, in the harbour here; and he stands in need of a sailing-master and a crew. You were once an officer in the Spanish navy – you speak English and Italian perfectly – you are thoroughly well acquainted with Naples and all that belongs to it. The rich young Englishman is ignorant of the language; and the interpreter who assists him, knows nothing of the sea. He is at his wits' end for want of useful help in this strange place; he has no more knowledge of the world than that child who is digging holes there with a stick in the sand; and he carries all his money with him in circular notes. So much for the person. As for the risk, estimate it for yourself.'

The greedy glitter in his eyes grew brighter and brighter with every word I said. He was plainly ready to face the risk, before I had done speaking.

'When can I see the Englishman?' he asked eagerly.

I moved to the seaward end of the fishing-boat, and saw that Armadale was at that moment disembarking on the shore.

'You can see him now,' I answered, and pointed to the place.

After a long look at Armadale walking carelessly up the slope of the beach, Manuel drew back again under the shelter of the boat. He waited a moment, considering something carefully with himself, and put another question to me – in a whisper this time.

'When the vessel is manned,' he said, 'and the Englishman sails from Naples, how many friends sail with him?'

'He has but two friends here,' I replied – 'that other gentleman whom you saw with me at the opera, and myself. He will invite us both to sail with him – and when the time comes, we shall both refuse.'

'Do you answer for that?'

'I answer for it positively.'

He walked a few steps away, and stood with his face hidden from me, thinking again. All I could see was, that he took off his hat, and passed his handkerchief over his forehead. All I could hear was, that he talked to himself excitedly in his own language.

There was a change in him when he came back. His face had turned to a livid yellow, and his eyes looked at me with a hideous distrust.

'One last question,' he said, and suddenly came closer to me, suddenly spoke with a marked emphasis on his next words. *'What is your interest in this?'*

I started back from him. The question reminded me that I *had* an interest in the matter, which was entirely unconnected with the interest of keeping Manuel and Midwinter apart. Thus far, I had only remembered that Midwinter's fatalism had smoothed the way for me, by abandoning Armadale beforehand to any stranger who might come forward to help him. Thus far, the sole object I had kept in view was to protect myself, by the sacrifice of Armadale, from the exposure that threatened me. I tell no lies to my Diary. I don't affect to have felt a moment's consideration for the interests of Armadale's purse, or the safety of Armadale's life. I hated him too savagely to care what pitfalls my tongue might be the means of opening under his feet. But I certainly did *not* see (until that last question was put to me) that, in serving his own designs, Manuel might – if he dared go all lengths for the money – be serving my designs too. The one overpowering anxiety to protect myself from exposure before Midwinter, had (I suppose) filled all my mind, to the exclusion of everything else.

Finding that I made no reply for the moment, Manuel reiterated his question, putting it in a new form.

'You have cast your Englishman at me,' he said, 'like the sop to Cerberus. Would you have been quite so ready to do that, if you had not had a motive of your own? I repeat my question. *You* have an interest in this – what is it?'

'I have two interests,' I answered. 'The interest of forcing you to respect my position here; and the interest of ridding myself of the sight of you, at once and for ever!' I spoke with a boldness he had not yet heard from me. The sense that I was making the villain an instrument in my hands, and forcing him to help my purpose blindly, while he was helping his own, roused my spirits, and made me feel like myself again.

He laughed. 'Strong language, on certain occasions, is a lady's privilege,' he said. 'You may, or may not, rid yourself of the sight of me, at once and for ever. We will leave that question to be settled in the future. But your other interest in this matter puzzles me. You have told all I need know about the Englishman and his yacht, and you have made no conditions before you opened your lips. Pray, how are you to force me, as you say, to respect your position here?'

'I will tell you how,' I rejoined. 'You shall hear my conditions first. I insist on your leaving me in five minutes more. I insist on your never again coming near the house where I live; and I forbid your attempting to communicate in any way, either with me, or with that other gentleman whom you saw with me at the theatre—'

'And suppose I say no?' he interposed. 'In that case, what will you do?'

'In that case,' I answered, 'I shall say two words in private to the rich young Englishman – and you will find yourself back again among the chorus at the opera.'

'You are a bold woman to take it for granted that I have my designs on the Englishman already, and that I am certain to succeed in them. How do you know—?'

'I know *you*,' I said. 'And that is enough.'

There was a moment's silence between us. He looked at me – and I looked at him. We understood each other.

He was the first to speak. The villainous smile died out of his face, and his voice dropped again distrustfully to its lowest tones.

'I accept your terms,' he said. 'As long as your lips are closed, my lips shall be closed too – except in the event of my finding that you have deceived me; in which case the bargain is at an end, and you will see me again. I shall present myself to the Englishman to-morrow, with the necessary credentials to establish me in his confidence. Tell me his name?'

I told it.

'Give me his address?'

I gave it – and turned to leave him. Before I had stepped out of the shelter of the boats, I heard him behind me again.

'One last word,' he said. 'Accidents sometimes happen at sea. Have you interest enough in the Englishman – if an accident happens in his case – to wish to know what has become of him?'

I stopped, and considered on my side. I had plainly failed to persuade him that I had no secret interest to serve, in placing Armadale's money, and (as a probable consequence) Armadale's life, at his mercy. And it was now equally clear that he was cunningly attempting to associate himself with my private objects (whatever they might be), by opening a means of communication between us in the future. There could be no hesitation about how to answer him, under such circumstances as these. If the 'accident' at which he hinted did really happen to Armadale, I stood in no need of Manuel's intervention to give me the intelligence of it. An easy search through the obituary columns of the English papers would tell me the news – with the great additional advantage that the papers might be relied on, in such a matter as this, to tell the truth. I formally thanked Manuel, and declined to accept his proposal. 'Having no interest in the Englishman,' I said, 'I have no wish whatever to know what becomes of him.'

He looked at me for a moment with steady attention, and with an interest in me which he had not shown yet.

'What the game you are playing may be,' he rejoined, speaking slowly and significantly, 'I don't pretend to know. But I venture on a prophecy nevertheless – *you will win it!* If we ever meet again, remember I said that.' He took off his hat, and bowed to me gravely. 'Go your way, madam. And leave me to go mine!'

With those words, he released me from the sight of him. I waited a minute alone, to recover myself in the air – and then returned to the house.

The first object that met my eyes on entering the sitting-room, was – Armadale himself!

He was waiting on the chance of seeing me, to beg that I would exert my influence with his friend. I made the needful inquiry as to what he meant, and found that Midwinter had spoken as he had warned me he would speak when he and Armadale next met. He had announced that he was unable to finish his work for the newspaper as soon as he had hoped; and he had advised Armadale to find a crew for the yacht without waiting for any assistance on his part.

All that it was necessary for me to do, on hearing this, was to perform the promise I had made to Midwinter, when he gave me my directions how to act in the matter. Armadale's vexation on finding me resolved not to interfere, expressed itself in the form of all others that is most personally offensive to me. He declined to believe my reiterated assurances that I possessed no influence to exert in his favour. 'If I was married to Neelie,' he said, 'she could do anything she liked with me; and I am sure, when you choose, you can do anything you like with Midwinter.' If the infatuated fool had actually tried to stifle the last faint struggles of remorse and pity left stirring in my heart, he could have said nothing more fatally to the purpose than this! I gave him a look which effectually silenced him so far as I was concerned. He went out of the room grumbling and growling to himself. 'It's all very well to talk about manning the yacht. I don't speak a word of their gibberish here – and the interpreter thinks a fisherman and a sailor mean the same thing. Hang me if I know what to do with the vessel, now I have got her!'

He will probably know by to-morrow. And if he only comes here as usual, I shall know too!

October 25th, Ten at night. – Manuel has got him!

He has just left us, after staying here more than an hour, and talking the whole time of nothing but his own wonderful luck in finding the very help he wanted, at the time when he needed it most.

At noon to-day, he was on the Mole,[5] it seems, with his interpreter, trying vainly to make himself understood by the vagabond population of the water-side. Just as he was giving it up in despair, a stranger standing by (Manuel had followed him, I suppose, to the Mole from his hotel) kindly interfered to put things right. He said, 'I speak your language and their language, sir. I know Naples well; and I have been professionally accustomed to the sea. Can I help you?' The inevitable result followed. Armadale shifted all his difficulties on to the shoulders of the polite stranger, in his usual helpless, headlong way. His new friend, however, insisted, in the most honourable manner, on complying with the customary formalities before he would consent to take the matter into his own hands. He begged leave to wait on Mr Armadale, with his testimonials to character and capacity. The same afternoon he had come by appointment to the hotel, with all his papers, and with 'the saddest story' of his sufferings and privations as 'a political refugee'[6] that Armadale had ever heard. The interview was decisive. Manuel left the hotel, commissioned to find a crew for the yacht, and to fill the post of sailing-master on the trial cruise.

571

I watched Midwinter anxiously, while Armadale was telling us these particulars; and afterwards, when he produced the new sailing-master's testimonials, which he had brought with him for his friend to see.

For the moment, Midwinter's superstitious misgivings seemed to be all lost in his natural anxiety for his friend. He examined the stranger's papers – after having told me that the sooner Armadale was in the hands of strangers the better! – with the closest scrutiny and the most business-like distrust. It is needless to say that the credentials were as perfectly regular and satisfactory as credentials could be. When Midwinter handed them back, his colour rose: he seemed to feel the inconsistency of his conduct, and to observe for the first time that I was present noticing it. 'There is nothing to object to in the testimonials, Allan: I am glad you have got the help you want at last.' That was all he said, at parting. As soon as Armadale's back was turned, I saw no more of him. He has locked himself up again for the night, in his own room.

There is now – so far as I am concerned – but one anxiety left. When the yacht is ready for sea, and when I decline to occupy the lady's cabin, will Midwinter hold to his resolution, and refuse to sail without me?

October 26th. – Warnings already of the coming ordeal. A letter from Armadale to Midwinter, which Midwinter has just sent in to me. Here it is:

> DEAR MID, – I am too busy to come to-day. Get on with your work, for heaven's sake! The new sailing-master is a man of ten thousand. He has got an Englishman whom he knows, to serve as mate on board already; and he is positively certain of getting the crew together in three or four days' time. I am dying for a whiff of the sea, and so are you, or you are no sailor. The rigging is set up, the stores are coming on board, and we shall bend the sails to-morrow or next day. I never was in such spirits in my life. Remember me to your wife, and tell her she will be doing me a favour if she will come at once, and order everything she wants in the lady's cabin. – Yours affectionately, A. A.

Under this was written in Midwinter's hand, – 'Remember what I told you. Write (it will break it to him more gently in that way), and beg him to accept your apologies, and to excuse you from sailing on the trial cruise.'

I have written without a moment's loss of time. The sooner Manuel knows (which he is certain to do through Armadale) that the promise not to sail in the yacht is performed already, so far as I am concerned, the safer I shall feel.

October 27th. – A letter from Armadale, – in answer to mine. He is full of ceremonious regret at the loss of my company on the cruise; and he politely hopes that Midwinter may yet induce me to alter my mind. Wait a little, till he finds that Midwinter won't sail with him either! . . .

October 30th. – Nothing new to record, until to-day. To-day, the change in our lives here has come at last!

Armadale presented himself this morning, in his noisiest high spirits, to announce that the yacht was ready for sea, and to ask when Midwinter would be able to go on board. I told him to make the inquiry himself in Midwinter's room. He left me, with a last request that I would reconsider my refusal to sail with him. I answered by a last apology for persisting in my resolution; and then took a chair alone at the window, to wait the event of the interview in the next room.

My whole future depended, now, on what passed between Midwinter and his friend! Everything had gone smoothly up to this time. The one danger to dread was the danger of Midwinter's resolution, or rather of Midwinter's fatalism, giving way at the last moment. If he allowed himself to be persuaded into accompanying Armadale on the cruise, Manuel's exasperation against me would hesitate at nothing – he would remember that I had answered to him for Armadale's sailing from Naples alone; and he would be capable of exposing my whole past life to Midwinter before the vessel left the port. As I thought of this, and as the slow minutes followed each other, and nothing reached my ears but the hum of voices in the next room, my suspense became almost unendurable. It was vain to try and fix my attention on what was going on in the street. I sat looking mechanically out of the window, and seeing nothing.

Suddenly – I can't say in how long, or how short a time – the hum of voices ceased; the door opened; and Armadale showed himself on the threshold, alone.

'I wish you good-by,' he said roughly. 'And I hope, when I am married, my wife may never cause Midwinter the disappointment that Midwinter's wife has caused *me!*'

He gave me an angry look, and made me an angry bow – and, turning sharply, left the room.

I saw the people in the street again! I saw the calm sea, and the masts of the shipping in the harbour where the yacht lay! I could think, I

could breathe freely once more! The words that saved me from Manuel
– the words that might be Armadale's sentence of death – had been
spoken. The yacht was to sail without Midwinter, as well as without
Me!

My first feeling of exultation was almost maddening. But it was the
feeling of a moment only. My heart sank in me again, when I thought
of Midwinter alone in the next room.

I went out into the passage to listen, and heard nothing. I tapped
gently at his door, and got no answer. I opened the door, and looked in.
He was sitting at the table, with his face hidden in his hands. I looked
at him in silence – and saw the glistening of the tears, as they trickled
through his fingers.

'Leave me,' he said, without moving his hands. 'I must get over it by
myself.'

I went back into the sitting-room. Who can understand women? – we
don't even understand ourselves. His sending me away from him in that
manner cut me to the heart. I don't believe the most harmless and most
gentle woman living could have felt it more acutely than I felt it. And
this, after what I have been doing! this, after what I was thinking of, the
moment before I went into his room! Who can account for it? Nobody –
I, least of all!

Half an hour later, his door opened, and I heard him hurrying down
the stairs. I ran out without waiting to think, and asked if I might go
with him. He neither stopped nor answered. I went back to the
window, and saw him pass, walking rapidly away, with his back turned
on Naples and the sea.

I can understand now, that he might not have heard me. At the time,
I thought him inexcusably and brutally unkind to me. I put on my
bonnet, in a frenzy of rage with him; I sent out for a carriage, and told
the man to take me where he liked. He took me, as he took other
strangers, to the Museum to see the statues and the pictures. I flounced
from room to room, with my face in a flame, and the people all staring
at me. I came to myself again, I don't know how. I returned to the
carriage, and made the man drive me back in a violent hurry, I don't
know why. I tossed off my cloak and bonnet, and sat down once more
at the window. The sight of the sea cooled me. I forgot Midwinter, and
thought of Armadale and his yacht. There wasn't a breath of wind;
there wasn't a cloud in the sky – the wide waters of the Bay were as
smooth as the surface of a glass.

The sun sank; the short twilight came, and went. I had some tea, and
sat at the table thinking and dreaming over it. When I roused myself

and went back to the window, the moon was up – but the quiet sea was as quiet as ever.

I was still looking out, when I saw Midwinter in the street below, coming back. I was composed enough by this time to remember his habits, and to guess that he had been trying to relieve the oppression on his mind by one of his long solitary walks. When I heard him go into his own room, I was too prudent to disturb him again – I waited his pleasure, where I was.

Before long, I heard his window opened, and I saw him, from my window, step into the balcony, and after a look at the sea, hold up his hand to the air. I was too stupid, for the moment, to remember that he had once been a sailor, and to know what this meant. I waited, and wondered what would happen next.

He went in again; and, after an interval, came out once more, and held up his hand as before, to the air. This time, he waited, leaning on the balcony rail, and looking out steadily, with all his attention absorbed by the sea.

For a long, long time, he never moved. Then, on a sudden, I saw him start. The next moment, he sank on his knees, with his clasped hands resting on the balcony rail. 'God Almighty bless and keep you, Allan!' he said fervently. 'Good-by for ever!'

I looked out to the sea. A soft steady breeze was blowing, and the rippled surface of the water was sparkling in the quiet moonlight. I looked again – and there passed slowly, between me and the track of the moon, a long black vessel with tall shadowy ghost-like sails, gliding smooth and noiseless through the water, like a snake.

The wind had come fair, with the night; and Armadale's yacht had sailed on the trial cruise.

CHAPTER III

THE DIARY BROKEN OFF

London, November 19th. – I am alone again in the Great City; alone, for the first time, since our marriage. Nearly a week since, I started on my homeward journey; leaving Midwinter behind me at Turin.

The days have been so full of events since the month began, and I have been so harassed, in mind and body both, for the greater part of the time, that my Diary has been wretchedly neglected. A few notes, written in such hurry and confusion that I can hardly understand them myself, are all that I possess to remind me of what has happened, since the night when Armadale's yacht left Naples. Let me try if I can set this right, without more loss of time – let me try if I can recall the circumstances in their order as they have followed each other, from the beginning of the month.

On the third of November[1] – being then still at Naples – Midwinter received a hurried letter from Armadale, dated 'Messina'. 'The weather,' he said, 'had been lovely, and the yacht had made one of the quickest passages on record. The crew were rather a rough set to look at; but Captain Manuel, and his English mate,' (the latter described as 'the best of good fellows'), 'managed them admirably.' After this prosperous beginning, Armadale had arranged, as a matter of course, to prolong the cruise; and, at the sailing-master's suggestion, he had decided to visit some of the ports in the Adriatic, which the captain had described as full of character, and well worth seeing.

A postscript followed, explaining that Armadale had written in a hurry to catch the steamer to Naples, and that he had opened his letter again, before sending it off, to add something that he had forgotten. On the day before the yacht sailed, he had been at the banker's to get 'a few hundreds in gold', and he believed he had left his cigar-case there. It was an old friend of his, and he begged that Midwinter would oblige him by endeavouring to recover it, and keeping it for him till they met again.

That was the substance of the letter.

I thought over it carefully when Midwinter had left me alone again, after reading it. My idea was then (and is still) that Manuel had not persuaded Armadale to cruise in a sea like the Adriatic, so much less frequented by ships than the Mediterranean, for nothing. The terms, too, in which the trifling loss of the cigar-case was mentioned, struck me as being equally suggestive of what was coming. I concluded that Armadale's circular notes had not been transformed into those 'few hundreds in gold', through any forethought or business-knowledge of his own. Manuel's influence, I suspected, had been exerted in this matter also – and once more not without reason. At intervals, through the wakeful night, these considerations came back again and again to me; and time after time they pointed obstinately (so far as my next movements were concerned) in one and the same way – the way back to England.

How to get there, and especially how to get there unaccompanied by Midwinter, was more than I had wit enough to discover, that night. I tried, and tried, to meet the difficulty, and fell asleep exhausted towards the morning, without having met it.

Some hours later, as soon as I was dressed, Midwinter came in, with news received by that morning's post from his employers in London. The proprietors of the newspaper had received from the editor so favourable a report of his correspondence from Naples, that they had determined on advancing him to a place of greater responsibility and greater emolument at Turin. His instructions were enclosed in the letter; and he was requested to lose no time in leaving Naples for his new post.

On hearing this, I relieved his mind, before he could put the question, of all anxiety about my willingness to remove. Turin had the great attraction, in my eyes, of being on the road to England. I assured him at once that I was ready to travel as soon as he pleased.

He thanked me for suiting myself to his plans, with more of his old gentleness and kindness than I had seen in him for some time past. The good news from Armadale on the previous day seemed to have roused him a little from the dull despair in which he had been sunk since the sailing of the yacht. And now, the prospect of advancement in his profession, and, more than that, the prospect of leaving the fatal place in which the third Vision of the Dream had come true, had (as he owned himself) additionally cheered and relieved him. He asked, before he went away to make the arrangements for our journey, whether I expected to hear from my 'family' in England, and whether he should give instructions for the forwarding of my letters with his own to the *poste restante* at Turin. I instantly thanked him, and accepted the offer. His proposal had suggested to me, the moment he made it, that my fictitious 'family circumstances' might be turned to good account once more, as a reason for unexpectedly summoning me from Italy to England.

On the ninth of the month we were installed at Turin.

On the thirteenth,[2] Midwinter – being then very busy – asked if I would save him a loss of time by applying for any letters which might have followed us from Naples. I had been waiting for the opportunity he now offered me; and I determined to snatch at it, without allowing myself time to hesitate. There were no letters at the *poste restante* for either of us. But, when he put the question on my return, I told him that there had been a letter for me, with alarming news from 'home'. My 'mother' was dangerously ill; and I was entreated to lose no time in hurrying back to England to see her.

It seems quite unaccountable – now that I am away from him – but it is none the less true, that I could not, even yet, tell him a downright premeditated falsehood, without a sense of shrinking and shame, which other people would think, and which I think myself, utterly inconsistent with such a character as mine. Inconsistent or not, I felt it. And what is stranger – perhaps, I ought to say, madder – still, if he had persisted in his first resolution to accompany me himself to England, rather than allow me to travel alone, I firmly believe I should have turned my back on temptation for the second time, and have lulled myself to rest once more in the old dream of living out my life happy and harmless in my husband's love.

Am I deceiving myself in this? It doesn't matter – I daresay I am. Never mind what *might* have happened. What *did* happen is the only thing of any importance now.

It ended in Midwinter's letting me persuade him that I was old enough to take care of myself on the journey to England, and that he owed it to the newspaper people, who had trusted their interests in his hands, not to leave Turin just as he was established there. He didn't suffer at taking leave of me as he suffered when he saw the last of his friend. I saw that, and set down the anxiety he expressed that I should write to him, at its proper value. I have quite got over my weakness for him at last. No man who really loved me would have put what he owed to a pack of newspaper people before what he owed to his wife. I hate him for letting me convince him! I believe he was glad to get rid of me. I believe he has seen some woman whom he likes at Turin. Well, let him follow his new fancy, if he pleases! I shall be the widow of Mr Armadale of Thorpe-Ambrose, before long – and what will his likes or dislikes matter to me then?

The events on the journey were not worth mentioning, and my arrival in London stands recorded already on the top of the new page.

As for to-day, the one thing of any importance that I have done, since I got to the cheap and quiet hotel at which I am now staying, has been to send for the landlord, and ask him to help me to a sight of the back numbers of *The Times* newspaper. He has politely offered to accompany me himself to-morrow morning to some place in the City where all the papers are kept, as he calls it, in file. Till to-morrow, then, I must control my impatience for news of Armadale as well as I can. And so good-night to the pretty reflection of myself that appears in these pages!

November 20th. – Not a word of news yet, either in the obituary column

578

or in any other part of the paper. I looked carefully through each number in succession, dating from the day when Armadale's letter was written at Messina, to this present 20th of the month – and I am certain, whatever may have happened, that nothing is known in England as yet. Patience! The newspaper is to meet me at the breakfast-table every morning till further notice – and any day now may show me what I most want to see.

November 21st. – No news again. I wrote to Midwinter to-day, to keep up appearances.

When the letter was done, I fell into wretchedly low spirits – I can't imagine why – and felt such a longing for a little company, that, in despair of knowing where else to go, I actually went to Pimlico, on the chance that Mother Oldershaw might have returned to her old quarters.

There were changes since I had seen the place during my former stay in London. Doctor Downward's side of the house was still empty. But the shop was being brightened up for the occupation of a milliner and dress-maker. The people, when I went in to make inquiries, were all strangers to me. They showed, however, no hesitation in giving me Mrs Oldershaw's address, when I asked for it – from which I infer that the little 'difficulty' which forced her to be in hiding in August last, is at an end, so far as she is concerned. As for the doctor, the people at the shop either were, or pretended to be, quite unable to tell me what had become of him.

I don't know whether it was the sight of the place at Pimlico that sickened me, or whether it was my own perversity, or what. But now that I had got Mrs Oldershaw's address, I felt as if she was the very last person in the world that I wanted to see. I took a cab, and told the man to drive to the street she lived in, and then told him to drive back to the hotel. I hardly know what is the matter with me – unless it is that I am getting more impatient every hour for information about Armadale. When will the future look a little less dark, I wonder? To-morrow is Saturday. Will to-morrow's newspaper lift the veil?

November 22nd. – Saturday's newspaper *has* lifted the veil! Words are vain to express the panic of astonishment in which I write. I never once anticipated it – I can't believe it or realize it now it has happened. The winds and waves themselves have turned my accomplices! The yacht has foundered at sea, and every soul on board has perished!

Here is the account cut out of this morning's newspaper:

DISASTER AT SEA. – Intelligence has reached the Royal Yacht Squadron[3] and the insurers, which leaves no reasonable doubt, we regret to say, of the total loss, on the fifth of the present month, of the yacht *Dorothea*, with every soul on board. The particulars are as follow: At daylight, on the morning of the sixth, the Italian brig *Speranza*, bound from Venice to Marsala for orders, encountered some floating objects off Cape Spartivento (at the southernmost extremity of Italy) which attracted the curiosity of the people of the brig. The previous day had been marked by one of the most severe of the sudden and violent storms, peculiar to these southern seas, which has been remembered for years. The *Speranza* herself having been in danger while the gale lasted, the captain and crew concluded that they were on the traces of a wreck, and a boat was lowered for the purpose of examining the objects in the water. A hencoop, some broken spars, and fragments of shattered plank were the first evidences discovered of the terrible disaster that had happened. Some of the lighter articles of cabin furniture, wrenched and shattered, were found next. And, lastly, a memento of melancholy interest turned up, in the shape of a life-buoy, with a corked bottle attached to it. These latter objects, with the relics of cabin-furniture, were brought on board the *Speranza*. On the buoy the name of the vessel was painted as follows: – '*Dorothea*, R.Y.S.' (meaning Royal Yacht Squadron). The bottle, on being uncorked, contained a sheet of note-paper, on which the following lines were hurriedly traced in pencil: – 'Off Cape Spartivento; two days out from Messina. Nov. 5th, 4 P.M.' (being the hour at which the log of the Italian brig showed the storm to have been at its height). 'Both our boats are stove in by the sea. The rudder is gone, and we have sprung a leak astern which is more than we can stop. The Lord help us all – we are sinking. (Signed) John Mitchenden, mate.' On reaching Marsala, the captain of the brig made his report to the British consul, and left the objects discovered in that gentleman's charge. Inquiry at Messina showed that the ill-fated vessel had arrived there from Naples. At the latter port it was ascertained that the *Dorothea* had been hired from the owner's agent, by an English gentleman, Mr Armadale, of Thorpe-Ambrose, Norfolk. Whether Mr Armadale had any friends on board with him has not been clearly discovered. But there is unhappily no doubt that the ill-fated gentleman himself sailed in the yacht from Naples, and that he was also on board of the vessel when she left Messina.

Such is the story of the wreck, as the newspaper tells it in the plainest and fewest words. My head is in a whirl; my confusion is so great that I think of fifty different things, in trying to think of one. I must wait – a day more or less is of no consequence now – I must wait till I can face my new position, without feeling bewildered by it.

November 23rd, Eight in the Morning. – I rose an hour ago, and saw my way clearly to the first step that I must take, under present circumstances.

It is of the utmost importance to me to know what is doing at Thorpe-Ambrose; and it would be the height of rashness, while I am quite in the dark in this matter, to venture there myself. The only other alternative is to write to somebody on the spot for news; and the only person I can write to is – Bashwood.

I have just finished the letter. It is headed 'private and confidential', and signed 'Lydia Armadale'. There is nothing in it to compromise me, if the old fool is mortally offended by my treatment of him, and if he spitefully shows my letter to other people. But I don't believe he will do this. A man at his age forgives a woman anything, if the woman only encourages him. I have requested him, as a personal favour, to keep our correspondence for the present strictly private. I have hinted that my married life with my deceased husband has not been a happy one; and that I feel the injudiciousness of having married a *young* man. In the postscript I go farther still, and venture boldly on these comforting words, – 'I can explain, dear Mr Bashwood, what may have seemed false and deceitful in my conduct towards you, when you give me a personal opportunity.' If he was on the right side of sixty I should feel doubtful of results. But he is on the wrong side of sixty, and I believe he will give me my personal opportunity.

Ten o'clock. – I have been looking over the copy of my marriage-certificate, with which I took care to provide myself on the wedding-day; and I have discovered, to my inexpressible dismay, an obstacle to my appearance in the character of Armadale's widow, which I now see for the first time.

The description of Midwinter (under his own name) which the certificate presents, answers in every important particular, to what would have been the description of Armadale of Thorpe-Ambrose, if I had really married him. 'Name and Surname' – Allan Armadale. 'Age' – twenty-one, instead of twenty-two, which might easily pass for a mistake. 'Condition' – Bachelor. 'Rank or Profession' – Gentleman.

'Residence at the time of Marriage' – Frant's Hotel, Darley-street. 'Father's Name and Surname' – Allan Armadale. 'Rank or Profession of Father' – Gentleman. Every particular (except the year's difference in their two ages) which answers for the one, answers for the other. But, suppose when I produce my copy of the certificate, that some meddlesome lawyer insists on looking at the original register? Midwinter's writing is as different as possible from the writing of his dead friend. The hand in which he has written 'Allan Armadale' in the book, has not a chance of passing for the hand in which Armadale of Thorpe-Ambrose was accustomed to sign his name.

Can I move safely in the matter, with such a pitfall as I see here, open under my feet? How can I tell? Where can I find an experienced person to inform me?[4] I must shut up my diary, and think.

Seven o'clock. – My prospects have changed again since I made my last entry. I have received a warning to be careful in the future, which I shall not neglect; and I have (I believe) succeeded in providing myself with the advice and assistance of which I stand in need.

After vainly trying to think of some better person to apply to in the difficulty which embarrassed me, I made a virtue of necessity, and set forth to surprise Mrs Oldershaw by a visit from her darling Lydia! It is almost needless to add that I determined to sound her carefully, and not to let any secret of importance out of my own possession.

A sour and solemn old maid-servant admitted me into the house. When I asked for her mistress, I was reminded with the bitterest emphasis, that I had committed the impropriety of calling on a Sunday. Mrs Oldershaw was at home, solely in consequence of being too unwell to go to church! The servant thought it very unlikely that she would see me. I thought it highly probable, on the contrary, that she would honour me with an interview in her own interests, if I sent in my name as 'Miss Gwilt', – and the event proved that I was right. After being kept waiting some minutes I was shown into the drawing-room.

There sat mother Jezebel, with the air of a woman resting on the high-road to heaven, dressed in a slate-coloured gown, with grey mittens on her hands, a severely simple cap on her head, and a volume of sermons on her lap. She turned up the whites of her eyes devoutly at the sight of me, and the first words she said were – 'Oh, Lydia! Lydia! why are you not at church?'[5]

If I had been less anxious, the sudden presentation of Mrs Oldershaw, in an entirely new character, might have amused me. But I was in no humour for laughing, and (my notes-of-hand being all paid), I was under no obligation to restrain my natural freedom of speech. 'Stuff and nonsense!' I said. 'Put your Sunday face in your pocket. I have got some news for you, since I last wrote from Thorpe-Ambrose.'

The instant I mentioned 'Thorpe-Ambrose', the whites of the old hypocrite's eyes showed themselves again, and she flatly refused to hear a word more from me on the subject of my proceedings in Norfolk. I insisted – but it was quite useless. Mother Oldershaw only shook her head and groaned, and informed me that her connection with the pomps and vanities of the world was at an end for ever. 'I have been born again, Lydia,' said the brazen old wretch, wiping her eyes. 'Nothing will induce me to return to the subject of that wicked speculation of yours on the folly of a rich young man.'

After hearing this, I should have left her on the spot, but for one consideration which delayed me a moment longer.

It was easy to see, by this time, that the circumstances (whatever they might have been) which had obliged Mother Oldershaw to keep in hiding, on the occasion of my former visit to London, had been sufficiently serious to force her into giving up, or appearing to give up, her old business. And it was hardly less plain that she had found it to her advantage – everybody in England finds it to their advantage, in some way – to cover the outer side of her character carefully with a smooth varnish of Cant. This was, however, no business of mine; and I should have made these reflections outside, instead of inside the house, if my interests had not been involved in putting the sincerity of Mother Oldershaw's reformation to the test – so far as it affected her past connection with myself. At the time when she had fitted me out for our enterprise, I remembered signing a certain business-document which gave her a handsome pecuniary interest in my success, if I became Mrs Armadale of Thorpe-Ambrose. The chance of turning this mischievous morsel of paper to good account, in the capacity of a touchstone, was too tempting to be resisted. I asked my devout friend's permission to say one last word, before I left the house.

'As you have no further interest in my wicked speculation at Thorpe-Ambrose,' I said, 'perhaps you will give me back the written paper that I signed, when you were not quite such an exemplary person as you are now?'

The shameless old hypocrite instantly shut her eyes and shuddered.

'Does that mean Yes, or No?' I asked.

'On moral and religious grounds, Lydia,' said Mrs Oldershaw, 'it means No.'

'On wicked and worldly grounds,' I rejoined, 'I beg to thank you for showing me your hand.'

There could, indeed, be no doubt, now, about the object she really had in view. She would run no more risks and lend no more money – she would leave me to win or lose, single-handed. If I lost, she would not be compromised. If I won, she would produce the paper I had signed, and profit by it without remorse. In my present situation it was mere waste of time and words to prolong the matter by any useless recrimination on my side. I put the warning away privately in my memory for future use, and got up to go.

At the moment when I left my chair, there was a sharp double knock at the street-door. Mrs Oldershaw evidently recognized it. She rose in a violent hurry and rang the bell. 'I am too unwell to see anybody,' she said, when the servant appeared. 'Wait a moment, if you please,' she added, turning sharply on me, when the woman had left us to answer the door.

It was small, very small, spitefulness on my part, I know – but the satisfaction of thwarting Mother Jezebel, even in a trifle, was not to be resisted. 'I can't wait,' I said; 'you reminded me just now that I ought to be at church.' Before she could answer, I was out of the room.

As I put my foot on the first stair the street-door was opened; and a man's voice inquired whether Mrs Oldershaw was at home.

I instantly recognized the voice. Doctor Downward![6]

CHAPTER III. – *continued*

THE DIARY BROKEN OFF

The doctor repeated the servant's message in a tone which betrayed unmistakable irritation at finding himself admitted no farther than the door.

'Your mistress is not well enough to see visitors? Give her that card,' said the doctor, 'and say I expect her, the next time I call, to be well enough to see *me*.'

If his voice had not told me plainly that he felt in no friendly mood towards Mrs Oldershaw, I daresay I should have let him go without claiming his acquaintance. But, as things were, I felt an impulse to speak to him or to anybody who had a grudge against Mother Jezebel. There was more of my small spitefulness in this, I suppose. Anyway, I slipped downstairs; and, following the doctor out quietly, overtook him in the street.

I had recognized his voice, and I recognized his back as I walked behind him. But when I called him by his name, and when he turned round with a start and confronted me, I followed his example, and started on my side. The doctor's face was transformed into the face of a perfect stranger! His baldness had hidden itself under an artfully grizzled wig. He had allowed his whiskers to grow, and had dyed them to match his new head of hair. Hideous circular spectacles bestrode his nose in place of the neat double eyeglass that he used to carry in his hand; and a black neckerchief, surmounted by immense shirt-collars, appeared as the unworthy successor of the clerical white cravat of former times. Nothing remained of the man I once knew but the comfortable plumpness of his figure, and the confidential courtesy and smoothness of his manner and his voice.

'Charmed to see you again,' said the doctor, looking about him a little anxiously, and producing his card-case in a very precipitate manner. 'But my dear Miss Gwilt, permit me to rectify a slight mistake on your part. Doctor Downward of Pimlico is dead and buried; and you will infinitely oblige me if you will never, on any consideration, mention him again!'

I took the card he offered me, and discovered that I was now supposed to be speaking to 'Doctor Le Doux, of the Sanatorium, Fairweather Vale, Hampstead'!

'You seem to have found it necessary,' I said, 'to change a great many things since I last saw you? Your name, your residence, your personal appearance, —?'

'And my branch of practice,' interposed the doctor. 'I have purchased of the original possessor (a person of feeble enterprise and no resources) a name, a diploma, and a partially completed sanatorium for the reception of nervous invalids. We are open already to the inspection of a few privileged friends – come and see us. Are you walking my way? Pray take my arm, and tell me to what happy chance I am indebted for the pleasure of seeing you again?'

I told him the circumstances exactly as they had happened, and I added (with a view to making sure of his relations with his former ally at Pimlico) that I had been greatly surprised to hear Mrs Oldershaw's door shut on such an old friend as himself. Cautious as he was, the doctor's manner of receiving my remark satisfied me at once that my suspicions of an estrangement were well founded. His smile vanished, and he settled his hideous spectacles irritably on the bridge of his nose.

'Pardon me if I leave you to draw your own conclusions,' he said. 'The subject of Mrs Oldershaw is, I regret to say, far from agreeable to me under existing circumstances. A business difficulty connected with our late partnership at Pimlico, entirely without interest for a young and brilliant woman like yourself. Tell me your news! Have you left your situation at Thorpe-Ambrose? Are you residing in London? Is there anything, professional or otherwise, that I can do for you?'

That last question was a more important one than he supposed. Before I answered it, I felt the necessity of parting company with him and of getting a little time to think.

'You have kindly asked me, doctor, to pay you a visit,' I said. 'In your quiet house at Hampstead, I may possibly have something to say to you which I can't say in this noisy street. When are you at home at the Sanatorium? Should I find you there later in the day?'

The doctor assured me that he was then on his way back, and begged that I would name my own hour. I said, 'Towards the afternoon;' and, pleading an engagement, hailed the first omnibus that passed us. 'Don't forget the address,' said the doctor, as he handed me in. 'I have got your card,' I answered – and so we parted.

I returned to the hotel, and went up into my room, and thought over it very anxiously.

The serious obstacle of the signature on the marriage register still stood in my way as unmanageably as ever. All hope of getting assistance from Mrs Oldershaw was at an end. I could only regard her henceforth as an enemy hidden in the dark – the enemy, beyond all doubt now, who had had me followed and watched when I was last in London. To what other counsellor could I turn for the advice which my unlucky ignorance of law and business obliged me to seek from some one more experienced than myself? Could I go to the lawyer whom I consulted when I was about to marry Midwinter in my maiden name? Impossible! To say nothing of his cold reception of me when I had last seen him, the advice I wanted this time, related (disguise the facts as I might) to the commission of a Fraud – a fraud of the sort that no prosperous lawyer would consent to assist, if he had a character to lose. Was there any other competent person I could think of? There was one, and one only – the doctor who had died at Pimlico, and had revived again at Hampstead.

I knew him to be entirely without scruples; to have the business experience that I wanted myself; and to be as cunning, as clever, and as far-seeing a man as could be found in all London. Beyond this, I had made two important discoveries in connection with him that morning. In the first place, he was on bad terms with Mrs Oldershaw, – which would protect me from all danger of the two leaguing together against me, if I trusted him. In the second place, circumstances still obliged him to keep his identity carefully disguised, – which gave me a hold over him in no respect inferior to any hold that *I* might give him over *me*. In every way he was the right man, the only man, for my purpose; and yet I hesitated at going to him – hesitated for a full hour and more, without knowing why!

It was two o'clock before I finally decided on paying the doctor a visit. Having, after this, occupied nearly another hour in determining to a hair's breadth how far I should take him into my confidence, I sent for a cab at last, and set off towards three in the afternoon for Hampstead.

I found the Sanatorium with some little difficulty.

Fairweather Vale proved to be a new neighbourhood,[7] situated below the high ground of Hampstead, on the southern side. The day was overcast, and the place looked very dreary. We approached it by a new road running between trees, which might once have been the park-avenue of a country house. At the end we came upon a wilderness of open ground, with half-finished villas dotted about, and a hideous litter of boards, wheel-barrows, and building materials of all sorts scattered in every direction. At one corner of this scene of desolation stood a great overgrown dismal house, plastered with drab-coloured stucco, and surrounded by a naked unfinished garden, without a shrub or a flower in it – frightful to behold. On the open iron gate that led into this enclosure was a new brass plate, with 'Sanatorium' inscribed on it in great black letters. The bell, when the cabman rang it, pealed through the empty house like a knell; and the pallid withered old manservant in black, who answered the door, looked as if he had stepped up out of his grave to perform that service. He let out on me a smell of damp plaster and new varnish; and he let in with me a chilling draught of the damp November air. I didn't notice it at the time – but writing of it now, I remember that I shivered as I crossed the threshold.

I gave my name to the servant as 'Mrs Armadale', and was shown into the waiting-room. The very fire itself was dying of damp in the grate. The only books on the table were the doctor's Works, in sober drab covers; and the only object that ornamented the walls was the foreign Diploma (handsomely framed and glazed), of which the doctor had possessed himself by purchase, along with the foreign name.

After a moment or two, the proprietor of the Sanatorium came in, and held up his hands in cheerful astonishment at the sight of me.

'I hadn't an idea who "Mrs Armadale" was!' he said. 'My dear lady, have *you* changed your name, too? How sly of you not to tell me when we met this morning! Come into my private snuggery – I can't think of keeping an old and dear friend like you in the patients' waiting-room.'

The doctor's private snuggery was at the back of the house, looking out on fields and trees, doomed but not yet destroyed by the builder. Horrible objects in brass and leather and glass, twisted and turned as if they were sentient things writhing in agonies of pain, filled up one end of the room. A great book-case with glass doors extended over the whole of the opposite wall, and exhibited on its shelves long rows of glass jars, in which shapeless dead creatures of a dull white colour floated in yellow liquid. Above the fireplace hung a collection of photographic portraits of men and women, enclosed in two large frames hanging side by side with a space between them. The left-hand frame illustrated the effects of nervous suffering as seen in the face; the right-hand frame exhibited the ravages of insanity from the same point of view; while the space between was occupied by an elegantly-illuminated scroll, bearing inscribed on it the time-honoured motto, 'Prevention is better than Cure.'

'Here I am, with my galvanic apparatus,[8] and my preserved specimens, and all the rest of it,' said the doctor, placing me in a chair by the fireside. 'And there is my System mutely addressing you just above your head, under a form of exposition which I venture to describe as frankness itself. This is no madhouse, my dear lady.[9] Let other men treat insanity, if they like – *I* stop it! No patients in the house as yet. But we live in an age when nervous derangement (parent of insanity) is steadily on the increase; and in due time the sufferers will come. I can wait as Harvey waited, as Jenner waited.[10] And now, do put your feet up on the fender, and tell me about yourself. You are married, of course? And what a pretty name! Accept my best and most heartfelt congratulations. You have the two greatest blessings that can fall to a woman's lot; the two capital H's, as I call them – Husband and Home.'

I interrupted the genial flow of the doctor's congratulations at the first opportunity.

'I am married; but the circumstances are by no means of the ordinary kind,' I said seriously. 'My present position includes none of the blessings that are usually supposed to fall to a woman's lot. I am already in a situation of very serious difficulty – and before long I may be in a situation of very serious danger as well.'

The doctor drew his chair a little nearer to me, and fell at once into his old professional manner and his old confidential tone.

'If you wish to consult me,' he said softly, 'you know that I have kept some dangerous secrets in my time, and you also know that I possess two valuable qualities as an adviser. I am not easily shocked; and I can be implicitly trusted.'

I hesitated even now, at the eleventh hour, sitting alone with him in his own room. It was so strange to me to be trusting to anybody but myself! And yet, how could I help trusting another person, in a difficulty which turned on a matter of law?

'Just as you please, you know,' added the doctor. 'I never invite confidences. I merely receive them.'

There was no help for it; I had come there not to hesitate, but to speak. I risked it, and spoke.

'The matter on which I wish to consult you,' I said, 'is not (as you seem to think) within your experience as a professional man. But I believe you may be of assistance to me, if I trust myself to your larger experience as a man of the world. I warn you, beforehand, that I shall certainly surprise and possibly alarm you before I have done.'

With that preface, I entered on my story, telling him what I had settled to tell him – and no more.

I made no secret, at the outset, of my intention to personate Armadale's widow; and I mentioned without reserve (knowing that the doctor could go to the office and examine the will for himself) the handsome income that would be settled on me in the event of my success. Some of the circumstances that followed next in succession, I thought it desirable to alter or conceal. I showed him the newspaper account of the loss of the yacht – but I said nothing about events at Naples. I informed him of the exact similarity of the two names; leaving him to imagine that it was accidental. I told him, as an important element in the matter, that my husband had kept his real name a profound secret from everybody but myself; but (to prevent any communication between them) I carefully concealed from the doctor what the assumed name under which Midwinter had lived all his life really was. I acknowledged that I had left my husband behind me on the Continent; but when the doctor put the question, I allowed him to conclude – I couldn't with all my resolution tell him positively! – that Midwinter knew of the contemplated Fraud, and that he was staying away purposely so as not to compromise me by his presence. This difficulty smoothed over – or, as I feel it now, this baseness committed, – I reverted to myself, and came back again to the truth. One after another, I mentioned all the circumstances connected with my private marriage, and with the movements of Armadale and Midwinter, which rendered any discovery of the false personation (through the evidence of other people) a downright impossibility. 'So much,' I said, in conclusion, 'for the object in view. The next thing is to tell you plainly of a very serious obstacle that stands in my way.'

The doctor, who had listened thus far without interrupting me, begged permission here to say a few words on his side before I went on.

The 'few words' proved to be all questions – clever, searching, suspicious questions, – which I was, however, able to answer with little or no reserve, for they related, in almost every instance, to the circumstances under which I had been married, and to the chances for and against my lawful husband if he chose to assert his claim to me at any future time.

My replies informed the doctor, in the first place, that I had so managed matters at Thorpe-Ambrose as to produce a general impression that Armadale intended to marry me; in the second place, that my husband's early life had not been of a kind to exhibit him favourably in the eyes of the world; in the third place, that we had been married without any witness present who knew us, at a large parish church in which two other couples had been married the same morning, to say nothing of the dozens on dozens of other couples (confusing all remembrance of us in the minds of the officiating people) who had been married since. When I had put the doctor in possession of these facts – and when he had further ascertained that Midwinter and I had gone abroad among strangers immediately after leaving the church; and that the men employed on board the yacht in which Armadale had sailed from Somersetshire (before my marriage) were now away in ships voyaging to the other end of the world – his confidence in my prospects showed itself plainly in his face. 'So as far as I can see,' he said, 'your husband's claim to you (after you have stepped into the place of the dead Mr Armadale's widow) would rest on nothing but his own bare assertion. And *that* I think you may safely set at defiance. Excuse my apparent distrust of the gentleman. But there might be a misunderstanding between you in the future, and it is highly desirable to ascertain beforehand exactly what he could or could not do under those circumstances. And now that we have done with the main obstacle that *I* see in the way of your success, let us by all means come to the obstacle that *you* see next!'

I was willing enough to come to it. The tone in which he spoke of Midwinter, though I myself was responsible for it, jarred on me horribly, and roused for the moment some of the old folly of feeling which I fancied I had laid asleep for ever. I rushed at the chance of changing the subject, and mentioned the discrepancy in the register between the hand in which Midwinter had signed the name of Allan Armadale, and the hand in which Armadale of Thorpe-Ambrose had been accustomed to write his name, with an eagerness which it quite diverted the doctor to see.

'Is *that* all?' he asked, to my infinite surprise and relief, when I had done. 'My dear lady, pray set your mind at ease! If the late Mr Armadale's lawyers want a proof of your marriage, they won't go to the church-register for it, I can promise you!'

'What!' I exclaimed in astonishment; 'do you mean to say that the entry in the register is not a proof of my marriage?'

'It is a proof,' said the doctor, 'that you have been married to somebody. But it is no proof that you have been married to Mr Armadale of Thorpe-Ambrose. Jack Nokes or Tom Styles (excuse the homeliness of the illustration!) might have got the Licence, and gone to the church to be married to you under Mr Armadale's name – and the register (how could it do otherwise?) must in that case have innocently assisted the deception. I see I surprise you. My dear madam, when you opened this interesting business you surprised *me* – I may own it now – by laying so much stress on the curious similarity between the two names. You might have entered on the very daring and romantic enterprise in which you are now engaged, without necessarily marrying your present husband. Any other man would have done just as well, provided he was willing to take Mr Armadale's name for the purpose.'

I felt my temper going at this. 'Any other man would *not* have done just as well,' I rejoined instantly. 'But for the similarity of the names, I should never have thought of the enterprise at all.'

The doctor admitted that he had spoken too hastily. 'That personal view of the subject had, I confess, escaped me,' he said. 'However, let us get back to the matter in hand. In the course of what I may term an adventurous medical life, I have been brought more than once into contact with the gentlemen of the law, and have had opportunities of observing their proceedings in cases of, let us say, Domestic Jurisprudence. I am quite sure I am correct in informing you that the proof which will be required by Mr Armadale's representatives will be the evidence of a witness present at the marriage, who can speak to the identity of the bride and bridegroom from his own personal knowledge.'

'But I have already told you,' I said, 'that there was no such person present.'[11]

'Precisely,' rejoined the doctor. 'In that case, what you now want, before you can safely stir a step in the matter, is – if you will pardon me the expression – a ready-made witness, possessed of rare moral and personal resources, who can be trusted to assume the necessary character, and to make the necessary Declaration before a magistrate. Do you know of any such person?' asked the doctor, throwing himself back in his chair, and looking at me with the utmost innocence.

'I only know You,' I said.

The doctor laughed softly. 'So like a woman!' he remarked, with the most exasperating good-humour. 'The moment she sees her object, she dashes at it headlong the nearest way. Oh, the sex! the sex!'

'Never mind the sex!' I broke out impatiently. 'I want a serious answer – Yes or No?'

The doctor rose, and waved his hand with great gravity and dignity all round the room. 'You see this vast establishment,' he began; 'you can possibly estimate to some extent the immense stake I have in its prosperity and success. Your excellent natural sense will tell you that the Principal of this Sanatorium must be a man of the most unblemished character—'

'Why waste so many words,' I said, 'when one word will do? You mean No!'

The Principal of the Sanatorium suddenly relapsed into the character of my confidential friend.

'My dear lady,' he said, 'it isn't Yes, and it isn't No, at a moment's notice. Give me till to-morrow afternoon. By that time, I engage to be ready to do one of two things – either to withdraw myself from this business at once, or to go into it with you heart and soul. Do you agree to that? Very good – we may drop the subject then till to-morrow. Where can I call on you when I have decided what to do?'

There was no objection to my trusting him with my address at the hotel. I had taken care to present myself there as 'Mrs Armadale'; and I had given Midwinter an address at the neighbouring post-office to write to, when he answered my letters. We settled the hour at which the doctor was to call on me; and, that matter arranged, I rose to go, resisting all offers of refreshment, and all proposals to show me over the house. His smooth persistence in keeping up appearances after we had thoroughly understood each other, disgusted me. I got away from him as soon as I could, and came back to my diary and my own room.

We shall see how it ends to-morrow. My own idea is that my confidential friend will say Yes.

November 24th. – The doctor has said Yes, as I supposed – but on terms which I never anticipated. The condition on which I have secured his services amounts to nothing less than the payment to him, on my stepping into the place of Armadale's widow, of half my first year's income – in other words, six hundred pounds!

I protested against this extortionate demand in every way I could think of. All to no purpose. The doctor met me with the most engaging frankness. Nothing, he said, but the accidental embarrassment of his position at the present time would have induced him to mix himself up in the matter at all. He would honestly confess that he had exhausted his own resources, and the resources of other persons whom he described as his 'backers', in the purchase and completion of the Sanatorium. Under those circumstances, six hundred pounds in prospect *was* an object to him. For that sum he would run the serious risk of advising and assisting me. Not a farthing less would tempt him – and there he left it, with his best and friendliest wishes, in my hands!

It ended in the only way in which it could end. I had no choice but to accept the terms, and to let the doctor settle things on the spot as he pleased. The arrangement once made between us, I must do him the justice to say that he showed no disposition to let the grass grow under his feet. He called briskly for pen, ink, and paper, and suggested opening the campaign at Thorpe-Ambrose by to-night's post.

We agreed on a form of letter which I wrote, and which he copied on the spot. I entered into no particulars at starting. I simply asserted that I was the widow of the deceased Mr Armadale; that I had been privately married to him; that I had returned to England on his sailing in the yacht from Naples; and that I begged to enclose a copy of my marriage-certificate, as a matter of form with which I presumed it was customary to comply. The letter was addressed to 'The representatives of the late Allan Armadale, Esq., Thorpe-Ambrose, Norfolk.' And the doctor himself carried it away, and put it in the post.[12]

I am not so excited and so impatient for results as I expected to be, now that the first step is taken. The thought of Midwinter haunts me like a ghost. I have been writing to him again – as before, to keep up appearances. It will be my last letter, I think. My courage feels shaken, my spirits get depressed, when my thoughts go back to Turin. I am no more capable of facing the consideration of Midwinter at this moment than I was in the bygone time. The day of reckoning with him, once distant and doubtful, is a day that may come to me now, I know not how soon. And here I am, trusting myself blindly to the chapter of Accidents still!

November 25th. – At two o'clock to-day the doctor called again by appointment. He has been to his lawyers (of course without taking them into our confidence) to put the case simply of proving my marriage. The result confirms what he has already told me. The pivot on which the whole matter will turn, if my claim is disputed, will be the question of identity; and it may be necessary for the witness to make his Declaration in the magistrates' presence before the week is out.

In this position of affairs, the doctor thinks it important that we should be within easy reach of each other, and proposes to find a quiet lodging for me in his neighbourhood. I am quite willing to go anywhere – for, among the other strange fancies that have got possession of me, I have an idea that I shall feel more completely lost to Midwinter if I move out of the neighbourhood in which his letters are addressed to me. I was awake and thinking of him again last night. This morning I have finally decided to write to him no more.

After staying half an hour, the doctor left me – having first inquired whether I would like to accompany him to Hampstead to look for lodgings. I informed him that I had some business of my own which would keep me in London. He inquired what the business was. 'You will see,' I said, 'to-morrow or next day.'

I had a moment's nervous trembling when I was by myself again. My business in London, besides being a serious business in a woman's eyes, took my mind back to Midwinter in spite of me. The prospect of removing to my new lodging had reminded me of the necessity of dressing in my new character. The time had come now for getting *my widow's weeds*.

My first proceeding, after putting my bonnet on, was to provide myself with money. I got what I wanted to fit me out for the character of Armadale's widow, by nothing less than the sale of Armadale's own present to me on my marriage – the ruby ring! It proved to be a more valuable jewel than I had supposed. I am likely to be spared all money anxieties for some time to come.

On leaving the jeweller's, I went to the great mourning shop in Regent Street.[13] In four and twenty hours (if I can give them no more) they have engaged to dress me in my widow's costume from head to foot. I had another feverish moment when I left the shop; and, by way of further excitement on this agitating day, I found a surprise in store for me on my return to the hotel. An elderly gentleman was announced to be waiting to see me. I opened my sitting-room door – and there was old Bashwood!

He had got my letter that morning, and had started for London by the next train to answer it in person. I had expected a great deal from him, but I had certainly not expected *that*. It flattered me. For the moment, I declare it flattered me!

I pass over the wretched old creature's raptures and reproaches, and groans and tears, and weary long prosings about the lonely months he had passed at Thorpe-Ambrose, brooding over my desertion of him. He was quite eloquent at times – but I don't want his eloquence here. It is needless to say that I put myself right with him, and consulted his feelings before I asked him for his news. What a blessing a woman's vanity is sometimes! I almost forgot my risks and responsibilities, in my anxiety to be charming. For a minute or two, I felt a warm little flutter of triumph. And it *was* a triumph – even with an old man! In a quarter of an hour, I had him smirking and smiling, hanging on my lightest words in an ecstasy, and answering all the questions I put to him, like a good little child.

Here is his account of affairs at Thorpe-Ambrose, as I gently extracted it from him bit by bit:

In the first place, the news of Armadale's death has reached Miss Milroy. It has so completely overwhelmed her that her father has been compelled to remove her from the school. She is back at the cottage, and the doctor is in daily attendance. Do I pity her? Yes! I pity her exactly as much as she once pitied me!

In the next place, the state of affairs at the great house, which I expected to find some difficulty in comprehending, turns out to be quite intelligible, and certainly not discouraging so far. Only yesterday, the lawyers on both sides came to an understanding. Mr Darch (the family solicitor of the Blanchards, and Armadale's bitter enemy in past times) represents the interests of Miss Blanchard, who is next heir to the estate, and who has, it appears, been in London on business of her own for some time past. Mr Smart, of Norwich (originally employed to overlook Bashwood in the steward's office), represents the deceased Armadale. And this is what the two lawyers have settled between them.

Mr Darch, acting for Miss Blanchard, has claimed the possession of the estate and the right of receiving the rents at the Christmas audit, in her name. Mr Smart, on his side, has admitted that there is great weight in the family solicitor's application. He cannot see his way, as things are now, to contesting the question of Armadale's death, and he will consent to offer no resistance to the application, if Mr Darch will consent, on his side, to assume the responsibility of taking possession in Miss Blanchard's name. This Mr Darch has already done; and the estate is now virtually in Miss Blanchard's possession.

One result of this course of proceeding will be (as Bashwood thinks) to put Mr Darch in the position of the person who really decides on my claim to the widow's place and the widow's money. The income being charged on the estate, it must come out of Miss Blanchard's pocket; and the question of paying it would appear therefore to be a question for Miss Blanchard's lawyer. To-morrow will probably decide whether this view is the right one – for my letter to Armadale's representatives will have been delivered at the great house this morning.

So much for what old Bashwood had to tell me. Having recovered my influence over him, and possessed myself of all his information so far, the next thing to consider was the right use to turn him to in the future. He was entirely at my disposal, for his place at the steward's office has been already taken by Miss Blanchard's man of business, and he pleaded hard to be allowed to stay and serve my interests in London. There would not have been the least danger in letting him stay, for I had, as a matter of course, left him undisturbed in his conviction that I really am the widow of Armadale of Thorpe-Ambrose. But with the doctor's resources at my command, I wanted no assistance of any sort in London; and it occurred to me that I might make Bashwood more useful by sending him back to Norfolk to watch events there in my interests.

He looked sorely disappointed (having had an eye evidently to paying his court to me in my widowed condition!) when I told him of the conclusion at which I had arrived. But a few words of persuasion, and a modest hint that he might cherish hopes in the future if he served me obediently in the present, did wonders in reconciling him to the necessity of meeting my wishes. He asked helplessly for 'instructions' when it was time for him to leave me and travel back by the evening train. I could give him none, for I had no idea as yet of what the legal people might or might not do. 'But suppose something happens,' he persisted, 'that I don't understand, what am I to do, so far away from you?' I could only give him one answer. 'Do nothing,' I said. 'Whatever it is, hold your tongue about it, and write, or come up to London immediately to consult me.' With those parting directions, and with an understanding that we were to correspond regularly, I let him kiss my hand, and sent him off to the train.

Now that I am alone again, and able to think calmly of the interview between me and my elderly admirer, I find myself recalling a certain change in old Bashwood's manner which puzzled me at the time, and which puzzles me still.

Even in his first moments of agitation at seeing me, I thought that his eyes rested on my face with a new kind of interest while I was speaking to him. Besides this, he dropped a word or two afterwards, in telling me of his lonely life at Thorpe-Ambrose, which seemed to imply that he had been sustained in his solitude by a feeling of confidence about his future relations with me when we next met. If he had been a younger and a bolder man (and if any such discovery had been possible), I should almost have suspected him of having found out something about my past life which had made him privately confident of controlling me, if I showed any disposition to deceive and desert him again. But such an idea as this in connection with old Bashwood is simply absurd. Perhaps I am over-excited by the suspense and anxiety of my present position? Perhaps the merest fancies and suspicions are leading me astray? Let this be as it may, I have at any rate more serious subjects than the subject of old Bashwood to occupy me now. To-morrow's post may tell me what Armadale's representatives think of the claim of Armadale's widow.

November 26th. – The answer has arrived this morning, in the form (as Bashwood supposed) of a letter from Mr Darch. The crabbed old lawyer acknowledges my letter in three lines. Before he takes any steps, or expresses any opinion on the subject, he wants evidence of identity as well as the evidence of the certificate; and he ventures to suggest that it may be desirable, before we go any further, to refer him to my legal advisers.

Two o'clock. – The doctor called shortly after twelve to say that he had found a lodging for me within twenty minutes' walk of the Sanatorium. In return for his news, I showed him Mr Darch's letter. He took it away at once to his lawyers, and came back with the necessary information for my guidance. I have answered Mr Darch by sending him the address of my legal advisers – otherwise, the doctor's lawyers – without making any comment on the desire that he has expressed for additional evidence of the marriage. This is all that can be done to-day. To-morrow will bring with it events of greater interest – for to-morrow the doctor is to make his Declaration before the magistrate, and to-morrow I am to move to my new lodging in my widow's weeds.

November 27th. – *Fairweather Vale Villas.* – The Declaration has been made, with all the necessary formalities. And I have taken possession, in my widow's costume, of my new rooms.

I ought to be excited by the opening of this new act in the drama, and by the venturesome part that I am playing in it myself. Strange to say, I am quiet and depressed. The thought of Midwinter has followed me to my new abode, and is pressing on me heavily at this moment. I have no fear of any accident happening, in the interval that must still pass before I step publicly into the place of Armadale's widow. But when that time comes, and when Midwinter finds me (as sooner or later find me he must!) figuring in my false character, and settled in the position that I have usurped – *then*, I ask myself, What will happen? The answer still comes as it first came to me this morning, when I put on my widow's dress. Now, as then, the presentiment is fixed in my mind that he will kill me. If it was not too late to draw back— Absurd! I shall shut up my journal.

November 28th. – The lawyers have heard from Mr Darch, and have sent him the Declaration by return of post.

When the doctor brought me this news, I asked him whether his lawyers were aware of my present address; and, finding that he had not yet mentioned it to them, I begged that he would continue to keep it a secret for the future. The doctor laughed. 'Are you afraid of Mr Darch's stealing a march on us, and coming to attack you personally?' he asked. I accepted the imputation, as the easiest way of making him comply with my request. 'Yes,' I said, 'I am afraid of Mr Darch.'

My spirits have risen since the doctor left me. There is a pleasant sensation of security in feeling that no strangers are in possession of my address. I am easy enough in my mind to-day to notice how wonderfully well I look in my widow's weeds, and to make myself agreeable to the people of the house.

Midwinter disturbed me a little again last night; but I have got over the ghastly delusion which possessed me yesterday. I know better now than to dread violence from him when he discovers what I have done. And there is still less fear of his stooping to assert his claim to a woman who has practised on him such a deception as mine. The one serious trial that I shall be put to when the day of reckoning comes, will be the trial of preserving my false character in his presence. I shall be safe in his loathing and contempt for me, after that. On the day when I have denied him to his face, I shall have seen the last of him for ever.

Shall I be able to deny him to his face? Shall I be able to look at him and speak to him as if he had never been more to me than a friend?

How do I know till the time comes! Was there ever such an infatuated fool as I am, to be writing of him at all, when writing only encourages me to think of him? I will make a new resolution. From this time forth his name shall appear no more in these pages.

Monday, December 1st. – The last month of the worn-out old year, eighteen hundred and fifty-one! If I allowed myself to look back, what a miserable year I should see added to all the other miserable years that are gone! But I have made my resolution to look forward only, and I mean to keep it.

I have nothing to record of the last two days, except that on the twenty-ninth I remembered Bashwood, and wrote to tell him of my new address. This morning the lawyers heard again from Mr Darch. He acknowledges the receipt of the Declaration, but postpones stating the decision at which he has arrived until he has communicated with the trustees under the late Mr Blanchard's will, and has received his final instructions from his client, Miss Blanchard. The doctor's lawyers declare that this last letter is a mere device for gaining time – with what object they are of course not in a position to guess. The doctor himself says, facetiously, it is the usual lawyer's object of making a long bill. My own idea is that Mr Darch has his suspicions of something wrong, and that his purpose in trying to gain time—

Ten, at night. – I had written as far as that last unfinished sentence (towards four in the afternoon) when I was startled by hearing a cab drive up to the door. I went to the window, and got there just in time to see old Bashwood getting out with an activity of which I should never have supposed him capable. So little did I anticipate the tremendous discovery that was going to burst on me in another minute, that I turned to the glass, and wondered what the susceptible old gentleman would say to me in my widow's cap.

The instant he entered the room, I saw that some serious disaster had happened. His eyes were wild, his wig was awry. He approached me with a strange mixture of eagerness and dismay. 'I've done as you told me,' he whispered breathlessly. 'I've held my tongue about it, and come straight to *you*!' He caught me by the hand before I could speak, with a boldness quite new in my experience of him. 'Oh, how can I break it to you!' he burst out. 'I'm beside myself when I think of it!'

'When you *can* speak,' I said, putting him into a chair, 'speak out. I see in your face that you bring me news I don't look for from Thorpe-Ambrose.'

He put his hand into the breast-pocket of his coat, and drew out a letter. He looked at the letter, and looked at me. 'New-new-news you don't look for,' he stammered; 'but not from Thorpe-Ambrose!'

'Not from Thorpe-Ambrose!'

'No. From the sea!'

The first dawning of the truth broke on me at those words. I couldn't speak – I could only hold out my hand to him for the letter.

He still shrank from giving it to me. 'I daren't! I daren't!' he said to himself vacantly. 'The shock of it might be the death of her.'

I snatched the letter from him. One glance at the writing on the address was enough. My hands fell on my lap, with the letter fast held in them. I sat petrified, without moving, without speaking, without hearing a word of what Bashwood was saying to me, and slowly realized the terrible truth. The man whose widow I had claimed to be, was a living man to confront me! In vain I had mixed the drink at Naples – in vain I had betrayed him into Manuel's hands. Twice I had set the deadly snare for him, and twice Armadale had escaped me!

I came to my sense of outward things again, and found Bashwood on his knees at my feet, crying.

'You look angry,' he murmured helplessly. 'Are you angry with *me*? Oh, if you only knew what hopes I had when we last saw each other, and how cruelly that letter has dashed them all to the ground!'

I put the miserable old creature back from me – but very gently. 'Hush!' I said. 'Don't distress me now. I want composure – I want to read the letter.'

He went away submissively to the other end of the room. As soon as my eye was off him, I heard him say to himself, with impotent malignity, 'If the sea had been of my mind, the sea would have drowned him!'

One by one, I slowly opened the folds of the letter; feeling, while I did so, the strangest incapability of fixing my attention on the very lines that I was burning to read. But why dwell any longer on sensations which I can't describe? It will be more to the purpose if I place the letter itself, for future reference, on this page of my journal.

Mr Bashwood,   Fiume, Illyria, November 21st, 1851.

The address I date from will surprise you – and you will be more surprised still when you hear how it is that I come to write to you from a port on the Adriatic Sea.

I have been the victim of a rascally attempt at robbery and murder. The robbery has succeeded; and it is only through the mercy of God that the murder did not succeed too.

I hired a yacht rather more than a month ago at Naples; and sailed (I am glad to think now) without any friend with me, for Messina. From Messina I went for a cruise in the Adriatic. Two days out, we were caught in a storm. Storms get up in a hurry, and go down in a hurry, in those parts. The vessel behaved nobly – I declare I feel the tears in my eyes now, when I think of her at the bottom of the sea! Towards sunset it began to moderate; and by midnight, except for a long smooth swell, the sea was as quiet as need be. I went below, a little tired (having helped in working the yacht while the gale lasted), and fell asleep in five minutes. About two hours after, I was woke by something falling into my cabin through a chink of the ventilator in the upper part of the door. I jumped up, and found a bit of paper with a key wrapped in it, and with writing on the inner side, in a hand which it was not very easy to read.

'Up to this time I had not had the ghost of a suspicion that I was alone at sea with a gang of murderous vagabonds (excepting one only) who would stick at nothing. I had got on very well with my sailing-master (the worst scoundrel of the lot), and better still with his English mate. The sailors being all foreigners, I had very little to say to. They did their work, and no quarrels and nothing unpleasant happened. If anybody had told me, before I went to bed on the night after the storm, that the sailing-master and the crew and the mate (who had been no better than the rest of them at starting) were all in a conspiracy to rob me of the money I had on board, and then to drown me in my own vessel afterwards, I should have laughed in his face. Just remember that; and then fancy for yourself (for I'm sure I can't tell you) what I must have thought when I opened the paper round the key, and read what I now copy (from the mate's writing) as follows:

Sir, – Stay in your bed till you hear a boat shove off from the starboard side – or you are a dead man. Your money is stolen; and in five minutes' time the yacht will be scuttled, and the cabin-hatch will be nailed down on you. Dead men tell no tales – and the sailing-master's notion is to leave proofs afloat that the vessel has foundered with all on board. It was his doing to begin with, and we were all in it. I can't find it in my heart not to give you a chance for your life. It's a bad chance, but I can do no more. I should be murdered myself if I didn't seem to go with the rest. The key of your cabin-door is thrown back to you, inside this. Don't be alarmed when you hear the hammer above. I shall do it, and I shall have short nails in my hand as well as long, and use the short ones only. Wait till you hear the boat with all of us shove off, and then prize up the cabin-hatch with your back. The vessel will float a quarter of an hour after the holes are bored in her. Slip into the sea on the port side, and keep the vessel between you and the boat. You will find plenty of loose lumber, wrenched away on purpose, drifting about to hold on by. It's a fine night and a smooth sea, and there's a chance that a ship may pick you up while there's life left in you. I can do no more. – Yours truly, J. M.

As I came to those last words, I heard the hammering down of the hatch over my head. I don't suppose I'm more of a coward than most people – but there was a moment when the sweat poured down me like rain. I got to be my own man again, before the hammering was done, and found myself thinking of somebody very dear to me in England. I said to myself, 'I'll have a try for my life, for her sake, though the chances are dead against me.'

I put a letter from that person I have mentioned into one of the stoppered bottles of my dressing-case – along with the mate's warning, in case I lived to see him again. I hung this, and a flask of whisky, in a sling round my neck – and, after first dressing myself in my confusion, thought better of it, and stripped again, for swimming, to my shirt and drawers. By the time I had done that, the hammering was over, and there was such a silence that I could hear the water bubbling into the scuttled vessel amidships. The next noise was the noise of the boat and the villains in her (always excepting my friend the mate) shoving off from the starboard side. I waited for the splash of the oars in the water, and then got my back under the hatch. The mate had kept his promise. I lifted it easily – crept across the deck, under cover of the bulwarks, on all fours – and slipped into the sea on the port side. Lots of things were floating about. I took the first thing I came to – a hencoop – and swam away with it about a couple of hundred yards, keeping the yacht between me and the boat. Having got that distance, I was seized with a shivering fit, and I stopped (fearing the cramp next) to take a pull at my flask. When

I had closed the flask again, I turned for a moment to look back, and saw the yacht in the act of sinking. In a minute more there was nothing between me and the boat, but the pieces of wreck that had been purposely thrown out to float. The moon was shining; and, if they had had a glass in the boat, I believe they might have seen my head, though I carefully kept the hencoop between me and them.

As it was, they laid on their oars; and I heard loud voices among them disputing. After what seemed an age to me, I discovered what the dispute was about. The boat's head was suddenly turned my way. Some cleverer scoundrel than the rest (the sailing-master, I daresay,) had evidently persuaded them to row back over the place where the yacht had gone down, and make quite sure that I had gone down with her.

They were more than half way across the distance that separated us, and I had given myself up for lost, when I heard a cry from one of them, and saw the boat's progress suddenly checked. In a minute or two more, the boat's head was turned again; and they rowed straight away from me like men rowing for their lives.

I looked on one side, towards the land, and saw nothing. I looked on the other, towards the sea, and discovered what the boat's crew had discovered before me – a sail in the distance, growing steadily brighter and bigger in the moonlight the longer I looked at it. In a quarter of an hour more the vessel was within hail of me, and the crew had got me on board.

They were all foreigners, and they quite deafened me by their jabber. I tried signs, but before I could make them understand me, I was seized with another shivering fit, and was carried below. The vessel held on her course, I have no doubt, but I was in no condition to know anything about it. Before morning, I was in a fever; and from that time I can remember nothing clearly till I came to my senses at this place, and found myself under the care of a Hungarian merchant, the consignee (as they call it) of the coasting vessel that had picked me up. He speaks English as well or better than I do; and he has treated me with a kindness which I can find no words to praise. When he was a young man he was in England himself, learning business, and he says he has remembrances of our country which make his heart warm towards an Englishman. He has fitted me out with clothes, and has lent me the money to travel with, as soon as the doctor allows me to start for home. Supposing I don't get a relapse, I shall be fit to travel in a week's time from this. If I can catch the mail at Trieste, and stand the fatigue, I shall be back again at Thorpe-Ambrose in a week or ten days at most after you get my letter. You will agree with me that it is a terribly long letter. But I can't help that. I seem to have lost my old knack at putting things short, and finishing on the first page. However, I am near the end now – for I have nothing left to mention but the reason why I write about what has happened to me, instead of waiting till I get home, and telling it all by word of mouth.

I fancy my head is still muddled by my illness. At any rate, it only struck me this morning that there is barely a chance of some vessel having passed the place where the yacht foundered, and having picked up the furniture, and other things wrenched out of her and left to float. Some false report of my being drowned may, in that case, have reached England.[14] If this has happened (which I hope to God may be an unfounded fear on my part), go directly to Major Milroy at the cottage. Show him this letter – I have written it quite as much for his eye as for yours – and then give him the enclosed note, and ask him if he doesn't think the circumstances justify me in hoping he will send it to Miss Milroy. I can't explain why I don't write directly to the major, or to Miss Milroy, instead of to you. I can only say there are considerations I am bound in honour to respect, which oblige me to act in this roundabout way.

I don't ask you to answer this – for I shall be on my way home, I hope, long before your letter could reach me in this out-of-the-way place. Whatever you do, don't lose a moment in going to Major Milroy. Go, on second thoughts, whether the loss of the yacht is known in England or not.

Yours truly,
ALLAN ARMADALE.

I looked up when I had come to the end of the letter, and saw, for the first time, that Bashwood had left his chair, and had placed himself opposite to me. He was intently studying my face, with the inquiring expression of a man who was trying to read my thoughts. His eyes fell guiltily when they met mine, and he shrank away to his chair. Believing, as he did, that I was really married to Armadale, was he trying to discover whether the news of Armadale's rescue from the sea was good news or bad news, in my estimation? It was no time then for entering into explanations with him. The first thing to be done was to communicate instantly with the doctor. I called Bashwood back to me, and gave him my hand.

'You have done me a service,' I said, 'which makes us closer friends than ever. I shall say more about this, and about other matters of some interest to both of us, later in the day. I want you now to lend me Mr Armadale's letter (which I promise to bring back) and to wait here till I return. Will you do that for me, Mr Bashwood?'

He would do anything I asked him, he said. I went into the bed-room, and put on my bonnet and shawl.

'Let me be quite sure of the facts before I leave you,' I resumed, when I was ready to go out. 'You have not shown this letter to anybody but me?'

'Not a living soul has seen it but our two selves.'

'What have you done with the note enclosed to Miss Milroy?'

He produced it from his pocket. I ran it over rapidly – saw that there was nothing in it of the slightest importance – and put it in the fire on the spot. That done, I left Bashwood in the sitting-room, and went to the Sanatorium, with Armadale's letter in my hand.

The doctor had gone out; and the servant was unable to say positively at what time he would be back. I went into his study, and wrote a line preparing him for the news I had brought with me, which I sealed up, with Armadale's letter, in an envelope, to await his return. That done, I told the servant I would call again in an hour, and left the place.

It was useless to go back to my lodgings and speak to Bashwood, until I knew first what the doctor meant to do. I walked about the neighbourhood, up and down new streets and crescents and squares, with a kind of dull, numbed feeling in me, which prevented, not only all voluntary exercise of thought, but all sensation of bodily fatigue. I remembered the same feeling overpowering me, years ago, on the morning when the people of the prison came to take me into court to be tried for my life. All that frightful scene came back again to my mind, in the strangest manner, as if it had been a scene in which some other person had figured. Once or twice I wondered, in a heavy senseless way, why they had not hanged me!

When I went back to the Sanatorium, I was informed that the doctor had returned half-an-hour since, and that he was in his own room anxiously waiting to see me.

I went into the study, and found him sitting close by the fire, with his head down, and his hands on his knees. On the table near him, besides Armadale's letter and my note, I saw, in the little circle of light thrown by the reading-lamp, an open railway guide. Was he meditating flight? It was impossible to tell from his face, when he looked up at me, what he was meditating, or how the shock had struck him when he first discovered that Armadale was a living man.

'Take a seat near the fire,' he said. 'It's very raw and cold to-day.'

I took a chair in silence. In silence, on his side, the doctor sat rubbing his knees before the fire.

'Have you nothing to say to me?' I asked.

He rose, and suddenly removed the shade from the reading-lamp so that the light fell on my face.

'You are not looking well,' he said. 'What's the matter?'

'My head feels dull, and my eyes are heavy and hot,' I replied. 'The weather, I suppose.'

It was strange how we both got farther and farther from the one vitally important subject which we had both come together to discuss!

'I think a cup of tea would do you good,' remarked the doctor.

I accepted his suggestion; and he ordered the tea. While it was coming, he walked up and down the room, and I sat by the fire – and not a word passed between us on either side.

The tea revived me; and the doctor noticed a change for the better in my face. He sat down opposite to me at the table, and spoke out at last.

'If I had ten thousand pounds at this moment,' he began, 'I would give the whole of it never to have compromised myself in your desperate speculation on Mr Armadale's death!'

He said those words with an abruptness, almost with a violence, which was strangely uncharacteristic of his ordinary manner. Was he frightened himself, or was he trying to frighten me? I determined to make him explain himself at the outset, so far as I was concerned. 'Wait a moment, doctor,' I said. 'Do you hold me responsible for what has happened?'

'Certainly not,' he replied, stiffly. 'Neither you nor anybody could have foreseen what has happened. When I say I would give ten thousand pounds to be out of this business, I am blaming nobody but myself. And when I tell you next, that I, for one, won't allow Mr Armadale's resurrection from the sea to be the ruin of me without a fight for it, I tell you, my dear madam, one of the plainest truths I ever told to man or woman, in the whole course of my life. Don't suppose I am invidiously separating my interests from yours, in the common danger that now threatens us both. I simply indicate the difference in the risk that we have respectively run. *You* have not sunk the whole of your resources in establishing a Sanatorium; and *you* have not made a false declaration before a magistrate, which is punishable as perjury by the law.'

I interrupted him again. His selfishness did me more good than his tea — it roused my temper effectually. 'Suppose we let your risk and my risk alone, and come to the point,' I said. 'What do you mean by making a fight for it? I see a railway guide on your table. Does making a fight for it, mean — running away?'

'Running away?' repeated the doctor. 'You appear to forget that every farthing I have in the world is embarked in this establishment.'

'You stop here then?' I said.

'Unquestionably!'

'And what do you mean to do when Mr Armadale comes to England?'

A solitary fly, the last of his race whom the winter had spared, was buzzing feebly about the doctor's face. He caught it before he answered me, and held it out across the table in his closed hand.

'If this fly's name was Armadale,' he said, 'and if you had got him as I have got him now, what would *you* do?'

His eyes, fixed on my face up to this time, turned significantly, as he ended his question, to my widow's dress. I, too, looked at it when he looked. A thrill of the old deadly hatred, and the old deadly determination, ran through me again.

'I should kill him,' I said.

The doctor started to his feet (with the fly still in his hand), and looked at me — a little too theatrically — with an expression of the utmost horror.

'Kill him!' repeated the doctor in a paroxysm of virtuous alarm. 'Violence — murderous violence — in My Sanatorium! You take my breath away!'

I caught his eye, while he was expressing himself in this elaborately indignant manner, scrutinizing me with a searching curiosity which was, to say the least of it, a little at variance with the vehemence of his language and the warmth of his tone. He laughed uneasily, when our eyes met, and recovered his smoothly confidential manner in the instant that elapsed before he spoke again.

'I beg a thousand pardons,' he said. 'I ought to have known better than to take a lady too literally at her word. Permit me to remind you, however, that the circumstances are too serious for anything in the nature of — let us say, an exaggeration or a joke. You shall hear what I propose, without further preface.' He paused, and resumed his figurative use of the fly imprisoned in his hand. 'Here is Mr Armadale. I can let him out, or keep him in, just as I please — and he knows it. I say to him,' continued the doctor, facetiously addressing the fly, 'Give me proper security, Mr Armadale, that no proceedings of any sort shall be taken against either this lady or myself, and I will let you out of the hollow of my hand. Refuse – and be the risk what it may, I will keep you in.' Can you doubt, my dear madam, what Mr Armadale's answer is, sooner or later, certain to be? Can you doubt,' said the doctor, suiting the action to the word, and letting the fly go, 'that it will end to the entire satisfaction of all parties, in this way?'

'I won't say at present,' I answered, 'whether I doubt or not. Let me make sure that I understand you first. You propose, if I am not mistaken, to shut the doors of this place on Mr Armadale, and not to let him out again, until he has agreed to the terms which it is our interest to impose on him? May I ask, in that case, how you mean to make him walk into the trap that you have set for him here?'

'I propose,' said the doctor, with his hand on the railway guide, 'ascertaining first, at what time during every evening of this month the tidal trains from Dover and Folkestone reach the London Bridge terminus. And I propose next, posting a person whom Mr Armadale knows, and whom you and I can trust, to wait the arrival of the trains, and to meet our man at the moment when he steps out of the railway carriage.'

'Have you thought,' I inquired, 'of who the person is to be?'

'I have thought,' said the doctor, taking up Armadale's letter, 'of the person to whom this letter is addressed.'

The answer startled me. Was it possible that he and Bashwood knew one another? I put the question immediately.

'Until to-day, I never so much as heard of the gentleman's name,' said the doctor. 'I have simply pursued the inductive process of reasoning, for which we are indebted to the immortal Bacon.[15] How does this very important letter come into your possession? I can't insult you by supposing it to have been stolen. Consequently, it has come to you with the leave and licence of the person to whom it is addressed. Consequently, that person is in your confidence. Consequently, he is the first person I think of. You see the process? Very good. Permit me a question or two, on the subject of Mr Bashwood, before we go on any further.'

The doctor's questions went as straight to the point as usual. My answers informed him that Mr Bashwood stood towards Armadale in the relation of steward – that he had received the letter at Thorpe-Ambrose that morning, and had brought it straight to me by the first train – that he had not shown it, or spoken of it before leaving, to Major Milroy or to any one else – that I had not obtained this service at his hands by trusting him with my secret – that I had communicated with him in the character of Armadale's widow – that he had suppressed the letter, under those circumstances, solely in obedience to a general caution I had given him, to keep his own counsel if anything strange happened at Thorpe-Ambrose, until he had first consulted me – and lastly, that the reason why he had done as I told him, in this matter, was, that in this matter, and in all others, Mr Bashwood was blindly devoted to my interests.

At that point in the interrogatory, the doctor's eyes began to look at me distrustfully, behind the doctor's spectacles.

'What is the secret of this blind devotion of Mr Bashwood's to your interests?' he asked.

I hesitated for a moment – in pity to Bashwood, not in pity to myself. 'If you must know,' I answered, 'Mr Bashwood is in love with me.'

'Ay! ay!' exclaimed the doctor, with an air of relief. 'I begin to understand now. Is he a young man?'

'He is an old man.'

The doctor laid himself back in his chair, and chuckled softly. 'Better and better!' he said. 'Here is the very man we want. Who so fit as Mr Armadale's steward to meet Mr Armadale on his return to London. And who so capable of influencing Mr Bashwood in the proper way as the charming object of Mr Bashwood's admiration?'

There could be no doubt that Bashwood was the man to serve the doctor's purpose, and that my influence was to be trusted to make him serve it. The difficulty was not here – the difficulty was in the unanswered question that I had put to the doctor a minute since. I put it to him again.

'Suppose Mr Armadale's steward meets his employer at the terminus,' I said. 'May I ask once more how Mr Armadale is to be persuaded to come here?'

'Don't think me ungallant,' rejoined the doctor in his gentlest manner, 'if I ask, on my side, how are men persuaded to do nine-tenths of the foolish acts of their lives? They are persuaded by your charming sex. The weak side of every man is the woman's side of him. We have only to discover the woman's side of Mr Armadale – to tickle him on it gently – and to lead him our way with a silken string. I observe here,' pursued the doctor, opening Armadale's letter, 'a reference to a certain young lady, which looks promising. Where is the note that Mr Armadale speaks of as addressed to Miss Milroy?'

Instead of answering him, I started, in a sudden burst of excitement, to my feet. The instant he mentioned Miss Milroy's name, all that I had heard from Bashwood of her illness, and of the cause of it, rushed back into my memory. I saw the means of decoying Armadale into the

Sanatorium, as plainly as I saw the doctor on the other side of the table, wondering at the extraordinary change in me. What a luxury it was to make Miss Milroy serve my interests at last!

'Never mind the note,' I said. 'It's burnt, for fear of accidents. I can tell you all (and more) than the note could have told you. Miss Milroy cuts the knot! Miss Milroy ends the difficulty! She is privately engaged to him. She has heard the false report of his death; and she has been seriously ill at Thorpe-Ambrose ever since. When Bashwood meets him at the station, the very first question he is certain to ask—'

'I see!' exclaimed the doctor, anticipating me. 'Mr Bashwood has nothing to do but to help the truth with a touch of fiction. When he tells his master that the false report has reached Miss Milroy, he has only to add that the shock has affected her head, and that she is here under medical care. Perfect! perfect! We shall have him at the Sanatorium as fast as the fastest cab-horse in London can bring him to us. And mind! no risk – no necessity for trusting other people. This is not a madhouse; this is not a Licensed Establishment – no doctors' certificates are necessary here! My dear lady, I congratulate you; I congratulate myself. Permit me to hand you the railway guide, with my best compliments to Mr Bashwood, and with the page turned down for him, as an additional attention, at the right place.'

Remembering how long I had kept Bashwood waiting for me, I took the book at once, and wished the doctor good evening without further ceremony. As he politely opened the door for me, he reverted, without the slightest necessity for doing so, and without a word from me to lead to it, to the outburst of virtuous alarm which had escaped him at the earlier part of our interview.

'I do hope,' he said, 'that you will kindly forget and forgive my extraordinary want of tact and perception when – in short, when I caught the fly. I positively blush at my own stupidity in putting a literal interpretation on a lady's little joke! Violence in My Sanatorium!' exclaimed the doctor, with his eyes once more fixed attentively on my face, 'violence in this enlightened nineteenth century! Was there ever anything so ridiculous? Do fasten your cloak before you go out – it is so cold and raw! Shall I escort you? Shall I send my servant? Ah, you were always independent! always, if I may say so, a host in yourself! May I call to-morrow morning, and hear what you have settled with Mr Bashwood?'

I said yes, and got away from him at last. In a quarter of an hour more I was back at my lodgings, and was informed by the servant that 'the elderly gentleman' was still waiting for me.

*

I have not got the heart, or the patience – I hardly know which – to waste many words on what passed between me and Bashwood. It was so easy, so degradingly easy, to pull the strings of the poor old puppet in any way I pleased! I met none of the difficulties which I should have been obliged to meet in the case of a younger man, or of a man less infatuated with admiration for me. I left the allusions to Miss Milroy in Armadale's letter, which had naturally puzzled him, to be explained at a future time. I never even troubled myself to invent a plausible reason for wishing him to meet Armadale at the terminus, and to entrap him by a stratagem into the doctor's Sanatorium. All that I found it necessary to do was to refer to what I had written to Mr Bashwood, on my arrival in London, and to what I had afterwards said to him, when he came to answer my letter personally at the hotel.

'You know already,' I said, 'that my marriage has not been a happy one. Draw your own conclusions from that – and don't press me to tell you whether the news of Mr Armadale's rescue from the sea is, or is not, the welcome news that it ought to be to his wife!' That was enough to put his withered old face in a glow, and to set his withered old hopes growing again. I had only to add, 'If you will do what I ask you to do, no matter how incomprehensible and how mysterious my request may seem to be; and if you will accept my assurances that you shall run no risk yourself, and that you shall receive the proper explanations at the proper time – you will have such a claim on my gratitude and my regard as no man living has ever had yet!' I had only to say those words, and to point them by a look and a stolen pressure of his hand; and I had him at my feet, blindly eager to obey me. If he could have seen what I thought of myself – but that doesn't matter: he saw nothing.

Hours have passed since I sent him away (pledged to secrecy, possessed of his instructions, and provided with his time-table) to the hotel near the terminus, at which he is to stay till Armadale appears on the railway platform. The excitement of the earlier part of the evening has all worn off; and the dull, numbed sensation has got me again. Are my energies wearing out, I wonder, just at the time when I most want them?

Or is some foreshadowing of disaster creeping over me which I don't yet understand?

I might be in a humour to sit here for some time longer, thinking thoughts like these, and letting them find their way into words at their own will and pleasure – if my Diary would only let me. But my idle pen has been busy enough to make its way to the end of the volume. I have reached the last morsel of space left on the last page; and whether I like it or not, I must close the book this time for good and all, when I close it to-night.

Good-by, my old friend and companion of many a miserable day! Having nothing else to be fond of, I half suspect myself of having been unreasonably fond of *you*.

What a fool I am!

THE END OF THE FIFTH BOOK

BOOK THE LAST

CHAPTER I

AT THE TERMINUS

On the night of the second of December, Mr Bashwood took up his post of observation at the terminus of the South Eastern Railway for the first time. It was an earlier date, by six days, than the date which Allan had himself fixed for his return. But the doctor, taking counsel of his medical experience, had considered it just probable that 'Mr Armadale might be perverse enought, at his enviable age, to recover sooner than his medical advisers might have anticipated.' For caution's sake, therefore, Mr Bashwood was instructed to begin watching the arrival of the tidal trains, on the day after he had received his employer's letter.

From the second to the seventh of December, the steward waited punctually on the platform, saw the trains come in, and satisfied himself, evening after evening, that the travellers were all strangers to him. From the second to the seventh of December, Miss Gwilt (to return to the name under which she is best known in these pages) received his daily report, sometimes delivered personally, sometimes sent by letter. The doctor, to whom the reports were communicated, received them in his turn with unabated confidence in the precautions that had been adopted, up to the morning of the eighth. On that date, the irritation of continued suspense had produced a change for the worse in Miss Gwilt's variable temper, which was perceptible to every one about her, and which, strangely enough, was reflected by an equally marked changed in the doctor's manner when he came to pay his usual visit. By a coincidence so extraordinary, that his enemies might have suspected it of not being a coincidence at all, the morning on which Miss Gwilt lost her patience, proved to be also the morning on which the doctor lost his confidence for the first time.

'No news, of course,' he said, sitting down with a heavy sigh. 'Well! well!'

Miss Gwilt looked up at him irritably, from her work.

'You seem strangely depressed this morning,' she said. 'What are you afraid of now?'[1]

'The imputation of being afraid, madam,' answered the doctor, solemnly, 'is not an imputation to cast rashly on any man – even when he belongs to such an essentially peaceful profession as mine. I am not afraid. I am (as you more correctly put it in the first instance) strangely depressed. My nature is, as you know, naturally sanguine, and I only see to-day, what, but for my habitual hopefulness, I might have seen, and ought to have seen, a week since.'

Miss Gwilt impatiently threw down her work. 'If words cost money,' she said, 'the luxury of talking would be rather an expensive luxury, in your case!'

'Which I might have seen, and ought to have seen,' reiterated the doctor, without taking the slightest notice of the interruption, 'a week since. To put it plainly, I feel by no means so certain as I did, that Mr Armadale will consent, without a struggle, to the terms which it is my interest (and in a minor degree yours) to impose on him. Observe! I don't question our entrapping him successfully into the Sanatorium – I only doubt whether he will prove quite as manageable as I originally anticipated, when we have got him there. Say,' remarked the doctor, raising his eyes for the first time, and fixing them in steady inquiry on Miss Gwilt; 'say that he is bold, obstinate, what you please; and that he holds out – holds out for weeks together, for months together, as men in similar situations to his have held out before him. What follows? The risk of keeping him forcibly in conceal-ment – of suppressing him, if I may so express myself – increases at compound interest, and becomes, Enormous! My house is, at this moment, virtually ready for patients. Patients may present themselves in a week's time. Patients may communicate with Mr Armadale, or Mr Armadale may communicate with patients. A note may be smug-gled out of the house, and may reach the Commissioners in Lunacy.[2] Even in the case of an unlicensed establishment like mine, those gentle-men – no! those chartered despots in a land of liberty – have only to apply to the Lord Chancellor for an order, and to enter (by heavens, to enter My Sanatorium!) and search the house from top to bottom at a moment's notice! I don't wish to despond; I don't wish to alarm you; I don't pretend to say that the means we are taking to secure our own safety are any other than the best means at our disposal. All I ask you to do is to imagine the Commissioners in the house – and then to conceive the consequences. The consequences!' repeated the doctor, getting sternly on his feet, and taking up his hat as if he meant to leave the room.[3]

'Have you anything more to say?' asked Miss Gwilt.

'Have you any remarks,' rejoined the doctor, 'to offer on your side?'

He stood hat in hand, waiting. For a full minute the two looked at each other in silence.

Miss Gwilt spoke first.

'I think I understand you,' she said, suddenly recovering her composure.

'I beg your pardon,' returned the doctor, with his hand to his ear. 'What did you say?'

'Nothing.'

'Nothing?'

'If you happened to catch another fly this morning,' said Miss Gwilt, with a bitterly sarcastic emphasis on the words, 'I might be capable of shocking you by another "little joke".'

The doctor held up both hands, in polite deprecation, and looked as if he was beginning to recover his good humour again.

'Hard,' he murmured gently, 'not to have forgiven me that unlucky blunder of mine, even yet!'

'What else have you to say? I am waiting for you,' said Miss Gwilt. She turned her chair to the window scornfully, and took up her work again, as she spoke.

The doctor came behind her, and put his hand on the back of her chair.

'I have a question to ask, in the first place,' he said; 'and a measure of necessary precaution to suggest in the second. If you will honour me with your attention, I will put the question first.'

'I am listening.'

'You know that Mr Armadale is alive,' pursued the doctor; 'and you know that he is coming back to England. Why do you continue to wear your widow's dress?'

She answered him without an instant's hesitation, steadily going on with her work.

'Because I am of a sanguine disposition, like you. I mean to trust to the chapter of accidents to the very last. Mr Armadale may die yet, on his way home.'

'And suppose he gets home alive – what then?'

'Then there is another chance still left.'

'What is it, pray?'

'He may die in your Sanatorium.'

'Madam!' remonstrated the doctor in the deep bass which he reserved for his outbursts of virtuous indignation. 'Wait! you spoke of the chapter of accidents,' he resumed, gliding back into his softer conversational tones. 'Yes! yes! of course. I understand you this time. Even the healing art is at the mercy of accidents – even such a Sanatorium as mine is liable to be surprised by Death. Just so! just so!' said the doctor, conceding the question with the utmost impartiality. 'There *is* the chapter of accidents, I admit – if you choose to trust to it. Mind! I say emphatically, *if* you choose to trust to it.'

There was another moment of silence – silence so profound that nothing was audible in the room but the rapid *click* of Miss Gwilt's needle through her work.

'Go on,' she said; 'you haven't done yet.'

'True!' said the doctor. 'Having put my question, I have my measure of precaution to impress on you next. You will see, my dear madam, that I am not disposed to trust to the chapter of accidents on my side. Reflection has convinced me that you and I are not (locally speaking) so conveniently situated as we might be, in case of emergency. Cabs are, as yet, rare in this rapidly-improving neighbourhood. I am twenty minutes' walk from you; you are twenty minutes' walk from me. I know nothing of Mr Armadale's character; you know it well. It might be necessary – vitally necessary – to appeal to your superior knowledge of him at a moment's notice. And how am I to do that unless we are within easy reach of each other, under the same roof? In both our interests, I beg to invite you, my dear madam, to become for a limited period an inmate of My Sanatorium.'

Miss Gwilt's rapid needle suddenly stopped. 'I understand you,' she said again, as quietly as before.

'I beg your pardon,' said the doctor, with another attack of deafness, and with his hand once more at his ear.

She laughed to herself – a low, terrible laugh, which startled even the doctor into taking his hand off the back of her chair.

'An inmate of your Sanatorium?' she repeated. 'You consult appearances in everything else – do you propose to consult appearances in receiving me into your house?'

'Most assuredly!' replied the doctor, with enthusiasm. 'I am surprised at your asking me the question! Did you ever know a man of any eminence in my profession who set appearances at defiance? If you honour me by accepting my invitation, you enter My Sanatorium in the most unimpeachable of all possible characters – in the character of a Patient.'

'When do you want my answer?'

'Can you decide to-day?'

'No.'

'To-morrow?'

'Yes. Have you anything more to say?'

'Nothing more.'

'Leave me then. *I* don't keep up appearances. I wish to be alone – and I say so. Good morning.'

'Oh, the sex! the sex!' said the doctor, with his excellent temper in perfect working order again. 'So delightfully impulsive! so charmingly reckless of what thay say, or how they say it! "Oh, woman, in our hours of ease, uncertain, coy, and hard to please!"[4] There! there! there! Good morning!'

Miss Gwilt rose and looked after him contemptuously from the window, when the street-door had closed, and he had left the house.

'Armadale himself drove me to it the first time,' she said. 'Manuel drove me to it the second time. – You cowardly scoundrel! shall I let *you* drive me to it for the third time and the last?'

She turned from the window, and looked thoughtfully at her widow's dress in the glass.

The hours of the day passed – and she decided nothing. The night came – and she hesitated still. The new morning dawned – and the terrible question was still unanswered.

By the early post there came a letter for her. It was Mr Bashwood's usual report. Again he had watched for Allan's arrival, and again in vain.

'I'll have more time!' she determined passionately. 'No man alive shall hurry me faster than I like!'

At breakfast that morning (the morning of the ninth) the doctor was surprised in his study by a visit from Miss Gwilt.

'I want another day,' she said, the moment the servant had closed the door on her.

The doctor looked at her before he answered, and saw the danger of driving her to extremities plainly expressed in her face.

'The time is getting on,' he remonstrated in his most persuasive manner. 'For all we know to the contrary, Mr Armadale may be here to-night.'

'I want another day!' she repeated, loudly and passionately.

'Granted!' said the doctor, looking nervously towards the door. 'Don't be too loud – the servants may hear you. Mind!' he added, 'I depend on your honour not to press me for any further delay.'

'You had better depend on my despair,' she said – and left him.'

The doctor chipped the shell of his egg, and laughed softly.

'Quite right, my dear!' he thought. 'I remember where your despair led you in past times; and I think I may trust it to lead you the same way now.'

At a quarter to eight o'clock that night, Mr Bashwood took up his post of observation as usual on the platform of the terminus at London Bridge.

He was in the highest good spirits; he smiled and smirked in irrepressible exultation. The sense that he held in reserve a means of influence over Miss Gwilt, in virtue of his knowledge of her past career, had had no share in effecting the transformation that now appeared in him. It had upheld his courage in his forlorn life at Thorpe-Ambrose, and it had given him that increased confidence of manner which Miss Gwilt herself had noticed; but, from the moment when he had regained his old place in her favour, it had vanished as a motive power in him, annihilated by the electric shock of her touch and her look. His vanity – the vanity which in men at his age is only despair in disguise – had now lifted him to the seventh heaven of fatuous happiness once more. He believed in her again as he believed in the smart new winter over-coat that he wore – as he believed in the dainty little cane (appropriate to the dawning dandyism of lads in their teens) that he flourished in his hand. He hummed! The worn-out old creature who had not sung since his childhood, hummed as he paced the platform the few fragments he could remember of a worn-out old song.

The train was due as early as eight o'clock that night. At five minutes past the hour, the whistle sounded. In less than five minutes more, the passengers were getting out on the platform.

Following the instructions that had been given to him, Mr Bashwood made his way as well as the crowd would let him, along the line of carriages; and discovering no familiar face on that first investigation, joined the passengers for a second search among them in the custom-house waiting-room next.

He had looked round the room, and had satisfied himself that the persons occupying it were all strangers, when he heard a voice behind him, exclaiming, 'Can that be Mr Bashwood!'

He turned in eager expectation; and found himself face to face with the last man under heaven whom he had expected to see.

The man was MIDWINTER.

IN THE HOUSE

Noticing Mr Bashwood's confusion (after a moment's glance at the change in his personal appearance), Midwinter spoke first.

'I see I have surprised you,' he said. 'You were looking, I suppose, for somebody else? Have you heard from Allan? Is he on his way home again already?'

The inquiry about Allan, though it would naturally have suggested itself to any one in Midwinter's position at that moment, added to Mr Bashwood's confusion. Not knowing how else to extricate himself from the critical position in which he was placed, he took refuge in simple denial.

'I know nothing about Mr Armadale – oh dear, no, sir, I know nothing about Mr Armadale,' he answered with needless eagerness and hurry. 'Welcome back to England, sir,' he went on, changing the subject in his nervously talkative manner. 'I didn't know you had been abroad. It's so long since we have had the pleasure – since I have had the pleasure. – Have you enjoyed yourself, sir, in foreign parts? Such different manners from ours – yes, yes, yes, – such different manners from ours! Do you make a long stay in England, now you have come back?'

'I hardly know,' said Midwinter. 'I have been obliged to alter my plans, and to come to England unexpectedly.' He hesitated a little; his manner changed, and he added in lower tones, 'A serious anxiety has brought me back. I can't say what my plans will be until that anxiety is set at rest.'

The light of a lamp fell on his face while he spoke, and Mr Bashwood observed, for the first time, that he looked sadly worn and changed.

'I'm sorry, sir – I'm sure I'm very sorry. If I could be of any use—?' suggested Mr Bashwood, speaking under the influence, in some degree of his nervous politeness, and in some degree of his remembrance of what Midwinter had done for him at Thorpe-Ambrose in the bygone time.

Midwinter thanked him, and turned away sadly. 'I am afraid you can be of no use Mr Bashwood – but I am obliged to you for your offer, all the same.' He stopped, and considered a little, 'Suppose she should *not* be ill? Suppose some misfortune should have happened?' he resumed, speaking to himself, and turning again towards the steward. 'If she has left her mother, some trace of her *might* be found by inquiring at Thorpe-Ambrose.'

Mr Bashwood's curiosity was instantly aroused. The whole sex was interesting to him now, for the sake of Miss Gwilt.

'A lady, sir?' he inquired. 'Are you looking for a lady?'

'I am looking,' said Midwinter simply, 'for my wife.'

'Married, sir!' exclaimed Mr Bashwood. 'Married since I last had the pleasure of seeing you! Might I take the liberty of asking——?'

Midwinter's eyes dropped uneasily to the ground.

'You knew the lady in former times,' he said. 'I have married Miss Gwilt.'

The steward started back, as he might have started back from a loaded pistol, levelled at his head. His eyes glared as if he had suddenly lost his senses, and the nervous trembling to which he was subject shook him from head to foot.

'What's the matter?' asked Midwinter. There was no answer. 'What is there so very startling,' he went on, a little impatiently, 'in Miss Gwilt's being my wife?'

'*Your* wife?' repeated Mr Bashwood, helplessly. 'Mrs Armadale——!' He checked himself by a desperate effort, and said no more.

The stupor of astonishment which possessed the steward was instantly reflected in Midwinter's face. The name in which he had secretly married his wife had passed the lips of the last man in the world whom he would have dreamed of admitting into his confidence! He took Mr Bashwood by the arm, and led him away to a quieter part of the terminus than the part of it in which they had hitherto spoken to each other.

'You referred to my wife just now,' he said; 'and you spoke of *Mrs Armadale* in the same breath. What do you mean by that?'

Again there was no answer. Utterly incapable of understanding more than that he had involved himself in some serious complication which was a complete mystery to him, Mr Bashwood struggled to extricate himself from the grasp that was laid on him, and struggled in vain.

Midwinter sternly repeated the question. 'I ask you again,' he said, 'what do you mean by it?'

'Nothing, sir! I give you my word of honour I meant nothing!' He felt the hand on his arm tightening its grasp; he saw, even in the obscurity of the remote corner in which they stood, that Midwinter's fiery temper was rising, and was not to be trifled with. The extremity of his danger inspired him with the one ready capacity that a timid man possesses when he is compelled by main force to face an emergency – the capacity to lie. 'I only meant to say, sir,' he burst out, with a desperate effort to look and speak confidently, 'that Mr Armadale would be surprised—'

'You said *Mrs* Armadale!'

'No, sir – on my word of honour, on my sacred word of honour, you are mistaken – you are indeed! I said *Mr* Armadale – how could I say anything else? Please to let me go, sir – I'm pressed for time. I do assure you I'm dreadfully pressed for time!'

For a moment longer Midwinter maintained his hold, and in that moment he decided what to do.

He had accurately stated his motive for returning to England as proceeding from anxiety about his wife – anxiety naturally caused (after the regular receipt of a letter from her every other, or every third day) by the sudden cessation of the correspondence between them on her side for a whole week. The first vaguely-terrible suspicion of some other reason for her silence than the reason of accident or of illness, to which he had hitherto attributed it, had struck through him like a sudden chill the instant he heard the steward associate the name of 'Mrs Armadale' with the idea of his wife. Little irregularities in her correspondence with him, which he had thus far only thought strange, now came back on his mind and proclaimed themselves to be suspicious as well. He had hitherto believed the reasons she had given for referring him, when he answered her letters, to no more definite address than an address at a post-office. *Now* he suspected her reasons of being excuses, for the first time. He had hitherto resolved, on reaching London, to inquire at the only place he knew of at which a clue to her could be found – the address she had given him as the address at which 'her mother' lived. *Now* (with a motive which he was afraid to define even to himself, but which was strong enough to overbear every other consideration in his mind), he determined, before all things, to solve the mystery of Mr Bashwood's familiarity with a secret, which was a marriage-secret between himself and his wife. Any direct appeal to a man of the steward's disposition, in the steward's present state of mind, would be evidently useless. The weapon of deception was, in this case, a weapon literally forced into Midwinter's hands. He let go of Mr Bashwood's arm, and accepted Mr Bashwood's explanation.

'I beg your pardon,' he said, 'I have no doubt you are right. Pray attribute my rudeness to over-anxiety and over-fatigue. I wish you good evening.'

The station was by this time almost a solitude; the passengers by the train being assembled at the examination of their luggage in the custom-house waiting-room. It was no easy matter, ostensibly to take leave of Mr Bashwood, and really to keep him in view. But Midwinter's early life with his gipsy master had been of a nature to practise him in such stratagems as he was now compelled to adopt. He walked away towards the waiting-room by the line of empty carriages – opened the door of one of them, as if to look after something that he had left behind – and detected Mr Bashwood making for the cab-rank on the opposite side of the platform. In an instant, Midwinter had crossed, and had passed through the long row of vehicles, so as to skirt it on the side farthest from the platform. He entered the second cab by the left-hand door, the moment after Mr Bashwood had entered the first cab by the right-hand door. 'Double your fare, whatever it is,' he said to the driver, 'if you keep the cab before you in view, and follow it wherever it goes.' In a minute more both vehicles were on their way out of the station.

The clerk sat in his sentry-box at the gate, taking down the destinations of the cabs as they passed. Midwinter heard the man who was driving him, call out 'Hampstead!' as he went by the clerk's window.

'Why did you say "Hampstead"? he asked when they had left the station.

'Because the man before me said "Hampstead," sir,' answered the driver.

Over and over again, on the wearisome journey to the north-western suburb, Midwinter asked if the cab was still in sight. Over and over again, the man answered, 'Right in front of us.'

It was between nine and ten o'clock, when the driver pulled up his horses at last. Midwinter got out, and saw the cab before them, waiting at a house-door. As soon as he had satisfied himself that the driver was the man whom Mr Bashwood had hired, he paid the promised reward, and dismissed his own cab.

He took a turn backwards and forwards before the door. The vaguely terrible suspicion which had risen in his mind at the terminus, had forced itself by this time into a definite form which was abhorrent to him. Without the shadow of an assignable reason for it, he found himself blindly distrusting his wife's fidelity, and blindly suspecting Mr Bashwood of serving her in the capacity of go-between. In sheer horror of his own morbid fancy, he determined to take down the number of the house, and the name of the street in which it stood – and then, in justice to his wife, to return at once to the address which she had given him as the address at which her mother lived. He had taken out his pocket-book, and was on his way to the corner of the street, when he observed the man who had driven Mr Bashwood, looking at him with an expression of inquisitive surprise. The idea of questioning the cab-driver, while he had the opportunity, instantly occurred to him. He took a half-crown from his pocket and put it into the man's ready hand.

'Has the gentleman whom you drove from the station, gone into that house?' he asked.

'Yes, sir.'

'Did you hear him inquire for anybody when the door was opened?'

'He asked for a lady, sir. Mrs —' The man hesitated. 'It wasn't a common name, sir; I should know it again if I heard it.'

'Was it "Midwinter"?'

'No, sir.'

'"Armadale"?'

'That's it, sir. Mrs Armadale.'

'Are you sure it was "Mrs" and not "Mr"?'

'I'm as sure as a man can be who hasn't taken any particular notice, sir.'

The doubt implied in that last answer decided Midwinter to investigate the matter on the spot. He ascended the house-steps. As he raised his hand to the bell at the side of the door, the violence of his agitation mastered him physically for the moment. A strange sensation as of something leaping up from his heart to his brain, turned his head wildly giddy. He held by the house-railings, and kept his face to the air, and resolutely waited till he was steady again. Then he rang the bell.

'Is?' – he tried to ask for 'Mrs Armadale', when the maid-servant had opened the door, but not even his resolution could force the name to pass his lips, – 'Is your mistress at home?' he asked.

'Yes, sir.'

The girl showed him into a back parlour, and presented him to a little old lady, with an obliging manner and a bright pair of eyes.

'There is some mistake,' said Midwinter. 'I wished to see—' Once more he tried to utter the name, and once more he failed to force it to his lips.

'Mrs Armadale?' suggested the little old lady, with a smile.

'Yes.'

'Show the gentleman upstairs, Jenny.'

The girl led the way to the drawing-room floor.

'Any name, sir?'

'No name.'

*

Mr Bashwood had barely completed his report of what had happened at the terminus; Mr Bashwood's imperious mistress was still sitting speechless under the shock of the discovery that had burst on her – when the door of the room opened; and, without a word of warning to precede him, Midwinter appeared on the threshold. He took one step into the room; and mechanically pushed the door to behind him. He stood in dead silence, and confronted his wife, with a scrutiny that was terrible in its unnatural self-possession, and that enveloped her steadily in one comprehensive look from head to foot.

In dead silence on her side, she rose from her chair. In dead silence she stood erect on the hearth-rug, and faced her husband in widow's weeds.

He took one step nearer to her and stopped again. He lifted his hand and pointed with his lean brown finger at her dress.

'What does that mean?' he asked, without losing his terrible self-possession, and without moving his outstretched hand.

At the sound of his voice, the quick rise and fall of her bosom – which had been the one outward betrayal thus far of the inner agony that tortured her – suddenly stopped. She stood impenetrably silent, breathlessly still – as if his question had struck her dead, and his pointing hand had petrified her.

He advanced one step nearer and reiterated his words, in a voice even lower and quieter than the voice in which he had spoken first.

One moment more of silence, one moment more of inaction might have been the salvation of her. But the fatal force of her character triumphed at the crisis of her destiny, and his. White and still, and haggard and old, she met the dreadful emergency with a dreadful courage, and spoke the irrevocable words which renounced him to his face.

'Mr Midwinter,' she said, in tones unnaturally hard and unnaturally clear, 'our acquaintance hardly entitles you to speak to me in that manner.' Those were her words. She never lifted her eyes from the ground while she spoke them. When she had done, the last faint vestige of colour in her cheeks faded out.

There was a pause. Still steadily looking at her, he set himself to fix the language she had used to him in his mind. 'She calls me "Mr Midwinter",' he said slowly, in a whisper. 'She speaks of "our acquaintance".' He waited a little and looked round the room. His wandering eyes encountered Mr Bashwood for the first time. He saw the steward standing near the fireplace, trembling, and watching him.

'I once did you a service,' he said; 'and you once told me you were not an ungrateful man. Are you grateful enough to answer me if I ask you something?'

He waited a little again. Mr Bashwood still stood trembling at the fireplace, silently watching him.

'I see you looking at me,' he went on. 'Is there some change in me that I am not conscious of myself? Am I seeing things that *you* don't see? Am I hearing words that *you* don't hear? Am I looking or speaking like a man out of his senses?'

Again he waited, and again the silence was unbroken. His eyes began to glitter; and the savage blood that he had inherited from his mother rose dark and slow in his ashy cheeks.

'Is that woman,' he asked, 'the woman whom you once knew, whose name was Miss Gwilt?'

Once more his wife collected her fatal courage. Once more his wife spoke her fatal words.

'You compel me to repeat,' she said, 'that you are presuming on our acquaintance, and that you are forgetting what is due to me.'

He turned upon her, with a savage suddenness which forced a cry of alarm from Mr Bashwood's lips.

'Are you, or are you not My Wife?' he asked, through his set teeth.

She raised her eyes to his for the first time. Her lost spirit looked at him, steadily defiant, out of the hell of its own despair.

'I am *not* your wife,' she said.

He staggered back, with his hand groping for something to hold by, like the hands of a man in the dark. He leaned heavily against the wall of the room, and looked at the woman who had slept on his bosom, and who had denied him to his face.

Mr Bashwood stole panic-stricken to her side. 'Go in there!' he whispered, trying to draw her towards the folding-doors which led into the next room. 'For God's sake be quick! He'll kill you!'

She put the old man back with her hand. She looked at him with a sudden irradiation of her blank face. She answered him with lips that struggled slowly into a frightful smile.

'*Let* him kill me,' she said.

As the words passed her lips, he sprang forward from the wall, with a cry that rang through the house. The frenzy of a maddened man flashed at her from his glassy eyes, and clutched at her in his threatening hands. He came on till he was within arm's length of her – and suddenly stood still. The black flush died out of his face in the instant when he stopped. His eyelids fell, his outstretched hands wavered, and sank helpless. He dropped, as the dead drop. He lay as the dead lie, in the arms of the wife who had denied him.

She knelt on the floor, and rested his head on her knee. She caught the arm of the steward hurrying to help her, with a hand that closed round it like a vice. 'Go for a doctor,' she said, 'and keep the people of the house away till he comes.' There was that in her eye, there was that in her voice, which would have warned any man living to obey her in silence. In silence, Mr Bashwood submitted, and hurried out of the room.

The instant she was alone, she raised him from her knee. With both arms clasped round him, the miserable woman lifted his lifeless face to hers, and rocked him on her bosom in an agony of tenderness beyond all relief in tears, in a passion of remorse beyond all expression in words. In silence she held him to her breast, in silence she devoured his forehead, his cheeks, his lips, with kisses. Not a sound escaped her, till she heard the trampling footsteps outside, hurrying up the stairs. Then a low moan burst from her lips, as she looked her last at him, and lowered his head again to her knee, before the strangers came in.

The landlady and the steward were the first persons whom she saw when the door was opened. The medical man (a surgeon living in the street) followed. The horror and the beauty of her face as she looked up at him absorbed the surgeon's attention for the moment, to the exclusion of everything else. She had to beckon to him, she had to point to the senseless man, before she could claim his attention for his patient and divert it from herself.

'Is he dead?' she asked.

The surgeon carried Midwinter to the sofa, and ordered the windows to be opened. 'It is a fainting fit,' he said; 'nothing more.'

At that answer her strength failed her for the first time. She drew a deep breath of relief, and leaned on the chimney-piece for support. Mr Bashwood was the only person present who noticed that she was overcome. He led her to the opposite end of the room, where there was an easy chair – leaving the landlady to hand the restoratives to the surgeon as they were wanted.

'Are you going to wait here till he recovers?' whispered the steward, looking towards the sofa, and trembling as he looked.

The question roused her to a sense of her position – to a knowledge of the merciless necessities which that position now forced her to confront. With a heavy sigh she looked towards the sofa, considered with herself for a moment, and answered Mr Bashwood's inquiry by a question on her side.

'Is the cab that brought you here from the railway still at the door?'

'Yes.'

'Drive at once to the gates of the Sanatorium, and wait there till I join you.'

Mr Bashwood hesitated. She lifted her eyes to his, and, with a look, sent him out of the room.

'The gentleman is coming to, ma'am,' said the landlady, as the steward closed the door. 'He has just breathed again.'

She bowed in mute reply, rose, and considered with herself once more – looked towards the sofa for the second time – then passed through the folding-doors into her own room.

After a short lapse of time the surgeon drew back from the sofa, and motioned to the landlady to stand aside. The bodily recovery of the patient was assured. There was nothing to be done now but to wait, and let his mind slowly recall its sense of what had happened.

'Where is she?' were the first words he said to the surgeon and the landlady anxiously watching him.

The landlady knocked at the folding-doors, and received no answer. She went in, and found the room empty. A sheet of note-paper was on the dressing-table, with the doctor's fee placed on it. The paper contained these lines, evidently written in great agitation or in great haste: 'It is impossible for me to remain here to-night, after what has happened. I will return to-morrow to take away my luggage, and to pay what I owe you.'

'Where is she?' Midwinter asked again, when the landlady returned alone to the drawing-room.

'Gone, sir.'

'I don't believe it!'

The old lady's colour rose. 'If you know her handwriting, sir,' she answered, handing him the sheet of note-paper, 'perhaps you may believe *that*?'

He looked at the paper. 'I beg your pardon, ma'am,' he said, as he handed it back. 'I beg your pardon, with all my heart.'

There was something in his face as he spoke those words which more than soothed the old lady's irritation – it touched her with a sudden pity for the man who had offended her. 'I am afraid there is some dreadful trouble, sir, at the bottom of all this,' she said simply. 'Do you wish me to give any message to the lady when she comes back?'

Midwinter rose, and steadied himself for a moment against the sofa. 'I will bring my own message to-morrow,' he said. 'I must see her before she leaves your house.'

The surgeon accompanied his patient into the street. 'Can I see you home?' he said, kindly. 'You had better not walk, if it is far. You mustn't over-exert yourself; you mustn't catch a chill this cold night.'

Midwinter took his hand and thanked him. 'I have been used to hard walking and to cold nights, sir,' he said; 'and I am not easily worn out, even when I look so broken as I do now. If you will tell me the nearest way out of these streets, I think the quiet of the country and the quiet of the night will help me. I have something serious to do to-morrow,' he added, in a lower tone; 'and I can't rest or sleep till I have thought over it to-night.'

The surgeon understood that he had no common man to deal with. He gave the necessary directions without any further remark, and parted with his patient at his own door.

Left by himself, Midwinter paused and looked up at the heaven in silence. The night had cleared, and the stars were out – the stars which he had first learnt to know from his gipsy master on the hill-side. For the first time his mind went back regretfully to his boyish days. 'Oh, for the old life!' he thought, longingly. 'I never knew till now how happy the old life was!'

He roused himself and went on towards the open country. His face darkened as he left the streets behind him and advanced into the solitude and obscurity that lay beyond.

'She has denied her husband to-night,' he said. 'She shall know her master to-morrow.'

CHAPTER III

<h2 style="text-align:center">THE PURPLE FLASK</h2>

The cab was waiting at the gates as Miss Gwilt approached the Sanatorium. Mr Bashwood got out and advanced to meet her. She took his arm and led him aside a few steps, out of the cabman's hearing.

'Think what you like of me,' she said, keeping her thick black veil down over her face – 'but don't speak to me to-night. Drive back to your hotel as if nothing had happened. Meet the tidal train to-morrow as usual; and come to me afterwards at the Sanatorium. Go without a word, and I shall believe there is one man in the world who really loves me. Stay and ask questions, and I shall bid you good-by at once and for ever!'

She pointed to the cab. In a minute more it had left the Sanatorium and was taking Mr Bashwood back to his hotel.

She opened the iron gate and walked slowly up to the house door. A shudder ran through her as she rang the bell. She laughed bitterly. 'Shivering again!' she said to herself. 'Who would have thought I had so much feeling left in me?'

For once in his life the doctor's face told the truth, when the study door opened between ten and eleven at night, and Miss Gwilt entered the room.

'Mercy on me!' he exclaimed, with a look of the blankest bewilderment, 'what does this mean?'

'It means,' she answered, 'that I have decided to-night instead of deciding to-morrow. You, who know women so well, ought to know that they act on impulse. I am here on an impulse. Take me or leave me, just as you like.'

'Take you or leave you?' repeated the doctor, recovering his presence of mind. 'My dear lady, what a dreadful way of putting it! Your room shall be got ready instantly! Where is your luggage? Will you let me send for it? No? You can do without your luggage to-night? What admirable fortitude! You will fetch it yourself to-morrow? What extraordinary independence! Do take off your bonnet. Do draw in to the fire! What can I offer you?'

'Offer me the strongest sleeping-draught you ever made in your life,' she replied. 'And leave me alone till the time comes to take it. I shall be your patient in earnest!' she added fiercely as the doctor attempted to remonstrate. 'I shall be the maddest of the mad if you irritate me to-night!'

The Principal of the Sanatorium became gravely and briefly professional in an instant.

'Sit down in that dark corner,' he said. 'Not a soul shall disturb you. In half an hour you will find your room ready, and your sleeping-draught on the table. It's been a harder struggle for her than I anticipated,' he thought, as he left the room, and crossed to his Dispensary on the opposite side of the hall. 'Good heavens, what business has *she* with a conscience, after such a life as hers has been!'

The Dispensary was elaborately fitted up with all the latest improvements in medical furniture. But one of the four walls of the room was unoccupied by shelves, and here the vacant space was filled by a handsome antique cabinet of carved wood, curiously out of harmony, as

an object, with the unornamented utilitarian aspect of the place generally. On either side of the cabinet two speaking-tubes were inserted in
the wall, communicating with the upper regions of the house, and
labelled respectively, 'Resident Dispenser', and 'Head Nurse'. Into the
second of these tubes the doctor spoke, on entering the room. An elderly
woman appeared, took her orders for preparing Mrs Armadale's bedchamber, curtseyed, and retired.

Left alone again in the Dispensary, the doctor unlocked the centre
compartment of the cabinet, and disclosed a collection of bottles inside,
containing the various poisons used in medicine. After taking out the
laudanum wanted for the sleeping-draught, and placing it on the
dispensary-table, he went back to the cabinet – looked into it for a little
while – shook his head doubtfully – and crossed to the open shelves on
the opposite side of the room. Here, after more consideration, he took
down one out of the row of large chemical bottles before him, filled with
a yellow liquid: placing the bottle on the table, he returned to the
cabinet, and opened a side compartment, containing some specimens of
Bohemian glass-work. After measuring it with his eye, he took from the
specimens a handsome purple flask, high and narrow in form, and
closed by a glass stopper. This he filled with the yellow liquid, leaving a
small quantity only at the bottom of the bottle, and locking up the flask
again in the place from which he had taken it. The bottle was next
restored to its place, after having been filled up with water from the
cistern in the Dispensary, mixed with certain chemical liquids in small
quantities, which restored it (so far as appearances went) to the condition in which it had been when it was first removed from the shelf.
Having completed these mysterious proceedings, the doctor laughed
softly, and went back to his speaking-tubes to summon the Resident
Dispenser next.

The Resident Dispenser made his appearance shrouded in the necessary white apron from his waist to his feet. The doctor solemnly wrote a
prescription for a composing draught, and handed it to his assistant.

'Wanted immediately, Benjamin,' he said, in a soft and melancholy
voice. 'A lady-patient – Mrs Armadale, Room Number-one, Second-
floor. Ah, dear, dear!' groaned the doctor absently; 'an anxious case,
Benjamin – an anxious case.' He opened the brand-new ledger of the
establishment, and entered the Case at full length, with a brief abstract
of the prescription. 'Have you done with the laudanum? Put it back,
and lock the cabinet, and give me the key. Is the draught ready? Label
it "to be taken at bed-time", and give it to the nurse, Benjamin – give it
to the nurse.'

While the doctor's lips were issuing these directions, the doctor's hands were occupied in opening a drawer under the desk on which the ledger was placed. He took out some gaily-printed cards of admission 'to view the Sanatorium, between the hours of two and four, P.M.', and filled them up with the date of the next day, 'December tenth'. When a dozen of the cards had been wrapped up in a dozen lithographed letters of invitation, and enclosed in a dozen envelopes, he next consulted a list of the families resident in the neighbourhood, and directed the envelopes from the list. Ringing a bell this time, instead of speaking through a tube, he summoned the man-servant, and gave him the letters, to be delivered by hand the first thing the next morning. 'I think it will do,' said the doctor, taking a turn in the Dispensary when the servant had gone out; 'I think it will do.' While he was still absorbed in his own reflections, the nurse re-appeared to announce that the lady's room was ready; and the doctor thereupon formally returned to the study to communicate the information to Miss Gwilt.

She had not moved since he left her. She rose from her dark corner when he made his announcement, and, without speaking or raising her veil, glided out of the room like a ghost.

After a brief interval, the nurse came downstairs again, with a word for her master's private ear.

'The lady has ordered me to call her to-morrow at seven o'clock, sir,' she said. 'She means to fetch her luggage herself, and she wants to have a cab at the door as soon as she is dressed. What am I to do?'

'Do what the lady tells you,' said the doctor. 'She may be safely trusted to return to the Sanatorium.'

The breakfast hour at the Sanatorium was half-past eight o'clock. By that time Miss Gwilt had settled everything at her lodging, and had returned with her luggage in her own possession. The doctor was quite amazed at the promptitude of his patient.

'Why waste so much energy?' he asked, when they met at the breakfast-table. 'Why be in such a hurry, my dear lady, when you had all the morning before you?'

'Mere restlessness!' she said, briefly. 'The longer I live, the more impatient I get.'

The doctor, who had noticed before she spoke that her face looked strangely pale and old that morning, observed when she answered him that her expression – naturally mobile in no ordinary degree – remained quite unaltered by the effort of speaking. There was none of the usual animation on her lips, none of the usual temper in her eyes. He had never seen her so impenetrably and coldly composed as he saw her now.

'She has made up her mind at last,' he thought. 'I may say to her this morning, what I couldn't say to her last night.'

He prefaced the coming remarks by a warning look at her widow's dress.

'Now you have got your luggage,' he began gravely, 'permit me to suggest putting that cap away, and wearing another gown.'

'Why?'

'Do you remember what you told me, a day or two since?' asked the doctor. 'You said there was a chance of Mr Armadale's dying in my Sanatorium?'

'I will say it again, if you like.'

'A more unlikely chance,' pursued the doctor, deaf as ever to all awkward interruptions, 'it is hardly possible to imagine! But as long as it *is* a chance at all, it is worth considering. Say then that he dies, – dies suddenly and unexpectedly, and makes a Coroner's Inquest necessary in the house. What is our course in that case? Our course is to preserve the characters to which we have committed ourselves – you as his widow, and I as the witness of your marriage – and, *in* those characters, to court the fullest inquiry. In the entirely improbable event of his dying just when we want him to die, my idea – I might even say, my resolution – is, to admit that we knew of his resurrection from the sea; and to acknowledge that we instructed Mr Bashwood to entrap him into this house, by means of a false statement about Miss Milroy. When the inevitable questions follow, I propose to assert that he exhibited symptoms of mental alienation shortly after your marriage – that his delusion consisted in denying that you were his wife, and in declaring that he was engaged to be married to Miss Milroy – that you were in such terror of him on this account, when you heard he was alive and coming back, as to be in a state of nervous agitation that required my care – that at your request, and to calm that nervous agitation, I saw him professionally, and got him quietly into the house by a humouring of his delusion perfectly justifiable in such a case – and lastly, that I can certify his brain to have been affected by one of those mysterious disorders, eminently incurable, eminently fatal, in relation to which medical science is still in the dark. Such a course as this (in the remotely possible event which we are now supposing) would be, in your interests and mine, unquestionably the right course to take – and such a dress as *that* is, just as certainly, under existing circumstances, the wrong dress to wear.'

'Shall I take it off at once?' she asked, rising from the breakfast-table, without a word of remark on what had just been said to her.

'Any time before two o'clock to-day, will do,' said the doctor.

She looked at him, with a languid curiosity – nothing more. 'Why before two?' she inquired.

'Because this is one of my "Visitors' Days". And the Visitors' time is from two to four.'

'What have I to do with your visitors?'

'Simply this. I think it important that perfectly respectable and perfectly disinterested witnesses should see you, in my house, in the character of a lady who has come to consult me.'

'Your motive seems rather far-fetched. Is it the only motive you have in the matter?'

'My dear, dear lady!' remonstrated the doctor; 'have I any conceal-ments from *you*? Surely, you ought to know me better than that?'

'Yes,' she said, with a weary contempt. 'It's dull enough of me not to understand you by this time. – Send word upstairs, when I am wanted.' She left him, and went back to her room.

Two o'clock came; and in a quarter of an hour afterwards the Visitors had arrived. Short as the notice had been, cheerless as the Sanatorium looked to spectators from without, the doctor's invitations had been largely accepted nevertheless by the female members of the families whom he had addressed. In the miserable monotony of the lives led by a large section of the middle classes of England, anything is welcome to the women which offers them any sort of harmless refuge from the established tyranny of the principle that all human happiness begins and ends at home. While the imperious needs of a commercial country limited the representatives of the male sex, among the doctor's visitors, to one feeble old man and one sleepy little boy, the women, poor souls, to the number of no less than sixteen – old and young, married and single – had seized the golden opportunity of a plunge into public life. Harmoniously united by the two common objects which they all had in view – in the first place, to look at each other, and in the second place, to look at the Sanatorium – they streamed in neatly dressed procession through the doctor's dreary iron gates, with a thin varnish over them of assumed superiority to all unlady-like excitement, most significant and most pitiable to see!

The proprietor of the Sanatorium received his visitors in the hall with Miss Gwilt on his arm. The hungry eyes of every woman in the company overlooked the doctor as if no such person had existed; and, fixing on the strange lady, devoured her from head to foot in an instant.

'My First Inmate,' said the doctor, presenting Miss Gwilt. 'This lady only arrived late last night; and she takes the present opportunity (the only one my morning's engagements have allowed me to give her) of going over the Sanatorium. – Allow me, ma'am,' he went on, releasing Miss Gwilt, and giving his arm to the eldest lady among the visitors. 'Shattered nerves – domestic anxiety,' he whispered confidentially. 'Sweet woman! sad case!' He sighed softly, and led the old lady across the hall.

The flock of visitors followed; Miss Gwilt accompanying them in silence, and walking alone – among them, but not of them – the last of all.

'The grounds, ladies and gentlemen,' said the doctor, wheeling round and addressing his audience, from the foot of the stairs, 'are, as you have seen, in a partially unfinished condition. Under any circumstances, I should lay little stress on the grounds, having Hampstead Heath so near at hand, and carriage-exercise and horse-exercise being parts of my System. In a lesser degree it is also necessary for me to ask your indulgence for the basement floor, on which we now stand. The waiting-room and study on that side, and the Dispensary on the other (to which I shall presently ask your attention), are completed. But the large drawing-room is still in the decorator's hands. In that room (when the walls are dry – not a moment before) my inmates will assemble for cheerful society. Nothing will be spared that can improve, elevate, and adorn life, at these happy little gatherings. Every evening, for example, there will be music for those who like it.'

At this point there was a faint stir among the visitors. A mother of a family interrupted the doctor. She begged to know whether music 'every evening' included Sunday evening; and, if so, what music was performed?

'Sacred music, of course, ma'am,' said the doctor. 'Handel on Sunday evening – and Haydn occasionally, when not too cheerful. But, as I was about to say, music is not the only entertainment offered to my nervous inmates. Amusing reading is provided for those who prefer books.'

There was another stir among the visitors. Another mother of a family wished to know whether amusing reading meant novels.

'Only such novels as I have selected and perused myself, in the first instance,' said the doctor. 'Nothing painful, ma'am! There may be plenty that is painful in real life – but, for that very reason, we don't want it in books. The English novelist[1] who enters my house (no foreign novelist will be admitted) must understand his art as the healthy-minded English reader understands it in our time. He must know that our purer modern taste, our higher modern morality, limits him to doing exactly two things for us, when he writes us a book. All we want of him is – occasionally to make us laugh; and invariably to make us comfortable.'

There was a third stir among the visitors – caused plainly this time, by approval of the sentiments which they had just heard. The doctor, wisely cautious of disturbing the favourable impression that he had produced, dropped the subject of the drawing-room, and led the way upstairs. As before, the company followed – and, as before, Miss Gwilt walked silently behind them, last of all. One after another, the ladies looked at her with the idea of speaking, and saw something in her face, utterly unintelligible to them, which checked the well-meant words on their lips. The prevalent impression was, that the Principal of the Sanatorium had been delicately concealing the truth, and that his first inmate was mad.

The doctor led the way – with intervals of breathing-time accorded to the old lady on his arm – straight to the top of the house. Having collected his visitors in the corridor, and having waved his hand indicatively at the numbered doors opening out of it on either side, he invited the company to look into any or all of the rooms at their own pleasure.

'Numbers one to four, ladies and gentlemen,' said the doctor, 'include the dormitories of the attendants. Numbers four to eight are rooms intended for the accommodation of the poorer class of patients whom I receive on terms which simply cover my expenditure – nothing more. In the cases of these poorer persons among my suffering fellow-creatures, personal piety and the recommendation of two clergymen are indispensable to admission. Those are the only conditions I make; but those I insist on. Pray observe that the rooms are all ventilated, and the bedsteads all iron; and kindly notice as we descend again to the second floor, that there is a door shutting off all communication between the second story and the top story, when necessary. The rooms on the second floor, which we have now reached, are (with the exception of my own room) entirely devoted to the reception of lady-inmates – experience having convinced me that the greater sensitiveness of the female constitution necessitates the higher position of the sleeping apartment, with a view to the greater purity and freer circulation of the air. Here the ladies are established immediately under my care, while my assistant-physician (whom I expect to arrive in a week's time) looks after the gentlemen on the floor beneath. Observe, again, as we descend to this lower, or first floor, a second door, closing all communication at night between the two stories to every one but the assistant-physician and myself. And now that we have reached the gentlemen's part of the house, and that you have observed for yourselves the regulations of the establishement, permit me to introduce you to a specimen of my system of treatment next. I can exemplify it practically, by introducing you to a room fitted up, under my own directions, for the accommodation of the most complicated cases of nervous suffering and nervous delusion that can come under my care.'

He threw open the door of a room at one extremity of the corridor, numbered Four. 'Look in, ladies and gentlemen,' he said; 'and, if you see anything remarkable, pray mention it.'

The room was not very large, but it was well lit by one broad window. Comfortably furnished as a bedroom, it was only remarkable among other rooms of the same sort, in one way. It had no fireplace. The visitors having noticed this, were informed that the room was warmed in winter by means of hot-water; and were then invited back again into the corridor, to make the discoveries, under professional direction, which they were unable to make for themselves.

'A word, ladies and gentlemen,' said the doctor; 'literally a word, on nervous derangement first. What is the process of treatment, when, let us say, mental anxiety has broken you down, and you apply to your doctor? He sees you, hears you, and gives you two prescriptions. One is written on paper, and made up at the chemist's. The other is administered by word of mouth, at the propitious moment when the fee is ready; and consists in a general recommendation to you to keep your mind easy. That excellent advice given, your doctor leaves you to spare yourself all earthly annoyances by your own unaided efforts, until he calls again. Here, my System steps in, and helps you! When *I* see the necessity of keeping your mind easy, I take the bull by the horns and do it for you. I place you in a sphere of action in which the ten thousand trifles which must, and do, irritate nervous people at home, are expressly considered and provided against. I throw up impregnable moral entrenchments between Worry and You. Find a door banging in *this* house, if you can! Catch a servant in *this* house, rattling the tea-things when he takes away the tray! Discover barking dogs, crowing cocks, hammering workmen, screeching children *here* – and I engage to close My Sanatorium to-morrow! Are these nuisances laughing matters to nervous people? Ask them! Can they escape these nuisances at home? Ask them! Will ten minutes' irritation from a barking dog or a screeching child, undo every atom of good done to a nervous sufferer by a month's medical treatment? There isn't a competent doctor in England who will venture to deny it! On those plain grounds my System is based. I assert the medical treatment of nervous suffering to be entirely subsidiary to the moral treatment of it. That moral treatment of it, you find here. That moral treatment, sedulously pursued throughout the day, follows the sufferer into his room at night; and soothes, helps, and cures him, without his own knowledge – you shall see how.'

The doctor paused to take breath; and looked for the first time since the visitors had entered the house, at Miss Gwilt. For the first time, on her side, she stepped forward among the audience, and looked at him in return. After a momentary obstruction in the shape of a cough, the doctor went on.

'Say, ladies and gentlemen,' he proceeded, 'that my patient has just come in. His mind is one mass of nervous fancies and caprices, which his friends (with the best possible intentions) have been ignorantly irritating at home. They have been afraid of him, for instance, at night. They have forced him to have somebody to sleep in the room with him, or, they have forbidden him, in case of accidents, to lock his door. He comes to me the first night, and says, "Mind, I won't have anybody in my room!" – "Certainly not!" – "I insist on locking my door." – "By all means!" In he goes, and locks his door; and there he is, soothed and quieted, predisposed to confidence, predisposed to sleep, by having his own way. "This is all very well," you may say; "but suppose something happens, suppose he has a fit in the night, what then?" You shall see! Hullo, my young friend!' cried the doctor, suddenly addressing the sleepy little boy. 'Let's have a game. You shall be the poor sick man, and I'll be the good doctor. Go into that room, and lock the door. There's a brave boy! Have you locked it? Very good. Do you think I can't get at you if I like? I wait till you're asleep, – I press this little white button, hidden here in the stencilled pattern of the outer wall – the mortice of the lock inside falls back silently against the door-post – and I walk into the room whenever I like. The same plan is pursued with the window. My capricious patient won't open it at night, when he ought. I humour him again. "Shut it, dear sir, by all means!" As soon as he is asleep, I pull the black handle hidden here, in the corner of the wall. The window of the room inside noiselessly opens, as you see. Say the patient's caprice is the other way – he persists in opening the window when he ought to shut it. Let him! by all means let him! I pull a second handle when he is snug in his bed, and the window noiselessly closes in a moment. Nothing to irritate him, ladies and gentlemen – absolutely nothing to irritate him! But I haven't done with him yet.

Epidemic disease, in spite of all my precautions, may enter this Sanatorium, and may render the purifying of the sick-room necessary. Or the patient's case may be complicated by other than nervous malady – say, for instance, asthmatic difficulty of breathing. In the one case, fumigation is necessary: in the other, additional oxygen in the air will give relief. The epidemic nervous patient says, "I won't be smoked under my own nose!" The asthmatic nervous patient gasps with terror at the idea of a chemical explosion in his room. I noiselessly fumigate one of them; I noiselessly oxygenize the other, by means of a simple Apparatus fixed outside in the corner here. It is protected by this wooden casing; it is locked with my own key; and it communicates by means of a tube with the interior of the room. Look at it!'

With a preliminary glance at Miss Gwilt, the doctor unlocked the lid of the wooden casing, and disclosed inside nothing more remarkable than a large stone jar, having a glass funnel, and a pipe communicating with the wall, inserted in the cork which closed the mouth of it. With another look at Miss Gwilt, the doctor locked the lid again, and asked in the blandest manner, whether his System was intelligible now?

'I might introduce you to all sorts of other contrivances of the same kind,' he resumed, leading the way downstairs – 'but it would be only the same thing over and over again. A nervous patient who always has his own way, is a nervous patient who is never worried – and a nervous patient who is never worried, is a nervous patient cured. There it is in a nutshell! – Come and see the Dispensary, ladies; the Dispensary and the kitchen next!'

Once more, Miss Gwilt dropped behind the visitors, and waited alone – looking steadfastly at the Room which the doctor had opened, and at the Apparatus which the doctor had unlocked. Again, without a word passing between them, she had understood him. She knew as well as if he had confessed it, that he was craftily putting the necessary temptation in her way, before witnesses who could speak to the superficially-innocent acts which they had seen, if anything serious happened. The Apparatus, originally constructed to serve the purpose of the doctor's medical crotchets, was evidently to be put to some other use, of which the doctor himself had probably never dreamed till now. And the chances were that before the day was over, that other use would be privately revealed to her at the right moment, in the presence of the right witness. 'Armadale will die this time,' she said to herself as she went slowly down the stairs. 'The doctor will kill him, by my hands.'

The visitors were in the Dispensary when she joined them. All the ladies were admiring the beauty of the antique cabinet; and, as a necessary consequence, all the ladies were desirous of seeing what was inside. The doctor – after a preliminary look at Miss Gwilt – good-humouredly shook his head. 'There is nothing to interest you inside,' he said. 'Nothing but rows of little shabby bottles containing the poisons used in medicine which I keep under lock and key. Come to the kitchen, ladies, and honour me with your advice on domestic matters below stairs.' He glanced again at Miss Gwilt as the company crossed the hall, with a look which said plainly, 'Wait here.'

In another quarter-of-an-hour, the doctor had expounded his views on cookery and diet, and the visitors (duly furnished with prospectuses) were taking leave of him at the door. 'Quite an intellectual treat!' they said to each other, as they streamed out again in neatly-dressed procession through the iron gates. 'And what a very superior man!'

The doctor turned back to the Dispensary, humming absently to himself, and failing entirely to observe the corner of the hall in which Miss Gwilt stood retired. After an instant's hesitation, she followed him. The assistant was in the room when she entered it – summoned by his employer the moment before.

'Doctor,' she said, coldly and mechanically, as if she was repeating a lesson; 'I am as curious as the other ladies about that pretty cabinet of yours. Now they are all gone, won't you show the inside of it to *me*?'

The doctor laughed in his pleasantest manner.

'The old story,' he said. 'Blue-Beard's locked chamber, and female curiosity! (Don't go, Benjamin, don't go.) My dear lady, what interest can you possibly have in looking at a medical bottle, simply because it happens to be a bottle of poison?'

She repeated her lesson for the second time.

'I have the interest of looking at it,' she said, 'and of thinking if it got into some people's hands, of the terrible things it might do.'

The doctor glanced at his assistant with a compassionate smile.

'Curious, Benjamin,' he said; 'the romantic view taken of these drugs of ours by the unscientific mind. My dear lady,' he added, turning again to Miss Gwilt, 'if *that* is the interest you attach to looking at poisons, you needn't ask me to unlock my cabinet – you need only look about you round the shelves of this room. There are all sorts of medical liquids and substances in those bottles – most innocent, most useful in themselves – which, in combination with other substances and other liquids, become poisons as terrible and as deadly as any that I have in my cabinet under lock and key.'

She looked at him for a moment, and crossed to the opposite side of the room.

'Show me one,' she said.

Still smiling as good-humouredly as ever, the doctor humoured his nervous patient. He pointed to the bottle from which he had privately removed the yellow liquid on the previous day, and which he had filled up again with a carefully-coloured imitation, in the shape of a mixture of his own.

'Do you see that bottle?' he said; 'that plump, round, comfortable-looking bottle? Never mind the name of what is inside it; let us stick to the bottle, and distinguish it, if you like, by giving it a name of our own. Suppose we call it "our Stout Friend"? Very good. Our Stout Friend,[2] by himself, is a most harmless and useful medicine. He is freely dispensed every day to tens of thousands of patients all over the civilized world. He has made no romantic appearances in courts of law; he has excited no breathless interest in novels; he has played no terrifying part on the stage. There he is, an innocent, inoffensive creature, who troubles nobody with the responsibility of locking him up! *But* bring him into contact with something else – introduce him to the acquaintance of a certain common mineral Substance, of a universally accessible kind, broken into fragments; provide yourself with (say) six doses of our Stout Friend, and pour those doses consecutively on the fragments I have mentioned, at intervals of not less than five minutes. Quantities of little bubbles will rise at every pouring; collect the gas in those bubbles; and convey it into a closed chamber – and let Samson himself be in that closed chamber, our Stout Friend will kill him in half-an-hour! Will kill him slowly, without his seeing anything, without his smelling anything, without his feeling anything but sleepiness. Will kill him, and tell the whole College of Surgeons nothing, if they examine him after death, but that he died of apoplexy or congestion of the lungs! What do you think of *that*, my dear lady, in the way of mystery and romance? Is our harmless Stout Friend as interesting *now* as if he rejoiced in the terrible popular fame of the Arsenic and the Strychnine which I keep locked up there? Don't suppose I am exaggerating! Don't suppose I'm inventing a story to put you off with, as the children say. Ask Benjamin, there,' said the doctor, appealing to his assistant, with his eyes fixed on Miss Gwilt. 'Ask Benjamin,' he repeated, with the steadiest emphasis on the next words, 'if six doses from that bottle, at intervals of five minutes each, would not, under the conditions I have stated, produce the results I have described?'

The Resident Dispenser, modestly admiring Miss Gwilt at a distance, started and coloured up. He was plainly gratified by the little attention which had included him in the conversation.

'The doctor is quite right, ma'am,' he said, addressing Miss Gwilt, with his best bow, 'the production of the gas, extended over half an hour, would be quite gradual enough. And,' added the Dispenser, silently appealing to his employer to let him exhibit a little chemical knowledge on his own account, 'the volume of the gas would be sufficient at the end of the time – if I am not mistaken, sir? – to be fatal to any person entering the room, in less than five minutes.'

'Unquestionably, Benjamin,' rejoined the doctor. 'But I think we have had enough of chemistry for the present,' he added, turning to Miss Gwilt. 'With every desire, my dear lady, to gratify every passing wish you may form, I venture to propose trying a more cheerful subject. Suppose we leave the Dispensary, before it suggests any more inquiries to that active mind of yours? No? You want to see an experiment? You want to see how the little bubbles are made? Well, well! there is no harm in that. We will let Mrs Armadale see the bubbles,' continued the doctor, in the tone of a parent humouring a spoilt child. 'Try if you can find a few of those fragments that we want, Benjamin. I daresay the workmen (slovenly fellows!) have left something of the sort about the house or the grounds.'

The Resident Dispenser left the room.

As soon as his back was turned, the doctor began opening and shutting drawers in various parts of the dispensary, with the air of a man who wants something in a hurry, and doesn't know where to find it. 'Bless my soul!' he exclaimed, suddenly stopping at the drawer from which he had taken his cards of invitation on the previous day, 'what's this? A key? A duplicate key, as I'm alive, of my fumigating Apparatus upstairs! Oh dear, dear, how careless I get,' said the doctor, turning round briskly to Miss Gwilt. 'I hadn't the least idea that I possessed this second key. I should never have missed it. I do assure you I should never have missed it, if anybody had taken it out of the drawer!' He bustled away to the other end of the room – without closing the drawer, and without taking away the duplicate key.

In silence, Miss Gwilt listened till he had done. In silence, she glided to the drawer. In silence, she took the key and hid it in her apron pocket.

The Dispenser came back, with the fragments required of him, collected in a basin. 'Thank you, Benjamin,' said the doctor. 'Kindly cover them with water, while I get the bottle down.'

As accidents sometimes happen in the most perfectly regulated families, so clumsiness sometimes possesses itself of the most perfectly-disciplined hands. In the process of its transfer from the shelf to the doctor, the bottle slipped, and fell smashed to pieces on the floor.

'Oh, my fingers and thumbs!' cried the doctor, with an air of comic vexation, 'what in the world do you mean by playing me such a wicked trick as that? Well, well, well – it can't be helped. Have we got any more of it, Benjamin?'

'Not a drop, sir.'

'Not a drop!' echoed the doctor. 'My dear madam, what excuses can I offer you? My clumsiness has made our little experiment impossible for to-day. Remind me to order some more to-morrow, Benjamin – and don't think of troubling yourself to put that mess to rights. I'll send the man here to mop it all up. Our Stout Friend is harmless enough now, my dear lady – in combination with a boarded floor and a coming mop! I'm so sorry; I really am so sorry to have disappointed you.' With those soothing words, he offered his arm, and led Miss Gwilt out of the dispensary.

'Have you done with me for the present?' she asked when they were in the hall.

'Oh dear, dear, what a way of putting it!' exclaimed the doctor. 'Dinner at six,' he added with his politest emphasis, as she turned from him in disdainful silence, and slowly mounted the stairs to her own room.

A clock of the noiseless sort – incapable of offending irritable nerves – was fixed in the wall, above the first-floor landing, at the Sanatorium. At the moment when the hands pointed to a quarter before six, the silence of the lonely upper regions was softly broken by the rustling of Miss Gwilt's dress. She advanced along the corridor of the first-floor – paused at the covered Apparatus fixed outside the room numbered Four – listened for a moment – and then unlocked the cover with the duplicate key.

The open lid cast a shadow over the inside of the casing. All she saw at first, was what she had seen already – the jar, and the pipe and glass funnel inserted in the cork. She removed the funnel; and, looking about her, observed on the window-sill close by, a wax-tipped wand used for lighting the gas. She took the wand, and, introducing it through the aperture occupied by the funnel, moved it to and fro in the jar. The faint splash of some liquid, and the grating noise of certain hard substances which she was stirring about, were the two sounds that caught her ear. She drew out the wand, and cautiously touched the wet left on it with the tip of her tongue. Caution was quite needless in this case. The liquid was – water.

In putting the funnel back in its place, she noticed something faintly shining in the obscurely-lit vacant space at the side of the jar. She drew it out, and produced a Purple Flask. The liquid with which it was filled showed dark through the transparent colouring of the glass; and, fastened at regular intervals down one side of the Flask, were six thin strips of paper which divided the contents into six equal parts.

There was no doubt now, that the Apparatus had been secretly prepared for her – the Apparatus of which she alone (besides the doctor) possessed the key.

She put back the Flask, and locked the cover of the casing. For a moment, she stood looking at it, with the key in her hand. On a sudden, her lost colour came back. On a sudden, its natural animation returned, for the first time that day, to her face. She turned and hurried breathlessly upstairs to her room on the second floor. With eager hands, she snatched her cloak out of the wardrobe, and took her bonnet from the box. 'I'm not in prison!' she burst out impetuously. 'I've got the use of my limbs! I can go – no matter where, as long as I am out of this house!'

With her cloak on her shoulders, with her bonnet in her hand, she crossed the room to the door. A moment more – and she would have been out in the passage. In that moment, the remembrance flashed back on her of the husband whom she had denied to his face. She stopped instantly, and threw the cloak and bonnet from her on the bed. 'No!' she said. 'The gulph is dug between us – the worst is done!'

There was a knock at the door. The doctor's voice outside, politely reminded her that it was six o'clock.

She opened the door, and stopped him on his way downstairs.

'What time is the train due to-night?' she asked in a whisper.

'At ten,' answered the doctor, in a voice which all the world might hear, and welcome.

'What room is Mr Armadale to have when he comes?'

'What room would you like him to have?'

'Number Four.'

The doctor kept up appearances to the very last.

'Number Four let it be,' he said graciously. 'Provided, of course, that Number Four is unoccupied at the time.'

The evening wore on, and the night came.

At a few minutes before ten, Mr Bashwood was again at his post; once more on the watch for the coming of the tidal train.

The inspector on duty, who knew him by sight, and who had personally ascertained that his regular attendance at the terminus implied no designs on the purses and portmanteaus of the passengers, noticed two new circumstances in connection with Mr Bashwood that night. In the first place, instead of exhibiting his customary cheerfulness, he looked anxious and depressed. In the second place, while he was watching for the train, he was to all appeareance being watched in his turn, by a slim, dark, undersized man, who had left his luggage (marked with the name of Midwinter,) at the custom-house department the evening before, and who had returned to have it examined about half an hour since.

What had brought Midwinter to the terminus? and why was he, too, waiting for the tidal train?

After straying as far as Hendon during his lonely walk of the previous night, he had taken refuge at the village inn, and had fallen asleep (from sheer exhaustion) towards those later hours of the morning, which were the hours that his wife's foresight had turned to account. When he returned to the lodging, the landlady could only inform him that her tenant had settled everything with her, and had left (for what destination neither she nor her servant could tell) more than two hours since.

Having given some little time to inquiries, the result of which convinced him that the clue was lost so far, Midwinter had quitted the house, and had pursued his way mechanically to the busier and more central parts of the metropolis. With the light now thrown on his wife's character, to call at the address she had given him as the address at which her mother lived would be plainly useless. He went on through the streets, resolute to discover her, and trying vainly to see the means to his end, till the sense of fatigue forced itself on him once more. Stopping to rest and recruit his strength at the first hotel he came to, a chance dispute between the waiter and a stranger about a lost portmanteau reminded him of his own luggage, left at the terminus, and instantly took his mind back to the circumstances under which he and Mr Bashwood had met. In a moment more, the idea that he had been vainly seeking on his way through the streets flashed on him. In a moment more, he had determined to try the chance of finding the steward again on the watch for the person whose arrival he had evidently expected by the previous evening's train.

Ignorant of the report of Allan's death at sea; uninformed, at the terrible interview with his wife, of the purpose which her assumption of a widow's dress really had in view, Midwinter's first vague suspicions of her fidelity had now inevitably developed into the conviction that she was false. He could place but one interpretation on her open disavowal of him, and on her taking the name under which he had secretly married her. Her conduct forced the conclusion on him that she was engaged in some infamous intrigue; and that she had basely secured herself beforehand in the position of all others in which she knew it would be most odious and most repellent to him to claim his authority over her. With that conviction he was now watching Mr Bashwood, firmly persuaded that his wife's hiding-place was known to the vile servant of his wife's vices – and darkly suspecting, as the time wore on, that the unknown man who had wronged him, and the unknown traveller for whose arrival the steward was waiting, were one and the same.

The train was late that night, and the carriages were more than usually crowded when they arrived at last. Midwinter became involved in the confusion on the platform, and in the effort to extricate himself he lost sight of Mr Bashwood for the first time.

A lapse of some few minutes had passed before he again discovered the steward talking eagerly to a man in a loose shaggy coat, whose back was turned towards him. Forgetful of all the cautions and restraints which he had imposed on himself before the train appeared, Midwinter instantly advanced on them. Mr Bashwood saw his threatening face as he came on, and fell back in silence. The man in the loose coat turned to look where the steward was looking, and disclosed to Midwinter, in the full light of the station-lamp, Allan's face!

For the moment they both stood speechless, hand in hand, looking at each other. Allan was the first to recover himself.

'Thank God for this!' he said fervently. 'I don't ask how you came here – it's enough for me that you have come. Miserable news has met me already, Midwinter. Nobody but you can comfort me, and help me to bear it.' His voice faltered over those last words, and he said no more.

The tone in which he had spoken roused Midwinter to meet the circumstances as they were, by appealing to the old grateful interest in his friend which had once been the foremost interest of his life. He mastered his personal misery for the first time since it had fallen on him, and gently taking Allan aside, asked what had happened.

The answer – after informing him of his friend's reported death at sea – announced (on Mr Bashwood's authority) that the news had reached Miss Milroy, and that the deplorable result of the shock thus inflicted, had obliged the major to place his daughter in the neighbourhood of London, under medical care.

Before saying a word on his side, Midwinter looked distrustfully behind him. Mr Bashwood had followed them. Mr Bashwood was watching to see what they did next.

'Was he waiting your arrival here to tell you this about Miss Milroy?' asked Midwinter, looking back again from the steward to Allan.

'Yes,' said Allan. 'He has been kindly waiting here, night after night, to meet me, and break the news to me.'

Midwinter paused once more. The attempt to reconcile the conclusion he had drawn from his wife's conduct with the discovery that Allan was the man for whose arrival Mr Bashwood had been waiting, was hopeless. The one present chance of discovering a truer solution of the mystery, was to press the steward on the one available point in which he had laid himself open to attack. He had positively denied on the previous evening that he knew anything of Allan's movements, or that he had any interest in Allan's return to England. Having detected Mr Bashwood in one lie told to himself, Midwinter instantly suspected him of telling another to Allan. He seized the opportunity of sifting the statement about Miss Milroy on the spot.

'How have you become acquainted with this sad news?' he inquired, turning suddenly on Mr Bashwood.

'Through the major of course,' said Allan, before the steward could answer.

'Who is the doctor who has the care of Miss Milroy?' persisted Midwinter, still addressing Mr Bashwood.

For the second time the steward made no reply. For the second time, Allan answered for him.

'He is a man with a foreign name,' said Allan. 'He keeps a Sanatorium near Hampstead. What did you say the place was called, Mr Bashwood?'

'Fairweather Vale, sir,' said the steward, answering his employer as a matter of necessity, but answering very unwillingly.

The address of the Sanatorium instantly reminded Midwinter that he had traced his wife to Fairweather Vale Villas the previous night. He began to see light through the darkness, dimly, for the first time. The instinct which comes with emergency, before the slower process of reason can assert itself, brought him at a leap to the conclusion that Mr Bashwood – who had been certainly acting under his wife's influence the previous day – might be acting again under his wife's influence now. He persisted in sifting the steward's statement, with the conviction growing firmer and firmer in his mind that the statement was a lie, and that his wife was concerned in it.

'Is the major in Norfolk?' he asked, 'or is he near his daughter in London?'

'In Norfolk,' said Mr Bashwood. Having answered Allan's look of inquiry, instead of Midwinter's spoken question, in those words, he hesitated, looked Midwinter in the face for the first time, and added, suddenly, 'I object, if you please, to be cross-examined, sir. I know what I have told Mr Armadale, and I know no more.'

The words, and the voice in which they were spoken, were alike at variance with Mr Bashwood's usual language and Mr Bashwood's usual tone. There was a sullen depression in his face – there was a furtive distrust and dislike in his eyes when they looked at Midwinter, which Midwinter himself now noticed for the first time. Before he could answer the steward's extraordinary outbreak, Allan interfered.

'Don't think me impatient,' he said. 'But it's getting late; it's a long way to Hampstead. I'm afraid the Sanatorium will be shut up.'

Midwinter started. 'You are not going to the Sanatorium to-night!' he exclaimed.

Allan took his friend's hand, and wrung it hard. 'If you were as fond of her as I am,' he whispered, 'you would take no rest, you could get no sleep, till you had seen the doctor, and heard the best and the worst he had to tell you. Poor dear little soul! who knows, if she could only see me alive and well—' The tears came into his eyes, and he turned away his head in silence.

Midwinter looked at the steward. 'Stand back,' he said. 'I want to speak to Mr Armadale.' There was something in his eye which it was not safe to trifle with. Mr Bashwood drew back out of hearing, but not out of sight. Midwinter laid his hand fondly on his friend's shoulder.

'Allan,' he said, 'I have reasons—' He stopped. Could the reasons be given before he had fairly realized them himself; at that time, too, and under those circumstances? Impossible! 'I have reasons,' he resumed, 'for advising you not to believe too readily what Mr Bashwood may say. Don't tell him this, but take the warning.'

Allan looked at his friend in astonishment. 'It was you who always liked Mr Bashwood!' he exclaimed. 'It was you who trusted him, when he first came to the great house!'

'Perhaps I was wrong, Allan, and perhaps you were right. Will you only wait till we can telegraph to Major Milroy and get his answer? Will you only wait over the night?'

'I shall go mad if I wait over the night,' said Allan. 'You have made me more anxious than I was before. If I am not to speak about it to

Bashwood, I must and will go to the Sanatorium, and find out whether she is or is not there, from the doctor himself.'

Midwinter saw that it was useless. In Allan's interests there was only one other course left to take. 'Will you let me go with you?' he asked.

Allan's face brightened for the first time. 'You dear, good fellow!' he exclaimed. 'It was the very thing I was going to beg of you myself.'

Midwinter beckoned to the steward. 'Mr Armadale is going to the Sanatorium,' he said, 'and I mean to accompany him. Get a cab and come with us.'

He waited, to see whether Mr Bashwood would comply. Having been strictly ordered, when Allan did arrive, not to lose sight of him, and having, in his own interests, Midwinter's unexpected appearance to explain to Miss Gwilt, the steward had no choice but to comply. In sullen submission he did as he had been told. The keys of Allan's baggage were given to the foreign travelling servant whom he had brought with him, and the man was instructed to wait his master's orders at the terminus hotel. In a minute more the cab was on its way out of the station – with Midwinter and Allan inside, and with Mr Bashwood by the driver on the box.

Between eleven and twelve o'clock that night, Miss Gwilt, standing alone at the window which lit the corridor of the Sanatorium on the second floor, heard the roll of wheels coming towards her. The sound, gathering rapidly in volume through the silence of the lonely neighbourhood, stopped at the iron gates. In another minute she saw the cab draw up beneath her, at the house door.

The earlier night had been cloudy, but the sky was clearing now, and the moon was out. She opened the window to see and hear more clearly. By the light of the moon she saw Allan get out of the cab, and turn round to speak to some other person inside. The answering voice told her, before he appeared in his turn, that Armadale's companion was her husband.

The same petrifying influence that had fallen on her at the interview with him of the previous day, fell on her now. She stood by the window, white and still, and haggard and old – as she had stood when she first faced him in her widow's weeds.

Mr Bashwood, stealing up alone to the second floor to make his report, knew, the instant he set eyes on her, that the report was needless. 'It's not my fault,' was all he said, as she slowly turned her head, and looked at him. 'They met together, and there was no parting them.'

She drew a long breath, and motioned to him to be silent. 'Wait a little,' she said; 'I know all about it.'

Turning from him at those words, she slowly paced the corridor to its furthest end; turned, and slowly came back to him with frowning brow and drooping head – with all the grace and beauty gone from her, but the inbred grace and beauty in the movement of her limbs.

'Do you wish to speak to me?' she asked; her mind far away from him, and her eyes looking at him vacantly as she put the question.

He roused his courage as he had never roused it in her presence yet.

'Don't drive me to despair!' he cried, with a startling abruptness. 'Don't look at me in that way, now I have found it out!'

'What have you found out?' she asked, with a momentary surprise in her face, which faded from it again before he could gather breath enough to go on.

'Mr Armadale is not the man who took you away from me,' he answered. 'Mr Midwinter is the man. I found it out in your face yesterday. I see it in your face now. Why did you sign your name, "Armadale", when you wrote to me? Why do you call yourself "Mrs Armadale" still?'

He spoke those bold words, at long intervals, with an effort to resist her influence over him, pitiable and terrible to see.

She looked at him for the first time with softened eyes. 'I wish I had pitied you when we first met,' she said gently, 'as I pity you now.'

He struggled desperately to go on, and say the words to her which he had strung himself to the pitch of saying on the drive from the terminus. They were words which hinted darkly at his knowledge of her past life; words which warned her – do what else she might; commit what crimes she pleased – to think twice before she deceived and deserted him again. In those terms he had vowed to himself to address her. He had the phrases picked and chosen; he had the sentences ranged and ordered in his mind; nothing was wanting but to make the one crowning effort of speaking them – and, even now, after all he had said, and all he had dared, the effort was more than he could compass! In helpless gratitude, even for so little as her pity, he stood looking at her, and wept the silent womanish tears that fall from old men's eyes.

She took his hand and spoke to him – with marked forbearance, but without the slightest sign of emotion on her side.

'You have waited already at my request,' she said. 'Wait till to-morrow, and you will know all. If you trust nothing else that I have told you, you may trust what I tell you now. *It will end to-night.*'

As she said the words, the doctor's step was heard on the stairs. Mr Bashwood drew back from her, with his heart beating fast in unutterable expectation. 'It will end to-night!' he repeated to himself, under his breath, as he moved away towards the far end of the corridor.

'Don't let me disturb you, sir,' said the doctor, cheerfully, as they met. 'I have nothing to say to Mrs Armadale but what you or anybody may hear.'

Mr Bashwood went on, without answering, to the far end of the corridor, still repeating to himself, 'It will end to-night!' The doctor passing him in the opposite direction, joined Miss Gwilt.

'You have heard, no doubt,' he began in his blandest manner and his roundest tones, 'that Mr Armadale has arrived. Permit me to add, my dear lady, that there is not the least reason for any nervous agitation on your part. He has been carefully humoured, and he is as quiet and manageable as his best friends could wish. I have informed him that it is impossible to allow him an interview with the young lady to-night – but that he may count on seeing her (with the proper precautions) at the earliest propitious hour, after she is awake to-morrow morning. As there is no hotel near, and as the propitious hour may occur at a moment's notice, it was clearly incumbent on me, under the peculiar circumstances, to offer him the hospitality of the Sanatorium. He has accepted it with the utmost gratitude; and has thanked me in a most gentlemanly and touching manner for the pains I have taken to set his mind at ease. Perfectly gratifying, perfectly satisfactory, so far! But there has been a little hitch – now happily got over – which I think it right to mention to you before we all retire for the night.'

Having paved the way in those words (and in Mr Bashwood's hearing) for the statement which he had previously announced his intention of making, in the event of Allan's dying in the Sanatorium, the doctor was about to proceed, when his attention was attracted by a sound below like the trying of a door.

He instantly descended the stairs, and unlocked the door of communication between the first and second floors, which he had locked behind him on his way up. But the person who had tried the door – if such a person there really had been – was too quick for him. He looked along the corridor, and over the staircase into the hall, and discovering nothing, returned to Miss Gwilt, after securing the door of communication behind him once more.

'Pardon me,' he resumed, 'I thought I heard something downstairs. With regard to the little hitch that I adverted to just now, permit me to inform you that Mr Armadale has brought a friend here with him, who bears the strange name of Midwinter. Do you know the gentleman at all?' asked the doctor, with a suspicious anxiety in his eyes, which strangely belied the elaborate indifference of his tone.

'I know him to be an old friend of Mr Armadale's,' she said. 'Does he—?' Her voice failed her, and her eyes fell before the doctor's steady scrutiny. She mastered the momentary weakness, and finished her question. 'Does he, too, stay here to-night?'

'Mr Midwinter is a person of coarse manners and suspicious temper,' rejoined the doctor, steadily watching her. 'He was rude enough to insist on staying here as soon as Mr Armadale had accepted my invitation.'

He paused to note the effect of those words on her. Left utterly in the dark by the caution with which she had avoided mentioning her husband's assumed name to him at their first interview, the doctor's distrust of her was necessarily of the vaguest kind. He had heard her voice fail her – he had seen her colour change. He suspected her of a mental reservation on the subject of Midwinter – and of nothing more.

'Did you permit him to have his way?' she asked. 'In your place, I should have shown him the door.'

The impenetrable composure of her tone warned the doctor that her self-command was not to be further shaken that night. He resumed the character of Mrs Armadale's medical referee on the subject of Mr Armadale's mental health.[3]

'If I had only had my own feelings to consult,' he said, 'I don't disguise from you that I should (as you say) have shown Mr Midwinter the door. But on appealing to Mr Armadale, I found he was himself anxious not to be parted from his friend. Under those circumstances, but one alternative was left, the alternative of humouring him again. The responsibility of thwarting him – to say nothing,' added the doctor, drifting for a moment towards the truth, 'of my natural apprehension, with such a temper as his friend's, of a scandal and disturbance in the house – was not to be thought of for a moment. Mr Midwinter accordingly remains here for the night; and occupies (I ought to say, insists on occupying) the next room to Mr Armadale. Advise me, my dear madam, in this emergency,' concluded the doctor, with his loudest emphasis. 'What rooms shall we put them in, on the first floor?'

'Put Mr Armadale in Number Four.'

'And his friend next to him, in number three?' said the doctor. 'Well! well! well! perhaps they *are* the most comfortable rooms. I'll give my orders immediately. Don't hurry away, Mr Bashwood,' he called out cheerfully as he reached the top of the staircase. 'I have left the assistant-physician's key[4] on the window-sill yonder, and Mrs Armadale can let you out at the staircase door whenever she pleases.[5] Don't sit up late, Mrs Armadale! Yours is a nervous system that requires plenty of sleep. "Tired nature's sweet restorer, balmy sleep."[6] Grand line! God bless you – good-night!'

Mr Bashwood came back from the far end of the corridor – still pondering, in unutterable expectation, on what was to come with the night.

'Am I to go now?' he asked.

'No. You are to stay. I said you should know all if you waited till the morning. Wait here.'

He hesitated and looked about him. 'The doctor,' he faltered. 'I thought the doctor said—'

'The doctor will interfere with nothing that I do in this house to-night. I tell you to stay. There are empty rooms on the floor above this. Take one of them.'

Mr Bashwood felt the trembling fit coming on him again as he looked at her. 'May I ask—?' he began.

'Ask nothing. I want you.'

'Will you please to tell me—?'

'I will tell you nothing till the night is over and the morning has come.'

His curiosity conquered his fear. He persisted.

'Is it something dreadful?' he whispered. 'Too dreadful to tell me?'

She stamped her foot with a sudden outbreak of impatience. 'Go!' she said, snatching the key of the staircase door from the window-sill. 'You do quite right to distrust me – you do quite right to follow me no farther in the dark. Go before the house is shut up. I can do without you.' She led the way to the stairs, with the key in one hand, and the candle in the other.

Mr Bashwood followed her in silence. No one, knowing what he knew of her earlier life, could have failed to perceive that she was a woman driven to the last extremity, and standing consciously on the brink of a Crime. In the first terror of the discovery, he broke free from the hold she had on him – he thought and acted like a man who had a will of his own again.

She put the key in the door, and turned to him before she opened it, with the light of the candle on her face. 'Forget me, and forgive me,' she said. 'We meet no more.'

She opened the door, and, standing inside it, after he had passed her, gave him her hand. He had resisted her look, he had resisted her words, but the magnetic fascination of her touch conquered him at the final

654

moment. 'I can't leave you!' he said, holding helplessly by the hand she had given him. 'What must I do?'

'Come and see,' she answered, without allowing him an instant to reflect.

Closing her hand firmly on his, she led him along the first-floor corridor to the room numbered Four. 'Notice that room,' she whispered. After a look over the stairs to see that they were alone, she retraced her steps with him to the opposite extremity of the corridor. Here, facing the window which lit the place at the other end, was one little room, with a narrow grating in the higher part of the door, intended for the sleeping-apartment of the doctor's deputy. From the position of this room, the grating commanded a view of the bed-chambers down each side of the corridor, and so enabled the deputy-physician to inform himself of any irregular proceedings on the part of the patients under his care, with little or no chance of being detected in watching them. Miss Gwilt opened the door and led the way into the empty room.

'Wait here,' she said, 'while I go back upstairs; and lock yourself in, if you like. You will be in the dark – but the gas will be burning in the corridor. Keep at the grating, and make sure that Mr Armadale goes into the room I have just pointed out to you, and that he doesn't leave it afterwards. If you lose sight of the room for a single moment, before I come back, you will repent it to the end of your life. If you do as I tell you, you shall see me to-morrow, and claim your own reward. Quick with your answer! Is it Yes or No?'

He could make no reply in words. He raised her hand to his lips, and kissed it rapturously. She left him in the room. From his place at the grating he saw her glide down the corridor to the staircase door. She passed through it, and locked it. Then there was silence.

The next sound was the sound of the women-servants' voices. Two of them came up to put the sheets on the beds in Number Three and Number Four. The women were in high good-humour, laughing and talking to each other through the open doors of the rooms. The master's customers were coming in at last, they said, with a vengeance; the house would soon begin to look cheerful, if things went on like this.

After a little, the beds were got ready, and the women returned to the kitchen-floor, on which the sleeping rooms of the domestic servants were all situated. Then there was silence again.

The next sound was the sound of the doctor's voice. He appeared at the end of the corridor, showing Allan and Midwinter the way to their rooms. They all went together into Number Four. After a little, the doctor came out first. He waited till Midwinter joined him, and pointed with a formal bow to the door of Number Three. Midwinter entered the room without speaking, and shut himself in. The doctor, left alone, withdrew to the staircase door and unlocked it – then waited in the corridor, whistling to himself softly, under his breath.

Voices pitched cautiously low became audible in a minute more in the hall. The Resident Dispenser and the Head Nurse appeared, on their way to the Dormitories of the Attendants at the top of the house. The man bowed silently, and passed the doctor; the woman curtseyed silently, and followed the man. The doctor acknowledged their saluta-tions by a courteous wave of his hand; and once more left alone, paused a moment, still whistling softly to himself – then walked to the door of Number Four, and opened the case of the fumigating apparatus fixed near it in the corner of the wall. As he lifted the lid and looked in, his whistling ceased. He took a long purple bottle out, examined it by the gaslight, put it back, and closed the case. This done, he advanced on tiptoe to the open staircase door – passed through it – and secured it on the inner side as usual.

Mr Bashwood had seen him at the apparatus; Mr Bashwood had noticed the manner of his withdrawal through the staircase-door. Again the sense of an unutterable expectation throbbed at his heart. A terror that was slow and cold and deadly crept into his hands, and guided them in the dark to the key that had been left for him in the inner side of the door. He turned it in vague distrust of what might happen next, and waited.

The slow minutes passed, and nothing happened. The silence was horrible; the solitude of the lonely corridor was a solitude of invisible treacheries. He began to count to keep his mind employed – to keep his own growing dread away from him. The numbers, as he whispered them, followed each other slowly up to a hundred, and still nothing happened. He had begun the second hundred; he had got on to twenty – when, without a sound to betray that he had been moving in his room, Midwinter suddenly appeared in the corridor.

He stood for a moment and listened – he went to the stairs and looked over into the hall beneath. Then, for the second time that night, he tried the staircase door, and for the second time found it fast. After a moment's reflection, he tried the doors of the bedrooms on his right hand next, looked into one after the other, and saw that they were empty, then came to the door of the end room in which the steward was concealed. Here again, the lock resisted him. He listened, and looked up at the grating. No sound was to be heard, no light was to be seen inside. 'Shall I break the door in,' he said to himself, 'and make sure? No; it

would be giving the doctor an excuse for turning me out of the house.'
He moved away, and looked into the two empty rooms in the row
occupied by Allan and himself, then walked to the window at the
staircase end of the corridor. Here, the case of the fumigating apparatus
attracted his attention. After trying vainly to open it, his suspicion
seemed to be aroused. He searched back along the corridor, and
observed that no object of a similar kind appeared outside any of the
other bedchambers. Again at the window, he looked again at the
apparatus, and turned away from it with a gesture which plainly
indicated that he had tried, and failed, to guess what it might be.

Baffled at all points, he still showed no sign of returning to his
bedchamber. He stood at the window, with his eyes fixed on the door of
Allan's room, thinking. If Mr Bashwood, furtively watching him through
the grating, could have seen him at that moment in the mind as well as
in the body, Mr Bashwood's heart might have throbbed even faster
than it was throbbing now, in expectation of the next event which
Midwinter's decision of the next minute was to bring forth.

On what was his mind occupied as he stood alone, at the dead of
night, in the strange house?

His mind was occupied in drawing its disconnected impressions
together, little by little, to one point. Convinced, from the first, that
some hidden danger threatened Allan in the Sanatorium, his distrust –
vaguely associated, thus far, with the place itself; with his wife (whom
he firmly believed to be now under the same roof with him); with the
doctor, who was as plainly in her confidence as Mr Bashwood himself –
now narrowed its range, and centred itself obstinately in Allan's room.
Resigning all further effort to connect his suspicion of a conspiracy
against his friend, with the outrage which had the day before been
offered to himself – an effort which would have led him, if he could have
maintained it, to a discovery of the Fraud really contemplated by his
wife – his mind, clouded and confused by disturbing influences, instinctively took refuge in its impressions of facts as they had shown themselves, since he had entered the house. Everything that he had noticed
below stairs suggested that there was some secret purpose to be answered
by getting Allan to sleep in the Sanatorium. Everything that he had
noticed above stairs, associated the lurking-place in which the danger
lay hid, with Allan's room. To reach this conclusion, and to decide on
baffling the conspiracy, whatever it might be, by taking Allan's place,
was with Midwinter the work of an instant. Confronted by actual peril,
the great nature of the man intuitively freed itself from the weaknesses
that had beset it in happier and safer times. Not even the shadow of the

old superstition rested on his mind now – no fatalist suspicion of himself disturbed the steady resolution that was in him. The one last doubt that troubled him, as he stood at the window thinking, was the doubt whether he could persuade Allan to change rooms with him, without involving himself in an explanation which might lead Allan to suspect the truth.

In the minute that elapsed, while he waited with his eyes on the room, the doubt was resolved – he found the trivial, yet sufficient, excuse of which he was in search. Mr Bashwood saw him rouse himself, and go to the door. Mr Bashwood heard him knock softly, and whisper, 'Allan, are you in bed?'

'No,' answered the voice inside, 'come in.'

He appeared to be on the point of entering the room, when he checked himself as if he had suddenly remembered something. 'Wait a minute,' he said, through the door, and, turning away, went straight to the end room. 'If there is anybody watching us in there,' he said aloud, 'let him watch us through this!' He took out his handkerchief, and stuffed it into the wires of the grating, so as completely to close the aperture. Having thus forced the spy inside (if there was one) either to betray himself by moving the handkerchief, or to remain blinded to all view of what might happen next, Midwinter presented himself in Allan's room.

'You know what poor nerves I have,' he said, 'and what a wretched sleeper I am at the best of times. I can't sleep to-night. The window in my room rattles every time the wind blows. I wish it was as fast as your window here.'

'My dear fellow!' cried Allan, 'I don't mind a rattling window. Let's change rooms. Nonsense! Why should you make excuses to *me*? Don't I know how easily trifles upset those excitable nerves of yours? Now the doctor has quieted my mind about my poor little Neelie, I begin to feel the journey – and I'll answer for sleeping anywhere till to-morrow comes.' He took up his travelling-bag. 'We must be quick about it,' he added, pointing to his candle. 'They haven't left me much candle to go to bed by.'

'Be very quiet, Allan,' said Midwinter, opening the door for him. 'We mustn't disturb the house at this time of night.'

'Yes, yes,' returned Allan, in a whisper. 'Good night – I hope you'll sleep as well as I shall.'

Midwinter saw him into Number Three, and noticed that his own candle (which he had left there) was as short as Allan's. 'Good night,' he said, and came out again into the corridor.

He went straight to the grating, and looked and listened once more. The handkerchief remained exactly as he had left it, and still there was no sound to be heard within. He returned slowly along the corridor, and thought of the precautions he had taken, for the last time. Was there no other way than the way he was trying now? There was none. Any openly-avowed posture of defence – while the nature of the danger, and the quarter from which it might come, were alike unknown – would be useless in itself, and worse than useless in the consequences which it might produce by putting the people of the house on their guard. Without a fact that could justify to other minds his distrust of what might happen with the night; incapable of shaking Allan's ready faith in the fair outside which the doctor had presented to him, the one safeguard in his friend's interests that Midwinter could set up, was the safeguard of changing the rooms – the one policy he could follow, come what might of it, was the policy of waiting for events. 'I can trust to one thing,' he said to himself, as he looked for the last time up and down the corridor – 'I can trust myself to keep awake.'

After a glance at the clock on the wall opposite, he went into Number Four. The sound of the closing door was heard, the sound of the turning lock followed it. Then, the dead silence fell over the house once more.

Little by little, the steward's horror of the stillness and the darkness overcame his dread of moving the handkerchief. He cautiously drew aside one corner of it – waited – looked – and took courage at last to draw the whole handkerchief through the wires of the grating. After first hiding it in his pocket, he thought of the consequences if it was found on him, and threw it down in a corner of the room. He trembled when he had cast it from him, as he looked at his watch, and placed himself again at the grating to wait for Miss Gwilt.

It was a quarter to one. The moon had come round from the side to the front of the Sanatorium. From time to time her light gleamed on the window of the corridor, when the gaps in the flying clouds let it through. The wind had risen, and sung its mournful song faintly, as it swept at intervals over the desert ground in front of the house.

The minute-hand of the clock travelled on half-way round the circle of the dial. As it touched the quarter-past one, Miss Gwilt stepped noiselessly into the corridor. 'Let yourself out,' she whispered through the grating, 'and follow me.' She returned to the stairs by which she had just descended; pushed the door to softly, after Mr Bashwood had followed her; and led the way up to the landing of the second-floor. There she put the question to him which she had not ventured to put below stairs.

'Was Mr Armadale shown into Number Four?' she asked.

He bowed his head without speaking.

'Answer me in words. Has Mr Armadale left the room since?'

He answered, 'No.'

'Have you never lost sight of Number Four since I left you?'

He answered, '*Never.*'

Something strange in his manner, something unfamiliar in his voice, as he made that last reply, attracted her attention. She took her candle from a table near, on which she had left it, and threw its light on him. His eyes were staring, his teeth chattered. There was everything to betray him to her as a terrified man – there was nothing to tell her that the terror was caused by his consciousness of deceiving her, for the first time in his life, to her face. If she had threatened him less openly when she placed him on the watch; if she had spoken less unreservedly of the interview which was to reward him in the morning, he might have owned the truth. As it was, his strongest fears and his dearest hopes were alike interested in telling her the fatal lie that he had now told – the fatal lie which he reiterated when she put her question for the second time.

She looked at him, deceived by the last man on earth whom she would have suspected of deception – the man whom she had deceived herself.

'You seem to be over-excited,' she said quietly. 'The night has been too much for you. Go upstairs, and rest. You will find the door of one of the rooms left open. That is the room you are to occupy. Good night.'

She put the candle (which she had left burning for him) on the table, and gave him her hand. He held her back by it desperately as she turned to leave him. His horror of what might happen when she was left by herself, forced the words to his lips which he would have feared to speak to her at any other time.

'Don't,' he pleaded in a whisper; 'oh, don't, don't, don't go downstairs to-night!'

She released her hand, and signed to him to take the candle. 'You shall see me to-morrow,' she said. 'Not a word more now!'

Her stronger will conquered him at that last moment, as it had conquered him throughout. He took the candle, and waited – following her eagerly with his eyes as she descended the stairs. The cold of the December night seemed to have found its way to her through the warmth of the house. She had put on a long heavy black shawl, and had fastened it close over her breast. The plaited coronet in which she wore her hair seemed to have weighed too heavily on her head. She had untwisted it, and thrown it back over her shoulders. The old man looked at her flowing hair, as it lay red over the black shawl – at her supple, long-fingered hand, as it slid down the banisters – at the smooth, seductive grace of every movement that took her farther and farther away from him. 'The night will go quickly,' he said to himself as she passed from his view; 'I shall dream of her till the morning comes!'

She secured the staircase door, after she had passed through it – listened, and satisfied herself that nothing was stirring – then went on slowly along the corridor to the window. Leaning on the window-sill, she looked out at the night. The clouds were over the moon at that moment; nothing was to be seen through the darkness but the scattered gaslights in the suburb. Turning from the window, she looked at the clock. It was twenty minutes past one.

For the last time, the resolution that had come to her in the earlier night, with the knowledge that her husband was in the house, forced itself uppermost in her mind. For the last time, the voice within her said, 'Think if there is no other way!'

She pondered over it till the minute-hand of the clock pointed to the half-hour. 'No!' she said, still thinking of her husband. 'The one chance left, is to go through with it to the end. He will leave the thing undone which he has come here to do; he will leave the words unspoken which he has come here to say – when he knows that the act may make me a public scandal, and that the words may send me to the scaffold!' Her colour rose, and she smiled with a terrible irony as she looked for the first time at the door of the Room. 'I shall be your widow,' she said, 'in half-an-hour!'

She opened the case of the apparatus, and took the Purple Flask in her hand. After marking the time by a glance at the clock, she dropped into the glass funnel the first of the six separate Pourings that were measured for her by the paper slips.

When she had put the Flask back, she listened at the mouth of the funnel. Not a sound reached her ear: the deadly process did its work, in the silence of death itself. When she rose, and looked up, the moon was shining in at the window, and the moaning wind was quiet.

Oh, the time! the time! If it could only have been begun and ended with the first Pouring!

She went downstairs into the hall – she walked to and fro, and listened at the open door that led to the kitchen stairs. She came up again; she went down again. The first of the intervals of five minutes was endless. The time stood still. The suspense was maddening.

The interval passed. As she took the Flask for the second time, and dropped in the second Pouring, the clouds floated over the moon, and the night-view through the window slowly darkened.

The restlessness that had driven her up and down the stairs, and backwards and forwards in the hall, left her as suddenly as it had come. She waited through the second interval, leaning on the window-sill, and staring, without conscious thought of any kind, into the black night. The howling of a belated dog was borne towards her on the wind, at intervals, from some distant part of the suburb. She found herself following the faint sound as it died away into silence with a dull attention, and listening for its coming again with an expectation that was duller still. Her arms lay like lead on the window-sill; her forehead rested against the glass without feeling the cold. It was not till the moon struggled out again that she was startled into sudden self-remembrance. She turned quickly, and looked at the clock; seven minutes had passed since the second Pouring.

As she snatched up the Flask, and fed the funnel for the third time, the full consciousness of her position came back to her. The fever-heat throbbed again in her blood, and flushed fiercely in her cheeks. Swift, smooth, and noiseless, she paced from end to end of the corridor, with her arms folded in her shawl, and her eye moment after moment on the clock.

Three out of the next five minutes passed, and again the suspense began to madden her. The space in the corridor grew too confined for the illimitable restlessness that possessed her limbs. She went down into the hall again, and circled round and round it like a wild creature in a cage. At the third turn, she felt something moving softly against her dress. The house-cat had come up through the open kitchen-door – a large, tawny, companionable cat that purred in high good temper, and followed her for company. She took the animal up in her arms – it rubbed its sleek head luxuriously against her chin as she bent her face over it. 'Armadale hates cats,' she whispered in the creature's ear. 'Come up and see Armadale killed!' The next moment her own frightful fancy horrified her. She dropped the cat with a shudder; she drove it below again with threatening hands. For a moment after, she stood still – then, in headlong haste, suddenly mounted the stairs. Her husband had forced his way back again into her thoughts; her husband threatened her with a danger which had never entered her mind till now. What, if he were not asleep? What if he came out upon her, and found her with the Purple Flask in her hand?

She stole to the door of number three, and listened. The slow, regular breathing of a sleeping man was just audible. After waiting a moment to let the feeling of relief quiet her, she took a step towards Number Four – and checked herself. It was needless to listen at *that* door. The doctor had told her that Sleep came first, as certainly as Death afterwards, in the poisoned air. She looked aside at the clock. The time had come for the fourth Pouring.

Her hand began to tremble violently, as she fed the funnel for the fourth time. The fear of her husband was back again in her heart. What if some noise disturbed him before the sixth Pouring? What if he woke on a sudden (as she had often seen him wake) without any noise at all?

She looked up and down the corridor. The end room, in which Mr Bashwood had been concealed, offered itself to her as a place of refuge. 'I might go in there!' she thought. 'Has he left the key?' She opened the door to look, and saw the handkerchief thrown down on the floor. Was it Mr Bashwood's handkerchief, left there by accident? She examined it at the corners. In the second corner she found her husband's name!

Her first impulse hurried her to the staircase-door, to rouse the steward, and insist on an explanation. The next moment, she remembered the Purple Flask, and the danger of leaving the corridor. She turned, and looked at the door of number three. Her husband, on the evidence of the handkerchief, had unquestionably been out of his room – and Mr Bashwood had not told her. Was he in his room now? In the violence of her agitation, as the question passed through her mind, she forgot the discovery which she had herself made not a minute before. Again, she listened at the door; again, she heard the slow regular breathing of the sleeping man. The first time, the evidence of her ears had been enough to quiet her. *This* time, in the tenfold aggravation of her suspicion and her alarm, she was determined to have the evidence of her eyes as well. 'All the doors open softly in this house,' she said to herself; 'there's no fear of my waking him.' Noiselessly, by an inch at a time, she opened the unlocked door, and looked in the moment the aperture was wide enough. In the little light she had let into the room, the sleeper's head was just visible on the pillow. Was it quite as dark against the white pillow as her husband's head looked when he was in bed? Was the breathing as light as her husband's breathing when he was asleep?

She opened the door more widely, and looked in by the clearer light.

There lay the man whose life she had attempted for the third time, peacefully sleeping in the room that had been given to her husband, and in the air that could harm nobody!

The inevitable conclusion overwhelmed her on the instant. With a frantic upward action of her hands she staggered back into the passage. The door of Allan's room fell to – but not noisily enough to wake him. She turned as she heard it close. For one moment she stood staring at it like a woman stupefied. The next, her instinct rushed into action, before her reason recovered itself. In two steps she was at the door of Number Four.

The door was locked.

She felt over the wall with both hands, wildly and clumsily, for the button which she had seen the doctor press, when he was showing the room to the visitors. Twice she missed it. The third time her eyes helped her hands – she found the button and pressed on it. The mortice of the lock inside fell back, and the door yielded to her.

Without an instant's hesitation she entered the room. Though the door was open – though so short a time had elapsed since the fourth Pouring, that but little more than half the contemplated volume of gas had been produced as yet – the poisoned air seized her, like the grasp of a hand at her throat, like the twisting of a wire round her head. She found him on the floor at the foot of the bed – his head and one arm were towards the door, as if he had risen under the first feeling of drowsiness, and had sunk in the effort to leave the room. With the desperate concentration of strength of which women are capable in emergencies, she lifted him and dragged him out into the corridor. Her brain reeled as she laid him down and crawled back on her knees to the room, to shut out the poisoned air from pursuing them into the passage. After closing the door, she waited, without daring to look at him the while, for strength enough to rise and get to the window over the stairs. When the window was opened, when the keen air of the early winter morning blew steadily in, she ventured back to him and raised his head, and looked for the first time closely at his face.

Was it death that spread the livid pallor over his forehead and his cheeks, and the dull leaden hue on his eyelids and his lips?

She loosened his cravat and opened his waistcoat, and bared his throat and breast to the air. With her hand on his heart, with her bosom supporting his head, so that he fronted the window, she waited the event. A time passed: a time short enough to be reckoned by minutes on the clock; and yet long enough to take her memory back over all her married life with him – long enough to mature the resolution that now rose in her mind as the one result that could come of the retrospect. As her eyes rested on him, a strange composure settled slowly on her face. She bore the look of a woman who was equally resigned to welcome the chance of his recovery, or to accept the certainty of his death.

Not a cry or a tear had escaped her yet. Not a cry or a tear escaped her when the interval had passed, and she felt the first faint fluttering of his heart, and heard the first faint catching of the breath at his lips. She silently bent over him and kissed his forehead. When she looked up again, the hard despair had melted from her face. There was something softly radiant in her eyes, which lit her whole countenance as with an inner light, and made her womanly and lovely once more.

She laid him down, and, taking off her shawl, made a pillow of it to support his head. 'It might have been hard, love,' she said, as she felt the faint pulsation strengthening at his heart. 'You have made it easy now.'

She rose, and, turning from him, noticed the Purple Flask in the place where she had left it since the fourth Pouring. 'Ah,' she thought quietly, 'I had forgotten my best friend – I had forgotten that there is more to pour in yet.'

With a steady hand, with a calm, attentive face, she fed the funnel for the fifth time. 'Five minutes more,' she said, when she had put the Flask back, after a look at the clock.

She fell into thought – thought that only deepened the grave and gentle composure of her face. 'Shall I write him a farewell word?' she asked herself. 'Shall I tell him the truth before I leave him for ever?'

Her little gold pencil-case hung with the other toys at her watch-chain. After looking about her for a moment, she knelt over her husband, and put her hand into the breast-pocket of his coat.

His pocket-book was there. Some papers fell from it as she unfastened the clasp. One of them was the letter which had come to him from Mr Brock's death-bed. She turned over the two sheets of note-paper on which the rector had written the words that had now come true – and found the last page of the last sheet a blank. On that page she wrote her farewell words, kneeling at her husband's side.

I am worse than the worst you can think of me. You have saved Armadale by changing rooms with him to-night – and you have saved him from Me. You can guess now whose widow I should have claimed to be, if you had not preserved his life; and you will know what a wretch you married when you married the woman who writes these lines. Still, I had some innocent moments – and then I loved you dearly. Forget me, my darling, in the love of a better woman than I am. I might, perhaps, have been that better woman myself, if I had not lived a miserable life before you met with me. It matters little now. The one atonement I can make for all the wrong I have done you is the atonement of my death. It is not hard for me to die, now I know you will live. Even my wickedness has one merit – it has not prospered. I have never been a happy woman.'[7]

She folded the letter again, and put it into his hand, to attract his attention in that way when he came to himself. As she gently closed his fingers on the paper and looked up, the last minute of the last interval faced her, recorded on the clock.

She bent over him, and gave him her farewell kiss.

'Live, my angel, live!' she murmured tenderly, with her lips just touching his. 'All your life is before you – a happy life, and an honoured life, if you are freed from *me*!'

With a last, lingering tenderness, she parted the hair back from his forehead. 'It is no merit to have loved you,' she said. 'You are one of the men whom women all like.' She sighed and left him. It was her last weakness. She bent her head affirmatively to the clock, as if it had been a living creature speaking to her – and fed the funnel for the last time, to the last drop left in the Flask.

The waning moon shone in faintly at the window. With her hand on the door of the room, she turned and looked at the light that was slowly fading out of the murky sky.

'Oh, God, forgive me!' she said. 'Oh, Christ, bear witness that I have suffered!'

One moment more she lingered on the threshold; lingered for her last look in this world – and turned that look on *him*.

'Good-by!' she said softly.

The door of the room opened – and closed on her. There was an interval of silence.

Then, a sound came dull and sudden, like the sound of a fall.

Then, there was silence again.

The hands of the clock, following their steady course, reckoned the minutes of the morning as one by one they lapsed away. It was the tenth minute since the door of the room had opened and closed, before Midwinter stirred on his pillow, and, struggling to raise himself, felt the letter in his hand.

At the same moment, a key was turned in the staircase-door. And the doctor, looking expectantly towards the fatal room, saw the Purple Flask on the window-sill, and the prostrate man trying to raise himself from the floor.

THE END OF THE LAST BOOK

EPILOGUE

CHAPTER I

NEWS FROM NOROLK

From Mr Pedgift Senior (Thorpe-Ambrose) to Mr Pedgift Junior (Paris)

High Street, December 20th.

MY DEAR AUGUSTUS, Your letter reached me yesterday. You seem to be making the most of your youth (as you call it) with a vengeance. Well! enjoy your holiday. I made the most of my youth, when I was your age; and, wonderful to relate, I haven't forgotten it yet!

You ask me for a good budget of news, and especially, for more information about that mysterious business at the Sanatorium.

Curiosity, my dear boy, is a quality, which (in our profession especially) sometimes leads to great results. I doubt, however, if you will find it leading to much on this occasion. All I know of the mystery at the Sanatorium, I know from Mr Armadale; and he is entirely in the dark on more than one point of importance. I have already told you how they were entrapped into the house, and how they passed the night there. To this I can now add that something did certainly happen to Mr Midwinter, which deprived him of consciousness; and that the doctor, who appears to have been mixed up in the matter, carried things with a high hand, and insisted on taking his own course in his own Sanatorium. There is not the least doubt that the miserable woman (however she might have come by her death) was found dead – that a coroner's inquest inquired into the circumstances – that the evidence showed her to have entered the house as a patient – and that the medical investigation ended in discovering that she had died of apoplexy. My idea is, that Mr Midwinter had a motive of his own for not coming forward with the evidence that he might have given. I have also reason to suspect that Mr Armadale, out of regard for him, followed his lead, and that the verdict at the inquest (attaching no blame to anybody), proceeded, like many other verdicts of the same kind, from an entirely superficial investigation of the circumstances.

The key to the whole mystery is to be found, I firmly believe, in that wretched woman's attempt to personate the character of Mr Armadale's widow, when the news of his death appeared in the papers. But what first set her on this, and by what inconceivable process of deception, she can have induced Mr Midwinter to marry her (as the certificate proves), under Mr Armadale's name, is more than Mr Armadale himself knows. The point was not touched at the inquest, for the simple reason that the inquest only concerned itself with the circumstances attending her death. Mr Armadale, at his friend's request, saw Miss Blanchard, and induced her to silence old Darch on the subject of the claim that had been made relating to the widow's income. As the claim had never been admitted, even our stiff-necked brother practitioner consented for once to do as he was asked. The doctor's statement that his patient was the widow of a gentleman named Armadale, was accordingly left unchallenged, and so the matter has been hushed up. She is buried in the great cemetery, near the place where she died. Nobody but Mr Midwinter and Mr Armadale (who insisted on going with him), followed her to the grave; and nothing has been inscribed on the tombstone, but the initial letter of her Christian name, and the date of her death. So, after all the harm she has done, she rests at last – and so the two men whom she has injured have forgiven her.

Is there more to say on this subject before we leave it? On referring to your letter, I find you have raised one other point, which may be worth a moment's notice.

You ask if there is reason to suppose that the doctor comes out of the matter with hands which are really as clean as they look? My dear Augustus, I believe the doctor to have been at the bottom of more of this mischief than we shall ever find out; and to have profited by the self-imposed silence of Mr Midwinter and Mr Armadale, as rogues perpetually profit by the misfortunes and necessities of honest men. It is an ascertained fact that he connived at the false statement about Miss Milroy, which entrapped the two gentlemen into his house, – and that one circumstance (after my Old Bailey experience) is enough for *me*. As to evidence against him, there is not a jot, – and as to Retribution overtaking him, I can only say I heartily hope Retribution may prove in the long run to be the more cunning customer of the two. There is not much prospect of it at present. The doctor's friends and admirers are, I understand, about to present him with a Testimonial, 'expressive of their sympathy under the sad occurrence which has thrown a cloud over the opening of his Sanatorium, and of their undiminished confidence in his integrity and ability as a medical man.' We live, Augustus, in an age eminently favourable to the growth of all roguery which is careful enough to keep up appearances. In this enlightened nineteenth century, I look upon the doctor as one of our rising men.

To turn now to pleasanter subjects than Sanatoriums, I may tell you that Miss Neelie is as good as well again, and is, in my humble opinion, prettier than ever. She is staying in London, under the care of a female relative – and Mr Armadale satisfies her of the fact of his existence (in case she should forget it) regularly every day. They are to be married in the spring – unless Mrs Milroy's death causes the ceremony to be postponed. The medical men are of opinion that the poor lady is sinking at last. It may be a question of weeks or a question of months, they can say no more. She is greatly altered – quiet and gentle, and anxiously affectionate with her husband and her child. But, in her case, this happy change is, it seems, a sign of approaching dissolution, from the medical point of view. There is a difficulty in making the poor old major understand this. He only sees that she has gone back to the likeness of her better self when he first married her; and he sits for hours by her bedside, now, and tells her about his wonderful clock.

Mr Midwinter, of whom you will next expect me to say something, is improving rapidly. After causing some anxiety at first to the medical men (who declared that he was suffering from a serious nervous shock, produced by circumstances about which their patient's obstinate silence kept them quite in the dark), he has rallied, as only men of his sensitive temperament (to quote the doctors again) *can* rally. He and Mr Armadale are together in a quiet lodging. I saw him last week, when I was in London. His face showed signs of wear and tear, very sad to see in so young a man. But he spoke of himself and his future with a courage and hopefulness, which men of twice his years (if he has suffered, as I suspect him to have suffered) might have envied. If I know anything of humanity, this is no common man – and we shall hear of him yet in no common way.

You will wonder how I came to be in London. I went up, with a return ticket (from Saturday to Monday) about that matter in dispute at our agent's. We had a tough fight – but, curiously enough, a point occurred to me just as I got up to go; and I went back to my chair, and settled the question in no time. Of course I stayed at Our Hotel in Covent Garden. William, the waiter, asked after you with the affection of a father; and Matilda, the chambermaid, said you almost persuaded her, that last time, to have the hollow tooth taken out of her lower jaw. I had the agent's second son (the young chap you nicknamed Mustapha, when he made that dreadful mess about the Turkish Securities) to dine with me on Sunday. A little incident happened in the evening which may be worth recording, as it connected itself with a certain old lady, who was not 'at home' when you and Mr Armadale blundered on that house in Pimlico in the bygone time.

Mustapha was like all the rest of you young men of the present day – he got restless after dinner. 'Let's go to a public amusement, Mr Pedgift,' says he. 'Public amusement? Why, it's Sunday evening!' says I. 'All right, sir,' says Mustapha. 'They stop acting on the stage, I grant you, on Sunday evening – but they don't stop acting in the pulpit. Come and see the last new Sunday performer of our time.' As he wouldn't have any more wine, there was nothing else for it, but to go.

We went to a street at the West End, and found it blocked up with carriages. If it hadn't been Sunday night, I should have thought we were going to the opera. 'What did I tell you?' says Mustapha, taking me up to an open door with a gas star outside and a bill of the performance. I had just time to notice that I was going to one of a series of 'Sunday Evening Discourses on the Pomps and Vanities of the World, by A Sinner Who Has Served Them,' when Mustapha jogged my elbow, and whispered, 'Half-a-crown is the fashionable tip.' I found myself between two demure and silent gentlemen, with plates in their hands, un-commonly well-filled already with the fashionable tip. Mustapha patronized one plate, and I the other. We passed through two doors into a long room, crammed with people. And there, on a platform at the farther end holding forth to the audience, was – not a man as I had expected – but a Woman, and that woman, MOTHER OLDERSHAW! You never listened to anything more eloquent in your life. As long as I heard her she was never once at a loss for a word anywhere. I shall think less of oratory as a human accomplishment, for the rest of my days, after that Sunday evening. As for the matter of the sermon, I may describe it as a narrative of Mrs Oldershaw's experience among dilapidated women, profusely illustrated in the pious and penitential style. You will ask what sort of audience it was. Principally women, Augustus – and, as I hope to be saved, all the old harridans of the world of fashion, whom Mother Oldershaw had enamelled in her time, sitting boldly in the front places, with their cheeks ruddled with paint, in a state of devout enjoyment wonderful to see! I left Mustapha to hear the end of it. And I thought to myself, as I went out, of what Shakespeare says somewhere, – 'Lord, what fools we mortals be!'

Have I anything more to tell you, before I leave off? Only one thing that I can remember.

That wretched old Bashwood has confirmed the fears I told you I had about him, when he was brought back here from London. There is no kind of doubt that he has really lost all the little reason he ever had. He is perfectly harmless, and perfectly happy. And he would do very well, if we could only prevent him from going out in his last new suit of clothes, smirking and smiling, and inviting everybody to his approaching marriage with the handsomest woman in England. It ends of course in the boys pelting him, and in his coming here crying to me, covered with mud. The moment his clothes are cleaned again, he falls back into his favourite delusion, and struts about before the church gates, in the character of a bridegroom, waiting for Miss Gwilt. We must get the poor wretch taken care of somewhere for the rest of the little time he has to live. Who would ever have thought of a man at his age falling in love? and who would ever have believed that the mischief that woman's beauty has done, could have reached as far in the downward direction as our superannuated old clerk?

Good-by, for the present, my dear boy. If you see a particularly handsome snuff-box in Paris, remember – though your father scorns Testimonials – he doesn't object to receive a present from his son.

Yours affectionately,
A. PEDGIFT Senr.

POSTSCRIPT. – I think it likely that the account you mention, in the French papers, of a fatal quarrel among some foreign sailors in one of the Lipari Islands, and of the death of their captain, among others, may really have been a quarrel among the scoundrels who robbed Mr Armadale, and scuttled his yacht.

Those fellows, luckily for society, can't always keep up appearances; and, in their case, Rogues and Retribution do occasionally come into collision with each other.[1]

CHAPTER II

MIDWINTER

The spring had advanced to the end of April. It was the eve of Allan's wedding-day. Midwinter and he had sat talking together at the great house till far into the night – till so far that it had struck twelve long since, and the wedding-day was already some hours old.

For the most part, the conversation had turned on the bridegroom's plans and projects. It was not till the two friends rose to go to rest, that Allan insisted on making Midwinter speak of himself. 'We have had enough, and more than enough, of *my* future,' he began, in his bluntly straightforward way. 'Let's say something now, Midwinter, about yours. You have promised me, I know, that if you take to Literature, it shan't part us, and that if you go on a sea voyage, you will remember when you come back that my house is your home. But this is the last chance we have of being together in our old way; and I own I should like to know—' His voice faltered, and his eyes moistened a little. He left the sentence unfinished.

Midwinter took his hand and helped him, as he had often helped him to the words that he wanted, in the bygone time.

'You would like to know, Allan,' he said, 'that I shall not bring an aching heart with me to your wedding-day? If you will let me go back for a moment to the past, I think I can satisfy you.'

They took their chairs again. Allan saw that Midwinter was moved. 'Why distress yourself?' he asked kindly – 'why go back to the past!'

'For two reasons, Allan. I ought to have thanked you long since for the silence you have observed, for my sake, on a matter that must have seemed very strange to you. You know what the name is which appears on the register of my marriage – and yet you have forborne to speak of it, from the fear of distressing me. Before you enter on your new life, let us come to a first and last understanding about this. I ask you – as one more kindness to me – to accept my assurance (strange as the thing must seem to you) that I am blameless in this matter; and I entreat you to believe that the reasons I have for leaving it unexplained, are reasons which, if Mr Brock was living, Mr Brock himself would approve.'

In those words, he kept the secret of the two names – and left the memory of Allan's mother, what he had found it, a sacred memory in the heart of her son.

'One word more,' he went on – 'a word which will take us, this time, from past to future. It has been said, and truly said, that out of Evil may come Good. Out of the horror and the misery of that night you know of, has come the silencing of a doubt which once made my life miserable with groundless anxiety about you and about myself. No clouds, raised by my superstition, will ever come between us again. I can't honestly tell you that I am more willing now than I was when we were in the Isle of Man, to take what is called the rational view of your Dream. Though I know what extraordinary coincidences are perpetually happening in the experience of all of us, still I cannot accept coincidences as explaining the fulfilment of the Visions which our own eyes have seen. All I can sincerely say for myself is, what I think it will satisfy you to know, that I have learnt to view the purpose of the Dream with a new mind. I once believed that it was sent to rouse your distrust of the friendless man whom you had taken as a brother to your heart. I now *know* that it came to you as a timely warning to take him closer still. Does this help to satisfy you that I, too, am standing hopefully on the brink of a new life, and that while we live, brother, your love and mine will never be divided again?'

They shook hands in silence. Allan was the first to recover himself. He answered in the few words of kindly assurance which were the best words that he could address to his friend.

'I have heard all I ever want to hear about the past,' he said; 'and I know what I most wanted to know about the future. Everybody says, Midwinter, you have a career before you – and I believe that everybody is right. Who knows what great things may happen before you and I are many years older?'

'Who *need* know?' said Midwinter, calmly. 'Happen what may, God is all-merciful, God is all-wise. In those words, your dear old friend once wrote to me. In that faith, I can look back without murmuring at the years that are past, and can look on without doubting to the years that are to come.'

He rose, and walked to the window. While they had been speaking together, the darkness had passed. The first light of the new day met him as he looked out, and rested tenderly on his face.

THE END

APPENDIX

NOTE. – My readers will perceive that I have purposely left them, with reference to the Dream in this story, in the position which they would occupy in the case of a dream in real life – they are free to interpret it by the natural or the supernatural theory, as the bent of their own minds may incline them. Persons disposed to take the rational view may, under these circumstances, be interested in hearing of a coincidence relating to the present story, which actually happened, and which in the matter of 'extravagant improbability', sets anything of the same kind that a novelist could imagine at flat defiance.

In November, 1865, – that is to say, when thirteen monthly parts of 'Armadale' had been published; and, I may add, when more than a year and a half had elapsed since the end of the story, as it now appears, was first sketched in my note-book – a vessel lay in the Huskisson Dock, at Liverpool, which was looked after by one man who slept on board, in the capacity of shipkeeper. On a certain day in the week, this man was found dead in the deck-house. On the next day, a second man, who had taken his place, was carried dying to the Northern Hospital. On the third day, a third shipkeeper was appointed, and was found dead in the deck-house which had already proved fatal to the other two. *The name of that ship was 'The Armadale'.* And the proceedings at the Inquest proved that the three men had been all suffocated *by sleeping in poisoned air!*[1]

I am indebted for these particulars to the kindness of the reporters at Liverpool, who sent me their statement of the facts. The case found its way into most of the newspapers. It was noticed – to give two instances in which I can cite the dates – in *The Times* of November 30th, 1865, and was more fully described in the *Daily News* of November 28th in the same year.

Before taking leave of 'Armadale', I may perhaps be allowed to mention for the benefit of any readers who may be curious on such points, that the 'Norfolk Broads' are here described after personal investigation in them. In this, as in other cases, I have spared no pains to instruct myself on matters of fact. Wherever the story touches on questions connected with Law, Medicine, or Chemistry, it has been submitted, before publication, to the experience of professional men. The kindness of a friend[2] supplied me with a plan of the Doctor's Apparatus – and I saw the chemical ingredients at work, before I ventured on describing the action of them in the closing scenes of this book.

NOTES

In these notes I make frequent use of Richard D. Altick's *The Presence of the Present* (Columbus: Ohio, 1991). References are abbreviated to the author's name. As in the Introduction I have abbreviated references to the principal biographical sources.

DEDICATION

1. *To John Forster.* John Forster (1812–76) was the author of a life of Goldsmith (1854) and was to be Dickens's biographer (1874). He was at this stage a friend of Collins's through Dickens and their mutual work in amateur theatricals. Forster was also a Commissioner in Lunacy (1861–72) and may well have provided Collins with some of the details for Dr Downward's sanatorium. Robinson (p. 190) assumes this dedication was in the nature of an 'olive branch' which Forster (who was envious of Collins's intimacy with Dickens in the 1850s) small-mindedly declined.

FOREWORD

1. This preface bears witness to a certain nervousness on Collins's part on the grounds of (1) hastiness of construction, and (2) immorality. The *Saturday Review* (16 June 1866) found it 'a little alarming to find Mr Wilkie Collins employed in heaving stones at imaginary reviewers before any of them have come in sight'.

2. *in more than one direction.* Collins first wrote, then crossed out, 'in all directions' – which was probably too aggressive.

BOOK THE FIRST

Chapter I

1. At the head of the first page of the manuscript is the note: 'First monthly part of Wilkie Collins's new story. No title decided on as yet.' The title was not in fact decided on until the third monthly part. Armadale is the name of a village in the Shetlands and, as Catherine Peters points out, the name was probably put in Collins's mind by a visit there which he made in 1842 (Peters, p. 59).

2. *the Baths of* WILDBAD. Collins visited this spa in summer 1863 for relief from his 'rheumatic gout'. As Robinson records:

> After a month [at Aix], though somewhat better in health, Wilkie was far from cured, and decided to move on to Wildbad. Situated by a mountain stream in the heart of the Black Forest, this little town, hardly more than a village, was dominated by palatial hotels and 'a Bath House as big as Buckingham Palace, and infinitely superior to it in architectural beauty'. It was strange, he reflected, to see all this magnificence, 'and stranger still to think that some of the acutest forms of human misery represent the dismal foundation on which the luxury and grandeur are built. Paralysis comes here and pays the bills . . . Here he underwent a month's course of a bath a day, which roused every lurking ache and pain . . . He left for home about the middle of June 1863, unquestionably better and on the road, I hope, to recovery at last'. It was a vain hope. (Robinson, pp. 177-8)

3. *Der Freischutz.* The opera by Carl Maria von Weber (1821). Altick notes this as a precise [1832] dating reference, culturally (Altick, p. 471).

4. *Death-in-Life.* An allusion to Coleridge's *Ancient Mariner*, Part Three, 'The Nightmare, Life-in-Death was she/ Who thicks man's blood with cold'. As Catherine Peters notes, the clear inference is that Armadale is dying of tertiary syphilis.

Chapter II

1. *replied the doctor, still vacillating between.* The manuscript has 'still preoccupied; still vacillating between' – probably a printer's error.

2. *rheumatic affection of the ankle-joint.* Collins's own affliction in Wildbad in 1863 (see Davis, p. 239).

3. *my own personal experience.* The manuscript continues:

> 'It may save your time and mine,' interrupted Mr Neal, 'if I remind you that I am quite ignorant of medical matters. Don't suppose I am at all importunate. I am only anxious to spare you unnecessary trouble.' With that explanation of his motive he sighed and resigned himself into his visitor's hands. 'I propose not to trouble you with professional mysteries,' said the doctor, 'I only wish to tell you what it is necessary to my purpose in coming here that you should know. In plain words Mr Armadale has been sent to Wildbad too late . . .

This was cut in proof, presumably, with the intention of making Neal's character less garrulous. Originally, the Scottish lawyer was evidently intended to have a much larger role in the novel as Ozias's wicked, Calvinistic stepfather. Collins

NOTES TO P. 15

may have been induced to close this line of development by George Smith's Scottish evangelical susceptibilities. As revised, Neal is a much more sympathetic character.

4. *and disease of the lower part of the spine has already taken place.* The manuscript reads, 'and congestion of the vessels about the lower part of the spine has already set in'. This was presumably changed in proof. Collins records that he corroborated medical and legal references with professional friends.

5. *which I despair of describing to you.* The manuscript continues:

> The Scotchman's cold grey eyes began to brighten with a growing interest. 'The scriptures have described it,' he broke out, warming to the subject for the first time. 'A man's terror may well overpower him, when he feels a taste of the worm that dieth not, and the fire that is not quenched! I am not a minister of the gospel, sir, as you appear to suppose. But I am an Elder of the Presbyterian Church of Scotland and I can well understand that spiritual help for a foreigner may be hard of attainment here. If there is no-one else to warn this dying sinner that his soul is in danger—.' 'You entirely mistake the nature of the request which I am making on Mr Armadale's behalf,' interposed the doctor more resolutely and more seriously than he had spoken yet. 'If you allow me to proceed I should have shown you that the fever of anxiety which is consuming this unhappy man in his last moments is not anxiety which the ministrations of a clergyman can allay. Give me one other minute of your patience, sir, and you will discover what the serious emergency that brings us here really is.'
>
> The ice reappeared in Mr Neal's face and manner more obstructively than ever. He objected to being put in the wrong by anybody; and he resented the absence of a strictly religious interest from a case which had been brought under his notice on strictly religious grounds. At the very point of the doctor's disclosures which would have stimulated all imaginative hearers to listen with the closest attention, the Scotchman's interest in the narrative began to ebb again steadily. He sighed in sullen protest, and resigned himself for the second time.
>
> 'You shall have the very words that passed between us,' said the doctor – 'I can hardly expect you to believe me, unless I report the words themselves. I took the liberty of asking Mr Armadale whether his affairs were unsettled . . .

This was deleted in proof, presumably. Kenneth Robinson notes (p. 180) that in 1863 Collins was invited to edit the new Scottish Evangelical magazine, *Good Words*. On the evidence of the above passage he would have been extremely unsuitable, had he been unwise enough to accept.

Chapter III

1. *a Writer to the Signet in Edinburgh.* The highest branch of the Scottish solicitors' profession.

2. *the marriage of an English lady of my acquaintance, in the island of Madeira.* The manuscript reads 'of Miss Jane Blanchard of Thorpe-Ambrose in Yorkshire'. This was presumably changed in proof, to fit in with changes made while writing the later part of the chapter (in which the wedding is made to take place in Madeira). One can plausibly speculate what put Yorkshire (rather than Norfolk) in Collins's mind as the county in which the 'great house' of Thorpe-Ambrose is located. As W. M. Clarke records: 'Wilkie's exploration of the Broads [in summer 1864, as research for *Armadale*] was interrupted by a brief trip to the Monckton-Milnes at Fryston hall in Yorkshire. Wilkie had known them for some years and was occasionally invited up for the weekend. He later described his host's house as "delightfully comfortable, with palatial rooms, a fine park, and perpetual company"' (Clarke, p. 111).

3. *more than one woman on the island whom I had wronged beyond all forgiveness.* He implies that some discarded lover has poisoned him. For the 1860s fascination with domestic poisoners (especially women) see Altick, p. 525.

4. *barely twelve years old.* Forgery was a capital offence in 1832. Ingleby evidently reasoned that, if caught, the law would be lenient on the twelve-year-old Lydia.

5. *Duelling had its received formalities . . . those days.* Duelling was largely abolished in England in the 1840s. The campaign against it was led by Prince Albert.

6. *a contemplated emancipation of the slaves.* There were uprisings in the West Indies in 1831 (the slaves mistakenly believing they had already been emancipated) with some loss of life among the white planters and much destruction of property. Emancipation followed two years later in 1833, and the process was completed in 1838. This, and the abolition of protection duty for Jamaica sugar in 1846, led to the collapse of the island's economy.

7. *on the Devonshire coast.* The manuscript has 'on the English coast'.

8. *changed no more.* Collins particularly wanted a funereal black line after 'changed no more'. This is one of the few occasions on which his instructions to the printer were overridden.

BOOK THE SECOND

Chapter I

1. *eighteen hundred and fifty-one.* The plot takes place in this pivotal year of Victoria's reign. But as Altick notes, specific references to the year are minimal (there is one reference to the Great Exhibition, see Book the Fourth, Chapter

IV, note 1). Catherine Peters plausibly suggests that the novel should be assumed to be taking place in the early 1860s.

2. *to say to him.* The manuscript continues:

> Mrs Armadale opened the proceedings by following the wise precedent established by her sex, on all occasions when they stand in need of a man to help them. She put herself in the first place, and kept her business waiting behind her.

This was deleted in proof, apparently.

3. *If Mrs Armadale . . . the responsibility of the son.* This paragraph was added at the proof stage.

4. *O. M.* The manuscript has 'O. M. 1846'. For the significance of the texts, see the Introduction.

5. *the yacht . . . doesn't eat up everything.* See Kenneth Robinson: 'In August 1864 [Wilkie Collins] was in Norfolk "studying localities" for *Armadale*, and taking time off to go sailing with Charles Ward and Pigott. About this time he was contemplating the purchase of a boat of his own, but never in fact acquired one' (Robinson, p. 187).

6. *socialist doctrines to a clergyman.* There were indeed socialist clergymen ('Christian Socialists') like F. D. Maurice and Charles Kingsley in the late 1840s, early 1850s. Collins wants the reader to understand that Brock is not one of their disreputable party.

7. *his tangled black beard.* Thus in the manuscript and the first edition of *Armadale*. Subsequent editions have 'rough black beard' because the illustrator, George Thomas, depicted Ozias with a very scanty growth on his face. Thomas may not have had proofs early enough to reflect Collins's description accurately.

8. *in a country town.* The manuscript has 'in a northern town'.

9. *the launch of the yacht.* The manuscript continues:

> On other occasions they had diverged to other subjects – among the rest the question how 'my friend Midwinter' (as Allan described him) was to get his living for the future. 'My friend Midwinter' was to make a new start as a sculptor; he was to begin (having a wonderful knack at catching likenesses in clay) by modelling a little portrait statue of Allan, which was to be kept a secret till it was done and was then to be made a present to Allan's mother. Nobody but a good fellow would have made such a proposal as that. What more did Mr Brock want to know about him? His relations? He had said nothing about his relations – except that they had not behaved well to him . . .

This was changed in proof, presumably. With the deletion Ozias's sculptural talents are removed from the novel. Clearly, he was originally intended to fashion the statuette in Allan's dream that symbolically breaks later in the action (see pp. 142, 398).

10. *wearing a gown and bonnet of black silk and a red Paisley shawl.* This sentence was added in proof. These articles of clothing are to feature significantly later as hallmark clues to Lydia Gwilt's identity (see p. 79).

11. *and had got it.* The manuscript continues:

> but the money mattered nothing. Was it long since Mrs Armadale had seen her last? Yes; as long as all Allan's lifetime – as long as one and twenty years.

The 1866 reprint reads:

> but the money was of no importance; the one thing needful was to get away before the woman came again. More and more surprised, Mr Brock ventured on another question. Was it long since Mrs Armadale and her visitor had last met? Yes; longer than all Allan's lifetime – as long ago as the year before Allan was born.

Collins evidently felt he had to be careful about dates here.

12. *Did she remain under your father's care?* The manuscript reads:

> 'Did your father bring her up?'
> 'I brought her up – I took her with me when we left England for Madeira. I had my father's leave . . .'

13. *continental travelling.* The manuscript reveals that Collins originally intended to send the men to Germany, and it was a page or two before he curtailed their trip.

14. *of his affliction.* The manuscript continues:

> and had received an answer, which he now put in Mr Brock's hands. He requested the rector to read the letter; to remember what Midwinter's conduct had been throughout under circumstances infinitely painful to himself; and then to say whether there was any harm (now that Allan was in London and on the spot) in his calling to say good-by before he started for Germany the next morning. What was Mr Brock to do? Midwinter's letter of sympathy was delicately and considerately written; and Midwinter's conduct had unanswerably . . .

This was dropped in proof, presumably.

15. *'Very oddly,' said the rector to the lawyers.* The manuscript reveals that Collins rewrote this section of the plot extensively. Most of his changes are irrecoverable, except for a deleted last paragraph:

> [Allan has just been speaking to the lawyers] in his own persistently original way.
> 'One thing at a time, gentlemen,' said the young philosopher to his legal advisers. 'I'm satisfied for the present with knowing that I've got the estate. I'll go and live there, if you please, when I know I can keep it. If it had been anywhere else I daresay I should have been in a violent hurry to go there at once. But they ill used my mother at Thorpe-Ambrose in

her lifetime; and they are ill using her there now after her death. I'll wait to be Squire of the Parish till I can set her memory right in the neighbourhood. When we have got our news from Madeira, let me know. While we are waiting for it, I shall go back to Somersetshire and finish my yacht.

Their client being at that moment legally in possession of the estate, the lawyers left him free to act on his own singular resolutions – merely stipulating that if he went cruising at sea, he should keep within easy reach of the English shore, and should inform them from time to time at what coast-towns a letter would reach him. So the matter rested for the present, while the commissioners on both sides were on their way to Madeira.

The dispute as to whether Allan's mother had been legally married would have taken the narrative in significantly different directions.

16. *Isle of Man.* In July–August 1863 Collins visited the island and found it 'the one inaccessible place left in the world'. He crossed the Sound to the Calf of Man which he described as 'wild and frightful, just what I wanted – everything made for my occult literary purposes' (Robinson, p. 182).

17. *to inquire for letters.* The manuscript continues: 'On the fifth day, the Rector found a letter from Somersetshire waiting for him at the hotel . . .' The striking detail of Allan ignoring the letter which will completely change his life was added in proof.

Chapter II

1. *Chapter II.* At this point in the manuscript there is a note: '3rd monthly Part – not complete yet. Another Chapter to follow. July 27th. WC.' The third monthly part was published in January 1865.

2. *the Broomielaw.* A street in Glasgow.

3. *the bridge at Bristol.* Isambard Brunel's famous suspension bridge over the Severn. Work on it was started in 1832 and it was finished in 1864 (which makes the reference slightly anachronistic here). Collins may intend the reader to remember (in view of Ozias being a Creole) that Bristol was a city enriched by the African slave trade.

4. *which brought me last night from my room to yours.* Later editions have 'which brought me from my room to yours'.

5. *If the conjecture . . . startling conclusion.* This sentence was added in proof.

Chapter III

1. *'a wet sheet . . . follows free.'* Slightly misquoted ('sail' should be 'sea') from the poem by Allan Cunningham (1784–1842). Catherine Peters points out that Cunningham was the biographer of Wilkie Collins's godfather, Sir David Wilkie.

2. *Governor Smelt.* More correctly the 'sub-governor'. Leonard Smelt (1719–1800) was a military engineer and expert in fortifications in service with the Royal Family.

3. *College of King William.* Boys' school on the Isle of Man made famous by Dean Farrar (1831–1903), who set his improving novel *Eric, or Little by Little* (1858) there, masked under the pseudonym 'Isle of Roslyn'.

4. *the wilds of Australia.* Collins may be recalling the Australian expedition of R. O. Burke and William J. Wills, described in the *Annual Register*, 1862. They eventually died of thirst.

Chapter IV

1. *while we are brothers still.* The abolitionists' slogan, 'Am I not a man and a brother?', would echo for many readers here, given the fact that Ozias is black and Allan white.

2. *Horrible, wasn't it?* As he records in his 'Appendix', Collins explored the Isle of Man for local colour for *Armadale* in summer 1863. According to Nuel Davis (working from Collins's later testimony to the Manx novelist, Hall Caine), while cruising in a yacht off the island's coast with Pigott,

> Collins saw a lunatic caper along the rocks pursued by a farmer and his wife. At Castletown, the capital, he learned that this sight was not so uncommon as one might think. Every Manx family was expected to take care of its own insane, with the result that many were kept chained in sheds. Wilkie, though he used the fact in *Armadale*, was not pleased to find material so perfectly suited to its mood. Sir James Gell, the Attorney General, later told Hall Caine about the results of Wilkie's visit. After several letters written by Wilkie to *The Times*, said Sir James, the Home Office told the insular Legislature that if they did not quickly make provision for their indigent lunatics the imperial authorities would do so for them. (Davis, p. 242)

This concern for lunatics was in line with Charles Reade's current, high-profile campaign for the abolition of private lunatic asylums. As Altick notes (p. 545), in 1858 there had been three highly publicized accounts of wrongful incarceration. Reade launched a series of letters to the press on '"Our Dark Places" – the unregulated mad-houses' (Altick, p. 546). A Commons Select Committee was appointed to look into the provision of care for lunatics and their property. Reade kept up the pressure with his novel *Hard Cash*, whose plot hinges on the (sane) hero's incarceration in a private lunatic asylum. Collins returns to the topic in his depiction of Dr Downward's 'Sanatorium' later in *Armadale*.

3. *hurts me.* The manuscript continues:

> The straightforward simplicity of Allan's appeal to that past time which his friend's memory held sacred seemed to work an instant revolution in Midwinter's mind. [The passage that follows in the text, down to 'dread

of wounding the sympathies of his friend', was added in proof. The manuscript then continues:] 'Why distress him?' he whispered to himself. 'Why resist him when the mischief's done, and the caution comes too late? What *is* to be *will* be. What have I to do with the future? and what has he? This ship—'

He rose and looked round him. Mr Brock's words of caution before the Confession was burnt recurred to his memory. There was no shadow of doubt in his mind now, that the woman whom the rector had met in Somersetshire, and the woman whose attempted suicide had opened Allan's way to Thorpe-Ambrose, were one and the same. 'Are we at the end here?' he asked himself. 'No we are only at another stage of the journey. There is worse than this to come – There is the woman behind us in the dark. Will Allan see her first or shall I?' He fell into deeper reflection – roused himself – and stepping hurriedly to the side of the vessel looked down at the channel of the Sound. 'No swimming *there!*' he thought. 'Would it be for Allan's good – would it be the saving of him in the future – if I jumped in?'

He laughed bitterly. 'As if that current would drown a man, as if those rocks would shatter him, before his time has come! No,' he said as he lowered himself again to the deck. 'Providence or Fate, I must see it out.'

He went back to Allan . . .

Collins deleted this powerful scene in proof, presumably. The suicidal tendency in Ozias suggests a gloomy end for him to which the author may not have wanted to commit himself so early.

4. *Address to the women of Norfolk posted in the park.* The manuscript reads 'notice posted in the park'.

Chapter V

1. The manuscript has a different version of the elements of the dream from 16 onwards:

16. From this time the darkness opened no more. I was left alone in it again; and I waited again.

17. Little by little, I felt something turning round and round me in the dense obscurity closer and closer at every turn.

18. It stopped. In the moment when it stopped, a cold hand touched my forehead, and chilled me to the heart.

19. For the first time in the dream my tongue was freed, and I spoke. I said or thought I said the words: 'Is the hand that touched me the Hand of Death?' Out of the darkness and the silence, there came softly an answering sigh. As I had known my father who appeared before me when the dream began – So I now knew the sigh that answered me when the dream ended. I had heard it, sitting by the bedside of the friend who was

with me on board the wreck. Night after night, when sleep fell on him in a weary illness, he sunk into his rest with that sigh.

20. So the dream left me; and I saw the morning sunshine once more.

Here again, there seems a stronger premonition of Ozias's death.

2. *my theory of dreams.* Jenny Bourne Taylor's *In the Secret Theatre of Home*, Chapter Five, records the Victorian psychologists from whom Collins derived (with some modifications) his theory of dreams: John Elliotson (the mesmerist, author of *Human Physiology*, 1840), Robert Macnish (*The Philosophy of Sleep*, 1830), John Abercrombie (*Inquiries Concerning the Intellectual Powers*, 1830) and J. A. Symonds (*Sleep and Dreams*, 1851). Taylor's research illumines this chapter of *Armadale* most usefully.

3. *Have you any reason to give.* In the manuscript there follows a deleted passage:

for going out of your way to reconcile such a mystical view as this with the unanswerably rational explanation of the dream which lies straight before you?'

'It is hard to tell how I reconcile it,' said Midwinter, 'but I will try. All supernatural influences which work on mortal creatures, must necessarily work by means of mortal perceptions. Acknowledging as I do that you have clearly traced the events of the dream to my friend's waking impressions, I go a step farther back when that point has been gained, and I ask next "If the waking impressions account for the dream, what accounts for the waking impressions?" I don't believe, sir, that Chance took us on the road from Castletown to this place. I don't believe that Chance caused our meeting with you. I see in that meeting, and in the events which grew out of it, a supernatural influence working its end with a mortal creature by mortal means, and producing those very waking impressions (about which we are all agreed) as the medium through which to convey the warning of the dream.'

The doctor looked at his watch . . .

BOOK THE THIRD

Chapter I

1. *Doctors' Commons.* As the *Oxford Companion to Law* records, the College of Doctors of Civil Law dealt with 'matrimonial, testamentary, and probate matters'. The College was dissolved in 1858.

2. *a good sixteen years older.* A chronological mistake. In the next number (April, p. 157) Collins printed a footnote entitled 'PRINTER'S ERROR' alerting the reader. The figure should be 'six years'.

3. *odious powders.* As a number of commentators have noted, Collins is alluding here to 'Madame' Rachel Leverson, the 'great lady renovator' who opened her beauty parlour at 47a New Bond Street in 1863. At her premises 'large sums of money were extracted from gullible women whose beauty she claimed to be able to preserve, or enhance, by means of various cosmetic preparations with romantic names'. Blackmail and procuring 'did not come amiss' (Altick, pp. 541–5). She was tried for fraud as early as December 1865 (see *The Times*, 13 December 1865). In 1867 she was sentenced to five years' penal servitude.

Chapter II

1. *wide-awake hat*: according to the *OED*, 'a soft felt hat with broad brim and low crown said to have been punningly named as not having a "nap".' It is a slight anachronism here as the fashion for this headgear did not catch on until the early 1860s.

2. *the dreadful justice of photography would have had no mercy on her*. Collins chooses his tense carefully. It is 1851: exchanging photographs (which became a rage in the 1860s) was not yet a widespread custom (see Altick, pp. 336–7).

3. *the famous clock at Strasbourg*. Catherine Peters quotes a letter of October 1853 from Wilkie Collins (touring Europe at the time) describing this famous cathedral clock and its elaborate puppetry to his mother. He was in Strasbourg also in June 1863 when he seems to have had his 'Idea' for *Armadale* (see Lonoff, p. 33). The major is an example of 'monomania', a variety of madness defined by the French psychologist Esquirol.

4. *Louis the Sixteenth*. As the *Encyclopaedia Britannica* (eleventh edition) records, Louis XVI, while in prison awaiting execution, 'amused himself in making locks and a little at masonry'.

5. *confined to her own room*. The manuscript continues:

> Allan made no reply; he was a little startled by a marked change in the speaker's manner. When Miss Milroy chanced to mention her mother in the course of their morning walk he had characteristically failed to notice that she spoke with a strange absence of any tenderness of feeling. But even he, careless as he was, observed the cloud that hovered over his host's face when Major Milroy described his wife's situation. Allan felt that he had inadvertently touched on something under the household surface which it was not desired that strangers should approach too closely. 'I have made a mistake already,' he thought to himself. 'The less I say in the future about Mrs Milroy, the better.'
>
> The Major turned away towards the breakfast table. 'Have we got everything we want on the table, my love?' he said, speaking to his daughter while he looked about the table with something of a return to his customary absence of manner. 'Will you come and make tea?'

This was cut in proof, presumably; possibly for reasons of length.

Chapter III

1. *Waverley novels ... Edgeworth ... Hemans.* The fiction of Walter Scott (1771–1832) was collected as the 'Waverley Novels' in 1829. Maria Edgeworth (1768–1849) was another popular novelist of the early nineteenth century. Felicia Hemans (1793–1835) was a highly respectable and admired poet.

2. *the Second Vision of the Dream.* There follows crossed out in the manuscript:

> He waited, thinking and looking mechanically at the statue, while he thought. There was little disturbance in his face; it had become suddenly steady and composed with the resignation of a great despair. He took the written narrative of the Dream from his pocket book and compared the scene described there with the scene before him. 'I said I would keep it till we got to Thorpe-Ambrose,' he whispered to himself as he put the paper back again. 'I was right.' A mounting impulse of curiosity stirred in his mind. He stepped out and looked along the whole row of windows, to see if another window of the French sort was among them. There was no other. He returned to the far side of the house – passed along the front of it – and returned again but the other side. Still this one window and the only window?

3. *the other fellow.* i.e. Abednego. In Daniel 3: 12–30, the three of them are cast into the burning furnace by Nebuchadnezzar, and are rescued from destruction by Jehovah.

4. *wants that little long.* From Edward Young's *Night Thoughts*, 4.118, 'man wants but little, nor that little long'.

5. *Darch is our friend the lawyer.* The manuscript reads:

> 'Darch is the lawyer,' said Allan, supposing Midwinter had forgotten the name, – 'the family lawyer who did all the Blanchards' business. Don't you remember the studious bachelor who offered for the cottage at the same time as the major?'
>
> Without making any reply ...

6. *a chimney-pot hat.* Sometimes called a stovepipe hat; a high, black, cylindrical item of headgear associated with Abraham Lincoln. It is probably slightly anachronistic for 1851.

7. *his personal influence next.* The manuscript continues:

> 'In the position you are now occupying, Allan, you *must* cultivate the good opinion of your neighbours,' he said. 'If this was only my idea, I wouldn't press it on you – but I know that Mr Brock thinks about it as I do. I know he has always felt uneasy at your living so entirely out of society. I know he wishes you to take your proper position in this place. Come! come! All I ask is the sacrifice of an hour or two. Only make the personal concession of calling on them first; only tell them (what you can say with perfect truth) that you were not aware their preparations had

advanced so far – and all this mischief will be set right.' He stopped and took Allan affectionately by the hand . . .

8. *Joe Miller. Joe Miller's Jests, or the Wit's Vade-mecum* was a famous (and ever expanding) collection of jokes in the eighteenth and nineteenth centuries.

Chapter IV

1. *a vagabond like me.* The manuscript reads 'a tramp like me'.

2. *at your friend's disposal.* In place of the passage that follows in the text, the manuscript continues:

'Who is he?' inquired Midwinter. 'One of the clerks?'

'Of course! how else should he be in the office? Wait a minute', said Allan, feeling in his pockets. 'I knew how particular you were and how little I was to be depended on in these matters of business – so I asked Pedgift to give me a memorandum to jog my memory. Here it is,' continued Allan, opening the memorandum and beginning to read from it. 'The man's name is Bashwood. He has been four years in Pedgift's service; and before that he was steward to Sir John Mellowship in the county. Steward – do you hear? Just the man you require at just the time you want him.'

'How came Mr Bashwood to drop from the position of steward on a gentleman's estate, to the position of clerk in a lawyer's, office?' asked Midwinter.

'Through troubles at home, poor wretch,' said Allan, consulting his memorandum. 'His wife was a drunkard. She died only lately at the county asylum here. Stop! that's not the reason he lost his place – here it is. He had a son whom he got into a merchant's office some years since, and who robbed his employers. Those employers came down on their clerk's security. Patience, patience, here's the point. Bashwood himself was the security. He was sold out of house and home to pay the money. Sir John was scandalized and Bashwood lost the steward's place. He came to Pedgift (whom he had done business with in former years) a broken-down man. Pedgift gave him a trial in his office. There he has stopped ever since; and that is the whole of his story.'

'Another question,' said Midwinter, 'When does Bashwood come here? Tomorrow?'

'No; he can't be spared – he won't come until two or three days before the rent-day dinner.' [The manuscript then continues as in the printed text until 'the new house', then reads:] The two young men dined together quietly; the rebuffed butler, benevolently forgetful of his injuries, presiding with undiminished grace and affability at the side-board. A man is none the worse a Christian because he happens to be afflicted with a bulbous nose. Let it be recorded to the butler's credit that he bore no malice, and that he let his master and his master's friend have the best wine in the cellar after all.

The one noticeable event . . .

It seems likely that Collins originally intended to do more with his bulbous-nosed butler.

3. *since yesterday*. The manuscript continues:

> A little dispirited, Allan sauntered about his gardens smoking and then returned to his house. There he discovered that his expedition to the cottage had not been entirely fruitless of satisfactory results. The resident gentry had all driven to Thorpe-Ambrose at the usual visiting hour to return Mr Armadale's call; and had all left their cards and gone away again, on finding that Mr Armadale was out.
>
> The next two days . . .

The manuscript reveals that Collins originally intended to make much more of Allan's difficulties with his Norfolk neighbours.

4. *watch for somebody*. The manuscript continues:

> 'Am I in luck's way at last?' thought Allan. 'Is it possible she's waiting for me?' She was waiting for him.
>
> She gave a little start when he appeared, and came forward without hesitation to meet him. Her complexion had suffered under confinement to her house. An expression of embarrassment clouded her pretty face; and the steady brightness of her smile, which had charmed Allan when she greeted him on the former occasion, was only a momentary lightness when she greeted him now.
>
> 'I hardly know . . .

5. *mentioned between them*. The manuscript continues:

> Depend on my acting for the best in his interests and in yours; and expect to hear from me again, as soon as I know how this strange discovery is to end. Very Truly Yours, Decimus Brock.

The chapter and the sixth monthly number finished at this point in the manuscript. Collins worked it up to get a better curtain line.

Chapter V

1. *venomous little quarrel*. The manuscript reads 'pretty little quarrel'.

2. *the mixed train*. i.e. with first, second and third class passengers.

Chapter VI

1. *Michael Angelo was to Sir Joshua Reynolds*. Collins quotes at length Sir Joshua Reynolds's eulogy on Michelangelo in his fifth lecture in 'To think, or be thought for' (1856), reprinted in Collins's *My Miscellanies* (1863). It seems likely that he may have re-read Reynolds's account of the Sistine ceilings in spring 1864, when he was in Rome and thinking out the plot of *Armadale*.

Chapter VIII

1. *He rides the whirlwind.* Quoted from Joseph Addison's eulogy of Marlborough ('who rides the whirlwind and directs the storm') in his poem *The Campaign* (1705).

2. *'The Death of Marmion', 'The Battle of the Baltic', 'The Bay of Biscay', 'Nelson'.* Marmion's death is an extract from Scott's poem on Bannockburn, 1808, The other recitations are appropriately nautical: the Scottish poet Thomas Campbell (1774–1844) wrote 'The Battle of the Baltic'; the Irish dramatist Andrew Cherry (1762–1812) wrote 'The Bay of Biscay'; the famous English tenor John Braham (1774–1856, see the 'late Braham' below) wrote 'Nelson'. Altick (pp. 467–8) cites this scene on the Broads as an illuminating example of Victorian entertainment.

3. *'The Mistletoe Bough'.* A ballad by Nathaniel Bayly (1797–1839). 'Poor Mary Anne' is a ballad by Braham, as Catherine Peters guesses. I am indebted to her for the identification of these songs.

4. *'Eveleen's Bower'.* From *Irish Melodies* (1801–34) by Thomas Moore (1779–1852). See Altick (p. 468) for the popularity of Moore in Victorian parlour entertainments.

Chapter IX

1. *Hurle Mere.* As Nuel Davis records:

> In the summer [1864] Collins cruised along the Norfolk coast in a yacht. [His brother] Charley joined him at Yarmouth in August and they explored one of the broads or marshes called Horsey Mere. Renaming it Hurle Mere, Wilkie introduced it into *Armadale* in one of the most dramatic and skilfully integrated bits of nature painting ever done in a novel.

For Martha Rudd's connection with Hurle Mere and nearby Winterton, see Clarke (pp. 110–11) and Peters (p. 267).

Chapter X

1. *said the voice of young Pedgift.* Crossed out in the manuscript there follows:

> 'And it's my opinion Miss Gwilt's place won't be a very easy one.'
> 'What do you mean?' asked Allan in return.
> 'Did you not notice how the Major and Miss Milroy looked?'
> 'They looked surprised; and well they might at getting such a handsome woman as a governess.'
> 'I don't mean how they looked at first, Mr Armadale. How did they look when Miss Gwilt made her excuses . . .'

2. *by the first train.* The manuscript continues much as the text:

> In any event – whether you succeed or whether you fail in confirming my

suspicions – write to me by return of post. If it is only to tell me you have received my letter, write! I am suffering under anxiety and suspense which, separated as I am from Allan, you alone can relieve.

Having said this, I know you well enough to feel that I need say no more.

This redundant information is dropped in subsequent editions.

3. *it was red!* Richard Altick notes the Victorian prejudice against red hair (particularly 'flaming red hair') and its 'association . . . with female villainy'. Collins, however (in alliance with the Pre-Raphaelites), cast a glamour over this hitherto dubious tint and, as Altick guesses, *Armadale* may even have inspired a fashion for false red hair (Altick, p. 323).

4. *to the Thorpe-Ambrose estate* – . The manuscript continues:

In her footsteps and in hers only could the March of Doom advance on the bearers of that fatal name.

Looking, under the influence of that one unalterable conviction, at events as they had just happened, his mind saw and seized its new conclusion . . .

This mood of inevitable fatalism was lightened systematically by Collins in revising his manuscript.

Chapter XI

1. *Miss Gwilt Among the Quicksands.* In the manuscript, this section is entitled 'Four Letters'.

2. *I have been proved not to be myself.* There was a spate of personation cases in the 1850s and 1860s, climaxing in the sensational Tichborne case, to whose early stirrings Collins may well refer in *Armadale*. In April 1854, Sir Roger Tichborne was lost at sea. His mother, the dowager Lady Tichborne, refused to believe he was dead, and advertised for information concerning her son. In late 1865, an Australian butcher from Wagga Wagga, Arthur Orton, claimed to be the Tichborne heir. The case dragged on with various trials until the 1870s when a totally discredited Orton was sent to prison.

3. *boa constrictor fed at the Zoological Gardens.* As Fred Kaplan (*Dickens*, New York, 1988, p. 359) records, Collins's friend Dickens had nightmares about the horrific sight of the boa constrictors being fed live rabbits at the Regent's Park Zoological Gardens.

Chapter XII

1. *her residence at Thorpe-Ambrose.* Crossed out in the manuscript, there follows:

Mr Brock's letter of the third of July had reached Mr Brock's correspondent that morning. He had read it, and had set it aside with the sense of relief from responsibility which the writer had desired to produce in him.

The subject had since dropped out of his thoughts, and had left his mind free to occupy itself with other and nearer objects of interest. As he now sat waiting for Allan, he looked round the room, seeking the object of his suspicious distrust, and noted, as composedly as a stranger might have noted, certain changes which had been made in it on that day . . .

2. *without knowing why.* The manuscript continues: ' "I suppose it's the weather," he said impatiently, as he took up his candle and went to bed.' In the manuscript the ninth number was to end here, but Collins wrote a better curtain line.

BOOK THE FOURTH

Chapter II

1. *Saturday.* The manuscript has 'yesterday'.

Chapter III

1. *Worth makes the Man . . . leather and prunella.* Proverbial, from Pope's *Essay on Man*, 4. 203.

2. *a ladies' medical man.* Collins's portraiture of Dr Downward seems to owe something to Thackeray's Dr Firmin, in *The Adventures of Philip*, which preceded *Armadale* in the *Cornhill Magazine*.

3. *absence of any other information, sir,' he resumed.* The manuscript continues:

and in the face of what the cabman has just said to us, I see only one other alternative. We must take it for granted that my notion about these people at Pimlico is wrong, and that they really *are* deceiving us for some purpose of their own. What do you say . . .

Chapter IV

1. *the Great Exhibition in Hyde Park.* The Crystal Palace which opened in 1851; the greatest public exhibition of its kind ever mounted in Britain. As Altick notes (p. 422), there are relatively few date markers of this kind in the narrative of *Armadale*.

2. *five shillingsworth of human labour and electric fluid.* i.e. electrical current ('fluid' was a common synonym at this period). This detail seems to have been put in Collins's mind by an article on the 'Electrical Telegraph' in *Cornhill*, July 1860. Wire telegraphs (run by, and alongside, the railroad system) had been widely used since the 1840s.

3. *learnt his profession at the Old Bailey.* A broad hint that Downward is an abortionist. Collins hints at Oldershaw's parallel procuring activities in a number of places in *Armadale* (see Altick, p. 543).

Chapter V

1. *a prison, in the present tender state of public feeling.* Collins is reflecting bitterly here on the recent acquittal of the Scottish arsenical poisoner, Madeleine Smith. Smith had an affair with, and became secretly affianced to, a Glasgow shipping clerk, Emile L'Angelier. A richer and older suitor came along. L'Angelier threatened to expose Smith, by means of her letters to him. In response Smith (as Collins, and many other observers firmly believed) poisoned him. The lovers' letters were introduced into evidence in the trial (which may have given Collins some ideas for *Armadale*). In her defence, Smith claimed she had bought arsenic, shortly before L'Angelier's death, for cosmetic purposes (which may have suggested to Collins the link between Lydia Gwilt and Maria Oldershaw). (See Mary S. Hartman, *Victorian Murderesses*, New York, 1977, Chapter Two and Altick, p. 525.)

Chapter VII

1. *I believe in mesmerism.* Mesmerism had been popularized by John Elliotson (1791–1868), a friend of Dickens and Collins's physician for a short period before *Armadale*. As Catherine Peters points out, Collins wrote sympathetic articles on the subject of mesmerism for the *Leader* (at a period when Elliotson was under attack for his theories). As William Clarke records, while Collins was preparing *Armadale*, Caroline Graves was regularly mesmerizing him to help him withdraw from his opium addiction (Clarke, p. 103).

2. *and left them.* The manuscript continues:

'I'll bet you another half-crown there's something wrong in that quarter,' said the first footman.

'Thank you,' said the second. 'When I've got half-a-crown to throw away I'll think of it.'

This was the end of the twelfth monthly part and Collins was working up his curtain line.

Chapter IX

1. *notes-of-hand.* IOUs, legally stamped, which would have to be renewed or retired by a certain date.

2. *wings of a dove.* From the 1662 Anglican Prayer Book, 'Oh that I had wings like a dove; for then would I flee away and be at rest.'

3. *fancy free.* A misquotation (on Oldershaw's part, not Collins's) from *A Midsummer Night's Dream*, II. i. 156.

4. *and tried in vain.* The manuscript continues:

There are times when one's wits seem to desert one – and it was this helpless time with me.

Monday morning . . .

5. *laudanum.* Collins was intermittently addicted to laudanum (a habit which he projects on to Lydia Gwilt). Laudanum – tincture of opium dissolved in alcohol – was an uncontrolled substance at this period.

6. *than you suppose.* Crossed out in manuscript there follows a partially legible passage:

> [I was] considering whether I had better not stop. When I began my letter, I was really angry enough to be bent on terrifying you with the whole truth. But the time I have passed in writing has calmed me down. My head aches and my hand is getting [?]

Chapter X

1. *The nursery . . . bread and butter.* Byron, *Beppo* (1818), 39. It should be 'leaps out' rather than 'lisps out'.

2. *It is for this, is it, Miss Milroy, that I resisted temptation.* i.e. the temptation to poison her. The manuscript reads:

> Well, well, Miss Milroy. I'm glad now that I resisted temptation, morning after morning, when I knew you were out alone in the park. I'm glad I waited till you yourself put the opportunity in my hands. Though you *did* take shelter from the thunderstorm under the tree, and though you *have* made the best use of your time since you forced him to ask you into his house, you are not Mrs Armadale yet . . .

3. *actually jealous of Armadale, at his age!* Both Collins and Dickens had recently fallen in love with much younger women: Martha Rudd (nineteen when Collins met her in 1864) and Ellen Ternan (twenty-seven when Dickens met her in 1857).

4. *domestic sentimentalists of the present day!* Collins attacks the sensation novel's critics, who valued instead the kind of domestic novel written by Anthony Trollope and Mrs Gaskell. Ironically, during its run in *Cornhill*, *Armadale* was accompanied by Gaskell's *Wives and Daughters* (August 1864–January 1866) and Trollope's *The Claverings* (February 1866–May 1867).

5. *On this hint, as the man says in the play, I spoke.* The reference is to *Othello*, I. iii. 166. There are many dramatic references in *Armadale*, presumably reflecting Collins's and Dickens's passionate interest in amateur theatricals in the late 1850s.

6. *a newspaper which is about to be started in London.* There were a large number of new newspapers started in the middle and late 1850s, following the lifting of the most burdensome of the old taxes ('taxes on knowledge') in 1855. The most successful of the new 1*d.* newspapers of the period was the *Daily Telegraph*, and Collins may be thinking here of the success that his former colleague on *Household Words*, G. A. Sala, had as a foreign correspondent for that paper.

7. *I will or will not go abroad.* Crossed out in the manuscript there follows:

> And suppose I put a kiss in the letter, and drew a line round it to sh‸

where it is? and suppose I write under it 'Patience, patience; and I'll send some more'? Who was the idiot who first said 'Beauty was only skin deep'? You can't see anything under the skin – why should you . . .

8. *Five o'clock*. The manuscript continues:

Another visitor! No less a person than Mrs Milroy's nurse! Her excuse (for it was plainly nothing else) for coming to see me, is that it is heavy on her conscience to tell me the truth. She is aware that I believe Miss Neelie to be responsible for sending Mr Armadale to my reference in London; and she wishes to apprise me, from her own personal knowledge, that Miss Neelie really knew nothing about it [the manuscript then continues as in text from 'and it all originated' to 'medical care']. Having favoured me with these particulars, the nurse finished with a little cough and looked as if she expected to be made the depository of some confidence on my side.

A little friendly talk between us soon satisfied me of two things. One, that she is so far as ignorant as the major of Miss Milroy's meetings with Armadale. The other, that she had some communication with the servants at the great house, and that she suspects me of stopping here with designs on Armadale, which might make a confidential person like herself a purchaseable bargain to me, in the character of go-between. I thought it wise not to undeceive her. She knows Miss Milroy's habits as well as I do; and her suspicions, if confided with me, might turn Miss Milroy [my way?] Without therefore saying anything positive one way or the other, I thanked her for coming, gave her some silver (which I can ill spare) and took down an address in London at which I can write to her if I pleased. I was not sorry to see the door close on her. She is a dangerous woman, and if she waits till I write, she will wait long enough.

As to what she told me about Mrs Milroy, even if it is true, which I persist in doubting – is of no importance now. I know that Miss Milroy and nobody *but* Miss Milroy – has utterly ruined my prospect of becoming Mrs Armadale of Thorpe-Ambrose – and I care to know nothing more. If her mother was really alone in the attempt to expose my false reference, the mother seems to me to be suffering for it any rate. And so, good bye to Mrs Milroy.

At an earlier stage, Collins apparently saw a part for the odious nurse in the subsequent narrative.

9. *I see* . . . he manuscript continues:

. . . . . . locked. I am afraid of the people of the house. If any of them
. . . . . . might see it in my face. I believe I look as I looked in the
. . . . . . en the people in authority came to me with their studied
. . . . . . r deadly calm, and said, 'This way, if you please. The
. . . . . . at and the court is waiting for you!'
. . . . . . going through all the unutterable horror of that
. . . . . . way again?

It came to me . . .

Collins evidently decided it would be more effective to bury all direct reference to Lydia's criminal past.

10. *I read the letters.* The manuscript continues:

> Most of them made me angry; but some of them made me cry. I daresay I am the wickedest woman breathing – the newspapers said it, I remember, at the time, and the newspapers are always right. I don't care. Most of them made me angry – but some of them made me cry.
>
> I came to the last . . .

11. *representing herself . . . drowned.* This seems to be another reference to the Tichborne case (see Book the Third, Chapter XI, note 2). Collins may also have been thinking of another sensational 'personation' case of the period, that of 'Mrs Longworth-Yelverton'. This case also seems to have suggested to Collins part of Lydia Gwilt's subsequent marriage-conspiracy schemes.

During the Crimean War, Captain Charles Yelverton, a combatant in the war and heir to the Marquis of Avonside, met Maria Theresa Longworth, who was nursing as a Catholic Sister of Mercy (i.e. a lay nun). They evidently fell in love, and he probably seduced her. In 1857 Major Yelverton (as he now was) became the 'husband' of Theresa Longworth by means of an irregular Scotch marriage. In the same year, the couple went through an unwitnessed form of service in a Roman Catholic church. In 1858, Major Yelverton left Theresa and 'married' another woman (this time with a more regular ceremony). Mrs Longworth-Yelverton subsequently brought a suit against the Major for the 'restitution of her conjugal rights'. Scottish and Irish courts declared her two 'marriages' valid. Yelverton appealed his case before the House of Lords, and on 28 July 1864 it found in his favour: 'Mrs Longworth-Yelverton' was merely personating his wife. The case aroused huge interest in England, and provoked a spate of 'bigamy' and 'is she or is she not his wife' novels – including one by Mrs Yelverton herself. (See 'Bigamy: The Rise and Fall of a Convention', Jeanne Fahnestock, *Nineteenth-Century Fiction*, June 1981, 47–71.)

12. *in your place.* The manuscript continues:

> I read no farther. When I had got on, line by line, to those words, it all burst on my mind in an instant. There is no doubting, no denying, what has happened to me. The frightful temptation under which I now feel myself sinking, has come straight out of that other temptation to which I yielded in the bygone time.

This was eliminated, in proof presumably, as were other references to Lydia's psychopathic criminality.

Chapter XI

1. *the blacksmith at Gretna Green.* Collins was intensely interested in the vagaries of British marriage law, and this section, *Love and Law*, hints at his later sensation novel on the subject, *Man and Wife* (1870). The situation in Scotland and

Ireland had long been anomalous. As Dougald B. McEachen points out, 'Easy Scotch marriages had been a source of irritation to the English ever since the passing of Lord Hardwicke's Marriage Act in 1753.' In the 1840s, Lord Brougham sponsored a bill that would eliminate irregular Scotch marriages. A law was finally enacted in 1856 (a year or two after the supposed action here) requiring that one of the parties in a Scotch marriage should have resided there for twenty-one days. As McEachen notes, 'This law put an end to quick Gretna Green marriages, but otherwise left the Scots law on irregular marriages essentially unchanged.' In 1868, a Royal Commission reported on Marriage Statutes and their anomalies. Irregular marriage figures centrally later in *Armadale*. (See D. B. McEachen, 'Wilkie Collins and the British Law', *Nineteenth-Century Fiction*, September 1950, 121–39.)

Chapter XIII

1. '*You mustn't bleed him, sir*'. Pedgift Junior has been reading Charles Reade's *Hard Cash*. In that novel, the Scottish Doctor Sampson, who treats his patients with unorthodox 'modern' methods, sends a telegram to the hero with a list of instructions:

> Out visiting when yours came. In apoplexy with a red face and stertorous breathing, put the feet in mustard bath and dash much cold water on the head from above. On revival give emetic; cure with sulphate of quinine. In apoplexy with a white face, treat as for a simple faint; here emetic dangerous. *In neither apoplexy bleed.*

There is a diatribe against bleeding in most of Reade's novels.

2. *harden once more.* The manuscript continues:

> His first suspicions of Mr Bashwood's motive – suspicions not even remotely approaching the truth – now dawned on his mind. After a moment's considering, he determined to state them openly, and to bring the interview in that way, if no other way, to an end.
> One of us . . .

3. *before he said anything more.* The manuscript continues:

> It was quite plain to him that in putting the question which had so violently agitated the Deputy Steward, he had unintentionally offered Mr Bashwood a chance of misleading him, which Mr Bashwood had eagerly – too eagerly – accepted on the spot.
> 'One thing is clear . . .

4. *and in making the discovery within a fortnight from the present time.* This detail was, apparently, added in proof.

Chapter XIV

1. *in my maiden name as 'Miss Gwilt'.* It is a nice question as to whether by doing this (and knowingly falsifying the banns) Lydia is invalidating the marriage. Her lawyer's advice, a little later, seems to follow the normal legal wisdom that so long as her husband is ignorant, and does not conspire with her, the marriage is valid – but vulnerable should he petition against its legality on the grounds that he was deceived. But Lydia is in murky legal waters. (See Fahnestock, pp. 58–9: 'Any error in the formalities could and in fact occasionally did annul an honestly intended marriage.') This situation was cleared up in the late 1860s, partly in response to pressure brought by novelists like Collins.

2. *go no further.* Crossed out in the manuscript there follows:

His engagements are too numerous to permit him being my friend; and in the event of legal advice being required, he begged I would recommend the lady to apply to some other person. The meaning of all this was plain to me. 'I can see plainly you are going the bad way again; and I won't run the risk of having anything to do with you.' If a lawyer's tongue ever went to the truth [illeg] that was what my lawyer would have said.

3. *he will tell me.* In the manuscript there continues, crossed out:

The major must have received my letter yesterday afternoon, and something must have been done on the same day. If Armadale wrote to Miss Milroy from the hotel (as I firmly believe he did) by yesterday's post, he ought to hear from her tomorrow – and if this result is to make any change in his plans, I must know what the change is. My whole future actually depends on what that booby may do, between this and my wedding day!

4. *After solemnly announcing.* The manuscript has 'After informing her disconsolate swain'.

5. *I hailed a passing omnibus, and was a free woman again.* In the late 1840s, horse-drawn omnibuses became more popular as taxes on them were lifted and various improvements were made in their design. Women were able to travel without hindrance in the lower, enclosed deck of the vehicle (men were expected to go to the open upper deck – or knifeboard – where they might smoke). As Altick notes, 'when London was flooded with Crystal Palace visitors in 1851, buses really came into their own as a democratic means of travel' (Altick, p. 374).

6. *from the hotel.* The manuscript continues:

It is not ten o'clock yet. How am I to get through the long lonely hours before he comes. I can't read. If I had a piano – no even if I had a piano I could not touch it. Oh, the weariness of this empty, solitary day! If I could sleep through it from now to the evening!
Five o'clock . . .

7. *Great Western . . . South Eastern . . . tidal train.* Lydia takes her cab from Paddington to London Bridge – the respective terminus stations of the two railway lines. The GPO head office was at Mount Pleasant, near King's Cross. Tidal trains (now called boat trains) were designed to meet ferries coming in, or leaving, at high tide. They would have appropriately flexible timetables through the year.

Chapter XV

1. *whose business is steadily enlarging.* The manuscript has a long, crossed-out passage emphasizing the despicable nature of the private detective, on the theme of 'People paid this man to be shameless and pitiless (when their interest required it) and he was shameless and pitiless.' Collins may well have been thinking about investigations into his and Dickens's private lives. The private-detective industry effectively began with the Matrimonial Causes Act of 1857, which for the first time made divorce generally available to the middle classes on the production of the necessary evidence of adultery and abuse. Collins draws a distinct line between the professional detectives of Scotland Yard (such as Sergeant Cuff in *The Moonstone*) and private detectives like James Bashwood.

2. *a travelling quack-doctor.* Catherine Peters points out that 'Madame Rachel Leverson's first husband was a chemist's assistant, who taught her to concoct cosmetics.'

3. *till she was eight years old.* This odd detail, which recalls *Great Expectations* (1861), suggests that Collins was holding in reserve the possibility of revealing Lydia Gwilt's mysterious origins later in the narrative.

4. *Miss Gwilt, in the character of a Nun.* Theresa Longworth was a lay nun when she met Captain Yelverton in the Crimea. (See Book the Fourth, Chapter X, note 11.)

5. *Women are queer creatures.* The manuscript continues: 'Nine out of ten of them don't know what of them is uppermost half the time.' This was presumably deleted because of the mildly indecent misconstructions that could arise.

6. *the Trial of the famous Mrs Waldron.* As Altick points out, Collins is conflating two sensational cases in the history of Lydia Gwilt, alias Mrs Waldron. In 1857, Madeleine Smith, the daughter of a Glasgow architect, was tried for killing her lover with arsenic-laced hot chocolate. She got off, on the Scottish legal technicality of 'Not Proven' (see Book the Fourth, Chapter V, note 1). The other case was that of Thomas Smethurst, tried for poisoning his wife the next year. As Altick records:

> The doctor was convicted but the evidence against him was so flimsy and the trial had been conducted with such palpable bias that there was a great outcry in the medical and legal professions and the press. The Home Secretary, with the reluctant acquiescence of the judge, was forced to turn the case over to Sir Benjamin Brodie, a highly respected surgeon – but not a forensic scientist, let alone a lawyer – who proceeded to adjudicate, not the controversial medical evidence alone but the jury's verdict itself ... The upshot was that Smethurst was granted a pardon, but since the proverbial pound of flesh had somehow to be extracted, he was rearrested and tried and convicted on a charge of bigamy.

Collins has Lydia convicted of poisoning her husband, pardoned by the Home Secretary, rearrested and convicted of the lesser charge of theft. As Altick points out, 'it is evident that Collins, bucking the tide of public opinion, thought Smethurst had been fairly convicted' of poisoning (Altick, pp. 526-7).

7. *the medical witnesses.* One concern arising from the sensational poison trials of the 1850s was the inadequacy of the forensic science and expert witnesses. The question was discussed in 'The Medical Evidence of Crime', *Cornhill Magazine*, March 1863. The article notes that recent poisoners had shown themselves 'alarmingly familiar with some of the most recondite secrets of toxicology'.

8. *the Scotch marriage.* Collins deliberately confuses the issue as to whether Lydia is bigamously married, or whether her marriage to Manuel is invalid (doubly suspect since he may be previously married, and his 'marriage' to Lydia is an irregular Scotch union).

BOOK THE FIFTH

Chapter I

1. *the cloud first rose between us.* The manuscript version of this section reads:

I only know that the cloud came; that he felt it, and kept the feeling a secret; that I felt it and kept the feeling a secret; that it has grown and darkened ever since that time; and that it is growing and darkening still, with every day that passes over our heads.

I could bear it . . .

2. *circular notes*: Instruments for raising cash in foreign banks (early versions of travellers' cheques). Collins had much trouble with currency on his spring 1864 visit to Italy (Robinson, p. 186).

3. *It is the vessel from Gibraltar.* The manuscript continues:

Armadale has kept his engagement to join us at Naples. Half an hour since, he walked into the room – having contrived to miss Midwinter in his usual blundering way. The first two questions he asked me, after we had shaken hands, were whether I had heard from Thorpe-Ambrose, and whether I could tell him any news of Miss Milroy.

Collins evidently did not at first intend an instalment break here.

4. *When you find . . . drop your pen.* Collins had been warned off writing in early 1863. He was continuously worried during the writing of *Armadale* that 'gout' was attacking his brain; 'the nervous misery is indescribable', he wrote in a letter of September 1864 (Clarke p. 102). Writing was particularly prone to bring on one of his nervous attacks. During his eighteen-month sabbatical from writing (1863-4) he went to various resorts on the Continent, including Naples, which he did not much like (Robinson, p. 184). The Irish doctor here is, apparently, a version of Collins's physician Frank Carr Beard.

Chapter II

1. *Bellini's lovely melodies.* They are apparently watching Vincenzo Bellini's *Norma.*

2. *tell me of it.* The manuscript continues:

'No words can say what a relief it would be to my mind, if you could satisfy me that I have deluded myself, in any important respect, as to what took place in the other room an hour since.'

3. *never mind what!* Lydia has presumably put a small amount of arsenic in Allan's drink, with the aim of poisoning him with a cumulative dose over a long period. This was a favoured method of domestic poisoners of the period.

4. *that he wished me to read.* Crossed out in the manuscript there follows:

'Read that', he said, 'and you will believe that my one anxiety in coming here was to test my recollection of the circumstances by yours. You will understand that the last desperate hope I had to cling to, was the hope that your memory of the night's events might yet prove to be wrong. Read that – and you will want no explanation of the direction that I gave you when I entered this room [illeg]'
I read these . . .

5. *the Mole.* i.e. breakwater.

6. *a political refugee.* Cuba in 1850–68 was seething with political opposition and uprising against the Spanish colonial regime.

Chapter III

1. *On the third of November.* The manuscript has 'On the second of November'.

2. *On the ninth . . . On the thirteenth.* The manuscript has 'On the eighth . . . On the fourteenth'.

3. *the Royal Yacht Squadron.* Formed in 1812 and based at Cowes it served as a general news service for amateur sailors.

4. *to inform me?* The manuscript continues:

I can't go to the lawyer whom I consulted when I was last in London, after such a reception as he then gave me; and it would be little less than madness to try a man whom I don't know. What is to be done? I must shut up my diary and think.
[white line]

5. *Oh Lydia! Lydia! why are you not at church?:* This was originally the end of the eighteenth monthly number.

6. *Doctor Downward!* Collins reshaped his manuscript to create a new instalment break here.

7. *Fairweather Vale . . . new neighbourhood.* Catherine Peters points out that this

706

description 'corresponds closely to the Vale of Health, Hampstead Heath, originally a small hamlet, where a number of new villas were built from 1862 onwards'. Altick (p. 413) also notes the topicality of this description.

8. *my galvanic apparatus.* Designed to give therapeutic electrical shocks. As Catherine Peters notes, Collins was treated at this period with 'electro-magnetic baths' for his gout.

9. *This is no madhouse, my dear lady.* Jenny Bourne Taylor notes the similarity of Downward's regime to that outlined in the (respectable) physician John Conolly's *Treatment of the Insane without Medical Restraints*, (1856). Conolly had an asylum for ladies from 1845 to 1866. There is also another more sinister aspect hinted at in Dr Le Doux's regimen. The 'nervous derangement (parent of insanity)' which he refers to may well be female masturbation, about which there was a panic in the 1860s. Extreme measures – such as clitoridectomy – were practised, as well as various kinds of laceration, scarification and mutilation (see Hartman, *Victorian Murderesses*, Chapter Three). The favoured, and less brutal, method was physical prevention via ingenious 'preservative belts', vigilant inspection, and institutionalized 'rest' (i.e. confinement) of the kind Downward specializes in (it is clear that his rooms have means by which occupants can be spied on). (See Alex Comfort, *The Anxiety Makers*, London, 1968.) This section of Collins's novel is also clearly influenced by Charles Reade's campaign against private asylums in *Hard Cash* (which invited anyone wrongfully incarcerated in an asylum in the last five years to get in touch with the author). In his sliminess, the character Dr Downward owes a lot to the crooked physician and confidence trickster, Dr Firmin, in Thackeray's *Philip* (1862).

10. *Harvey . . . Jenner.* William Harvey (1578–1657) made pioneering discoveries about the circulation of the blood; Edward Jenner (1749–1823) pioneered vaccination for smallpox. Collins is here echoing the Scottish physician Dr Sampson in Reade's *Hard Cash*, who boasts about his discovery of the principle of 'remittency' (a doctrine similar to Downward's 'rest' cure): 'And I discovered this, and the new paths to the cure of all diseases that it opens. Alone I did it; and what my reward? hooted, insulted, belied, and called a quack by the banded school of professional assassins who in their day hooted Harvey and Jenner'.

11. *no such person present.* The absence of witnesses to confirm the marriage ceremony had taken place was one of the problematic features of the Yelverton case. (See Book the Fourth, Chapter X, note 11.)

12. *in the post.* Crossed out in the manuscript a passage follows describing '. . . that other letter which I addressed privately to old Bashwood and I myself privately posted at an earlier period of the day. An appointment has been made for the Doctor to call here tomorrow, with a view to making further arrangements, and there the matter rests so far.'

13. *the great mourning shop in Regent Street.* As Catherine Peters points out, Jays', the London General Mourning Warehouse, 247–51 Regent Street.

14. *Some false report . . . England.* An apparent reference to the Tichborne case (see Book the Third, Chapter XI, note 2).

15. *the immortal Bacon.* Francis Bacon, Lord Verulam (1561–1626).

BOOK THE LAST

Chapter I

1. *afraid of now.* Crossed out in the manuscript there follows:

> . . .[illeg] No', said the Doctor, 'we have his own word for it that he is returning in a hurry, and he may therefore be trusted to come back by Dover, or by Boulogne and Folkestone. In other words, by the South Eastern route.'
> 'Then what are you afraid of?' asked Miss Gwilt.

2. *the Commissioners in Lunacy.* Inspectors charged to look after the welfare of mental patients in care. John Forster, dedicatee of *Armadale*, was a commissioner from 1861.

3. *leave the room.* The manuscript has 'leave the house'.

4. *and hard to please.* Scott, *Marmion*, 6. 30.

Chapter II

1. *Chapter II.* Collins initially intended this to be the beginning of the twentieth monthly number. 'In the House' is marked in the manuscript as 'first portion of the 20th monthly number, W C'. In the event, in *Cornhill Magazine*, 'The Purple Flask' (p. 630) opened the twentieth number. Collins was evidently only a few weeks ahead of the printer at this stage of his composition.

Chapter III

1. *The English novelist.* A polemic against the 'domestic novel'. Collins is defending his own genre of sensation fiction from critics such as the Reverend Henry Mansel in the *Quarterly Review* (April 1863) and Mrs Oliphant. Collins here echoes the sarcasm of a piece he had written with Dickens called 'Doctor Dulcamara MP' for *Household Words*, 18 December 1858. Dr Dulcamara is an itinerant physician and charlatan (based on a character in Donizetti's *The Elixir of Love*) who advocates the sedative virtues of the domestic novel for his patients.

2. *Our Stout Friend.* Catherine Peters notes the deliberate vagueness, but assumes Collins is referring to 'the production of carbonic acid gas by dissolving lime-stone'. She cites a book which Collins is known to have consulted, Alfred Taylor's *Medical Jurisprudence* (1849). Collins evidently had difficulty with the machinery of this section of his plot. He may have been influenced by two articles in *Cornhill Magazine*. In October 1862, there was a piece on 'Carbonic

Acid as an Anaesthetic' which described experiments undertaken by a French scientist on animals in 1858. Two years earlier, Thackeray had drawn on another article in *Cornhill* ('Under Chloroform') for *Philip*, where the villain, Dr Firmin, is rendered unconscious at the climax of the narrative. See Appendix, note 1, for more on the carbonic acid problem.

3. *Mr Armadale's mental health.* The manuscript reads 'health'.

4. *the assistant-physician's key.* The manuscript reads 'the duplicate key'.

5. *whenever she pleases.* Crossed out in manuscript there follows:

> I really don't mind (bless my soul, how late it is!) if you like to take refuge in one of the bedrooms on the top floor tonight, you are heartily welcome. The cab is dismissed – and how you are to get all the way back to London Bridge at past twelve – Well I'm sure I don't know. Once more, Mrs Armadale, what do *you* desire?'
>
> 'I advise Mr Bashwood to stay here for the night,' she said.
>
> 'A lady's advice, Mr Bashwood, to men of your breeding and mine, is equivalent to a command. Good night, my dear sir! Good night in case I don't see you again!' With those words, the doctor retired; forgetting to take away with him the duplicate key of the staircase door.
>
> His memory served him better, when he reached the ground floor. He locked the hall door, and put the key in his pocket. 'Now', thought the doctor, as he returned to the room in which Allan and Midwinter were waiting for him; 'I have got them all three safe in the house; and out of it they won't get till whatever this night may bring forth.'

6. '*Tired nature's sweet restorer, balmy sleep.*' The opening line of Edward Young's *Night Thoughts* (1742-5).

7. *Even my wickedness . . . I have never been a happy woman.* This pious sentiment was chosen by Collins as the novel's epigraph – to deflect moral criticism of the novel, presumably.

EPILOGUE

Chapter I

1. *each other.* The manuscript continues with the following crossed-out passage:

SECOND POSTSCRIPT (Dec. 22nd.)

Mr Armadale's letter has just come. It contains, as I thought it would, news of his friend. The doctors have decided that change is the only remedy that Mr Midwinter now wants, and that a sea voyage (if he can be prevailed on to take it) is the best form in which change can come to him. He is ready and willing to follow their advice, and in a week's time he will probably have sailed from London. 'I have only allowed him to go without me' (Mr Armadale adds) 'on two conditions, with which he has promised me to comply. He is to be back for my marriage and he is to consider my wife his sister and my house his home from that time forth. I am to see him on his voyage as far as the Downs; and then the Major is to have his daughter back at Thorpe-Ambrose, and we are all three to be very busy settling matters for the future at the great house.' There, for the present, ends Mr Armadale's news.

[a black line]

APPENDIX

1. *all suffocated by sleeping in poisoned air.* Altick quotes the relevant item in *The Times*, 30 November 1865:

POISONOUS GAS – At the Liverpool Coroner's Court yesterday an inquiry was held touching the deaths of three men who were suffocated within a few days of each other while acting as shipkeepers on board the ship *Armadale* lying in the Huskisson Dock. Dr Trench, medical officer of health, and Mrs Ayrton gave evidence to the effect that death had been caused by inhalation of carbonic acid gas, which, in consequence of the prevailing high winds, had been forced back into the deckhouse where the men slept, and where they had kindled fires. The jury returned a verdict 'That death resulted from suffocation caused by defective ventilation.'

Although Collins claims that he had the ending 'sketched in his notebook' years before, Altick suspects that the novelist may have been influenced by the news item to invent the finer chemical details of Miss Gwilt's ingenious murder technique (Altick pp. 86–7). It seems likely, too, that Collins was misled by a scientific error in *The Times* report. It is clear that the men on the *Armadale* were suffocated by the build-up of carbon monoxide from a fire in their bunkroom on board the ship. (This is still a hazard with such things as indoor barbeques.) 'Carbonic acid' seems to have been included in the report by mistake. Dissolving small amounts of limestone in carbonic acid (which is what Collins has in mind with Miss Gwilt's fiendish purple flask, apparently) would produce small amounts of carbon-dioxide. In very confined chambers this could have a narcotic, or even a fatal effect – but not in an area as large as a bedroom. A scientist tells me it would be like trying to poison someone with the emissions from a fizzing coke can. Lydia would need vast amounts of acid and huge chunks of limestone and a very sophisticated pumping mechanism. It seems that Collins was misled by this report in *The Times* into thinking that his carbonic acid idea was scientifically plausible.

2. *the kindness of a friend.* Catherine Peters guesses that the friend was Francis Carr Beard.

DRAMATIC VERSIONS OF *ARMADALE*

Collins was very interested in drama and the dramatization of his fiction in the late 1850s and early 1860s. With Dickens he had performed in successful amateur theatricals, and had written plays such as *The Lighthouse* (1855) and *The Frozen Deep* (1857).[1] (Both had exciting scenes at sea which may have inspired the wrecked ship episode, and the later reappearance of *La Grace de Dieu*, in *Armadale*.) In May 1866 (the month that *Armadale* was printed in volume form) *The Frozen Deep* was accepted for the London commercial stage.[2] Collins had written an essay for *Household Words* in 1858, 'Dramatic Grub Street', noting the fact that 'in France, the most eminent imaginative writers work, as a matter of course, for the stage as well as for the literary table'. In Britain, however, as Collins observed, the dramatist-novelist was not honoured. Collins and Charles Reade (and to a lesser extent Dickens and Bulwer Lytton) set out to remedy the situation by writing original plays, and by adapting their own work for the theatre.

The title page of the volume edition of *Armadale* declared that 'Rights of Translation and Dramatic Adaptation are Reserved'. In order to protect his property from the pirates, Collins dashed off a dramatized version of *Armadale* as soon as he had finished the last number. George Smith undertook to have it printed, so it could be registered at Stationers' Hall for copyright purposes. Collins sent proofs of Acts One and Two and the manuscript of Act Three of his dramatized *Armadale* to Smith on 14 June 1866. He intimated at this point that the play would be in four acts, although he evidently later changed his mind. The printed work was entitled '*Armadale*: a Drama in Three Acts'. As Collins told Smith, 'It has been a much harder task to turn the book into a play than I anticipated'.[3]

The action of the play is set in 'our own time' (unlike the novel, which is antedated to 1851). There is a severely curtailed dramatis personae: Allan Armadale, Ozias Midwinter, Dr Downward, Felix Bashwood, Lydia Gwilt, Miss Milroy and Mrs Oldershaw are the principal characters. The first act opens in a wooded glade in the park of Thorpe-Ambrose. In the background is a 'fancy fair' to raise funds for the local infirmary (an episode which Collins largely dropped from the novel). The infirmary aspect explains the presence, at this early stage, of Dr Downward. He and Mrs Oldershaw are really at Thorpe-Ambrose, however, to meet Miss Gwilt and conspire together to set a marriage trap for the new squire, Allan Armadale. Oldershaw has bills of Lydia's with which she blackmails her, and Downward wants money for his sanatorium. The play has a very cumbersome exposition with unnaturally long asides to the audience. Gwilt, it emerges, hates Allan Armadale 'because he is his mother's son'. At the age of twelve (as in the novel) she was forced to commit forgery by Allan's father. In another part of the park, the lovers Allan and Neelie Milroy play out their 'Blackstone' scene, in which they plan their elopement. The arrangement for Allan to go to London is overheard by Lydia. The first act ends with Ozias discovering Miss Gwilt onstage and confessing 'I love you'. With this in mind, Lydia hatches her plot: to start the rumour she has eloped with Allan Armadale, and to marry Ozias (in his true name).

The second act finds Miss Gwilt at home in her London lodgings. Once more, Oldershaw and Downward are in attendance. The false marriage between Ozias and Lydia has taken place and Allan has been 'killed' at sea. Lydia is masquerading as his widow. But Allan returns. Downward (borrowing one of the more dramatic scenes in the novel) kills a fly to intimate to Lydia what must now be done. On this cue, she hatches the murder plot. Ozias enters, only to be denied by Lydia, with the melodramatic line: 'I am *not* your wife.'

The third act takes place in Downward's sanatorium. It includes such episodes from the novel as the visitors' tour and the ruse to lure Allan into staying overnight on the grounds that Neelie is being treated there. As in the novel, Ozias and Allan exchange rooms, putting Ozias in the ominous Room Four. The act is dominated by a long, Lady Macbeth-like soliloquy by Lydia, in which she reflects 'How people would cry Fie upon the truth if I was put into a novel or a play.' The play ends with her farewell 'Good by, good by for ever' after which she enters the deadly bedchamber. The police break the door down and arrest Downward.

Smith obligingly printed twenty-five copies of *Armadale* the play. Collins sent one copy to Dickens, who replied with his opinion on 10 July 1866. While generally favourable, he pointed out how 'dangerous' the character of Gwilt was: 'I do not think any English audience would accept the scene in which Miss Gwilt in that widow's dress renounces Midwinter,'[4] he warned his friend. In the context of the savage reviews the novel received on the grounds of its immorality, Collins seems to have decided against trying to stage the play. Writing to an acquaintance some years later (24 February 1880) he recalled that 'My first attempt to adapt *Armadale* for performance . . . was [not] found suitable for this purpose and it has never been, and never can be, performed upon the stage.'[5] He evidently accepted that it was too immoral for Victorian England.

Armadale the play was a failure, but not a dead end. As Catherine Peters records, a French adaptation was made in 1867, in collaboration with Collins's friend François Régnier. Part of this version survives in manuscript. Although it was not, apparently, staged in Paris Collins was very hopeful that something would come of it. 'I am at work on the "dramatic" *Armadale*' he wrote (presumably in 1867), 'and I will take John Bull by the scruff of the neck, and force him into the theatre to see it – before or after it has been played in French, I don't know which – but into the theatre John Bull shall go'.[6]

It was to be a few years before John Bull saw the play. In 1875, Collins produced a third dramatic version of his story, now entitled *Miss Gwilt*. This was essentially an Englishing of the text produced with Régnier. It now had a five-act structure, shorter speeches, more stage action and more melodramatic emphasis. A production was mounted in Liverpool, for which Collins worked in the theatre with the cast. The play was now described as 'altered from the Novel of *Armadale*'. There survives in the Huntington Library a printed prompt copy with Collins's manuscript additions and corrections, which apparently date from a subsequent staging in 1877.[7] The play now has a slightly enlarged dramatis personae, giving a large role to Major Milroy (in the play a straightforward Victorian paterfamilias, not the monomaniac zany we encounter in the novel). Captain Manuel figures as a seductive villain (although Collins carefully does not make him a bigamist). Darch (played in Liverpool by Arthur Pinero, later a more famous dramatist than Collins) was also given a largish part in this new version of the plot. Mrs Oldershaw, however, was removed entirely. The action again opens in Thorpe-Ambrose park. Miss Milroy and her father are talking about their new governess. 'Is she a young woman,' Neelie asks; 'Yes,' answers Major Milroy (Lydia's age is indeed reduced from the thirty-five years that figures so prominently in the novel). Allan Armadale has just arrived as the new squire and their landlord. By a complicated twist of the plot, Ozias has earlier saved Miss Gwilt from drowning, and Downward has been involved as the physician called in after the episode. During the public welcome of Allan Armadale at Thorpe-Ambrose Ozias learns for the first time that he is the other Allan Armadale. This bombshell (in the form of his dead father's letter) is followed by the dramatic entrance of Miss Gwilt, which climaxes the act.

Act Two is set at the 'fishing house' of Thorpe-Ambrose. Miss Gwilt (more demure than in previous depictions) is engaged painting landscape. She is adored by her pupil, Neelie. Miss Gwilt has also entranced Allan Armadale and Ozias and Major Milroy. Ozias knows some guilty secrets in Miss Gwilt's past but has kept his knowledge secret for love. Lydia's mother, it emerges, was the cause of a fatal quarrel between the fathers of Allan Armadale and Ozias (this is a significant change from the novel). Meanwhile, Downward faces ruin if he cannot get Allan Armadale's money in three months. Enter Captain Manuel of the Brazilian Navy who will be Downward's tool. Allan and Miss Milroy declare their love. The Major banishes the young man for one year, to test his constancy. He rushes off to Cowes, to voyage round the world in his yacht. Downward now sees his opportunity: 'Armadale goes to the Mediterranean; and Midwinter marries Miss Gwilt; the three meet abroad, and Armadale dies!'

In pursuance of this scheme Downward, who owns a newspaper, sends Ozias to Naples. Ozias, meanwhile, has proposed marriage to Miss Gwilt (who has resigned her post at Thorpe-Ambrose). Downward is the only witness at the wedding. Miss Gwilt (or Mrs Midwinter, she now is) upbraids Downward: 'you have forced me into marrying him'. The way is open for Downward to conspire with Manuel to do away with Allan at sea.

Act Three opens in Naples, at the Midwinters' lodgings, six weeks later. Allan Armadale is in yachting gear. Lydia hates him, because she suspects Ozias loves him more than he does her. Manuel has ingratiated himself into the post of Allan's sailing master. Manuel and Lydia, it emerges, have been lovers in the past. He is now dying of consumption, and desperate. Midwinter unexpectedly goes off to sea with Allan. Lydia, who knows of Downward's plot, tearfully realizes that her husband (whom she now loves) has gone off to certain death. The fourth act moves to Lydia's lodgings in London. Allan Armadale and Ozias have drowned and the whole crew of the yacht are presumed lost with them. Downward persuades Lydia to personate Allan Armadale's widow, and thus inherit Thorpe-Ambrose and all its wealth. Lydia is attracted by 'the splendid wickedness of it'. At this point, Ozias and Allan Armadale return. They have not drowned after all (although Ozias has discovered about Lydia's earlier relationship with Manuel – who *has* drowned). In the face of their return, Downward plans the sanatorium murder.

The fifth act is set in the sanatorium. Lydia, who still hates Allan, proposes poisoning him. He is lured to the establishment by a false report of Neelie's being there. The 'vaporizer' poisoning technique is suggested by Lydia, collaborating with Downward (Bashwood, like Oldershaw, is absent from this version of the plot). There is the familiar change of rooms, and Lydia finds that she has poisoned (but not quite killed) Ozias. She discovers round his neck a locket containing some of her magnificent red hair. She kills herself in an agony of remorse.

Miss Gwilt in this last stage version is much less guilty than her namesake in the novel, or in the first dramatization. But it is not quite accurate to say, as Catherine Peters does, that 'she is not implicated in the plots to sink Allan's yacht and to murder him with poison gas'. Lydia is, albeit not always wholeheartedly, a clear accessory before the murder.

As Collins records, *Miss Gwilt* was 'put on for the first time at the Alexandra Theatre, Liverpool, 9 Dec 1875' and thereafter 'performed some hundreds of nights in England and in America'. It had its London opening in April 1876 at the Globe Theatre. It was not a critical success. The *Athenaeum*'s review (22 April 1876) was scathing:

> So favourable a reception had, according to report, been awarded *Miss Gwilt* on its first production in Liverpool, a success in London had been discounted beforehand. The best laid plans o' mice and managers 'gang oft agley' . . . To the faults which ordinarily attend dramatized versions of novels, *Miss Gwilt* adds some shortcomings which are specially characteristic of the author. It is long-winded, involved, oppressive in atmosphere, and artificial in treatment.

The reviewer liked Ada Cavendish, the actress who played Miss Gwilt, but thought the climactic murder wholly absurd.

Notes

1. For Collins's theatrical activities with Dickens in the 1850s see Robert L. Brannan, *Under the Management of Mr Charles Dickens* (Ithaca: New York, 1966).

2. Robinson, p. 195.

3. Huntington Library, call mark HM 33787.

4. Walter Dexter, ed., *The Letters of Charles Dickens* (London, 1938), III, p. 477.

5. Huntington Library, call mark HM 33789.

6. Robinson, p. 198.

7. B. A. Brashear has studied the various dramatic versions of *Armadale* in his doctoral thesis, 'Wilkie Collins: from novel to play' (Case-Western Reserve University, 1972).

BY THE SAME AUTHOR

The Moonstone
Edited by J. I. M. Stewart

The Moonstone, a yellow diamond of huge price, originally stolen from a shrine in India, is given to Rachel Verinder on her eighteenth-birthday present and, on the same night, stolen again . . .

T. S. Eliot described *The Moonstone* as 'The first, the longest, and the best of modern English detective novels.' In this and one or two others Wilkie Collins grasped the essential ingredients that the still more ingenious of a master. Few of his successors have attempted nothing on so magnificent a scale, few have matched his ability to create mystery, suspense, and atmosphere; and hardly any could be said to have tained the reader's interest so unfalteringly over so many pages.

The Woman in White
Edited . . .

There, as if it had that moment sprung out of the earth or dropped from heaven . . . stood the figure of a solitary woman, dressed from head to foot in white garments . . .

Thus began the story on a lonely moonlit road in north London of what is still the greatest mystery thriller in the English language. When *The Woman in White* . . . 1860 it received enormous and has never lost its . . . suspense and control.

No Name
Edited . . .

'Shall I tell you what a lady is? A lady is a woman who wears a silk gown, and has a house of her own . . .'

Ingenious and unscrupulous, Magdalen Vanstone is Wilkie Collins's most vividly-living heroine, one of the great . . . in Victorian fiction and a woman dazzlingly . . . Her powers of transformation, through her . . . 'No Name' proves how easily Magdalen . . . 'a social identity can be . . .

23032A